CONFESSOR

A Sword of Truth novel

Also by Terry Goodkind

SWORD OF TRUTH

Wizard's First Rule
Stone of Tears
Blood of the Fold
Temple of the Winds
Soul of the Fire
Faith of the Fallen
The Pillars of Creation
Naked Empire
Chainfire
Phantom

Debt of Bones

CONFESSOR

TERRY GOODKIND

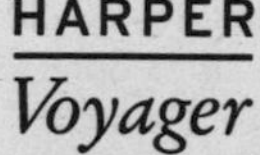

Harper*Voyager*
An Imprint of HarperCollins*Publishers*
77–85 Fulham Palace Road,
Hammersmith, London W6 8JB

www.harpercollins.co.uk

Published by *Voyager* 2008
1 3 5 7 9 8 6 4 2

A catalogue record for this book
is available from the British Library

ISBN 978 0 00 725083 7

Typeset in Janson by
Palimpsest Book Production Limited
Grangemouth, Stirlingshire

Printed and bound in Great Britain by
Clays Limited, St Ives plc

To my good friend Mark Masters, a man of remarkable creativity, determination, and achievement. He is living proof of all that I write about: that one man, through his joyful love of life, the valor of decency, and the calm grace of strength devoid of hate, can inspire all who know him with the nobility of the human spirit.

CONFESSOR

CHAPTER 1

For the second time that day, a woman stabbed Richard.

Jolted fully awake by the shock of pain, he instantly seized her bony wrist, preventing her from ripping open his thigh. A dingy dress, buttoned all the way up to her throat, covered her gaunt figure. In the dim light of distant campfires Richard saw that the square of cloth draped over her head and knotted under her angular jaw looked to be made out of a scrap of frayed burlap.

Despite her frail frame, her sunken cheeks, her stooped back, she had the glare of a predator. The woman who had stabbed him earlier that night had been heavier, and stronger. Her eyes, too, had burned with hate.

The slender blade this woman wielded was smaller as well. While it made a painful puncture wound, had she sliced across his thigh muscle, as she'd apparently intended by the way she was holding the knife, it would have been far worse. The army of the Imperial Order did not bother to care for slaves with crippling injuries; they would simply have put him to death. That had probably been her plan in the first place.

Gritting his teeth with awakened rage as he held the struggling woman's wrist in a viselike grip, Richard twisted her arm as he lifted her white-knuckled fist in order to withdraw the blade from his leg. A drop of blood dripped from the tip.

He easily muscled her under his control. She was not the powerful killer he had at first feared. Her desire, her intent, her lust, however, were just as vicious as that of any of the invading horde she followed. As she grunted in pain, vapor from each panting breath rose into the cold night air. Richard knew that to be gentle would only give her another opportunity to finish the job. Surprise had provided her with an opening; he would not foolishly grant her a second chance. Still firmly holding her wrist, he wrenched the knife from her grasp.

He didn't let up the pressure on her arm until he had possession of the blade. He could have broken her arm, and she deserved no less, but he didn't—this was not the time or place to create a disturbance. He merely wanted her away from him. Once he'd disarmed her, he shoved her back.

As soon as she stumbled to a halt, she spat at him. "You'll never beat the team of the great and glorious Emperor Jagang. You are dogs—all of you! All of you from up here in the New World are heathen dogs!"

Richard glared at her, watching to make sure she didn't pull another knife and renew the attack. He checked to the sides for an accomplice. Although there were soldiers not far away, just beyond the small enclosure of supply wagons, they were preoccupied with their own business. There didn't appear to be anyone with the woman.

When she started to spit at him again, Richard lunged at her. She gasped in fright as she flinched back. Having lost courage for the business of stabbing a man when he was awake and able to defend himself, she cast him one last hateful glare, then turned and escaped into the night. Richard had known that the length of heavy chain attached to the collar around his neck wasn't long enough to allow him to get to her, but she hadn't known that and so the threat had been convincing enough to scare her off.

Even in the middle of the night the vast army encampment into which she had vanished was ceaselessly busy. Like some great, churning beast it swallowed her up.

While many of the soldiers were sleeping, others seemed always to be at work repairing gear, making weapons, cooking, eating, or engaged in drinking and raucous stories around fires as they passed the time waiting for their next opportunity at murder, rape, and plunder. All night long, it seemed, there were men testing their strength against one another, sometimes with muscle, sometimes with knives. Small crowds gathered from time to time to watch such contests and to bet on the outcome. Patrolling guards looking for any signs of serious trouble, soldiers looking for entertainment, and camp followers looking for a handout prowled the encampment throughout the night. Occasionally men wandered by to size up Richard and his fellow captives.

Between gaps in the wagons Richard could see some of the camp followers, hoping to earn food or even a small coin, going from group to group offering to play a flute and sing for the men. Others offered to shave soldiers, wash and care for their clothes, or tattoo their flesh. A number of the shadowy figures, after brief negotiations, disappeared into tents with the men. Others wandered the camp looking to steal. And a few of those out in the night were intent on murder.

In the center of it all, in a prison island created out of a ring of supply wagons, Richard lay chained with other captive men brought in to play in the Ja'La dh Jin tournaments. Most of his team was made up of regular Imperial Order troops, but they were off sleeping in their own tents.

Hardly a city ruled by the Order was without a Ja'La team. As children these soldiers had played it almost from the time they could walk. They all expected that after the war was over Ja'La would endure for them. To many of the soldiers of the Order, Ja'La dh Jin—the Game of Life—was itself a matter of life and death, nearly equal to the cause of the Order.

Even to a scrawny old woman who followed her emperor to war and lived off the scraps of his conquest, murder was an acceptable means of helping her favored team to victory.

Having a winning Ja'La team was a source of great pride for an army division, just as it was for any city. Commander Karg, the officer responsible for Richard's team, was also intent on winning. A winning team could bring far more tangible benefits to those directly involved than mere glory. Those who ran the top teams became powerful men. Winning Ja'La players became heroes rewarded with riches of every sort, including legions of women eager to be with them.

At night Richard was chained to the wagons that held the cages that had transported him and the other captives, but in the games they had played along the way he was the point man for their team, trusted to carry Commander Karg's ambitions to glory in the tournaments at Emperor Jagang's main encampment. Richard's life depended on how well he did his job. So far he had rewarded Commander Karg's faith in him.

Richard's choice from the first had been to either join Commander Karg's effort, or be executed in the most gruesome manner possible.

Richard, though, had had other reasons for "volunteering." Those reasons were far more important to him than anything else.

He glanced over and saw that Johnrock, chained to the same transport wagon, lay on his back sound asleep. The man, a miller by trade, was built like an oak tree. Unlike the point men of other teams, Richard insisted on endless practice whenever they were not on the move. Not everyone on his team liked it, but they followed his instructions. Even in their cage as they had traveled to the Imperial Order's main force, Richard and Johnrock analyzed how they could have done better, devised and memorized codes for plays, and did endless push-ups and other exercises to build their strength.

Exhaustion had apparently overcome the noise and confusion of camp, and Johnrock was sleeping as peacefully as a baby, unaware that their reputation had brought people out into the night who wanted to end their team's chances before they reached the tournaments.

As tired as Richard was, he had only been dozing from time to time. He found himself having difficulty sleeping. Something was wrong, something not connected to all the myriad troubles swirling around him. It was not even anything to do with the immediate worldly dangers of being a captive. This was something different, something inside him, something deep within him. In a way it reminded him a little of the times he'd been sick with a fever, but that wasn't really it, either. No matter how carefully he tried to analyze it, the nature of the feeling remained elusive. He was so confused by the inexplicable sensation that he was left with nothing so much as an aching feeling of restless foreboding.

Besides that, he was too preoccupied thinking about Kahlan to be able to sleep. Held captive by Emperor Jagang himself, she was not all that far away.

Sometimes when he'd been alone with Nicci, late in the night sitting before a fire, she had stared into those flames and confided in him how Jagang had brutalized her. Those stories gnawed at Richard's insides.

He couldn't see the emperor's compound, but as they had rolled in through the sprawling encampment earlier that day he had seen the impressive command tents. To find himself looking into Kahlan's green eyes after all this time, even if for only a fleeting moment, had filled him with joy and relief. He had at long last found her, and she was alive. He had to find a way to get her out.

Reasonably sure that the latest woman to have stabbed him was no longer lurking in the shadows for another attempt, Richard finally pulled his hand away to inspect the wound. It wasn't as bad as it might have been. If he had been sound asleep, like Johnrock, it might have gone much worse.

He guessed that perhaps the odd feeling that had been keeping him awake had actually served him well.

As much as the wound in his leg stung, it wasn't serious. Holding his hand tightly over it had stopped the bleeding. The wound from earlier that night was also painful, but it, too, wasn't anywhere as bad as it might have been. His shoulder blade had caught the tip of the woman's knife and thwarted her attempt at murder.

Death had visited him twice that night and gone away empty-handed. Richard remembered the old saying that trouble sired three children. He hoped not to meet the third child.

He had just rolled onto his side to try again to get some sleep when he saw a shadow slipping up among the wagons. The stride appeared deliberate, though, rather than stealthy. Richard sat up as Commander Karg came to a halt over him.

In the dim light Richard could plainly see the tattooed scales covering the right side of the man's face. Without the leather shoulder plates and breastplates that the commander usually wore, or even a shirt, Richard could see that the pattern of scales ran down over his shoulder and covered part of his chest as well. The tattoo made him look reptilian. Among themselves, Richard and Johnrock referred to the commander as "Snake-face." The name fit in more ways than one.

"What do you think you're doing, Ruben?"

Ruben Rybnik was the name Johnrock—and everyone else on the team—knew Richard by. It was the name Richard had given when he'd been taken prisoner. If there was one place that his real name would surely get him killed, Richard now sat right in the middle of it.

"Trying to get some sleep."

"You have no business trying to force a woman to lie with you." Commander Karg pointed an accusatory finger. "She came to me and told me all about what you tried to do to her."

Richard's brow lifted. "Did she, now."

"I told you before, if you beat the emperor's team—if you beat them—then you will get your choice of a woman. But in the meantime you get no favors. I won't tolerate anyone disobeying my orders—least of all the likes of you."

"I don't know what she told you, Commander, but she came here with the intent of killing me. She wanted to make sure that the emperor's team wouldn't lose to us."

The commander squatted down, resting his forearm on his knee as he peered at the point man for his Ja'La team. He looked ready to murder Richard himself.

"A poor lie, Ruben."

The knife that only a short time ago he'd taken away from the woman was in Richard's hand, pressed up along the inside of his wrist. At this distance he could have gutted the commander before the man knew what had happened.

But this was not the time or place. It wouldn't help Richard get Kahlan back.

Without taking his gaze off the commander's eyes, Richard spun the knife through his fingers and caught the point between his first finger and thumb. It felt good to have a blade in his hand, any blade, even one this small. He held the handle of the knife out toward the commander.

"This is why my leg was bleeding. She stabbed me with it. Where else do you think I could get a knife?"

The significance—and the danger—of a knife being in Richard's possession was not lost on the man. He glanced at the wound on Richard's thigh and then took the knife.

"If you want us to win this tournament," Richard said with deliberate care, "then I need to get some rest. I would rest a lot easier if there were guards posted. If one skinny old woman, who probably has a bet on the emperor's team, kills me while I'm asleep, then your team will be without a point man and has no chance to win."

"Think a lot of yourself, don't you, Ruben?"

"You think a lot of me, Commander, or you would have killed me long ago back in Tamarang after I killed dozens of your men."

With his tattooed scales faintly lit by campfires, the commander looked like a snake considering a meal.

"It would appear that being point man is dangerous not just on the Ja'La field." He finally rose up over Richard. "I'll post a guard. Just keep in mind that a lot of people don't think you're so good—after all, you've already lost one game for us."

They had lost that game because Richard had tried to protect one of his men, a captive named York, whose leg had just been broken in a concentrated charge by the opposing team. He had been a valuable man, a good player, and therefore targeted. The way the Order played Ja'La, the rules allowed such things.

With a badly broken leg York had suddenly become useless as a player, and as a slave. After he had been carried from the field, Commander Karg had unceremoniously cut the man's throat. For protecting the downed player rather than continuing play by taking the broc upfield toward the opposing goal, the referee had penalized their team by banning Richard from the rest of the game. They had lost as a result.

"The emperor's team lost a game, too, as I hear tell." Richard said.

"His Excellency had that team put to death. His new team was created from the best men in all of the Old World."

Richard shrugged. "We lose players for various reasons, too, and they get replaced. Any number have been hurt and can't play. Not long ago one of our men broke a leg. You did no less than the emperor did with his losers.

"As I see it, the details of who used to be on his team don't matter all that much. We've each lost a game. That makes us even. That's all that really matters. We come into this contest on equal footing. They're no better than us."

The commander arched an eyebrow. "You think you are their equal?"

Richard didn't shrink away from the man's glare. "I am going to win us the chance to play the emperor's team, Commander, and then we will see what happens."

A sly smile curved into the scales. "Hoping for your choice of a woman, Ruben?"

Richard nodded without returning the smile. "As a matter of fact I am."

Commander Karg had no idea that Richard already knew the woman he wanted. He wanted Kahlan. He wanted her more than life itself. He intended to do whatever was necessary to get his wife away from the nightmare of captivity by Jagang and his Sisters of the Dark.

Staring down at Richard, Commander Karg finally conceded with a sigh. "I'll tell the guards that their lives depend on no one getting at my team while they sleep."

After the commander had vanished into the night, Richard lay back, at last letting his aching muscles relax. He watched guards in the distance rushing to set up a tight perimeter around the captive members of the team. The realization of what could be lost to nothing more than a conniving camp follower had spurred Commander Karg to action. At least the attack had served the purpose of making it possible for Richard to get the rest he needed. It wasn't easy sleeping when anyone who wanted to could sneak up and cut your throat.

Now, at least, he was temporarily safe, even if it had been necessary to surrender the knife. He still had the other one, though, the one he'd taken from the first woman. It was tucked away in his boot.

Richard curled into a ball on the bare ground in an effort

to stay warm as he tried to go to sleep. The ground had long ago lost any heat from the previous day. Without a bedroll or blanket, he was forced to bunch up the slack in the chain to make a pillow of sorts. The next sunrise was not far off. Out on the Azrith Plain it wasn't going to be getting warmer any time soon.

Dawn would bring the first day of winter.

The noise of the camp droned on. He was so tired. Thinking about Kahlan, about the first time he'd met her, about how it had lifted his heart to at last see her alive again, about how happy it made him to look into her beautiful green eyes, finally allowed sleep to gently quiet his mind and take him.

CHAPTER 2

It was a soft, otherworldly sound, like a doorway into the world of the dead opening, that woke Richard from a deep sleep.

He looked up and saw a figure in a hooded cloak looming over him. Something about its bearing, its very presence, made the hair on the backs of his arms stand on end.

This was no timid, frail woman. Something in the demeanor told him that this was not even a knife-wielding attacker.

This was something far worse.

Richard knew without doubt that this was the third child of trouble and it had just found him.

He sat up and scooted back a little, gaining some precious distance. Somehow, Commander Karg's guards had failed to stop the intruder. He glanced their way and saw them casually walking their patrol. As closely spaced as they were, Richard didn't see how anyone could have gotten through their perimeter, yet this latest visitor had managed it.

The hooded figure glided closer.

The cleansing has begun.

Startled, Richard blinked. The eerie voice echoed in his mind, but he wasn't at all sure that he had actually heard it. The words just seemed to be there, in his head.

He carefully slipped two fingers down into his boot, groping for the wooden handle of the knife. When he found it, he started drawing it out.

The cleansing has begun, the figure said again.

It wasn't like a real voice. It was neither male nor female. The words didn't seem to have been spoken aloud, as by a voice, but rather sounded like a thousand whispers joined together. The words seemed like they had come from another world. Richard couldn't imagine how anything dead could speak, but the words didn't sound at all as if they had come from anything living.

He feared to imagine just what it was that stood before him.

"Who are you?" he asked, stalling for time while he appraised the situation.

A quick glance to each side revealed no one else in plain sight; as far as he could tell the visitor had come alone. The guards were facing the other way. They were watching for anyone who might try to get at the sleeping captives; they weren't looking inside the circle of wagons for trouble.

The figure seemed suddenly to be closer yet, within a mere arm's length. Richard didn't know how it had gotten that close to him. He hadn't seen it move. He wouldn't have allowed it to get that close if he had seen it moving toward him. And yet, it had.

Having a chain attached to his collar didn't leave him much freedom to maneuver if he had to fight. With his fingers he carefully collected links of chain into his free hand. If he had to fight, he would loop the chain and use it as a noose. With his other hand he was still surreptitiously fishing out the knife.

Your time starts this day, Richard Rahl.

Richard's fingers on the knife paused. It had spoken his real name. No one in the camp knew his real name. Richard's heart hammered against his chest.

With as dark as it was, and the hood, the face inside was hidden from view. Richard could see only blackness, like death itself, staring out at him.

It crossed his mind that that just might be exactly what it was.

He reminded himself not to let his imagination get carried away. He summoned his courage.

"What did you say?"

An arm beneath the dark cloak rose toward him. He couldn't see the hand, just the drape of the cloth over it.

Your time starts this day, Richard Rahl, the first day of winter. You have one year to complete the cleansing.

An unsettling image of something all too familiar came to mind: the boxes of Orden.

As if reading his mind, a thousand whispers of the dead spoke.

You are a new player, Richard Rahl. Because of that, the time of the play is now reset. It starts anew from this day, the first day of winter.

Until a little more than three years before, Richard had been living a peaceful life in Westland. The entire chain of events had started when his real father, Darken Rahl, had finally gotten his hands on the boxes of Orden and first put them in play. That had been on the first day of winter four years ago.

The key to telling the three boxes of Orden apart and knowing the correct box to open was *The Book of Counted Shadows*. Richard had memorized that book as a young man. Because he had lost his link to his gift he could no longer remember the words of the book; to be able to read or remember books of magic required magic. But while he didn't recall the words, he did know from remembering his own actions some of the basic principles laid out in the book.

One of the most important elements of using *The Book of Counted Shadows* was verifying if the words Richard had memorized were spoken true—verifying if that key component to opening the boxes of Orden was genuine. The book itself stipulated the means of verification.

The means of verification was the use of a Confessor.

Kahlan was the last living Confessor.

Richard summoned his voice only with the greatest of difficulty.

"What you say is impossible. I have put nothing into play."

You are named as the player.

"Named? Named by who?"

That you have been named as a new player is what matters. You are forewarned that you have one year from this day—and not one day longer to complete the cleansing. Use your time well, Richard Rahl. Your life will be the price if you fail. All life will be the price if you fail.

"But it's impossible!" Richard cried out as he lunged, locking both hands around the throat of the figure.

The cloak collapsed.

There was nothing inside it.

He heard a small, soft sound, like a doorway into the world of the dead closing.

He could see the little clouds of his panting breath rising into the black winter night.

After what seemed an empty eternity, Richard finally lay back down, using the cloak to cover his trembling body, but he could not force himself to close his eyes.

To the west distant lightning flickered at the horizon. To the east the dawn of the first day of winter fast approached.

Between lightning and dawn, in the middle of an enemy numbering in the millions, Richard Rahl, leader of the D'Haran Empire, lay chained to a wagon thinking about his captive wife, and the third child of trouble.

CHAPTER 3

Kahlan lay on the floor in the near darkness, unable to sleep. She could hear Jagang's even breathing in the bed above her. On an ornately carved wooden chest against the far wall a single oil lamp, its wick turned down low, cast a weak glow through the gloom of the emperor's inner sanctum.

The burning oil helped, if only to a small degree, to mask the stench of the encampment: the smells of soot from fires, fetid sweat, rancid refuse, the latrines, the horses and other animals, and manure all mingled together into a ubiquitous stink. In much the same way that the horrific memory of all of the maggot-infested, rotting corpses she had seen along her journey invariably brought to mind the unforgettable, unmistakable, gagging smell of death, it was impossible to contemplate the Imperial Order encampment without it also bringing to mind its singular, pervasive stink, a thing as vile as the Imperial Order itself. Since arriving in the encampment she was always reluctant to draw a breath too deeply. The smell would forever be linked in her mind to the suffering, misery, and death that the soldiers of the Imperial Order visited upon on everything they touched.

As far as Kahlan was concerned, the people who believed in, supported, and fought for the convictions of the Imperial Order did not belong in the world of life among those who valued it.

Through the gauze fabric covering the vents in the top of the tent, Kahlan could see the furious flashes of lightning to the west illuminating the sky overhead to announce the approaching storms. The emperor's tent, with its hangings, carpets, and padded walls, was relatively quiet, considering the constant din of the sprawling encampment out beyond, so it was hard to hear the thunder, but she could occasionally feel rumbles of it through the ground.

With the cold weather settling in, the rain would make it all the more miserable.

As tired as she was, Kahlan couldn't stop thinking about the man from earlier that day, the man who had looked out from that cage as it had rolled through the camp, the man with the gray eyes, the man who had seen her—actually seen her—and had called out her name. It was a galvanizing moment for her.

For anyone to see her bordered on miraculous. Kahlan was invisible to almost everyone. *Invisible* wasn't really accurate, though, because they actually did see her. They simply forgot having seen her as soon as they had, forgot that they had been aware of her only an instant before. So, while she wasn't really invisible, she might as well have been.

Kahlan knew well the icy touch of oblivion. The same spell that made people forget her as soon as they'd seen her had also wiped out every memory she had of her past. Whatever there was to her life before the Sisters of the Dark, it was now lost to her.

Among the millions of troops sprawled out across the vast, barren plain, her captors had found only a handful of soldiers who could see her—forty-three, to be exact. These forty-three were men who, like the collar around her neck, the Sisters, and Jagang himself, stood between her and freedom.

Kahlan made it her business to know every one of those forty-three men, to know their strengths, their weaknesses. She studied them silently, mentally making notes about each of them. Everyone had habits—ways of walking, of observing what was going on around them, of paying attention or failing to pay attention, of doing their job. She had learned everything she could about their individual characteristics.

The Sisters believed that an anomaly in the spell they had used was responsible for a handful of people being aware of Kahlan. It was possible that out among the Order's vast army there were others who could see and remember her, but Jagang had so far not discovered any more. The forty-three soldiers were thus the only men able to serve as her guards.

Jagang, of course, could see her, as well as the Sisters who had used the spell in the first place. Much to the Sisters' horror they had been captured by Jagang and they, too, had ended up with Kahlan in the wretched encampment of the Imperial Order. Other than the Sisters and Jagang, none of those few who could see her really knew her—knew her from her forgotten past, a past that even Kahlan didn't know.

But that man in the cage was different. He had known her. Since she didn't remember ever seeing him before, that could only mean that he was someone who knew her from her past.

Jagang had promised her that when she finally had her past back and knew who she was, when she knew everything, then the real horror for her would begin. He delighted in explaining in vivid detail exactly what he intended to do to her, how he would make her life one of endless torment. Since she didn't remember her past, his promises of retribution didn't mean as much to her as he would have liked. Still, the things he'd promised were terrifying enough in and of themselves.

Whenever Jagang promised such vengeance, Kahlan returned only a blank look. It was a way of walling off her emotions from him. She didn't want to give him the satisfaction of seeing her emotions, her fear. Despite what it would mean for her, Kahlan was proud to have earned the contempt of such a vile man. It gave her the confidence that whatever she had done in her past, her convictions could only have placed her in direct opposition to the will of the Order.

Because of Jagang's ghastly oaths, Kahlan greatly feared remembering her past, yet after seeing the raw emotion in the captive man's eyes she longed to know everything about herself. His joyous reaction to seeing her stood out in sharp contrast to all those around her who despised and reviled her. She had to know who she was, who the woman was that could be held in such regard by that man.

She wished she could have looked at the man for longer than the brief glimpse she had gotten. She'd had to turn away. If she had been caught showing any interest in a captive, Jagang surely would have killed him. Kahlan felt protective of the man. She didn't want to inadvertently bring trouble to someone who knew her, someone so obviously overcome by the sight of her.

Yet again Kahlan tried to put her racing mind to rest. She yawned as she watched the flickers of lightning in the little patch of dark sky. Dawn was not far off and she needed sleep.

With that dawn, though, came the first day of winter. She didn't know why, but the very idea of the first day of winter made her uneasy. She couldn't imagine a reason. Something about the first day of winter seemed to knot her insides with anxiety. It seemed that beneath the surface of her ability to remember lurked dangers she could not begin to imagine.

Her head came up at the sound of something falling over. The noise had come from the outer room, the room outside Jagang's bedroom. Kahlan propped herself up on an elbow, but she dared not get up from her spot on the floor beside the emperor's bed. She knew well the consequences of disobeying his orders. If she was to endure the pain he could give her through the collar around her neck, it would have to be for something more than moving from the carpet.

In the darkness Kahlan heard Jagang, just above her on the bed, sit up.

Sudden cries and moans broke out on the other side of the padded walls of the bedroom. It sounded like it might have been Sister Ulicia. Since being captured by Jagang, Kahlan had had occasion enough to hear Sister Ulicia sobbing and crying. Kahlan herself had often enough been brought to tears, all because of those Sisters of the Dark, but especially Sister Ulicia.

Jagang threw the covers off. "What's going on out there?"

Kahlan knew that for the crime of disturbing Emperor Jagang Sister Ulicia was soon going to have even more reason to be moaning.

Jagang stepped down onto the floor, straddling Kahlan on the carpet beside his bed. He looked down deliberately, making sure that in the dim light of the lantern glowing atop the chest, she saw him naked and exposed over her. Satisfied with his silent, implied threat, he retrieved his trousers from a nearby chair. Hopping from one foot to the other he pulled them on as he started for the doorway. He didn't bother putting on anything more.

He paused before the thick hanging that covered the doorway and turned back, crooking a finger at Kahlan. He wanted to keep an eye on her. As Kahlan rose to her feet, Jagang drew back the heavy covering over the doorway. Kahlan glanced to the side and saw the latest captive woman to be brought in as a prize for the emperor cowering on the bed, the blanket held in her fists up under her chin. Like almost everyone, the woman didn't see Kahlan and had only been more confused and frightened the evening before when Jagang had spoken to the phantom in the room with him. That had been the least of the woman's cause for fright that night.

Kahlan felt a jolt of pain sizzle down the nerves of her shoulders and arms—Jagang's reminder through the collar not to linger in doing as she'd been told. Without letting him see how much it hurt, she hurried after him.

The sight that greeted her in the outer room was confusing. Sister Ulicia was rolling around on the floor, arms flailing as she babbled incoherently between moans and cries. Sister Armina, hunched over the woman at her feet, shuffled to and fro, following as Sister Ulicia writhed around on the floor, afraid to touch the woman, afraid not to, afraid of what might be the problem. She looked like she wanted to collect Sister Ulicia in her arms and quiet her lest she create a disturbance that would get the attention of the emperor. She didn't yet realize that it was too late for that. Usually when one of those two was in any kind of agony it was agony inflicted by Jagang through his control of their minds, but now he, too, stood watching the strange sight, apparently unsure of what could be causing such behavior.

Sister Armina, already bent over the woman floundering on the floor, suddenly noticed Emperor Jagang and bowed deeper yet. "Excellency, I don't know what is wrong with her. I'm sorry that she has disturbed your sleep. I will try to quiet her."

Jagang, being a dream walker, didn't need to speak to those whose minds were his domain. His consciousness wandered at will among their most intimate thoughts.

Sister Ulicia thrashed around, one wildly swinging arm knocking over a chair. Guards—the guards who had been specially selected because they were the few who could see and remember Kahlan—had all backed off in a circle around the woman rolling on the floor. They had been tasked with seeing to it that Kahlan didn't leave the tent without Jagang. Sisters were not their responsibility. Other guards, Jagang's personal elite guards, huge brutes all covered in tattoos and metal studs piercing their flesh, stood like statues near the doorway of the tent. The job of the elite guard was to see to it that no one entered the tent without invitation. They looked only mildly curious about what might be happening in their midst.

Off in the darker corners of the expansive tent, slaves waited in the shadows, always silently at the ready to carry out the emperor's wishes. They, too, would show little reaction no matter what might happen right before them. They were there to serve at the whim of the emperor and nothing more. It was unhealthy for any of them, individually, to distinguish themselves in any way that might bring them notice.

The Sisters, sorceresses all, were Jagang's personal weapons, his personal property and marked as such with rings through their lower lips. They were not the responsibility of any of the guards unless specifically instructed. Jagang could have cut Sister Ulicia's throat, or raped her, or invited her to tea, and his elite guards would not have batted an eye. If it had been tea the emperor wanted, the slaves would have dutifully fetched it. If a bloody murder had been committed right before their eyes, they would have waited until he was finished and then without a word cleaned up the mess.

When Sister Ulicia cried out again, Kahlan realized that it didn't look, as she had at first thought, like the woman was in pain. It looked more like she was . . . possessed.

Jagang's nightmare gaze passed among the dozen guards. "Has she said anything?"

"No, Excellency," one of the special guards said. The rest of the soldiers, those who could see Kahlan, shook their heads in agreement. The emperor's elite guard did not dispute the account of the lesser men.

"What's wrong with her?" Jagang asked the Sister, who looked ready to fall to the ground and grovel at his feet.

Sister Armina winced at the anger in his voice. "I don't have any idea, Excellency, I swear." She gestured toward the far side of the room. "I was asleep, waiting until I could be of service. Sister Ulicia was asleep as well. I woke when I heard her voice. I thought she was speaking to me."

"What was she saying?" Jagang asked.

"I couldn't understand her, Excellency."

Kahlan realized, then, that Jagang didn't know what Sister Ulicia had said. He always knew what the Sisters had said, what they'd thought, what they were planning. He was a dream walker. He wandered the landscape of their minds. He was always privy to everything.

And yet, he was not privy to this.

Or, Kahlan surmised, perhaps he didn't want to say aloud what he already knew. He liked to test people that way, asking questions to which he already knew the answers. It displeased him greatly whenever he caught anyone in a lie. Only the day before he had erupted in a rage and strangled the life out of a new captive slave who'd lied to him about having taken a bite to eat off a tray coming in for the emperor's dinner. Jagang, as heavily muscled as any of his elite guard, had accomplished the deed with one powerful hand around the gaunt man's throat. The rest of the slaves had waited patiently until the emperor had finished the gruesome murder, and then dragged the body away.

Jagang reached down and with one meaty fist hauled the Sister to her feet by her hair. "What's this about, Ulicia?"

The woman's eyes rolled, her lips moved, and her tongue wandered aimlessly in her open mouth.

Jagang seized her by the shoulders and shook her violently. Sister Ulicia's head whipped back and forth. Kahlan thought he very well might break her neck. She wished he would; then there would be one less Sister for Kahlan to worry about.

"Excellency," Sister Armina said in a confidential tone of discreet counsel, "we need her." When the emperor glared at her, she added. "She is the player."

Jagang considered Sister Armina's words, looking none too happy about them, but not arguing, either.

"First day . . ." Sister Ulicia moaned.

Jagang pulled her a little closer. "First day what?"

"Winter . . . winter . . . winter," Sister Ulicia mumbled.

Jagang looked around, frowning at those in the room, as if asking them to explain it. One of the soldiers lifted an arm, pointing toward the doorway out of the grand tent. "It's just dawn, Excellency."

Jagang fixed him in a glare. "What?"

"Excellency, it's just dawn of the first day of winter."

Jagang let go of Sister Ulicia. She dropped heavily to the carpets that covered the floor.

He stared at the doorway. "So it is."

Outside, through the slight slit of an opening at the side of the heavy covering hung over the doorway, Kahlan could see the first streaks of color in the sky. She could also see more of the ever-present elite guard who always surrounded Jagang. None of them could see Kahlan; they were totally unaware of her presence. The special guards inside the tent, the ones who were always at hand, could see her just fine, though. Outside, with Jagang's elite guard, there would be more of those special guards. Their job was to insure that Kahlan never came out of the tent alone.

On the floor, Sister Ulicia, as if in a trance, mumbled, "One year, one year, one year."

"One year what?" Jagang yelled. Several of the closer guards flinched back.

Sister Ulicia sat up. She began rocking back and forth. "Starts over. Year starts over. Starts over. One year. It must start over."

Jagang looked up at the other Sister. "What's she gibbering about?"

Sister Armina spread her hands. "I'm not sure, Excellency."

His glare darkened. "That's a lie, Armina."

Sister Armina, a little of the color draining from her face, licked her lips. "What I meant by that, Excellency, is that the only thing I can imagine is that she must be referring to the boxes. She is the player, after all."

Jagang's mouth twisted with impatience. "But we already know that we have a year from back when Ulicia put them in play"—he flicked a hand in the direction of the towering plateau—"right after Kahlan took them from the palace up there."

"New player!" Sister Ulicia shouted, eyes closed, as if to correct him. "New player! The year starts over!"

Jagang looked genuinely surprised at her words.

Kahlan wondered how it was that the dream walker could be surprised by such a thing. For some reason, though, he seemed to be unable, at the moment anyway, to use his ability on Sister Ulicia. Unless he was simply playing a trick. Jagang didn't always reveal exactly what he knew and what he didn't know. Kahlan had never felt that he could read her mind, but she always remained cautious that he might want her to think just that. What if all the time he was reading her every thought?

Still, she just didn't believe it was so. She couldn't put her finger on any one thing that made her think that he was unable to use his ability as a dream walker on her, but rather it was an impression based on the cumulative evidence of many small little things.

"How is it possible for there to be a new player?" Jagang asked in a tone that made Sister Armina begin to tremble just the slightest bit.

She had to swallow twice before she was able to speak. "Excellency, we don't have . . . all three boxes. We have but two. There is the the third box, after all, the one that Tovi had."

"You mean the box that was stolen because you stupid bitches sent Tovi off by herself rather than having her stay with the rest of you." It was an angry charge, not a question.

Sister Armina, on the verge of panic, thrust a finger out at Kahlan. "It was her fault! If she had done as we instructed and brought all three boxes out together, we would all have been together and we would have the three boxes. But she failed to bring them all out together. It's her fault!"

Sister Ulicia had told Kahlan to hide all three boxes in her pack and bring them out. All three wouldn't fit, so she brought one out first, intending to go back for the others. Sister Ulicia had not been pleased, to say the least. She had beaten Kahlan nearly to a bloody death for failing to somehow do the impossible and fit all three in a pack that was not big enough.

Kahlan didn't bother to speak up in her own defense. She refused to lower herself to trying to reason with people who didn't abide by reason.

Jagang looked back over his shoulder at Kahlan. She met his gaze with nothing but her blank countenance. He turned back to Sister Armina.

"So what? Sister Ulicia put the boxes in play. That makes her the player."

"Another player!" Sister Ulicia shouted up from the floor between them. "Two players now! The year starts over! It's impossible!" Sister Ulicia lunged. "Impossible!"

There was nothing there and her arms caught only air.

She sat back heavily on the floor, breathing rapidly. Trembling hands covered her face, as if she was overwhelmed by what had just taken place.

Jagang turned away, lost in thought as he considered. "Can there be two people who both have the boxes in play at the same time?" he asked himself.

Sister Armina's eyes darted about. She seemed unsure if she was supposed to attempt an answer. In the end she remained silent.

Sister Ulicia rubbed her eyes. "He vanished."

Jagang frowned down at her. "Who vanished?"

"I couldn't see his face." She gestured vaguely. "He was just there, telling me, but he vanished. I don't know who it was, Excellency."

The woman looked shaken to her core.

"What did you see?" Jagang asked.

As if jolted by an unexpected sudden shock, she shot to her feet. Her eyes had gone wide with pain. Blood trickled from one ear.

"What did you see?" Jagang repeated.

Kahlan had seen him give the Sisters pain in the past. Whether or not he was able to be in Sister Ulicia's mind before, it was clear that he now had no difficulty making his presence felt.

"It was someone—" Sister Ulicia said with a gasp. "Someone who was just here, in the tent, Excellency. He told me that there was a new player, and because of that the year must start anew."

Jagang's brow was drawn down in a tight knot. "A new player for the power of Orden?"

Sister Ulicia nodded, as if fearing to admit it. "Yes, Excellency. Someone else has also put the boxes of Orden in play. We are warned that the year must start over. We now have one year from today, the first day of winter."

Looking to be deep in thought, Jagang started toward the doorway. Two of the elite guards pulled open the double hanging, allowing their emperor to walk through the opening without pause. Kahlan, knowing that if she didn't stay close at hand the pain of the collar was only an instant away, followed him out before he gave her that reminder. Behind her, Sisters Ulicia and Armina hurried to keep up.

The big men of the elite guard outside the tent casually stepped away to each side, making way for the emperor. The other soldiers—Kahlan's special guards—marched back and forth just beyond them.

Standing close behind Jagang in the cold dawn, Kahlan rubbed her arms, trying to work up some warmth. A wall of dark clouds towered to the west. Even through the stink of the encampment, she could smell the rain carried on the damp air. The thin clouds fleeing to the east were stained bloodred in the sunrise of the first day of winter.

Jagang stood silently considering the immense plateau in the distance. Atop that towering tableland was the People's Palace. While certainly a palace, it was vast almost beyond belief. It was also a city, really, a city that was the seat of power for all of D'Hara. That city stood as the last vestige of resistance to the Imperial Order's lust to rule the world and enforce their beliefs on mankind. The army of the Order spread like a poisonous black sea across the Azrith Plain around the plateau, leaving it isolated from any hope of rescue or salvation.

The first rays of light were just touching the distant palace, making the marble walls, columns, and towers glow golden in the sunrise. It was a breathtakingly beautiful sight. To all these people of the Order, though, the sight of the palace, of such beauty yet untouched by their lecherous hands, only inspired jealousy and hate. They lusted to destroy the place, to blot such majesty out of existence, to insure that man never again aspired to such merit.

Kahlan had been up in that palace—Lord Rahl's palace—when the four Sisters had taken her there to have her steal the boxes out of the Garden of Life. The splendor of the place was awe-inspiring. Kahlan had hated to take those boxes from Lord Rahl's garden. They didn't belong to the Sisters, and, worse, the Sisters were driven by evil intent.

On that altar where the boxes had sat, Kahlan left in their place her most precious possession. It was a small carving of a woman, her head thrown back, her fists at her sides, her back arched as if opposition to a force trying to subdue her Kahlan could not imagine where she would have gotten such a beautiful thing.

She was heartbroken to have to leave that carving behind, but she had to in order to fit the last two boxes in her pack. Had she not, Sister Ulicia would have killed her. As much as she loved that small statue, she loved her life more. She hoped that Lord Rahl, when he saw it, would somehow understand that she was sorry for taking what was his.

Now Jagang had captured the Sisters and he had possession of the sinister black boxes. Two of them, anyway. Sister Tovi had started ahead with the first of the three boxes. Now she was dead and the box she'd had was missing. Kahlan had killed Sister Cecilia. That left Sisters Ulicia and Armina, out of her four original captors. Of course, Jagang had other Sisters under his control.

"Who could put a box in play?" Jagang asked as he stared off toward the palace atop the plateau. It wasn't entirely clear if he was asking the Sisters for an answer, or if he was merely thinking out loud.

Sisters Ulicia and Armina shared a look. The elite guards

stood like stone sentinels. The special guards marched slowly back and forth, the closest one taking note of Kahlan, giving her a superior, smug glance each time he turned to march in the opposite direction. Kahlan knew the man, knew his habits. He was one of her less intelligent guards, substituting arrogance for competence.

"Well," Sister Ulicia finally said into the uneasy silence, "it would take someone with both sides of the gift—both Additive and Subtractive Magic."

"Other than the Sisters of the Dark you have here, Excellency," Sister Armina added, "I'm not sure who could accomplish such a task."

Jagang shot a look back over his shoulder. The soldier was not the only one who foolishly harbored an attitude of arrogant superiority. Jagang was a lot smarter than Sister Armina; she just wasn't smart enough to know it. She was, however, smart enough to recognize the look in Jagang's eyes, the look that said he knew she was lying. She quailed, momentarily struck silent by the emperor's glare.

Sister Ulicia, also a great deal smarter than Sister Armina, quickly recognized the danger of the situation and spoke up.

"There are only a couple of people it could be, Excellency."

"It had to have been Richard Rahl," Sister Armina was quick to put in, eager to redeem herself.

"Richard Rahl," Jagang repeated in a flat tone of cold hatred. He didn't sound the least bit surprised by the Sister's suggestion.

Sister Ulicia cleared her throat. "Or Sister Nicci. She is the only Sister you don't have who is able to wield Subtractive Magic."

Jagang's glare fixed on her for a moment before he finally turned back to consider the People's Palace, now lit by the sun so that it glowed like a beacon above the dark plain.

"Sister Nicci knows everything you stupid bitches did," he finally announced.

Sister Armina blinked in surprise. She couldn't resist speaking. "How is that possible, Excellency?"

Jagang clasped his meaty hands behind his back. His heavily

muscled back and neck looked more like those of a bull than those of a man. Curly black body hair only added to the impression. His shaved head made him look all the more menacing.

"Nicci was there with Tovi when she was dying," Jagang said, "after she had been stabbed and the box stolen from her. It had been a very long time since I'd seen Nicci. I was surprised to see her show up out of the blue. I was there, in Tovi's mind, watching the whole thing. Tovi didn't know I was in her mind, though, the same as you two didn't know.

"Nicci didn't know I was there, either.

"Nicci questioned Tovi, used the woman's grievous wound to prod her into revealing your plan, Ulicia. Nicci told Tovi quite the story about wishing she could escape my control and with that lie gained Tovi's confidence. Tovi told her everything—everything about the Chainfire spell you ignited, the boxes you stole with Kahlan's help, how the boxes were meant to work in conjunction with the Chainfire spell, all of it."

Sister Ulicia was looking sicker by the moment. "Then it very well could be Nicci who did this. It has to be one or the other."

"Or Nicci and Richard Rahl together," Sister Armina suggested.

Jagang said nothing as he stared off at the palace.

Sister Ulicia leaned forward the slightest bit. "If I may ask, Excellency, why is it that you are unable to . . . well, why is Nicci not here, with you?"

Jagang's completely black eyes turned to the woman. Cloudy shapes shifted in those inky eyes, a storm of his own brewing.

"She was with me. She left. Unlike your clumsy and insincere attempt at trying to shield your minds from me with the bond to the Lord Rahl, the bond worked for Nicci. For reasons I can't begin to understand she was sincere, and so it worked. She gave up everything she had worked for her whole life—gave up her moral duty!"

He rolled his shoulders, pulling the mantle of calm authority back around himself. "The bond worked for Nicci. I can no longer enter her mind."

Sister Armina stood frozen in more than simple fear of the man; she was obviously baffled by what she'd just heard.

Sister Ulicia nodded to herself, staring off into memories. "I guess that, in retrospect, it's not a surprise. I guess I always knew that she loved Richard. She never said a word tous, of course, to the other Sisters of the Dark, but back at the Palace of the Prophets she gave up a great deal—things I would never have imagined her giving up—in exchange for me naming her to be one of his six teachers.

"The price she paid for that chance to be his teacher made me suspicious of her motives. A couple of the others were driven by greed. They simply wanted to suck the gift out of that man—have it for themselves. But not Nicci. That wasn't what she was after. So I watched her.

"She never gave it away—dear spirits, I don't think she was even aware of it herself at the time—but there was a look in her eyes. She was in love with him. I never really understood that look back then, probably because she seemed so sure of her hatred for the man and for all that he represented, but she was in love with Richard Rahl. Even back then, she was in love with him."

Jagang had gone crimson. Absorbed in her recollections, Sister Ulicia hadn't noticed his mute rage. Sister Armina surreptitiously touched the other woman's arm in warning. Sister Ulicia looked up and blanched at seeing the look on the emperor's face, and immediately changed the subject.

"Like I said, she never said any such thing, so perhaps I'm just imagining it. In fact, now that I think about it, I'm sure of it. She hated the man. She wanted him dead. She hated everything he represented. She hated him. Plain as day. She hated him."

Sister Ulicia closed her mouth, visibly forcing herself to stop babbling.

"I gave her everything." Jagang's voice rumbled like bottled thunder. "I made her as good as a queen. As Jagang the Just, I granted her the authority to be the fist of the Fellowship of Order. Those who opposed the righteous ways of the Order came to know her as Death's Mistress. She was able to fulfill that virtuous call to duty only because of my generosity. I was foolish to have given her so much latitude. She betrayed me. Betrayed me for him."

Kahlan didn't think that she would ever see Jagang in the grip of hot jealousy, but she was seeing it now. He was a man who took what he wanted. He was not used to being denied anything. Apparently, he couldn't have this woman Nicci. Apparently, Richard Rahl had her heart.

Kahlan swallowed back her own confused feelings over Richard Rahl—a man she had never met—and stared at her guards marching back and forth.

"But I'll have her back." Jagang held up a fist. Muscled cords stood out on his arms as the fist tightened. Veins in his temples bulged. "Sooner or later I will crush the immoral resistance offered by Richard Rahl, and then I'll deal with Nicci. She will pay for her sinful ways."

Kahlan and this Nicci had somethig in common. If Jagang ever got his hands on Nicci, Kahlan knew, he was going to do his worst to her as well.

"And the boxes of Orden, Excellency?" Sister Ulicia asked.

The arm dropped. He turned a grim smile on her. "Darlin, it doesn't matter if one of them has somehow managed to put the boxes of Orden in play. It will do them no good." He pointed a thumb back over his shoulder at Kahlan. "I have her. I have what we need to put the power of Orden to use for the cause of the Fellowship of Order.

"We have right on our side. The Creator is on our side. When we unleash the power of Orden we will wipe the blasphemy of magic from the world. We will make all men bow down before the teachings of the Order. All men will submit to divine justice and be of one faith.

"It will be a new dawn for mankind, the dawn of the age of man without magic to taint men's souls. All men will rejoice to be part of the glory that is the cause of the Order. In that new world of man, all men will be equal. All men can then dedicate themselves in service to their fellow man, as is the will of the Creator."

"Yes, Excellency," Sister Armina said, eager to find an opening to worm her way back into his favor.

"Excellency," Sister Ulicia ventured, "as I've explained before, while we may have many of the elements needed, as you have so rightly pointed out, we must still have all three boxes if we are to accomplish the goal of accessing the power of Orden for the cause of the Fellowship of Order. We still need that third box."

His grisly grin returned. "As I told you, I was there in Tovi's mind. I may have an idea about who was involved in taking it."

Sisters Ulicia and Armina looked not only surprised, but curious.

"You do, Excellency?" Sister Armina asked.

He nodded. "My spiritual advisor Brother Narev had a friend he had dealings with from time to time. I suspect she might be involved."

Sister Ulicia looked skeptical. "You think a friend of the Fellowship of Order might have been involved?"

"No, I didn't say a friend of the Fellowship. I said a friend of Brother Narev. A woman I, too, have had occasional dealings with in the past on Brother Narev's behalf. I think you may have heard of her." Jagang arched an eyebrow at the woman. "She goes by the name of Six."

Sister Armina gasped and went stiff.

Sister Ulicia's eyes widened and her jaw dropped. "Six . . . Excellency, surely you don't mean Six, the witch woman?"

Jagang looked pleased by the reaction. "Ah, so you know her."

"I had occasion to cross paths with her once. We had a talk, of sorts. It was not what I would describe as a pleasant conversation. Excellency, no one can deal with that woman."

"Well, you see, Ulicia, that's just one more are where you and I differ. You have nothing of value to offer her but your boneless carcass to feed to those with a taste for human flesh she keeps back in her lair. I, on the other hand, have a pretty good grasp on what the woman needs and wants. I'm in a position to grant her the kinds of indulgences she seeks. Unlike you, Ulicia, I can deal with her."

"But if Richard Rahl or Nicci put the box in play, that can only mean that they are now in possession of it," Sister Ulicia said. "So, even if Six really did once have the box after Tovi, it's now out of her grasp."

"So you think such a woman will abandon her burning desires? All the things she lusts after?" Jagang shook his head. "No, it will not sit well with Six that her plans were . . . interrupted. Six is a woman who will not be denied. She does not treat very kindly anyone who gets in her way. Am I correct, Ulicia?"

Sister Ulicia swallowed before nodding.

"I expect that a woman of her dark talents and boundless determination will not rest until she has corrected the injustice, and then she will have to deal with the Order. So, you see, I think everything is well in hand. That one of those two criminals, Nicci or Richard Rahl, put that box in play will mean nothing in the end. The Order will prevail."

Sister Ulicia, her fingers folded tightly together to stop them from trembling ever since she first heard the name Six, bowed her head. "Yes, Excellency. I can see that you do indeed have everything well in hand."

Jagang, seeing her defeated demeanor, snapped his fingers as he turned his attention toward one of the shirtless slaves standing back near the entrance to the royal tent.

"I'm hungry. The Ja'La tournaments start today. I want a hearty meal before going to watch the games."

The man bowed deeply from the waist. "Yes, Excellency. I will see to it at once."

After he'd run off to see to the task, Jagang gazed out over the sea of men. "For now, our brave fighters need a diversion from the difficult work. One of the teams out there will eventually win a chance to play my own team. Let's hope the team that eventually wins the right to play my team is good enough to at least make my men break a sweat in beating them."

"Yes, Excellency," the Sisters said together.

Jagang, looking annoyed by their groveling, gestured to one of the special guards as the man marched by.

"She's going to kill you first."

The man froze, panic in his eyes. "Excellency?"

Jagang tilted his head to indicate Kahlan only a half step behind him and to his right. "She's going to kill you first, and you deserve it."

The man dipped his head deferentially. "I don't understand, Excellency."

"Of course you don't—you're stupid. She's been counting your steps. You take the same number of paces each time before you turn to march in the opposite direction. Each time you turn you look to check on her, then march away.

"She's counted your paces. When it's time for you to turn, she doesn't have to be looking in your direction because she knows exactly when you will turn. She knows that just before you turn, you'll check on her and see her looking the other way. That will put you at ease.

"When you march up to us from the right and turn, you pivot the same way each time—to your right. Each time you turn, the knife on your belt at your right hip is on the side closest to her."

The man looked down at the knife on his belt. He covered it protectively with a hand. "But Excellency, I wouldn't let her get my knife. I swear. I would stop her."

"Stop her?" Jagang snorted a brief laugh. "She knows that she is but two strides from the spot where you turn, two strides from snatching your knife right out of its sheath." He snapped his fingers. "Quick as that, she'll have your knife. You probably won't even realize it before you die."

"But I would—"

"You will look to check on her, see her looking in another direction, and then turn. By the time you've taken your third step, she will have your knife. It will then be but an instant before she rams the entire length of the blade into your tender right kidney. You'll be as good as dead before you know what hit you."

Despite the cold, sweat beaded on the man's forehead.

Jagang glanced back at Kahlan. She showed him only a blank expression devoid of any emotion.

Jagang was wrong. The man would die second. He was stupid, just as Jagang had said. Stupid men were easier to kill. It was harder to kill smart, attentive men. Kahlan knew each of her special guards. She made it her business to learn everything she could about each one of them. The other man marching before the tent was one of the smartest among her special guard.

Wherever she was, she always analyzed the situation and envisioned how she would implement an attempt to escape. This was not the time, or place, but she still had thought it through.

She wouldn't kill the stupid one first, but she would take his knife, just as Jagang had said. Then she would turn to the smart one because he was more watchful and his reactions were far quicker. The special guards' task was to prevent her from escaping; they weren't supposed to use lethal force against her. When the smart one came at her to tackle her, she would already have the knife and would use their closing momentum as she spun toward him to slash his throat. She would sidestep his falling dead weight to his left side, spin, and plunge the knife into the kidney of the stupid fellow, just as Jagang had suggested.

"You have me dead to rights," Kahlan told the emperor in a flat tone. "Well done."

His left eye twitched just the slightest bit. He didn't know if she was telling the truth, or lying.

CHAPTER 4

Do you know the consequences of breaking the seal on those doors?" Cara asked.

Zedd looked back over his shoulder at the woman. "Need I remind you that I am First Wizard?"

Cara returned the glare in kind. "Well, excuse me. Do you know the consequences of breaking the seal on those doors, First Wizard Zorander?"

Zedd straightened. "That's not what I meant."

The woman was still glaring. "You haven't answered my question."

If there was one thing that was consistent about Mord-Sith, it was that they didn't like it when they asked questions and got evasive answers. They didn't like it one bit. It made them surly. As a rule Zedd considered it wise not to give Mord-Sith cause to be surly, but then, he didn't like being pestered when he was doing something important. That made him surly.

"Why does Richard put up with you, anyway?"

Cara's glare only deepened. "I have never offered Lord Rahl a choice. Now, answer my question. Do you know the consequences of breaking the seal on those doors?"

Zedd planted his fists on his hips. "Don't you suppose that I know a thing of two about magic?"

"I would have thought so, but I'm beginning to have my doubts."

"Oh, so you think you know more about it than I do?"

"I know that magic is trouble. It would seem that in this instance I very well might know more about it than you. I know better than to go barging through a seal of this kind.

Nicci would only have shielded this door for a good reason. I don't think it's too awfully wise, *First Wizard*, to go barging through her shield without knowing why it's there."

"Well, I think I know a thing or two about seals and shields and such."

Cara arched an eyebrow. "Zedd, Nicci can wield Subtractive Magic."

Zedd glanced at the door, then looked back at Cara. The way she was leaning over him he thought she very well might seize him by his collar and haul him back from the brass-clad doors if she decided that she had to.

"I suppose you have a point." He held up a finger. "But on the other hand I can sense that something serious is going on in there—something altogether ominous."

Cara sighed and finally withdrew her blue-eyed Mord-Sith glare. She straightened, drawing her long blond braid through her loose fist as she checked the hallway to both sides.

She tossed the braid back over her shoulder. "I don't know, Zedd. If I was in a room and had locked the door it would be for good reason and I'd not like you to pick the lock. Nicci wouldn't allow me to stay with her—and she's never asked that I leave her alone like that before. I didn't want to let her go in there by herself, but she insisted.

"She was in one of those spooky, quiet moods of hers. She's been like that a lot lately."

Zedd sighed. "That she has. But not without good reason. Dear spirits, Cara, we've all been in a mood lately, and we all have good reason."

Cara nodded. "Nicci said she needed to be alone. I told her I didn't care and that I intended to stay with her.

"I don't know what it is about her, but sometimes when she says to do something you all of a sudden find yourself doing it. Lord Rahl is the same way. I don't often pay a great deal of attention to his orders—after all, I know better than he does how to protect him—but sometimes he says something in that way he has and you just find yourself doing as he asked. I never know how he manages to do it. Nicci is the same way. They both have the odd ability to make you do things you have no intention of doing—and they don't even raise their voices.

"Nicci said that it involved magic—said it in a way that made it clear she wanted to be alone. The next thing I know, I'd told her that I would wait out here in case she needed anything."

Zedd tilted his head toward the woman, giving her a look from under his bushy brow. "I believe this has something to do with Richard."

Her Mord-Sith glare returned in an instant. Zedd could see her muscles tighten beneath her red leather.

"What do you mean?"

"Like you said, she was acting pretty strange. She asked me if I trusted everyone's life to Richard."

Cara stared at him a moment. "She asked me that very same thing."

"That's been eating at me, making me wonder what she meant." Zedd waggled a long finger back toward the door. "Cara, she's in there with that thing—with that box of Orden. I can sense it."

Cara nodded. "Well, you're right about that. I saw it in there just before she closed the door."

Zedd pushed a stray wave of white hair back from his face. "That's part of the reason I think this has something to do with Richard. Cara, I don't go through this kind of seal lightly, but I think this is important."

Cara sighed in resignation. "All right." Her mouth twisted with the displeasure of agreeing to his plan. "If she bites your head off I suppose I can always sew it back on for you."

Zedd smiled as he pushed his sleeves up his arms. Taking a deep breath, he hunched back to the business of unknotting the seal Nicci had woven with magic around the lever.

The immense, brass-clad doors were covered with engraved symbols that were specific to the containment field in that part of the Keep. Such a place was already hardened against tampering and shielded against casual entry, but he had grown up in the Keep and knew how various elements of the place functioned. He also knew a great many of the tricks associated with those elements. This particular field was tricky because, being a containment field for what might be inside, it was double-sided.

He gently glided the first three fingers of his left hand over the area of convergence. It made the nerve in his left arm tingle up to his elbow—not a good sign. Nicci had added something to the shield, making a personal shield out of something that had been generic. Zedd was beginning to think that Cara knew more than he had given her credit for.

This was a shield that seemed to respond in a unique way to the application of force. He paused a moment to consider. He would have to achieve what he wanted without applying force that would invoke that reaction. He carefully slipped a thin thread of innocent nothing through the snarl. With his right hand he eased the tangled restriction of power so that the whole thing would begin to loosen.

He knew all too well that it would do no good to simply try to break through the seal, because the containment field was constructed in such a way that force only caused it to lock tighter. Nicci had apparently added multipliers to that quality. If he applied too much force the shield would simply tighten, like pulling the ends of a knotted rope tighter. If that happened, he would never get it undone.

Besides that, Cara was right—Nicci had Subtractive Magic and there was no telling what elements of such sinister power she might have woven into the matrix to prevent the inner seal from being breached. He would not like to force his hand through the keyhole, so to speak, only to discover he had plunged it right into a cauldron of molten lead. Much less risky to untie the knot of magic than try to rip it apart.

Such difficulties only made Zedd all the more determined that he was going to find a way to get through. It was a personal trait of his that had in the distant past made his father surly—especially if it had been a shield that Zedd's father had constructed specifically to keep out his inquisitive son.

Zedd's tongue poked out the left corner of his mouth as he worked at threading his way through the fabric of the shield. He was already farther in than he had expected to get so quickly.

He extended the invisible probe of power through the inner workings so that he could control it from inside.

And then, even though he was being careful beyond all reason, the weave of the shield tightened, neatly snapping off the foray of magic. It was as if it had maneuvered him into an ambush.

Zedd stood hunched before the brass-clad doors, surprised that a shield would have been able to react in that way. He was, after all, not yet trying to breach it, but merely to probe its inner workings—having a look in the keyhole, as it were.

He had done the very same thing any number of times before. It always worked. It should have worked. It was the most confounding shield he had ever encountered.

He was still bent over the lever, considering his next move, when the door opened inward.

Zedd turned his head a little, peering up. Nicci, one hand on the inner lever, the other at her side, towered over him.

"Did you ever think of knocking?" she asked.

Zedd straightened, hoping his face wasn't going red but suspecting it had. "Well, actually, I did consider it, but then I discounted the idea. I thought you might have been working late on that book and might be asleep. I didn't want to disturb you."

Her blond hair was tumbled down over the shoulders of her black dress, a dress that hugged every curve of her perfect shape. Even though she looked as if she hadn't slept a wink all night, her blue eyes were as penetrating as those of any sorceress he had ever met. The combination of her alluring beauty, aloof dignity, and keen intellect—to say nothing of the fact that she possessed enough power to turn just about anyone to ash—was both disarming and intimidating.

"If I had been asleep," Nicci said in that calm, silken voice of hers, "then just how was breaking through a containment field that was buffered with a shield conjured from instructions in a three-thousand-year-old book and spiked with Subtractive counterlocks not going to wake me?"

Zedd's level of alarm rose. Such shields were not constructed lightly, nor for a private nap.

He spread his hands. "I only meant to have a peek to check up on you."

Her cool gaze was making him start to sweat. "I spent a very long time at the Palace of the Prophets teaching boy wizards how to behave themselves and school their powers. I know how to make shields that can't be picked. As a Sister of the Dark I've had a great deal of practice at it."

"Really? I'd be quite interested to learn about such arcane shields—from a strictly professional perspective, of course. Such things are rather a . . . hobby of mine."

She still had a hand on the door lever. "What is it you want, Zedd?"

Zedd cleared his throat. "Well, quite honestly, Nicci, I was worried about what might be going on in there with that box."

Nicci finally smiled just the slightest bit. "Ah. Somehow I didn't think you were hoping to catch me cavorting naked."

She stepped back into the library, implying permission to enter.

It was an immense room, with two-story-high round-top windows running the entire length of the far wall. Heavy dark green velvet draperies with gold fringe along with two-story polished mahogany columns rose up between each of the windows, each of those made of hundreds of thick squares of glass. Even the dawn light flooding in through those windows wasn't enough to banish the somber atmosphere from the room.

Some of the panes of refractory glass making up the windows that were part of the containment field in this section of the Keep had been broken in an unexpected battle back when Richard had been there. Nicci had invited lightning in through those windows to obliterate the underworld beast that had attacked Richard. Asked how she had been able to coax lightning to do her bidding, she had shrugged and said simply that she had created a void that the lightning needed to fill, so it had been compelled to do so. Zedd understood the principle, he just couldn't imagine how it could be accomplished.

While grateful that she had saved Richard's life, Zedd had not been pleased that such valuable and irreplaceable glass had been destroyed, leaving the containment field breached. Nicci had offered to help with the repairs. Zedd wouldn't have known how to accomplish such a thing by himself. He wouldn't have thought that there was anyone alive who would have known how to bend forces in the way she had done, or who would have had the required power to do so. Who would ever have thought that there would be anyone alive who could re-create the glass in those windows? And yet she had.

It had put Zedd in mind of nothing so much as a queen come down to the royal kitchens to deftly demonstrate how to make a rare bread with a long-forgotten recipe.

While Zedd had known some very powerful sorceresses, he had never known any who were the equal of Nicci. Some of the things she could do with seeming ease were so confounding that it left him speechless.

Of course, Nicci was far more than a mere sorceress. As a former Sister of the Dark she knew how to command Subtractive Magic. As a Sister of the Dark, she would have taken the power from a wizard and added it to her own, creating something altogether unique—not something he liked to contemplate.

To a certain extent she frightened him. Without Richard to show her the value of her own life she would still be devoted to the cause of the Order. With so much of her life a mystery to him, with all that she had done but never spoke of, with all that she had once been a part of, Zedd wasn't entirely sure of how far he could trust her.

Richard trusted her, though—trusted her with his life. She had proven worthy of that trust on numerous occasions. Other than himself and Cara, Zedd didn't know anyone as fiercely devoted to Richard as Nicci. Nicci would without question or a second thought go to the underworld itself if she had to in order to save him.

Richard had brought this remarkable woman back from the depths of evil, just as he had done with Cara and the other Mord-Sith. Who but Richard could accomplish such a thing? Who but Richard could even think to do such a thing?

How Zedd missed that boy.

Nicci glided back into the library, and Zedd saw, then, what was on the table. His ability had told him that it was there, but his ability had not told him what more there was to it.

Behind him, Cara let out a low whistle. Zedd sympathized with the sentiment.

The box of Orden, sitting atop one of the massive library tables, absent the decorative covering that once had contained it, was a bewitching black that seemed as if it might suck the light right out of the dawn, a black so black it almost appeared as if the box itself was nothing so much as a void in the world of life. Staring at it felt uncomfortably like looking right into the underworld, the world of the dead.

But it was the containment spell that had been drawn all around the box that had him alarmed. It had been drawn in blood. There were other charms, other spells, drawn on the tabletop, and they, too, were drawn in blood.

Zedd recognized some of the elements of the diagrams. He didn't know of anyone living who could have drawn such charms. Such things were not entirely stable, making them dangerous beyond belief. Any number of spells could kill in an instant if done improperly. These spells, drawn in blood no less, were among the most perilous spells in existence. Employing them successfully was not something Zedd himself, with a lifetime of knowledge, training, and practice, would ever consider attempting.

Zedd had seen such terrible spells drawn only once before. Those had been drawn by Darken Rahl—Richard's father—when Darken Rahl had been completing the conjuring involved in opening the boxes of Orden. Opening one of the boxes had cost him his life.

Around the box itself, in midair, lines of green and amber light traced yet more spells through space. They were somewhat reminiscent of the glowing green lines of the verification web they had done for the Chainfire spell in that very room, but this structure of three-dimensional formulas was materially different. And these glowing lines pulsed as if alive. He supposed that made sense. The power of Orden was the power of life itself.

Other lines, connected to intersections of the green and, in places, amber light, were as black as the box. Peering at them was like looking through slits into death itself. Subtractive Magic had been mingled with Additive to create a network of power the likes of which Zedd had never imagined he would see in his lifetime.

The whole web of light and darkness hung in space.

The box of Orden itself sat in the center of that web, like a fat black spider.

The Book of Life lay open nearby.

"Nicci," Zedd managed with only the greatest of difficulty, "what in the name of Creation have you done?"

When she reached the table, Nicci turned back and stared at him for an uncomfortably long moment.

"I have done nothing in the name of Creation. I have done it in the name of Richard Rahl."

Zedd pulled his gaze away from the terrible thing within the glowing lines to stare at her. He was having difficulty drawing a breath.

"Nicci, what have you done?"

"The only thing I could do. The thing that had to be done. The thing that only I could do."

The confluence of both sides of the gift holding the box of Orden within its glowing web was beyond imagining. It was the stuff of nightmares.

Zedd chose his words carefully. "Are you suggesting that you believe that you can put that box in play?"

The manner in which she slowly shook her head tightened his chest with dread. Her blue-eyed gaze riveted him in place.

"I have already put it in play."

Zedd felt as if the floor might come apart under him and he might never stop falling. He wondered for just an instant if any of this was real. The whole room seemed to be swirling around him. His legs felt wobbly.

Cara's hand came up under his arm to steady him.

"Are you out of you mind?" he asked, the heat rising in his voice as his legs stiffened.

"Zedd . . ." She took a step closer. "I had to."

He couldn't even make himself blink. "You had to? You *had* to?"

"Yes. I had to. It's the only way."

"The only way for what! The only way to end the world? The only way to destroy life itself?"

"No. The only way to give us a chance to survive. You know what the world is coming to. You know what the Imperial Order is going to do—what they are on the verge of doing. The world is at the brink. Mankind is staring into a thousand years of darkness at best. At worst, mankind may never again emerge into the light.

"You know that we are approaching paths in prophecy beyond which everything goes dark. Nathan has told you of those branches leading to a great void beyond which there is nothing. We stand staring into that void."

"And have you ever thought that what you have just done very well might be the cause of it—the very thing that takes mankind, all life, into that void of extinction?"

"Sister Ulicia has already put the boxes of Orden in play. Do you think she and her Sisters of the Dark care about life? They work to unleash the Keeper of the underworld. If she succeeds, the world of life is doomed. You know what the boxes are, you know their power, you know what will happen if she is the one to rule the power of Orden."

"But that doesn't mean—"

"We have no choice." Her gaze didn't waver. "I had to."

"And do you have any idea how to invoke Orden? How to command the boxes? How to know the correct box?"

"No, not yet," she admitted.

"You don't even have the other two!"

"We have a year to get them," she said with calm determination. "We have a year from the first day of winter. A year from today."

Zedd lifted his hands in fury and frustration. "Even if we could find them, you think that you would somehow be able to command the power of Orden? You think you can wield the power of Orden?"

"Not me," she said in a near whisper.

Zedd cocked his head, unsure he had actually heard what he thought he'd heard. His suspicion flared into hot dread.

"What do you mean, not you? You just said that you put the boxes in play."

Nicci stepped closer. She laid a hand gently on his forearm. "When I opened the gateway I was asked to name the player. I named Richard. I put the boxes of Orden in play on behalf of Richard."

Zedd stood thunderstruck.

He wanted to strike her dead.

He wanted to strangle her. He wanted to rip her limb from limb.

"You named Richard?"

She nodded. "It was the only way."

Zedd ran the fingers of both hands back into his unruly thatch of wavy white hair, holding his head for fear it might come apart.

"The only way? Bags, woman! Are you out of your mind?"

"Zedd, calm down. I know it's a surprise, but this is hardly a whim. I've thought it through. Believe me, I've thought it all through. If we are to survive, if those who care about life are to survive, if there is to be a chance for life, if there is to be a chance for a future, then this is the only way."

Zedd dropped heavily into one of the chairs at the table. Before he did something beyond retrieval, before he reacted out of blind rage, he told himself that he must keep his head. He tried to touch on all he knew about the boxes and what was happening, tried to remind himself of all the desperate things he'd had to do in his life. He tried to see it from her perspective.

He couldn't.

"Nicci, Richard doesn't know how to use his gift."

"He will have to find a way."

"He doesn't know anything about the boxes of Orden!"

"We will have to teach him."

"We don't know enough about the boxes of Orden. We don't know for sure which is the correct *Book of Counted Shadows*. Only the correct book works as the key to the boxes!"

"We will have to sort that out."

"Dear spirits, Nicci, we don't even know where Richard is!"

"We know that the witch woman tried to capture him in the sliph and failed. We know from what Rachel told us that Six apparently cut Richard off from his gift by drawing spells in the sacred caves in Tamarang. Rachel says that Six lost him when he was captured by the Imperial Order. For all we know, by now he may have escaped them as well and be on his way here. If not, we will have to find him."

Zedd couldn't seem to find a way to make her see and understand all that stood in their way. "What you're suggesting is impossible!"

She smiled then, a sad smile. "A wizard I know and respect, a wizard who taught Richard to be the man he is, also taught him to think of the solution, not the problem. Such advice has always served him well."

Zedd was having none of it. He shot to his feet. "You had no right to do such a thing, Nicci. You have no right to decide this for his life. You had no right to name Richard to this!"

Her smile vanished to reveal the iron beneath. "I know Richard. I know how he fights for life. I know what it means to him. I know that there is nothing he would not do to preserve the value of life. I know that if he knew all the things I know, he would have wanted me to do as I have done."

"Nicci, you don't—"

"Zedd," she said in a commanding tone of voice that cut him off. "I asked you if you trusted Richard with your life, with all life. You said that you did. Those words have meaning. You did not hem and haw, qualifying the bounds of your trust. Trusting someone with your life is as unequivocal as trust can be.

"Richard is the only one who can lead us in the final battle. While Jagang and the Order might be part of it, the battle over the power of Orden *is* the final battle. The Sisters of the Dark who command those boxes will make it so. One way or another, they will make sure of it. The only way Richard can lead us is for him to have the boxes in play. In that way, he truly is the fulfillment of prophecy: *fuer grissa ost drauka*—the bringer of death.

"But this is more than prophecy. Prophecy only expresses what we already know, that Richard is the one who has been leading us in defending the values we hold dear, the values that promote life.

"Richard himself named the terms of the engagement when he spoke to the D'Haran troops. As the Lord Rahl, the leader of the D'Haran Empire, he told those men how the war would be fought from now on: All or nothing.

"This can be no different. Richard is true to the core and would not expect everyone else to do what he himself would not do. He is the heart of all we believe. He would not betray us.

"We are now in it all the way. It now truly is all or nothing."

Zedd threw his arms up. "But naming Richard the player is not the only way he can lead this battle, not the only way for him to succeed—but it very well might instead be the cause of him failing. What you have done could lead us all to ruin."

Nicci's blue eyes filled with the kind of conviction, resolve, and rage that told him she might reduce him to ash if he stood in the way of what she believed was necessary. For the first time he was seeing Death's Mistress as those who stood in her way, stood before her full fury, saw her.

"Your love for your grandson is blinding you. He is more than your grandson."

"My love for him doesn't—"

Nicci thrust an arm out to point to the east, toward D'Hara. "Those Sisters of the Dark ignited the Chainfire event! Chainfire is burning unchecked through all of our memories. Such an event means far more than simply losing our memory of Kahlan.

"Who we are, what we are, what we can be, is moment by moment disintegrating. It's not just about forgetting Kahlan. The vortex of that spell grows daily. The damage is multiplying on itself. We are unaware of the full extent of all we have lost already while day by day we lose yet more. Our very minds, or ability to think, to reason, are being eroded by that vile spell.

"Worse, the Chainfire spell is contaminated. Richard himself showed it to us. The contamination of the chimes is buried deep within the Chainfire spell that has infected everyone. The contamination carried by the Chainfire spell is burning through the world of life. Besides destroying the nature of who and what we are, it's destroying the fabric of magic itself. Without Richard we wouldn't even be aware of it.

"The world not only stands at the brink due to Jagang and the Imperial Order, but it is being destroyed by the silent, unseen work of the Chainfire spell and the contamination within it."

Nicci jabbed a finger at her temple. "Has that contamination already destroyed your ability to see what is at stake? Has it already taken your ability to think?

"The only counter to the Chainfire event is the boxes of Orden. That is the reason the boxes were created—they were created specifically as the only salvation should the Chainfire event ever be ignited.

"Those Sisters ignited Chainfire. To compound what they did, to make it irreversible, they themselves put the boxes in play, put the counter in play, naming themselves as the player. They believe that there is now no way for anyone to stop them. They may be right. I've read *The Book of Life*, the instructions for how Orden functions. It provides no way to halt the play once initiated. We can't shut down Chainfire. We can't halt the play of Orden. The world of life is about to spin out of control—just as they want.

"What is Richard fighting for? What are we all fighting for? Should we simply give up, say that it's too hard, too risky to try to prevent our total annihilation? Should we shrink from the only chance we have? Shall we surrender everything that matters? Should we let Jagang slaughter all those who wish to be free? Let the Fellowship of order enslave the world? Allow Chainfire to run rampant and destroy our memory of everything good? Let the contamination within that spell wipe magic from the world along with everything that depends on it for life? Shall we just sit down and give up? Shall we let the world end at the hands of people who would destroy it all?

"Sister Ulicia opened the gateway to the power of Orden. She put the boxes in play. What is Richard supposed to do? He has to have the weapons he needs to fight this battle. I have just given him what he needs.

"The struggle is now truly in balance. The two sides of this battle are now fully engaged in the struggle that will decide it all.

"We have to trust Richard in this struggle.

"There was a time a few years back when you were faced with similar decisions. You knew your choices, your responsibilities, the risks, and the lethal consequences of inaction. You named Richard the Seeker of Truth."

Zedd nodded, hardly able to summon his voice. "Yes, I did indeed."

"And he lived up to everything you believed of him, and more, didn't he?"

He couldn't make himself stop trembling. "Yes, the boy did all I ever expected and more."

"This is no different, Zedd. The Sisters of the Dark no longer have exclusive access to the power of Orden." She brought an arm up and made a fist. "I have given Richard a chance—I have given us all a chance. In that sense, I have just put Richard into play, giving him what he must have to win this struggle."

Through his watery vision Zedd gazed into her eyes. Besides the resolve, the fury, the determination, there was something else. He saw there in her blue eyes a shadow of pain.

"And . . . ?"

She drew back. "And what?"

"As complete as your rationale has been, there is something more to this, something that you have not said."

Nicci turned away, the fingers of one hand trailing along the tabletop, trailing through spells drawn in her own blood, spells she had risked her life to invoke.

Her back to him, Nicci gestured vaguely, a self-conscious flick of her hand, a simple motion gracefully betraying unimaginable anguish.

"You're right," she said in a voice on the ragged edge of control. "I have given Richard one other thing."

Zedd stood for a moment, considering the woman turned away from him. "And what would that be?"

She turned back. A tear traced a slow path down her cheek.

"I have just given him the only chance he has of getting back the woman he loves. The boxes of Orden are the only counter to the Chainfire spell that took Kahlan from him. If he is to have her back, the boxes of Orden are the only way.

"I have given him the only chance he has to have what he loves most in life."

Zedd sank back down in the chair and put his face in his hands.

CHAPTER 5

Nicci stood, her back stiff and straight, as Zedd, slumped in the chair before her, wept into his hands.

She had locked her knees for fear that her legs would give way beneath her. She told herself that she would not allow a single tear to escape her control.

She had almost succeeded.

When she had invoked the power of Orden, putting the box in play in Richard's name, that power had done something to her. It had, to a degree, countered the damage of the Chainfire spell infecting her.

When Nicci named Richard the player, completing the links to the power she had invoked, Nicci had suddenly known Kahlan.

It was not a rebuilding of her lost memory of Kahlan—that was gone—but rather it was a simple reconnection to the awareness of the reality of Kahlan's existence, to the here and now.

For ages, it seemed, Nicci had thought that Richard was deluded in his belief in the existence of a woman no one but he remembered. Even later, when Richard had found the Chainfire book and had proven to them what had really happened, Nicci had at last believed him, but she had based that belief only on her belief in Richard and the facts he had uncovered. It was an intellectual conviction based on indirect evidence alone.

That conviction had no basis in her own memories or perceptions. She had no personal recollection of Kahlan, only Richard's memory to go on, his word, and the evidence at hand. In that secondhand manner she believed in the existence of this woman, Kahlan, because she believed Richard.

But now Nicci knew—really knew—that Kahlan was real.

Nicci still had no memory of anything about the woman, but she viscerally knew that Kahlan was real, that she existed. She no longer needed to rely on Richard's word to know it. It was self-evident, almost as if she perceived it directly. It was somewhat like remembering meeting someone in the past but not being able to remember their face. While that person's face would not be recalled, that person's existence was not in doubt.

Nicci knew that, now, because of the connection to the power of Orden, because of what it had done within her, Kahlan would no longer seem to be invisible. Nicci would be able to see her just as she could see everyone else. The Chainfire spell still resided within Nicci, but Orden had at least partially countered the spell, halted the continuing damage, allowing her to be aware of the truth. Her memory of Kahlan was still not vital, but Kahlan was.

Nicci now knew, really knew, that Richard's love was real. Nicci felt an aching joy for Richard's heart, even as her own had broken.

Cara stepped up close beside her and did something Nicci could never have imagined a Mord-Sith doing: she put an arm gently around Nicci's waist, drawing her close.

At least, it was something no Mord-Sith would ever have done until Richard had come along. Richard had changed everything. Cara, like Nicci, had been brought back from the brink of madness by Richard's passion for life. The two of them shared a unique understanding of Richard, a special connection, a perspective that Nicci doubted anyone else, even Zedd, could truly appreciate.

More than that, no one but Cara could grasp all that Nicci had just given up.

"You did good, Nicci," Cara whispered.

Zedd rose. "Yes, she did. I'm sorry, my dear, if I've been unfairly hard on you. I can see now that you did in fact think it through. You did what you thought was right. I must admit that, given the circumstances, you did the only thing that made sense.

"I apologize for jumping to foolish assumptions. I've had

reason to know many of the profound dangers surrounding the use of the power of Orden—I probably know more about it than anyone alive today. I've even seen the magic of Orden called forth by Darken Rahl. Because of that, I have a somewhat different view than you've presented.

"While I don't necessarily completely agree with you, what you did was an act of great intellect and courage, to say nothing of desperation. I'm familiar, too, with acts of desperation in the face of incredible odds and I can appreciate how they are sometimes necessary.

"I hope you are right in what you've done. Even if it means I am wrong, I would choose for you to be the one who was right.

"But it doesn't matter, now. Done is done. You have put the boxes of Orden in play and named Richard the player. Despite what I may believe, we are all of a mind in our cause. Now that it is done, we must do our best to see to it that this works. We will all need to do our utmost to help Richard. If he fails, we all fail. All life fails."

Nicci couldn't help but feel a certain degree of relief. "Thank you, Zedd. With your help, we will make this work."

He shook his head sadly. "My help? Perhaps I'm merely a hindrance. I just wish you had consulted me first."

"I did," Nicci said. "I asked you if you trusted Richard with your life, with all life. What more consultation could there be than that?"

Zedd smiled through the sadness lingering on his face. "I guess you're right. It could just be that the combination of the Chainfire spell and the contamination of the chimes has already eroded my ability to think."

"I don't believe that for a moment, Zedd. I think it's that you love Richard and are worried for him. I wouldn't have sought your counsel had it not been important. You told me what I needed to know."

"If you get confused again," Cara said to him, "I'll straighten you out."

Zedd scowled at the woman. "How reassuring."

"Well, Nicci made a long story of it," Cara said, "but it's

not really all that complicated. Anyone should be able to see it—even you, Zedd."

Zedd frowned. "What do you mean?"

Cara shrugged one shoulder. "We are the steel against steel. Lord Rahl is the magic against magic."

To Cara, it was no more complicated than that. Nicci wondered if the Mord-Sith didn't really grasp that she was only scratching the surface, or if she understood the entire concept better than anyone. Perhaps she was right and it really wasn't any more complicated than that.

Zedd laid a hand gently on Nicci's shoulder. It reminded her of Richard's gentle touch.

"Well, despite what Cara says, this may be the death of us all. If it is to have a chance to work, though, we have a lot of work to do. Richard is going to need our help. You and I know a great deal about magic. Richard knows next to nothing."

Nicci smiled to herself. "He knows more about it than you think he does. It was Richard who deciphered the taint in the Chainfire spell. None of us understood all that business about the language of symbols, but Richard picked it up on his own. By himself he learned to understand ancient drawings, designs, and emblems.

"I could never teach him anything about his gift, but he often surprised me with how much he grasped that was beyond the conventional understanding of magic. He taught me things I could never have imagined."

Zedd was nodding. "He drives me crazy, too."

Rikka, the other Mord-Sith living at the Wizard's Keep, stuck her head in the doorway. "Zedd, I just thought you ought to know about something." She pointed a finger skyward. "I was a few levels up and there must be some kind of broken window or something. The wind is making a strange noise."

Zedd frowned. "What kind of noise?"

Rikka put her hands on her hips and stared at the floor, thinking it over. "I don't know." She looked up again. "It's hard to describe. It reminded me a litle of wind blowing through a narrow passage."

"A howling noise?" Zedd asked.

Rikka shook her head. "No. More like the way it sounds out on the ramparts when the wind blows through the crenellations."

Nicci glanced toward the windows. "It's just dawn. I've been casting webs. The wind hasn't come up yet."

Rikka shrugged. "I don't know what it could have been, then."

"The Keep sometimes makes noises when it breathes."

Rikka wrinkled her nose. "Breathes?"

"Yes," the wizard said. "When the temperature changes, like now when the nights are getting colder, the air down in the thousands of rooms will move around. Forced into the constrictions of the passageways it sometimes moans through the halls of the Keep when there is no wind outside."

"Well, I haven't been here long enough to have experienced such a thing, but that must be it, then. The Keep must be breathing." Rikka started away.

"Rikka," Zedd called, waiting for her to halt. "What were you doing up there in that section anyway?"

"Chase is looking for Rachel," Rikka said back over her shoulder. "I was just helping out. You haven't seen her, have you?"

Zedd shook his head. "Not this morning. I saw her last night before she went off to bed."

"All right, I'll tell Chase." Rikka peered into the room a moment and then leaned a hand against the doorway. "What's that thing on the table, anyway? What are you three up to?"

"Trouble," Cara said.

Rikka nodded knowingly. "Magic."

"You have that right," Cara said.

Rikka tapped the palm of her hand against the doorframe. "Well, I'd better go find Rachel before Chase finds her first and gives her a talking-to for going off exploring in such a place."

"That child is a born Keep rat." Zedd sighed. "Sometimes I think she knows the Keep as well as I do."

"I know." Rikka said. "I've been on patrol and have come across her in places I couldn't believe. Once I thought for certain that she had to be lost. She insisted she wasn't. I made her lead me back to prove it. She marched back to her room without ever making a wrong turn, then grinned up at me and said 'See?'"

Smiling, Zedd scratched his temple. "I had a similar experience with her. Children are quick to learn such things. Chase encourages her to learn things, to know where she is so that she isn't so easily lost. I guess, since I grew up here, that's why I don't get lost in the place."

Rikka turned toward the hallway but then turned back when Zedd called her name.

"The wind noise?" He waggled a finger toward the ceiling. "You said it was up there?"

Rikka nodded.

"Do you mean the speckled hallway that runs past the row of libraries? The place with the sitting areas spaced along the hall outside the rooms?"

"That's the place. I was checking the libraries for Rachel. She likes to look through books. As you said, it must be the Keep breathing."

"The only problem is that that's one of several areas where the Keep doesn't tend to make any sound when it breathes. The dead ends off that hall divert the movement of air elsewhere, preventing enough air moving through that area fast enough to make much of a sound."

"It might have been coming from farther away and I only thought it was in those halls."

Zedd planted a fist on one bony hip as he considered. "And you say it sounded like a moaning sound?"

"Well, now that I think about it, it seemed more of a growl."

Zedd's brow creased. "A growl?" He crossed the thick carpet and poked his head out of the doorway, listening.

"Well, not a growl like an animal," Rikka said. "More of a rolling rumble. Like I mentioned—it reminded me of the sound the wind makes going through the crenellations. You know, a rumbling, fluttering kind of sound."

"I don't hear anything," Zedd muttered.

Rikka made a face. "Well, you can't hear it way down here."

Nicci met them at the doorway. "Then why do I feel something vibrating in the center of my chest?"

Zedd stared at Nicci for a moment. "Perhaps something to do with all the conjuring involving the box?"

Nicci shrugged. "Could be, I suppose. I've never dealt with some of those elements before. Much of it was new to me. There is no telling what some of the ancillary effects might be."

"Do you remember when Friedrich accidentally set off that alarm?" he asked, turning to Rikka. She nodded. "Did it sound anything like that?"

Rikka shook her head adamantly. "Not unless you put the alarm under water."

"The alarms are constructed magic." Zedd rubbed his chin in thought. "You can't put them under water."

Cara spun her Agiel up into her fist. "Enough talk." She pushed between them to make it through the doorway. "I say we go have a look."

Zedd and Rikka followed after her. Nicci didn't.

She gestured toward the box of Orden sitting on the table within the glowing web of light. "I'd better stay close."

Besides watching over the box, she needed to study *The Book of Life*, along with other volumes, further. There were still parts of Ordenic theory that she hadn't been able to fully understand. She was distracted by a number of unanswered questions. If she was eventually to be of any help to Richard she would need to know the answers to those questions.

What concerned her most was an issue at the center of Ordenic theory having to do with the connections between Orden and the subject of the Chainfire event—Kahlan. Nicci needed to better understand the nature of requirements for connections based on primary foundations. She needed to fully grasp how those foundations were established. She was troubled by the constraints on predetermined protocols—their need of a sterile field in order to re-create memory. She also needed to learn more about the precise conditions in which the forces needed to be applied.

At the center of it all, though, was that cautionary requirement of a sterile field. She needed to understand the precise nature of the sterile field Orden required and, more importantly, why Ordenic protocols needed it.

"I have all the shields up," Zedd told her. "The entrances to the Keep are scaled. If anyone had entered without permission alarms would be going off all over the place. We'd all be plugging our ears until we found the cause."

"There are gifted people who know about such things," Nicci reminded him.

Zedd didn't need to consider for long. "You have a point. Considering all that's going on, and all we don't yet know, we can't be too careful. It wouldn't be a bad idea for you to keep an eye on the box."

Nicci nodded as she followed them out of the doorway. "Let me know as soon as all is clear."

The towering hall outside, while not more than a dozen feet wide, rose nearly out of sight high overhead. The passageway formed a long, narrow rift deep within the mountain down in the lower part of the Keep. To the left side rose a natural rock wall that had been chiseled right out of the granite of the mountain itself. Even thousands of years later, the marks left by cutting tools could still be seen.

The wall on the side with the rooms was made up of tightly fit, enormous stone blocks. They formed the wall opposing the chiseled granite, rising up together sixty or more feet. That seemingly endless split through the mountain constituted part of the boundary of the containment field. The rooms within the containment area were all lined up along the very outer edge of the Keep that rose up out of the mountain itself.

Nicci followed the others only a short way through the seemingly endless hall, watching them until they reached the first intersection.

"This is no time to get sloppy or lenient," she called after them. "Too much is at risk."

Zedd accepted her warning with a nod. "We'll be back after I look into it."

Cara cast Nicci a look back over her shoulder. "Don't worry, I'll be there and I'm not in the mood to be lenient. In fact. I'm not going to be in a good mood again until I see Lord Rahl alive and safe."

"You have good moods?" Zedd asked as they hurried away.

Cara scowled at him. "I'm frequently cheerful and pleasant. Are you suggesting that I'm not?"

Zedd held up his hands in surrender. "No, no. *Cheerful* describes you perfectly."

"Good, then."

"In fact, *cheerful* would come even before *bloodthirsty* in my book."

"Come to think of it, I think I like *bloodthirsty* even better."

Nicci couldn't share the spirit of their banter. She wasn't good at making people laugh. She frequently found herself perplexed by the way Zedd and others could ease tension with such exchanges.

Nicci knew all too well the nature of the people who were trying to kill them. She had once been one of those people of the Order. She had been as merciless as she had been deadly.

She had never once seen Emperor Jagang being jovial or lighthearted. He was hardly a man given to repartee. She had spent a great deal of time with him, and he was never anything but consistently lethal. His cause was deadly serious to him and he was fanatically dedicated to it. Knowing the kind of people coming for them, people like she herself had once been, and understanding their heartless nature, Nicci didn't feel that she could be any less serious than they.

She watched Zedd, Cara, and Rikka hurry down the first hall to the right, heading for the stairway.

As they started up, Nicci suddenly understood the sound, the vibration she felt.

It was an alarm, of sorts.

She knew why Rikka didn't recognize it.

She opened her mouth to call out to the others just as the world seemed to come grinding to a halt.

A dark cloud poured down the stairwell. It was like a million-speckled suggestion of a snake in midair, rolling, turning, twisting, thinning, thickening as it came roaring down the stairwell. The rolling, fluttering rumble was deafening.

Thousands of bats poured around the corner, a fat snake of them in midair, a thing alive made up of untold numbers of the little creatures. The sight of so many thousands of them coalesced into a single moving shape was riveting. The racket reverberated off the walls, filling the split in the mountain with a riot of noise. The bats seemed to be flying in a panic, their fused form coiling around the corner in a rush as they bolted from something.

Zedd, Cara, and Rikka seemed frozen where they had begun to climb the stairs.

And then the fleeing bats were gone, driven before some terror coming through the Keep behind them. The soft, fluttering sound they left in their wake echoed its muted alarm through the hall as the bats fled into deeper darkness.

That distant sound was what Rikka had heard but not understood.

Staring at the stairs from where the bats had come, Nicci felt as if she were frozen and immobile in an expectant, silent moment in time, waiting to breathe, waiting for something unimaginable. With a rising sense of panic, she realized that in fact she really couldn't move.

And then a dark shape came sweeping down the stairs like an ill wind. Yet, at the same time, it inexplicably appeared to hang motionless. It seemed composed of swirling black shapes and flowing shadows, creating an inky eddy of obscurity. The dizzying shape of it, the entwining currents of darkness, implied movement that it didn't have.

Nicci blinked, and it was gone.

She urgently renewed her effort to move, but she felt as if she was suspended in warm wax. She could breathe to a small extent, and make headway, but only in the most impossibly slow fashion. Every inch took monumental effort and seemed to take an eternity. The world had become impossibly thick as everything slowed toward a halt.

In the passageway, just behind the others in the hall at the bottom of the stairs, the shape appeared again, suspended in midair above the stone floor. It looked like a woman in a flowing black dress floating underwater.

Even in the midst of growing terror, Nicci found the exotic sight strangely fascinating. The others, with the intruder already past them, were in mid-stride ascending the stairs, as still as if caught in a painting.

The woman's wiry black hair lifted lazily out all around her bloodless face. The loose fabric of the black dress swirled as if in whirls of water. Within the slow turbulence of black cloth and hair, the woman herself seemed nearly unmoving.

It looked like nothing so much as if she were floating under murky water.

Then the figure was gone again.

No, not underwater, Nicci realized.

In the sliph.

That's how Nicci felt, too. It was that kind of strange, otherworldly, suspended sensation of drifting. It was impossibly slow and at the same time blindingly fast.

The figure suddenly appeared again, closer this time.

Nicci tried to call out, but she couldn't. She tried to lift her arms to cast a web, but she drifted too slowly. She thought it might take an entire day just to lift her arm.

Sparkling shards of light glimmered and flashed in the air between Nicci and the others. Magic, she knew, cast by the wizard. It fell far short of the intruder. Even though the brief spate of power sputtered out without having any effect, Nicci was astounded that Zedd had managed to ignite it at all. She had tried much the same thing without any result.

Dark trailers of cloth drifted, fluidly flapping through the hallway. Snaking shapes and shadows curled around as they moved ever so slowly. The figure wasn't walking, or running. It glided, floated, flowed, almost unmoving within the swirling cloth of the dress.

Then it was gone again.

In a blink, it reappeared, much closer yet. The ghostlike skin stretched tight over a bony face looking as if it had never been touched by sunlight. Snarls of weightless black hair rose up with wisps of the flowing black dress.

It was as disorienting a sight as Nicci had ever seen. She felt as if she were drowning. Panic welled up in her at the feeling of not being able to breathe fast enough, of trying to get the air she needed. Her burning lungs were unable to work any faster than the rest of her.

When Nicci focused her gaze, the figure of the woman was gone. It occurred to her that her eyes, too, were too slow. The hallway was empty again. It seemed that her focus could not keep up with the movement.

Nicci thought that maybe she was having some kind of hallucination brought on by the spells she had cast, by the power of Orden she had tapped into. She wondered if it could be some kind of aftereffect of the spells. Maybe it was Orden itself come to claim her for tampering with such forbidden powers.

That had to be it—something to do with all the dangerous things she had conjured.

The woman appeared again, as if floating up through the murky deep, emerging suddenly into view out of the dark abyss.

This time Nicci could clearly see the woman's austere, angular features.

Blanched blue eyes fixed on Nicci as if there was nothing else in her world. That scrutiny touched Nicci's very soul with icy dread. The woman's eyes were so pale that they seemed as if they had to be sightless, but Nicci knew that this woman could see just fine, not only in the light, but also in the blackest cave, or under a rock where the light of day never touched her.

The woman smiled as wicked a grin as Nicci had ever seen. It was the smile of someone who had no fear but enjoyed causing it, a woman who knew she had everything under her mastery. It was a smile that sent a slow shiver through Nicci.

And then the woman was gone.

In the distance more of Zedd's magic sparked and sputtered briefly before it died out.

Nicci struggled to move, but the world was too thick, the way it sometimes felt in those terrible dreams she had, dreams where she struggled to move but simply couldn't despite how hard she tried. It was the dream where she was trying to run from Jagang. He was always close, coming for her, reaching for her. He was like death itself, intent on the most unimaginable cruelty, as he came toward her. She always wanted desperately to run in those dreams but, despite extraordinary effort, her legs wouldn't move nearly fast enough.

Those dreams always put her in a state of trembling panic. It was a dream that made death so real she could taste its terror.

She'd had that dream one time in camp. Richard had been there. He woke her, asking what was wrong. She gasped back tears as she told him. He cupped her face and told her that it was only a dream and she was all right. She would have given anything to have had him hold her in his arms and tell her that she was safe, but he didn't. Still, his hand on her face, covered with both of hers, and his gentle words, his empathy, had been a comfort that calmed her terror.

This, though, was no dream.

Nicci tried to gasp a breath, to call out to Zedd, but could do neither. She tried to call her Han, her gift, but couldn't seem to connect to it. It was as if her gift was impossibly fast and she was impossibly slow. The two wouldn't mesh.

The woman, her flesh the pallid color of the freshly dead, her hair and dress as black as the underworld, was suddenly right there, right beside Nicci.

The woman's arm floated out, reaching through the swirling black cloth. Parched flesh stretched tightly over her knuckles served to emphasize the skeleton beneath. Her bony fingers brushed along the underside of Nicci's jaw. It was a haughty touch, an arrogant act of triumph.

At the touch, the vibration in Nicci's chest felt as if it might tear her apart.

The woman laughed a hollow, slow, burbling underwater laugh that echoed painfully through the stone halls of the Keep.

Nicci knew without doubt what the woman wanted, what she had come for. Nicci tried desperately to ignite her power, to grab the woman, to lunge, to do anything to stop her, but she could do nothing. Her power seemed impossibly distant, crackling so far away that it would take forever to reach it.

As the finger brushed along the length of Nicci's jaw, the

woman was gone again, vanishing gently back into the dark depths.

The next time she appeared, she was back at the brass-clad doors standing open to the room with the box. The woman drifted through the doorway, her feet never touching the ground, her dress washing lightly all around her.

Again she vanished out of Nicci's focus.

The next time she appeared, she was between the room and Nicci.

She had the box of Orden under an arm.

As that terrible laughter echoed through Nicci's mind, the world melted into blackness.

CHAPTER 6

Rachel didn't know who the horse belonged to, and she didn't really care. She wanted it.

She had been running all night and she was exhausted. She had never stopped to consider why she might be running. It somehow didn't seem important. It mattered only that she keep going, keep making progress. She needed to hurry. She needed to keep going.

She needed to go faster.

She needed the horse.

She was certain of the direction in which she had to go. She didn't know why she felt so certain about it. She didn't give that matter any serious thought. It remained only a question from somewhere deep in the back of her mind that never completely surfaced into full conscious concern.

As she crouched in the dry, brittle brush, she tried to remain still as a shadow as she figured out what to do. It was hard to stay still because she was so cold. She tried not to shiver for fear of giving herself away. She wanted to rub her arms, but she knew not to because any movement might draw attention. As cold as she was, what concerned her the most was getting the horse.

Whoever owned the horse didn't seem to be nearby at the moment. At least, if he was, she couldn't see him. He might be sleeping in the long, brown grass and be too low for her to see where he was. He might be off scouting.

Or, he might be waiting, watching for her, maybe with an arrow nocked and at the ready so that once she bolted from cover he could take aim and shoot her down. As scary as such a thought was, her fear of such a thing couldn't compare to her need to keep going, her need to hurry.

Rachel checked the sun off through the thick stand of trees, checking her bearings, making sure she knew the direction she needed to go. She surveyed her choices of escape routes. There was a wide path, not quite a road, that would be a good place for a fast getaway. There was also a shallow, gravel-bottomed stream that ran through part of the open meadow. On the other side of the meadow the stream joined the road and ran beside it as both made their way southeast through the trees.

The sun, low, huge-looking, and red, hung just above the horizon. The color matched the color of the scratches all over her arms from running through the brush.

Before Rachel realized it, before she had finished thinking it through, her legs were moving. They almost seemed to have a mind of their own. Only a few steps out of the brush she was running, bolting out across the open ground toward the horse.

Out of the corner of her eye Rachel caught sight of the man as he suddenly sat up in the tall grass. Just as she had suspected, he had been sleeping. With his leather vest and studded straps holding knives, he looked like one of those Imperial Order men. He appeared to be alone. Probably on a scouting mission. That's what Chase had taught her. Imperial Order troops out alone were likely scouts.

She didn't really care who he was. She wanted the horse. She thought that maybe she should be afraid of the man, but she wasn't. She was afraid only of not getting the horse, of not hurrying.

The man threw his blanket aside as he shot to his feet. He scrambled into a dead run. He was coming fast, but Rachel's legs had grown long over the summer and she was a fast runner. The soldier yelled at her. She paid him no never mind as she raced toward the bay mare.

The man threw something at her. She saw it streak by over her left shoulder. It was a knife. At such a distance she knew that it had been a foolish throw—a throw-and-pray, as Chase called it. He taught her to focus, to aim. He'd taught her a lot about knives. She also knew that a running target was difficult to hit with a knife.

She was right. The knife missed her by a good margin. With a soft thunk it stuck in a fallen log lying along the way between her and the horse. She yanked the knife out of the rotting log as she ran by and stuck it through her belt as she slowed.

The knife was hers now. Chase had taught her to take the enemy's weapons whenever possible and be prepared to use them, especially if the weapon was superior to what she had. He had taught her that in a survival situation she had to use whatever was at hand.

Gulping air, she ran under the horse's nose, snatching up the loose ends of the reins, but they were tied to a branch of the fallen log. Her fingers worked frantically to undo the tight knot, but they were numb with cold. They sliped on the leather as she clawed at it. She wanted to scream with frustration, but instead she kept tugging, working the knot. It seemed to take forever to get it loose. As soon as the reins were free she gathered them together in one hand.

It was then that she noticed the saddle not far away. She glanced up as the man yelled again, calling her a name. He was coming fast. She wouldn't have near enough time to even think about saddling the horse. Saddlebags—probably full of supplies—leaned against the saddle.

She slipped her arm under the flat piece of leather connecting the two halves of the saddlebag and ducked under the startled horse's neck.

Rounding the far side she grabbed a fistful of mane and hung on tightly to help her vault up onto the animal's bare back. The saddlebags were heavy and she almost dropped them, but she held on tight and pulled them up behind her. Even though the horse hadn't been saddled, at least it had on its bridle. Somewhere in the dim recesses of her mind Rachel relished the warmth of the animal.

She laid the hefty packs across the horse's withers in front of her legs. There would be food and water inside. She would need both if she was to be able to continue for long. She just assumed that it would be a long journey.

The horse snorted, tossing its head. Rachel didn't take the time to gentle the animal as Chase had taught her. She laid the reins over as she thumped the horse's ribs with her heels. The horse danced sideways, not sure about its strange new rider. Rachel glanced over a shoulder and saw the man almost there. Holding a fistful of mane tightly with one hand and the reins with the other, Rachel leaned forward and again thumped her heels into the horse's sides, farther back. The horse bolted into a dead run.

The man, cursing, made a frantic dive for the bridle. Rachel jerked the reins to the side and the horse followed. The soldier flew past them and landed on his face, grunting with the force of the impact. Suddenly seeing the thundering hooves so close he cried out, his anger switching to fright as he rolled out of the way. He missed being trampled by inches.

Rachel felt no sense of triumph. She felt only the compulsion to hurry, to run southeast. The horse obliged.

She guided the racing mare to the stream at the far side of the grassy clearing. Trees closed in around them as they ran up the wide swath of shallow water, the man disappearing far behind. Water splashed as the horse ran. The gravel bottom seemed to suit the horse's gait.

Chase had taught her how to use water to hide her tracks.

Every galloping stride was one stride closer, and that was all that mattered.

CHAPTER 7

When the soldier walking past the wagons tossed the hard-boiled eggs, Richard caught as many as he could. As soon as he had scooped the rest of them up off the ground he gathered them all in the crook of his arm and crawled back under the wagon to get out of the rain. It was a cold, miserable excuse for a shelter, but it was still better than sitting in the rain.

After having collected his own booty of eggs, Johnrock, pulling his chain behind, scurried back under the other end of the wagon.

"Eggs again," Johnrock said in disgust. "That's all they ever feed us. Eggs!"

"It could be worse," Richard told him.

"How?" Johnrock demanded, not at all happy about his diet.

Richard wiped eggs on his pants, trying to clean the mud off the shells as best he could. "They could be feeding us York."

Johnrock frowned over at Richard. "York?"

"Your teammate who broke his leg," Richard said as he started peeling one of his eggs. "The one Snake-face murdered."

"Oh. That York." Johnrock considered a moment. "You really think these soldiers eat people?"

Richard glanced over. "If they run out of food they will turn to eating the dead. If they are hungry enough and run out of dead, they will harvest a new crop."

"You think they will run out of food?"

Richard knew they would, but he didn't want to say so. He had instructed the D'Haran forces not only to destroy any supply train from the Old World, but to destroy the Old World's ability to provide for their massive invasion force to the north.

"I'm just saying that it could be worse than eggs."

Johnrock looked at his eggs in a new light, finally grumbling his agreement.

As Johnrock started in peeling an egg of his own, he changed the subject. "You think they'll make us play Ja'La in the rain?"

Richard swallowed a mouthful of egg before he answered. "Probably. But I'd rather be playing a game and get warm than sit here freezing all day."

"I suppose," Johnrock said.

"Besides," Richard told him, "the sooner we can start defeating the teams come for the tournaments, the sooner we work our way up in the standings, and the sooner we get to play the emperor's team."

Johnrock grinned at that prospect.

Richard was starving, but he forced himself to slow down and savor the meal. As they peeled shells and ate in silence, he kept an eye on the activity in the distance. Even in the rain, men were busy at every sort of work. The sound of hammers at forges rang through the drone of rain and clamor of conversation, yelling, arguing, laughing, and orders being shouted.

The vast encampment spread across the flat Azrith Plain to what Richard could see of the horizon. Sitting on the ground it was hard to see a great deal of the larger camp out beyond. He could see wagons and a little farther away the larger tents in the middle distance. Horses rode past while wagons pulled by mules made their way through the milling masses. Men on foot, looking miserable in the rain, stood in lines waiting for food at cook tents.

In the distance the People's Palace, sitting on a high plateau, towered over everything. Even in the murk of the gray day, the magnificent stone walls, grand towers, and tiled roofs of the palace stood out above the grimy army come to destroy it. With the steamy vapor rising from the Imperial Order camp, along with the rain and the overcast, the plateau and the palace atop it looked like a distant, noble apparition. There were times when cloud and mist drew across like a curtain and the entire plateau vanished in the gray gloom, as if it had seen enough of the seething horde come to defile it.

There was no easy way for any enemy to attack the palace high on the plateau. The road up the side of the cliff walls was far too narrow for any kind of meaningful assault. Besides that, there was a drawbridge that Richard was certain would have already been raised and, even if it weren't, there were massive walls at the top that were formidable in their own right and little space outside of them to gather any sizable assault force.

Except in times of war, the People's Palace drew commerce from all over D'Hara. Supplies for all the people living there were constantly being brought in. Because it was a trade center, great numbers of people came to the palace to buy and sell goods. For all those people, the primary way up to the city palace was through the inside of the plateau itself. Stairs and walkways accommodated the large number of visitors and vendors. There were also wide ramps for horses and wagons. Because so many people traveled up the inside of the plateau, there were shops and stands all along the way. Large numbers of people came for those market stands and never made the journey all the way up to the city at the top.

The entire inside of the plateau was honeycombed with rooms of every sort. Some of the interior spaces were public, but some were not. There were large numbers of soldiers of the First File—the palace guard—barracked there.

The problem, from the perspective of the Imperial Order, was that the great doors to those inner access areas were closed. Those doors had been made to stand against any kind of attack, and there were enough supplies stored inside for a long siege.

Outside, the Azrith Plain was not at all a hospitable place for forces to gather for a siege. While deep wells inside the plateau provided water for the inhabitants, outside on the Azrith Plain there was no steady supply of water nearby, except the occasional rain, and there was no close source of firewood. On top of that, the weather out on the plain was harsh.

The Imperial Order did have plenty of gifted with them, but they couldn't be much help in breaching the palace defenses. The very construction of the palace was in the form of a protection spell that magnified the power of the ruling Lord Rahl while at the same time hindering the power of others. Inside that plateau, and in the city atop it, the ability of any gifted but a Rahl was severely blunted by that spell.

Because he was a Rahl, such a spell would ordinarily be a benefit for Richard, if it were not for the fact that he had somehow been cut off from his gift. He was pretty sure how that had been accomplished. Chained to a wagon, in the middle of an enemy force numbering in the millions, though, he couldn't do a whole lot about it.

Other than the plateau and the palace atop it, the thing that stood out highest of all out on the Azrith Plain was the ramp that the Imperial Order was constructing. Without an easy way to attack the seat of power of the D'Haran Empire, the last obstacle standing in the way of their total domination of the New World, Jagang had apparently come up with a plan to build an enormous ramp to get enough forces to the top of the plateau to breach the walls. He planned not simply to besiege the People's Palace, but to assault it.

At first Richard had thought such a task impossible, but as he had studied what Jagang's army was doing, he'd quickly become disheartened to realize that it just might work. While the plateau was an imposing height, towering high above the Azrith Plain, the Imperial Order surrounding it had millions of men to devote to the undertaking.

From Jagang's perspective, this was his last objective, the last place he needed to crush in order to establish the unopposed rule of the Imperial Order. As far as the emperor was concerned, he had no other battles to fight, no more armies to destroy, no more cities to capture. The city on top of the plateau was all that stood in their way.

The Imperial Order—the brutes who enforced the faith demanded by the Fellowship of Order—could not allow the people of the New World to live outside the control of the Order, because it put the lie to the teachings of their spiritual leaders. The Brothers of the Order taught that individual choice was immoral because it was ruinous to mankind. The very existence of a prosperous, independent, free people stood in stark contrast to the foundational doctrines of the Order. The Order had condemned the people of the New World as selfish and evil, and required them to convert to the beliefs of the Order, or die.

Having millions of soldiers with time on their hands as they waited to enforce faith in the Order's beliefs was no doubt troublesome. Jagang had found a task to keep them all busy, a sacrifice to the cause; they were all now devoted to working in shifts every hour of the day and night at the construction of the ramp.

While Richard couldn't see the men down lower, he knew that they had to be digging dirt and rock. As those excavation pits grew ever larger, other men carried the dirt to the site of the ramp. In such massive numbers, working without pause, they were up to such a daunting undertaking. Richard hadn't been in the camp for long, but he imagined that day by day he would soon be able to see the sloping ramp growing inexorably toward the top of the plateau.

"How will you die?" Johnrock asked.

Richard was sick of watching the distant ramp, of contemplating the dark and savage future the Order would enforce on everyone. Johnrock's question, though, wasn't exactly a ray of sunshine in the gloom. Richard slumped back against the inside of the wheel on the far side of the wagon as he ate eggs.

"You think I will have a choice?" he finally asked. "A say in the matter?" Richard rested a forearm over his knee, gesturing with half an egg. "We make choices about how we will live, Johnrock. I don't think we have nearly so much say about how we will die."

Johnrock looked surprised by the answer. "You think we have a choice about how we live? Ruben, we have no choice."

"We have choices," Richard said without explanation. He popped the half of an egg in his mouth.

Johnrock lifted the chain attached to his collar. "How can I make any choice?" He gestured out at the encampment. "They are our masters."

"Masters? They have chosen not to think for themselves and instead to live according to the teachings of the Order. In so doing they are not even the masters of their own lives."

Johnrock shook his head in astonishment. "Sometimes, Ruben, you say the strangest things. I am a slave. I am the one with no choice, not them."

"There are chains stronger than those attached to the collar around your neck, Johnrock. My life means a great deal to me. I would give my life to save the life of someone I hold dear, someone I value.

"Those men out there have chosen to sacrifice their lives to a mindless cause that produces only suffering—they have already given up their lives and gotten nothing of any value in return. Is that choosing to live? I don't think so. They wear chains that they have put around their own necks, chains of a different kind, but chains nonetheless."

"I fought when they came to take me. The Imperial Order won. Now I am chained here. Those men live, but if we try to be free we will die."

Richard wiped the remaining bits of shell off an egg. "We all have to die, Johnrock—every one of us. It is how we choose to live that matters. After all, it's the only life each one of us will ever have, so how we live is of paramount importance."

Johnrock chewed for a moment as he thought it over. Finally, with a grin, he seemed to dismiss the whole matter. "Well, if I do end up having to choose how I will die, I wish it to be to the cheers of the crowd for how well I played the game." He glanced over at Richard. "And you, Ruben? If you have to choose?"

Richard had other things on his mind—important things. "I hope not to have to decide the matter this day."

Johnrock sighed heavily. The eggs looked tiny in the man's meaty fists. "Maybe not today, but I think this place is the end of the games . . . I think that in this place we finally lose our lives."

Richard didn't answer, so Johnrock spoke again into the drone of the downpour. "I'm serious." He frowned. "Ruben, are you listening, or are you still dreaming about that woman you think you saw when we came into camp yesterday?"

Richard realized that he was, and that he was smiling. Despite everything, he was smiling. Despite how true Johnrock's words were—that they very well might die in this place—he was smiling. Still, he didn't want to discuss Kahlan with the man.

"I saw a lot of things when we rolled into this camp."

"Soon enough, after the games," Johnrock said, "and if we do well, there will be women enough. Snake-face has promised us. But now there are just soldiers and more soldiers. You must have been seeing phantoms yesterday."

Richard stared off at nothing, nodding. "I guess you're far from the first to think that she's a phantom."

Johnrock heaved a length of chain out of his way and scooted closer to Richard. "Ruben, you'd better get your head straight or we're going to get ourselves killed before we even get a chance to play the emperor's team."

Richard looked up. "I thought you were ready to die."

"I don't want to die. Not today, anyway."

"There you go, Johnrock, you have made a choice. Even chained up, you have made a choice about your life."

Johnrock shook a thick finger at Richard. "Look here, Ruben, if I end up getting killed playing Ja'La, I don't want it to be because you have your head in the clouds, dreaming of women."

"Just one woman, Johnrock."

The big man leaned back and flicked eggshells off his fingers. "I remember. You said that you saw the woman you want to be your wife."

Richard didn't correct him. "I just want for us to play well and win all our games so that we can have the chance to play the emperor's team."

Johnrock's grin returned. "Do you really think we can beat the emperor's team, Ruben? Do you think we can survive such a game with those men?"

Richard cracked the shell of another egg on the side of his heel. "You're the one who wants to die to cheers of the crowds for how well you've played."

Johnrock gave Richard a sidelong glance. "Maybe I will do as you say and choose to live free, yes?"

Richard only smiled before biting the egg in half.

Not long after Richard and Johnrock had finished the last

of their meal, Commander Karg appeared, his boots splashing as he marched toward them through the mud.

"Get out here! All of you!"

Richard and Johnrock crawled out from under the wagon into the drizzle. Other captives at wagons to either side stood up, waiting to hear what the commander wanted. Soldiers who were on the team gathered closer.

"We're going to have visitors," Commander Karg announced.

"What kind of visitors?" one of the soldiers asked.

"The emperor is touring the teams that arrived for the tournament. Emperor Jagang and I go way back. I expect you to show him that I've done well in selecting a worthy team. Any man who doesn't reflect well on me, or who fails to show the proper respect for our emperor, will be of no use to me."

Without further word, the commander hurried away.

Richard could feel himself swaying on his feet as his heart pounded. He wondered if Kahlan would be with Jagang, as she had been the day before. While he desperately wanted to see her again, he hated to think of her being anywhere near that man. For that matter, he hated to think of her being anywhere near any of these men.

Over the winter, when Nicci had captured Richard and taken him down to the Old World, Kahlan, in his place, had led the D'Haran forces. She was the one responsible for keeping Jagang from having the victory back then that he might otherwise have had. She had been responsible for whittling down the ranks of Order soldiers, even if the endless supplies from the Old World had included reinforcements that more than replenished all the men lost. Kahlan had not only delayed the invaders, but earned their undying hatred for all the pain she had inflicted upon them. Were it not for Kahlan the Order probably would have caught the D'Haran army and slaughtered them. She had kept them one step ahead of Jagang and just out of his reach.

Trying to look composed, Richard leaned back against the wagon and folded his arms as he waited. Before long he caught sight of an entourage off to the left making their way through the encampment. They were moving down the line of teams in the distance, pausing at regular intervals along the way to take a closer look.

Judging by the types of soldiers Richard could see making up the group, it could be none other than the emperor that they escorted. Richard recognized the royal guard from the day before when he had rolled through the camp and right past Jagang. That was when he had briefly seen Kahlan. The emperor's guards were intimidating in their mail and leather and with their well-made weapons, but it was the size of the men and their bulging, rain-slicked muscles that was truly daunting.

These were men who even struck fear into the hearts of the regular brutes of the Order. Those regular troops all fell back well clear of the royal guard. Richard didn't imagine that such men were at all tolerant of anything they believed might potentially be a threat to the emperor.

Johnrock stepped forward to join the other men waiting in a line for the emperor to review them.

It was when Richard saw Jagang's shaved head off in the center of the ranks of muscled guards that the sudden realization hit him.

Jagang would recognize him.

Jagang, as a dream walker, had been in the minds of various people and he had seen Richard though their eyes.

Richard could hardly believe how careless he had been not to even consider that when he played the emperor's team in order to get close enough to Kahlan, Jagang would be there, and Jagang would recognize him. Distracted by the thought of actually getting to Kahlan, he hadn't taken such a prospect into consideration.

Richard noticed something else, then—a Sister.

It looked like Sister Ulicia, but if it was, she had aged a great deal since he'd last seen her. She was farther away, back at the tail end of all the guards following Jagang, but Richard could still see the sagging creases in her face. The last time he had seen her she'd been an attractive woman, although Richard had difficulty separating a person's looks from their personality and Sister Ulicia was one sinister woman. No matter how superficially attractive a person was, a cruel personality tainted Richard's image of them. Corrupt character colored his appraisal of a person to such an extent that he could not see them as attractive separate from their vicious nature.

That was also one of the reasons Kahlan was so beautiful to him—she was not simply stunningly attractive, but exemplary in every way. Her intelligence and insight were matched by her passion for life. It was as if her captivating looks perfectly reflected everything else about her.

Sister Ulicia, despite how physically attractive she once had been, now appeared to reflect only the rot at her core.

Richard realized then that not only would Jagang and Sister Ulicia recognize him, but there would be other Sisters in the camp who also knew him.

He suddenly felt very vulnerable. Any of those Sisters could happen by at any time. He had nowhere to hide.

When he got close enough, Jagang would not fail to see that Lord Rahl, the very man he was after, was right there in his midst. Chained as he was, without his ability to use his Han, even as difficult as it had been for him to call forth his gift when'd he'd had access to it, Richard would be at Jagang's mercy.

He had a sickening flash of a vision that Shota the witch woman had given him. It had been a vision of being executed. It had been raining in that vision, much as it was raining now. Kahlan had been there. In tearful terror she had watched as his wrists had been bound behind his back and he was made to kneel in the mud. As he knelt there, with Kahlan screaming his name, a big brute of a soldier came up behind him, promising to have Kahlan for himself as he brought a long knife around before Richard's face, and then with a mighty effort cut deep through his throat.

Richard realized that he was touching his throat, as if to comfort the gaping wound. He was panting in a panic.

He felt a hot wave of nausea welling up through him. Was this to be Shota's vision come to life? Was this what she had been warning him about? Was this to be the day he died?

It was all happening too fast. He hadn't been ready for this. But what could he have done to get ready?

"Ruben!" Commander Karg yelled. "Get up here!"

Richard struggled to get control of his emotions. He took a deep breath and worked to calm himself as he started moving, knowing that if he didn't it was only going to get ugly even faster.

Not far away, the clot of men had stopped at the next team up the line. Richard could hear only the murmur of conversation over the sound of rain.

His mind raced, trying to think of what he could do before Jagang recognized him. He knew that he couldn't hide behind the other men. He was point man. Jagang would want to see the team's point man.

And then he caught a glimpse of Kahlan.

Richard moved as if in a dream. The whole cluster of men around the emperor and Kahlan had started turning in the direction of Richard and his team.

Knowing that he had to get up with the other men, Richard started to step over the chain attached to Johnrock's collar. Just then he had an idea. He hurried forward and deliberately let his foot catch the chain. He fell face-first in the mud.

Commander Karg went red with rage. "Ruben—you clumsy idiot! Get on your feet!"

Richard scrambled to his feet as Jagang's guards began parting for the emperor. Richard stood up tall next to Johnrock. With a finger, he wiped mud from his eyes.

He blinked to clear his vision. It was then that he spotted Kahlan. She was walking just behind Jagang. The hood of her cloak, pulled up to protect her against the rain, partially hid her face. Richard recognized every familiar movement of her body. No one moved quite the way she moved.

Their eyes met. He thought his heart might stop.

He remembered the first time he had seen her. She had looked so noble in that white dress. He remembered the way she had looked directly at him without speaking—a gaze that was questioning and at the same time guarded, a gaze that instantly and clearly conveyed her intelligence. He had never seen anyone before that moment who looked so . . . valiant.

He thought that he had probably been in love with her from

that first instant, from that first look into her beautiful green eyes. He had been sure that in that first look into those eyes he had seen her soul.

Now there was all that, along with a hint of confused concern in her expression. Because of the way his gaze fixed on her, followed her, she was aware that he could see her. Being the object of the Chainfire spell, she wouldn't remember who he was or, for that matter, who she was. Other than Richard and the Sisters who had taken her prisoner and ignited the Chainfire spell, no one could remember her. Obviously, Jagang was not affected by the spell. Richard surmised that it probably had something to do with a connection to the Sisters. But Kahlan would be invisible to everyone else.

She recognized, though, that Richard could see her. In the isolation imposed by the spell, that had to be something profoundly important and meaningful for her. In fact, by the look on her face, he could see that it was.

Before Jagang could begin to get close enough to inspect the team, a man called out as he ran up to the group. The emperor gestured him forward in a manner that suggested the man was well known. The guards parted for him as he made his way through their inner circle of protection. Since he carried only minimal weapons—a couple of knives—Richard reasoned that he was probably a messenger. He was winded but seemed to be in a great hurry.

When he made it to the emperor, the man bent close, speaking excitedly but in a low voice. At one point in his report, he gestured across the camp toward the area where the construction of the ramp was taking place.

Kahlan, pulling her gaze from Richard, looked over at the man speaking with Jagang.

Richard surveyed a cadre of other guards, closer in, who surrounded her. They weren't the royal guard, and in fact they were careful to stay out of the way of the imposing royal guards. These men looked more like the regular soldiers of the camp. Their weapons weren't well made. They had no chain mail or armor. Their clothes seemed to be a collection of whatever they could find that looked the part of the rest of the army.

They were big men, young and strong, but they were not the match of the emperor's guards. They looked more like common thugs.

Richard realized, then, that they could only be guarding Kahlan.

Unlike Jagang's guards, who seemed unmindful of her presence, these men frequently glanced at Kahlan, checking on her every move. That could only mean that these men could see her. Jagang's guards never looked at Kahlan, but these men did. Somehow, they were able to see her. Somehow, Jagang had found men to guard her who were not affected by the spell.

At first questioning if he was really right that they could see her, and confused by how such a thing was possible, Richard finally realized that it actually did make sense. The Chainfire spell, like the world of magic itself, had been contaminated by the chimes. That contamination croded the ability of magic to function. The whole purpose of the chimes was to destroy magic. Because of the taint left by their presence in the world of life, the Chainfire spell's very makeup had been impaired. When Zedd and Nicci had run the verification web, Richard had discovered the damage to the structure of the spell itself.

Because of that contamination within the Chainfire spell, it didn't function as designed. It was flawed. It only made sense that such a flaw might allow a few people to escape its effects.

Richard remembered how the plague, sweeping through the population like a wildfire, didn't touch everyone. There were a few people—even some who cared for the sick and dying—who never contracted the plague themselves. This must be something like that. There were bound to be a few people who weren't affected by the Chainfire event and would therefore be able to see Kahlan. It would certainly explain why there were guards who could see her.

As those special guards, distracted by the man speaking to Jagang with such urgency, turned to try to see better what was happening with the emperor, Kahlan made a small move to turn with them. It looked perfectly natural; Richard knew it was anything but. As she turned, Kahlan adjusted the hood of her cloak against the rain, and as her hand came back down it passed close to one of her guards. Richard saw that the sheath at the man's belt was empty. As Kahlan's hand disappeared back under her cloak, Richard caught a brief glint of reflection off the blade. He wanted to laugh out loud, to cheer, but he didn't dare move a muscle.

Kahlan caught him looking at her and realized that he had to have seen what she'd just done. She watched him a moment to see if he might betray her. She was using the hood of her cloak to hide her face from those guarding her, to prevent them from seeing that she was looking obliquely at Richard. When he didn't move, she turned and along with the guards watched what was going on between the messenger and the emperor.

Jagang suddenly swung around and started away, returning back the way he'd come, the messenger right on his heels. Kahlan briefly glanced back over a shoulder to catch one last glimpse of Richard before the guards could all close in around the emperor and his captive.

As she did so, and the hood of her cloak moved just enough, Richard saw the dark bruise on her left cheek.

Hot anger blazed through him. Every fiber of his being wanted to do something, to act, to get her away from Jagang, to get her out of this camp. His mind raced to come up with something, anything, but, chained as he was, there was nothing he could do. This was not the time or place he could act.

Worse, he knew that if he did nothing Jagang's abuse of her would only continue. If he did nothing, and Kahlan suffered worse, Richard knew that he would never forgive himself. Despite how desperately he wanted to do something, though, he could do nothing.

He stood silent and still, enduring the rage storming through him, a wrath that was the twin to the Sword of Truth, the sword he'd given up in order to find Kahlan.

Kahlan, the emperor, and all the guards vanished back into the churning grime of the encampment. Curtains of mist seemed to draw in behind them.

Richard stood trembling in bitter frustration. Not even the cold rain could cool his bottled fury. Even as his min through every possible action, he knew that there was nothing he could do. Not now, anyway.

At the same time his heart ached for Kahlan. Agony for what she must be facing at the hands of such a man knotted his insides. His knees felt weak with his fear for her. He had to stiffen his resolve to keep himself from falling to the ground in tears.

If only he could get his hands on Jagang. If only . . .

Commander Karg strode up close in front of Richard. "You're lucky," he growled. "The emperor obviously had more important things to do than review my team and my clumsy point man."

"I need some paint," Richard said.

Commander Karg blinked in surprise. "What?"

"Paint. I need some."

"You expect me to fetch paint for you?"

"Yes. I told you, I need it."

"What for?"

Richard wagged a finger at the man's face, resisting mightily the urge to whip a length of chain around the commander's neck and strangle the life out of him. "Why do you have those tattoos?"

Confused, Commander Karg hesitated for a moment, considering the question as if it might have thorns in it.

"To make me look all the more fierce to the enemy," he said at last. "Such a look gives me power. When the enemy sees our men, they see ferocious fighters. It strikes terror into their hearts. When they freeze for a moment in fear, we triumph."

"That's why I want the paint," Richard said. "I want to paint the faces of our team so that it strikes fear into the hearts of our opponents. It will help us defeat them. It will help your team to triumph."

Commander Karg studied Richard's eyes for a moment, as …uge if he was serious or up to something.

… a better idea," the commander said. "I will have …me around and tattoo my entire team." He …he scales covering the side of his face. "I …all with scales and such all over your faces. It will make you all look like my men. When you all have tattoos like mine you will look like my team. Everyone will know you belong to me."

The commander gave Richard a grim smile, pleased with his idea. "I will have you all pierced as well. You all will have tattoos and metal studs in your faces. You will all look like inhuman animals."

Richard waited until the man was finished and then shook his head. "No. That won't do. It's not good enough."

Commander Karg planted his fists on his hips. "What do you mean it's not good enough?"

"Well," Richard said, "you can't see those kinds of tattoos from far enough away. I'm sure that they work just fine in battle, when you are in a face-to-face confrontation with the enemy, but it won't be that way in the Ja'La games. Such tattoos would too easily be missed."

"You are often as close on the Ja'La field as you are in battle," Commander Karg said.

"Maybe," Richard conceded, "but I want us to stand out not only to our opponents at the moment, not just to the men on the field, but also to other teams who will be watching—to everyone who is watching. I want everyone to see our painted faces and instantly recognize us. I want such a sight to plant fear in the minds of other teams. I want them to remember us and to worry."

Commander Karg folded his muscled arms. "I want you to be tattooed so that you look like my team. So that all will know that it is Commander Karg's team."

"And if we lose? If we lose in a humiliating fashion?"

The commander leaned in a little as he glared. "Then you will be whipped at the least, and no longer of any use to me at worst. I think you know by now what becomes of captives who are of no use."

"If that happens," Richard said, "everyone will remember that the team you put to death for being inferior were all tattooed just like you. If we fail, they will remember the snake pattern of your tattoo on all of us. It would link us to you, but also you to us. If we lose, you will be stigmatized by that tattoo.

If we lose, every time they see your tattooed face they will laugh at you.

"If we should for some reason happen to lose, paint can be washed off before we are whipped or worse."

Commander Karg was beginning to grasp just what Richard meant. He visibly cooled as he scratched his jaw.

"I'll see if I can't come up with some paint."

"Make it red."

"Red? Why?"

"Red stands out. It will be memorable. Red also reminds people of blood. I want them to see us and before anything else wonder why we want to look like we are painted in blood. I want the other teams to worry about that the night before a game. I want them to sweat and lose sleep thinking about it. When they finally come to play us they will be tired and then we will make them bleed."

A slow smile spread on Commander Karg's face. "You know, Ruben, were you born on the right side of this war, along with me, I bet we would be good friends."

Richard doubted that the man truly understood the concept of friendship, or could even appreciate such values.

"I'll need enough paint for all the men," Richard said.

Commander Karg nodded as he started away. "You will have it."

CHAPTER 8

Kahlan hurried to stay close to Jagang as he marched though the camp lest he give her a stunning shock of pain through the collar. Of course, as he had demonstrated any number of times, he needed no excuse. She knew, though, that right then she had better not even look like she might give him cause, because he was in a hurry due to the strange news the man had brought.

She didn't care so much about the news, though. Her mind was on the man she had finally seen again, the captive who had been brought in the day before.

As she moved through the encampment, thinking about the man, she watched not only her guards but also the common soldiers in the camp, looking for reactions that might indicate that they could see her, listening for any obscene remark that would betray them. All around, startled men stared at the heavily armed group making their way through the midst of their daily life, but she didn't see a single man look directly at her, or show any other signs of seeing her.

Despite being men in an army led by the emperor himself, these men had probably never seen Jagang this close before. The army, all in one place, constituted a population that was larger than almost any city. If these men had ever seen the emperor before, it was likely only at a great distance. Now, as he passed close by, they stared at him in open awe.

Kahlan noted in their reaction, and Jagang's attitude toward them, the contradiction to the Order's teachings of the absolute equality of all men. For his part, Jagang never showed any penchant for sharing the common life of his men, a daily existence in the filth and mud. They lived in a camp that was virtually lawless, involved in crimes of every sort with their unruly fellows, while Jagang always enjoyed protection from those theoretically equal to him in every way. Kahlan supposed that if they shared one thing, it was that they, like their emperor, lived lives of almost constant, irrational violence and complete indifference to human life.

Kahlan, invisible to the soldiers all around, stepped carefully over puddles and dung. She clutched the knife tightly in a fist under her cloak, unsure, yet, exactly what she would do with it. The opportunity to take the knife had suddenly presented itself and she had acted.

In such rough surroundings it felt good to have a weapon. The encampment was a frightening place, despite how invisible she was to nearly all the soldiers. Even though she knew that she had no hope of using the knife to escape Jagang, all of her special guards, and the Sisters, it still felt good to have a weapon. A weapon gave her a modicum of control, a way to defend herself—at least to a degree. More than that, though, a weapon symbolized how much she valued her life. Having it was a declaration to herself that she had not, and would not, give up.

If she had a chance, Kahlan would use the knife to try to kill Jagang. She knew that if she were to actually accomplish such a deed it would mean a sure death for her as well. She knew, too, that the Order would not falter because of the loss of the man. They were like ants. Stepping on one would not send the colony into retreat.

Still, she knew that sooner or later she was going to be put to death—and probably made to suffer greatly along the way by Jagang's own hand. She had already seen him murder several people for little or no excuse, so putting an end to him would at least serve to satisfy her sense of justice. Kahlan's memory of her past life was gone. Her total awareness since the Sisters had taken that memory was that of a world gone mad. She might not be able to set the world right, but if she could kill Jagang she might be able to see justice done in one little part of it.

It wouldn't be easy, though. Jagang was not only physically powerful and skilled at combat, he was a very clever individual. Sometimes Kahlan thought that he really could read her mind. In another way, since Jagang was a warrior and he was often able to anticipate what she would do next, Kahlan thought that in the past she could not remember she must have been a warrior, too.

Alerted by the urgent whispers of their friends, men in the camp all around came out of tents, rubbed sleep from their eyes, and stood in the drizzle staring at the swift procession in their midst. Other men turned from work at caring for animals to watch. Riders reined in their horses to wait until the emperor passed. Wagons rumbled to a halt.

No matter where she was in the camp it stank, but in among the men it was a degree worse. The cook fires added greasy soot to the smell of the latrines. She didn't think that the hastily dug latrines were going to be adequate for long. By the foul look of the little streams of water wending their way through the camp, they were already overflowing. The smell proclaimed that she was right. She couldn't imagine how much worse it was going to become over the coming months of the siege.

Even with the stench and the revolting sights of some of the things going on in the camp, Kahlan noted it all only dimly in the back of her mind. Her thoughts were on other things. Or rather, on one thing: that man with the gray eyes.

She hadn't known which team he would be with. When she had seen his face the day before he had been in a cage on a transport wagon. She knew only, from catching bits of Jagang's conversations with officers, that the cages held some of the men who were on a team come to play in the tournaments.

Jagang had been eager to tour the teams before any of the games were to begin. As they went from team to team, she had been looking for the man. At first, she hadn't even realized that she was doing it. She found herself staying close to Jagang as he inspected the players so that she could also see them.

He knew a great deal about some of the teams. He commented to his guards about what he expected he would see before he reached each new team. When he arrived at a new group he would ask to see the point man, along with the wing men. Several times he wanted to have a look at the men of the blocking line. It reminded Kahlan of a housewife at market, inspecting cuts of meat.

Kahlan had searched all the faces she saw, looking at every man. She had not been gauging their height, weight, and muscle, as Jagang had been doing. She had found herself looking at their faces, trying to find the man she had seen in the cage the day before. She was beginning to lose heart, thinking that he must not be among the teams. She had begun to suppose that maybe he had ended up being sent to work as slave labor at the ramp site along with many other captives.

And then when she finally did spot the man, he did the strangest thing: he fell face-first into the mud. They were still some distance off and no one but Kahlan had really been looking at him yet. Everyone else thought the man was just clumsy as he tripped over the chain lying there on the ground. As they'd approached the team some of the guards had laughed, whispering among themselves about how quickly such a man was going to get his neck broken on the Ja'La field.

Kahlan hadn't thought it was funny, though. She alone had been looking at the man and she knew that he hadn't tripped accidentally. She knew that it had been deliberate.

The fall had looked real enough. No one else imagined that it had been by design. Kahlan knew it was. She knew what it was to be a captive and have to instantly do something no matter how risky because you had no choice.

She just couldn't imagine why the man had done it.

What could be the purpose of such a thing? What danger could he have been trying to avoid? In some circumstances people did such things to get a laugh—and some of the guards had laughed—but that wasn't the purpose behind what this man had done.

To Kahlan's mind it had been not only deliberate, but done with haste, as if he thought of it only a second before and there was no time to come up with something better. It had been an act of desperation. But why? Why fall on your face in the mud? What could it possibly accomplish?

It suddenly hit her. It was in a way something like what she had been doing—using the hood of her cloak to hide what she was doing, where she was looking, who she was looking at. He must have wanted to cover his face. It could only be because he thought that someone would recognize him. It must have been that the man feared that Jagang himself would recognize him. Or possibly Sister Ulicia. At any rate, it had to be that he was trying to keep from being recognized.

She supposed that it did make some sense. After all, the man was a captive. Only enemies of the Order would be captives. She wondered if he was a high-ranking officer or something like that.

And he had known Kahlan. From the first instant their eyes met the day before, when he had been in that cage, she could see that he recognized her.

As she had approached his team with Jagang, she and the man had shared a look. In that look she saw that they both knew the plight the other was in, and they both had done nothing to betray the other, as if they'd made a silent pact.

It lifted Kahlan's heart to know that among all these murderous men, there was one who was not an enemy.

At least, she didn't think he was. She reminded herself not to substitute her imagination for the truth. With her memory gone she had no real way of knowing if he was an enemy or not. She supposed that he could be someone who had been hunting her. She wondered if it could be possible that he, like Jagang, had some motive to want to see her suffer. That he was a captive of Jagang didn't automatically mean that he was on her side. After all, the Sisters had hardly been on Jagang's side.

But if he was trying to hide his face to keep from being recognized, what was going to happen once the Ja'La games started? He might be able to stay muddy for a day or two, but once the rain stopped the mud was going to dry up. She wondered what he would do then. She couldn't help feeling a pang of worry for him.

At the end of visiting the teams, as they had left to see what the messenger had to show Jagang, she had seen one other thing in the man's eyes; rage. As she had turned back for a last, quick look at him, the hood of her cloak had pulled back and he had seen the black bruise Jagang had left on her face.

Kahlan had thought that he looked like he might use his bare hands to rip apart the chain holding him. She was at least relieved that he was smart enough not to try to do anything. Commander Karg would have killed him in a blink.

From the conversations between Jagang and the commander as Jagang had started out to inspect the teams, the two were old acquaintances. They mentioned battles they had been in together. In that brief conversation she had taken appraisal of the commander. Like Jagang himself, the commander was not a man to be underestimated. Such a man would not have wanted to be embarrassed before his emperor, and would have killed his point man without hesitation had he allowed his anger to slip its bounds.

She supposed that it was that, his anger at seeing what Jagang had done to her, that made her think the man could not be her enemy.

But the man was dangerous as well. The way he stood, the way he balanced, the way he moved, told Kahlan a great deal about him. She could clearly see the intelligence in his raptor gaze. In the measured way he moved she saw that he also was a man not to be underestimated. She would know for sure if she was correct once the games started, but a man like Commander Karg would not have a captive be his point man unless there was a very good reason. Kahlan would know soon enough when she saw the man play, but to her he looked like coiled fury, and like he knew how to uncoil.

"Over this way, Excellency," the messenger said as he pointed off through the gray drizzle.

They followed the messenger, leaving the dark sea of the camp, emerging out onto the open ground of the Azrith Plain. Kahlan had been so preoccupied thinking about the man with the gray eyes that she hadn't even noticed that they were coming up on the site of the construction. The ramp rose high overhead. Beyond, the plateau towered above them. Up this close the plateau truly was imposing. Up this close she could see far less of the magnificent palace atop it.

When it had started to rain she had hoped that maybe it would cause the ramp to collapse, but she could see, now that they were there beside it, that it was not only reinforced with rock but being well compacted as material was added. Gangs of men with heavy weights tamped the dirt and rock as it was placed.

This was not a haphazard effort. While the soldiers in camp—like the ones guarding her—were little more than ignorant brutes mindlessly devoted to a senseless cause, there were some men among the Imperial Order who were intelligent. They were the ones supervising the construction; the brutes merely handled the dirt.

As ignorant and unaware as the general population of soldiers was, Jagang surrounded himself with competent men. His personal guards, as big and powerful as they were, were hardly idiots. Those overseeing the construction of the ramp were likewise intelligent men.

The men supervising the project knew what they were doing and were confident enough to contradict Jagang when he suggested something that wouldn't work. Jagang had initially wanted to make the base of the ramp narrower so that they could build height more quickly. While respectful, they were not afraid to tell him that it wouldn't work, and why. He had listened carefully and, when satisfied that they were right, let them proceed with their plans even though those plans had been contrary to his initial desire. When Jagang thought he was right, though, he was as determined as a bull to have his way.

Numerous lines of men, each twelve or fifteen men deep, stretched back away from the colossal ramp. Some of the men passed baskets filled with dirt and rock, and some passed back empty baskets. Other men wheeled carts carrying rock. Mules pulled trains of wagons hauling larger rock. The project was massive almost beyond belief, but with so many men constantly adding to it, the ramp grew steadily.

Kahlan followed as the emperor hurried through the site, the messenger constantly pointing the way among the confusion of activity. The lines of men parted as the royal procession marched through, then melted back together.

As they made their way past throngs of workers, Kahlan finally saw the pits where men in astounding numbers dug material for the ramp. There seemed to be countless numbers of vast pits in the ground, each with one sloping end where men were carrying material out as others brought empty baskets, carts, and wagons back down in to be loaded. The array of pits stretched as far as she could see into the gray drizzle.

Jagang and his party made their way along the wide tracks between the pits arranged in a grid across the plain. Those pathways between were wide enough to accommodate wagons going in opposite directions.

"Down here, Excellency. This is the place."

Jagang paused, peering down the long, sloping ramp into the pit. It appeared to be the only excavation that was deserted. He looked around at the other pits nearby.

"Clear this one, here, as well," he said, gesturing at the next pit lying in the direction of the plateau. "And don't start any new digging beyond in the same direction."

Some of the supervisors who had gathered hurried to carry out his instructions.

"Let's go," Jagang said. "I want to see if this is really something or not."

"I'm sure you will find it as I described, Excellency."

Jagang ignored the angular messenger as he started down the sloping track into the pit. Kahlan stayed close. A glance back revealed Sister Ulicia not a dozen steps behind. The Sister, without a hood on her cloak and with her wet hair plastered to her head, did not look at all pleased to be out in the rain.

Kahlan turned back to watch her footing on the slick, muddy slope.

The bottom of the pit was an uneven mess where thousands of men had toiled at digging and loading. Since some of the ground was softer and easier to dig, those places were deeper. In other spots, where it was more rocky and harder to dig, there were mounds nearly twice Kahlan's height that had yet to be reduced.

Following the messenger through the disorder, Jagang descended into one of the deeper areas. Kahlan followed them down into the muck, her guards staying close around her. She wanted to stay close to Jagang in case he became distracted by whatever was in the pit. If she got a chance, no matter the risk, she would try to kill him.

The messenger squatted down as they came to a halt. "This is it, Excellency."

He slapped his hand on something just peeking up from the ground. Kahlan frowned, looking along with everyone else at the smooth expanse that had been exposed.

The messenger had been right, it definitely did not look natural. She could see what looked like joints. It did look like a structure buried deep in the ground.

"Clean it off," Jagang said to some of the foremen from the project who had come down into the pit.

Apparently, as per standing orders, when the structure had been discovered all work was abandoned and the workers pulled out until Jagang could personally inspect the find. The form was slightly rounded, as if they had uncovered the very top portion of a massive, long, rounded shape.

As men worked with shovels and brooms, Jagang directing where they dug, it quickly became apparent that the messenger had been accurate in his report: it did look like the exterior of a barrel-vaulted ceiling.

As the men cleaned it off, Kahlan could see that the structure was made of large stones cut to precise shapes to make up the curve of the arch. It reminded her of nothing so much as a buried building, except that there was no roof, just the exposed outer structure of an interior vaulted ceiling.

Kahlan could not imagine what such a thing could be doing buried all the way out here on the Azrith Plain. There was no telling how many hundreds of even thousands of years whatever was inside had been entombed.

When enough of the dirt and debris had been cleared off, Jagang crouched down and ran his hand over the wet stone. His fingers traced a few of the joints. They were so tight that not even a thin knife blade would have slipped between them.

"Get some tools down here—pry bars and such," he said. "I want this opened. I want to know what's down inside it."

"At once, Excellency," one of the construction bosses said.

"Use your assistants instead of the laborers." Jagang stood, sweeping an arm around at the general area. "I want this whole place cordoned off. I don't want any of the regular soldiers anywhere near here. I will have some of my guards stationed here to watch the site at all times. This area is to be as restricted as my own tents."

Kahlan knew that if any of the soldiers were to get into a tomb—or whatever ancient thing it was that they'd found—they would loot everything of value. The plundered rings he wore said that Jagang knew the same thing.

Kahlan glanced up when she noticed some of Jagang's guards rushing down the slope into the pit. They pushed their way through the construction foremen and other guards to get in near the emperor.

"We got her," one of the breathless men reported.

Jagang smiled a slow, wicked grin. "Where is she?"

The man pointed. "Just up there, Excellency."

Jagang glanced briefly at Kahlan. She didn't know what he was up to, but the look he gave her ran a chill up her spine.

"Bring her down here, now," Jagang told the man.

He and another of the guards hurried back up the slope to get whoever it was they had. Kahlan could not imagine who the men had been talking about, and why it gave Jagang such satisfaction.

As they waited, the construction supervisors continued to expose more of the buried structure. In short order, a stretch of the stone nearly fifty feet long had been exposed. All of it that they had uncovered ran in a straight line, the arch uniform along the entire length.

Other men worked at widening the excavation around the smooth stonework. The more of it they uncovered, the more the shape—and scale—of it came into view. This was no small thing. If the stone really was a ceiling of something beneath, then that room, or tomb, would have to be nearly twenty feet across. Since it showed no sign of terminating, there was no telling how long it was. From what she could see of it, it looked something like a buried hallway.

At the sounds of muted cries and a scuffle, Kahlan looked up. The big guards were bringing a struggling, slender figure down the muddy slope.

Kahlan's eyes went wide. Her knees went weak.

The men each held a thin, spindly arm of a girl not half their height.

It was Jillian, the girl from back in the ancient ruins in the city of Caska, the girl Kahlan had helped to escape. Kahlan had killed two of Jagang's guards and Sister Cecilia so that Jillian could get away.

As the guards brought the helpless girl forward, her copper-colored eyes finally caught sight of Kahlan. Those eyes filled with tears at all that had been lost, at her failure to evade the men of the Order.

The guards brought her in close and stood her up before the emperor.

"Well, well," Jagang said with a shallow, gruff chuckle, "look what we have here."

"I'm sorry," the girl whispered up at Kahlan.

Jagang glanced over at Kahlan. "I've had men searching for your little friend, here. Quite the dramatic escape you pulled off for her." Jagang cupped Jillian's chin, his thick fingers squeezing her cheeks. "Too bad it was all for nothing."

Kahlan thought that it wasn't for nothing. She had at least killed two of his guards and Sister Cecilia. She had at least done her best to gain freedom for Jillian. She had tried her best. Her efforts had cost her dearly, but she would do the same thing again.

Jagang seized the girl's thin arm in his big hand and pulled her forward. Again he grinned at Kahlan. "Do you know what we have here?"

Kahlan didn't answer. She was not about to join his game.

"What we have here," he said in answer to his own question, "is someone who can help you behave."

She gave him a blank look and didn't ask.

Jagang unexpectedly pointed at the waist of one of Kahlan's special guards, the one standing just to her right. "Where's your knife?"

The man looked down at his belt as if he was afraid a snake might be about to sink its fangs into him. He looked back up from the empty scabbard.

"Excellency . . . I, I must have lost it."

Jagang's icy look made the man's face pale. "You lost it, all right."

Jagang spun and backhanded Jillian hard enough to send her flying through the air. She landed in the mud, screaming in shock and pain. A red stain spread in the puddle around her face.

Jagang turned back to Kahlan and held out his hand. "Give me the knife."

His completely black eyes were so deadly-looking that Kahlan thought she might have to take a step back out of sheer fright.

Jagang waggled his fingers. "If I have to ask again, I'll kick her teeth in."

In a flash Kahlan ran though everything she could think of. She felt like the man with the gray eyes must have felt when he deliberately fell face-first into the mud. She had no choice either.

Kahlan laid the knife in Jagang's upturned palm.

He grinned in triumph. "Why, thank you, darlin."

Without pause he turned, as if driving his fist in a mighty blow, and slammed the knife right though the face of the man it belonged to. The damp air rang with a loud crack as bone shattered. The man collapsed dead into the mud. The flood of blood was shocking in the gray light. The man never even had time to scream before he died.

"There's your knife back," Jagang called down to the corpse.

His attention focused on the stunned faces of Kahlan's special guards. "I'd suggested that you keep better track of your weapons than he did. If she takes a weapon from any of you, and she doesn't kill you with it, I will. Is that simple enough for you all to understand?"

As one they all said, "Yes, Excellency."

Jagang bent and yanked the sobbing Jillian to her feet. He effortlessly held her up so that only her toes were touching the ground.

"Do you know how many bones are in the human body?"

Kahlan choked back her tears. "No."

He shrugged. "Neither do I. But I have a way to find out. We can start breaking her bones, one at a time, counting each one as it snaps."

"Please . . ." Kahlan begged, trying mightily to contain her sob.

Jagang shoved the girl at Kahlan as if he were giving her a life-size doll.

"You are now responsible for her life. Whenever you give me any cause to be displeased, I am going to break one of her bones. I don't know the exact number of bones in her frail little body, but I'm sure that it's a great many." He arched an eyebrow. "And I do know that I'm easily displeased.

"If you do more than simply displease me I will have her tortured before your eyes. I have men who are experts in the fine art of torture." The storms of gray shapes shifted in his inky eyes. "They are very good at keeping people alive for a long time as they endure unimaginable agony, but if she should happen to die under torture, then I will have to start in on you."

Kahlan clutched the poor girl's bleeding head tightly to her chest. Jillian sobbed softly to Kahlan how sorry she was for getting caught. Kahlan gently shushed her.

"Do you understand me?" Jagang demanded in a deadly calm voice.

Kahlan swallowed. "Yes."

He grabbed Jillian's hair in his big fist and started pulling her back. Jillian screamed with renewed terror.

"Yes, Excellency!" Kahlan shouted.

Jagang smiled as he released the girl's hair. "That's better."

Kahlan wanted more than anything for the nightmare to end, but she knew that it was only just beginning.

CHAPTER 9

Stop being a big baby and hold still," Richard said.

Johnrock blinked frantically. "Don't get it in my eyes."

"I'm not going to get it in your eyes."

Johnrock took an anxious breath. "Why do I have to be first?"

"Because you are my right wing man."

Johnrock didn't have an immediate answer. He pulled his chin away from Richard's grip. "Do you really think this will help us win?"

"It will," Richard said as he straightened, "if we all follow through with the rest of it. Paint all by itself isn't going to win games for us, but the paint will add something important, something that merely winning could not accomplish—it will help to forge a reputation. That reputation will unsettle those who have to face us next."

"Come on, Johnrock," one of the other men said as he impatiently folded his arms.

The rest of the team gathered around watching nodded their agreement. None of them really wanted to be first. Most of them, but not all, had at least been won over by Richard's explanation of what the paint would do for them.

Johnrock, looking around at all the men waiting, finally grimaced. "All right, go ahead."

Richard glanced past his wing man to the guards with arrows nocked and at the ready. Now that the chains had been removed from the captives, the guards watched for any sign of trouble as they waited to take the team to their first match. Commander Karg always stationed a heavy guard whenever Richard and the other captives were not chained. Richard noted, though, that most of the arrows were pointed in his direction.

Focusing again on Johnrock, he spread his fingers and grabbed the top of the man's head to hold him still.

Richard had been fretting about what he would paint on the faces of the team. When he'd first come up with the idea, he had thought that maybe he would simply have each man paint his own face in whatever manner he wanted. After brief consideration he realized that he couldn't leave it up to the men. Too much was at risk.

Besides that, they all wanted Richard to do it. He was the point man. It had been his idea. He figured that most of them had been hesitant because they believed that they were going to be laughed at, and so they had wanted it to be by his hand rather than their own.

Richard dipped his finger in the small bucket of red paint. He had decided against using the brush Commander Karg had brought along with the paint.

Richard wanted to feel the act of drawing directly.

In the little time he'd had, he'd given a great deal of thought to what he would paint. He knew that it had to be something that would accomplish what he'd intended in the first place.

In order to make it work the way he'd described, he had to draw the things he knew.

He had to draw the dance with death.

The dance with death, after all, was ultimately centered on life, yet the meaning of the dance with death was not merely the singular concept of survival. The purpose of the forms was to be able to meet evil and destroy it, in that manner enabling one to preserve life, even one's own. It was a fine distinction, but an important one: it required recognizing the existence of evil in order to be able to fight for life.

While the vital necessity of recognizing the existence of evil was obvious to Richard, it was clearly a concept that many people willfully refused to face. They chose to be blind, to live in a fantasy world. The dance with death would not allow such lethal fantasies. Survival required the clear and conscious recognition of reality; therefore the dance with death required that one recognize truth. It was all part of a whole and would not succeed if parts were ignored or left out.

The elements of the dance with death—their forms—were at their base the components of every manner of combat, from a debate, to a game, to fighting to the death. Drawn in a language of emblems, those components built the concepts making up the dance. Using those concepts involved seeing what was really happening—in part and in whole—in order to counter it. The ultimate purpose of the dance with death was winning life. The translation of Ja'La dh Jin was "the Game of Life."

The things that belonged to a war wizard all played some part in the dance with death. In that way a war wizard was devoted to life. Among other items, the symbols on the amulet Richard had worn were a picture, a condensed diagram, forming the core concept of the dance. He knew those moves from fighting with the Sword of Truth.

Even if he didn't have the sword any longer, he grasped the totality of what was involved in the meaning of the dance with death, and therefore the knowledge he'd gained from using the sword remained with him whether or not he had the sword itself. As Zedd had often reminded him in the beginning, the sword was just a tool; it was the mind behind the weapon that mattered.

Along the way, since Zedd had first given Richard the sword, he had come to understand the language of emblems. He knew their meaning. They spoke to him. He recognized the symbols belonging to a war wizard, and understood what they meant.

Using his finger, Richard began laying down those lines on Johnrock's face. They were the lines of parts of the dance, the forms used to meet the enemy. Each combination of lines making up an element had meaning. Cut, sidestep, thrust, twist, spin, slash, follow through, deliver death swiftly even as you prepare to meet the next target. The lines he put on Johnrock's right cheek were admonitions to watch for all that would come at you, without focusing too narrowly.

Besides the elements of the dance, Richard found himself drawing parts of spells he had seen. At first he didn't realize he was doing it. At first, as he drew those components, he had trouble recalling where he'd seen them before. Then he remembered that they were parts of the spells that Darken Rahl had drawn in the sorcerer's sand in the Garden of Life as he had invoked the magic necessary to open the boxes of Orden.

Richard realized only then that the visit by the strange, ghostly figure the previous night still weighed heavily on his mind. The voice had told him that he'd been named a player. This was the first day of winter. He had one year to open the correct box of Orden.

Richard had been exhausted, but he could think of little else after that encounter. He had been unable to get much sleep. Being distracted by the pain of the wound in his leg and the one on his back kept him from fully devoting his mind to reasoning it out. The first day of winter had brought the inspection by Jagang. With his sudden concern over how to avoid being recognized by Jagang and all the Sisters in the Order's encampment, Richard hadn't been able to consider how it was possible for him to be a player for the boxes of Orden.

He wondered if it could be some kind of mistake—some misdirection of magic caused by the contamination left by the chimes. Even if he had the knowledge, which he didn't, his gift had been cut off by that witch woman, Six, so he didn't see how he could have somehow inadvertently put the boxes in play. He couldn't imagine how such a thing as opening the correct box would be able to be accomplished without his gift. He wondered if Six could be at the center of it all, if it could be some part of a plot he didn't yet understand.

Back when Darken Rahl had been drawing those spells just before he opened one of the boxes, Richard had not understood anything about their composition. Zedd had told him that drawing such spells was dangerous in the extreme, and that one misplaced line, drawn by the right person, in the right circumstance, in the right medium, could invoke disaster. At the time all the drawings had seemed like arcane motifs executed with mysterious elements that were all part of some complex foreign language.

As Richard had come to learn more about magical designs

and emblems, he had come to grasp the meaning behind some of their elements—in much the same way he had at first learned the ancient language of High D'Haran by first coming to recognize individual words. As his understanding of words grew, he was able to grasp the ideas the words were expressing.

In much that same way, he had come to learn that some of the parts of the spells Darken Rahl had drawn to open the boxes of Orden were also parts of the dance with death.

In a way that made sense. Zedd had once told him that the power of Orden was the power of life itself. The dance with death was really about preserving life, and Orden itself was centered around life and preserving it from the rampages of the Chainfire spell.

Richard dunked his finger back in the red paint and laid down an arcing line across Johnrock's forehead, then supported it with lines that created a symbol for centering strength. He was using elements he understood, but combining them in new ways to alter them. He didn't want a Sister to see the drawings and recognize their direct meaning. While the designs he was painting were composed of elements he knew, they were original.

The men who had gathered all around leaned in a little, spellbound by not just the process, but by the drawing itself. It had a kind of poetry to it. While they didn't understand the meaning of the lines, they experienced the totality of them as expressive of meaningful purpose, as important, and as exactly what they were: threatening.

"You know what this whole thing, this drawing, reminds me of?" one of the men asked.

"What?" Richard murmured as he added more to the emblem that stood for a powerful strike meant to break an opponent's strength.

"In a way it reminds me of the play of the game. I don't know why, but the lines kind of look like the movements of certain attacks in Ja'La."

Surprised that the man—another captive—could pick up such a significant trait from the drawing, Richard shot the man a questioning frown.

"When I was a farrier," the man explained, "I had to understand horses if I was to shoe them. You can't ask a horse what's bothering him, but if you pay attention you can learn to pick up on things, like the way the horse moves, and after a time you start to understand the meaning behind certain body language. If you pay attention to those little movements you can avoid getting kicked, or bitten."

"That's very good," Richard said. "That's something like what I'm doing. I'm going to give each of you a kind of visual picture of power."

"And how would you know so much about drawing symbols of power?" one of the men, Bruce, asked in a suspicious tone. He was one of the Order soldiers on the team—one of the men who slept in his own tent and resented having to follow the orders of a point man who was an unenlightened heathen, a man who was kept chained at night like an animal. "You people up here put a lot of stock in the outdated beliefs of magic and such, rather than devoting your minds to proper things, to matters of the Creator, to your responsibilities and duty to your fellow man."

Richard shrugged. "I guess that what I meant by that is that it's my vision, my idea, of symbols of power. My intention is to draw on each man what I think makes them look more powerful, that's all."

Bruce didn't look satisfied by the answer. He gestured at Johnrock's face. "What makes you think all them squiggly lines and such look like visions of power?"

"Well, I don't know," Richard said, trying to come up with something to make the man stop asking questions without having to actually reveal anything important, "the form of the lines just seem powerful to me."

"That's nonsense," Bruce said. "Drawings don't mean anything."

Some of the soldiers on the team watched Bruce and waited for Richard's answer as if considering a rebellion against their point man.

Richard smiled. "If you think so, Bruce, if you're convinced that drawings don't mean anything, then how about if I paint a flower on your forehead."

All the men laughed—even the soldiers.

Bruce, suddenly looking a little less sure of himself as his gaze darted around at his chuckling teammates, cleared his throat.

"I guess, now that you put it that way, I can see some of what you mean. I guess I'd like to have some of your power drawings, too." He thumped his chest with a fist. "I want the other teams to fear me."

Richard nodded. "They will, if you all do as I say. Keep in mind that before this first game the men on the other teams will probably see this red paint on all our faces and think it's foolish. You have to be prepared for that. When you hear them laughing at you, let that laughter make you angry. Let it fill your hearts with the desire to jam that laughter right back down their throats.

"In that very first moment when we step onto the field, the other team, as well as many of those watching, will probably not just laugh, but call us names. Let them. We want that. Let them underestimate us. When they do that, when they laugh at you or call you names, I want you to save up the anger you're feeling. Fill your hearts with it."

Richard met the eyes of each man in turn. "Keep in mind that we are here to be victorious in the tournaments. We are here to win the chance to play the emperor's team. We alone are worthy of that chance. Those men who are laughing at you are the worthless dregs of Ja'La players. We must sweep them aside so that we can get at the emperor's team. The men in the first games are in our way. They are in our way and they are laughing at us.

"When you step onto the field of play let their laughter ring in your ears. Soak it in, but keep silent. Let them see no emotion from you. Hold it inside until the right moment.

"Let them think us fools. Let them be distracted by believing that we will be easy marks, rather than focusing on how to play us. Let them lower their guard.

"Then, the instant the game begins, in a focused, coordinated manner unleash your rage against those who laughed at you. We have to hit them with our full force. We have to crush them. We have to make this game as important as if it were the emperor's team we were playing.

"We can't simply win this first game by a point or two as is usually the way it goes. That's not good enough. We can't be satisfied with that kind of piddling victory. We must be unyielding. We must overwhelm them. We must hammer them into the ground.

"We must beat them by at least ten points."

The men's jaws dropped. Eyebrows went up. Such lopsided victories happened only in children's mismatched games. A Ja'La team on this level winning by more than four or five points was virtually unheard of.

"Every member of the losing team gets a lash of the whip for each point they lose by," Richard said. "I want that bloody whipping to be on every tongue of every other team in this camp.

"From that moment on, no one will laugh. Instead, each team who has to face us will worry. When men worry, they make mistakes. Every time they make one of those mistakes we will be ready to pounce. We will make their worry warranted. We will bring their worst fears to life. We will prove every sleepless moment of cold sweat to have been justified.

"The second team we beat by twelve points.

"And then, the next team will be even more fearful of us."

Richard waved his red finger in the direction of the soldiers on the team. "You know the effectiveness of such tactics. You crushed any city that stood against you so that those yet to be conquered trembled in fear as they waited for you to come. Those people knew your reputation and they greatly feared your arrival. Their fear allowed you to more easily conquer them."

The soldiers grinned. They could now put Richard's plan in a frame of reference that they understood.

"We want to make all the other teams afraid of the team with the red, painted faces." Richard fisted his free hand. "Then, we will crush each of them in turn."

In the sudden silence, the men all made fists to match his and thumped them to their chests in oaths that they would make it so. These men all wanted to win, each for his own reason.

None of those reasons was anything like Richard's reason.

He hoped not to ever have to play the emperor's team—he hoped to get his chance long before then—but he had to be prepared to go that far, if necessary. He knew that a good chance might not come along before then. Should it not, he had to insure that they reached the final game of the tournament, when he was more confident of getting the chance he would need.

Richard finally turned back to Johnrock and in short order completed the drawing with a few emblems that symbolized massive weight behind an attack, drawing them down each of Johnrock's heavily muscled arms.

"Do me next, will you, Ruben?" one of the men asked.

"Then me," another called out.

"One at a time," Richard said. "Now, as I'm working, we need to go over our strategy. I want each man to go into this game knowing exactly what to do. We all have to know the plan so that we can all follow it. We all have to know the signals. I want for us to be ready to rush the opponent from the first instant. I want to knock the wind out of them while they're still laughing."

Each man in turn sat on the overturned bucket and let Richard paint his face. Richard approached each man as if the drawing was a matter of life and death. In a way it was.

The men had all been pulled in by Richard's sober lecture. A solemn mood settled over them as they sat silently watching their point man draw what only Richard knew were some of the most deadly concepts he knew how to create. Even if they didn't understand the language behind those symbols, they understood the meaning behind what Richard was doing. They could see that each man looked fearsome.

As each man was completed, Richard realized that it was like looking at a nearly complete collection of the designs that made up the dance with death, with elements of the boxes of Orden thrown in for good measure.

The only symbols he'd left out were the ones he was saving

for himself, the elements of the dance that invoked the most deadly of cuts—the ones that cut into the enemy's very soul.

One of the soldiers on his team offered Richard a polished piece of metal so that he could see himself as he began to apply the elements of the dance with death. He dunked his finger in the red paint, thinking of it as blood.

The men all watched in rapt attention. This was their leader in battle, the one they followed in Ja'La dh Jin. This was his new face and they were all serious about learning it.

As a final element, Richard added the lightning bolts of the Con Dar, the symbols representing a power Kahlan had invoked when the two of them had been trying to stop Darken Rahl from opening the boxes of Orden and she thought that Richard had been killed. It was a power meant for vengeance.

Thinking about Kahlan, her memory lost, her identity taken from her, being at the mercy of Jagang and the evil beliefs of the Order, as well as picturing her in his mind with that lurid bruise on her face, made his blood boil with rage.

Con Dar meant "Blood Rage."

CHAPTER 10

Kahlan kept an arm protectively around Jillian as they followed closely behind Jagang. The emperor's entourage made its way through the sprawling encampment to the silent awe of some, and the cheers of many. Some chanted Jagang's name as he passed, shouting encouragement for his leadership in their fight to exterminate opposition to the Imperial Order, while many more lauded him as "Jagang the Just." It never failed to dishearten her that so many could view him—or the Fellowship of Order itself—as custodians of justice.

From time to time Jillian's trusting, copper-colored eyes gazed up at Kahlan with gratitude for the shelter. Kahlan felt somewhat ashamed of her pretense of protection when she knew that in reality she could offer little safety to the girl. Worse, Kahlan might very well end up being the cause of any harm that came to Jillian.

No. She reminded herself that she would not be the cause of such harm, should it come to pass. Jagang, as advocate for the corrupt beliefs of the Fellowship of Order and the champion of unjust justice, would be the cause. The twisted beliefs of the Order justified, in their minds, any injustice in aid to their ends. Kahlan was not responsible—in part or in whole—for evil committed by others. They were answerable for their own actions.

She told herself that she mustn't allow herself to shift blame from the guilty to the victim. One of the hallmarks of the people playing evil beliefs was to always blame the victim. That was their game and she would not allow herself to play it.

Still, it broke Kahlan's heart that Jillian was once more a

terrified captive of these brutes. These people from the Old World who would harm innocent people in the name of a greater good were traitors to the very concept of good. They were not capable of sincere feelings of heartache because they did not value good; they resented it. Rather than seeking values, it was a kind of corrosive envy that guided their actions.

Kahlan's only real satisfaction since being captured by Jagang had been that she had managed to engineer an escape for Jillian. Now even that was lost.

As they marched through the camp, Jillian's arm tightly circled Kahlan's waist, her fingers clutched at Kahlan's shirt. It was obvious that while the sinister nature of the soldiers all around them frightened her, she was more terrified of Jagang's personal guards. It had been men like these who had hunted her down. She had managed to evade them for quite a while but, despite how well she knew the deserted ruins of the ancient city of Caska, she was still a child and no match for a search carried out by such determined and experienced men. Now that Jillian was a prisoner in the sprawling encampment, Kahlan knew that she had little chance of again helping the girl escape the clutches of the Order's men.

As they walked through the mud and refuse, weaving around the disorder of tents, wagons, and piles of gear and supplies, Kahlan turned Jillian's face up and saw that at least the cut had stopped bleeding. One of the collection of plundered rings that Jagang wore had been responsible for the jagged gash over the bone of Jillian's cheek. If only that were her biggest worry. Kahlan smoothed her hand over the girl's head in response to a brave smile.

Jagang had momentarily been quite pleased to have back a girl who had dared escape from him—and to have yet another means to torment and control Kahlan—but he had been more interested in learning all he could about the discovery down in the pit. It seemed to Kahlan that he knew something more about whatever it was that was buried than he was revealing. For one thing, he had not been as surprised by the find as she would have expected. He seemed to take the discovery in stride.

Once he had seen to it that the area had been cordoned off

and cleared of the regular soldiers, he gave strict instructions to the officers to seek him out immediately once they had breached the stone walls and gotten inside whatever it was that was planted so deep in the Azrith Plain. Once he was satisfied that everyone understood exactly how he wanted the discovery handled, and that everyone there was working diligently toward those ends, his attention had quickly turned to seeing a bit of the opening games of the tournaments. He was eager to appraise some of the eventual competition to his own team.

Kahlan had been forced to go with him to Ja'La games before. She wasn't looking forward to going again, primarily because the excitement and violence of the games put him in a stormy mood laced with savage carnal desires. Ordinarily the man was terrifying enough, capable of instantaneous and brutal violence, but when he was in an agitated, aroused mood after a day at Ja'La games he was altogether more intractable and willful.

After the first time they'd gone to watch games the focus of his depraved lust had been Kahlan. She had fought her panic, finally coming to accept that he was going to do what he was going to do and there was nothing she could do to stop it. She had finally gone numb to the terror of being under him, resigning herself to the inevitable. She had turned her eyes away from his lecherous gaze and freed her mind go to another place, telling herself that she would save her hot rage until the time was right, until a time when it would serve some purpose.

But then he'd stopped short.

"*I want you to know who you are when I do this*," he had told her. "*I want you to know what I mean to you when I do this. I want you to hate this more than you have ever hated anything in your entire life.*

"*But you have to remember who you are, you have to know everything, if this is to truly be rape . . . and I intend it to be the worst rape you can suffer, a rape that will give you a child that he will see as a reminder, as a monster.*"

Kahlan didn't know who the "he" was.

"*For it to be all of that*," Jagang had told her, "*you have to be fully aware of who you are, and everything this will mean to you, everything it will touch, everything it will harm, everything it will taint for all time."*

The idea of how much worse such a violation would be for her then was more important to him than sating his immediate urges. That alone spoke volumes about the man's craving for revenge, and about how much she had engendered his lust for it.

Patience was a quality that made Jagang all the more dangerous. He could easily be impulsive, but it was a mistake to think that he could be lured into becoming reckless.

Feeling the need to make her understand his greater purpose, Jagang had explained that it was much the same as the way he punished people who angered him. If he killed such people, he'd pointed out, they would be dead and unable to suffer, but if he made them endure agonizing pain then they would wish for death and he could deny it. Witnessing their endless torment, he could be sure of their great regret for their crimes, of their insufferable grief for all that was lost to them.

That, he'd told her, was what he had in store for her: the torture of regret and utter loss. Her lack of memory left her dead to those things, so he would wait until the proper time. Having reined in his immediate urges in favor of greater ambitions when she finally remembered everything, he had filled his bed with a variety of other women captives.

Kahlan hoped that Jillian was too young for his tastes. She wouldn't be, Kahlan knew, if she were to do anything to give him cause.

As they moved through crowds of soldiers cheering for a game already under way, the royal guards forcefully shoved any men out of the way they judged to be too close to the emperor. Several men who didn't move willingly enough, or quickly enough, got an elbow that nearly cracked their skulls. One burly drunk in a sour disposition, who didn't intend on being shoved aside for anyone, even an emperor, turned on the advancing royal guards. As the soldier stood his ground, growling bold threats, he was eviscerated with one swift scything cut from a curved knife. The incident didn't slow the royal party a single step. Kahlan shielded Jillian's eyes from the sight of the man's insides spilled in their path.

Since it had stopped raining, Kahlan pushed the hood of her cloak back off her head. Dark clouds scudded low over the Azrith Plain, adding to the suffocating feeling of being closed in. The thick, murky overcast suggested that the first damp, cold day of winter would offer no chance of sunlight. It felt like the whole world was gradually descending into a cold, numb, everlasting gloom.

When they reached the edge of the Ja'La field, Kahlan rose up on her toes, looking over or around the shoulders of the guards, trying to see the faces of the men already in the thick of play. When she realized that she was stretching in order to see the game, she immediately lowered herself back down. The last thing she wanted was for Jagang to ask her why she was suddenly so interested in Ja'La.

She wasn't really interested in the game, but she was interested in seeing if she could spot the man with the gray eyes, the man who had deliberately tripped and fallen in the mud so as to hide his face from Jagang—or maybe Sister Ulicia.

If the rain didn't return, it was soon going to be hard for the man to maintain a muddy face to hide his identity. Even with rain and mud Jagang would quickly become suspicious if the point man for Commander Karg's team walked around all the time with a muddy face. Then the man would find that the mud, rather than hiding him, only attracted Jagang's suspicion. Kahlan fretted about what would happen then.

Many of the men watching the game cheered and shouted encouragement when the point man for one of the teams made it into the opposing team's territory. Blockers rushed in to prevent the man from gaining any more ground. The onlookers roared as the players toppled one another while other men scrambled to protect their territory.

Ja'La was a game in which men ran, dodged, and darted past one another, or blocked, or chased the man with the broc—a heavy, leather-covered ball a little smaller than a man's head—trying to capture it, or attack with it, or score with it. Men often fell or were knocked from their feet. Rolling across the ground without shirts, many were soon left slick not just with sweat, but with blood.

The square Ja'La fields were marked out in a grid. In each corner was a goal, two for each team. The only man who could score, and only when it was his team's timed turn, was the point man, and even then he had to do so from within a specific section of the grid on the opponents' side of the field. From that scoring zone, an area running across the width of the field, he could throw the broc toward either of the rivals' goal nets.

It wasn't easy to score. It was a throw of some distance and the goal nets weren't large.

To make it all the more difficult, the opposing players could block the throw of the heavy broc. They could also knock the point man back out of the shooting zone—or even tackle him—as he tried to score. The broc could also be used as a kind of weapon to knock interfering players out of the way. The point man's team could try to clear the opposing players from in front of a goal net, or they could protect him from blockers so that he could try to find an opening in one net or the other so that he could make a shot, or they could split up and try to do both. Each strategy for each side had its advantages and disadvantages.

There was also a line far back from the regular shooting zone from where the point man could attempt a throw. If such a shot went in, his team scored two points rather than the usual single point, but shots were rarely wasted at such a distance because the chance for interception was so much greater, while at the same time the chance of making such the shot was negligible. Such attempts were usually made only out of desperation, such as a last-ditch effort by the team that was behind, trying to score before time ran out.

If the opposing team tackled the point man, then, and only then, were his wing men allowed to recover the broc and attempt to score. If any attempt to score missed the net and the broc went out of bounds, then the team on offense got the broc back, but it was returned to them on their own side of the field. From there they had to start the running attack all over again. All the while their timed turn with the broc continued to run down.

On a few squares on the field the attacking point man was safe from the threat of being tackled and having the broc stripped away from him. Those squares, though, could easily become dangerous islands where he could become trapped and unable to advance. He could, though, pass the broc to a wing man and once on the charge get it back again.

On the rest of the squares, and in the regular scoring zone, the defending team could capture or steal the broc in an attempt to prevent the attacking team from scoring. If the defending team captured the broc, though, they couldn't score with it until their turn of the hourglass, their turn at attack, but they could try to keep possession in order to deny the team whose turn it was a chance to score. The attacking team had to get it back if they were to score. Fights over possession of the broc could get bloody.

An hourglass timed each team's turn of play—each side's timed chance to score. If an hourglass wasn't available, other timing means, such as a bucket of water with a hole in it, could be used. The rules of the game could in certain instances be rather complicated, but in general they were very loose. It often seem to Kahlan that there were no rules—other than the major rule that a team could score only during their timed turn.

The timed-play rule prevented any one team from dominating the possession of the broc and kept the game moving. It was a fast-paced, exhausting game, with constant back-and-forth play and no real time to rest.

Because it was so difficult to make a point, teams rarely scored more than three or four points in a game. At this level of play the concluding gap in the final score was usually only a point or two.

A prescribed number of turns of the hourglass for each side made up the official time of the game, but if the score was even at the end of those turns then play continued, no matter how many more turns of the hourglass were needed, until one team scored another point. When that finally happened the other team then had but one turn of the hourglass to try to match the point. If they failed, the game was over. If they made the point, the other team got another turn. The extended play went on in that fashion until a team scored without an answering point within the one-following-play rule. For that reason, no

Ja'La dh Jin game could ever end in a tie. There was always a winner, always a loser.

With or without tie-breaking play, when the game was over the losing team was brought out onto the field and each man was flogged. A terrible whip made up of a bundle of knotted leather cords bound together at the handle end was used to mete out the punishment. Each of those leather cords was tipped with heavy nuggets of metal. The men were given one lash for each point by which they'd lost. The crowd enthusiastically counted out each lash to each man on the losing team kneeling in the center of the field. The winners often cavorted around the perimeter of the field, showing off for the crowd, while the losers, with bowed heads, received their whipping.

With such bitter rivalry between teams the flogging always ended up being a grim sight. The players, after all, had been selected specifically for their belligerent brutality, not merely their skill at playing.

The crowds who watched the Ja'La games expected bloody matches. The female camp followers watching from the sidelines weren't in the least bit put off by the blood. If anything, it made them all the more eager to catch the attention of favorite players. To the people of the Old World, blood and sex were inextricably linked—whether it was a Ja'La match, or the sacking of a city.

If there wasn't much blood during the game the crowd could get riled, believing that the teams weren't really trying hard enough. Kahlan once saw Jagang order the execution of a team because he thought they hadn't fought hard enough. The teams who had played on the bloody field after the executions had thrown themselves into the match.

The more brutal the players were—from the crowd's standpoint—the better. Legs and arms were frequently broken, as were skulls. Those who had previously killed an opponent in a Ja'La match were well known and widely acclaimed. Such men were idolized and entered the field at the beginning of games to the wild cheers of the spectators. The women seeking to be with the players after a match strongly favored being with such dominant men.

To the Imperial Order, the Game of Life was a blood sport.

Kahlan moved up close behind Jagang as he stood near the edge of the field at midpoint. The game had already gotten under way while they had still been back at the construction site.

The royal guards flanked Jagang's sides and guarded his back. Kahlan's own special guards surrounded her close enough to be sure she didn't try to wander away. She suspected that the heated emotions of the fans, as well as their drinking, held the potential for more than a little trouble.

Still, Jagang, despite the show of force by his guards, was a man who did not fear trouble. He had won rule by brute force; he held on to it by being absolutely ruthless. There were few, even among the largest of his guard, who were his equal in sheer brawn, to say nothing of his skill and experience as a warrior. Kahlan suspected that he could easily crush a man's skull in one bare hand. On top of that, the man was a dream walker. He could probably have strolled alone among the meanest of drunken soldiers and had nothing to fear.

Out on the field the teams came together in a great crash of bone and muscle. Kahlan watched the point man as he lost the broc when hit from both sides at once. On one knee, he held a hand over his ribs as he panted, trying to catch his breath. He wasn't the man she was looking for.

The horn blew, signifying the end of that turn of play. The fans of the other team cheered wildly at the failure to score. The referee walked the broc to the other end of the field and gave it to the point man on the other team. Kahlan let out a silent sigh. That wasn't him, either. As the hourglass was turned over the horn blew again. The point man and his team started their run downfield. The opposing team started their run to defend their goals.

The crash of flesh was horrific. One of the players screamed in pain. Jillian, behind the wall of guards and unable to see much of what was happening on the field, still shrank from the sound of the screams. She pressed herself all the harder against Kahlan. Play continued even as the fallen player was dragged from the field by the referee's assistants.

Jagang, having seen enough, turned and started off toward the next Ja'La field. The men in the crowd, all pushing and shoving as they tried to see the game, parted for the emperor leaving their game. The crowd was huge, even though in such a camp it constituted only a small fraction of the men.

The construction of the ramp continued despite the games. Most of the men working on it would have plenty of time, once their shift was over, to see other games that were to go on throughout the day and evening. From what Kahlan could gather from bits of conversation, there were a lot of teams contending for the right to eventually play the emperor's team. The tournaments constituted a welcome diversion for men with nothing to do but endure endless days of working and the interminable siege of the People's Palace.

It was a long trek through the cheering, shouting, booing men watching the game the emperor was leaving behind. Making their way through the muddy, filthy, reeking camp, they eventually arrived at the next Ja'La field. An area had been roped off for the emperor and his party of guards. Jagang and a number of officers who had joined him talked at length about the teams who were about to play. Apparently, the game they'd left was between lesser-ranked teams. This game, though, was supposed to be between men who were for some reason expected to offer a better show.

The two point men were just arriving at center field to draw straws to determine which team would get the chance at first play. A hush fell over the crowd as they waited. The point men both drew a straw from a bunch the referee held out in his fist. The two men held up their straws. The man with the short straw cursed. The winning point man held the straw high as he cried out in triumph. His fellow players and the crowd favoring his team sent up a thunderous cheer.

The long straw give him the choice of taking the broc on the first play or giving it to the man who had pulled the short straw. Of course, no team ever gave up their chance to be first to score a point. Scoring first augured well for their prospect of victory.

From what Kahlan overheard from the soldiers and guards

around her, it was believed by most that the Game of Life was won or lost by that very first draw of a straw. That straw, they believed, revealed what fate had in store.

Neither point man was the one Kahlan was looking for.

As the game started, it became obvious that these men were better than those playing in the last game. The tackles were wild efforts. Men threw themselves through the air in desperate attempts to make contact—either to take out the point man or to protect him. The point man, besides running with the broc, used its weight to help knock a man out of his way. As another man closed on him, he heaved the broc with all his might at close range. The blocker grunted with the weight of the impact of the broc and fell. The fans rooted and hooted. One of the wing men scooped up the broc and tossed it to the point man as they charged across the field.

"I'm sorry," Jillian whispered up to Kahlan while the guards, officers, and Jagang all watched the game, some of them commenting on the players.

"It wasn't your fault, Jillian. You did your best."

"But you did so much. I wish I was as good as you and then—"

"Shush, now. I'm a captive, too. We both are no match for these men."

Jillian smiled just a little, then. "I'm at least glad to be with you."

Kahlan returned the smile in kind. She glanced at her guards. They were caught up in watching the excitement of the game.

"I'll try to think of a way to get us out of this," she whispered.

From time to time Jillian peeked out between the big men to try to see what was happening on the field. When Kahlan noticed Jillian rubbing her bare arms and that she was beginning to shiver in the cold, she wrapped her cloak protectively around the girl, sharing her warmth with her.

As time wore on, each team scored a point. With the game tied, time almost out, and both teams unable to gain much of an advantage, Kahlan knew that it might last quite a while in overtime play until a winner was decided.

It didn't take as long as she'd thought it would nor did it need to go into overtime. The point man of one team was tackled low from behind while at the same time another blocker, in a coordinated attack, flew in from the front, hitting him square in the chest with a lowered shoulder. The point man went limp and hit the ground hard. The tackle looked like it might very well have broken the man's back. The crowd went wild.

Kahlan turned Jillian's face away and pressed it in against her instead. "Don't watch."

Jillian, on the edge of tears, nodded. "I don't know why they like such cruel games."

"Because they are cruel people," Kahlan murmured.

Another man was designated point man as their fallen leader was carried away to a deafening roar of satisfaction on the one side, and angry yells on the other. The two sides of onlookers seemed on the verge of combat, but when play swiftly resumed they were quickly caught up in the fast-paced action.

The team who had lost the point man fought desperately, but it soon became apparent that they were fighting a losing battle. The new point man was not the equal of the man they'd lost. When the last regular play of the hourglass was finished they had lost by two points—a resounding victory for the other team. Such a point spread, as well as eliminating the opposing point man in such savage fashion, would add greatly to the winning team's reputation.

Jagang and the officers looked to be pleased with the results of the game. It had proven to have had all the elements of brutality, blood, and ruthless triumph that they believed Ja'La dh Jin should have. The guards, intoxicated with the murderous ferocity of the play, whispered among themselves, going over what they had liked best about some of the more violent clashes. The crowd, already worked up by the game, was excited all the more by the ensuing whippings. They were fired up, eagerly anticipating the next game.

As they waited, they began a rhythmic chant, impatiently urging the next teams out. They clapped their hands in time to their monotone cries for action.

One of the teams emerged from the crowd at the far end of the field on the right. By the way they cheered, the crowd recognized a favored team. Each player raised a fist over his head as they strutted in a circle around the field, showing off for their fans. Men in the crowd, as well as the women camp followers, cheered the team they knew and supported.

One of Jagang's guards standing not far in front of Kahlan commented to the man next to him that this team was more than merely good, and he expected that they would badly maul their foe. By the hooting of the crowd, most onlookers seemed to be of the same mind. Apparently, this was a popular team with the kind of hostile reputation the men of Imperial Order liked and remembered. After the previous game, the mob of soldiers was aroused and eager for blood.

The vast crush of soldiers all stretched, craning their necks to see the other team as they finally made their way out through the crowd on the left. They emerged in single file, no fists raised, no show of bravado.

Kahlan stared in surprise along with everyone else. A hush fell over the crowd. No one cheered.

They were too astonished to cheer.

CHAPTER 11

The men, all without shirts, marched in single file out from the middle of a thick knot of grim guards, all with arrows at the ready. Each man in the column making his way toward the center of the field was painted with strange red symbols. The lines, whorls, circles, and arcs covered their faces, chests, shoulders, and arms.

They looked like they had been marked in blood by the Keeper of the underworld himself.

Kahlan noticed that the man at the lead had designs drawn on him that, while similar, were slightly different. In addition, he alone had twin lightning bolts on his face. Starting from the temple on each side, in a mirror image of each other, the top part of each bolt zigzagged over the eyebrow, the center lobe of each lightning bolt passing over the eyelid, with the bottom of the zigzag slashing over the cheekbones, finally terminating in a point at the hollow of each cheek.

Kahlan found the effect viscerally frightening.

Glaring out from the raptor gaze at the center of those twin lightning bolts were penetrating gray eyes.

It was hard to make out what the man looked like beneath the distraction of lines. The strange symbols, and especially the lightning bolts, confused the features beneath. Kahlan suddenly realized that he had found a way to hide his identity without the mud. She didn't let so much as a smile slip onto her features. While relieved, at the same time she wished that she could see his face, really see it, see what he looked like.

He was not as big as some of the other hulking players, but he was still a big man—tall and muscular, but not muscled the way some of the thick, heavy, bull-like men were muscled. This man was built in a way that was all the right proportions.

As she stared at him, Kahlan suddenly feared that everyone might see her transfixed by the man. She could feel her face flushing.

Still, she stared. She couldn't seem to help herself. This was the first time she'd really gotten a good look at the man. He looked exactly the way she somehow knew he would. Or maybe it was that he looked just the way she dreamed he would. The cold first day of winter suddenly felt warm to her.

She wondered who this man was to her. She made herself rein in her imagination. She dared not daydream about things that she knew could never be.

While the other point man laughed, the man with the gray eyes waited before the referee, his cutting gaze fixed on his counterpart.

She had known the instant she'd seen the painted designs that it would be viewed by these soldiers as empty bravado. The painted designs were the sort of visual statement that, if not backed up by a man of the right nature, would in such circumstances be the worst kind of presumption, the kind of provocation that would bring him brutal, if not lethal, treatment.

Hiding his face was one thing, but this was altogether something else. He was putting himself and his team at great risk by making such a proclamation in paint. It almost seemed that the lightning bolts were meant to insure that no one could miss that he was the point man, as if he meant to direct the other team's focus and attention to him. She couldn't imagine why he would do such a thing.

Following their point man's lead, the team that wasn't painted had all started laughing. The crowd, too, had joined in, laughing, hooting, and calling the painted men, and in particular the point man with the lightning bolts, names.

Kahlan knew without a doubt that there was no more dangerous mistake to be made than to laugh at this man.

The painted team stood as still as stone, waiting while the crowd went into a riot of laughter and mockery. The other team shouted insults and taunts. Some of the women camp followers threw small things—chicken bones, rotten food, and even dirt when nothing else could be found.

The players on the other team called the man with lightning bolts the kind of names that caused Kahlan to absently cover Jillian's ear with a hand, pressing her head to Kahlan's chest. She wrapped her cloak around Jillian. She didn't know what was going to happen, but she knew for sure that this game was not going to be a place for a girl.

The point man with the twin lightning bolts stood with an expressionless look that showed nothing of what he might be feeling. It reminded Kahlan of herself when she put on a blank expression when facing certain kinds of terrible challenges, a blank look that betrayed nothing of what was building inside her.

And yet, in this man's calm demeanor Kahlan saw coiled fury.

He never looked her way—his gaze was fixed on his counterpart—but just seeing him standing there, seeing all of him, seeing his face, even though it was covered in painted lines, seeing the way he held himself, seeing him at length without having to quickly look away . . . made Kahlan's knees weak.

Commander Karg nudged his way in through the wall of guards to join Emperor Jagang at the side of the field. He folded his muscled arms, apparently not at all concerned about the uproar his team was causing. Kahlan noticed that Jagang was not laughing along with everyone else. He didn't even smile. The commander and the emperor tipped their heads close together and spoke in words Kahlan couldn't hear over the jeering, laughing, and vulgar insults being shouted by the crowd.

As Jagang and Commander Karg spoke at length, the other team took to dancing around the field, arms raised, the recipients of the mob's esteem even though they had yet to score a point. They had become heroes without having done anything.

These soldiers, devoted to dogmatic beliefs, were motivated by hate. They saw any individual's quiet confidence as arrogance, his competence as unjust, and such inequity as oppression. Kahlan recalled Jagang's words: "*The Fellowship of Order teaches us that to be better than someone is to be worse than everyone.*"

The men watching believed in that creed and so they hated men for appearing to proclaim with paint that they were better. At the same time, they were there to see a team triumph, to see men best other men. It was unavoidable that beliefs as irrational as those taught by the Fellowship of Order would produce endless tangles of contradictions, desires, and emotions. Shortcomings made evident by even the most basic common sense were plastered over with a liberal application of faith. Anyone who questioned matters of faith was held to be a sinner.

These men were here in the New World to eliminate sinners.

Order was finally restored by the referee calling for the crowd to settle down so that the game could start. As the spectators quieted, to a degree at least, the man with the gray eyes gestured to the referee's fistful of straws, inviting his opponent to draw first. The man drew a straw, smiling at his choice when it came out looking like it surely had to be a winning length.

The man with the gray eyes drew a straw that was longer.

As the crowd hooted their disapproval, the referee gave the broc to the point man with the painted face.

Instead of going to his side of the field to start his charge, he waited a moment until the crowd quieted a little and then graciously handed the broc to the other point man, forfeiting the first turn at an attempt to score. The crowd erupted in wild laughter at such an unexpected turn of events. They clearly thought the painted point man was a fool who had just handed victory to the other team. They cheered as if their team had just been victorious.

None of the painted team showed any reaction to what their point man had just done. Instead, they moved off in a businesslike manner, taking up their places on the left side of the field, ready to defend against the first attack.

When the hourglass was turned over and the horn blew, the attacking team wasted no time. Eager to score quickly, their charge was instantaneous. They all yelled battle cries as they rushed across the field. The painted team raced toward the center of the field to meet the charge. The roar from the crowd was deafening.

Kahlan's muscles tensed in anticipation of a terrible collision of flesh and bone.

It didn't happen the way she expected.

The painted team—the red team as the guards had already taken to calling them—deviated in their direction of charge, splitting in two and pouring to either side around the advance blockers, going instead for the rear guard. Such an unexpected and amateurish mistake was a stroke of luck for the team trying to score. Following his blockers and wing men, the point man with the broc went through the gap the red team had left open, racing straight up the field.

In an instant both wings of the red team pivoted and the opening snapped closed like great jaws, tumbling the charging blockers inward. The painted point man charged right up the middle—toward the center blockers coming for him. Just as they were about to tackle him, he sidestepped one man and whirled around, slipping between two others.

Kahlan blinked in disbelief at what she had just seen. It looked as if he had squirted like a melon seed right through half a dozen men converging on him.

One of the bigger men on the red team, likely one of the wing men, went for the charging point man with the broc. Just before reaching him, though, he dove at him too soon, so that his diving block was too low. The man with the broc jumped right over him. The crowd cheered at how deftly their man had just evaded a tackle.

But the man with the twin lightning bolts also made a flying leap over his downed wing man, using his back like a step to launch himself. He met the other point man in midflight, hooking him with an arm and upending him in midair. The reversal of direction was forceful enough to dislodge the broc. As he came crashing to the ground the man with the gray eyes caught the loose broc while it was still in the air. His foot came down on the back of the fallen point man's head, driving his face into the mud.

Kahlan knew without a doubt that he could have easily broken the man's neck, but he had deliberately avoided doing so.

Blockers from every direction dove for the painted man who now had their broc. He pivoted, changing direction. They landed where he had been but he was already gone. They crashed down instead atop their own point man.

The red team now had possession of the broc. Even though they couldn't score until it was their turn, they could keep the other team from scoring. For some reason, though, the man with the gray eyes charged across the field, flanked by his two wing men and half his blockers. They were formed into a perfect wedge as they crossed the field. When the painted men reached the scoring area on the opposite side of the field, the point man heaved the broc into one of the nets—even though it was not their turn and the point would not count.

He followed the broc, recovered it from the net, and then, rather than keeping possession in an effort to deny the other team an opportunity to score, he trotted back up the field and with an easy underarm throw tossed the broc back to the point man still on his knees spitting out mud.

The crowd gasped in confused astonishment.

What Kahlan had just seen confirmed what she had believed from the first moment she'd looked into the man's raptor gaze—this was the most dangerous man alive. More dangerous than Jagang, dangerous in a different way, but more dangerous than Jagang. More dangerous than anyone.

This was a man too dangerous to be allowed to live. Once Jagang realized what she already knew—if he didn't already know it—he might very well decide to have this man put to death.

The team with first turn took the broc back to their starting point on the right and, in a fury to redeem themselves and score a point that would count, charged across the field. Surprisingly, the red team waited rather than running to stop the advance as far away from their goal as possible. A mistake, it would seem, but Kahlan didn't think so.

When the attackers reached the red team they threw themselves into the defenders. The red team abruptly bolted in every direction, evading the overconfident blockers. As they ran, the red team came around and their own blockers formed into a crescent formation. As they raced across the field they seythed down the opposing wing men and blockers, as well as the point man. The big painted wing man stripped the broc from him, then tossed it as high as he could into the air. The man with the lightning bolts, who had already dodged, darted, and threaded his way through the line of charging men, came through at a dead run and caught the broc before it hit the ground.

By himself he had outrun all the men of the other team chasing him. When he reached the opposite end of the field he heaved the broc into the net in the corner opposite to the one he'd thrown it into the first time. The blockers dove for him but he effortlessly sidestepped and they crashed to the ground in a heap beside him. He trotted to the net and retrieved the broc.

"Who is that man?" Jagang asked in a low voice.

Kahlan knew that Jagang meant the point man with the lightning bolts painted on his face, the man with the gray eyes.

"His name is Ruben," Commander Karg said.

It was a lie.

Kahlan knew that wasn't the man's name. She didn't have any idea what his name really was, but it was not Ruben. Ruben was a disguise, just like the mud had been, just like the red paint was now. Ruben was not his real name.

She suddenly wondered what made her think such a thing.

She knew from the way he'd looked at her that first time their eyes had met the day before that he knew her. That meant that he probably had to be someone from her past. She didn't remember him, and she didn't know his real name, but she knew it was not Ruben. The name just didn't fit him.

The horn blew, marking the end of the first play. The hourglass was turned over and the horn blew again. The red team was already down at their end of the field, back beyond their starting point. They didn't bother to give themselves the advantage of getting up to the sections of the grid where they were allowed to start their attack.

Instead, the man Commander Karg had said was named Ruben, already in possession of the broc, gave a slight hand signal to his men. Kahlan's brow twitched as she watched carefully. She had never seen a point man use such hand signals.

Men playing Ja'La usually seemed to function as a loosely coordinated mob, carrying out the designated job of their position—blockers, or wing men, or guards, as seemed fitting to each man in each circumstance that came up. The prevailing wisdom was that only if each man acted as he saw fit could the team expect to deal with the unexpected variations that came about during play. They were, in a way, each reacting to what fate dealt them.

Ruben's team was different. At the completion of the signal, they pivoted and in a coordinated fashion charged ahead of him in formation. They were not acting as a loosely coordinated mob; they were behaving like a well-disciplined army going into a battle.

The men of the other team, by now enraged, each man driven by the desire for revenge, rushed to intercept the team with the broc. Crossing midfield, the red team turned as one, going for the net to their right. The defending team all went for them like bears on a tear. Their blockers knew that their job was to block, and they meant to stop the advancing red team before they could reach the scoring zone.

But Ruben didn't follow his men. He broke left at the last moment. All by himself, without even his wing men for protection, he alone went diagonally the other way across the field, heading for the net to the left. The bulk of the two teams collided in a great heap, some of the defenders not even aware that the man they were after wasn't under the pile.

Only one guard had been lagging back, saw what Ruben was doing, and was able to turn in time to block. Ruben lowered a shoulder and caught the guard square in the chest, knocking the wind from him and sending him sprawling. Without pause as he reached the scoring area of the field, Ruben heaved the broc into the net.

The red team sprinted back to their side of the field, forming up for a second attack while they still had time left. As they waited for the referee trolling with the broc across the field, they all looked to their panting leader for his hand signal. It was quick and simple, a sign that, to Kahlan, didn't look like it meant anything. When the referee tossed Ruben the broc he immediately broke into a dead run. His team was ready and sprang out ahead to fan out in a short, tight line before him.

When the angry, disorderly cluster of men of the other team were almost upon them, the red team pivoted left, scooping up the blocking charge, deflecting its momentum left. Ruben, not far behind his line of men, broke right and raced alone across open ground. Before any of the blockers could reach him, he yelled with the effort of heaving the broc from way behind the regular scoring zone. It was exceedingly difficult to make a shot from that far back. Thrown from there, a shot that went in was worth two points rather than one.

The broc arced through the air over the heads of net guards jumping wildly for it. Confused by the strange single-line charge, they hadn't expected such a long-shot attempt to score and hadn't been ready for it.

The broc just made it into the net.

The horn blew, signifying the end of the red team's scoring period.

The crowd stood stunned, mouths hanging agape. In their first turn at play, the red team had scored three points—not to mention the two points Ruben had made that didn't count.

A hush fell over the field as the other team huddled in a confidential discussion of what to do about the sudden turn of events. Their point man made what appeared to be an angry proposal. All his men, grinning at what he suggested, nodded and then broke up to begin their turn with the broc.

Seeing that they had obviously cooked up a plan, the crowd again started cheering encouragement. Over the cheers, the point man growled orders to his men. Two of his guards nodded at words Kahlan couldn't hear.

At his yell, they charged across the field, gathering into a tight knot of muscle and fury. Rather than going for the scoring zone, the point man abruptly hooked right, leading the charge oddly off course. Ruben and his defenders shifted to meet the charge but weren't able to bring their full weight to bear in time. It was a brutal impact. The strike had deliberately targeted Ruben's left wing man to the exclusion of all the other men, abandoning even the show of an attempt to score in favor of doing damage to one man in order to harm the red team's ability to play effectively.

As the crowd cheered in anticipation of first blood, the pile of men got up one at a time. Players painted red yanked their opponents back out of the way, trying to reach the men at the bottom of the heap. The left wing man for the red team was the only man who did not get up.

As the team with the broc ran back to form up another charge, Ruben knelt beside the downed man, checking on him. It was obvious by his lack of urgency that there was nothing to be done. His left wing man was dead. The crowd cheered as the fallen player was dragged away, leaving a thick trail of blood across the field.

Ruben's raptor gaze swept the sidelines. Kahlan recognized the appraisal. She could almost feel what he was thinking because she had also appraised opposition and weighed odds. The guards with arrows put tension to their bows as Ruben rose up.

"What's going on?" Jillian whispered as she peeked out from under Kahlan's cloak. "I can't see past all of Jagang's guards."

"A man was hurt," Kahlan said. "Just stay warm, there's nothing worth seeing."

Jillian nodded and remained huddled under Kahlan's protective arm and the warmth of her cloak.

The play of Ja'La was not halted for anything, even a death on the field. Kahlan felt great sadness that the death of a man was all part of the game, and cheered by the spectators.

The men with bows stationed around the field, watching over the captives who played on the red team, all seemed to be pointing their nocked arrows toward one man. She and the man with the lightning bolts painted on his face had something in common: they each had their own special guards.

As the crowd chanted for play, Kahlan felt an odd, tense, foreboding in the air.

The broc was returned to the team with time left in their turn at play. As they formed up, she knew that the moment had passed.

Kahlan saw a grim Ruben give his men a stealthy signal. Each of his men returned a slight nod. Then, just enough for them to catch his meaning, Ruben stealthily showed them three fingers. The men immediately assembled up into an odd formation.

They waited briefly as the other team started across the field at a dead run, yelling battle cries inspired by their brutal accomplishment. They believed they now had a tactical advantage that gave them the upper hand. They were confident that they could now dictate the course of the game.

As the team with the broc charged across the field, the red team broke into three separate wedges. Ruben led the smaller center wedge, heading for the point man with the broc. His two wing men—his big right wing man and the newly designated left wing man—led the majority of the blockers in the two side wedges. Some of the men on the team with the broc shifted to each side as they charged ahead to block the odd outrigger formation should they try to turn in toward their point man.

The strange defensive tactic drew scorn from Jagang's guards. From the comments Kahlan could hear they were convinced that the red team, by splitting up into three groups, would not have the weight of enough blockers left in the center to stop the point man with the broc, much less handle all the men coming at them. The guards thought that such an in-effective defense would give the aggressors an easy score and probably cost the life of another member of the red team in the center group—very possibly the point man himself, since he was now virtually unprotected.

The two outer red-team wedges cut through the sides of the charge, not blocking in the expected manner. The legs of men on the attacking team flipped up through the air as men were violently upended. Ruben's center wedge smashed into the main group of blockers defending the point man with the broc. He tucked the broc tightly against his stomach and, following behind some of his guards, leaped over the lumbling tangle of men.

Ruben, at the rear of the center wedge, running at full speed, deftly evaded the onrushing line of guards and sprang over the pileup of his blockers. As he jumped, he pushed off with one foot, twisting as he leaped off from the ground so that he spiraled through the air. In midair, as they came together, Ruben hooked his right arm around the other point man's head as if to tackle him, but the momentum of his spin suddenly and violently twisted the man's head around.

Kahlan could hear the sound of the pop as the point man's neck broke. They both crashed to the ground, Ruben on top, his arm still around the other man's neck.

When men from both teams scrambled to their feet, two men from the attacking team were down, one on each side of the field. Both men rolled in pain with broken limbs.

Ruben rose up over the point man lying dead in the center of the field. The man's head lay twisted back at a gruesome angle.

Ruben scooped the loose broc up off the ground, trotted through the stunned, confused players, and threw a point that didn't count.

The meaning of what he'd just done was clear: if another team played specifically to harm anyone on his team, then he would retaliate with a withering response. He was giving notice that by their own actions they were choosing for themselves what would happen to them.

Kahlan now knew without doubt that Ruben's red paint was no hollow display. The men on the other team lived only by his grace.

Surrounded by nearly uncountable captors, with dozens of arrows pointed at him, this one man had just laid down his own laws, laws that could not be avoided or dismissed. He had just told his opponents how they would play against him and his team. It was a clear message that, by their own actions, Ruben's opponents chose their own fate.

Kahlan had to school her features and keep herself from smiling, from shouting with joy at what he had just accomplished—from being the only one in the crowd to cheer this one man.

She wished he would look at her, but he never did.

With their point man dead and two other players now out of play—the ones primarily responsible for what could only be described as the murder of the red team's left wing man—it looked like the favored team was on the verge of an unprecedented loss.

Kahlan wondered just how many points the red team was going to win by. She expected it was going to be a rout.

Just then, out of the corner of her eye, she spotted the messenger rushing up, waving an arm to get the emperor's attention as he shoved his way through the big guards.

"Excellency," the excited man said in a breathless voice, "the men have gotten in. The Sisters there at the site asked for you to come at once."

Jagang asked no questions and wasted no time. As the play on the field resumed he started away. Kahlan glanced back just in time to see Ruben tackle the new opposing point man hard enough to rattle his teeth. All of the big guards swarmed around the emperor, opening a clear pathway before him. Kahlan knew better than to draw his attention by not following close behind.

"We're leaving," she said to Jillian, still huddling for warmth under Kahlan's cloak.

Holding hands so that they wouldn't become separated, they turned to follow Jagang. Kahlan looked back over her shoulder.

For a brief moment, their eyes met. In that fleeting instant, Kahlan realized that even though he hadn't looked her way once throughout the game, he had known exactly where she had been the entire time.

CHAPTER 12

Nicci's eyes popped open. She gasped in panic.

Dim shapes swam in her vision. She could make no sense of the indistinct forms she saw. In an effort to get her bearings her mind snatched at memories of every sort, frantically searching through their ever-changing essence, trying to find ones that seemed relevant, ones that fit. The great store of all of her thoughts seemed in as much disarray as a library full of books scattered by the twisting winds of a thunderstorm. Nothing seemed to make sense to her. She couldn't understand where she was.

"Nicci, it's me, Cara. You're safe. Calm down."

A different voice in the murky, blurry distance said, "I'll go get Zedd." Nicci saw the dark shape move and then vanish into yet more darkness.

She realized that it had to be the person who had spoken going through a doorway. That was the only thing that made sense. She thought she might cry with relief at finally being able, out of all the shapes and shadows, to grasp the simple concept of a doorway, and the vastly more complex concept of a person.

"Nicci, calm down," Cara repeated.

Nicci only then realized that she was struggling mightily, trying to move her arms, and that she was being held down. It was as if her mind and body were both jumbled, trying to function through turmoil and confusion, trying to get a grip on something solid.

But she was beginning to make sense of things.

"Six," she said with great effort. "Six."

The black memory loomed up in her mind as if she had summoned it and it had returned to finish her.

She fixated on the meaning of that word, that name, that dark form floating there in her mind. She pulled random bits inward, building them together around it. When one memory fit—the memory of the hallway with Rikka, Zedd, and Cara up ahead frozen in place on the stairs—she went on to the next and worked to add another piece.

By the sheer force of her will, order began tumbling into place. Her thoughts fused into coherence. Her memories began to coalesce.

"You're safe," Cara said, still holding Nicci's arms. "Be still, now."

Nicci wasn't safe. None of them were safe. She had to do something.

"Six is here," she managed through gritted teeth as she struggled to push Cara out of the way. "I have to stop her. She has the box."

"She's gone, Nicci. Just calm down."

Nicci blinked, still trying to clear her vision, still trying to catch her breath. "Gone?"

"Yes. We're safe for the time being."

"Gone?" Nicci clutched a fistful of red leather, pulling the Mord-Sith closer. "Gone? She's gone? How long has she been gone?"

"Since yesterday."

The memory of the dark figure seemed to stretch away into the distance, out of reach.

"Yesterday," Nicci breathed as she sank back against the pillow. "Dear spirits."

Cara finally straightened. Nicci no longer cared if she got up.

Everything had been for nothing.

She thought she might not ever want to get up again.

She stared off at nothing. "Was anyone else hurt?"

"No. Just you."

"Just me," Nicci repeated in a flat tone. "She should have killed me."

Cara frowned. "What?"

"Six should have killed me."

"Well, I'm sure she probably would have liked to, but she didn't manage to accomplish it. You're safe."

Cara hadn't understood what Nicci had meant.

"All for nothing," Nicci mumbled to herself.

Everything was lost. All the work had been for nothing. All that Nicci had accomplished had unraveled, melting away in a dark shadow's echoing laughter. All the studying, the piecing together, the monumental effort to finally understand how it all actually functioned, the work to invoke such power, to control it, to direct it—all of it had been in vain.

It had been one of the most difficult things she had ever done . . . and now it was all in ashes.

Cara dunked a cloth in a basin of water on a side table. Water ran back as she wrung the cloth. The sound of each drop falling back into the basin was pronounced, penetrating, painful.

Rather than a blur of shapes and shadows, as it had been when she'd first awakened, now everything had focused into raw sharpness. Colors seemed blindingly bright, sounds strident. The dozen candles in the nearby stand shone like twelve little suns.

Cara pressed the damp cloth to Nicci's forehead. The red color of the Mord-Sith's leather outfit hurt Nicci's eyes, so she closed them. The cloth felt like a thorned hedge being pressed against her tender flesh.

"There is other trouble," Cara said in a quiet, confidential voice.

Nicci opened her eyes. "Other trouble?"

Cara nodded as she blotted the cloth on the sides of Nicci's neck.

"Trouble with the Keep."

Nicci glanced past the foot of her bed to the heavy dark blue and gold drapes over the narrow window. The drapes were drawn closed, but there was no light at all leaking in, so she realized that it had to be nighttime.

As she looked back at Cara, Nicci frowned even though doing so hurt. "What do you mean, trouble with the Keep? What sort of trouble?"

Cara opened her mouth to speak, but then turned at the sound of a commotion coming from behind her across the room.

Zedd swooped into the room without knocking, his elbows pumping up and out to the sides in time with each long stride, his simple robes billowing behind him as if he were the king of the place come to see to kingly business. Nicci supposed that, in a way, he was.

"Is she awake?" he demanded of Cara before he had even arrived at the bedside. His wavy white hair seemed especially disheveled.

"I'm awake," Nicci answered for herself.

Zedd came to an abrupt halt, looming over her. He leaned down, scowling, having a look for himself as if not trusting her word for it.

He pressed the tips of his long, bony fingers to her forehead. "Your fever has broken," he announced.

"I had a fever?"

"Of a sort."

"What do you mean, of a sort? A fever is a fever."

"Not always. The fever you had was induced by the exertion of forces, rather than by illness. In this case, to be precise, your own forces. The fever was your body's reaction to the stress of it. Rather like the way a piece of metal gets hot when you bend it back and forth."

Nicci pushed herself up on her elbows. "You mean I had a fever caused by what Six did to me?"

Zedd straightened his robes on his angular shoulders. "In a way. The stress of exerting force against all that witchery she was doing threw your body into a feverish condition."

Nicci looked from one to the other. "Why weren't you affected? Or Cara?"

Zedd impatiently tapped his temple. "Because I was smart enough to cast a web. It protected Cara and me, but you were too far away. At that distance its protective properties weren't adequate to keep you from harm, but I dared not try any harder. Even though it wasn't enough to protect you from all harm, it was enough to at least save your life."

"Your spell protected me?"

Zedd shook a finger at her as if she had misbehaved. "You certainly weren't doing anything to defend yourself."

Nicci blinked in surprise. "Zedd, I was trying. I don't think I've ever tried harder to use my Han. I tried with all my strength to cast my power—I swear. It just wouldn't work."

"Of course not." He threw his arms up in exasperation. "That was your problem."

"What was my problem?"

"You were trying too hard!"

Nicci sat up the rest of the way. The world suddenly started spinning. She had to put a hand over her eyes. The spinning was making her sick to her stomach.

"What are you talking about?" She lifted her hand just enough to squint up at him in the candlelight. "What do you mean I was trying too hard?"

She thought she might throw up. As if annoyed by the distraction, Zedd pushed his sleeves up his arms and then reached out, pressing a finger of each hand to the opposite sides of her forehead. Nicci recognized the tingling sensation of Additive Magic crawling under her skin. It felt a little odd to her not to feel any of the Subtractive side as an element of his power, but he had no Subtractive Magic.

The sick feeling lifted.

"Better?" he asked in a tone that suggested he thought it had all been her own fault.

Nicci turned her head this way and that, stretching the muscles of her neck, testing her equilibrium. She tried to feel the nausea, fearing it would well up suddenly, but it didn't.

"Yes, I guess I am."

Zedd smiled at the small triumph. "Good."

"What do you mean I was trying too hard?"

"You can't fight a witch woman the way you were trying to do it—especially not a witch woman as powerful as that one. You were pushing too hard."

"Pushing too hard?" She felt as uncomfortable as she had as a novice when she'd been unable to grasp a lesson being taught by an impatient Sister. "What do you mean?"

Zedd gestured vaguely. "When you use your force to try to

push against what she's doing, she simply turns it back around on you. You can't reach her with your power because the force you use hasn't yet established a foundational link between the two of you, between principal and object; it's still in its free-floating, formative stage."

Nicci understood what he was saying, in theory, she just didn't know if it fit in this case.

"Are you trying to say that it's like lightning needing to find a tree, or something tall, to another its connection to the ground so it can ignite? That if there is no place within range to link to, it simply jumps back and ignites within the cloud? Turns in on itself?"

"I never thought of it in those terms, but I guess you could say that it's something like that. You might say that your power turned back in on you, like lightning turns back within a cloud when it isn't able to make it to ground. A witch woman is one of the few people who instinctively understands the precise nature of the exertion of force, the intricacies of its needs for connections, and the ways in which specific spells link at both ends."

"You mean she knows how lightning works," Cara said, "and she pulled the rug out from under Nicci."

Zedd shot the woman a dumbfounded look. "You really don't know anything about magic, do you? Or about a mixed-up token turn of a phrase."

Cara's expression darkened. "If I pull that rug out from under you, I think you'll understand it well enough."

Zedd rolled his eyes. "Well, it's an oversimplification, but I guess you could put it that way . . . Sort of," he added under his breath.

Nicci wasn't really listening; her mind was elsewhere. She remembered that she herself had done something involving those same relationships of power and connections when the beast had been attacking Richard in the shielded part of the Keep. She had created a linking node but denied that link the power to complete it. That expectancy, without being fulfilled, drew the nearest power—lightning—to the beast, eliminating it for the moment. Because the beast was not really alive, though, it couldn't actually be destroyed, in much the same way a corpse, because it was already dead, couldn't be killed, or made any more dead.

But this was different. This was well beyond what Nicci had done with the beast. This, in a way, was the opposite of what she had done.

"Zedd, I don't understand how such a thing is possible. It's like throwing a rock; once thrown, the trajectory is set. The rock would follow that trajectory to a termination point."

"She hit you on the head with your own rock before you'd even thrown it," Cara said.

Zedd fixed her in a murderous scowl, as if she were an impetuous student who had just spoken out of turn. Cara's mouth took on an obstinate twist, but she kept it closed.

Nicci ignored the interruption as she went on. "She would have needed to act on specific power as it was engendered—before it was even fully formed—as it began to ignite. That's when the foundational node is formed as well. At that point the full nature and power of the spell wouldn't even have come into being, yet."

Zedd gave Cara a sidelong glance to make sure she intended to keep quiet. When she folded her arms and remained mute, Zedd turned back to Nicci.

"That's precisely what she does," he said.

Having never actually encountered a witch woman before, the explicit mechanisms they used were a mystery to Nicci. "How?"

"A witch woman rides eddies of time. She sees the flow of events into the future. Their ability is in many ways an ancillary form of prophecy. That means she is ready for the spell before you cast it. She knows what is coming. Her own ability, her own gift, allows her to act against you before you can complete what you are doing to her.

"It all comes naturally to them—like lifting an arm when someone throws a punch at you. Her block is there as your web forms—as you begin to throw your punch. She is denying you a foundational link so that your web can't even begin to form. As I said, she has the ability to turn it back before that link between principal and object is established. Your power falls inward on itself—on you.

"It doesn't take great power on her part. Her strength is your strength. The harder you try to do something, the more difficult it becomes. She doesn't increase her effort, she merely denies yours a completing node. The harder you push, the more force it feeds back at you from her block.

"A witch woman uses you. That force, your force, folds back in on you, over and over, as you try all the harder. Much the way bending a piece of metal back and forth makes it hot, your own force bent back in on you, over and over as you tried to conjure your ability to overpower her, sent your body into a fever."

"Zedd, that can't be. You used magic. I saw you, I saw the web you cast and it didn't harm you. It merely fizzled out."

The old wizard smiled. "No, it did not fizzle out. It was a fizzle from the beginning. I was using so little power that she couldn't draw strength from it. Since she couldn't draw strength from it, she couldn't block it or bend it back. There wasn't enough for her to grab hold of."

"What kind of spell can do such a thing?"

"I cast a protection web laced inside a simple tranquillity spell. You should have done the same."

Nicci wiped a hand across her face. "Zedd, I've been a sorceress for a very long time. I've never even heard of a tranquillity spell."

He shrugged. "Well, I guess you don't know everything, now, do you? I used a tranquillity spell for the shell because if I misjudged and made it just a little too strong, and she cast it back at me, well, she would simply be making me more tranquil. Being even more calm would have helped me. I would then know the threshold had been surpassed, and I would be more calm to try again and have a better chance at success the second time."

Nicci shook her head in amazement. "It's for sure that I didn't know enough to deal with the likes of Six. What you did may not have been able to reach me, but at least it was enough to keep her from killing me."

Zedd only smiled.

She looked up at him. "Where did you learn such a trick?"

He shrugged. "Harsh experience. I've dealt with witch women before, so I knew that there was only one thing I could do."

"You mean Shota?"

"In part," he said. "When I took the Sword of Truth back from her I had a great deal of trouble. That woman is cunning, clever, and trouble behind sparkling eyes and a crafty smile. I found out that doing things the usual way simply didn't work. She found my struggles amusing. The more force I used, the worse I made things for myself, and the wider she smiled."

He smiled himself as he leaned in a little. "That was her mistake—smiling." He lifted a finger to make his point. "Her smile tipped me off that what I was doing was my own undoing. I realized in that instant that my use of force was what was giving her the power she needed."

"So you didn't use force."

He spread his hands as if she had finally grasped the lesson. "Sometimes doing what you would most like to do can be the very worst thing to do. Sometimes to accomplish what you want in the end, you have to hold back in the beginning."

As the concept he'd expressed sank in, yet more of her disordered memories—perplexing pieces of some grand puzzle that had never before fit anywhere—having been freed from where they languished in the dark corners of her mind, tumbled into place. It was as if she was seeing everything in a new light.

The sudden realizations were jolting.

Nicci's jaw fell open. Her eyes went wide.

"I understand, now. I know what it meant. Dear spirits, I understand. I know the purpose of the sterile field."

CHAPTER 13

Sterile field?" Zedd's bushy white brow drew down. "What are you talking about?"

Nicci pressed her fingertips to her forehead as she reasoned it all out. She could hardly believe she hadn't realized it sooner. She looked up at the wizard.

"There is a complex order of events required for the power of Orden to work. Like you said, connections based on primary foundations must be established—just as in any magic. It was, after all, created by wizards and they would have had to have based anything they did on what they knew about the nature of the things they were manipulating.

"For the most part, at its core, Orden is a complex constructed spell. Like any constructed spell, in the right conditions it is triggered by a specific set of events. It then runs according to its predetermined protocols. Yet, no matter how complex it is, once begun it still functions according to basic principles."

"And the sun rises in the east," Zedd growled. "What are you getting at?"

"It all correlates," she said to herself as she stared off at nothing for a moment.

She abruptly turned her attention back to the wizard. "*The Book of Life* explains how to put the power of Orden in play. It lays out the protocols. It's basically an operating manual; it doesn't explain the theory behind Orden—that's not its purpose. To understand the whole thing you have to look elsewhere.

"While that power, like all forms of power, can be misappropriated and looted for the objective of dominion, it was created and intended for a specific purpose: to counter the Chainfire spell. Central elements of Orden are a constructed spell so, once ignited, it runs through established routines. Those routines in turn require specific conditions—such as properly using the key, *The Book of Counted Shadows*."

Her mind was still racing through all the new connections as she fit together pieces from different sources that she had never before connected.

"Yes, yes," Zedd said as he rolled his hand impatiently. "The boxes of Orden were created specifically to counter the Chainfire spell. We already know that. What's more, it is self-evident that certain conditions must be met and that then the power will function in a given manner. That's all stone-cold obvious."

Nicci threw off the covers and stood in a rush, no longer feeling that she belonged in bed. She looked down and saw that she was in a pink nightdress. She hated pink. Why did they always end up putting her in a pink nightdress? She imagined that it must have been all they had at hand.

She ignited a razor-thin flow of Subtractive Magic almost without a thought and directed it downward through the fabric of the nightdress. With that power she scavenged through the fabric itself, allowing the Subtractive flow to seek only the elements of the dye, and eliminate it. The color in the nightdress, starting at the neckline, faded away in a wave that went through the entire garment. Eliminating the pink color left behind a simple, off-white color to the cloth.

Incredulous, Zedd stared at the nightdress. "Did you just use Subtractive Magic, the power of the underworld, the power of death itself, to take the color out of that thing?"

"Yes. Much better, don't you think?" She wasn't really paying much attention to the question as her mind was already on other things.

Zedd lifted a hand in protest. "Well, I don't think it's a good idea to—"

"What is the purpose of it all?" Nicci asked, cutting off the objection she hadn't really heard and cared even less about.

Zedd's hand paused. He was starting to look exasperated. "That is the purpose. To counter Chainfire."

"No, no. I mean what is the specific function of the counter to the spell?"

His impatience with things that seemed only too obvious was curdling into annoyance. "To make us all remember the object of the spell." His eyes flashed with that agitation. "In this case, that would be Kahlan."

"Yes, in a sense, but that is an oversimplification of the process, an expression of the terminal objective." Nicci lifted a finger, now the teacher instead of the student. "In order to do as you just said it has to restore what was destroyed in us. It has to re-create our memories.

"It's not a matter of the power of Orden making us remember things we've forgotten but, rather, of needing to reconstruct what is no longer there.

"Those lost memories are gone. It isn't that we've forgotten things and we can't recall the people and events. There is nothing there in our minds for us to recall because those memories are nonexistent, not merely forgotten. They have been eroded and destroyed by the Chainfire event. It's not that we just aren't able to remember things. The reality is that those parts of our minds—of our memories—have been destroyed.

"In actual fact, there is nothing there for us to remember.

"Re-creating from scratch what is gone is altogether different from helping us to remember things. It's the difference between someone who is asleep, and someone who is dead. On the surface both may look much the same, but having their eyes closed is about the only thing they have in common.

"The end objective may be the same in both instances, but both the problem and the means to solve it have nothing in common. In order for Orden to counter Chainfire and restore us to the way we were before, it needs to incarnate in our minds knowledge, awareness, of what has happened in the past. It needs to create new memories to replace those that were destroyed. It needs to bring our memories back to life."

As he considered her words, tension had settled in Zedd's brow, replacing the impatience that had been there. His gaze tracked her as she paced. "Well, yes, there somehow has to be a reestablishment to real events from the past." He scratched his temple as he viewed her askance. "Are you saying that you think that you now understand how such a thing could work?"

Nicci's bare feet padded across the carpets as she paced. "From what I've pieced together from what I've read, those who created the boxes of Orden, even though they intended them to be a counter to Chainfire, weren't themselves convinced that such a thing could actually be done."

Nicci halted to look at him. "Can you even imagine how monumentally complex such a thing would have to be? How complicated it would be to rebuild and restore memories in everyone? How convoluted?

"I mean, those wizards back then must have driven themselves crazy trying to sort out how such a thing could rebuild what no longer has a template. How is Orden to know what you are supposed to remember? Or Cara? Or me? What's worse, people believe all the time that they correctly recall things but their recollections are in error. How will Orden rebuild memories that once were but no longer are, when those memories themselves, when we had them, weren't always true, or accurate?

"From what I read in the books on Ordenic theory, even the wizards who created Orden weren't certain that it would work."

She started pacing again as she went on. "Don't forget, they couldn't test it against an actual Chainfire event. Chainfire itself was never tested, either—no one dared to—so, while they had confidence in their syllogism, they still couldn't be completely certain of how Orden would work in the real world. Because they couldn't observe an actual Chainfire event play out, they couldn't be positive that their counter would work as they intended it to, even if all the complicated elements functioned perfectly and according to plan—and there was even cause for doubt in that part of it as well.

"All that said, there is an even more important aspect to the protocols they established and that is the need to counter the Chainfire spell in the subject—in this case, Kahlan. The subject is the vortex of the whole thing, the center of the entire Chainfire event. She is the center of an enormously complex equation.

"Therefore, the counter to the entire event must anchor itself there, in her. The element of constructed magic in the elaborate system of Orden must ignite in her."

"She is the foundational link . . ." Zedd said, half to himself, as he stared off, following along with Nicci's reasoning.

"That's right." Nicci said. "And for Orden to do such a thing, for it to repair the damage done starting from the center of that storm, it requires that such a foundational link be a sterile field."

"A sterile field?" Zedd asked, still frowning as he listened intently. "You mentioned that before."

Nicci nodded. "It's a shadowy element that the wizards wrestled with throughout the work on the creation of the Ordenic counter to Chainfire. I didn't understand the importance of it before, didn't grasp the significance of the issue they were grappling with, didn't see why they were so concerned about it, but what you've explained about a witch woman's ability finally allowed me to comprehend the concept at the center of Ordenic theory."

Zedd planted his fists on his bony hips. "You didn't understand part of Ordenic theory? And yet you put it in play—in Richard's name? Even when you didn't understand it?"

Nicci ignored the heated tone of the question. "Just the part about the sterile field. I realize now that it's much the same as what you explained about how I needed a link when I cast a spell at Six, but she denied me that place to anchor the spell. Orden must initiate magic in a similar manner. Like all magic, it, too, needs a connection. That connection is Kahlan. But it needs that target of the connection to be a blank slate."

"A blank slate?" Zedd tilted his head in toward her. "Nicci, need I remind you that the person is a blank slate? The Chainfire spell erases everything from their past. It renders them blank, in a manner of speaking. Orden thus has what it needs."

Nicci shook her head insistently. "No. You have to consider it all together in the context of the *Chainfire* book, *The Book of Life*, and those obscure books you found for me on Ordenic theory. You have to look at it all, at the larger picture, to see it."

"See what?" Zedd roared in exasperation.

"The subject must be emotionally blank, or the whole thing is tainted."

"Emotionally blank?" Cara asked when Zedd fell to muttering to himself as he wiped a hand down his face. "What does that mean?"

"It means that knowledge of her previous emotional condition would contaminate the effort to restore what was within her. She has to remain emotionally blank for Orden to be able to do its job. The subject has to be kept blank. Care must be taken not to introduce emotional links."

"Nicci, you are a bright woman," Zedd said, trying to remain calm, "but this time you've driven the wagon off the bridge and into the river."

He started in pacing himself. "What you're saying doesn't make any sense. How can the subject be prevented from finding out anything at all about their past? The wizards who created the boxes of Orden must have realized that the chances were the subject would find out any number of things about their past before Orden could be brought to bear. They couldn't expect the person to be locked in a dark room until Orden could be employed."

"That's not what I mean. You're missing my point. Details don't matter—in fact details learned by anyone with lost memories only help because they are like guide pins on which to fit the template of the restoration process of Orden. But great emotional experiences within the subject of Chainfire do matter. Emotions are the sums created by details, whether those details are true or not."

Cara looked focused on trying to understand what Nicci was saying. "How can emotions be created by false details?"

"Take me, for example," Nicci said. "The things that I was taught by the Fellowship of Order caused me to hate anyone who resisted the teachings of the Order, hate anyone who accomplished anything. I believed as I was taught, that such people were selfish heathens who didn't care about their fellow man.

"I was taught to have an emotional response of hatred to all those who didn't believe as I did. I was taught to hate you and everything you did without actually knowing anything about you. I had a visceral, emotional hatred for the value of life itself. I would have killed Richard based on those emotional drives. My emotions were based on lies and indoctrination, not anything true."

Cara sighed. "I see what you mean. You and I were both taught similar things and made to feel similar emotions, and those emotions were completely mistaken."

"But emotions, when based on valid things, can be a faithful and consistent sum of truths."

"Valid things?" Cara asked.

"Of course," Nicci said. "Such as worthwhile values. Love—proper love, true love—is a response to those things we value in others. It's an emotional response to life-affirming values held by another person. We value the good nature of that other person. In those cases that emotion is a central, powerful part of our humanity."

Zedd, still pacing, came to an impatient halt. "What does this have to do with anything?"

Nicci spread her hands. "Keep in mind that Ordenic theory is just that, theory, so I can't say that I know for certain because even those who created it didn't know it for certain, either, but it all fits. While they were convinced they were correct, they had no actual experience of foreknowledge tainting magic in which to ground their theory, but I think they were right."

Zedd leaned in, peering at her with one eye. "Right about what, exactly?"

"Emotions interjected into the subject without the underlying cause will corrupt the countering of the Chainfire spell."

Cara frowned. "You lost me."

"They were convinced that foreknowledge of a certain emotional nature would taint the magic they were using, taint Orden." Nicci looked from Zedd's troubled hazel eyes to Cara. "What it means is that if Kahlan were to learn the truth of her emotions—her dominant emotions—before the correct box of Orden is opened, then Orden will not be able to restore those emotions. The field where Orden must ignite would be contaminated by that foreknowledge. Kahlan would be lost in the tangle of the spell."

Cara put her hands on her hips. "What *are* you talking about?"

"Well, let's say, for example, that Richard found Kahlan and he told her about the two of them, about their emotional connection, their love for one another. In that case Orden would be prevented from working."

The wizard's face had gone unreadable. "Why?" he asked in a tone that sent a shiver up her spine.

"It's kind of like the way my spells didn't work against Six because the strength of my power first needed to establish anchors, foundations, in order to do its work."

"You mean that if Richard ever gets the chance to actually open one of the boxes of Orden," Zedd asked, "he must do so with the subject completely unaware of her ties to him?"

Nicci nodded. "Her deepest emotional ties, anyway. We have to be sure Richard understands that if we find Kahlan before he gets the chance to open the correct box of Orden, he can't interject any causeless emotion or it will corrupt the field."

"Causeless emotion?" Cara's nose wrinkled. "Are you trying to say that Lord Rahl can't tell Kahlan that she loves him?"

"Exactly," Nicci said.

"But why?"

"Because right now, she doesn't," Nicci said. "Those things that caused her to fall in love with him are no longer in her. The foundation of her love—the memory of the things that happened, the things she did with him, the reasons that she fell in love with him—are no longer there in her. Chainfire destroyed those memories. Right now, it's as if she never met him before. She does not love him. She has no reason to love him. She is a blank slate."

Zedd poked a long thin finger through his thatch of wavy hair and scratched his scalp. "Nicci, I think the fever may have done more damage than I thought. What you're saying makes no sense. Kahlan's problem is that Chainfire made her forget her past. Orden was created to counter Chainfire. There is nothing as powerful as Orden. It's the power of life itself. Revealing to Kahlan something as simple as her love for Richard is not going to cause the restoration to become scrambled."

"Oh, but it would." Nicci paced a few steps and returned to stand before him. "Zedd, with all your power as First Wizard, why couldn't you stop a mere witch?"

"Because she turns your power back around on you."

"That's the key," Nicci said. "That's the part I needed to add in, why I was finally able to put together everything I've been reading in those books. I was finally able to understand what the wizards who created Orden meant about the sterile field. The force of emotions will turn back the power applied to the person.

"It's something like the way that trying to convince those who believe in the teachings of the Order that they are wrong in their feelings only strengthens those feelings, makes them even more resistant to casting off those false beliefs. If you tell them that the Order is evil they will hate you all the more, not the Order. Their belief in the Imperial Order is steeled, rather than broken."

"So what?" Cara said. "It wouldn't be contradictory for Kahlan, like in your example. If Lord Rahl were to tell Kahlan that she loves him, that would be what the magic of Orden would do anyway, so it's not really a problem."

"Oh, but it is a problem," Nicci said, waggling a finger. "A very big problem. The whole thing would be backwards. The effect would be there without the cause. Emotions are the end result, the sum, of things learned. Putting emotions in first would be like trying to construct a two-story building by starting at the roof and working your way down to the foundation. Or, like me trying to push a powerful spell at a witch woman.

"The emotions that Orden would otherwise put back where they belong would be turned away by the emotions that were placed there by foreknowledge. Foreknowledge would interfere with the protocols."

"That's what I mean," Cara insisted. "Kahlan would already have been told that she loves Lord Rahl, so it couldn't possibly matter."

"But it does. You see, that foreknowledge would be empty. The emotions revealed ahead of time have no meaning, no substance. They aren't real. If she were to be told of her love for Richard, then Orden wouldn't be able to restore her true emotions of love."

Cara looked like she was ready to pull her hair out in exasperation. "But Lord Rahl would already have told her, so it's the same difference. She would know. She would already know that she loves him."

"No. One would be true, the other not. Don't forget, right now she doesn't love him. The real emotions Orden would be trying to build would already have been replaced by something that isn't real—emotions without cause. Those emotions would be empty and untrue. The reasons she loves him would be missing, so while the foreknowledge of her love might be there it would be empty knowledge. It would be empty love, love based on nothing. Love without everything supporting it would be meaningless."

Cara lifted her arms and then let them flop back to her sides. "I just don't get it."

Nicci halted her pacing and turned back to Cara. "Imagine that I bring a man you've never seen before into the room and I tell you that you love him. Would you love him because I told you that you did? No, because you can't inject such emotions without something to support them.

"That's what Orden does; it builds support for the real emotions from the knowledge of past events that it restores. It establishes the causes. Putting the emotions there first—the end result of past events—taints that process. According to the wizards who created Orden, her foreknowledge of loving him would contaminate the field, taint her mind, so that the incarnation of the real events—the reasons behind why she loves him—couldn't be engendered in her. They would be blocked, the way the witch woman blocked my spells. She would be left with nothing but the hollow information. She couldn't retrieve her past. It would remain lost to her."

Zedd scratched his jaw. He looked up. "But, as you say, this is only theory."

"The wizards who dreamed up Ordenic theory in order to counter Chainfire, and from that theory created the boxes of Orden, came to believe they were right. I also believe that their conclusions are correct."

"What would happen if, if, I don't know," Cara said, "if Lord Rahl told Kahlan first—about her loving him and that she was his wife—and then later he was finally able to get the boxes of Orden, and get his power back, and learn what was necessary, and he finally opened the correct box, invoking the counter to the Chainfire event? Would the counter to Chainfire still work?"

"Yes, the counter would still work."

Cara looked truly confused. "So, what's the problem?"

"It's a constructed spell, so the protocols would run just the same. If the theory is sound, and I think it is, all the other components of Orden would still function. The Chainfire spell would be countered and everyone's memories would be restored—with one exception. Orden would be unable to rebuild Kahlan's past. That element of the spell would be blocked. The one at the center of the storm would be lost to it.

"We would all be restored, our memories would be what they once were, we would all remember Kahlan, but Kahlan would forever be without her past. You might say she would be like a soldier injured in battle who, because of a head injury, no longer is who he once was. She would only be able to go on from her life after the Chainfire spell had taken her identity from her. She would only be aware of things from that point on. She would be a different person, a person who would have to build a new life for herself.

"All the while she would have the knowledge that she was supposed to love this person, Richard, whom she doesn't know and for whom she has no real feeling."

"So, then she would be the only casualty," Cara said. "The rest of us would be restored."

Nicci sighed. "Well, that's my belief from my understanding of the theory."

Zedd was looking suspicious again. "But there is an alternate possibility?"

Nicci nodded. "Not one I'd like to contemplate. One of the lines of reasoning in the books of Ordenic theory postulates that absent the anchor it needs in a sterile field, the counter would be unable to run its protocols and collapse in on itself. That line of reasoning suggests that in such a circumstance the counter would fail and the Chainfire event would burn on out of control. Life as we know it would be lost. Our ability to reason would crumble as the inferno of Chainfire continued to burn, until our minds would be unable to support our own existence. Savagery would sustain some people for a short time, but the inevitable outcome would be the extinction of mankind.

"I think you can see why the wizards who created Orden were so concerned about preserving the sterile field."

Zedd frowned in thought. "But the predominant theory is that if something were to go wrong, and she were to gain such foreknowledge before Orden could be brought to play, she would forever remain a casualty of Chainfire but that wouldn't really interfere with Chainfire in everyone else being countered."

"That's right. In a way, as much as Kahlan means to Richard, I'm afraid that in this she has become secondary to the Chainfire event. It may have started with her, but now everyone is infected. If that event is not stopped, everything is lost. Countering Chainfire has become more important than Richard and Kahlan's love for each other. It would be wonderful if her love for him could be restored, but it isn't necessary in order to counter the Chainfire event.

"Regardless of what it means for this one person, for Kahlan, or what it means for Richard, personally, the power of Orden must be invoked to counter Chainfire in order to purge the infection from everyone else.

"There's one other alternate theory, besides the one about the whole thing not working if the field is tainted. A few wizards believed that Ordenic theory might indicate that pouring so much power into the subject of the Chainfire event in anything but a sterile field—one contaminated with foreknowledge—would kill the person."

"What about everyone else in such a mishap?" Zedd asked.

"By the time she hits the floor dead, the trigger for the constructed portion of Orden would already have been initiated and the rest of the spell would run through its protocols. Orden would ripple outward from the core and do its job.

"If that happens, if Kahlan is lost in the effort, it will be a terrible personal loss for Richard, but it will mean nothing more than that for the rest of us. The introduction of Orden would destroy the Chainfire contamination and restore everyone else."

Zedd gave her a hard look. "We may not remember Kahlan, but there is no doubt in any of us what she means to Richard. He has already shown us that he would be willing to go to the underworld if he thought doing so could save her life. If he knew that opening one of the boxes and releasing the power of Orden would kill her . . ."

Nicci didn't shy from his look, or the implication. "Richard must open the correct box of Orden and initiate the constructed spell that will counter Chainfire . . . even if it means that it will kill Kahlan. It's as simple as that."

The room was silent for a moment.

Zedd rubbed a finger back and forth on his chin as he gazed off into the shadows. "It would seem wise, in view of such dangers—whether real or not—to see to it that if Kahlan is found she be kept in the dark about her former feelings for Richard. Best to let Orden restore her emotions."

"That makes the most sense to me, too," Nicci said. "When we get Richard back we have to convince him that should he find her, he must not reveal the truth to her."

Zedd clasped his hands behind his back as he shook his head. "Considering everything at stake, I agree that such a thing is wise, and that it should be our plan, but I don't know that I really believe such a thing as simple foreknowledge could cause such a personal tragedy. I don't know if I can believe that such a simple thing as foreknowledge can cause such great harm."

"If it's any consolation to you, there were wizards involved in the creation of the boxes of Orden who held the same view. But then it seemed impossible to me that using power against a witch woman would bring me to harm."

Zedd stared off, absently, as he considered. "You have a point. Great harm can sometimes result from the best of intentions.

"When we find the boy we can tell him all this. But we're an awfully long way from any of this ever happening. We no longer have even one of the boxes of Orden."

Nicci sighed. "True enough. What worries me the most, though, is convincing Richard of this." Nicci cleared her throat. "When we find him, I think it best if such a thing came from you, Zedd. He might take it better coming from you. He might be more open to listening."

Zedd glanced her way before resuming his pacing. "I understand." He halted and turned to Nicci. "But I'm still not sure I buy the whole theory about emotional foreknowledge being able to taint . . ."

In midsentence, Zedd's mouth snapped closed with a startled expression.

"What?" Nicci asked. "Did you think of something?"

Zedd sank down to sit on the edge of the bed. "Yes, I most certainly did."

The power, the fire, had gone out of him.

"Dear spirits," he whispered, sounding as if the weight of his years had just settled on his slumped shoulders.

Nicci leaned down and touched his arm. "Zedd, what's wrong?"

He looked up at her with haunted eyes. "Foreknowledge can affect how magic works. It's not a theory. It's true."

"Are you sure? How do you know?"

"I don't remember Kahlan, or anything about her. When Richard was here, though, he told me about her. He filled me in on my missing memories of how he came to love her, and she him.

"Kahlan is a Confessor. A Confessor's gift destroys the mind of the person she touches with her power. Confessors release their restraint on their power to unleash it. The rest of the time they must keep it under their tight control."

"I know, I've heard about their ability." Nicci said. "But what does that have to do with their love?"

"A Confessor always chooses her mate from among those they don't really care about because if she were to be intimate with a man she loved she would unintentionally lose control of that power. So released, her power would take the man. He would stand no chance. He would no longer be who he was. He would be lost, his mind destroyed. He would be a hollow shell, left with a blind, mindless devotion to the Confessor. She would have him, have his love and devotion, but it would be meaningless, empty love.

"For this reason Confessors always choose a man they don't care about, and then take him with their power. They choose a mate for what kind of father he would be, for the daughter he could produce, but they never choose a man they love. Men fear an unmarried Confessor in search of a mate, fear being chosen, fear losing who they are to her power."

"But there obviously must be a way for it to work," Nicci said. "How did Richard accomplish it?"

Zedd looked up. "There is only one way. I can't tell you what it was. I couldn't tell Richard, either. I couldn't even tell him that a way existed."

"Why not?" she asked.

"Because the foreknowledge would have tainted him and her magic, when first she unleashed it on him without intending to, would have taken him. He had to be totally unaware of the solution to it, or that a solution even existed, or that solution would not have worked."

Zedd stared at the floor. "It is no theory. Foreknowledge can taint a sterile field, as you put it. Richard himself proved the central question of Ordenic theory: foreknowledge can affect the function of magic."

Nicci padded barefoot across the carpet to stand before him. She frowned down at the old wizard. "You knew of this beforehand, before Richard and Kahlan were married? You knew that the foreknowledge of the solution would cause it to fail in Richard?"

"I did. But I dared not tell him that a solution existed that would enable him to be with his love. Even that much foreknowledge, even the knowledge that there might be a solution, would ruin his chance of it working."

"How did you know about this?"

Zedd lifted a hand and then let it fall back to his lap. "The very same thing happened to the first Confessor, Magda Searus, and the man who loved her, Merritt. They, too, ended up in love and married. Since that time, Richard was the first to ever again solve the problem. Since Magda Searus was the first Confessor, no one knew that there was a solution; therefore, there was not yet any foreknowledge to taint him. Without such foreknowledge he was able to solve the paradox of loving a Confessor without her power destroying him."

Nicci pulled at a strand of blond hair as she considered. "Then the reality of foreknowledge alone being able to taint magic is true." She frowned down at Zedd. "But the wizards who created Orden knew of no example of foreknowledge tainting a spell. It was only a theory for them."

Zedd shrugged. "That probably means that Confessors were created after Orden. First Wizard Merrit proved the concept, so maybe it happened after Orden had already been created."

Nicci sighed at it all. "I suppose that might be the answer."

She gestured vaguely as she went on to other business. "Cara said something, before, about there being a problem. A problem with the Keep."

Zedd finally looked up from his private thoughts and stood. The creases in his face drew into a grave expression.

"Yes, there is trouble."

"What sort of trouble?" Nicci asked.

He started for the door. "Come with me, and I'll show you."

CHAPTER 14

Zedd led Nicci and Cara toward an area of the Keep that Nicci knew to be a labyrinth of halls and passageways heavily guarded by layers of shields. Glass spheres in iron brackets brightened in turn as they approached each one, then faded back into darkness as they passed. The Keep felt like a great, silent, gloomy place to Nicci. It was not only immense, but immensely complex, and she couldn't imagine what could be the trouble with it that so concerned Zedd.

Before they had gone far, Rikka; Tom, the big blond-headed D'Haran from Lord Rahl's elite guard; and Friedrich the old gilder emerged from a reading room to join in the quiet procession. Nicci guessed that they had all been waiting there for her to awake from her encounter with Six. That Zedd had probably asked them to stand by and wait for Nicci to wake only heightened her growing sense of concern.

"You look a lot better than you did last night," Rikka said as they started through a cozy room hung with hundreds of paintings of every size. The paintings, each in a rich gold-leaf frame, covered every bit of the walls.

"Thanks. I'm fine now."

Nicci noticed that the paintings hung throughout the room were all portraits, though the styles varied greatly. The subjects in some, dressed in ceremonial robes, sat in formal poses while in others the people stood casually in beautiful gardens, met in conversation among grand columns, or relaxed on benches in courtyards.

She saw that in many of the portraits the Keep, or parts of it, were visible in the background. It was a somewhat startling and sad thought to realize that all of these people had probably once lived in the Keep, a place that had been alive with life. It made the place now seem all the more deserted and empty.

Rikka cast a sidelong glance down the length of Nicci. "That nightdress was pink, before."

"I hate pink." Nicci said.

Rikka looked disappointed. "Really? When Cara and I put you in it I thought that it made you look even prettier."

At first startled by such a statement coming from a Mord-Sith, Nicci suddenly grasped the whole pink nightgown thing. This was a woman trying to find her way out of the dark wasteland of madness. She was trying to throw off the shackles of emotions that had been drilled into her since she had been a girl. Everything in her life, her world, had been ugly and violent. The pink nightdress represented something innocent and lovely—the kind of thing forbidden to the likes of a Mord-Sith. By appreciating such a simple thing on Nicci, she was testing the possibility of enjoying something attractive and harmless—testing dreams. It was much the same as a young girl making a pretty dress for a doll. It was a considered examination of aesthetics and, more than that, it was practice at aspirations.

"Thank you," Nicci said. After a moment's consideration she added. "It is a pretty nightdress, it's just that it's the wrong color for me, that's all. How about if after I'm dressed I return the color to the nightdress and you can have it."

Rikka's expression turned suspicious. "Me? I don't know if—"

"It would look beautiful on you. Honest. The pink color would go well with your skin tones."

Rikka looked a bit flustered and uncertain. "Really?"

Nicci nodded. "It would be perfect for you. I'd like you to have it."

Rikka hesitated a moment. "Well, I'll think about it," she finally said.

"I'll clean it and make sure the color is just the right shade of pink for you."

Rikka smiled. "Thanks."

Nicci wished that Richard could have been there to see the small smile that was such a great risk for a Mord-Sith. He would have understood that such a seemingly tentative step was really a rather big shift for such a woman. Nicci realized, too, that it warmed her own heart to see such a positive, if tiny, step back toward the simple joys of life.

She comprehended at seeing Rikka's smile how Richard must feel at such things.

As a yet larger realization dawned on her, she almost laughed out loud. Richard would not merely have appreciated Rikka's growth, he would also have seen Nicci—Death's Mistress—learning herself how to connect another person with the joy of life, if only in a small matter. She hadn't even realized that she and Rikka had just taken a step together. Nicci couldn't imagine how Richard must have felt to have brought her back from the dark existence she had lived for her whole life.

For just an instant, she had a glimpse, a vision, of life through Richard's eyes. It was a staggeringly joyous perspective, a view of how each person's choices could make their own life better. It was a vision of the possible, of how things could and should be.

How she missed him. She would have given anything at that moment just to see his smile, that smile that seemed to reflect all that was good and decent. She missed him so much that she thought she might burst into tears.

Rikka cast Nicci a sidelong glance. "Are you all right? The witch woman didn't do you any lasting harm, did she? You look a little, I don't know . . . distressed."

Nicci dismissed the concern with a flick of a hand and changed the subject. "Did you find Rachel?"

As they emerged from a stone room lined with tapestries of country scenes and into a broad hall with wood-paneled walls, the Mord-Sith gave Nicci an unreadable look. "No. Early this morning Chase came back and told us that he found her tracks outside the Keep. He went off looking for her."

Rachel was another of those connections back to the simple joys of life for Rikka. Nicci knew that Rikka was quite fond of the girl, even though she never came close to admitting it.

"I don't know what in the world could have gotten into her," Zedd said back over his shoulder as he led them around a corner and into a narrower hallway. "It's just not like her to run off."

"Do you think it could have anything to do with Six being here?" Nicci suggested. "Maybe she's responsible."

Rikka shook her head. "Chase said that Rachel's tracks are all alone. He said that he didn't see any of Six's tracks."

"Are you thinking what I'm thinking?" Cara asked Nicci.

"You mean about the lesson Richard gave us one time about tracks?"

Cara nodded. "He talked about magic being able to hide tracks."

"True enough." Zedd put in. "But Rachel disappeared before Six showed up. If Six were trying to hide her tracks with some sort of magic, what would be the point of hiding her own tracks if she didn't hide Rachel's as well?"

Nicci halted abruptly. She turned back to the opening they had just passed through. A gilded pillar stood to each side of the small portal in the passageway. The pillars held up a stout beam with symbols carved in it.

She frowned at the pillars. "Wasn't there a shield there, before?"

Zedd's dark look told her that she was right. As he started away again they all rushed to catch up. At the end of the hall, he turned down a short passageway to the right that led to a spiral stairway.

Compared with some of the grand staircases in the Keep, the spiral stairs were small, but compared with typical spiral stairs, these were remarkable. They were wide enough for two people to walk side by side in the center of the tread, where its run was comfortable and a proper relation to the rise. The stairwell was so large, though, that the outer end of each wedge of tread would have required a person to take several steps before reaching each leading edge. The stairs also wandered with an odd twist, winding downward in an oblong corkscrew. The whole thing was disorienting and required her to pay attention lest she trip and fall on the unconventional configuration. As they descended she was able at last to see that the stairs were designed so as to make their way around and then under a formation of rock veined with sparkling minerals.

At the bottom of the stairs a short passageway spilled into the familiar split in the mountain that separated the rooms of the containment field from the bedrock of the mountain itself. This was very near the place where the witch woman had caught them unexpectedly. Nicci thought that the halls felt especially quiet after the violation of the witch woman roaming unfettered through them. Knowing as much as she did about shields, she didn't think that such a thing should have been possible. The wizards who had created this place and its defenses would certainly have made provisions to protect against all forms of magic, including that of a witch woman.

"Here," Zedd announced as he came to a halt. "This is where it first appeared."

He gestured up at the precisely fit stone blocks of the wall opposite the raw, carved-out, natural granite wall of the mountain itself.

Nicci looked along the length of the wall and noticed dark stains that didn't look natural. She scanned dozens of feet up along the rise of stone, picking out here and there the same dark patches. It seemed as if something might be weeping out of the stone itself.

"What is it?" She asked.

Zedd swiped a finger through one of the dark places. He held the finger up before her.

"Blood."

Nicci blinked. She stared at the thick, wet, red substance on his finger. She looked back at the wizard's eyes.

"Blood?"

He nodded solemnly. "Blood."

"Real blood?"

"Real blood," he confirmed.

"Blood from some kind of animals?" Nicci remembered all the

bats that had fled through these very halls, driven before the witch woman. "Maybe the bats?"

"Human blood," the wizard said.

Nicci was momentarily struck speechless. She looked at Cara.

"Yes, we're sure," the Mord-Sith said in answer to the unspoken question.

"I give up," Nicci finally said. "What is human blood doing oozing out of the stone of this wall?"

"Not just this wall here in this hallway," Zedd said. "It's leaking out of stone in different places all over the keep. There seems to be no pattern to where it appears."

Nicci looked again at some of the thick drips of blood running down the wall. She didn't want to touch it.

"Well," she finally said, "this certainly qualifies as trouble. I just don't know what kind of trouble." She turned her attention back to Zedd. "Do you have any idea what it means?"

"It means that the Keep itself is bleeding, in a way. It means that it's dying."

Nicci could only blink at what she'd just heard. "Dying?"

Looking grim, Zedd nodded. "That shield back there that you asked about? It has stood in that hallway for thousands of years. Now it's down. There are shields all over the Keep that are failing. The whole fabric of the Keep is in grave trouble.

"Six, as talented as she is, should not have been able to get in here without alarms going off, but they didn't. The alarms have failed. That's why we didn't know she was in the Keep. That's how she snuck up on us.

"If the Keep were well, and even if the alarms for some reason failed or were somehow defeated, the shields would have prevented her not only from moving freely but from getting this far into the interior of the Keep. This is a secure area. She simply should not have been able to get down here, but she was able to find ways around the working shields to go where she wanted.

"It's only because of this disorder"—he lifted a hand toward the bleeding walls—"that she was able to enter the Keep without the alarms sounding and the shields stopping her. The

Keep was too sick to prevent her entry or to stop her once inside.

"As far as I know, a violation of this nature has never happened before. People have gotten into the Keep in the past, but not because the Keep itself failed in its role. Those entries were successful because the trespasser was clever, or exceedingly talented, or because they had help from inside. Six danced in here all by herself without the alarms sounding or the defenses stopping her. She merely had to take some detours to get around shields that are still functioning."

"The chimes . . ." Nicci breathed, suddenly understanding.

Zedd conceded with a nod. "Richard was right."

"Can anything be done?"

"Yes," Zedd said. "If we can find Richard we can get him to open the correct box of Orden. The Chainfire spell is also contaminated by the chimes. This is confirmation that the taint left by the chimes is corrupting all magic—not only the Chainfire spell—just as Richard told us it was. He needs to unleash Orden and hope that its power will be able to purge the world not only of Chainfire but of the taint left by the chimes having been loose in the world of life."

Nicci cocked her head. "Zedd, Orden is designed for a specific purpose: to counter Chainfire. Orden isn't going seek out other magic plaguing us and purge it as well. It's not designed to do that."

Zedd smoothed back some stray wisps of white hair as he chose his words carefully. "You yourself spoke of how Orden's power, like any power, can be used for aims other than its narrow, intended purpose. Richard needs to use the power of Orden not only to purge us of the taint of Chainfire, but in a broader manner to eliminate the taint left by the chimes."

Nicci didn't know if such a profound course of action was at all wise, or even possible, but she didn't think that this was the time or place to debate it. They were a very long way from having Richard attempt such a thing. They first had to find Richard before anything else could even be considered. After that, there were difficulties with Richard opening a box of Orden that Nicci had not even begun to reveal to Zedd because she hadn't wanted to worry him any more than was necessary. There were, after all, enough immediate problems they had to solve.

"In the meantime," Zedd said, "we must evacuate the Keep."

Nicci was taken aback. "But if the Keep is weakened, then we must do just the opposite; we must defend it. There are invaluable things here that we dare not allow to fall into the wrong hands. We can't risk Jagang and the Sisters gaining possession of the powerful things of magic in here—the ones that still work, anyway, to say nothing of the libraries."

"That is precisely why we must leave," Zedd insisted. "If we leave, I can put the entire Keep in a state that will keep everyone out. It's something that as far as I know has never been activated before, but I can see no other solution."

Nicci gazed up at the blood staining the stone wall. "Well, if the Keep is sick, and its magic is failing, how can you possibly do such a thing and expect it to work?"

"The ancient books that explained the defensive design of the Keep explained about the walls bleeding. A warning in blood, being as gruesome as it is, signifies how grave the trouble with the Keep itself really is. As far as I know such a thing has never happened before. This is the first time such a drastic warning has ever been necessary. It's just one of the things about this place that I had to learn about when I became First Wizard.

"Those same sources also described emergency procedures in the event such a thing did happen. There is a way to lock down the Keep with an elevated state of power that is not yet degraded."

Nicci found the very thought troubling. "Elevated state of power?"

"It was in storage—took me most of the day to find it."

"What was?"

Zedd gestured to the nearby brass doors where the box of Orden had been until Six stole it. "A bone box. It's waiting in there. It's about the size of one of the boxes of Orden. While it's bone, I don't know what beast the bone came from. Ancient symbols are carved all over the outside.

"It contains a constructed spell said to be keyed to the Keep's nature. It was constructed by the same wizards who invested the Keep with its many defenses. You might compare it to a small bit of starter dough you set aside so that you always have a bit of the original in order to continue to make the same kind of bread. This spell contains elements of the original magic of the Keep. Quite remarkable, when you think about it."

"How long will such a constructed spell last, once activated, before the taint of the chimes begins to degrade it as well?"

Zedd made a face as he shook his head. "I have no idea. From the things I've read and the tests I've run, I believe that such a state will last quite a while, but there is no way to know for certain. All we can do is try."

"What if it's already been corrupted by the chimes?" Friendrich asked. "After all, if the Keep is infected, and this spell is part of the Keep's original power, what's to say it's not corrupted as well?"

Friedrich, having been married to a sorceress most of his life, knew quite a bit about magic even though he was not himself gifted.

"I tried to run verification webs on some of the corrupted aspects of the Keep, such as the alarms. The corruption prevented the verification from functioning. The verification on the spell in the bone box worked without any difficulty. From my tests it's still viable."

"Why can't we stay here and put the Keep in this protective state?" Cara asked.

"It's too dangerous," Zedd told her. "The emergency procedure has never been employed before. I'm not sure of its precise nature or exactly how it works, but the information I reviewed said that such a state will prevent anyone from entering. I can only assume that such an emergency condition, by necessity, would deal harshly with any intruders. It appears that it's a form of light spell. From the limited amount that I know about the conditions of the interior of the Keep in such a state, it would be very dangerous for anyone to be in the place.

"After all, how can we know that there aren't intruders in the Keep right now?"

Cara straightened. "Now?"

"Yes. If the Keep's defenses are failing, and the alarms aren't working, how would we know if there were people wandering about who don't belong in here? For all we know, Six could still be lurking about. Chase said he didn't find any tracks of her leaving. Sisters of the Dark could have snuck in as well. There's no longer a dependable way for us to know.

"Even more concerning is that enemies could enter through the sliph. Richard is the only one who could put the sliph back to sleep; we can't. The sliph isn't designed to deny her services to anyone who asks and has the proper power. Jagang could send Sisters of the Dark in through the sliph. There aren't enough of us to guard the sliph all the time, at least not enough of us with enough power to have a chance to defend against an attack from Sisters of the Dark.

"Without the ability to put the sliph back to sleep, or to be able to depend on alarms and shields to protect the Keep, it remains vulnerable to intrusion of all sorts. It must be assumed that such a spell, by its very nature, would eliminate anyone in the Keep. Since it's a measure of last resort we have to assume that it could be as fatal for us to be in here as it would be for an intruder.

"Therefore, we have to leave and then ignite the protective state."

"How will be get back in?" Cara asked.

"I will have to shut the thing down. I know the sequence necessary to inactivate the spell. Once I shut it down, though, I don't believe it can be reactivated, so we dare not shut it down unless it's absolutely necessary for some reason, or until the taint of the chimes can be eliminated from the world of life."

Nicci heaved a sigh. "I can't think of any argument against the plan. It seems the only way to preserve the Keep for the time being."

"Besides that," Zedd said, "we can't just continue to sit here."

"No," Nicci said, "I don't suppose we can."

She was already thinking of things that had to be done. There were any number of places she needed to go.

"It seems to me," Zedd said as he looked around at those waiting for his pronouncement, "that the first thing to be done is to try to get Richard his power back. If he was reconnected with his gift perhaps it would help him.

"We have reason to believe that it was cut off by a spell drawn in the sacred caves in Tamarang. Unless anyone has a better idea, I say we go to Tamarang and help Richard by eliminating whatever is blocking him from his gift."

Both Mord-Sith nodded. "If it would help Lord Rahl, I say let's get going," Cara said.

"I agree," Tom said.

"I'm afraid that I'd slow you down," Friedrich said. "I'm not as young as I used to be. Perhaps it would be best if I stayed in the area in case Richard shows up. He'll need to know what's happening. I can stay close, watch the Keep from the outside."

"That makes sense," Zedd told the man.

"I think I had better go to the People's Palace," Nicci said.

Zedd frowned. "Why?"

"Well, I can use the sliph. From the People's Palace I can take the sliph down to the area of Tamarang and meet you there. The sliph is much faster, so I will have time at the palace to check into some things."

"Like what?" Zedd asked.

"Well, with Richard missing and cut off from his power, Nathan is acting in the capacity of Lord Rahl. That bond is all that stands between us and the dream walker being able to enter our minds. I want to see how he's doing."

Zedd nodded in thought.

"There are defenses at the palace that are powered by magic, much the same as here at the Keep," Nicci said. "Ann and Nathan need to know that the chimes are corrupting that magic. They need to know what happened here so they will be prepared if it happens there as well, and not caught unaware as we were.

"But most of all we need to get the box of Orden back. Six

was from the Old World. Ann and Nathan lived there a very long time. They said they didn't know anything about Six but maybe they've thought of something by now or can offer a clue. Six was secretive when she lived down there in the Old World, but maybe someone knows something about her. Ann and Nathan may be able to point me in the direction of such a person. Right now we know next to nothing about the witch woman. We need information.

"I'm at a loss to know where to look for Six. This is at least a place to start asking questions."

Zedd sighed. "That makes sense. But if you find anything out, you come to Tamarang first—come to me first before you think to go after her yourself. We may need your help to deal with whatever is going on down there in Tamarang, and you will definitely need my help to come up with a way to deal with Six. She has already proven how dangerous she is. You're not going to be able to sneak up on her and take back the box. If we get a lead on where she might be, we're going to have to put our heads together and come up with a plan."

"Agreed," Nicci said. "What about the sliph—after I've gone through, I mean? Will anyone be able to sneak back into the Keep?"

"The protective spell takes special precautions at the points of entry. The sliph will draw branches of the spell, hardening that entry point just like any other. Once you leave through the sliph I'll activate the spell."

"I'm going with you," Cara said to Nicci. It wasn't a request.

"I'll go with Zedd, then," Rikka said. "He'll need one of us looking after him."

Zedd shot her a sour glare but didn't say anything.

Cara drew her blond braid through a loose fist. "Makes sense. It's decided, then."

It was as if the two of them were settling how the operation would be conducted. Nicci was beginning to appreciate Richard's remarkable forbearance.

"Let's get our things together," Zedd said. "It will be light soon."

Nicci took Rikka by the elbow and pulled her aside. "As

soon as I change into my clothes, I'll fix up the nightdress for you so that you can pack it with your things."

Rikka smiled. "All right."

Nicci thought that the woman looked quietly excited at the prospect of having something pretty, something that had nothing to do with the outfit of a Mord-Sith.

Nicci concentrated on that happy thought, rather than on how nervous she was about again traveling in the sliph. This time, Richard would not be with her to help her.

CHAPTER 15

What is it?" Jennsen whispered to the young woman ahead of her as they both crawled through the tall, dry grass.

"Shh" was Laurie's only answer.

Laurie and her husband had been out in the desolate place picking a late crop of wild figs that grew among the low hills. In the course of their work, as they had picked farther and farther afield, they had separated. As the afternoon drew to a close Laurie had wanted to head back to town but she hadn't been able to find her husband. He seemed to have vanished.

Increasingly distraught, she'd eventually run back to the town of Hawton seeking Jennsen's help. Needing to rush, Jennsen had decided to leave her pet goat, Betty, in her pen. Betty hadn't been happy about it, but Jennsen was more concerned about finding Laurie's husband. By the time they had returned with a small search party the sun had long since gone down.

As Owen, his wife Marilee, Anson, and Jennsen had spread out searching in among the low hills for Laurie's missing husband, Laurie had found something she hadn't expected. It had clearly shaken her. She wouldn't say what it was; she wanted Jennsen to hurry to see it for herself, and she wanted Jennsen to be quiet about it.

Laurie cautiously lifted her head just enough to look off into the night.

She pointed and at the same time leaned back so that Jennsen could hear her whisper. "There."

By now infected with Laurie's obvious sense of alarm,

Jennsen carefully stretched her neck up to peer into the darkness.

The tomb was open.

The great granite monument to Nathan Rahl had been slid to the side. Light shone up from under the ground, creating a softly glowing beacon in the dark heart of the starlit night.

Jennsen knew, of course, that it was not really Nathan Rahl's tomb. Laurie wouldn't know that, though.

Back when Nathan and Ann had been staying with them, Nathan had discovered the tomb with his name on it. He had also discovered that what appeared to be a rather extravagant tomb in the ancient graveyard was actually an entrance to secret underground rooms filled with books. He and Ann had told Jennsen that the stash was thousands of years old and had been protected all that time by magic.

Jennsen wouldn't know; she had no magic. She was pristinely ungifted—a hole in the world, as it was sometimes called because those with magic were unable to use their gift to sense those like Jennsen. She was a rare creature—a pillar of Creation.

She and the people with her down in Bandakar were all pillars of Creation. In ancient times it had been learned that when the pristinely ungifted mingled with normal people, all of whom possessed at least a small spark of the gift, every child of such unions would be pristinely ungifted. Roaming free in the world they forever carried the latent potential to breed the gift itself out of mankind. In antiquity the solution to the ever-growing numbers of the pristinely ungifted had been to gather them all together and banish them.

The pristinely ungifted trait originated in the offspring of the Lord Rahl. Pristinely ungifted births were exceedingly rare, but once those with the trait became adults, the anomaly was spread forth into the general population. After the ancestors of these people in Bandakar had been banished, every child of a Rahl was tested. If found to be born pristinely ungifted such a child would immediately be put to death to prevent the trait from ever again spreading into the general population.

Jennsen, the offspring of rape by Darken Rahl, had managed to defy the odds and escape detection. Since Richard was now the Lord Rahl, eliminating any such flaw in his lineage fell to him.

But Richard found the very thought abhorrent and would not do such a thing. He believed that Jennsen and those like her had the same right to life as did he. He had actually been happy to discover that he had a half sister—pristinely ungifted or not. He had greeted her with open arms rather than murderous intent, as she had once expected.

Richard had broken the banishment and freed these people to live their own lives. Since Richard had become the Lord Rahl, they were no longer banished but welcomed into the world, as was Jennsen. Despite what it would eventually mean for the existence of magic within mankind, he had destroyed the barrier barring these people from the rest of the world.

Since the barrier had come down, many of the people from Bandakar had been captured by the Imperial Order and taken away to be used for breeding stock to hasten the end of magic. After the Imperial Order had been driven from Bandakar, most of the rest of these people had chosen to remain in their ancestral homeland for the time being. They wanted to take some time to learn about the outside world before deciding what they would do.

Jennsen felt a kinship with these people. Having been in hiding her whole life for fear of being put to death for the crime of her birth, she had in a way suffered under her own form of banishment. She had wanted to remain with these people as they all learned to be a part of their new, wider world. That new beginning, that excitement of building a new life for themselves full of possibilities, was a passion shared by them all.

Laurie obviously felt a sense of dread that their world was again being threatened. But with the Imperial Order on the march everyone's world was threatened. In that sense there was nothing especially unique about the pristinely ungifted.

Jennsen wasn't sure who it was that was now down in the

tomb. She reasoned that it might be Nathan and Ann returned to retrieve books they needed from the long-forgotten underground library. Those books, too, had been banished to their hiding place behind boundaries that none had been able to cross until Richard had come along.

Jennsen reasoned that it might also be Richard down in the tomb. Nathan and Ann had long ago set off with Tom to find him. If they had succeeded they would have told him about the underground library. Perhaps he'd returned to see the ancient library for himself, or maybe he'd returned looking for something specific. Jennsen would dearly love to see her brother again. The very idea of it gave her a flutter of excitement.

She realized, though, that it could be someone else—someone who could harm them all. It was that thought that kept her from rushing down into the tomb.

Despite how much she wanted to go and see if it was Richard, Jennsen's life on the run with her mother had given her a finely honed sense of caution, so she crouched motionless, watching for any sign of who it might be down in the tomb.

Mockingbirds in the distance repeated calls into the still darkness, trying to outdo one another in a kind of endless nightly argument. As she idly listened to the strident calls, Jennsen knew that it would be best to remain hidden and wait for whoever was down inside the tomb to appear, but she worried that the others might return from their search and inadvertently give them away, so she decided that as she kept an eye on the tomb it would be best to send Laurie to find the others and warn them about the unknown intruders.

Before Jennsen could crawl in close and whisper instructions to Laurie, the young woman abruptly started crawling forward. Apparently, she'd decided that it might be her husband down in the tomb. Jennsen lunged, snatching at the young woman's ankle, but it was out of reach.

"Laurie!" Jennsen whispered. "Stop!"

Laurie ignored the command, instead skittering off through the dry grass. Jennsen immediately crawled after her, wending her way among ancient grave markers scattered about on the uneven ground. The dry grass made far too much noise for Jennsen's liking. Laurie wasn't being especially careful, or quiet. Jennsen had been schooled in evasion and escape by her mother. Laurie didn't know much about such things.

Some distance ahead in the darkness, Laurie gasped in fright.

Jennsen lifted her head just enough to try to see if anyone was nearby, but in the darkness it was hard to see much of anything. For all Jennsen knew there could be a dozen men spread out around them. If they remained still it would be difficult, if not impossible, to see them.

Laurie suddenly rose up on her knees as she let out a wail of horror that sent a ripple of goose bumps up the nape of Jennsen's neck. The scream shattered the quiet of the night. The mockingbirds fell silent.

In the dead of night, such a scream would carry great distances. No longer having to worry about giving herself away, Jennsen scrambled to her feet and raced to cover the remaining distance to the woman. Overcome with abject misery, Laurie held her hair in her fists as she threw her head back and cried in desolation.

The body of a man lay sprawled in the grass before her. Even though it was too dark for Jennsen to make out the face, it was only too obvious who it had to be.

Jennsen pulled the silver-handled knife from the sheath at her waist.

Just as she did so, the dark shape of a big man, sword in hand, loomed up out of the darkness. He had probably been the one who had killed Laurie's husband. After that he'd likely crouched somewhere nearby to be on watch for anyone else who might approach the open tomb.

Just as Jennsen reached Laurie, but before she could knock the young woman out of harm's way, the man swung the sword. The dark blur of the blade slashed across Laurie's throat, nearly decapitating her. Splatters of warm blood splashed across the side of Jennsen's face.

Her horror was instantly banished by a flash of anger. She might have expected dread, fear, or even panic, but it was a rush of hot rage that erupted through her. It was an anger first ignited by others who had so long ago come out of nowhere and brutally murdered her mother.

Before the sword had even finished the murderous slash, Jennsen was already leaping toward the man.

She leaped out of the darkness, hitting him square in the chest with her knife. Before he could even flinch back in surprise, she pulled the knife back and, gripping it tightly in her fist, stabbed it into his neck three times in rapid succession. Atop him, she rode him to the ground, still furiously stabbing him. Only when his breath gurgled to a halt did she stop.

In the sudden stillness, she panted, catching her breath. She struggled to not allow herself to become paralyzed by the shock of what had just happened. If there was one guard, there would likely be others. She knew for certain that there was someone down in the tomb. She had to get away from the place where Laurie had screamed.

Jennsen told herself to move. Moving was her best defense, now. Moving was life.

Crouching low, she started slipping away to the side, the whole time keeping an eye on the shaft of light rising up from the tomb, watching for anyone who might emerge to investigate the noise and discover the bodies.

A second man seemed suddenly to materialize out of the black night, rising up out of the grass right in front of her.

Jennsen flipped the knife in her hand, getting a fighting grip on it, rather than the stabbing grip she'd had when she'd taken the other man down. Her heart pounded wildly as she looked around for other threats.

She ignored the man's command to stop and instead quickly feinted left. As he lunged in that direction, grabbing for her, Jennsen instead rolled to the right.

Another man appeared out of the darkness, responding to the yells of the first man, blocking any escape to that side. The light coming from the tomb glinted softly off links of the chain mail covering the man's broad chest and the axe gripped in a meaty fist. Long greasy strings of hair hung down over his shoulders.

She reminded herself to remember his chain mail in case she had to fight him off. Her knife would be largely ineffective against such armor. She would need to find vulnerable spots. She realized that she had been lucky that the man she'd fought, the man who had killed Laurie, hadn't been wearing chain mail.

Jennsen's frantic urge was to turn and run in blind panic but she knew that running would be a mistake. Running aroused the instinct to chase. Once in a chase, that instinct took over and men like this wouldn't stop until they had a kill.

Both men expected her to run in the direction that seemed open to her—away to her left. Instead, she bolted for them, intending to slip right between them and out of their snare before they could close in. The closest man, the one she knew to be wearing mail, had his axe at the ready. Before he could raise it and strike, she slashed the exposed inside of his arm. Her razor-sharp knife sliced across the meat of the underside of his forearm, just up from the wrist. She could hear the soft snap of tendons under tension parting as they were cut.

The man cried out. Unable to hold his axe, he dropped it to the ground. Jennsen snatched it up as she ducked under the second man diving for her. She spun and slammed the weapon into his back as he flew past.

Jennsen scrambled away as one of the men held his useless right arm and the other wheeled toward her with an axe handle jutting up at an angle from his back. He staggered a few steps, still coming for her, before he dropped to a knee gasping for breath. By the gurgling sound of his breathing, she knew that she had punctured his lung at the least. It was clear that he was in no condition to fight, so she turned her attention elsewhere.

If she was going to escape, this was her chance. Without hesitation, she took it.

Almost immediately a wall of men loomed up before her. Jennsen skidded to a stop. Men appeared all around her. From the corner of her eye she saw shadows twisting through the shaft of light as figures raced up from within the tomb.

"If you want," the man in front of her said in a gruff voice, "we'd be happy to cut you down. Otherwise, I'd suggest you just hand me that knife."

Jennsen stood frozen, considering her options. He mind didn't seem to want to work.

In the distance she could see figures, silhouetted by the light, rushing toward her from the tomb.

The man held out a hand. "The knife," he said with menace.

Jennsen wheeled her arm and stabbed him through the palm of his hand. As he flinched back at the same time Jennsen pulled, the blade parted his hand between his two middle fingers. The night air rang with a rage of profanity. Jennsen took the chance to dart through the biggest opening in the wall of men and into the darkness beyond.

Before she had run three steps an arm hooked her around the middle. He yanked her back so violently that it drove the air from her in a whoosh. The soldier slammed her back against his leather armor. Jennsen gasped for breath.

Before he was able to corral her flailing arms, she drove her knife into his thigh. The tip hit bone and stuck. Cursing, he finally collected her arms, pinning them to her sides.

Tears of terror and frustration stung at her eyes. She was going to die here in the middle of a graveyard without ever seeing Tom again. At that moment, he was all that seemed important, all she wanted. He would never know what had happened to her. She would never be able to tell him one last time how much she loved him.

The soldier jerked the knife from his leg. She gasped back a sob at all that was lost to her, all that was lost to these people.

Before the men could tear her apart as she expected them to do, someone appeared with a lantern. It was a woman. She had something else in the same hand as the lantern. She came to a halt before Jennsen, scowling as she took charge of the situation.

"Be quiet," the woman said to the man holding his bloody hand and still cursing.

"The bitch stabbed my hand!"

"And my leg!" the man holding her added.

The woman glanced to the bodies lying nearby. "Looks like you got off lucky."

"I guess," the man holding Jennsen finally grumbled, clearly uncomfortable under her implacable scrutiny. He handed the woman Jennsen's knife.

"She cut my hand nearly in two!" the other interrupted, not yet content to submit to the woman's indifference to their pain. "She must be made to pay!"

The woman turned a withering glare on him. "Your only purpose is to serve the ends of the Order. What good do you think you will be in that service if you are a cripple? Now, shut your mouth or I won't even consider healing you."

When he hung his head in mute agreement, the woman finally withdrew her glare and turned her attention to Jennsen. Holding the lantern up, she leaned in to get a better look at Jennsen's face. Jennsen saw then that it was a book she was holding in the hand along with the lantern. She had probably stolen the book from the underground stash.

"Amazing," she said, as if speaking to herself as she studied Jennsen's eyes. "You're right there in front of me, and yet my gift says you are not."

Jennsen realized that the woman had to be a sorceress, probably one of Jagang's Sisters. Jennsen could not be directly harmed by the powers of such a woman, or anyone with magic, but under the circumstances, that hardly meant that she wasn't a threat. After all, she didn't need magic to order the soldiers to put Jennsen to death.

The woman held out the knife, peering at what was on the handle. Her brow drew down as she grasped the significance of the ornate letter "R," the symbol standing for the House of Rahl, engraved on the silver handle.

Her eyes turned up to Jennsen, this time filled with a kind of grim recognition. Unexpectedly, she dropped the knife. It stuck in the ground at her feet as she put the fingers of one hand to her forehead, wincing as if in pain. The silent soldiers shared troubled looks.

When she looked up again, the woman's face had gone blank. "Well, well, well. If it isn't Jennsen Rahl." Her voice sounded different. It was deeper, and carried a threatening, masculine tone.

It was Jennsen's turn to frown. "You know me?"

"Oh yes, darlin, I know you," the woman said in a voice that had turned deep and husky. "Seems I recall you swearing to me that you would kill Richard Rahl."

Jennsen understood, then. It was Emperor Jagang, seeing her through the eyes of this woman. Jagang was a dream walker. He could do such seemingly impossible things.

"And what of your promise?" the woman asked in a voice that wasn't entirely her own. Her movements were puppetlike and appeared to be painful.

Jennsen didn't know if she was talking to the woman or to Jagang. "I failed."

The woman's lip curled derisively. "You failed."

"That's right. I failed."

"And what of Sebastian?"

Jennsen swallowed. "He died."

"He died," she said in a mocking tone. She took a step closer and cocked her head, peering with one angry eye. "And how did he die, darlin?"

"By his own hand."

"And why would a man like Sebastian take his own life?"

Jennsen would have taken a step back had she not already been pressed up against the chest of hulking soldier. "I guess it was his way of saying that he no longer wanted to be a strategist to the emperor of the Imperial Order. Maybe he realized that his life had been wasted, that it had been for nothing."

The woman glared but said nothing.

Jennsen saw then a soft gold glint off the book the woman was holding in the same hand as the lantern. Jennsen could just make out the title in faded, worn gold lettering.

It said *The Book of Counted Shadows*.

Everyone turned at the sound of a commotion. Yet more men were dragging other captives closer. When they reached the light Jennsen's heart sank. The big soldiers had Anson, Owen, and Owen's wife, Marilee. All three were disheveled and bloody.

The woman bent and retrieved Jennsen's knife at her feet.

"His Excellency has decided that he may have a use for these people," the woman said as she straightened. She gestured with Jennsen's knife. "Bring them along."

CHAPTER 16

Nicci paused and turned at the sound of her name called out from behind. It was Nathan. Ann followed close on his heels. For every one of Nathan's long strides Ann had to take three just to keep up.

Their footsteps echoed off the golden-yellow and brown marble floor of the empty hallway. The rather simple hall was part of the private complex within the palace, used by the Lord Rahl, staff and officials, and, of course, Mord-Sith. It was a passageway of unadorned utility, making no pretense of grandeur.

In her modest gray dress buttoned to her throat, Ann looked about the same to Nicci as she had when Nicci had been a child. Short and compact, like a dense thundercloud scudding across the landscape, she always seemed about to throw off lightning. The woman had loomed as an imposing figure in Nicci's mind from the time she'd first been sent to the Palace of the Prophets to become a young novice.

Annalina Aldurren had always been the kind of woman who could elicit a babbling confession with nothing more than a stony stare. She struck terror into novices, fear into young wizards, and trepidation into most of the Sisters. As a novice, Nicci had suspected that the Creator Himself would walk on eggshells in the presence of the forbidding prelate, and mind his manners as well.

"We got the message that you've just arrived from the Keep," the tall prophet said in a deep, powerful voice as he and Ann caught up with Nicci and Cara.

Considering that he was nearly a thousand years old, Nathan

was still ruggedly handsome. He had Rahl features in common with Richard, including a hawklike brow. His eyes, though, were a beautiful azure color, while Richard's were gray. Despite his age, the prophet had a vigorous, purposeful stride.

His age, like Nicci's, was relevant only to those who at the time had lived outside the spell of the Palace of the Prophets. Those in the palace aged just like anyone else, but at a slower rate only when compared to those who lived outside the spell. Time had moved differently within the palace. Now that the palace, the home of the Sisters of the Light for thousands of years, had been destroyed, Nathan, Ann, Nicci, and all the others who had once called the place home would age at the same rate as everyone else.

Nicci remembered the prophet as always wearing robes when he'd lived as a captive in his apartments at the Palace of the Prophets. As a Sister of the Light, it had sometimes been required that she visit him in those apartments to write down anything he claimed to be prophecy. Nicci never really thought one way or the other about the task; it was just one of many required of her. There were Sisters, though, who would not go down into Nathan's apartments alone.

Now he was in brown trousers and a ruffled white shirt under a dark green vest. The hem of his maroon cape hovered just above the floor, swirling around his black boots after he came to a halt. Dressed as he now was, he cut an imposing figure.

Nicci couldn't imagine why, but at his hip he wore a sword sheathed in an elegant scabbard. Wizards hardly needed swords. Being the only prophet those at the palace had known of in recent centuries, he had always been an unfathomable character.

Many of the Sisters at the palace used to believe that Nathan was crazy. Many feared him. It wasn't so much that Nathan gave them cause for their fear as it was that their imagination provided colorful terrors that the mere sight of him somehow seemed to confirm. Nicci didn't know if very many of the Sisters now thought any differently, but she did know that a number of them were greatly worried because he was no longer locked up behind powerful shields. While a few thought he was rather harmless, if a little odd, most of the Sisters considered him to be the most dangerous man alive. Nicci had come to see him differently.

Moreover, he was now the Lord Rahl, standing in for Richard.

"Where is Verna?" Nicci asked. "I need to talk with her as well."

Coming to a halt beside Nathan, Ann tipped her head back toward the empty hallway. "She and Adie are off meeting with General Trimack about security issues. Since it's getting late I told Berdine to let them both know that you and Cara just arrived from the Keep and that we will all shortly meet them in the private dining room."

Nicci nodded. "That sounds like a good idea."

"In the meantime," Nathan pressed, "what news is there?"

Nicci was still disoriented from traveling in the sliph. It was a distracting experience in which time seemed to lose all meaning. On top of that, being in the People's Palace only added to her discomfort. The entire palace existed within a spell that amplified the power of the Lord Rahl. At the same time, the spell diminished the power of every other gifted person. Nicci wasn't used to the feeling. It made her restless and uneasy.

Being in the sliph also reminded her of Richard. She supposed that everything made her think of Richard. It seemed that her nerves were always on edge with worry for him.

It took a moment for Nicci to focus her mind on the question as she struggled to put thoughts of Richard aside. As improbable as it seemed, this man, not Richard, was now the Lord Rahl. Ann, the former prelate, his former jailer, stood beside him waiting to hear the answer to his question.

"I'm afraid that the news is not very good," Nicci admitted.

"You mean about Richard?" Ann asked.

Nicci shook her head. "We've had no news about him, yet."

Nathan's brow took on an even more suspicious slant. "Then what news are you talking about?"

Nicci took a deep breath. It still felt strange breathing air after being in the sliph. Despite having traveled in the strange creature before, she didn't think she would ever get used to breathing into her lungs the liquid silver essence that was the sliph.

Mentally gathering her thoughts, she gazed out over the short section of balcony railing. The particular portion of the hallway that they were in bridged a complex of expansive halls below. Overhead, out through the opening with the balcony, late-day light flooded into the palace through skylights above. The short balcony, between rather dark runs of the hallway beyond in either direction, was almost like a window looking out into the People's Palace. Nicci imagined that, being a rather small opening, it was probably meant to allow a covert place to watch the halls below.

Now, far below, people filling the various passageways hurried in every direction. Their movements looked purposeful. Nearly all of the benches were empty. Nicci didn't see people gathered in casual conversation the way they had in the past. This was a time of war; the People's Palace was under siege. Worry was everyone's constant companion. Guards patrolled, watching not just every person, but every shadow.

Trying to decide how to sum up the troubling news, Nicci ran her fingers through her hair, sweeping it back away from her face. "Remember Richard telling us about how the taint left by the chimes having been in the world of life was causing magic to fail?"

Ann flicked her hand in a dismissive gesture as she heaved a sigh, apparently annoyed to revisit an old topic. "We remember. But I hardly think that it's our most pressing problem."

"Maybe not," Nicci said, "but it has begun to cause some very real trouble."

Nathan lifted a hand, the backs of his fingers touching Ann's shoulder, as if to implore her to let him handle the matter. "How so?"

"We've been forced to abandon the Wizard's Keep," Nicci told him. "For the time being, at least."

Nathan's eyebrows lifted. As he tilted his head toward her

some of his long white hair fell forward over his broad shoulders. "Why? What happened?"

Nicci smoothed the black dress at her hips. "The magic of the Keep is beginning to fail."

"How do you know?" Ann demanded.

"The witch woman, Six, got into the Keep," Nicci said. "The alarms failed to warn us. A number of the shields are down. She was able to go where she pleased within the Keep without the shields stopping her."

Ann poked a loose strand of gray hair back into the knot of hair at the back of her head as she considered Nicci's words. "That isn't necessarily convincing evidence that the magic of the Keep is failing," she finally said, "or even that magic is tainted by the chimes and failing. It's difficult telling just how talented a woman like Six is liable to be. Just because there is some sort of problem with the Keep there is no way to know its cause, much less know that the chimes are the cause. With a place as complicated as the Keep it's difficult to really know if it really is all that serious. It could simply be a temporary—"

"Blood is coming out of the stone walls of the Keep," Nicci said in a tone that made it clear she didn't want to debate it. She didn't appreciate being treated like a novice frightened by shadows on her first night away from home. She needed to get on to other matters. "It's worse down in the lower areas, in the foundation."

Ann and Nathan both straightened.

Ann opened her mouth to say something, but Cara spoke first, apparently as disinterested in having to argue the point as Nicci. "The blood oozing out of the stone in various places all over the Keep is all human blood."

Again, both the prophet and the former prelate went mute with surprise.

"Well now," Nathan finally said as he scratched under his jaw with one finger, "that certainly is serious." He gestured up the hall. "Where are you headed?"

"Cara and I need to go out to see how Jagang's ramp is progressing. I also want to have a look at the Order's army and see if I can tell how they're doing. I'm hoping that Richard's plan will work, that the D'Haran troops sent to the Old World will be able to cut the supply lines. If they succeed, Jagang is going to have a problem. If all those men down there can't be supplied, they can't sit there all winter. They'll starve. I think it may turn out to be a race between the ramp and their supplies running out."

Nathan nodded as he stepped past Nicci and Cara. "Come on, then. We'll go with you and you can tell us about your encounter with this witch woman."

Nicci stood her ground, not following after the prophet. "She took the box of Orden."

Nathan turned back and stared at her. "What?"

"She stole the box of Orden we had. The one that the witch woman's companion, Samuel, stole from Sister Tovi and that Rachel had then managed to get ahold of and bring to us. We thought it was safe in the Keep. Turns out it wasn't."

"It's gone?" Ann seized Nicci's sleeve. "Do you have any idea where she went with it?"

"I'm afraid not," Nicci said. "I'm hoping that you two can give us some clues about the witch woman. We need to find her. Anything you can tell me about her, no matter how insignificant it seems, might be of help. We need to get that box back."

"At least Nicci was able to put the power of Orden in play before the box was taken," Cara said.

Nathan and Ann could not have looked more stunned.

"She did what?" Nathan whispered, seemingly unable to stop staring at Cara, as if hoping he might have heard her wrong or, if he hadn't, that she might think better of what she'd said and recant the claim.

"Nicci put the power of Orden in play," Cara said.

Nicci thought that the Mord-Sith sounded a bit proud of the accomplishment, proud of Nicci.

"Are you out of your mind!" Ann roared as she rounded on Nicci, her face going scarlet. "You named yourself a player for the power of Orden!"

"No, that's not at all what happened," Cara said, once more drawing the attention of the prophet and the former prelate. "She named Richard the player."

Cara smiled just the slightest bit, as if pleased to prove that Nicci was better than Nathan and Ann seemed to think. For their part, Nathan and Ann stood thunderstruck.

While it had indeed been quite an accomplishment, Nicci didn't feel any pride for having done such a thing—she had been driven to it out of desperation.

Standing there in the hallway in the vast complex of the People's Palace, acutely aware of the interlocking layers of problems they faced, Nicci suddenly felt overwhelmingly weary, and it wasn't from her power being drained by the spell around the People's Palace. Besides the recent events, exhaustion was beginning to take its toll. There was so much to do and so little time.

Worse, only she had the necessary knowledge or ability to deal with many of the problems they faced. Who but she had a chance to teach Richard about the use of Subtractive Magic that was necessary to open the boxes of Orden? There was no one else. Nicci felt the terrible weight of that responsibility.

There were moments when the enormity of the battles facing them stood out for her in stark clarity. Sometimes when that happened Nicci's courage wavered. She sometimes feared that she was deluding herself that they could actually solve the monumental problems they faced.

She remembered how, as a little girl, her mother had forced her to go out with bread to feed the poor and, later, how Brother Narev of the Fellowship of Order had shamed her into working tirelessly to serve the endless needs of people. No matter how much effort she put into solving the problems of all those who were needy, their problems only seemed to grow, outpacing her ability to satisfy them, binding her ever tighter in slavery to the growing ranks of those in need. She was taught that, because she had the ability, it was her duty to ignore her own wants and needs and to sacrifice her life to the wants and needs of others. Their inability, or unwillingness to try, made them her masters.

In those moments when she thought their present problems were insurmountable, she felt again the way she had as a child, like a slave to the problems. In those dark moments of self-doubt she wondered if she could ever really shed the mantle Jagang himself had laid around her shoulders when he named her the Slave Queen. He'd had no idea how apt the title really was.

In a way, that was how she sometimes felt in this struggle. While she knew that this cause was right, it still seemed hopeless to think that they could win when they were up against so many who sought to crush them.

Sometimes, in the face of the seemingly insurmountable, Nicci wanted nothing so much as to sit down and give up. In private moments in the past, Richard had confessed to having the same self-doubts as she felt, and yet she'd seen how he still forged ahead. Whenever Nicci felt discouraged, she thought of Richard, of how relentless he was, and she once again made herself get to her feet if for no other reason than to make him proud of her.

She believed in and fought for their cause, but that cause was crystallized in Richard.

They needed him. She didn't know how they were ever going to find him or, if they did, how they would get him back. That was assuming he was still alive.

Richard being dead, though, was a thought that she refused to contemplate and so she immediately shoved the very idea aside.

Ann seized Nicci's upper arm in a firm grip, bringing her out of her dark thoughts. "You put the boxes of Orden in play, and you named Richard the player?"

Nicci wasn't in the mood to address the denouncement within the rhetorical question, to yet again have the same argument she'd already had with Zedd.

"That's right. I had no choice. Zedd at first had the same reaction as you. When I explained it all to him, explained why I had to do as I had done, and once he'd calmed down, he came to see that there truly is no other way."

"And who are you to decide such a thing?" Ann demanded.

Nicci chose not to rise to the insult and instead kept her voice, if not deferential, at least civil. "You yourself said that Richard is the one who must lead us in this battle. You and

Nathan have waited nearly five hundred years for Richard to be born and worked to make sure that he could lead us. You yourself saw to it that he had *The Book of Counted Shadows* so that he could fight this fight. You seem to have decided a great deal for him before I ever came along.

"The Sisters of the Dark have already put Orden in play. I hardly need to tell you what their goal is. That makes this the final battle—the battle for life itself. Richard is the one who must lead us. If he is to succeed he must have the ability to fight them. You gave him a mere book. I gave him the power, the weapon, that he needs to win."

Nathan laid a big hand on Ann's shoulder. "Perhaps Nicci has a point."

Ann glanced up at the prophet. She visibly cooled as she considered his words. Back when she'd lived at the Palace of the Prophets, Nicci would never have expected the prophet, of all people, to be able to bring the prelate to see reason. There had been few at the palace who thought that Nathan had the ability to reason.

"Well, done is done," Ann said, her voice considerably calmer. "We'll have to give some thought to what we must do next."

"What about Zedd?" Nathan asked. "Does he have any ideas to help Richard?"

Nicci tried to keep her voice, as well as her expression, from betraying her level of concern. "Since Zedd believes that spells cast in the sacred caves in Tamarang are responsible for blocking Richard from the use of his gift, he, Tom, and Rikka are on their way there now. They hope to be able to help Richard by finding a way to eliminate whatever spell is barring him from his gift."

"You make it sound simple," Nathan said as he considered the problem. "Such a thing will be far from simple."

Nicci lifted an eyebrow. "I doubt that standing around wishing for a solution will work better."

Nathan grunted his agreement. "What about the Keep?"

Nicci turned and started down the hall, talking back over her shoulder. "After Cara and I left in the sliph, and before he started out for Tamarang, Zedd was going to use a spell to close down the Keep."

"What about the others—Chase, Rachel, and Jebra?" Nathan asked.

"Jebra vanished a while back. Zedd thinks it's possible that she regained consciousness and because of everything she's been through, she simply ran away."

"Or the witch woman has been influencing her mind yet again," Nathan suggested.

Nicci opened her hands. "That's possible too. We just don't know. Rachel vanished as well, just the other night, the night before Six arrived. Chase went looking for her."

Nathan shook his head in frustration. "I hate being stuck here when so much is going on."

"Zedd wanted you two to know about the trouble with the magic of the Keep," Nicci said. "He said that there are defenses protecting the People's Palace that may be similar to those at the Keep, so he wants you to be aware of the problem. There's no telling how the contamination from the chimes will affect magic, whether it will hamper all similar power, or whether it's a function of location—if the contamination might be confined to a specific area."

"After we're finished here," Cara put in, "Nicci and I are going to travel in the sliph down to the Tamarang area to help Zedd get Lord Rahl's power back. Then we're going after Lord Rahl."

Nathan didn't object that he presently held the title of Lord Rahl. He, of all people, knew that Richard was the one that prophecy had named to lead them. Nathan was the one, after all, who had originally revealed that prophecy said they stood a chance against the coming storm only if Richard led them.

Cara's plan that they were "going after Lord Rahl" was news to Nicci. If they knew where Richard was, Nicci would already be headed there.

As Nicci continued to answer Ann's steady barrage of questions, Nathan led them through several rather simple passageways until they finally came to one with a heavy oak door at the end. As Nathan pulled the door open for them, cold air rushed in.

A bloodred sky greeted Nicci as she stepped out onto a platform high above the rampart of the outer wall. "Dear spirits," she whispered to herself. "Every time I see them it's a terrible shock."

Nathan squeezed out beside her. There was room for only two people on what was apparently an observation platform. Ann and Cara watched from just inside the doorway.

The height was dizzying. Nicci gripped the waist-high iron railing as she leaned out a little, peering over the side. She could see over the edge of the outer wall, and the plateau itself, all the way down to the Azrith Plain.

The ground immediately around the plateau was deserted. The Imperial Order had camped some distance back, apparently not wanting to chance drawing any unpleasant attention from the gifted up in the palace before absolutely necessary. While the Imperial Order had Sisters and even several young wizards who could shield them from any conjuring from above, Jagang would want to keep them in reserve, keep them healthy, strong, and alive until he began his final attack.

A thick red overcast hung above the distant plain black with the invading army. They spread all the way to the horizon in every direction. Nicci rubbed her shoulders with the chill she felt from within. While from this distance it was hard to see much detail, she knew what it was like to be among such men. She knew all too well what they were like. She knew all too well what their officers were like. She knew all too well what their leader was like.

It made Nicci's skin crawl to think of being down among those men.

When she had served with that army she had not given a great deal of thought to how not only physically filthy but spiritually squalid it was. As the Slave Queen she had been willfully blind to it. She had believed that brutes like Jagang and his men were necessary in order to impose higher ideals on mankind. Benevolence enforced through brutality. Looking back on such a thought, she could hardly believe how contradictory those convictions really were, and that she had accepted them without question. Not just accepted them, but helped enforce them. She had been so effective at enforcing the Order's will that she had become known as Death's Mistress.

She could hardly believe that Richard had put up with her. Of course, she had given him no choice in the matter.

She felt tears sting at her eyes at the memory of all the times she had tried to force Richard to join her in service to their vile cause and how, instead, he had shown her something noble. She swallowed back a sob at how much she missed him, missed the light in his eyes.

The sight below made the silence up on the platform seem all the more bleak. These men, these millions of men spread out across the plain, were all there for one purpose: to kill everyone in the People's Palace, anyone who opposed the rule of the Order. This was their last obstacle to imposing their beliefs on all of mankind.

Nicci stared out at the ramp rising up in the distance. It was larger than the last time she'd seen it. Beyond the ramp she could just make out scars in the ground where the material for the ramp was being dug. The top slope of the ramp aimed in a straight line right for the top of the plateau. Even though it was getting dark, there were snaking lines of men carrying dirt and rock to the construction site.

If anyone described such an undertaking to her she doubted that she would believe it was possible, but seeing it was different. Seeing it filled her with dread. It was only a matter of time until that ramp was completed and the dark sea of the Imperial Order flooded up it to assault the palace.

Standing at the edge of the platform, hugging her shoulders tightly, she knew that she was looking out onto more than a dark army. Nicci knew that she was looking out on a thousand years of darkness.

Having been a Sister of the Dark, and having been raised under the teachings of the Fellowship of Order, she knew, perhaps better than anyone, just how real the threat was. She knew how vehemently the followers of the Order believed in their cause. Their faith defined them. They were more than willing to die for it. After all, death was their goal; they had been promised glory in the afterlife. They believed that this life was only a test, a means to gain entry into everlasting life. If the Order required them to die, then they would die. If the Order required that they kill those who did not believe, then they would make the world a sea of blood.

Nicci understood precisely what it would mean for everyone if the Order won this war. It was not the army that would bring those thousand years of darkness, but the ideas that had spawned that army. Those ideas would cast the world into a living nightmare.

"Nicci, there is something you need to know about," Nathan said, breaking the uneasy silence.

Nicci folded her arms and glanced over at the prophet. "What's that, Nathan?"

"We've been studying books of prophecy here at the People's Palace. Just like all the books of prophecy everywhere else, the Chainfire spell has caused sections of these books, sections that apparently touch on Kahlan, to vanish. But there is still useful information as of yet untouched by Chainfire. Some of those books are new to me. They've helped me to connect things I've read about in the past. They've helped me to see the larger picture."

With the Chainfire spell having erased so much of their memories, she didn't know how he could know if he really was seeing the larger picture—or how she could know if she was. Instead of saying so, Nicci waited silently, the cold wind ruffling her hair, watching Nathan look away to gaze out at the forces spread out across the Azrith Plain below.

"There is a place in the prophecies, a cardinal root, that leads to a determinative fork," he said at last. "Beyond that fork, down one of its two branches, is a place the prophecies call the Great Void."

Nicci frowned into her recollections. There had always been a great deal of speculation surrounding that portion of prophecy.

"I've heard mention of it," she said. "Do you finally know what that means?"

"One of the two branches after that crucial fork leads to

areas of yet more branches, offshoots, and forks farther on." Nathan flicked his wrist offhandedly, as if indicating those things unseen to anyone but him. "There are a few books of prophecy that I've been able to identify as having to do with issues that lie beyond on that branch. I'm sure that a concerted search would reveal others. So, you might say that down that fork lies the world as we know it."

He tapped the palm of one hand on the railing as he gathered his thoughts. "On the other branch of that mantic root lies only the Great Void. There are no books of prophecy for what lies beyond. That is the reason it is called the Great Void. You might say that there is nothing on that branch for prophecy to see—no magic, no world as we know it, and thus no prophecy to illuminate it."

He cast her a brief glance. "That is the world the Imperial Order wants. If they take us down that fork, mankind will go forever into the unknown of the Great Void, a place without magic and thus without prophecy.

"Some of my predecessors have speculated that since there is no prophecy for what lies beyond, it could only mean that the Great Void augurs the end of everything, the end of all life."

Nicci could find no words. She didn't think that there could be anything but darkness if the Order won, so this news wasn't really all that surprising to her.

"From the books here that I have been studying, from the information they have given me—and from recent events—I have been able to fix us on the chronology of this prophetic root."

Nicci's gaze darted to the wizard. "Are you sure?"

Nathan held a hand out toward the army below. "Jagang's army being here as they are, surrounding us, is one of a number of events that tells me that we are now on the cardinal root that takes us toward that fateful fork.

"I've known for centuries about the Great Void being in prophecy, but I didn't know if it was significant because I was never sure precisely where it fit in the chronology of prophecy. As far as I knew it was always possible that we might end up following an altogether different arm of the tree of prophecy, never setting foot in the area containing that particular cardinal root with the Great Void.

"There was always the possibility that the Great Void would turn out to be somewhere beyond any one of hundreds of false forks, down a dead branch on the tree of prophecy. Ages ago, when I first started studying it, it had seemed to me that it would turn out to be nothing more than false prophecy, eventually to be left in the forgotten dust of history along with so much of the other dead wood of the possible things that never came to pass.

"Slowly, though, events have inexorably carried us to where we find ourselves today. I am now sure that we are on that trunk of prophecy, on that particular branch, on that cardinal root, about to encounter the determinative fork.

"You," Nathan said to Nicci, "have irrevocably placed us there by putting the power of Orden in play in Richard's name. The boxes of Orden were the final node on the mantic root.

"There is no longer any possibility for mankind but to face that fork."

CHAPTER 17

Cara stuck her head out of the doorway far enough that the wind coming up the walls of the palace lifted her blond braid. "You mean, if Richard takes us down one of those two forks we will survive, but if he doesn't, and we go down the other . . ."

"There is only the Great Void," Nathan finished for her. He turned back to Nicci, laying a hand on her shoulder. "Do you understand the significance of what I'm telling you?"

"Nathan, I may not know everything that prophecy has had to say about it, but I certainly know what is at stake. The boxes of Orden were put into play by Sisters of the Dark, after all. I hardly see any outcome should they win except for the end of everything good. As far as I can see, Richard is the only one who has a chance to stop that from happening."

"Quite so," Nathan said with a sigh. "This is why Ann and I have been waiting five hundred years for Richard to come into the world. He was the one meant to navigate the forks that would successfully carry us through a dangerous tangle of shrouded knots within prophecy. If he succeeded, which he has so far done, then he is the one who must lead us in this final battle. We've known that for a long time, now."

Nathan rubbed a finger along the side of his temple. "We've always understood that the boxes of Orden were the final node upon which this cardinal root forks."

Nicci frowned as his words sunk in. She suddenly understood.

"That's where you made the mistake, before," she said, half to herself.

Ann leaned through the doorway a little, her eyes narrowing. "What?"

"You were tracing the wrong root in prophecy," Nicci said, even as parts of the puzzle were still falling into place in her own mind. "You were aware of the importance of the boxes of Orden, but your chronology was jumbled and as a result you ended up tracing a false fork. You mistakenly thought that it was Darken Rahl who, by using the boxes of Orden, created the terminal node. You thought it was Darken Rahl who would lead us into the Great Void."

Understanding the gravity of the mistake, Nicci turned to stare at the former prelate. "You thought that you had to prepare Richard to deal with that threat, thinking it was this fork of prophecy—the one we find ourselves on right now—so you stole *The Book of Counted Shadows* and gave it to George Cypher, meaning it for Richard when he got older. You thought Darken Rahl was the final battle, the terminal node in prophecy. You wanted Richard to fight Darken Rahl. You thought you were giving him the tools he needed to fight the final battle.

"But you had mistakenly taken a wrong turn—you ended up on a barren branch of prophecy and you didn't realize it. You were preparing him for the wrong battle. You thought that you were helping him, but you got it all wrong and in the end your misjudgment only ended up causing Richard to bring down the great barrier that allowed Jagang to become the threat that the prophecies had warned of in the first place. Because of you, the Sisters of the Dark were at last able to get their hands on the boxes of Orden. Because of you, the Keeper of the underworld has them to do his bidding. Without what you did, none of that would have been possible."

Nicci blinked at the former prelate as the magnitude of what they had done sank in. The realization gave her goose bumps.

"You inadvertently caused all of this. You tried to use prophecy to avert a disaster and instead you only served to fulfill prophecy. Your decision to interfere is what made the disaster possible."

Ann's face twisted with a sour expression. "While it would seem that we—"

"All that work, all that planning, all that waiting for centuries, and you messed it up." Nicci pulled wind-whipped hair back from her face. "Turns out I was the one prophecy needed—because of what you would do."

Nathan cleared his throat. "Well, that's a pretty big—and somewhat misleading—oversimplification, but I must admit that it's not entirely untrue."

Nicci suddenly saw the Prelate, a woman she had always thought of as next to infallible, a woman always ready to point out the tiniest mistakes made by others, in a new light. "You made a mistake. You got it all wrong.

"While you worked to insure that Richard could play his part as the linchpin who might be able to save us, you ended up being the pivotal element that brought the potential for destruction upon us all."

"If we hadn't—"

"Yes, we made some mistakes." Nathan said, cutting Ann off before she could even begin. "But it seems to me that we all make mistakes. After all, here you stand, a woman who fought your whole life for the beliefs of the Order, only to give yourself over to becoming a Sister of the Dark. Shall I invalidate everything you now say and do because you've made mistakes in the past? Do you wish to invalidate everything we've learned and have been able to accomplish on the grounds that there have been times when we've made mistakes?

"It could even be that our mistakes were not really mistakes, but rather a tool of prophecy, a part of a larger design, because all along you were the one meant to be close enough to Richard to help him. Perhaps the things we did are what allowed you to get close enough to him to play such a vital role, a role that only you would be able to play."

"Free will is a variable in prophecy," Ann said. "Without it, without all that happened because of the events that Richard tumbled into place, where would you be? What would you be had we never acted when we did? Where would you be had you never met Richard?"

Nicci didn't want to consider such a possibility.

"How many more, like you, in the end might be saved because events turned out this way," the Prelate added, "rather than if none of this had ever happened?"

"It could very well be," Nathan said, "that, had we not done the things we did, for reasons right or wrong, prophecy would simply have found another way to accomplish the very same results. It's likely, by the way these roots intertwine, that what is happening right now, one way or another, had to happen."

"Like water finding a route to lower ground?" Cara asked.

"Precisely," Nathan said, smiling proudly at her power of observation. "Prophecy is to a degree self-healing. We may think we understand the details, but in fact we may be unable to see the totality of events on a grander scale, so that when we take it upon ourselves to interfere prophecy must find other roots to nourish the tree, lest it die.

"In some ways, since prophecy can be self-healing, any attempt to influence events is ultimately futile. And yet, at the same time, prophecy is intended to be used, intended to spur action, otherwise what would be its purpose? Any intervention in events, though, is a dangerous thing to do. The trick is knowing when and where to act. It's an imprecise discipline, even for a prophet."

"Perhaps because we are so painfully aware of our own well-intentioned mistakes," Ann said, "you can see why we would be so distraught that you would take it upon yourself to make such a choice for Richard—a central figure in prophecy—as to name him a player for the power of Orden. We know the magnitude of harm that can result by interfering with even relatively minor issues in prophecy. The boxes of Orden are a determinative node, just about as far from a minor element within prophecy as one can get."

Nicci hadn't meant it the way it had come out. She never thought of herself as free of fault—quite the opposite. Her whole life she had felt inferior, if not outright evil. Her mother, Brother Narev, and later Emperor Jagang had always told her as much, constantly driving into her how inadequate she was. It was just that it had been surprising to learn that the Prelate could be so . . . human.

Nicci's gaze fell away. "I didn't mean it the way it sounded. I just never thought you made mistakes."

"While I do not agree with your characterization of events that have spanned five centuries and countless years of toil and effort," Ann said, "I'm afraid that we all make mistakes. One of the things that defines our character is how we handle our mistakes. If we lie about having made a mistake, then it can't be corrected and it festers. On the other hand, if we give up just because we made a mistake, even a big mistake, none of us would get far in life.

"As to your version of our interaction with prophecy, there are many factors you've not taken into account, to say nothing of those elements of which you are ignorant. You are connecting events in ways that are simplistic, if not entirely inaccurate. The assumptions made on the basis of those connections take great leaps over intervening circumstances."

When Nathan cleared his throat, Ann went on. "That is not to say, however, that we haven't at times misjudged things. We have made mistakes. Some of our errors involve events you have just pointed out. We are trying to correct them."

"So," Cara asked, somewhat impatiently, "what about this prophecy of no prophecy, the Great Void? You claim that we need to insure that Lord Rahl fights the final battle because prophecy says he must, and yet at the same time part of the prophecy says that prophecy itself is blank? That makes no sense—by prophecy's own admission, part of the prophecy in question is missing."

Ann pursed her lips. "Now even Mord-Sith have become experts on prophecy?"

Nathan looked back over his shoulder at Cara. "It's not so easy to understand the context of events as they relate to prophecy. Prophecy and free will, you see, exist in tension, in opposition. Yet, they interact. Prophecy is magic and all magic needs balance. The balance to prophecy, the balance that allows prophecy to exist, is free will."

"Oh, that makes a lot of sense," Cara sniped from the doorway. "If what you're saying is true, that would mean that they cancel each other out."

The prophet held up a finger. "Ah, but they don't. They are interdependent and yet they are antithetical. Just as Additive and Subtractive Magic are opposite forces, they both exist. They each serve to balance the other. Creation and destruction, life and death. Magic must have balance to function. So must the magic of prophecy. Prophecy functions by the presence of its counter: free will. That's one of the major difficulties we've had in the whole matter—understanding the interplay between prophecy and free will."

Cara's nose wrinkled. "You're a prophet, and you believe in free will? Now, *that* makes no sense."

"Does death invalidate life? No, it defines it, and in so doing creates its value."

Cara didn't look at all convinced. "I don't see how free will can even manage to exist within prophecy."

Nathan shrugged. "Richard is a perfect example. He ignores prophecy and balances it at the same time."

"He ignores me, too, and when he does he always gets in trouble."

"We have something in common," Ann said.

Cara let out a sigh. "Well anyway, Nicci got it right. And I don't think it was prophecy, but her free will that brought her to do the reasoned thing. That's why Lord Rahl trusts her."

"I don't disagree," Nathan said with a shrug. "As nervous as it makes me, we sometimes must let Richard do as he thinks best. Perhaps that is ultimately what Nicci has done—given him the tools to have the freedom to truly exercise his free will."

Nicci wasn't really listening anymore. Her mind was elsewhere. She abruptly turned to Nathan.

"I need to see Panis Rahl's tomb. I think I know why it's melting."

From in the distance, a rumbling roar rolled up through the gathering gloom, drawing their attention.

Cara stretched her neck out to see. "What's going on?"

Nicci looked out over the sea of men. "They're cheering for a Ja'La game. Jagang uses Ja'La dh Jin as a distraction, both for the people in the Old World and for his army. The rules used in the army games are quite a bit more brutal, though. It satisfies the blood lust of his soldiers."

Nicci remembered Jagang's devotion to Ja'La. He was a man who understood how to control and direct the emotions of his people. He distracted them from the daily misery of their lives by continually blaming every common trouble they faced on those who refused to put their faith in the Order, the latest of those being the heathens to the north. That distraction kept the people from questioning the teachings of the Order, since all their troubles were blamed on those who questioned.

Nicci knew, because she did that very thing herself as Death's Mistress. Any suffering was blamed on those who were selfish. Anyone who questioned was attacked as selfish.

Jagang won widespread passion for war by building hatred for an imagined oppressor that was condemned for causing every problem the people lived with daily. Personal responsibility was abandoned to the disease of assigning fault for all hardships, and every hardship was blamed on the greedy who failed to do their part. In that way, their daily problems were a constant reminder of the enemy who they believed caused those problems.

The demands for Jagang to destroy the heathens that the people of the Old World believed were the cause of all their troubles served Jagang's ends. He also needed to destroy a free and prosperous people because their very existence put the lie to the Order's beliefs and teachings. The truth would ultimately threaten his rule.

The distraction of blaming others for the people's misery came full circle, being the means to turn attention elsewhere, and to let the people themselves demand of him that he go off to fight this battle against evil. Who could complain about the cost and sacrifice of a war they themselves demanded?

Ja'La, too, was a distraction that served his ends. In the cities the somewhat more civilized games were a focal point that funneled the emotions and energy of the populace into rather meaningless events. It helped give his people a common cause to rally around, to cheer for, promoting a mentality that steeped people in the concept of being joined in opposition to others.

In his army, Ja'La served to distract his men from the misery of service in the army. Since the audience of soldiers was made up of aggressive young men, those games were played under a more brutal set of rules. The violence of such games gave frustrated, combative, hostile men an outlet for their pent-up passions. Without Ja'La, Jagang understood that he might not be able to maintain discipline and control over such a vast and unwieldy force. Without Ja'La they might turn their idle hostility inward, among themselves.

Jagang had his own team, which served to demonstrate the indomitable supremacy of the emperor. They were an extension of his power and might, an object of awe. They reflected that awe onto the emperor. His Ja'La team connected the emperor to his men, made him like them, while at the same time stressing his superiority.

Having spent so much time with him, as his Slave Queen, Nicci knew that despite all of those calculated factors, Jagang, like his men, had actually become caught up in the game. For Jagang, combat was the ultimate game. Ja'La dh Jin was a kind of combat he could enjoy when he was not engaged in actual combat. It kept his own aggressive juices flowing. Since assembling his new team of unbeatable men, a team universally feared, he had come to feel that he, personally, was the master of Ja'La dh Jin.

It had become more than a game to Jagang. It had become an extension of his persona.

Nicci turned away from the sight of the Imperial Order forces gathered below. She could no longer endure the sight, or the thought of the bloody games she so hated. The muffled roars washed over her, a building blood lust that would eventually be turned loose on the People's Palace.

Once back inside, Nicci waited until Nathan pushed the heavy door closed against the cold night descending on the outside world.

"I need to go down to see Panis Rahl's tomb."

He looked back over his shoulder as he forced the latch into place. "So you said. Let's go, then."

As they started away, Ann hesitated. "I know how much you hate going down in that tomb," she said to Nathan as she caught his arm, bringing him to a halt. "Verna and Adie will be waiting. Perhaps you could see to that while I take Nicci down to the tomb."

Nathan cast her a suspicious look. He was about to say something when Ann gave him a look of her own. He seemed to grasp her meaning.

"Yes, that's a good idea, my dear. Cara and I will go speak with Verna and Adie."

The leather of Cara's outfit creaked as she folded her arms. "I'll stay with Nicci. In Lord Rahl's absence it's my job to protect her."

"I really think that Berdine and Nyda would like to talk over some issues of palace security with you," Ann said. When Cara didn't look at all inclined to agree to the plan, Ann hastily added, "For when Richard gets back. They want to be certain that everything is being done to insure his security when he returns to the palace."

Nicci thought that there were few people as wary as a Mord-Sith. They seemed to be constantly suspicious and to assume the worst. Nicci could tell that Ann simply wanted to speak with her alone. She didn't know why she didn't just tell Cara that. She guessed that Ann probably wasn't convinced that such an approach would work.

Nicci placed a hand on the small of Cara's back and leaned toward her. "It's all right, Cara. Go on with Nathan and I'll join you shortly."

Cara looked from Nicci's eyes to Ann's. "Where?"

"You know the dining room between the Mord-Sith

quarters and the devotion square beside the small grouping of trees?"

"Of course."

"That is where Verna and Adie are to meet us. We'll catch up with you there after Nicci has had her look at the tomb."

Only when Nicci gave Cara a nod did she finally agree.

CHAPTER 18

As they started away, Nicci just caught a parting look that Ann gave Nathan. It was an intimate gaze warmed by a child-like smile, a look of shared understanding and affection. Nicci almost felt embarrassed to be witness to such a private moment. At the same time, it revealed a quality of both Ann and Nathan that she found captivating. It was the kind of simple thing that almost anyone who saw it would understand and appreciate.

The brief glimpse into their feelings gave Nicci a sense of comfort and peace. This was not just the prelate she had feared for so much of her life, but a woman who shared the same feelings, longings, and values as most anyone.

As they made their way back along the hallway while Nathan and Cara vanished down a stairwell, Nicci glanced over at Ann.

"You love him, don't you?"

Ann smiled. "Yes."

Nicci stared, unable to think of what to say.

"Surprised that I would admit it?" Ann asked.

"Yes," Nicci confessed.

Ann chuckled. "Well, I guess there would have been a time when I would have been surprised as well."

Nicci loosely intertwined her fingers. "When did all this happen?"

Ann stared off into memories. "Probably centuries ago. I was just too foolish, too caught up in being the Prelate, to recognize what was right there before me. Maybe I thought I had a duty which came first. But I think that's just an excuse for being a fool."

Nicci was struck dumb by such a frank admission from this woman.

A look of amusement overcame Ann when she saw the look on Nicci's face. "Shocked to find me human?"

Nicci smiled. "That's not a very flattering way to put it, but I guess that must be the heart of it."

They turned down a long flight of stairs with evenly spaced landings in the square stairwell descending through the palace. The railing all the way down was vinelike wrought iron, held in place by masterfully worked iron made to mimic leafy branches.

"Well," Ann sighed, "I guess that I, too, was shocked to find out that I was human. At the same time, at first anyway, it made me quite sad."

"Sad?" Nicci frowned. "Why?"

"Because I had to admit to myself that I had thrown away most of my life. I've been blessed by the Creator with a very long life, but I realized only as I approach the end of it that I had lived very little of that life." She looked up at Nicci as they reached a landing. "Doesn't it make you feel remorse to realize how much of your life you wasted without ever realizing what was really important about that life?"

Nicci swallowed back a pang of regret of her own as they reached the edge of a landing and started down the next flight of stairs. "We have that in common."

Together they listened in silence to the whisper of their footsteps as they made their way down the rest of the stairs. When they finally reached the bottom they took a broad hallway leading straight ahead rather than one of the passageways branching off to sides. The hallway carried the spiced scent from the evenly spaced oil lamps.

Cherrywood squares paneled the walls to each side, each panel separated by straw-colored draperies spaced at uniform intervals. Each set of draperies was swagged with a golden rope terminated with gold and black tassels. The reflector lamps hung in every other opening between the drapes lent the hall a warm glow.

In every other warmly paneled square hung a painting. Most

were ornately framed, as if the works of art were beloved. Each painting had a panel to itself.

While the subject matter varied greatly, from a late-day mountain scene beside a lake, to a barnyard scene, to a towering waterfall, the thing that all the paintings had in common was an achingly beautiful use of light. The mountain lake sat between soaring mountains with light from beyond hazy mountains breaking through billowing, golden clouds. A shaft of that glorious light spilled across the shoreline. The forest all around fell back into a cozy darkness, while in the center, the distant couple standing on a rocky prominence were bathed in the warmth of the shaft of light.

In the barnyard scene the chickens scratched on stone pavers littered with straw and lit by an unseen source of muted light that, without the harsh touch of direct sunlight, made the whole painting all the more vibrant. Nicci had never before thought of a barnyard as beautiful, but this artist had seen the beauty in it, and brought it forth.

In the foreground of the painting with the towering waterfall spilling over a distant, lofty ridgeline, the arch of a natural stone bridge emerged from dark woods to either side. A couple faced each other across that bridge, backlit by the setting sun, which had turned the majestic mountains a deep purple. Standing in that light the two people had a nobility about them that was transfixing.

Nicci found it interesting to note that so much about the People's Palace was devoted to beauty. From the design of the interior, to the variety of stones used for the floors, stairs, and pillars, to the statues and artwork, the place seemed to be filled with a celebration of the beauty of life. Everything from the structure of the palace itself to its contents seemed intent on displaying the highest accomplishments of man. It was almost a setting dedicated to virtuosity meant to inspire.

What was perhaps even more intriguing was that these masterful paintings would be seen by few people. This was a private corridor, down in the depths of the palace on the way to the tombs of past leaders. It would be used almost exclusively by the Lord Rahl.

Some might see it as a display of greed, a private show of possessions, but that would be a mistake born of cynicism.

Nicci knew that different sorts of men had been the Lord Rahl. Richard's own father had been a brutal tyrant. His ancestors, much farther back, had been anything but. Original intent was often twisted and corrupted by following generations just as the original intent of these works of art had probably been lost, warping into entitlement of the elite. Wise leaders were often followed by fools who threw away all that had been won by their ancestors. Nicci supposed that all that could be hoped for was for each generation to be raised to be sensible enough to learn from the past, not to lose sight of the things that mattered, and to understand why they mattered.

Still, every person had to make choices for themselves. Those who lost sight of the values fought for and won in the past usually came to lose those values, leaving subsequent generations to have to fight to win them back, only for them to be squandered by their heirs, who didn't have to face the struggle to gain them.

Nicci saw the paintings along this long walk to visit the dead as messages from past generations meant to remind the latest to become Lord Rahl of the value of life. As he went to visit tombs of those passed away, this hall was intended to remind him where his attention belonged. In a way, this was the Lord Rahl's reminder of his proper duty: to life.

Many who had taken this long walk had lost sight of that, and in so doing, generations of people also lost what their ancestors had enjoyed, and they had taken for granted.

That was why the entire palace was created in the form of a spell to give the House of Rahl more power, and why the place was so filled with beauty—to remind him of what was important, and give him the power to keep hold of it for his people.

None of it, though, as breathtaking as it all was, was as beautiful to Nicci as the statue Richard had carved down in Altur' Rang. That statue had been so powerfully filled with the vitality of life that it had touched Nicci's soul and changed her for all time.

Richard was a Lord Rahl who carried that sense of life within him. He understood what could be lost.

"You love him, don't you?"

Nicci blinked. She looked over at Ann as they marched down the passageway.

"What?"

"You love Richard."

Nicci turned her eyes back ahead. "We all love Richard."

"That's not what I mean and you know it."

Nicci maintained her composure. On the outside, anyway.

"Ann, Richard is married. Not just married, but married to a woman he loves. Not just loves, but loves more than life itself."

Ann didn't say anything.

"Besides," Nicci added into the awkward silence, "I could have ruined his life—all of our lives—when I took him away down to the Old World. I nearly did. By all rights he should have killed me back then."

"Perhaps," Ann said, "but that was then, this is now."

"What do you mean?"

She shrugged as they turned at an intersection toward another set of stairs that would take them down to the level with the tombs. "Well, I guess that Nathan had every reason to hate me, in much the same way that Richard had every reason to hate you. As it happens, things just didn't turn out that way.

"As I mentioned a little while ago, we all make mistakes. Nathan was able to forgive mine. Since you're still alive, Richard obviously forgave yours. He must care about you."

"I told you, Richard is married to the woman he loves."

"A woman who may or may not exist."

"I put Orden in play. Believe me, I now know that she exists."

"That's not exactly what I meant."

Nicci slowed. "Then what do you mean?"

"Look, Nicci . . ." Ann paused as if distracted. "Do you have any idea how difficult it is for me not to call you 'Sister' Nicci?"

"You're going off the subject."

Ann flashed a brief smile. "Quite so. What I mean is that this is all larger than one man."

"What is?"

Ann threw her arms up. "All of it. This whole war, him being Lord Rahl, his gift, the war with the Imperial Order, the problems with magic caused by the chimes, the Chainfire spell, the boxes of Orden—all of it. Right now, who knows what trouble he's in. Look at all he faces. He's just one man. One lonely man. One man without anyone to help him."

"I can't deny the truth of that," Nicci said.

"Richard is a pebble in the pond—an individual at the center of so many things. He touches so many things. He has turned out to be a core element in all of our lives. Everything turns on what he does, on the decisions he makes. If he takes a wrong step, we all fall down.

"And look at the poor boy, the first born in three thousand years with Subtractive Magic, raised without learning to use his gift. Born a war wizard without even knowing how to use his own ability."

"I suppose. What of it?"

"Nicci, can you even imagine what it must be like for him? Can you imagine the pressure he must feel? He grew up in Westland in a small place and became a woods guide. He grew up without knowing anything about magic. Can you imagine what it must be like to have so much responsibility placed on your shoulders without even knowing how to call forth your gift? And on top of that, he is now a player for the power of Orden.

"When he finds out that the power of Orden is in play—in his name—can you imagine how such a thing will terrify him? He doesn't even know how to connect with his Han and now he is expected to manipulate what is perhaps the most complex bit of magic ever conceived by the mind of man?"

"That is what I'm for," Nicci said as she once more started down the hall. "I will teach him. I will be his guide."

"That's what I mean. He needs you."

"He has me. I would do anything for him."

"Would you?"

Nicci frowned over at the prelate's unreadable look. "What do you mean by that?"

"Would you do anything? Would you be the person he needs most?"

"And what would that be?"

"His partner."

Nicci's nose wrinkled with her frown. "Partner?"

"His partner in life."

"He has a partner. He has a—"

"Can she use magic?"

"She's the Mother Confessor."

"Yes, but can she use magic? Can she call upon her Han the way you can?"

"Well, I don't—"

"Can she use Subtractive Magic? You can. Richard was born with the gift for Subtractive Magic. You know how to wield such power. I don't, but you do. You are the only one on our side who does. Have you ever thought that you ended up near him for a reason?"

"A reason?"

"Of course. He can't do this alone. You are perhaps the only person alive who can be what Richard needs most—a partner who loves him, is able to teach and guide him, and who is able to be his proper mate."

"His proper mate?" Nicci could hardly believe her ears. "Dear spirits, Ann, he loves Kahlan. What are you talking about, his proper mate?"

"His proper mate." She gestured vaguely with one hand. "His equal. His equal in the feminine sense, anyway. Who better than you to be what Richard really needs? What we really need?"

"Look, I know Richard," Nicci said, bringing up a hand to halt the conversation before it went any farther. "I know that if he loves Kahlan then she must be someone remarkable. She must be his equal. You love what you admire. It is the Order's way to do the opposite, to say that you must love what is loathsome.

"She may not be able to use magic in the same ways that

he can, but she has to be someone he admires, someone who completes and complements him. He would not be so devoted to her were she not. Richard wouldn't love anyone who was less.

"You are discounting her without the benefit of remembering anything about her. We don't remember Kahlan or what she's like, but you only have to know Richard to understand just how remarkable a woman she has to be.

"Besides, she's the Mother Confessor—a very powerful woman. She may not be able to do the same kinds of things with her power that a sorceress can, but a Confessor can do what no sorceress can.

"Before the boundaries and barriers came down, the Mother Confessor oversaw the Midlands. Queens and kings bowed to her. Could we do such a thing? You ruled a palace. I am nothing but the Slave Queen. Kahlan is a real ruler, a ruler her people depended on, a ruler who fought for them, fought to keep them free. A woman who, according to Richard, crossed the boundary itself—crossed through the underworld—to get help for her people. While I had Richard down in the Old World she stood in for Richard. She fought with and directed the D'Haran forces, slowing Jagang's advance to buy time to try to find a way to stop him.

"Richard loves Kahlan. That says it all—it says everything."

Nicci could hardly believe what she was finding herself forced to argue.

"Yes, all you say may well be true. He may indeed love this woman, this Kahlan, but who knows if she's alive? You know far better than I the vile nature of the Sisters who have her. There is no telling if Richard will ever see her again."

"If I know Richard, he will."

Ann opened her hands. "And if he does, then what? What can there ever be of it?"

The fine hairs at the back of Nicci neck stiffened. "What do you mean?"

"I've read the *Chainfire* book. I know how the spell works. Face it: the woman who Kahlan was no longer exists. Chainfire obliterated all that. Chainfire does not simply make people forget their past, it destroys those memories, destroys their past. For all practical purposes the Kahlan that was, is no more."

"But she—"

"You love Richard. Put him foremost in your mind. Think of his needs. Kahlan is gone—her mind, anyway. All you say about how much she meant to him, how wonderful she must have been, may very well be true, but that woman, that woman Richard loved, is no more. Even if Richard were to find her it would only be the body of the woman he loved, an empty shell. There is no longer anything there within her for him to love.

"The mind that made her Kahlan is gone. Is Richard the kind of man who would love her form alone, just want her for her body? Hardly. It is the mind that makes the person who they are, and it is the mind that Richard loved, but that mind is gone.

"Are you going to throw away your life the way I threw away mine? I lost out on a lifetime of what I could have had with Nathan, a man I loved, had I not been so devoted to a sense of duty. Don't throw your life away as well, Nicci. Don't allow any chance for Richard's happiness to slip away from him as well."

Nicci squeezed her trembling fingers tightly together. "Are you forgeting who you are talking to? Do you realize that you are trying to push a Sister of the Dark on Richard, the man you say is the hope for everyone's future?"

"Baa," Ann scoffed. "You are no Sister of the Dark. You are different than the other Sisters of the Dark. They were real Sisters of the Dark. You are not." She tapped Nicci's chest. "In here, you are not.

"They became Sisters of the Dark because they were greedy. They wanted what they could not earn. They wanted power and the fulfillment of dark promises.

"You were different. You became a Sister of the Dark not because you were greedy for power, but for the opposite reason. You thought that you were unworthy of your own life."

It was true. Nicci was the only Sister of the Dark who had not converted in order to gain power or promises of rewards for herself, but rather out of a sense that she was not worthy of anything good. She hated having to be selfless, having to sacrifice herself to everyone else's wants and needs, hated not having her own life to herself. She thought that those feelings made her selfish, made her an evil person. Unlike the other Sisters of the Dark, she didn't really think that she deserved anything but everlasting punishment.

That motivation of guilt, rather than greed, troubled the other Sisters of the Dark. They didn't trust Nicci. She was not really one of them.

"Dear spirits," Nicci whispered, hardly able to believe that this woman whom she hardly ever saw, for what seemed decades at a time while they lived at the Palace of the Prophets, could so clearly understand the way it had been.

"I didn't know that I had been so transparent."

"It was always a source of sadness for me," Ann said in a soft voice, "that a creature as beautiful, as talented, as you, would think so little of herself."

Nicci swallowed. "Why didn't you ever try to tell me that?"

"Would you have believed me?"

Nicci paused at the head of the stairs, resting a hand on the white marble newel post. "I guess not. It took Richard to make me see it."

Ann sighed. "Perhaps I should have brought you in and tried to make you think more of yourself, but I always feared to be seen as too gentle lest through familiarity my authority come to be dismissed. I also feared that telling novices what I really thought of them might cause them to become full of themselves. You were not as transparent as you might think, though. I never realized the depth of your feelings. I thought that what I saw as your modesty would serve you well as you became a woman. I was mistaken about that as well."

"I never knew," Nicci said, her thoughts seemingly lost back in that distant time.

"Don't think it was only you, though. Others, because I thought so much of them, I treated worse. I trusted Verna perhaps more than anyone. I never told her that. Instead, I sent her on a blind chase for twenty years because she was the only person I dared trust in such a mission. All part of my involvement with various events in prophecy." Ann shook her head. "How she hated me for those twenty frustrating years."

"You're talking about her journey to find Richard?"

"Yes." Ann smiled to herself. "It was a journey in which she also found herself."

After being lost in memories for a moment, she smiled up at Nicci. "Remember when Verna finally brought him in? Remember that first day, in the big hall, when all the Sisters were gathered to greet the new boy Verna had brought in and it was Richard, grown into a man?"

"I remember," Nicci said as she, too, smiled at the memory. "I doubt that you would believe all that was sparked on that day. When I saw him that first day I swore to myself that I would become one of his teachers."

She had become his teacher, and in the end Richard had become hers.

"Richard needs you now, Nicci. He needs someone to stand with him, now. In this battle he needs a partner. It is all too much of a burden for one man. He needs a woman who loves him. Kahlan is gone. If she is alive she is only a shell of who she once was. She doesn't remember Richard or love him; he is a stranger to her. The sad fact of the matter is that Richard has lost her to this war. He needs someone, now, to be his partner in life.

"Richard needs you, Nicci, to whisper in his ear at night those things he must hear. Whether he knows it or not, he needs you more than anything."

Nicci was on the verge of bursting into sobs. Finding herself arguing against the thing for which she would give her life was tearing her apart inside. There was nothing in life she could want more than Richard.

But because she loved him, she couldn't do as Ann wanted.

Nicci started down the stairwell, and changed the subject. "I need to see the tomb and then I need to talk with Verna and Adie. I don't have any time to waste. I have to get down to Tamarang to help Zedd get the witch woman's spell off Richard. Right now that's what Richard needs the most.

"To help me in that, I need to know everything about Six. You may not have known the woman, but you had a network of spies spread throughout the Old World."

"You knew about the spies?" Ann asked, following Nicci down the stairs.

"Suspected. A woman such as you does not hold on to power for as long as you held on to power without help. Under your rule the Palace of the Prophets was an island of stability and calm in a world of turmoil, a world falling under the spell of the Fellowship of Order. You had to have had your web spread far and wide to keep yourself aware of all that was happening in the outside world, to keep you aware of any potential threats. After all, you kept the palace safe and free to do its work for hundreds of years."

Ann lifted an eyebrow. "I was not so good at it as you think, my dear. Otherwise, the Sisters of the Dark would not have become established right under my nose."

"But you suspected, and you look precautions."

"Not enough, on either account, as it turns out."

"No one can be perfect, and no one is invincible. It remains true that you did a very good job for a very long time of keeping them at bay. You had a network of informants to help you stay abreast of what was happening in the outside world. I know that the Sisters of the Dark were always looking over their shoulders. They feared you.

"With the kind of web that only the Prelate can spin, you must have heard something about Six over the years."

"I don't know, Nicci. Over the years there were a great many important things going on. Rumors of a witch woman were not of much interest to me. There were more important problems. As far as Six, I didn't really hear anything of note."

"I'm not interested in getting you to betray confidences, Ann. I'm only interested in anything at all you might know about her. For some reason she took the box of Orden. I need to get it back for Richard. Any bit of information at all might help me to that end."

"I simply never heard anything about her from my sources." Ann finally nodded, almost as if to herself. "But I know about her in a general sense, and I also know that she can't put Orden in play."

"Then why would she take it?"

"While I don't know any specifies about her, other than what Shota told us, I do know that the desire to destroy the good in life is what defines some people. The particular twisted beliefs they adopt are merely their internal justification for their overriding hatred of the good. That core drive gives them an affinity with others having the same goal of crushing anyone who lives free, who seeks to better themselves. It is the end—destroying anything good—that inflames and impassions them.

"Ultimately, it is life they hate. They feel inadequate at facing the challenges of life. They loath the necessity of dealing with the world the way it really is, so they grasp at shortcuts to existence. Instead of working hard, they choose to destroy those who do. Instead of creating something worthwhile, they want to steal what someone else has created."

"So," Nicci suggested, "you're saying that while you don't know anything specific about Six, you think that because of her nature she will seek others driven by hatred."

"That's right," Ann said. "And what does that mean?"

As they reached the bottom of the stairs, Nicci paused, resting a wrist over the newel post, tapping a fingernail on the white marble as she stared off in thought. "It means that, ultimately, she will seek an alliance with the ones who have the other two boxes: the Sisters of the Dark. They may believe very different things, but they are sisters in hate."

Ann smiled to herself. "Very good, child."

"She can't use the box herself," Nicci finally said, thinking out loud. "That means she had to have taken it as a bargaining tool. She wanted it in order to gain power for herself. When the great barrier came down she saw the New World as vulnerable. She schemed and eventually stole what Shota had created up here in the New World, but ultimately that isn't enough for her. She intends to have power in exchange for the box she now has."

Ann was nodding. "She is insuring that when Orden is unleashed she will be included. She is drawn to the potential for the massive destruction of all that is good. She may want power for herself, but I think her real passion is to be part of the dismantlement of values and order."

"There is one thing about it, though, that doesn't make sense." Nicci shook her head as she stared off down the long passageway. "The Sisters of the Dark are not likely to want to deal with the witch woman. They fear her."

"They fear the Keeper more. They must have the box if they are to unleash Orden. Don't forget, now that they have put the boxes in play, their lives will be forfeit if they fail to open the correct box. They will be forced to deal with Six."

"I suppose," Nicci said.

Something seemed to be missing, she just couldn't figure out what. It seemed that there had to be something more to it.

CHAPTER 19

Nicci's hand slipped from the newel post and dropped to her side as they started away. The floors, walls, and ceiling of the quiet hallway stretching into the distance were made entirely of polished slabs of white marble. Soft tendrils of gray and gold veining meandered through the marble, giving the entire stone corridor a faintly wispy look.

Torches in iron brackets spaced evenly along the walls cast the solemn corridor in a flickering light. The dead air carried the heavy smell of pitch and a pale haze of acrid smoke. At varying places along the passageway were other halls leading off to tombs.

"It's a dangerous time we are in," Ann said, the sounds of their footsteps echoing off the stone. "We approach the most dangerous place in prophecy that I know of. We approach what holds the potential to be our end."

Nicci glanced over at the old prelate. "That's why I have to help Zedd and then find Richard. At the same time Six has to be stopped before she can unite all three boxes. She has already shown me how dangerous she is, but if we can find her Zedd might be able to help with handling the witch woman.

"I think it might be more important for me to get my hands on Sisters Ulicia and Armina. They have the other two boxes. If they unite all three boxes of Orden, I don't think that the Sisters of the Dark intend to let Richard have until the first day of winter next year to try to open one of the boxes of Orden. They will certainly try to open them as soon as they have all three. I have this uneasy feelign that we may be running out of time."

"I agree," Ann said as they passed a hissing torch. "That is why it's so important for you to be there for Richard—so important for you to help him."

"I intend to help him."

Ann glanced up at Nicci. "A man needs a woman to temper his choices, especially when those choices can change the course of life itself."

Nicci watched their shadows rotate around them as they passed another torch. "I'm not sure I know what you're talking about."

"Only a woman who loves him, who stands at his side, who is trusted implicitly, can be the kind of woman who can be a positive influence."

"I do love him and I will stand at his side."

"You need to do more than stand at his side, Nicci, to be the woman who can have the influence needed."

Nicci glanced over out of the corner of her eye. "And what influence is it, exactly, that you think is needed?"

"A child needs the strength of a father as well as the nurturing of a mother." She held up her first two fingers pressed tightly together. "Male and female working together shape us, define us, guide us. In this it is no different. A man needs the feminine element in his life if he is to be a proper ruler to guide the growth of mankind.

"A powerful general without a woman can fight battles and win wars. Jagang can crush those in his way, but he can do nothing more than that—nothing worthwhile, anyway.

"Our side, our cause, is different. It takes more not only to win such a war as we face, but the future that we hope to be the result. Richard doesn't simply need someone who loves him, but someone he can love. Living by the sword alone is not enough. He needs that investment of his own emotion. He needs to give love as well as receive it."

Nicci didn't want to go down this line of argument again. "I am not that woman."

"You can be," Ann pressed in a soft voice.

"I'm sure that Kahlan is a woman who deserves Richard's love. I am not. I have done terrible things, things which I can never undo. I've walked a very dark path. All that I can do is to fight to stop the evil ideas for which I once fought. If I can do that, then I can earn redemption in my own heart. But I could never deserve Richard's love. Kahlan is that kind of woman. I am not."

"Nicci, Kahlan is not an option for us. It is pointless to frame it as a choice between you and Kahlan being there for him; she can no longer fill that role. Chainfire took that woman. Only you can fill the role, now. You must marry Richard and be that woman for him."

"Marry him!" Nicci let out a brief, bitter laugh as she shook her head. "Richard doesn't love me. He would have no reason to want to marry me."

"Did you learn nothing at the Palace of the Prophets?" Ann clicked her tongue impatiently. "How did you ever get to be a Sister?"

Nicci threw up her hands. "Now what are you talking about?"

"Men have needs." Ann shook a finger at Nicci. "Attend to them with all your talent as a woman—as the beautiful woman the Creator made you—and he will want more. He will marry you to get it."

Nicci wanted to slap the woman. Instead, she said, "Richard isn't like that. He understands that love is what makes passion between a man and a woman meaningful."

"In the end that is what he will have. You would merely be helping that meaningful passion come to be. A man's heart will follow his needs. Are you so backward as to think that all couples marry for love? The wisdom of elders often creates a better match. In the absence of Kahlan, that is what we must do.

"It is your job to urge him into your bed and show him what you can do for him, what he is missing, what he needs. If you tend to his passions, his heart will be yours and he will, in the end, have that meaningful passion."

Nicci could feel her face going scarlet. She couldn't believe they were having this conversation. She had to change the subject but she couldn't seem to find her voice.

Nicci knew that she had Richard's friendship and trust. To do as Ann suggested would violate that friendship and void that trust. Richard was safe in her friendship. The sincerity and shelter of Nicci's friendship in some ways qualified her for his love, but to do as Ann suggested would breach the trust of his friendship and in so doing disqualify her from ever really being worthy of it.

"You must not allow this chance to pass you by, child, to pass us by."

Nicci seized Ann's arm and pulled her to a halt. "Pass us by?"

Ann nodded. "You are our link to Richard."

Nicci narrowed her eyes. "What link?"

Ann's face tightened, looking more and more like the prelate Nicci remembered. "The link those of us who teach young wizards need to have with such men."

"Richard is our leader—not by birth, but by his own ability and force of will to see this through. He may not have set out to become the Lord Rahl, to become the one to lead us in this war, but along the way he grew into that role. He decided that life meant enough to him that he had to fight for his right to live it as he saw fit. He has inspired others who feel the same. It is only because of that that we have made it this far.

"He is not a boy at the Palace of the Prophets with a Rada'Han around his neck. He is his own man."

"Is he? Step back, child, and look at the larger picture. Yes, Richard is our leader—and I am sincere in saying that—but he is also a man who has the gift and knows nothing about it. More than that, he is a wizard with both sides of the gift. Lightning is bottled up in that man. What is the purpose of a Sister of the Light if not to teach such men how to control their ability and to—"

"I am not a Sister of the Light."

Ann flicked a hand dismissively. "Semantics. Wordplay. Denying it will not change it."

"I am not—"

"You are." Ann jabbed an insistent finger against the center of Nicci's chest. "In there, you are. You are a person who, by whatever course, has embraced life. That is the Creator's calling. Call yourself what you will, Sister of the Light, or simply Nicci. It matters not; it changes nothing. You fight for our cause—the Creator's cause of life itself. You are a Sister, a sorceress, who can guide a man in what he needs to do."

"I am not a whore, not for you, not for anyone."

Ann rolled her eyes. "Did I ask you to bed a man you don't love? No. Did I ask you to trick him out of anything? No. I asked you to go to a man you love, give him love, and be the woman he so desperately needs, be the woman who can receive his love. That is what he needs—a woman to be the link for his need to love. That is the completing link to his humanity."

Nicci glared. "A minder from the Palace of the Prophets, that's what you really want me to be."

Ann muttered a prayer for strength toward the ceiling. "Child," she said, her gaze finally coming down to fix on Nicci, "I am only asking you not to waste any more of your life. You don't fully grasp what it is you are not seeing. You may think that this is about love, but you don't really know love, now do you? You know only its beginning: longing.

"The circumstances may not be what you would ask for in a perfect world, but this is the chance the Creator has given you, your chance to have the greatest joy possible to us in this life—love. Complete love. Your love right now is one sided, incomplete, deficient. It is merely sweet longing and imagined bliss. You can't know what love really is unless those feelings within your heart are returned in kind and set free. Only then is it real love, complete love. Only then can the heart truly soar. You don't yet know the joy of that most human of emotions."

Nicci had been kissed by rutting brutes. There was no joy in such things. Ann was right: Nicci didn't think that she could truly understand what it would be like to be kissed by a man she loved, truly loved, a man who loved her in return and held her above all else in his heart. She could only imagine such bliss. What a pity for those who didn't know the difference.

Ann opened a hand in a gesture of appeal. "If in that joy of complete love—for both of you—you can help guide the man you love to make choices that are nothing more than the right choices, what is wrong with that?"

She let the hand drop. "I'm not asking you to cause him to do wrong, but to do right, to do what he himself would want. I'm only asking you to save him from the kind of pain that risks him making a mistake, a mistake that will take us all down with him."

Nicci again felt the fine hair on the back of her neck stiffen.

"What are you talking about?"

"Nicci, when you were with the Order—when you were known as Death's Mistress—what did you feel like?"

"Feel like?" Nicci cast about in her mind for an answer to the unexpected question. "I don't know. I don't know what you mean. I guess I hated myself, hated life."

"And in your hatred of yourself did you care if Jagang killed you?"

"Not really."

"Would you act the same today? Act out of disinterest for yourself, for the future?"

"Of course not. Back then I didn't care what happened to me. What future could there be? I didn't think that I deserved any happiness—I didn't think that I could ever have any happiness—so nothing really mattered to me, not even my own life. I just didn't think that anything mattered."

"Didn't think that anything mattered," Ann repeated. She tsked concern to herself before continuing her theatrical dismay at what Nicci had said. "You didn't think you could have any happiness, and so you didn't think anything mattered." She held up a finger for a point of clarity. "You didn't make the same kinds of decisions back then that you would make today because you didn't care about yourself. Am I right?"

Nicci suspected that she was nearing the unseen jaws of a trap. "That's right."

"And how do you suppose a man like Richard is going to feel when he finally realizes that Kahlan is lost to him—when the finality of it really and truly sinks in? Will he think that life is worth living? Do you think he will feel the same connection to us—feel the same sense of the importance of life—if he is lost, alone, despairing, despondent . . . hopeless? If he thinks he can never have any happiness, do you think he will care as much what happens to him? You know what that feels like, child. You tell me."

Goose bumps tingled up Nicci's arms. She feared to answer the question.

Ann waggled a finger. "If he has no one, no love, do you think he will care so much if he lives or dies?"

Nicci swallowed, forcing herself to face the truth. "I suppose it's possible that he might not."

"And if he has no hope for himself, will he make the right choices for us? Or will he simply give up?"

"I don't think Richard would give up."

"You don't think he would." Ann leaned closer. "Are you eager to put that to the test? Put our lives, our world, existence itself, to such a test?"

The intensity of Ann's expression seemed to have frozen Nicci in place. "Child, if we lose Richard, then we are all lost."

She went on in a soft voice, making Nicci feel as if the trap were finally closing around her. "You yourself know his central importance—that is why you put the boxes of Orden in play in his name. You know that he is the only one who can lead us in this battle. You know that without him the Sisters of the Dark will unleash the Keeper of the underworld. Without Richard to stop them they will unleash death upon life itself. They will end the world of life. They will take us into the Great Void.

"Without Richard we are all lost," she said again, as if hammering the final nail into a coffin.

Nicci swallowed back the lump in her throat. "Richard wouldn't ever abandon us."

"Maybe not intentionally. But if he goes into this battle alone, having lost love and hope, he may make the kind of decisions that he wouldn't make if he held in his care the heart of a woman he loved. That love could be the stitch that holds the whole thing together, holds him together.

"That kind of love can be the single thing, the only thing, that keeps a man from giving up when he has no strength to go on."

"That all may be true, but it still does not give you the right to decide his heart."

"Nicci, I don't think—"

"What are we fighting for, if not the sanctity of life?"

"I am fighting for the sanctity of life."

"Are you? Are you really? Your whole life has been devoted to molding others to what you wanted, not to what they wanted. While it might not be out of a hatred for the good, it certainly has been out of your notion of how others ought to live, and what they should live for. You molded novices into Sisters so that they could serve in the duty you assigned them. You used Sisters to shape young men into wizards who would likewise follow what you believe the Creator wants.

"Everyone you've had control over has been forced to your vision of how they ought to live their lives and what beliefs they must follow. You rarely let people make reasoned choices for themselves. You often didn't allow them to learn about life; you instead told them what aspects of it mattered and how they would live it. The only partial exception that I know of is Verna, when you sent her away for twenty years.

"You have been planning Richard's life for hundreds of years before he was even born. You laid out plans for how he must live out his existence—his only life. You, Annalina Aldurren, based on your own interpretation of what you read into prophecy, decided how Richard would spend his existence in the world of life. Now you are planning his emotions for him. You've probably even planned his place in the spirit world.

"You imprisoned Nathan nearly his whole life, even though he spent centuries helping you to your ends. Even though you came to love him, you condemned him to a life of imprisonment for the crime of what you feared the might possibly do.

"Ann, what are we fighting for, if it is not the ability to live our own lives? You simply can't decide what others will do or not do. You can't set yourself up as the good version of Jagang, the flip side of the same coin."

Ann blinked in sincere surprise. "Is that what you think I'm doing?"

"Aren't you? You're deciding Richard's life for him now the

same as you did before he was even born. It's his life. He loves Kahlan. What good is his life to him if he can't have sovereignty over his own heart, if he must do as you say? Who are you to decide that he must abandon what he wants most and instead love me?

"How could I be the kind of woman he really could love if I were to manipulate him in the way you want? If I did what you ask I would automatically invalidate any emotions I created in him, make a sham of any such feelings."

Ann looked disheartened. "But I don't want you to love him against your will. I only want what is best for you as well."

"I would give anything to be able to use your urging as an excuse to do this, but I would never again respect myself. Richard loves Kahlan. It is not for me to replace that love with anything. It is because I love him that I could never betray his heart."

"But I don't think—"

"Would you be happy to have Nathan's love as a prize for a calculated trick? Would that be satisfactory to you? Would that bring you happiness?"

Ann's gaze drifted away, tears starting to fill her eyes. "No, it wouldn't."

"Then how can you think that I would be satisfied to seduce Richard at the expense of my self-respect? Love, real love, is something you earn for who you are; it's not a prize for your performance in bed."

Ann's gaze searched without settling. "But I only . . ."

"When I took Richard down to the Old World, when I took him captive, I wanted to force him to accept the Order's beliefs. But I also wanted to make him love me. To that end I thought to do something very similar to what you are asking me to do now. Richard refused.

"That's one of the reasons I so respect him. He was unlike any of the men I'd known who simply wanted me in their bed. I thought I could have him by the same means. He proved that his mind was what ruled him. He wasn't an animal like others who allowed their passion to rule them. He is a man ruled by reason. That is why he is our leader, not, as you seem to think, because you have pulled the proper strings.

"Had he given in to me I would never have respected him in the same way I do now. How could I truly love him if he would have proven such weakness of character? Even if I were to agree to your plan, Richard would not. He would remain the same Richard now as he was then. All that would happen is that he would lose his respect for me. In the end the plan would fail. It would fail because, ultimately, you failed to respect him as well.

"But would you really want it to work? Would you really want a man who is ruled by passion rather than reason to be our leader? Do you want merely to install a puppet of your wishes?"

"No, I suppose not."

"Me neither."

Ann smiled then, and took Nicci's arm, starting her down the white marble corridor.

"I hate to admit it, but I see your point. I guess that I have been guilty of allowing my passion for doing the Creator's work to get carried away into believing that I alone could decide how that should be accomplished, and how others should live."

They walked in silence for a moment, accompanied by flickering light and the soft hiss of the torches.

"I am sorry, Nicci. In spite of me, you have turned out to be a woman of true character."

Nicci stared into the distance. "It seems destined to be a lonely path."

"Richard would be wise were he to love you for who you are, just the way you are."

Nicci swallowed, unable to bring forth words.

"I guess that, in all the urgency of everything, I started to forget much the same lesson I'd already learned from Nathan."

"Perhaps all this really isn't your fault," Nicci allowed. "Perhaps it has more to do with Chainfire, and how much of what we knew is being lost to us."

Ann sighed. "I'm not sure I can blame my actions of a lifetime on a spell that has only recently happened."

Nicci glanced over at the former prelate. "What lesson from Nathan are you talking about?"

"He one day convinced me of very much the same things you have just brought back to my attention. In fact, he used much the same reasoning as you have just used. I misjudged Nathan, just as I have misjudged you, Nicci. You have my apology, child, not just for this, but for so much more I have robbed you of."

Nicci shook her head. "No, don't apologize for my life. I made the choices I made. Everyone, to one extent or another, must face life's trials. There will always be those who try to influence or even dominate us. We cannot allow such things to be an excuse for making the wrong choices. Ultimately, each of us lives our own life and we are responsible for it."

Ann nodded. "The mistakes that we spoke of before." She laid a hand tenderly against Nicci's back. "But you have made amends for yours, child. You have come to be responsible for yourself. You have done good."

"While I've come to see the grievous errors in my thinking, and I've tried to correct my mistakes, I don't think that counts as amends, but I promise you, Ann, if Richard needs anything, he will have it from me. That is what a true friend would do."

Ann smiled. "I guess you really are his friend, Sister."

"Nicci."

Ann chuckled. "Nicci, then."

They walked in silence past a dozen torches. Nicci was relieved that Ann had finally understood. She supposed that one could never be too old to come to new understandings. She hoped that Ann truly did understand, and that this was not just another strategy, another way to wield her influence over events. Maybe Nathan had actually changed her, as Ann had suggested.

To Nicci, it felt sincere. It also felt like this had been a conversation with Ann that she had been waiting her whole life to have.

"Which reminds me," Ann said, "in regard to Nathan and the terrible thing I had intended for him just before he helped me come to my senses. There is something important I left down in the dungeons."

Nicci glanced over at her squat companion. "And what would that be?"

"I was intending—"

"Well, well, well," a voice said.

Nicci froze in place, looking up just in time to see three women step out of a hallway ahead and to the left.

Ann stared in confusion. "Sister Armina?"

Sister Armina wore a haughty smirk. "If it isn't the dead prelate—once again alive, it would seem." She lifted an eyebrow. "I believe we can remedy that problem."

Ann used her weight to pull Nicci behind her. "Run, child. It's upon you now to protect him."

There was no doubt in Nicci's mind who Ann meant.

CHAPTER 20

Having been in countless deadly confrontations, Nicci knew that running right then would be a fatal mistake. Instead, she fell back on instinct and lifted a hand over Ann's shoulder, summoning every bit of dark power she possessed. Nicci fully committed herself to visiting unrestrained violence upon the three women down the hall.

In the same bewildering instant that she felt the failure of that dynamic connection—and nothing happened—she realized that within the People's Palace her power was, for the most part, useless. The dead weight of dread descended on her.

From down the corridor lightning ignited. The sudden sound within the confines of the hall was deafening. The blazing light of it arcing through the white passageway nearly blinded her.

Dark ropes of inky blackness tangled with the flare of lightning, creating a snarling mix that cracked and popped where it touched. Sparks flew. The air burned. So black was the Subtractive element that it seemed like a void in existence. In effect, it was.

Marble covering the floor, ceiling, and walls ripped open in ragged rifts at the contact. Stone chips shot through the hall, ricocheting everywhere. Marble dust billowed as the air itself convulsed with the violence of the discharge of power. The concussion snuffed the light of several of the closer torches.

Despite her power being so diminished that the commitment of force failed, in that instant of connecting with her Han, Nicci still had enough use of her gift to feel the familiar shift in her perception of time.

Her arms and legs felt like lead. The world, within the tunnel of her vision, seemed to slow almost to a stop.

She could see every bit of stone tumbling as it flew toward her through the smoky passageway. She would have had ample time to have counted them all while suspended in midair. She could see each chip, flake, and speck rotating as it flew. All the while the lightning thrashed wildly, lashing ever so slowly back and forth, leaving a dazzling tracing of afterglow in Nicci's vision. The lightning blasted through stone wherever it touched.

At the same time as the world slowed, her mind raced, trying to think of a way to stop what was inexorably coming toward them. But there was nothing within her ability to conjure that could stop Additive and Subtractive Magic laced together in such a violent mix. The power of it cut through stone down to bedrock. The air itself sizzled.

As the rope of liquid light twisted unchecked across the passageway, Ann dove in front of Nicci. Nicci knew all too well what was coming. She knew the nature of the three woman facing them. She knew the sort of lethal power they had invoked.

With no time to scream a command, Nicci instead stretched out to grab the Prelate and throw her down out of harm's way. She caught the gray dress. Her fingers started the ever so slow labor of closing.

It was a race between getting a firm grip and the flickering lightning that seemed to be raging out of control. But Nicci knew that it wasn't really out of control.

The crackling discharge of power jumped sideways and slammed squarely into the short woman. The blinding flash ripped right through her, coming out her back. The impact was of such power that it yanked the Prelate from Nicci's tenuous grasp.

Ann's squat body crashed into the wall with enough force to crack the marble slab. Such an impact would certainly have broken nearly every bone in her body.

Nicci could see, though, that Annalina Aldurren had been dead before she'd hit the wall.

The lightning abruptly cut off. The clap of thunder left Nicci's ears ringing. The afterglow burned in her vision.

Ann, her dead eyes staring, slid to the floor and fell over face-first. A pool of blood grew under her, flooding across the white marble.

The three woman down the hall, like three vultures perched on a dead limb, stood shoulder-to-shoulder, watching Nicci.

Nicci knew how they had just accomplished what she could not: they had linked their power. She herself, when they had first been captured by Jagang, had linked her ability with Sisters of the Dark. The three of them had acted as one and by that means had just managed to use their power inside the palace.

What Nicci didn't know was how they had gotten in.

She expected that at any second the lightning would again ignite and she would suffer the same fate as Ann. There had been a time when she hadn't cared one way or the other if she died. Now she cared. She cared greatly. She regretted that she would not have the opportunity to fight back before the end. At least it would be swift.

Sister Armina smiled a wicked smile. "Nicci, dear. How good to see you again."

"Bad company you keep," said Sister Julia, standing close on Sister Armina's right.

A stocky Sister Greta, close on her left, glared.

All three were Sisters of the Dark. Sister Armina had been free of Jagang, along with Ulicia, Cecilia, and Tovi. On their own those four had ignited Chainfire, captured Kahlan, and put the boxes of Orden in play.

But Sisters Julia and Greta, whom Nicci also knew well, had long been captives of Jagang. Sister Armina being with the other two made no sense.

Without having the time to consider the implications of those three being together, Nicci decided that if she was to die, she would at least try to fight. She abruptly flung an arm around in an arc, casting the strongest shield she could summon, knowing how weak it would be but hoping it might hold long enough. She bolted in the opposite direction—back toward the stairs.

She hadn't gone three steps when a rope of compacted air whipped around, sweeping her feet out from under her. She smacked the floor hard. Her shield had proven useless against the power of those three linked.

She was somewhat startled that they had not used the same kind of deadly power that they had on Ann. Not waiting to contemplate why, or for what might follow, Nicci rolled to the left and then scrambled to her feet. She dove through an opening into another hallway. Behind, she could hear the three Sister running toward her.

With simple, empty halls made of smooth marble, there was no place to hide. Nicci knew that if she ran they would simply ignite a bolt of power to take her down. She had no real chance to outrun them and escape the reach of their power. But, since they were already running after her, they would probably be expecting her to run, so Nicci instead pressed her back up against the wall just around the corner of the next intersection, on the side closest to the three coming for her.

She panted, catching her breath, trying to keep as quiet as possible. From where she waited she couldn't see Ann's body, but she could see the bright stain of blood running across the white marble floor.

It was hard to believe that Ann was dead. She had been witness to the rise and fall of kingdoms and the passing of countless generations over a vast march of time. It seemed she had been alive forever. It was numbing to try to imagine a world without Annalina Aldurren.

Although the Prelate had not been beloved by Nicci, she still felt a pang of grief for her. The woman had finally seemed to come to terms with some of her mistakes. After all this time, after such a long life, she had finally come to have real love in her life.

As Nicci heard the footsteps rushing close she gathered her wits. This was no time to grieve.

Nicci was hardly a stranger to violence and death, but she was not at all used to this manner of combat. As Death's Mistress she had been witness to thousands of deaths, and had killed more people than she could count or recall, but she had never done it with her bare hands. Now, without her power, that was her only option. She tried to think of how Richard would do such a thing.

As the three Sisters charged around the corner, Nicci used all her strength to ram her elbow into the face of the closest woman. She heard teeth snap. Her heart was pumping so fast she didn't even feel the blow in her elbow. Sister Julia was knocked sprawling on her back.

Without pause, even as Sister Julia was still sliding across the floor, Nicci sprang at Sister Armina, grabbing her by the hair. She used the women's forward momentum to propel her across the hall and slam her head into the wall. Her skull made a sickening *thwack* against the stone. Nicci hoped to at least knock the woman out, if not kill her. If there was only one Sister left standing she wouldn't be able to use her power any better than Nicci could.

But Sister Armina was still very conscious. She screamed curses as she struggled to get free. Nicci pulled her back, while she had the initiative, lifting her by the hair in order to get another swing to bash her face against the wall.

Before she could accomplish the task, the stout Sister Greta crashed into Nicci's middle, knocking her to the side, off Sister Armina. The flying weight of the Sister whacked Nicci against the wall with enough force to knock the wind out of her. She blindly clawed at the woman tackling her, trying to get her off.

Sister Greta, holding Nicci tightly around the middle, twisted to the side, easily throwing her face-first to the ground. Nicci flipped over to kick Sister Greta away.

Sister Armina, blood running down her face, planted a boot on Nicci's chest. Sister Greta rose up next to her, catching her breath.

Before Nicci could struggle to get up, a jolt of pain seared up through her body, exploding at the base of her skull. The shock of it drove the air from her lungs. The two of them joining their gift was enough to incapacitate Nicci.

"Not a very gracious way to greet your Sisters," Sister Greta said.

Nicci tried to ignore the pain. Her arms flailed as she tried to get up, but Sister Armina put more weight on her foot and at the same time expanded the sharp barbs of pain. Nicci's vision blurred down to a small spot at the center of a dark tunnel of blackness, her back arched as her muscles convulsed into knots. Her fingers clawed at the floor. She thought that she might do anything to make it stop.

"I suggest that you stay where you are," Sister Armina said, "or, if you prefer, we'll remind you just how much more agony we can deliver." She arched an eyebrow at Nicci. "Hmm?"

Nicci couldn't speak. Tears of torment streaming from her eyes, she instead nodded.

Sister Julia stumbled close, both hands held tightly over her mouth as she bawled in pain and anger. Blood hung in strings from her chin, covered the front of her faded blue dress, and dripped from her elbows.

Sister Armina, her foot still on Nicci's chest, leaned down, resting an arm across her knee.

In a voice only partly her own, she said, "Returned to us at long last, darlin?"

Nicci's blood flashed icy cold.

She realized that it was Jagang's gaze looking down at her.

Had she not been in such agony, had it not been all she could do just to breath, she surely would have run, even if it would have meant sudden death. Sudden death would be preferable.

Unable to run, she instead envisioned gouging out Sister Armina's eyes—Jagang's window.

"I'm going to kick your teeth in for this!" Sister Julia said in a muffled voice from behind the hands clamped over her mouth. "I'm going to—"

"Shut up," Sister Armina said in that terrible voice only half her own, "or I'll not allow them to heal you."

Sister Julia's eyes flashed with terror at recognizing Jagang addressing her. She fell silent.

Sister Armina held a hand out to her. "Give it to me."

Sister Julia slipped bloody fingers into a pocket and brought out something unexpected, something that made Nicci's breath catch with fright. Sister Julia handed it to Sister Armina.

Sister Armina removed her foot and went down on one

knee, leaning over a prostrated Nicci. Nicci knew what was coming. She struggled with all her might, all her panic, but she couldn't manage to make her body respond. Her muscles were locked rigid with the tingling power searing through her nerves.

Sister Armina bent forward and forced the blood-slicked collar around Nicci's neck.

Nicci felt the Rada'Han snap closed.

In the same instant, she lost the link to her Han.

She had been born with the gift. Most of the time she never gave it any thought. Now she was cut completely off from her ability. Like her eyesight or hearing, it had always been there, always been something she used without thought. Now there was only a terrifyingly unfamiliar void.

Such an abrupt separation from her gift stunned her. To be without it was to be without a part of her, without the very core of her, of who she was, of what she was.

"On your feet," Sister Armina said.

When the pain at last eased off, Nicci's whole body sagged against the floor. She didn't know if her muscles would work, or if she would have the strength to get up, but she knew Sister Armina well enough not to hesitate. She flopped over and pushed herself up onto her hands and knees. When she didn't move fast enough for Sister Armina, a stunning shock of pain slammed into the small of Nicci's back. She sucked back a scream. Her arms and legs shot out straight involuntarily and she dropped flat to the floor.

Sister Greta chuckled.

"Get up," Sister Armina said, "or I will show you some real pain."

Nicci pushed herself up on her hands and knees again. She gasped, getting her breath. Tears dripped onto the dusty floor. Knowing better than to delay, she struggled to her feet. Her legs wobbled, but she managed to stay upright.

"Just kill me," Nicci said. "I'm not going to cooperate, no matter how much you make it hurt."

Sister Armina cocked her head, peering closely at Nicci with one eye. "Oh, darlin, I think you're wrong about that."

It was once again Jagang speaking.

A blinding shimmer of agony, delivered by the collar around her neck, cascaded down through Nicci's core. The pain was so stunning that it dropped her to her knees.

She had endured pain from Jagang before, when he had been able to enter her mind, before she learned how to stop him. It was her devotion to Richard—the bond—that had protected her just as it protected those from D'Hara and those who followed the Lord Rahl. But before that, when he had been able to enter her mind, just as he could enter the minds of these Sisters, now, he had been able to make it feel like he was pushing thin iron spikes deep into Nicci's ears, then send the pain ripping downward through her insides.

This was worse.

She stared at the floor, fully expecting blood to run from her ears and nose and begin carpeting the stone. She blinked as she gasped in utter agony, but she saw no blood. She wished she did. If she bled enough she would die.

She knew Jagang well enough, though, to know that he would not allow her to die. Not yet, anyway.

The dream walker didn't like a swift death for people who angered him. Nicci knew that there was probably no one Jagang wanted to make suffer more than her. He would eventually kill her, of course, but he would extract his vengeance first. He would no doubt give her to his men for a time, just to humiliate her, then send her to the torture tents. That part of it, she knew, would last a very long time. When he eventually became bored with her suffering, she would spend her final days having her intestines pulled slowly out of a slit in her belly. He would want to be there to see her finally die, to make sure that the last thing she saw before the end was him smiling in triumph.

The one thing that she regretted at that moment, in the realization of what was about to befall her, was that she would never see Richard again. She thought that if she could only see him one more time she could endure what was to come.

Sister Armina stepped closer, close enough to be sure that Nicci could see her superior smile. She was now in control of the collar around Nicci's neck. Jagang, too, could now dominate her through that connection as well.

The Rada'Han was meant to control young wizards. It acted on the gift. Though the People's Palace diminished her gift—prevented the projection of power—it would not impede the collar, because the Rada'Han worked internally. The device could cause unimaginable pain—enough pain that a boy would do anything to make it stop.

Nicci, on her knees, trembled as she gasped in agony. Her vision went darker and darker until she could hardly see anything. Her ears rang.

"Do you now fully understand what will happen should you disobey us?" Sister Armina asked.

Nicci couldn't answer. She had no voice. She managed a slight nod.

Sister Armina leaned down. The blood had finally stopped running from her scalp. "Then get to your feet, Sister."

The pain finally lifted enough for Nicci to be able to stand.

She didn't want to stand. She wanted them to kill her. Jagang was not going to allow that, though. Jagang wanted to get his hands on her.

As her vision began to clear, she saw that Sister Greta was back across the hall, rummaging through Ann's pockets. She pulled something from a pocket hidden under Ann's belt. She looked it over and then held it up.

"Guess what I found," she said, waving it for the other two to see. "Should we take it?"

"Yes," Sister Armina said, "but be quick about it."

Sister Greta shoved the small item in her pocket and returned to the other two. "There's nothing else on her."

Sister Armina nodded. "We'd best be quick."

The three stood shoulder to shoulder, facing back down the hall toward Ann. Nicci could tell that, even with the link, they were still having difficulty using their power. Without the spell of the People's Palace draining their Han, any of the three of them, by herself, could have easily wielded the kind of power that had killed Ann.

The air cracked with the ignition of Subtractive Magic. The

hallways dimmed as several more torches were blown out by the blast. Inky darkness undulated thorough the passageway, back toward the Prelate, finally enveloping the dead woman. The hum of power made Nicci again momentarily lose her vision under the oppressive blanket of blackness.

When her sight returned, Ann was gone. Even her blood was gone. Every trace of her existence had been wiped away by Subtractive Magic. It seemed impossible that nearly a thousand years of life could be gone in an instant.

No one would ever know what had happened to her.

While the body and the blood had been eliminated, the shattered marble was not so easily fixed. The Sisters didn't seem to care.

To Nicci, it felt as if everything, even all hope, had just died.

Sister Armina seized Nicci under the arm and shoved her down the passageway. Nicci stumbled but regained her footing before she fell. She walked woodenly ahead of the three, prodded to keep moving by sharp reminders the collar sent into her tender kidneys.

They hadn't gone far before Nicci was directed to turn down a hallway to the left. She numbly followed their orders, making turns and taking several smaller passageways when told to until at the end of a lesser hallway they ended at an entrance to a tomb. Rather simple brass-clad doors stood closed. They weren't nearly as massive, or ornately decorated, as some of the others she'd seen when she'd visited the tomb of Richard's grandfather, Panis Rahl, located in a distant area.

Nicci thought that it was odd to be going to a tomb. She wondered if the the Sisters were intending to hide until they could think of a way to make good their escape from the heavily guarded palace. Since it was night, perhaps they intended to wait until a busier time of day so they wouldn't be as easily noticed. How they had gotten in, Nicci couldn't imagine.

Each door was embossed with a simple circle-within-a-circle motif. Sister Greta pulled one door open and ushered the others in, Nicci in the lead.

Inside, the Sisters used a spark of power to light a single torch. An ornately decorated coffin rested on a raised floor in the center of the small room. The walls above the height of the coffin were covered in stone of swirling browns and tans. Black granite that in the torchlight sparkled with copper flakes covered the lower portion of the walls.

It was an odd arrangement, almost making the upper portion, above coffin height, seem like the world of life, while the area below covered in black stone was reminiscent of the underworld.

Cut into the upper, lighter stone were the primary invocations in High D'Haran. They ran in bands around the room. Nicci scanned the script, seeing that it appeared to be rather common appeals to the good spirits to welcome this Rahl leader into the ranks of the good spirits along with others who had come before him. It spoke of the man's life and the things he had done for his people.

Nothing of any particular significance in the writing stood out to Nicci. It seemed to be the tomb of a Lord Rahl from the distant past who had served his people by ruling during a rather peaceful time in D'Haran history. The words called it a time of "transition."

Inscribed in the black granite covering the lower walls was a rather odd admonition to remember the foundation that made all that lay above them possible. That foundation, it said, had been laid by all the countless souls long forgotten.

The coffin itself, made of smooth stone in a simple shape, was covered with inscriptions advising those who visited to keep in mind all those who had passed from this life and into the next.

Sister Armina, surprisingly, put her weight against one end of the coffin. With a grunt of effort, she pushed, and the coffin moved a few inches, exposing a lever. She reached down into the narrow slot, grapsed the lever, and pulled it up until it clicked into place.

The coffin pivoted, making only a whisper of sound.

Once the coffin had turned aside, Nicci was surprised to see a dark opening. This was no tomb. It was a hidden entrance to whatever lay below.

When Sister Julia shoved her, Nicci stepped forward onto

the raised platform until she saw stairs, roughly hewn from rock, descending into darkness.

Sister Greta stepped down into the opening. She lit one of a dozen torches stuck in a row of holes in the rough stone wall and then took it with her as she started down. Sister Julia went next, also taking a torch.

"Well," Sister Armina said, "what are you waiting for? Get going."

CHAPTER 21

Lifting the skirts of her black dress, Nicci stepped over the raised edge of the pedestal that held the coffin. She gripped the edge of the opening to steady herself as she started down the steep run of stairs. The first two Sisters were already making their way down. The wavering glow of their torches showed nothing but a nearly vertical shaft of steps.

Once Sister Armina had climbed in after Nicci, she pushed a lever back into the wall, then took a torch for herself. Overhead, the coffin pivoted back into place, sealing them in.

It looked to Nicci like they were about to descend into the underworld itself.

The stairs wound downward haphazardly. The shaft was only wide enough for one person at a time. Descending at a steep angle, the steps turned at small landings only to continue tunneling downward in what seemed to be random directions. The stairs themselves had been crudely hewn; they were uneven and not all the same size, making the descent treacherous. It appeared that whoever had carved the stairs had followed softer veins in the rock whenever they were available. Such work resulted in a meandering, crooked route.

The stairs dropped so sharply that Nicci found herself having to breathe the smoke of the two torches carried by the Sisters right under her. As her mind raced, trying to think out her options, she briefly gave consideration to throwing herself down the precipitous shaft in the hope that she could break her neck, maybe even taking the two below her down as well, but with as narrow as the opening was she expected that she would probably get wedged to a stop before falling far. The landings, too, were numerous, so while the stairs were steep they paused frequently to make turns. She would probably only break an arm, not her neck.

They climbed downward for what began to feel to Nicci like hours. Descending at such a steep angle made her thighs burn. By the way they labored to breathe, the three Sisters were feeling the strain as well. They clearly weren't up to the demanding effort and were tiring.

While Nicci was getting tired as well, she wasn't having the trouble the others were. The Sisters had to pause a number of times to take brief rests. When they stopped, they would sit on a step, leaning back against the wall, panting as they caught their breath. They made Nicci stand.

None of the three liked Nicci. As she had told Ann, she was different from the rest of the Sisters of the Dark. They'd always thought that they deserved eternal rewards. Nicci always thought that she deserved eternal punishment. It was a grim irony that only after she had finally realized the value of her life, would she have the punishment she'd thought she deserved—Jagang would see to that.

When it seemed she could not make it down another flight, they came to a flat spot. At first, Nicci thought that it might only be another landing, but it turned out to be a level passageway.

The way ahead burrowed in a wandering course in much the same way the stairs had, only it was flat. In places the tight tunnel was so low that they had to duck down under low hanging rock. The walls had been carved from that same rock, and were irregular, making it almost look like nothing so much as a cave. Some spots were a tight squeeze to get through. In the small places the choking smoke from the torches made Nicci's eyes burn.

The narrow tunnel abruptly widened into a proper passageway easily wide enough for two people to walk side by side. The walls, rather than being hewn from bedrock, were made of blocks of stone. The ceiling, made of huge stone blocks spanning the width of the passageway, was low and blackened by soot from torches, but at least it wasn't so low that Nicci had to bend.

Before long they began encountering intersections and halls to the sides. It quickly became apparent that there was a warren of passageways branching in every direction. As they passed bisecting intersections, the light of the torches briefly illuminated long, dark halls. In some of the side openings, though, Nicci saw rooms with low niches carved into the walls to the sides.

Her curiosity got the better of her. She glanced back over her shoulder at Sister Armina.

"What is this place?"

"Catacombs."

Nicci hadn't known that there were catacombs beneath the People's Palace. She wondered if anyone up above them knew—Nathan, Ann, Verna, the Mord-Sith. At the same time the question came to mind she knew the answer. No one knew.

"Well, what are we doing down here?"

Sister Julia turned back to give Nicci a bloody, toothless grin. "You'll find out soon enough."

Now that she knew what the place was, Nicci realized that what she had seen stacked in some of the rooms to the sides were bodies, bodies in the thousands, wrapped in burial shrouds and covered with dust over the dark, still, silent centuries. As they passed other tightly spaced rooms she began to see recesses in the walls that held not individual remains, but mounds of bones. The bones were stacked in staggering numbers, all fit neatly into the recesses, filling them completely. As the torchlight fell into rooms to each side, Nicci saw skulls stacked together from floor to ceiling. The orderly rows of skulls went as far back as the light penetrated. There was no telling how far those rooms of snugly stacked skulls ran into the darkness.

Nicci found it appalling to contemplate all the individuals she was seeing. These had all once been living people who had been born, grown up, and lived lives probably filled with family and love. Now there were only bones to say that they had ever existed.

Nicci swallowed at the frightening thought that she would soon end up yet another anonymous skull that someone might one day see and wonder about. Just as she didn't know anything about these people, what they dreamed, what they believed, what they loved, or even how they had looked in life, she would be nameless bones slowly crumbling to dust.

She had such a short time ago been up among the beauty of the palace, among color and life. Now she found herself among nothing but dust and dirt and death, on her way to her own.

The two Sisters in front lead them through a confusing series of intersections. Some of the passageways they took sloped downward. In several areas they had to descend yet more flights of stairs to halls even deeper in the ground.

Everywhere there were rooms filled with bones, some with skulls, some with other bones stacked neatly in every available space, all bearing silent witness to lives once lived. Some of the passageways they passed through were made of brick but most had been constructed of stone. By the varying sizes of stone and styles of construction it seemed like they were passing from one era to another, each age preferring a different method to add to the ever-growing catacombs for their dead.

The next turn took them past a room with a different kind of entrance. Thick stone slabs that had closed off the cavern beyond had been slid aside. Nicci was surprised to see another Sister standing guard there. Beyond, back inside, in the shadows, there were big Imperial Order guards. Judging by their size, the type of chain mail they wore, the leather straps crossing their chests, along with the tattoos back across their shaved heads, these were some of Jagang's most trusted, and skilled, soldiers.

Back behind them Nicci saw that the low room was tightly packed with shelves holding countless books. Beyond, behind the rows in various places, the light from lamps revealed where people were searching through the volumes. Jagang had teams of scholars devoted to scouring caches of books for him. They were specially trained and knew the sorts of things Jagang was looking for.

The place reminded Nicci of nothing so much as the catacombs down in Caska. That was where, with the help of Jillian, Richard had discovered the *Chainfire* book. Nicci realized that these catacombs as well were liable to have a number of rooms with books.

"You," Sister Armina said to one of the guards, "come here."

When the man came to a stop out in the hall and leaned on his lance, she gestured back the way they had come. "Get some workmen together and—"

"What kind of workmen?" the man interrupted. Men like these were not intimidated by Sisters of the Dark—mere captives, slaves of the emperor.

"Men who know how to work with stone," she said, "with marble slabs. Sister Greta will go with you and show you what must be done. His Excellency doesn't want anyone to know that we've discovered a way into the palace."

Jagang, being a dream walker, frequently entered the minds of the Sisters. It was becoming increasingly obvious to the soldier that Sister Armina was operating under the direction of the emperor himself, so he nodded without objection as she went on.

"There is a place right near where we entered up top where the stone has been damaged. It's a small secondary network of halls. You will need to pull some of the undamaged slabs off the walls in the area with the damage and use them to block off that branch of halls. From the other side it needs to look like part of the wall of the main corridor. It needs to fool anyone who goes down that corridor into thinking there is not supposed to be an opening there. It needs to be done immediately." She tipped her head toward Nicci. "Before anyone looking for her discovers the damage."

"Won't people who know the place realize that an intersection has been blocked off?"

"Not if it looks seamless, if it looks like it's always been that way. It's the tomb area of the palace. The Lord Rahl uses it to visit his ancestors, but only if he ever wishes to do such a thing. It's likely to be rare for anyone else to go down there, so no one else is likely to notice that an intersection is missing—at least, not until it's too late."

The man cast a forbidding look at Nicci. "Then what was she doing down there?"

When Sister Armina turned a questioning look at her, Nicci felt a sudden shock of pain caused by the collar.

Sister Armina lifted an eyebrow. "Well? Answer the man's question."

Nicci gasped in a breath against the razor-sharp pain searing down her back and legs. "Just going for a walk . . . to have a private conversation . . . where no one would bother us," she managed between gasps of agony.

The Sister seemed indifferent to Nicci's explanation. She turned back to the soldier. "See? It's mostly an unused area. But before anyone goes down there looking for her, and the woman we killed, it needs to be done. Work as swiftly as possible."

The man smoothed a hand back over his bald, tattooed head. "All right. But it seems a lot of work to hide some damage." He shrugged. "After all, if they see it, they won't know why it's damaged. They'll probably think it's from before. There have been battles in the palace in the recent past."

Sister Armina did not look pleased to have the man second-guess her. "His Excellency does not want anyone up there to know that we've found a way in. This is of paramount importance to him. Would you like me to tell him that you suggest the work is not worth the effort and he should simply not worry?"

The man cleared his throat. "No, of course not."

"Besides that, it will give us a place to assemble and prepare without anyone knowing that we are all right there, just on the other side of a thin veneer of marble."

He dipped his head. "I will see to it at once, Sister."

Nicci felt sick. Once that opening was covered with marble slab the Order would be able to gather a sizable assault force veiled from those in the palace. No one would know that the enemy had found a way in. They were expecting the Order to have to finish the ramp before they could attack. The defending forces within the palace would be caught off guard.

A jab of pain started Nicci moving again. Sister Armina guided her with that pain, rather than simply telling her where she needed to turn. They walked down endless corridors, all made of stone block and with barrel ceilings, that seemed to connect clusters of rooms and networks of corridors.

As they rounded a corner, Nicci saw a knot of people in the distance lit by torches. As they got closer she saw a ladder ascending into darkness. She had long since understood where they had to be, and where they were going.

Royal guards had massed around a place broken open in the barrel ceiling. These men were the elite. They knew their business.

At the thought of what was up that ladder, Nicci feared her legs might give out.

One of the royal guard, who obviously recognized Nicci, stepped aside, never taking his eyes off her.

"Start climbing," Sister Armina said.

CHAPTER 22

Nicci emerged into what appeared to be a vast pit gouged into the ground of the Azrith Plain. She couldn't see what was up beyond the dirt and rock walls, but she didn't need to see it to know what was up there.

Out past the rim of the pit, the imposing ramp, lit by torches, rose up into the cold night sky. In the distance the dark shadow of the plateau that held the People's Palace, looking like it touched the stars themselves, towered over the dirt and gravel ramp.

The floor of the pit was a confusing maze of various elevations, apparently the result of different gangs of workers laboring to scoop up material for the ramp. Those workers were nowhere to be seen. It had to be that when they were digging in the area where she stood they had discovered the catacombs.

While the laborers may have been long gone, there were now soldiers everywhere. The ones she saw weren't regular Imperial Order troops, who were little more than an organized mob of thugs. These were the professional soldiers, the experienced men closest to Jagang. These were the trusted core of men who had fought with him in various campaigns over the years.

Because these were men who had always been closest to the emperor, Nicci recognized many of them. Although she didn't see any individuals she knew by name, she knew many of the faces watching her. These men all recognized her as well.

A woman like Nicci, with her fall of blond hair and shapely figure, hardly went unnoticed in the Imperial Order camp.

More than that, though, she was recognized by every one of these men as Death's Mistress.

They knew her by that name because she had in the past commanded many of them. They feared her. She had killed some of their comrades who had failed to follow her orders in the way she had expected of them. Belief in the Order called for selfless sacrifice for the greater good—the sacrifice of this life for the afterlife—yet when she had brought that righteous sacrifice upon them, ushering them into their longed-for afterlife, the very core of the beliefs for which they fought, they hated her for it.

Every one of these men also knew that she was Jagang's woman. In a movement dedicated to the greater good over individual rights, to ideals of absolute equality of all, he enjoyed making it clear that she was his personal possession.

Like the common soldiers, not one of these men ever dared to touch her. Jagang had in the past, however, given her as a favor to some of his inner circle of officers, men such as Commander Kadar Kardeef.

Many of these men had been there the day Nicci had ordered Kardeef burned to death. Some of them, at her command, had helped tie their commander to a stake and put him over the fire. Despite their reluctance, they dared not contradict her orders.

She kept her previous status in mind as she stood in the frigid night with all eyes upon her. Like a protective cloak, she once again wrapped that former persona around herself. That image of her was her only protection. She held her head erect, her back straight. She was Death's Mistress and she wanted everyone to know it.

Rather than wait for Sister Armina to direct her, Nicci started up the ramp. She had surveyed the encampment from up on the observation platform in the palace and knew how it was laid out. She knew where to find the command tents. She would have no trouble making her way to Jagang's tent. Since Jagang was probably watching Nicci through Sister Armina's eyes, the woman did not object to Nicci striking out on her own.

There was no use being dragged kicking and screaming to the emperor's feet. It wouldn't change anything. She might as well go to her fate under her own power and with her head held high.

More than that, though, Nicci wanted Jagang to see her in the same way as he had always seen her. She wanted him to see what he knew, see her as the same, even if she wasn't. Even if he suspected she might be somehow different, she wanted to present him with the familiar.

In the past her safety had been in her indifference to what he might do to her. That indifference gave Jagang pause. It infuriated him, it frustrated him, and it fascinated him. She had been someone who had fought on his side, fought for his goals, and yet she had been someone he could have only by force.

Even if she didn't have command of her power, she did have command of her mind, and it was her mind that was her true power—that was what Richard had taught her. With or without her gift, she could still be indifferent to what Jagang might do to her. That indifference gave her power.

Once up and out of the pit and past the heavily armed perimeter guards, she began encountering row upon row of workers hauling dirt and rock from other pits. Hundreds of mules, pulling every sort of wagon, plodded along in long lines through the darkness. Torches showed the rows of men the way to the ramp. The men, the average soldiers in the Imperial Order, the young, the strong, the pride of the Old World, had become common laborers. Not exactly the glory for which they had gone off to fight.

Nicci paid the activity little heed. It no longer mattered to her what they were doing with the ramp—the ramp was only a diversion. She felt sick at the thought of the brutes spread out in the camp getting up inside the palace.

She had to think of a way to stop them.

For a brief moment the very thought of her stopping them struck her as absurd. What was she going to do to stop them? She stiffened her resolve, along with her back. She would fight them with her last breath if need be.

Sisters Armina and Julia both trailed behind as Nicci marched through all the activity of the camp. Sister Armina would only make herself look silly if she pushed her way out front, now. By taking the lead, Nicci had already retaken her place as the Slave Queen.

Old patterns were hard to break. Now that they were entering the camp, neither Sister wished to challenge what Nicci was doing, at least not for the moment. She was, after all, stalking off toward where they would have taken her anyway. They would have no way of knowing for sure if Jagang was in her mind or not. They knew, the same as the soldiers knew, that she was Jagang's woman. That gave her unspoken rank over them. Even back at the Palace of the Prophets, she had always been a mystery to them. They had always been resentful and jealous of her—which meant that they feared her.

For all they knew, it was possible that the emperor had merely sent them to bring his stubborn and defiant queen back to him. Jagang, no doubt watching Nicci through their eyes, seemed to be making no effort to change that perception in their minds. It could even be that Jagang really did look at it that way, that he really did think that he could have her back.

She noticed but didn't acknowledge the large contingent of guards who had formed up into a train behind her. A queen did not acknowledge her attendants. They were beneath her. Fortunately, they couldn't hear her heart hammering.

As they entered the camp proper, where the regular soldiers had set up their tents in squalid clusters, men stood mute, looking like beggars watching a royal procession passing before them. Others rushed up from the darkness to see what was happening. Hushed whispers passed through the crowd; Death's Mistress had at long last returned.

To many of these men, even though they feared her, she was a heroine of the Order, a powerful weapon for their side. They had seen her rain down death on those who opposed the teachings of the Fellowship of Order.

Even though it felt strange to be back, the camp itself was no different than she remembered. It was the usual jumble of men, tents, animals, and equipment. The only difference was that as it sat unmoving for so long it was all beginning to take on the look of rot and decay. Firewood out on the Azrith Plain was virtually nonexistent, so fires were few and small, leaving the whole place gripped by a kind of grim gloom. Sloppy midden heaps growing everywhere among the men drew clouds of flies. With so many animals and men in the same place for so long the smell was worse than the usual stench.

The crush of unkempt men crowding in all around, which she had never paid a great deal of attention to in the past, was unnerving. They barely looked human. In many ways they weren't. In the past, not caring what happened to her, Nicci had been indifferent to these brutes. Now, since she cared about her life, it was different. More than that, though, in the past she had always known that she had the use of her power if their fear of her for some reason didn't keep them away. Now she could only count on their fear to keep them at arm's length.

It was a long walk through hundreds of thousands of men to reach her destination, but because the camp had been in place for so long trails had become established. In places trails had widened into roads that had gradually pushed aside tents and corrals. Now, as Nicci walked those roads, trailed by her entourage, wide-eyed men lined the way, watching.

Beyond the immediate silence of the men standing close by staring at her as she passed, the camp was a noisy place, even at this late hour. Behind her was the sound of the work on the ramp, wagons rolling, rock scraping and tumbling, and men calling out in unison as they pulled on heavy lines. In the camp all around the voices of soldiers laughing, talking, and arguing carried through the cold night air. She heard orders being yelled over the rhythmic sound of hammers ringing.

She could also hear the distant roar of crowds cheering for Ja'La games still going on even at this late hour. Sometimes collective boos of disapproval rose into the night air, only to be drowned out by wild yells of support. During runs with the broc men sometimes chanted shouts for their team to score.

As she made her way past a corral filled with huge warhorses, and then a line of empty supply wagons, the command tents came into view. Beneath a starlit sky flags atop the tents fluttered in the cold breeze. The sight of the largest tent, the emperor's tent, threatened to drain her of courage. She wanted to run, but she was not going to be able to run ever again.

This was the place where Nicci's whole life caught up with her.

This was the place where it all ended.

Rather than avoid the inevitable, she marched purposefully toward it. She didn't slow for the first of the checkpoints in the outer rings of protection around the command area. The big men standing watch eyed her as she approached. Their gazes also took in the contingent of the emperor's personal guard marching behind her. She was glad that she happened to be wearing a black dress because that was what she had always worn when these men would have seen her in the past. She wanted them to recognize her. A brief glare insured that none accosted her.

Each successive layer of men in closer to the center of the compound was more trusted. Each ring of men around the command tents had their own units, methods, and equipment. Each wanted to be the ones to stop any harm from reaching their emperor. They each had different protocol for entering their area of responsibility.

Nicci ignored those protocols. She was Death's Mistress, the emperor's Slave Queen. She stopped for no one. No one challenged her.

Jagang's tent was set back in a grouping of larger tents but, unlike all the other tents in the camp, it had ample space around it. Sisters patrolling the area took note of Nicci, as did the gifted young men she saw, but their gazes fell away when Nicci fixed them in her glare. The guards, too, all watched her but tried to be less obvious about it.

Nicci was encouraged to see that none of these people saw her as anything but what she had been when last among them.

She saw then a strange sight. Besides a cadre of Jagang's personal guards standing to either side of the heavy hanging covering the opening into his tent, there were other soldiers as well—regular soldiers. Pacing back and forth, they, too, appeared to be guarding the tent. She couldn't imagine why in the world regular soldiers would be inside the emperor's compound, much less guarding his tent. Such men had never before been trusted inside the command area.

Ignoring the curiosity of regular soldiers being there in the compound, Nicci headed straight for the heavy hanging over the opening into Jagang's tent. The two Sisters, already lagging behind, reluctantly followed Nicci toward the emperor's tent. Color drained from their faces. No one, least of all a woman, was eager to enter Jagang's private sanctuary. While he was sometimes pleasant to some of his trusted officers, he did not treat others indulgently.

Two big men, each holding a pike, their faces tattooed with animalistic designs, drew back the hanging. The small silver discs attached to the lambskin made soft metallic ringing sounds, letting the emperor know that someone was entering his tent. She recognized both men holding the hanging out of the way for her but didn't acknowledge them as she lifted her skirts to step over the threshold and into the darkness beyond.

Inside, slaves were busy clearing plates and platters from the emperor's table. The aroma of all the food reminded Nicci that she hadn't eaten. The knot of anxiety in her middle masked her hunger.

Dozens of candles gave the place a dimly lit, cozy warmth. Thick carpets covered the floor so that footsteps of slaves going about their work would not disturb the emperor. Some of the slaves, all with heads bowed, were new. Some she remembered. Jagang appeared to have already finished his meal and was not in the outer areas.

The two Sisters, having entered behind her, edged their way into the shadows toward the far walls of the tent. This was apparently as far as they were to go, and within the outer room they wanted to be as far away as possible.

Knowing where Jagang would be, Nicci headed across the room. Slaves scurried to stay out of her way. At the hanging over the opening into the bedroom, she lifted the covering aside and ducked through.

Inside the emperor's bedchamber Nicci at last saw him. He was sitting facing away from her on the other side of the plush bed covered with gold-colored silk. Points of light from the candles and oil lamps reflected off his shaved head. His bull neck spread into broad, powerful shoulders. He was wearing a lamb's-wool vest, and his massive arms were bare.

He was occupied with thumbing through a book, absorbed in scanning the text. While easily given to violence, Jagang was, in certain areas, an intelligent man who prized the knowledge to be found in books or sifted from the minds he inhabited. Emotionally convinced of the veracity of his beliefs, he never troubled himself to subject those beliefs to reasoning. In fact, he viewed such questioning to be heresy. Instead, his efforts were spent collecting information in narrow areas. He knew that the right kind of knowledge could be a valuable weapon. He was a man who liked to be well armed—with every form of weapon.

Something caught Nicci's eye. She looked to her left.

That was when she saw her, sitting on the floor, resting on one hip and leaning on an arm. She was the most sublimely beautiful creature Nicci had ever seen.

She knew without doubt who this woman was.

It was Kahlan, Richard's wife.

Their eyes met. The intelligence, the nobility, the life in those green eyes was riveting.

This was a woman the equal of Richard.

Ann had been wrong. This was the only woman who could by right stand at his side.

CHAPTER 23

Nicci saw that there was a Rada'Han around Kahlan's neck. That would explain why she seemed to be planted on the faded blue and beige carpet. Her gaze didn't miss the collar that Nicci wore. Nicci didn't think that this woman's gaze missed much.

A tentative look haunted Kahlan's green eyes as they stared at each other. It was a ghost of cautious encouragement brought about by her awareness that Nicci could actually see her. They were instantly sisters in more than one way, sharing more than just having collars around their necks.

How lonely and forlorn it must be to exist unseen and forgotten at the center of such a wicked spell.

Unseen, anyway, by anyone other than Sisters of the Dark—and, apparently, Jagang. It had to be a cause for hope that another person, even a stranger, could see her.

Looking at her now, Nicci could hardly believe that she could ever have forgotten this woman, even with the Chainfire spell. She could clearly see why Richard had never for an instant given up on finding her.

This woman, even discounting her exquisite beauty, had a presence about her, an insightful awareness, that Nicci instantly recognized from the statue that Richard had carved. That statue, called Spirit, had not been meant to look like Kahlan, but to represent her abiding strength, her inner courage. It did that in a way that, seeing the real thing, nearly took Nicci's breath.

She was beginning to see why, even at her relatively young age, Kahlan had been named the Mother Confessor. Now, though, there were no other Confessors. She was the last.

At first surprised to find Kahlan there, Nicci realized that it only made sense. Sister Armina had been one of the Sisters who had captured Kahlan and ignited the Chainfire spell. Sister Tovi had told Nicci that they had managed to evade Jagang by using the bond to Richard. While she supposed that Jagang might have somehow managed to get past that bond, Nicci thought that it made more sense that the bond had never actually protected them in the first place.

If Jagang had captured Sister Armina he would have Sisters Ulicia and Cecilia as well. That had to be why Kahlan was there; she had been held by those Sisters so she, too, would have been swept up in Jagang's net.

Nicci saw that Jillian was there as well. The girl's copper-colored eyes blinked in surprise to see Nicci standing there before her. While it made sense for Kahlan to be there, Nicci couldn't fathom why Jillian was.

Jillian leaned in close to Kahlan, cupped a hand to her ear, and whispered something—undoubtedly Nicci's name. Kahlan responded only with a slight nod, but her eyes revealed a great deal more. She had heard Nicci's name before.

When Jagang tossed the book he was studying on a bedside table, Nicci quickly pointed with two fingers between Kahlan's eyes and her own, then used one to cross her lips, urging silence. Nicci didn't want Jagang knowing that she could see Kahlan, or even that she knew Jillian. The less he knew, the safer those two would be—if being a captive of Emperor Jagang could in any sense be said to be safe. Without waiting for confirmation, Nicci looked away from Kahlan and Jillian to face Jagang.

When he turned around, fixing his black gaze on her, Nicci thought she might faint. It was one thing to remember him, quite another to be standing there before him.

To once again find herself under the scrutiny of those nightmare eyes crushed her courage.

She knew what lay ahead for her.

"Well, well," Jagang said as he made his way around the bed, his gaze fixed on her. "Look who has returned at long last." He smiled broadly. "You are as beautiful as every dream I've had of you since you were last here with me."

Nicci wasn't surprised by the approach he'd taken, nor did it indicate anything meaningful. Never knowing how he would react kept those around him in a state of constant dread. His anger could be sparked at any time by the smallest thing, or nothing at all. Nicci had seen him strangle a slave to death for dropping a breadboard, and yet on another occasion she'd seen him pick up a dropped plate of lamb and casually hand it back to the servant who had dropped it without missing a beat in his conversation.

In no small sense, this capricious quality in the emperor only reflected the same irrational, unpredictable, incomprehensible behavior of the Order itself. The virtue—the very adequacy—of one's self-sacrifice for the cause was measured against unseen, inscrutable, unknowable standards. Fortune or misfortune always seemed to hang on a whim. For a population, that perpetual gnawing doubt was debilitating. The deadweight of constant tension left people ready to accuse anyone of sedition—even friends or family—if only it would keep the talons of fate at bay.

Like any number of other men, Jagang also thought he could win Nicci's affection with a little empty flattery. He liked to imagine that he could be charming. The form his praise took, though, revealed more about his values than hers.

Nicci did not bow. She was acutely aware of the metal collar around her neck that prevented her from using her gift. While she had no defense against this man, she wasn't going to pretend respect by bowing, nor would she fawn at his finely framed lust.

In the past, despite her ability to use her Han, her real safety had always been her indifference to what he might do to her. During those times when he had been able to enter her mind, and she'd had no collar around her neck, her abilities as a sorceress had been of no help to her, just as his other captive Sisters were now helpless despite the fact that none of them wore a collar.

Her protection had always been in her attitude, not her gift.

Before, Nicci simply hadn't cared if he hurt her, or even if he might at any time decide to kill her. She thought she deserved any suffering he might inflict and she didn't care if she died. That left her indifferent to the ever-present possibility that the whim of murder might strike him.

Even though all of that had changed because of Richard, she couldn't allow Jagang to know how much it had changed. Her only chance, her only defense, was to make him think that nothing had changed in her attitude, that she cared no more about what might happen to her now than she had in the past.

Death's Mistress would not care if she could use her power or not. To Death's Mistress a collar meant nothing.

Jagang lightly drew the long braided hair growing under his lower lip between his finger and thumb. His gaze took in the length of her. He let out a deep breath, as if considering what he would do with her first.

She didn't have long to wait.

He abruptly backhanded her hard enough to send her flying. When she landed her head hit the floor but, fortunately, the thick carpets cushioned the impact. It felt as if the muscles of her jaw had been ripped and the bone shattered. The shock of the blow stunned her senseless.

Even though the room seemed to be spinning and tilting, she was determined to make herself return to her feet. Death's Mistress did not cower. Death's Mistress faced death indifferently.

Once up on her knees, she wiped the blood from the corner of her mouth with the inside of a wrist as she worked to find her balance. Her jaw, despite the pain, seemed to be intact. She struggled to get her feet under her.

Before she managed to stand, Jillian rushed up between Nicci and Jagang.

"You leave her be!"

As Jagang planted his fists on his hips, glaring at the girl, Nicci stole a glance at Kahlan. Nicci recognized the glaze of pain in the woman's eyes. By the way her fingers trembled, Nicci knew exactly what kind of pain Jagang was giving her through the collar. Such preemptive agony was meant to keep her where she was, keep her from interfering.

Nicci judged it to be, from Jagang's perspective, a wise decision.

As far back as she could remember, Nicci had been able to appraise people and to do so quickly. It had become a valuable talent, since survival in violent encounters often depended on the accurate evaluation of those she faced. Nicci could tell just by looking at Kahlan that she was a dangerous woman, a woman who was used to interfering.

Jagang snatched Jillian by the back of her neck and lifted her like a troublesome kitten. She squealed—more in fright than pain—as he held her aloft and marched her across the room. She clawed at his big hands to no effect. Her feet kicked at empty air. Jagang lifted aside the heavy, padded wool hanging covering the opening into his bedchamber and tossed Jillian out.

"Armina! Watch the child. I want to be alone with my queen."

Nicci could just see Sister Armina corral Jillian in her arms and draw her back into the darkness. A quick glance revealed Kahlan still in the same place on the rug, her whole body trembling slightly. A tear of agony ran down across her cheek. Nicci wondered if Jagang was even aware of how much pain he was giving Kahlan. He didn't know his own strength—in more ways than one. His unchecked anger tended to be universal, encompassing not just his muscle, but his mental ability as well.

In the past he'd frequently beat Nicci more severely than he'd intended or, in a blind rage, used his ability as a dream walker to inflict what could easily have been a lethal dose of pain. Later, after he realized how close he'd come to killing her, he would apologize but eventually end up by saying that it had been her own fault for making him so angry.

As Jagang dropped the hanging, closing off his bedchamber, Kahlan's tense muscles suddenly slackened. She sagged, panting in relief, looking hardly able to move after the silent ordeal.

"So," Jagang said as he turned back to Nicci, "do you love him?"

Nicci blinked. "What?"

His face went red with rage as he closed on her. "What do

you mean, what! You heard me!" He seized a fistful of her hair as he leaned to within inches of her. "Don't try to pretend you didn't understand me or I'll rip your head off!"

Nicci smiled, lifting her chin as best she could, exposing her throat to him. "Please do. It will save us both a great deal of trouble."

He glared a moment before releasing her hair. He smoothed it down, back into place, before he turned and moved off a few paces.

"Is that what you want? To die?" He turned back. "To abandon your duty to the Creator and the Order? To abandon your duty to me?"

Nicci shrugged indifferently. "Doesn't matter much what I want, now, does it?"

"What's that supposed to mean?"

"You know very well what it means. Since when has it mattered to you in the least what I want? You're going to do what you want regardless of what I might have to say about it. After all, I am just a subject of the Order, am I not? I'd say that what you want is what you've always wanted—to finally kill me."

"Kill you?" He spread his arms. "What makes you think I want to kill you?"

"Your self-indulgent actions."

"Self-indulgent?" He glared at her askance. "I am hardly self-indulgent. I am Jagang the Just."

"Are you forgetting that it was I who gave you that title? I did so not because it reflected any truth, but to counter the truth—to create an image that would serve the purposes of the Order. I am the one who created that image for you, knowing that unthinking people would believe it simply because we proclaimed it. You wouldn't know how to fill the role if your life depended on it."

The cloudy shapes in his eyes shifted in an inky darkness that reminded her of the underworld-black box of Orden she had put into play in Richard's name.

"I don't know how you can say such things, Nicci. I have always been more than just with you. I have given you things

I have given no other. Why would I do that if I wanted to kill you?"

Nicci sighed impatiently. "Just say what you want to say, or bash in my skull, or send me off to the torture tents. I'm not much interested in playing this game with you. You believe what you wish to believe regardless of reality. You know and I know that what I might have to say about anything is not really going to make any difference."

"What you say has always made a difference." He lifted a hand toward her as the heat in his voice also rose. "Look at what you just said about naming me Jagang the Just. That was your idea. I listened to it and used it because it was a good idea. It served our ends. You did well. I told you before that when this war is won you will sit at my side."

Nicci didn't answer him.

He clasped his hands behind his back as he took a few steps away.

"Do you love him?"

Nicci stole a glance to the side. Kahlan sat on the carpet, watching her. Kahlan's face was etched with concern for the sense of threat in the air. It looked as if she would like to tell Nicci to stop provoking the man. Yet, while she obviously looked worried for what Jagang was going to do, she also looked interested in the answer to the emperor's question.

Nicci's head spun as she tried to think of how to respond—not out of concern for what Jagang might think of the answer, but out of worry for what Kahlan might. There was the Chainfire spell to consider, the need for a sterile field that Nicci had to take into account. The way it now seemed she would likely be dead by then, but if Richard ever somehow managed to get a chance to use Orden to counter the Chainfire event, Kahlan had to remain a sterile field if he was to have a chance to restore her to who she once had been.

"Do you?" Jagang repeated without looking back at her.

Nicci finally concluded that, for the purpose of maintaining a sterile field, it wouldn't make any difference how she answered the question. It would not introduce any emotional precondition on Kahlan. It was Kahlan's emotional connection with Richard, not Nicci's, that mattered.

"My feelings have never burdened you before," Nicci finally said, irritably. "What difference could it make to you?"

He turned back to stare at her. "What difference? How can you ask such a thing? I made you as good as my queen. You asked me to trust you and allow you to go off to eliminate Lord Rahl. I wished you to remain here but instead I let you go. I trusted you."

"So you say. If you really trusted me then you would trust me, not interrogate me. It would seem that you have difficulty understanding the concept represented by the word."

"That was a year and a half ago. I haven't seen you since. I've had no word."

"You saw me with Tovi."

He nodded. "I saw a lot of things through Tovi's eyes—through the eyes of all four of these women."

"They thought they were clever enough to use the bond to the Lord Rahl." Nicci smiled slightly. "But you were watching them the whole time. You knew everything."

He smiled with her. "You always were smarter than Ulicia and the rest of them." He arched an eyebrow. "I trusted you when you said that you were going off to kill Richard Rahl. Instead, you end up having no trouble making the bond work for you. How is that possible, darlin? Such a bond would only work if you were devoted to him. Would you like to explain it to me?"

Nicci folded her arms. "I fail to see how it could be at all difficult to grasp. You destroy; he creates. You offer an existence devoted to death; he offers life. They aren't empty words—from either of you. He never beat me bloody, or raped me."

Jagang's face, and his shaved head, went scarlet with rage. "Rape? If I wanted to rape you I would—and by right—but it isn't rape. You wanted it. You're just too stubborn to admit it. You hide your lustful desires for me behind feigned outrage."

Nicci's arms slipped to her sides as she leaned toward him as she spoke through rage of her own. "You can invent things to justify your actions all you want, but that does not make them true."

With a murderous expression twisting his features, he turned away from the sight of her. Nicci fully expected him to suddenly round on her and hit her hard enough to break her skull. She wanted him to. A quick end was far preferable to drawn-out torture on the way to a slow death.

The myriad strident sounds from out in the night all around were muted by the thickly padded tent walls. To be out of the constant din of the camp was a luxury. Outside, the ground crawled with vermin. Inside the emperor's tent there were slaves who constantly plucked up the roaches. The scented oils in the tent also covered some of the stench that hung thick in the air.

In a certain sense the emperor's tent might seem to be a peaceful refuge, but it wasn't. It was actually one of the most dangerous places in the entire camp. The emperor held absolute power of life and death. No matter what Jagang chose to do, he would never be questioned or challenged.

"So," Jagang finally said, his back still to her, "answer my question. Do you love him?"

Nicci wiped a weary hand over her brow. "Since when have you cared what my feelings were? It's never interfered with your ability to rape me."

"Why this nonsense about rape all of a sudden!" he roared as he took a long stride back toward her. "You know that I have feelings for you! And I know that you have feelings for me!"

Nicci didn't bother to answer. He was right in that she had never presented such objections to him before. She hadn't known how to object. In that past she hadn't believed that her life was her own. How could she object to the Order using her to their ends? Further, how could she object to the leader of the Order using her to his ends?

Because of Richard she had come to grasp that her life was her own. That meant that her body, too, was her own and she didn't have to give it to anyone if she didn't want to.

"I know what you're doing, Nicci." His hands fisted again.

"You're just using him to try to make me jealous. You're using your womanly ways to get me to throw you on that bed and rip off your clothes—that's what you're really after and we both know it! You're using him as a way to lure me into heated passion for you. It's really me you want, but you hide your true passions behind protests of rape."

Nicci coolly appraised his heated expression. "You are getting bad advice from your testicles."

He drew back a fist. She stood her ground, glaring into the cloudy shapes shifting across the midnight landscape of his eyes.

The hand finally dropped to his side. "I have offered you what I have offered no other—to be as good as my queen, to be above all others. Richard Rahl can offer you nothing. Only I can offer you all that an emperor can offer. Only I can offer you a part in the power that will rule the world."

Nicci swept an arm around at the royal tent. "Ah, the glamour of embracing evil. All mine if only I will give up my thinking mind and proclaim utter inequity to be a virtue."

"I offered you the power to rule with me!"

Nicci shot him a cold glare as she let her arm drop. "No, you offered me the duty of being your whore and the chore of killing those who would not bow to your rule."

"It is the Order's rule! This war is not about bringing glory to me and you know it! This conflict is in the cause of the Creator—for the salvation of mankind. We bring the true will of the Creator to heathens. We bring the teachings of the Order to those hungering for meaning and purpose in their lives."

Nicci stood mute. He was right. He might have greatly enjoyed the trappings of power but she knew that he sincerely believed that he was merely the champion of a greater good, a warrior who was serving the Creator's true wishes by enforcing the Order's teachings in this life so that mankind could go on to glory in the next.

Nicci knew very well what it was to believe. Jagang believed.

It struck her as almost laughable, though, how the ideology she herself had once advanced now seemed so profoundly foolish. Unlike Jagang, and most people who embraced the Order's beliefs. Nicci had accepted them because she thought she had to, that it was the only way for her to achieve a moral life. She endured the yoke of servitude to others, all the while hating herself for not being happy about it. The Sisters of the Light had really been no better, offering her only a different flavor of the same selfless call to duty, so she remained in the helpless grip of the Fellowship of Order. As a numb subject of the Order, being used by Jagang was one of the many sacrifices she had believed was necessary in order to be a good and moral person.

And then all that had changed.

How she missed Richard.

"All you are going to bring to mankind is a thousand years of darkness," she said, weary of arguing the truth to a true believer whose theological construct was based on what the Order preached, not on reality. "All you are going to do is cast the world into a long, dark, savage age."

He glared at her a moment. "That's not you talking, Nicci. I know it's not. You're just saying those things because Lord Rahl spouts such hate for his fellow man. You are repeating it to make me think you love him."

"Maybe I do."

He grinned. "No." He shook his head. "No, you merely want to use him to twist me around your little finger. That's the way of women—trying to maneuver and exploit men."

Rather than letting him take her down the path of what her true feelings for Richard might be, Nicci changed the subject. "Your plans of rule, your plans for the Order to bring its ideas to all the world, are not going to work. You need all three boxes of Orden. I was there when Sister Tovi died. She had the third box but it was stolen from her."

"Ah yes, the brave Seeker, wielding the sword of truth"—he parodied a sword thrust—"stepping in to liberate the box of Orden from a wicked Sister of the Dark." He gave her a sour look. "I was there, watching through her eyes, after all."

He had been watching Nicci through Tovi's eyes as well.

"The fact remains that the Sisters had all three boxes. You may now have those Sisters, but you only have two boxes."

A sly smile replaced his annoyance. "Oh, I don't think that's going to be as much of a problem as you think. Nor will it matter that you placed that box in play. I have ways around such petty difficulties."

Nicci was somewhat alarmed to learn that he knew that she had put the box in play, but she tried not to let on.

"What ways?"

The smile only widened. "What kind of emperor would I be if I didn't have plans for every eventuality? Don't you worry, darlin, I have everything well in hand. All that matters is that in the end I will see to it that all three boxes are reunited. When they are once again together then I will at last use the power of Orden to end all resistance to the Order's rule."

"If you survive that long."

His annoyance returned as he studied her blank expression. "What's that supposed to mean?"

She gestured into the distance. "Richard Rahl has loosed the wolves on your beloved flock."

"Meaning?"

She arched an eyebrow. "The army you chased up here is gone. You weren't able to destroy it, were you? Guess where that army is, now."

"Scattered in fear for their lives."

Nicci smiled at his scowl. "Not exactly. The D'Haran army has been charged with taking the war to those in the Old World who support that war, to those who gave birth to aggression with their teachings and set it upon the innocent. Those people are going to have to face the consequences of sending surrogate murderers north. They, no less than you, have the blood of innocent people on their hands. They think that distance sanitizes them, but being far removed from the evil they directly bring about will not absolve them of their crimes. They will pay the price."

"I am aware of Lord Rahl's latest sins." The muscles in Jagang's jaw flexed as he gritted his teeth. "Richard Rahl is a coward who goes after innocent women and children because he cannot bear to face real men."

"That would be the worst kind of willful ignorance if you actually believed it, but you don't. You want others to believe it, so you pluck carefully selected half-truths out of the context of reality in order to cloak your cause in pseudomorality. You seek to craft an excuse for the inexcusable. In a manner of speaking you hide behind women's skirts as you shoot arrows so that when arrows come back at you, you can feign outrage at an atrocity.

"Your true purpose, though, is to strip the absolute right of self-defense from those you wish to destroy.

"Richard is a man who understands the reality of the threat represented by the beliefs of the Order. He is not sidetracked by rigged issues meant to obscure the truth. He understands that to survive he must be strong enough to eliminate the threat, no matter what form it takes—even if it is to destroy the fields that grow the food that gives your men the strength to slit the throats of people peacefully living their own lives. Anyone defending those fields is a party to murder.

"Richard knows the simple truth that without victory there is no survival for his people."

"Those people bring suffering on themselves by resisting the righteous teachings of the Order," Jagang said.

The muscles in his arms tightened along with his fists as he paced, looking on the verge of violence. He didn't like it when anyone disputed his assertions, so he rounded on Nicci and repeated them more forcefully, as if his raised voice, and the threat in it, would settle the matter.

"Richard Rahl proves his depravity, and the immorality of those he leads, by sending his men off to kill the innocent women and children of the Old World instead of standing and fighting our soldiers. His atrocities against women and children prove what a cowardly criminal he really is. We have an obligation to rid the world of such sinful people."

Nicci folded her arms as she fixed him in the kind of glare once reserved for those who would not bow to the will of the Order. It was a look that had frequently preceded actions that had earned her the title Death's Mistress. It was a look that gave even the emperor pause.

"All the people of the New World are innocent," she said. "They did not bring war to the Order, the Order brought war to them. It's true that people in the Old World—including children—will be hurt or killed in the fighting. What choice is there for these people? Continue to be slaughtered and enslaved out of fear of harming someone innocent? They are all innocent. Their children are all innocent. They are being harmed, now.

"You know from being in the mind of Sister Ulicia the tactic she thought would deliver her the safety of the bond to Richard and protect her mind from you. Sister Ulicia knew that life is Richard's highest value, so she hatched the scheme that when she used the power of Orden to free the Keeper of the underworld from his prison in the world of the dead, she would grant Richard Rahl eternal life. That Richard wouldn't believe such a bargain was possible, much less accept it, was irrelevant in Ulicia's mind. She thought that until the offer was made and refused, her intentions to grant him eternal life gave her immunity from your ability as a dream walker.

"But you were already secretly embedded in Ulicia's mind. That's how you learned what matters most to Richard, his greatest value: life.

"That's a foreign concept to you. Life is not a value to the Order. They teach that our lives are a meaningless transitory state on our way to an eternal afterlife. They believe that this life is a mere vessel, a shell, to hold our soul until it can reach a higher plane of existence. The Order teaches that glory in the afterlife is our greatest value, and that that glory is earned through the sacrifice of this life to their cause. The Order, therefore, values death.

"You see those who value life as weak, inferior. You can't understand what life, all life, means to someone like Richard, but you do know how to use what you learned.

"You use that value to try to intimidate Richard from facing the larger challenge of defending all of life. By advancing the propaganda that he is a killer of women and children you believe that you can cow his courage, shame him out of attacking for fear that civilians might be killed, and thus limit him to defending himself.

"As an experienced warrior you are well aware that wars are not won defensively. Without the total commitment of the force necessary to crush the vicious beliefs of an aggressor, you can never hope to win a war because those beliefs are what bring about war in the first place.

"Richard also knows that wars are not won defensively, that to end war as quickly as possible and with the smallest possible loss of life, the only way is to stop the aggressor's ability to harm you and crush their devotion to beliefs that caused them to attack in the first place.

"Your aim, with such sensationalized charges against a man who so values life, is to discredit, dishonor, and disgrace him into fearing to act as he must if he is to win.

"You create a diversion with half-truths in order to turn all eyes away from the real implications of your beliefs and to win converts to the Order's twisted ideology. You accuse others of the things you are actually guilty of, knowing that it will stir emotions.

"But in the end, such dramatic charges are merely a cover—an attempt to latch onto an excuse to legitimize your routine killing of unimaginable numbers of people.

"You and I both know the truth of the endless corpses of women and children the Order leaves in its wake, but those are ignored in your contrived moral outrage. Your brutality, savagery, and cruelty against those who have done nothing to the people in the Old World frame the true nature of your beliefs. The enormity of your depravity is only compounded by blaming the victim with the crimes you bring to his people, the same as you blame me for my own rape.

"I was there the day Richard gave those troops their orders. I know the truth.

"The truth is that the minds of most people of the Old World have been irrevocably blackened by their fanatical devotion to ideas that result only in suffering and death. Those people are beyond redemption by reason. Richard knows that the only way to deal with evil, to break a people's bond to it, is to make holding on to such beliefs unendurable.

"The Order itself has made this a war to the end. Richard knows that his people cannot survive by trying to coexist with such evil, or by excusing those who nurture it.

"The Order seeks to exterminate liberty. The knife that the Order is trying to thrust into his heart is driven by devotion to the corrupt beliefs of the Order. Richard understands that he must eliminate the source of those beliefs or freethinking people everywhere will all die, murdered by men encouraged and fed by the people of the Old World.

"War is a terrible business. The faster it is ended the less suffering and death there will be. That is Richard's goal. The weak-minded would shrink from what must be done for fear of being criticized by the wicked. Richard is not going to be deterred by the words of hypocrites and haters.

"The truth is that his orders were that, whenever possible, his soldiers should avoid harming people, but ending the war is their overriding objective. To do that, they must destroy the Order's ability to wage war. As soldiers, that is the responsibility Richard Rahl charged them with—they are defending their people's right to exist. He told them that anything else is just whistling on the way to their graves.

"This war is merely an extension of the great war that raged so long ago, but never really ended. The Old World again has fallen prey to the evil ideas of the Order. How many lives have been wasted because of those beliefs? How many yet will be?

"The last time, those defending against such teachings did not have the courage to crush them into cold, lifeless ashes and as a result this ancient war has once again rekindled at the hands of the Fellowship of Order. Just as back then, it is sparked by those same mindless ideas that everyone must believe the same as they do or die.

"Richard understands that this time it must be ended once and for all, that the world of life must be liberated from the poison of the Order. He has the courage to do just that. He will not be dissuaded by your taunts. He doesn't care what other people think of him. He only cares that they can't again harm him and those he cares about.

"To make sure of that, those who preach the Order's hate will be hunted down and killed.

"The D'Haran army may not be anywhere near as large as the Imperial Order, but they will still strangle you. They will burn crops and orchards, destroy mills and stables, break dams and canals. Anyone who gets in the way of their halting the Old World's ability to wage war will be eliminated.

"Most importantly, those soldiers will cut the supply lines headed north. Ending your ability to kill these people is Richard's only objective. Unlike you, he does not need to teach anyone a lesson in dominance—but he will end yours.

"There will be no final battle to decide it all, as was your plan. Richard does not care how your men are stopped, only that they are—once and for all.

"Without supplies, your army will wither and die out here on this barren plain. That is victory enough."

Jagang smiled in a way that in turn gave Nicci pause. "Darlin, the Old World is a big place. They waste their efforts attacking crops. They can't be everywhere."

"They don't have to be."

He shrugged. "They may be able to attack supply trains from here and there, but that is simply the sacrifice our people make for the advancement of our cause. Casualties, no matter how many, are the cost of achieving moral ends.

"Because I understand the price that must be paid to take us to our final victory, I had already ordered a dramatic increase in the numbers of supplies being sent north to our valiant troops. We can send more men and supplies than Richard Rahl can hope to stop.

"The people of the Old World will sacrifice what they must in order to see to it that we have what we need to persevere. The price has been raised, but our people will gladly pay it. I expect that you're right, that many of those supply trains will be destroyed, but the D'Haran forces do not have enough men to stop them all."

Nicci's insides tightened. "A bold boast."

"If you don't believe me you can judge for yourself if I'm telling the truth. Another new train will arrive soon, a supply train so long that you would have to stand in one place for two days just to watch it all pass before your eyes. Don't you worry, our brave men will have enough supplies to press this war to its conclusion."

Nicci shook her head. "You're not seeing the whole of it. If you can't catch and defeat the D'Haran forces, you can't win this war. There are people in the Old World, just like anywhere else, who long to live their own lives as they wish. The Order may blind a great many with its teachings, but there are individuals everywhere who use their minds and understand the truth of life. There are such people all over the Old World who will turn against the Order.

"You have only to look at Altur'Rang. I was there when it fell. It had been a place of widespread suffering under the rule of the Imperial Order. Now that it has thrown off those shackles, the people there prosper. Other people will see such a change and be encouraged to have their own life. They, too, will want to prosper."

Jagang looked outraged at such talk. "Prosper? They are merely heathens dancing on the ground that will be their graves. They will be crushed. That is what people will see—that the Order will rightly punish those who turn away from their duty to their fellow man. The punishment they suffer for their selfishness will be remembered for the next thousand years."

"And the D'Haran forces? The wolves set loose on your flock? They will not be so easily eliminated. They will continue to break the hold of the Order. They will continue to hound those who have sent war north, eviscerating the very core of the Fellowship of Order."

Jagang grinned. "Oh, darlin, you are so wrong about that. You forget the boxes of Orden."

"You have only two."

"At the moment, maybe, but I will have all three. When I do, then I will unleash the power of Orden to do our bidding. With the power of Orden under my control, all opposition will be swept away in the firestorm of our righteous cause.

I will use the power of Orden to burn the flesh from every one of those D'Haran troops, and leave each one to die a slow, agonizing death. Hunted by the power of Orden, there will be nowhere for them to hide. Their screams will be the sound of sweet justice to our people now suffering under their brutality. I will also make each one of those heathen traitors from Altur'Rang suffer for betraying our teachings.

"The power of Orden will serve the cause of the Fellowship of Order and in the end strike the D'Harans down—no matter where they are.

"I will grind Richard Rahl's bones to dust. He is a dead man, he just doesn't know it, yet."

Jagang's grim grin gave Nicci goose bumps. "But first," he said with obvious delight, "I want him to live long enough to see it all, live long enough to truly suffer. You know how much I like those who have opposed me to live so that they may endure the pain of proper suffering."

His voice lowered to a growl. "To that end, I have something very, very dear to Richard Rahl. When I unleash the power of Orden I will at long last be able to bring him pain he can't begin to imagine. It will bring him the kind of emotional anguish that will crush his spirit, crush his very soul, before I crush his worldly body."

Nicci knew that Jagang was talking about Kahlan, but she dared not let him know what she knew about it. It took all her will power not to glance at her, not to give away what she knew.

"We will prevail," he said. "I offer you the opportunity to return to my side—to the Order's side. In the end, you have no choice in the matter but to accept the Creator's will. It is time for you to accept your moral responsibility to your fellow man."

She had known from the moment she had entered the camp that she had no chance to escape the inevitable. She would never again see Richard, or freedom.

Jagang gestured dismissively. "You can accomplish nothing with your childish affection for Richard Rahl."

Nicci knew what was going to happen if she did not submit

to his authority and accept his offer. If she did not accept, he was going to make it all that much more agonizing for her.

But her life was hers, now, and she would not throw it away willingly.

"If you are going to grind Richard Rahl to dust," she said in her most condescending tone, "if he is nothing more than a petty problem to you, then why are you so concerned about him?" She arched an eyebrow. "More to the point, why are you so jealous of him?"

His face flushing red with rage, Jagang seized her by the throat. With a roar he heaved her onto the bed. She drew a sharp breath just before he landed on her. He straddled her middle, then leaned to the side and retrieved something. With his weight atop her she could hardly breathe.

One meaty hand grabbed her face to hold her head still even though she made no effort to resist. With the thumb and knuckle of the other hand he pulled her lower lip out. When he released her face she saw that he was holding a sharpened awl.

He stabbed it through her lower lip, twisting it around, making a hole. Tears of pain stung at her eyes. She dared not move lest he rip her lip off.

After he pulled the awl out he pushed a split gold ring through her freshly pierced lip.

Bending forward, he used his teeth to close the ring.

His stubble scraped against her cheek as he pressed close and whispered in her ear. "You are mine. Until the day I decide you are to die, your life belongs to me. You might as well forget any thoughts of Richard Rahl. When I've finished with you the Keeper will have you for betraying me."

When he straightened, he slapped her. The powerful wallop felt like it rattled her teeth. "Your whoring with Richard Rahl is ended. You will soon enough be begging to admit that you were only trying to make me jealous and that my bed is where you really wanted to be all along. Isn't that right?"

Nicci stared up at him without showing any emotion or saying anything.

He hit her across the face with a closed fist. "Admit it!"

With all her strength, Nicci steadied her voice. "You can't make someone care about you by hitting them."

"You make me hit you! It's your own fault! You say things that you know will make me angry. I wouldn't hit you if you wouldn't keep pushing me into it. You bring it on yourself."

As if to prove his point, he delivered two mighty blows across her face. She did her best to ignore the pain. She knew that this was only the beginning.

Nicci stared up at him. She said nothing. She had been beneath him enough times to know very well what was coming.

She was already going off to that faraway place in her mind. She no longer focused on the man atop her, hitting her. Her gaze drifted to the ceiling of the tent.

As his fists pounded her, she hardly felt it. It was only her body, somewhere distant, that was hurting.

She had to breathe through a burble of blood.

She knew that he was pulling off her dress, knew that his big hands were groping her, but she ignored that, too.

Instead—as Jagang beat her, pawed her, climbed on top of her, forced her legs open—she thought about Richard, about how he always treated her with respect.

As the nightmare started, she dreamed of other things.

CHAPTER 24

With the back of her wrist, Rachel wiped sweat from her forehead. She knew that as soon as she stopped working she would get cold, but at the moment she was sweating. It was hard to stop, because she was in a hurry. She knew that she couldn't hurry when she was stopped for the night, but she still felt driven to rush, so she raced to as she built her shelter.

She didn't like to think about what would happen to her if she didn't hurry.

The pine boughs she had cut and leaned up against the low rock wall would help block the cold wind. She'd braced them with a support made of dead cedar saplings she had found nearby. Cutting fresh pine branches with a knife wasn't easy. Chase had taught her how to build a shelter. He probably wouldn't think much of this one, but without at least a hatchet it was the best she could do. At least, it was the best she felt like doing. All she really felt like doing was hurrying.

She'd picketed the horse close, after letting it drink its fill from a nearby brook. She had been careful to give it enough line to be able to crop at the bunches of grass growing along the bank.

Using the flint from the saddlebags, she'd built a fire just inside the protection of the wind block she'd made. It was terrifying being out alone in the countryside at night. There could be bears, or mountain lions, or wolves. A fire helped her to feel safe while she got some sleep waiting for first light. She needed it to be light so that she could start out again. She needed to get going. She needed to hurry.

When she started getting cold, Rachel put another piece of the driftwood she'd collected on the fire and then sat on the small blanket she'd laid over pine boughs. Chase had taught her that a fresh cushion of pine or spruce branches would keep her up off the ground and help keep her warm. She put her back to the rock wall so that nothing could sneak up behind her. With it getting darker, she was feeling afraid.

Rather than think about being afraid, she pulled the saddlebags closer and retrieved a piece of dried meat. She tore off a small bite with her teeth and sucked on it for a time, letting the taste start to satisfy her gnawing hunger. She didn't have a lot of food left, so she was trying to conserve what she had. It wasn't long, though, until she was chewing and swallowing.

She broke off a piece of hard biscuit and, holding it in her palm, dribbled a little water from the waterskin onto it to try to soften it up a bit before she tried to chew it. The biscuits were as hard as rocks. The dried meat was easier to chew than the biscuits, but she had more biscuits.

She'd searched for berries as she rode, but it was too late in the year for there to be any left. One day she had spotted a wild apple tree. Even though they were shriveled they had looked like they might make a meal, but she knew better than to eat red fruit. Red fruit was poisonous. As hungry as she was for something other than dried meat and dried biscuits, she didn't want to get poisoned.

Rachel sat quietly for a time, chewing on the tough meat as she stared into the fire. She kept listening for things that might be out in the darkness beyond the fire. She didn't want to be surprised by a hungry animal that might think she'd make a good meal.

When she looked up, there was a woman standing before her, on the opposite side of the fire.

Rachel gasped. She tried to back up, but the rock wall was right there behind her. She thought that she might be able to slip away to the side if she had to. She snatched up her knife.

"Please, don't be afraid."

Rachel thought that it was just about the most pleasing,

gentle, kind voice she had ever heard. Still, she knew better than to be taken in by kind-sounding words.

She stared up at the woman, trying to decide what to do, as the woman stared down at her. She didn't look threatening. She didn't do anything that seemed unfriendly. She had, though, shown up out in the middle of nowhere.

There was something about her that looked faintly familiar. Her pleasant voice still sang in Rachel's mind. The woman was pretty enough, with plain, cropped blond hair. Her arms hung slack, hands joined before her, fingers loosely knitted together. She wore simple flaxen robes that reached all the way to the ground. The shawl around her shoulders looked to be dyed from henna.

Her modest dress made her look like she must be a commoner, rather than a woman of noble rank. From having lived at the palace in Tamarang Rachel knew a lot about noble women. Noble women were usually trouble for someone like Rachel.

"Please, may I sit and share your fire?" the woman asked in that voice that had Rachel hanging on every word.

"No."

"No?"

"No. I don't know you. Keep back."

The woman smiled a little. "Are you sure you don't know me, Rachel?"

Rachel swallowed. Goose bumps tingled up her arms.

"How do you know my name?"

The smile widened a little—not in a cunning way, but in a gentle, kindhearted manner. The woman's eyes, too, had a softness about them that made it seem like they could never intend harm. Still, that did not do much to diminish Rachel's caution. She'd been fooled by nice looking ladies in the past.

"Would you like something to eat other than that dry traveling food?"

"No. I'm fine," Rachel said. "I mean, I appreciate your offer, it's very kind of you, but I'm fine, thank you."

The woman bent and picked up something lying on the ground behind her. When she stood again, Rachel saw that it was a string of small trout.

She held them up. "Would it be all right if I just used your fire to cook these for myself, then?"

Rachel was having trouble trying to think. She had to hurry. That was all she seemed able to focus on—that she had to hurry. But she couldn't hurry at camp. She couldn't leave until it was light.

"I suppose it would be all right if you cooked your fish on the fire."

The woman smiled again. It was a smile that for some reason lifted Rachel's heart.

"Thank you. I'll not be any trouble to you."

Quick as a wink, she turned and disappeared into the night. Rachel had no idea where she went, or why. The string of fish still lay nearby. Rachel sat listening into the darkness as the fire hissed and popped. She clutched her knife tightly in her fist as she strained to hear off into the darkness for any sign that the woman might have other people with her.

When she returned, the woman had a pile of big moose maple leaves, a number of them covered with a thick layer of mud. The woman said nothing as she squatted down and went about preparing the fish. She rolled each fish in a clean moose maple leaf, then lined them all up in the mud, layered mud on top, and finally wrapped it all in leaves. When she was finished making the rolled up mud oven she carefully placed it on the fire.

The whole time, Rachel watched her. It was hard not to. In fact, Rachel couldn't take her eyes off the woman. There was something about her that just kind of made Rachel ache with longing to be closer to her. Still, her sense of caution wouldn't allow it.

Besides, she was in a hurry.

The woman backed away a few paces, apparently so as not to frighten Rachel, and sat on the ground, folding her legs under her, to wait for her fish to cook. Flames danced in the cold night air, and sparks swirled up whenever the wood popped. From time to time the woman warmed her hands at the fire.

Rachel was having a hard time not thinking about the fish.

It smelled delicious. She could imagine how good it would taste. But she had said that she didn't want any.

Rachel realized, then, that she had asked a question before and never gotten an answer.

"How do you know my name?"

The woman shrugged one shoulder. "The good spirits must have whispered it in my ear."

Rachel thought that was about the silliest thing she had ever heard. She couldn't help giggling, though.

"In truth," the woman said, looking more serious, "I remember you."

The goose bumps returned. "From the castle in Tamarang?"

The woman rolled a finger. "No. From before then."

Rachel frowned. "From the orphanage?"

The woman made a little sound to confirm it. She suddenly looked sad.

Together they watched the flames waver and dance, and throw light against the rock wall and lean-to of pine boughs. In the distance coyotes howled in long, lonely wails. Whenever the coyotes started in to howling Rachel was glad for the fire. She could easily be prey for wolves and such if not for the fire.

The bugs nearby chirped and buzzed while moths whirled in circles through the light. Swirling sparks ascended into the night sky, looking as if they were eager to join the stars. It was all making Rachel sleepy.

"I bet the fish are ready," the woman said in a bright voice.

She scooted forward and used a stick to roll the little mud oven out of the fire. Spreading the leaves open on the ground, she finally exposed the fish inside. They were steaming hot, and flaky.

She broke off a piece and tasted it, then moaned with delight at how good it tasted.

Then she put the rest of the little trout on a moose maple leaf and offered it to Rachel. Rachel sat staring at the hand. She had said that she didn't want any of the woman's fish.

"Thank you, but I have my own things to eat. You should have your fish."

"Nonsense, there's more than enough. Please, won't you eat some with me? Just a little? After all, I used the fire you worked to build, so it's the least I can do."

Rachel stared at the delicious looking fish on the leaf in the palm of the woman's hand.

"Well, if you don't mind, then, I'll have one."

The woman smiled and the world suddenly seemed a better place. Rachel thought that it must be a smile like a mother would have—filled with simple delight at the wonder of life.

She tried not to devour the fish. That it was steaming hot helped to slow her down. That, and the sharp little bones. It felt so good to eat hot food that she almost cried with joy. When she finished the fish, the woman handed her another. Rachel took it without hesitation. She so needed to eat. She told herself that she needed to be strong so that she could hurry. The tender fish warmed the pang of hunger lodged deep in the pit of her stomach, making the ache melt away. Rachel ate four more before she was full.

"Don't push your horse so hard tomorrow," the woman said. "If you do, it will die."

Rachel blinked. "How do you know that?"

"I introduced myself to your animal when I came across your camp. Your horse is in sorry shape."

Rachel felt bad for the horse, but she had to hurry. She couldn't slow for anything. She had to hurry.

"If I go any slower, they'll get me."

The woman cocked her head. "Who will get you?"

"The ghostie gobblies."

"Ah, I see."

"The ghostie gobblies are after me. Whenever I slow they start to get closer." Tears stung Rachel's eyes. "I don't want the ghostie gobblies to get me."

The woman was there, then, right next to her, circling an arm around her, sheltering her. It felt so good that Rachel started to cry in the comfort of that protection. She had to hurry. She was so afraid.

"If you kill the horse," the woman said in a soft, gentle

voice, "then the ghostie gobblies will get you, now, won't they? Take it just a little slower. You have time."

Rachel snuggled in the nook of the woman's arm. "Are you sure?"

"I'm sure. You need to let the horse get its strength back. It won't do you any good to kill the animal. Trust me, you don't want to be out in the deserted countryside without a horse."

"Because then the ghostie gobblies will get me?"

The woman nodded. "Because then the ghostie gobblies will get you."

When a shiver ran up Rachel's back, the woman squeezed her tight until it went away. Rachel realized that she had the hem of her dress in her mouth, just like she used to do when she was little.

"Hold out your hand," the woman said in that soothing voice she had. "I have something for you."

"What is it?"

"Hold out your hand."

When Rachel held out her hand the woman laid something small in it. Rachel held it up closer, trying to see it better. It was short, and straight.

"Put it in your pocket."

Rachel looked up at the gentle face watching her. "Why?"

"For when you need it."

"Need it? What will I need it for?"

"You will know when the time comes. You will know when you need it. When you do, remember that it's there, in your pocket."

"But what is it?"

The woman smiled that wonderful smile. "It's what you need, Rachel."

As baffled as she was, Rachel couldn't think of how to solve the riddle. She slipped the small thing into her pocket.

"Is it magic?" Rachel asked.

"No," the woman said. "It's not magic. But it's what you will need."

"Will it save me?"

"I have to go now," the woman said.

Rachel felt a lump raising in her throat. "Couldn't you sit by the fire a little while?"

The woman gazed at her with knowing, gentle eyes. "I suppose I could."

Rachel felt goose bumps tingling up her arms again.

She knew who the woman was.

"You're my mother, aren't you?"

The woman smoothed a hand down Rachel's hair. She had a sad smile. A tear rolled down her cheek.

Rachel knew that her mother was dead, or, at least she had been told that she was.

Maybe this was her mother's good spirit.

Rachel opened her mouth to speak again, but her mother gently shushed her, then tipped Rachel's head against her. "You need rest. I'll watch over you. Sleep. You're safe with me."

Rachel was so tired. She listened to the wonderful sound of her mother's heart beating. She stretched her arms around her mother's ribs, and nuzzled against her.

Rachel had a thousand questions, but she didn't think that she would be able to get a single word past the lump in her throat. Besides, she didn't really want to talk. She just wanted to be held in the shelter of her mother's arms.

As much as she loved Chase, this was something that felt so special that she knew it was unfair to compare it to anything else. She loved Chase fiercely. This was wonderful in its own way. It was like two halves that made a whole.

Rachel only realized that she'd been asleep because when she opened her eyes it was just first light. Dark purple clouds looked as if they were trying to hide the approaching light in the eastern sky.

She sat up abruptly.

All that was left of the fire was cold ashes.

She was alone.

Before she could think of anything else, before she had time to be sad, she knew that she had to hurry.

With frantic effort she quickly gathered up her few things—the blanket, the flint and steel, the waterskin—stuffing them into the saddlebags. She saw the horse not far away, watching her.

She had to make sure not to run the horse too hard. If she ran the horse and it died, then Rachel would be on foot.

And then the ghostie gobblies would get her.

CHAPTER 25

Kahlan tenderly closed both of her hands around Nicci's trembling, loose fist. She hoped that through that connection, that simple act, the woman covered in blood, lying in Jagang's bed, could at least take a small measure of solace. As much as Kahlan ached with empathy, she could offer little help.

It had been a frightening, dreadful night. Jagang often brought women captives to his bed. He frequently hurt them, either simply by not taking into account his own strength, or because he intended them harm when they failed to cooperate.

This was different. With Nicci, he was venting hot jealousy.

He had never hurt any of those other women the way he hurt Nicci. In his own mind, Kahlan knew, he was getting even, settling a score, making Nicci pay the price of being unfaithful to him.

But, in some ways, Jagang was also showing Kahlan what kind of treatment she could look forward to once her memory was finally restored. Kahlan tried to shut the things she'd seen and heard from her mind lest she be sick. She focused instead on the present, and the future.

She let go with one hand and turned to retrieve a waterskin lying on the floor nearby. Nicci lightly caught the remaining hand, apparently fearful of losing the human compassion in that connection.

"Here," Kahlan said in little more than a whisper as she lifted the waterskin to Nicci's lips. Splatters of dried blood masked her face and hair.

Other than loosely holding on to Kahlan's hand, Nicci didn't respond.

"Drink," Kahlan urged. "It's water."

Nicci didn't make any effort to drink, so Kahlan let a little of the water trickle across the woman's cracked lips and into her mouth. She swallowed, then turned her head away from the waterskin with a cry of pain.

"Shh," Kahlan urged. "I know it hurts, but try to stay quiet. You need to try to take a drink. You need water. When you're hurt your body needs water so you can get better."

As much as he had choked her while he railed in fury, it was a miracle that Jagang hadn't crushed Nicci's windpipe. His powerful hands had left behind lurid bruises, though, and not just on her neck.

Nicci's blue eyes slowly opened, focusing on Kahlan's face. Kahlan was down low, sitting on the floor beside the bed. She was leaning in close to Nicci, trying to keep her voice low so that it wouldn't carry to those outside the bedchamber. She didn't want anyone to hear her talking to Nicci. Nicci hadn't wanted Jagang to know that she could see Kahlan. Kahlan thought it wise to never let an enemy know anything more than was absolutely necessary. Apparently, Nicci thought much the same thing.

As awkward as it was leaning over the edge of the bed, Kahlan didn't dare get up off the carpet. She knew the consequences of getting up when Jagang had told her to stay on the floor.

A jagged gash at Nicci's scalp line on the right side of her forehead was still bleeding. A glancing blow from Jagang's ringed fist had ripped up a flap of scalp. Kahlan snatched up a small cloth, folded it, and gently pressed it against the wound on Nicci's forehead, fitting the loose chunk of flesh in place as she applied pressure to stop the bleeding. In mere moments the cloth soaked through with blood. As much as she ached to help, there was little more she could think to do other than try to stop some of the bleeding and offer a drink of water.

The wound from the gold ring pierced through Nicci's lower lip still oozed, leaving a trail of blood down her jaw and the side of her neck, but it wasn't serious, like the wound on her forehead, so Kahlan didn't try to do anything for it.

She carefully pulled a lock of blond hair back off Nicci's face. "I'm so sorry for what he did to you."

Nicci nodded slightly, her jaw trembling slightly as she held back tears.

"I wanted so much to stop him," Kahlan said.

With the back of a finger Nicci caught the tear running down Kahlan's cheek.

"There was nothing you could do," the woman managed. "Nothing."

Her voice was weak but, despite that, it still carried the same silken grace as before. It was a voice that matched the rest of her perfectly. Kahlan would never have guessed that such a lovely voice could also carry such righteous contempt as she'd shown Jagang.

"Nothing any of us can do," Nicci whispered as her eyelids slid closed. "Except maybe Richard."

Kahlan studied the woman's blue eyes a moment. "You really think that Richard Rahl can do something?"

Nicci smiled to herself. "Sorry. I didn't realize that I'd said the last part aloud. Where's Jagang?"

Kahlan checked and saw that the wound under the cloth she had pressed to Nicci's head had at last stopped the bleeding.

"You didn't hear him when he left?" she asked as she set the blood-soaked cloth aside.

Nicci rocked her head side to side to say that she hadn't. Kahlan lifted the waterskin in question. Nicci nodded. She winced as she swallowed, but she drank.

"Well," Kahlan said when Nicci finished drinking, "someone called out for him. He went to the doorway and a man spoke to him in a low voice. I couldn't hear all of it, but it sounded like he said that they'd found something. Jagang came back and put on his clothes. As fast as he got dressed, he was obviously in a hurry to have a look at the discovery. He told me to stay where I was.

"Then he put one knee on the bed, leaned over you, and whispered to you that he was sorry."

Nicci huffed a laugh, but it was cut short when she winced in pain. "He isn't capable of feeling sorry for anyone but himself."

"You'll get no argument from me," Kahlan said. "Anyway, he promised to bring back a Sister to heal you. He ran a hand down your face and again said that he was sorry. Then he paused, looking down at you with a worried look. He leaned a little closer to you and said, 'Please don't die, Nicci.' After that he rushed away, telling me again to stay on the floor.

"I don't know how long he will be gone, but I suspect that a Sister, at least, will be in at any moment."

Nicci nodded, not seeming to really care if she was healed or not. Kahlan could understand, in a way, how Nicci would rather slip into the dark forever of death than face what would be her life from now on.

"I'm terribly sorry that you've been caught up by him, but you don't know how good it is to have another person be able to see me—someone who isn't with them."

"I can only imagine," Nicci said.

"Jillian said that she's seen you before. With Richard Rahl. She told me a little about you. You're as beautiful as she said you were."

"My mother used to tell me that being beautiful was only useful to whores. Perhaps she was right."

"Perhaps she was jealous of you. Or just a fool."

Nicci smiled so broadly that it looked like she might laugh. "It was the latter. She hated life."

Kahlan's gaze drifted away from Nicci as she picked at a loose thread on the bedcover.

"So you know Richard Rahl pretty well, then?"

"Pretty well," Nicci said.

"Are you in love with him?"

Nicci looked over, gazing into Kahlan's eyes for a long moment. "It's more complicated than that. I have responsibilities."

Kahlan smiled a little. "I see." She was glad that Nicci hadn't tried to lie by denying it.

"You have a beautiful voice, Kahlan Amnell," Nicci whispered as she stared at Kahlan. "You really do."

"Thank you, but it doesn't seem beautiful to me. Sometimes I think I sound like a frog."

Nicci smiled. "Hardly."

Kahlan frowned. "You know me, then?"

"Not really."

"But you know my name. Do you know anything about me? About my past? Who I really am?"

Nicci's blue eyes watched her in a most curious fashion. "Just what I've heard."

"And what have you heard?"

"That you are the Mother Confessor."

Kahlan hooked some hair behind her ear. "I heard that myself."

She checked the doorway again and, seeing the hanging still in place and hearing no voices close, turned back to Nicci. "I'm afraid that I don't know what it means. I don't know very much at all about myself. As I'm sure you can probably imagine, it's pretty frustrating. Sometimes, I get so dispirited by not being able to remember anything . . ."

Kahlan's voice trailed off as Nicci's eyes closed against a pang of agony. She was having trouble breathing.

Kahlan laid a hand on the woman's shoulder. "Hold on, Nicci. Please hold on. A Sister will be in to heal you any moment. I've been hurt by them before—hurt terribly—and they healed me, so I know they can do it. You'll be all right after they get in here."

Nicci nodded slightly, but she didn't open her eyes. Kahlan wished that one of the Sisters would hurry. In the absence of anything she could do, Kahlan gave Nicci another drink, then wet the piece of cloth again and gently mopped her brow.

Kahlan was torn between staying where she'd been told to stay and rushing to the opening out of the bedchamber to demand that someone go get a Sister. She knew, though, that the collar she wore around her neck would drop her before she would be able to take two steps. It was somewhat surprising that there wasn't a Sister already outside. There was usually at least one of them at hand.

"I've never seen anyone stand up to Jagang the way you did," Kahlan said.

"It wouldn't really have mattered if I did or not." Nicci

paused to get her breath. "He was going to do what he wanted to do. But I wasn't about to agree to it."

Kahlan smiled at Nicci's spirit of defiance.

"Jagang was already angry at you long before you arrived. Sister Ulicia told him how you're in love with Richard. She was going on and on about it."

Nicci's eyes were open, but she said nothing as she stared up at the ceiling.

"That's why Jagang was questioning you—because of what Sister Ulicia told him. He was jealous."

"He has no reason to be jealous. He should be more concerned that someday I'm going to kill him."

Kahlan smiled at that. Then, she wondered if Nicci meant that Jagang had no reason to be jealous because there was nothing between her and Richard, or because there was but the emperor had no right to have a claim on her heart.

"Do you think you will ever get a chance to kill him?"

In frustration, Nicci lifted a hand just a little bit, then let it drop back down to her side. "Probably not. I think I'm the one who is going to be killed."

"Maybe we can think of something before that happens," Kahlan said. "How did he manage to capture you, anyway?"

"I was in the palace."

"They found a way in?"

"Yes. Through forgotten catacombs that run underneath the Azrith Plain and under the plateau. The underground chambers and tunnels appear to have been abandoned millennia ago.

"I think it was a reconnaissance expedition that caught me. They haven't begun to invade the palace, yet, but as soon as they have what they need in place I'm sure they will."

Kahlan realized that that was what had been discovered buried in the pit. With a way in, it was only a matter of time until they stormed the palace and slaughtered everyone up there. She knew that when that happened all hope would be lost. Jagang would have defeated the last holdout against the Imperial Order. He would rule the world.

At least, he would if he could get his hands on the third box of Orden. Kahlan didn't doubt his word, though, that he would soon accomplish that as well. It seemed that time was not just running out for Richard Rahl, but for any hope of freedom surviving.

Nicci, her chin trembling, looked over at Kahlan. "Please, cover me?"

"Sorry," Kahlan said. "I should have thought of that."

Actually, she had, but she had thought that maybe it might be worse if she covered Nicci and the sheet stuck to the wounds. She could certainly understand, though, why Nicci would want to be covered.

Kahlan stretched, caught the edge of the gold bedcover and pulled it up. Ever mindful of the collar, she had to be careful not to let herself get up from the floor.

"Thanks," Nicci said as she at last was able to pull the silk cover the rest of the way over herself.

"Don't be ashamed," Kahlan said.

Nicci frowned a little. "What do you mean?"

"You should never be ashamed to be a victim. It wasn't through any fault of yours. The only thing you should feel is anger at such a violation. You didn't do anything to encourage it. It was rape, just as you said it was."

Nicci smiled a little as she touched Kahlan's cheek. "Thanks."

Kahlan took a deep breath. "Jagang has promised to do much the same to me as he did to you."

Nicci's hand tightened on Kahlan's, offering in turn some solace.

Kahlan hesitated, but then went on. "The only reason he hasn't yet is because he wants it to be worse than it would be if he did it now. He told me that he wants to wait until I know who I am. He says that when I remember my past and who I am it will be all the worse for me. He says that he wants 'him' to see it. Jagang says that he wants to destroy us both in that way, to destroy everything."

Nicci closed her eyes, covering them with a hand as if unable to bear the thought of it.

"It seems pretty obvious that he has to be talking about someone from my past. Do you know who this 'he' is?"

Nicci's answer was a long moment in coming. "I'm sorry,

but I don't remember you, or your past. All I know is the things I've heard, like your name and that you are the Mother Confessor."

Kahlan nodded. She didn't think she was getting the whole truth. She felt pretty confident that Nicci knew more than she was admitting. Kahlan thought it best, though, not to press her on the subject. At that moment, forcing her to do anything she didn't want to do seemed too cruel to contemplate. Maybe she had her own reasons for not wanting to say more. Maybe those reasons were strictly personal and none of Kahlan's business.

Kahlan smiled, determined to steer away from the gloom of such a dark subject. "I liked all the things you said about Richard Rahl. This Richard sounds like my kind of man."

Nicci smiled the slightest bit. "You are both good people."

Kahlan rubbed a thumb back and forth on the edge of the bedcover. "What's he like? I keep hearing things about him. Every time I turn around, in fact, it seems as if the phantom of Richard Rahl is somehow haunting my life." Kahlan looked up. "What's he really like?"

"I don't know. He's just . . . Richard. He's a man who cares deeply for those he loves."

"From what you told Jagang you seem to know how he feels about a great many things. You seem to be there at his side a lot. It sounds like he cares a great deal for you."

Nicci dismissed the suggestion with a flick of a hand. She looked over at Kahlan.

"There are regular soldiers outside Jagang's tent. Do you know why?"

The abrupt change of topic told Kahlan that she was probing into things Nicci didn't want to talk about. Kahlan wondered why not.

She turned her attention to Nicci's question. "The soldiers are there because they can see me. Very few people can. Sister Ulicia told Jagang that she thinks it's just an anomaly. After I killed two of his guards and Sister Cecilia—"

Her expression intense, Nicci lifted her head a little. "You killed Sister Cecilia?"

"Yes."

"How did you manage to kill a Sister of the Dark?"

"It was back in Caska, the place where you and Richard saw Jillian."

"Who told you that?"

"Jillian."

Nicci's head sank back down. "Oh."

"Jillian said she helped Richard find the *Chainfire* book he was hunting for down in the catacombs of Caska. That's also where Jagang finally captured Sisters Ulicia, Armina, and Cecilia. They thought they were going to meet up with Sister Tovi when they got there. As it turned out, Tovi was already dead and it was Jagang who was there waiting for them. They were pretty surprised."

"I bet they were," Nicci said.

"Like just about everyone else, Jagang's guards couldn't see me, so while the dream walker was busy with the Sisters, arguing over a book, I pulled the guards knives out of their sheaths. Since they couldn't see me, they had no idea the danger they were in. As they stood silently watching over their emperor I used their own weapons to run them through.

"Before they even hit the floor I pushed Jillian out ahead of me into the maze of tunnels. As everyone came rushing out the doorway behind us I threw a knife. I'd been hoping to get Jagang with the knife but it was Sister Cecilia who came through the doorway first. They caught me after that, but it had been enough to help Jillian escape."

Kahlan let out a heavy sigh. "In the end it didn't do any good. Jagang returned to the encampment with the other two Sisters and me, but he sent men to search for Jillian. They finally found her and brought her back.

"She is Jagang's way of making me comply with his wishes. He promised me that if I make him angry by not doing as I'm told he will do terrible things to her."

"He is a ruthless man."

Kahlan nodded. "After what I did, though, Jagang realized that he needed some guards who could see me, so he searched the camp looking for men who could. He found a number of them. There are thirty-eight left."

Nicci glanced over at Kahlan. "You mean there were more at first?"

"Yes."

"Then what happened to the rest?"

Kahlan stared resolutely into Nicci's eyes. "Whenever I get the chance I kill them."

Nicci smiled broadly. "Good girl."

Kahlan smiled with her, but then the smile faded. "Now, if I kill any more, it will mean torture for Jillian."

Nicci's expression reflected her concern for Jillian. "Don't ever doubt him. He will do it without hesitation."

"I know. Do you have any idea why there are a few people who can see me when almost no one can? Do you know if it's really an anomaly, as Sister Ulicia says?"

"The Sisters used a Chainfire spell on you. It made everyone forget you. Richard discovered that there is a defect in the spell and it—"

"See what I mean? Richard again, tied up in my life." She shook her head. "Sometimes I don't know if it's a good thing or not." When Nicci said nothing, she urged her to go on. "So, how did he ever discover the defect?"

"It's a long story. Basically, we were trying to find a way to undo the Chainfire spell."

"You were trying to help me? But you said you don't remember me. Why would you be doing such a thing if no one remembers me?"

When Nicci had to lie back, laboring to breathe, Kahlan said, "Sorry. I know I ask a lot of questions, it's just that . . ."

"We're trying to stop the damage being done to everyone," Nicci finally managed after enduring a shiver of pain. "The whole problem is broader than people only forgetting you. The Chainfire spell has tangled us all up in it. If it runs free it could even end life itself."

Kahlan silently reprimanded herself for even fantasizing that Richard Rahl had actually been trying to save her, that maybe he knew her and she meant something to him.

"I was running a verification web," Nicci said. "Richard saw indications in the spell—unique designs—that told him that it was contaminated. It explained a lot. We need to undo the Chainfire spell because, while it does make everyone forget you, it causes larger problems."

"What kind of larger problems?"

Nicci paused to draw a few rattling breaths, wincing in pain, before going on. "Since it's contaminated, the damaging effects of the spell expanded in unexpected ways. We fear that, unchecked, it will destroy the minds of those it has infected. I think that the contamination may be responsible for the spell not working as intended. As a result, there are a few isolated instances of people who apparently aren't affected."

"Why am I at the center of all of this?"

In the silence Kahlan could hear an oil lamp hissing softly. The sounds of the camp outside the tent seemed like they were in another world altogether.

"The Sisters used the spell on you so they could send you into the palace, unseen, to steal the boxes of Orden for them. The key to the boxes is a book called *The Book of Counted Shadows*. They need a Confessor to confirm if the book they are using is the true key to the boxes."

"I've seen the book," Kahlan said. She knew that Nicci was telling the truth about that much of it, because Jagang had already demanded that Kahlan confirm if the book was a true copy or a fake. She had proclaimed it a false copy.

She knew that there also had to be more to it, but for some reason Nicci was carefully dancing around secrets.

Kahlan pulled at a string on the bedcover. "I wish I could talk to Richard Rahl. I wonder if he might have answers for me."

"I wish you could meet him. But that now seems unlikely to ever happen."

Kahlan wanted to ask if it had actually been likely until recent events. She thought that maybe Nicci had just revealed more than she thought she had, or had intended.

"I hate to say it, but I think that you and I are not ever going to be able to see the outcome of this struggle, but do you really think that Richard Rahl is going to be able to stop this madness? For other people, I mean."

"I don't know, Kahlan. But I can tell you that he's the only one who can."

Kahlan took up Nicci's hand again. "Well, if he can, I hope he can rescue you. You should be with him. You love him."

Nicci squeezed her eyes closed. She turned her face away as a tear leaked out, tracing a slow path through the splotches of dried blood.

"I'm sorry," Kahlan said. "I shouldn't have said anything. You must miss him beyond endurance."

"No," Nicci managed as she rocked her head, "it isn't that. It's just that what Jagang did hurts, that's all. I'm having trouble breathing. I think my ribs are broken."

"They are," Kahlan said. "Some of the ones on this side, anyway. I heard them crack when he punched you there. If I'd had a knife I'd have castrated the bastard."

Nicci smiled. "I believe you could do it, Kahlan Amnell. It's too late for me, but if you get the chance, do it before he starts in on you."

"Nicci, don't give up hope."

"There's not much cause for hope."

"Yes, there is. As long as there's life, there's the potential that we can change things for the better. After all, didn't you or Richard put the boxes of Orden in play?"

"I did," Nicci said. "In Richard's name."

"What are these boxes, anyway? Why is there a magic power that is just meant to be able to, to, I don't know, vanquish all opposition and rule the world?"

"That's not their intended purpose. They were created as a counter to the Chainfire spell."

Kahlan realized, then, that Richard Rahl must have been trying to help her. Even if he was now trying to save others from the effects of the spell, he hadn't discovered the defect that was causing that damage to other people until after he was already trying to figure out how he could restore Kahlan's memory.

Having difficulty breathing, Nicci fell to a fit of coughing that was obviously agonizingly painful. She started gasping for air. Kahlan could hear the rattle of fluid in her lungs. Nicci was beginning to panic with the unsuccessful effort to breathe. She gripped the bedcover in her fists and her back arched as she tried desperately to pull a breath.

Kahlan quickly pulled the bedcover down a ways and placed a hand directly on Nicci's upper abdomen. "Nicci, listen to me. Breathe to my hand. Slowly."

Nicci's confused eyes sought Kahlan's but she couldn't speak through her gasping attempts to get a breath. Tears began to flow.

Kahlan gently rubbed her hand around in a small circle, speaking as calmly as she could. "Slow down, Nicci. Focus your mind on my hand. Feel where it is. Pull your breath slowly and evenly toward it. You're going to be fine. You're trying to breathe too fast, that's all.

"You're not alone. Everything is all right. I promise. Take slow breaths and you'll be able to breathe just fine. Let them reach down toward where you feel my hand."

Kahlan could feel Nicci's heart galloping under her hand. She continued to rub slowly and talk in a reassuring voice.

"Everything is fine. You can get plenty of air if you just let yourself slow down and take it in."

Nicci watched Kahlan as if hanging on her every word.

"You're doing good. You're all right. I won't let you die. Just think about my hand. Let your breath reach down to my hand. Slower. Slower. That's it, easy . . . easy. That's it. You're doing good. Just think about my hand and keep breathing slowly."

Nicci's breathing slowed. She seemed like she was at last getting the air she so desperately needed. Kahlan continued to gently rub Nicci's abdomen just below her ribs and to urge her to slow down. The whole time Nicci tightly held Kahlan's other hand. After a short time the crisis passed and Nicci was more comfortably getting her breath. She needed more help, though, than Kahlan could offer her. She wished that a Sister would arrive.

"Look, Nicci, we may not get a chance to talk again, but don't give up. There's a man here who I think is going to do something."

Nicci swallowed as she regained her equilibrium. "What are you talking about? What sort of man?"

"He's a Ja'La player. He's the point man on a team belonging to Commander Karg."

"Karg," she said with disgust. "I know him. The things he does to women are more vile in their invention than Jagang. Karg is a twisted bastard. Stay away from him."

Kahlan arched an eyebrow. "You're saying that at the next gala ball if he asks me to dance I should decline the offer?"

Nicci smiled a little. "That would be best."

"Anyway, there's something about this point man for Commander Karg's team. He knows me. I can see it in his eyes. You should see him play Ja'La."

"I hate Ja'La."

"That's not what I mean. This man is different. He's . . . dangerous."

Nicci frowned over at Kahlan. "Dangerous? In what way?"

"I think he's up to something."

"Like what?"

"I don't know. He doesn't want anyone in the camp to recognize him."

"How in the world would you know that?"

"It's a long story, but he found a way around anyone recognizing him. He painted his face in wild designs—with red paint—along with the faces of all the men on his team." Kahlan leaned closer. "Maybe he's an assassin or something. It could be that he's intending to kill Jagang."

Nicci closed her eyes again, losing interest. "I wouldn't get my hopes up about such a thing if I were you."

"You would if you saw this man's eyes."

Kahlan wanted to ask Nicci a thousand questions, but she heard voices beyond the doorway coming closer. Then she heard a woman outside dismiss a slave.

"I think the Sister is coming." Kahlan squeezed Nicci's hand. "Be strong."

"I don't think—"

"Be strong for Richard."

Nicci stared, unable to speak.

Kahlan hurriedly scooted away from the bed. The covering over the doorway opened and Sister Armina stepped through, pulling Jillian in behind her.

CHAPTER 26

Well, what do you expect me to do?" Verna asked as they marched past a smoking torch in an iron bracket. "Pull Nicci out of thin air?"

"I expect you to find out where she and Ann went," Cara said. "That's what I expect."

Despite the Mord-Sith's innuendo, Verna wanted to find Nicci and Ann as much as Cara did. She just wasn't as vocal about it.

The red leather outfit Cara wore stood out like blood against the virtuous white of the marble walls. The Mord-Sith's mood, which seemed to match the color of her outfit, had only gotten worse as the day had worn on and the search had turned up nothing. Several other Mord-Sith followed some distance back, along with a contingent of the First File—the Palace Guard. Adie was not far behind while Nathan was out by himself in the lead.

Verna understood Cara's feelings, and in an odd way was cheered by them. Nicci was more than Cara's charge, more than a woman Richard had wanted Cara to protect. Nicci was Cara's friend. Not that she would openly admit as much, but it was clear enough by her smoldering rage. Nicci, like Cara herself, had long been someone lost to a dark purpose. They had both come back from that terrible place because Richard had given them not only the chance to change, but a reason to.

It wasn't so much when a Mord-Sith shouted and yelled that alarmed Verna, it was when their questions became quiet and terse. That was what lifted the hackles on the back of her neck—when it was clear that they meant business, and the business of Mord-Sith was not at all pleasant. It was best not to find yourself in the way of a Mord-Sith when she meant to have answers. Verna only wished that she had them.

She understood Cara's frustration. She felt no less anxious and bewildered at what could have happened to Nicci and Ann. She knew, though, that repeating the same questions and insisting on answers would not produce those answers any more than it would produce the two missing women. She supposed that Mord-Sith fell back on their training when there seemed no other solution.

Cara stopped, hands on hips, and looked back down the marble hallway. Behind them a few hundred men of the First File slowed to a halt so that they wouldn't overrun those in the lead. The echo of boots on stone slowly dwindled to a whisper. Several of the soldiers had crossbows with red fletched arrows at the ready. Those arrows made Verna sweat. She almost wished that Nathan had never found them. Almost.

The seemingly endless maze of halls behind the heavily armed soldiers was empty and silent but for the hissing torches. Cara frowned in thought for a moment, then started out once again. This was the fourth time since Ann and Nicci had disappeared the night before that they had been down in the halls that led to the tombs. Verna couldn't begin to imagine what the Mord-Sith could be trying to figure out. Empty passageways were empty passageways. The two missing women were hardly likely to pop out of the marble walls.

"They had to have gone somewhere else," Verna finally said, even though no one had seen them.

Cara turned back. "Like where?"

Verna lifted her arms and finally let them flop back down to her sides. "I don't know."

"It be a big palace," Adie said. The torchlight lent the sorceress's completely white eyes a disturbing, translucent quality.

Verna gestured down the silent passageway. "Cara, we've spent hours going up and down these halls and it's just as obvious now as it was the last time we were down here—or the first time for that matter—that they are empty. Nicci and Ann have to be somewhere up in the palace. We're wasting our time down here. I agree that we need to find them, but we need to look elsewhere."

Cara's eyes looked like blue fire. "They were down here."

"Yes, I'm sure you're right. But *were* is the word in what you said that matters. Do you see any trace of them? I don't. You're no doubt correct that they were down here. It's obvious, though, that they've since gone elsewhere." Verna sighed impatiently. "We're wasting valuable time marching up and down empty halls."

As everyone waited where they stood, Cara paced up the hallway a short distance. When she returned she again planted her fists on her hips.

"There's something wrong down here."

Nathan, out by himself in the lead and keeping his own counsel, stared back at them, for the first time curious. "Wrong? What do you mean . . . wrong?"

"I don't know," Cara admitted. "I can't put my finger on it but there's something down here that doesn't feel right to me."

Verna spread her hands, searching for understanding. "You mean some kind of . . . essence of magic, or something?"

"No," Cara said, waving off the very notion. "I don't mean anything like that." She returned the hand to her red leather-clad hip. "It's just that it seems like something is wrong—I don't know what, but something."

Verna glanced about. "Do you think something is missing?" She gestured ahead, up the empty passageway. "Decorations, furnishings, something of that nature?"

"No. As I recall there never was any decorations down in most of these halls. But I haven't been down here to the tombs much—no one has.

"Darken Rahl would visit his father's tomb from time to time, but as far as I know he didn't have any interest in visiting the others. The area down here with the tombs is private and he made it off-limits. When he went to his father's tomb he usually took his bodyguards, not Mord-Sith, so I'm just not all that familiar with the place."

"Maybe that's all it is," Verna suggested, "an uneasy feeling brought on by unfamiliarity."

"I suppose that could be it," Cara said, her mouth twisting with annoyance at having to admit it was a possibility.

Everyone stood silently, considering what they should do next, if anything. It was always possible, after all, that the two missing women could show up at any moment and wonder what all the fuss was about.

"You said Ann and Nicci had wanted to be alone to have a private conversation," Adie said. "Perhaps they went off somewhere private."

"All night?" Verna asked. "I can't imagine that. The two of them didn't have much in common. They weren't friends. Dear Creator, I don't think they even liked each other all that much. I can't imagine them chatting the night away."

"Me neither," Cara said.

Verna looked up at the prophet. "Do you have any idea what Ann might have wanted to talk to Nicci about?"

Nathan's long white hair brushed his shoulders when he shook his head. "Ann naturally took a dim view of Nicci, considering that she turned to the Sisters of the Dark. I know that always bothered her—and not without sound reason. It was more than a betrayal of the cause of the Light; it was a personal betrayal and a betrayal of the palace. Ann might have wanted to get Nicci alone so she could counsel her about coming back to the Creator."

"That would have been a brief conversation," Cara said.

"I suppose so," Nathan admitted. He scratched the bridge of his nose as he considered. "Well, knowing Ann, it very well might be something about Richard."

Cara's blue eyes narrowed as they turned up toward the prophet. "What about Richard?"

Nathan shrugged. "I don't know for certain."

Cara's brow tightened. "I didn't say that it had to be for certain."

Nathan looked somewhat reluctant to speak of it, but he finally did. "Ann sometimes mentioned how she thought that Nicci might be able to guide him."

Verna joined Cara in frowning. "Guide him? Guide him how?"

"You know Ann." Nathan smoothed the front of his white shirt. "She always thinks she needs to have a hand in guiding everything. She has often mentioned to me how uneasy it makes her to have so tenuous a connection to Richard."

"Why does she think she needs a 'connection' to Lord Rahl?" Cara asked, ignoring the fact that it was now Nathan who was Lord Rahl and not Richard.

Verna couldn't say that she was any more comfortable with the thought of Nathan being the Lord Rahl than was Cara.

"She has always thought she needed to control what Richard might do," Nathan said. "She is always calculating and planning. She has never liked leaving anything to chance."

"True enough," Verna said. "The woman always did have a network of spies to help her insure that the world was revolving properly. She had connections in the most far-flung places in order to exert influence toward what she saw as the cause of her life. She never liked leaving anything important to others, much less to chance."

Nathan heaved a deep sigh. "Ann is a determined woman. She believes that Nicci—since renouncing the Sisters of the Dark—has no other choice, now, except to return her devotion to the cause of the Sisters of the Light."

"What cause? Why does she think Nicci has to be devoted to the Sisters of the Light?" Cara asked.

Nathan leaned a little toward the Mord-Sith. "She thinks that us wizards need a Sister of the Light to guide our every thought and action. She has always believed that we should not be allowed to think for ourselves."

Verna's gaze wandered off down the empty passageway. "I guess that I used to believe much same thing. But that was before Richard."

"Keep in mind, though, that you've spent far more time with Richard than Ann ever did." Nathan shook his head sadly. "While she had to have come to much the same understanding about Richard needing to act on his own as most of us agree he must, she seems lately to be reverting to her old ways, her old beliefs. I'm not sure that the Chainfire spell hasn't wiped away those changes in Ann, crased the things she had learned."

Verna had suspected much the same. "We must let Ann speak for herself, but I think that it's clear that the Chainfire spell is affecting us all. We know that, unchecked, it will likely continue to run rampant through our minds and very possibly destroy our ability to reason. The problem is, none of us is aware of how we are changing. Each of us feels that we are the same as we've always been. I doubt that to be true. There is no telling how much any one of us has changed. Any of us could unwittingly lead our cause astray."

"You can discuss all that with Ann when we find them," Cara said, impatient to get back to the issue at hand. "They're not down here. We need to spread our search."

"Maybe they're not done with whatever they had to talk about," Nathan suggested. "Maybe Ann doesn't want to be found until after she is finished with trying to convince Nicci of what she must do."

"That sounds like a possibility," Verna agreed.

Nathan fussed with the edge of his cape. "I wouldn't put it past the woman to abscond with Nicci, intent on being alone with her so she can browbeat her into Ann's way of thinking."

Cara flicked a hand dismissively. "Nicci is devoted to helping Richard, not Ann. She wouldn't go along and Ann couldn't make her—Nicci can wield Subtractive Magic, after all."

"I agree." Verna said. "I can't imagine the two of them just wandering off for this long without letting us know where they are."

Adie turned to Verna. "Why not ask her where she be?"

Verna frowned at the old sorceress. "You mean use the journey book?"

Adie gave a single, firm nod. "Yes. Ask her."

Verna was skeptical. "Being here in the palace it's hardly likely that she would look in her journey book for a message from me."

"Maybe she not be in the palace," Adie said. "Perhaps the two of them had to leave for some sudden, important reason and she already sent you a message in the journey book."

"How in the world could the two of them leave the palace?" Verna asked. "We're surrounded by the army of the Imperial Order."

Adie shrugged. "It not be impossible. I can see with my gift, not my eyes. It be dark last night. Maybe in the dark they had to slip away for some reason. Maybe it be important and they didn't have time to tell us."

"You could do that?" Cara asked. "You could go out in the dark and make it through the enemy?"

"Of course."

Verna was already thumbing through her journey book. As she had expected, it was completely blank. "There is no message." She tucked the small book back behind her belt. "I'll try your suggestion, though, and write Ann a message. Perhaps she will look in her journey book and reply."

With a flourish of his cape, Nathan once again started away. "Before we go off to look elsewhere I want to check the tomb again."

"Post a guard up here," Cara called back to the soldiers. "The rest of you come with us."

Already some distance off down the hall, Nathan turned down a stairway. The rest of them all followed behind, their footsteps echoing as they hurried to catch up. Nathan, Cara, Adie, Verna, and the soldiers bringing up the rear all descended down to the next level.

The walls of the lower level were stone block, rather than marble. In places they were stained by centuries of water seeping through. The seepage left behind yellowish formations that made the stone look as if it were melting.

They soon enough arrived at stone that really had melted.

Nathan came to a halt before the opening to Panis Rahl's tomb. The tall prophet, his face grim and drawn, stared past melted stone into the tomb. It was the fourth time he had returned to look into the tomb and this time it looked no different than on previous visits.

Verna was worried about the man. While he was worried and wanted to find answers, there was a kind of rage simmering just below the surface. She had never seen him like this before. The only person she could think of who had same quality of quiet, bottled fury that could make her heart race was Richard. Such focused anger had to be, she thought, a Rahl quality.

Whatever doors had once guarded the crypt had been replaced with a kind of white stone intended to seal the large tomb. It appeared to have been hastily constructed, but it hadn't succeeded in halting the strange conditions overcoming Panis Rahl's tomb.

Inside, fifty-seven cold torches rested in ornate gold brackets. Nathan cast out a hand, using magic to light several of them. As they burst into flame the walls of the crypt came alive with flickering light that reflected off the polished pink granite of the vaulted room. Beneath each of the torches was a vase meant to hold flowers. By the fifty-seven torches and vases, Verna guessed that Panis Rahl must have been fifty-seven when he died.

A short pillar in the center of the cavernous room supported the coffin itself, making it look as if it floated above the floor of white marble. The gold-enshrouded coffin glowed softly in the wavering, warm light of the four torches. The way the walls were covered in polished crystalline granite that ran up and completely across the vaulting, Verna imagined that when all the torches around the room were lit the coffin must glow in golden glory as it floated all by itself in the center of the room.

Words carved in the ancient language of High D'Haran covered the sides of the coffin. Cut into the granite beneath the torches and gold vases, an endless ribbon of words in the same nearly forgotten language ringed the room. The deeply incised letters shimmered in the torchlight, almost making them look as if they were lit from within.

Whatever was causing the white stone that had once blocked the entrance to the tomb to melt was beginning to affect the room itself, although not to the same extent. Verna suspected that the white stone used to wall over the entrance was a stopgap, a sacrificial substance deliberately selected to draw and absorb the invisible force responsible for the trouble. Now that the white stone was almost all melted away those forces were beginning to attack the tomb itself.

The stone slabs of the walls and floor hadn't melted or cracked, but they were just beginning to distort, as if they were being subjected to great heat or pressure. Verna could see that the joints between the ceiling and walls out in the hall were splitting open under the pressure of the deformation from within the room itself. Whatever was causing such an event, it was obvious that it was not a construction defeet, but rather some kind of external force.

Nicci had said that she wanted to see the tomb because she thought she knew why it was melting. Unfortunately, she hadn't revealed the nature of her suspicion. There was no sign that she and Ann had visited the tomb.

Verna was impatient to find both women so that the whole mystery could be solved. She couldn't imagine what the trouble with the tomb of Richard's grandfather could be, or how much worse it would get, but she didn't think it would turn out to be anything good. Nor did she think that there was much time left to answer the riddle—any part of it.

"Lord Rahl," a voice called.

They all turned back. A messenger came to a halt not far away. All the messengers wore while robes trimmed around the neck and down the front with a design of intertwined purple vines.

"What is it?" Nathan asked.

Verna thought that as long as she lived she would never get used to hearing people call Nathan "Lord Rahl."

The man bowed briefly. "There is a delegation from the Imperial Order waiting on the other side of the drawbridge."

Nathan blinked in surprise. "What do they want?"

"They want to speak to Lord Rahl."

Nathan glanced to Cara and then Verna. Both were just as surprised as he.

"It could be a trick," Adie said.

"Or a trap," Cara added.

Nathan's face bent into a sour expression. "Whatever it is, I think I'd better go look into it."

"I'm going, too." Cara said.

"As am I," Verna added.

"We'll all go," Nathan said as he started away.

Verna and the small clutch of people with her followed Nathan out of the grand entrance of People's Palace and into the bright late-afternoon sunlight. Long shadows cast by the towering columns cascaded down the hillside of steps before them. In the distance, across the expanse of grounds, the great outer wall stood at the edge of the plateau. Men patrolled a walkway between crenellated battlements along the top of the massive wall.

It had been a long journey up from the tombs deep within the palace and they were all winded. Verna shaded her eyes with a hand as they descended the grand stairs in the wake of the long-legged prophet. Guards posted on each of the expansive landings saluted the Lord Rahl with a fist to their hearts. There were greater numbers of soldiers in the distance patrolling the broad sweep of grounds leading to the outer wall.

The stairs ended in a broad area of bluestone that took them to a roadway winding up from around the side where stables and carriages would be. Tall cypress trees lined the short road as it led toward the outer walls.

Beyond the gates through the massive wall the road was less grand as it followed the the sheer walls of the plateau down in a series of switchbacks. Each turn gave the silent company an unbroken view of the Imperial Order spread out far below.

The drawbridge was guarded by hundreds of troops of the First File. These were all well-trained, heavily armed soldiers committed to insuring that no one came up the road to assault the People's Palace. There was little chance of that, though. The road was too narrow to mount any kind of meaningful attack. In such tight confines a few dozen good men could hold off an entire army. More than that, though, the drawbridge was up. The sheer drop was dizzying. It was too far across for assault ladders or ropes with grappling hooks. Without the bridge down no one could cross the chasm and approach the palace.

Beyond the drawbridge a small delegation waited. By their simple dress they looked to be messengers. Verna did see a few dozen lightly armed soldiers, but they remained well back from the messengers so as not to appear threatening.

Nathan, his cloak buttoned back on one shoulder even though it was a cold day, came to a halt at the edge of the chasm, feet spread, fists on his hips, looking imposing and commanding.

"I am Lord Rahl," he announced to the party across the drop. "What do you want?"

One of the men, a slender fellow wearing a simple tunic of darkly dyed leather, shared a look with his comrades and then stepped a little closer to his side of the brink.

"His Excellency, Emperor Jagang, has sent me with a message for the D'Haran people."

Nathan glanced around at the others behind him. "Well, I'm Lord Rahl, so I speak for the D'Haran people. What is the message?"

Verna eased up beside the prophet.

The messenger was looking more displeased by the moment. "You are not the Lord Rahl."

Nathan eyed the man with a Rahl scowl. "Would you like me to use a bit of conjured wind and blow you off that road? Would that settle the matter to your satisfaction?"

The men across the way stole glances down the drop.

"It's just that we were expecting someone else," the messenger said.

"Well, I'm Lord Rahl so I'm what you get. If you have something to say, then say it, otherwise I'm busy. We have a banquet to attend."

The man finally bowed slightly. "Emperor Jagang is prepared to make a generous offer to those in the People's Palace."

"What sort of offer?"

"His Excellency has no desire to destroy the palace or its inhabitants. Surrender peacefully, and you will be allowed to live. Fail to surrender and each of them will die a slow and agonizing death. Their bodies will be thrown off the walls to the plain below, where they will feed the vultures."

"Wizard's fire," Cara said under her breath.

Nathan frowned back over his shoulder. "What?"

"Your power works here. Theirs, if they are gifted, wouldn't work as well up here, so their shields would be less effective. You can incinerate the lot of them from here."

Nathan waved his arm in a grand gesture to those across the way. "Will you excuse me for a moment?"

The man bowed his head indulgently.

Nathan led Cara and Verna back up the road to where Adie, several other Mord-Sith, and the escort of soldiers waited.

"I agree with Cara," Verna said before the prophet could say anything. "Give them our answer in the only way the Order understands."

Nathan's bushy brow drew down over his azure eyes. "I don't think that's such a good idea."

Cara folded her arms. "Why not?"

"Jagang is probably watching our reaction through the eyes of those men," Verna said. "I agree with Cara. We need to show him strength."

Nathan frowned. "I'm surprised at you, Verna." He smiled politely at Cara. "I'm not surprised at you, however, my dear."

"Why are you so surprised?" Verna asked.

"Because it would be the wrong thing to do. You usually don't give such poor advice."

Verna restrained herself. This was not the time to launch into a heated lecture—especially not in front of Jagang's eyes. She also recalled all too vividly how she had thought for most of her life that the prophet was mad. She wasn't entirely sure that her assessment had been wrong. She also knew from past experience that lecturing Nathan was like trying to talk the sun out of setting.

"You can't seriously be considering surrender," she said in a low voice that those across the way wouldn't hear.

Nathan made a sour face. "Of course not. But that doesn't mean that we should kill them for asking."

"Why not?" Cara spun her Agiel up into her fist as she

leaned toward the prophet. "I, for one, think that killing them is an excellent idea."

"Well, I don't," Nathan huffed. "If I incinerate them that will tell Jagang that we have no intention of considering his offer."

Verna contained her fury. "Well, we don't."

Nathan turned an intense look on her. "If we tell them that we have no intention of considering the offer then the negotiations are ended."

"We're not going to negotiate," Verna said with rising impatience.

"But we don't have to tell them that," Nathan explained with exaggerated care.

Verna straightened and fussed with her hair, using the moment to take a deep breath. "What would be the purpose of not telling them that we have no intention of seriously considering their offer?"

"To buy time," Nathan said. "If I blast them off that road Jagang would have his answer, now wouldn't he? But if I take the offer under consideration we can string out the negotiations."

"There can be no negotiations," Verna said through gritted teeth.

"To what end?" Cara asked, ignoring Verna. "Why would we want to do such a thing?"

Nathan shrugged as if it were obvious and they were all idiots for not seeing it. "Delay. They know how difficult it is going to be to take the palace. With every foot of elevation that ramp of theirs gains it becomes exponentially more difficult to construct. It could easily take them the winter, and possibly a great deal longer, to build that thing. Jagang can't be looking forward to an army that massive sitting out there on the Azrith Plain for the entire winter. They are a long way from home and supplies. He could lose the whole army to starvation or a virulent sickness, then where would he be?

"If they think we might consider surrender then they might put thought and effort into winning the palace in that way. Our surrender would solve their problem. But if they think there is no way but to rout us from the place then they will put all their efforts into that method. Why push them to it?"

Verna's mouth twisted. "I suppose that makes some sense." When Nathan smiled at the small triumph, she added, "Not a lot, but some."

"I'm not at all sure it does," Cara said.

Nathan spread his arms. "Why turn them down? There is nothing to be gained by doing so. We should keep them guessing, keep them wondering if we might be considering giving up without a fight. Enough cities have surrendered to make it seem like a reasonable possibility that we might do the same. If they think there is a chance we might surrender then that hope will keep them from being fully committed to finishing their ramp and ending it with a rout of the palace."

"I must admit," Cara said, "there is value in stringing people along so that they fall into waiting for an answer they really want."

Verna finally gave him a nod. "I guess that for now it can't hurt to let them wonder."

Finished with the task of bringing them around to his way of thinking, Nathan brushed his hands together. "I will tell them that we will take their offer under advisement."

Verna wondered if Nathan had another reason for wanting to say he would consider the offer. She wondered if he could actually be contemplating surrendering the palace. While Verna held no illusions that Jagang would actually keep his word not to harm those in the palace if they surrendered, she wondered if Nathan was thinking of secretly arranging his own surrender deal, a deal that would leave him as the permanent Lord Rahl of a vanquished D'Hara under the authority of the Imperial Order.

After all, once the war was over Jagang would need people to rule far-flung conquered lands.

She wondered if Nathan was capable of such treason.

She wondered how much his resentment had grown over nearly a lifetime of imprisonment in the Palace of the Prophets for no more of a crime than what the Sisters of the Light thought him capable of. She wondered if he could be thinking of revenge.

She wondered if the Sisters of the Light, by their well-intentioned treatment of a man who had done them no harm, might have sown the seeds of destruction.

As Verna watched a smiling Lord Rahl marching back to the edge of the chasm, she wondered if the prophet was scheming to throw them all to the wolves.

CHAPTER 27

Richard was growing ever more concerned. He had expected that at one of the games he would see his chance. But after Jagang and Kahlan had come to the first Ja'La match a dozen days before, the emperor had not again shown up to watch a game.

Richard was frantic with worry over the reason. He tried not to think about what Jagang might be doing to Kahlan, and yet he couldn't keep himself from imagining the worst.

Sitting chained to the wagon, surrounded by a ring of guards, there was not much Richard could do about it. Despite how desperately he wanted to act, he had to use his head and look for the right opportunity. It had always been a risk that a good opportunity might not come along and then he would be forced to act, but doing something out of frustration alone was not likely to accomplish anything except maybe ruin any chance he would otherwise have of getting the opportunity he needed. Still, waiting was driving him crazy.

As sore as he was from the Ja'La match that day, he longed to lie down and get some rest. He knew, though, that his anxiety was going to keep him from getting much sleep, just as it had kept him from getting sleep for days. He was going to need the sleep, though, because the next day was their most important game yet—a game that he hoped would get him to the opportunity he was looking for.

He glanced up when he heard the soldier coming with their evening meal. As hungry as Richard was, even the usual hard-boiled eggs sounded good. The soldier, pulling the small cart he always used to haul their food, made his way through the ring of guards around the captive members of Richard's team. The soldiers gave the man only a cursory look. The wheels of the cart squeaked with a familiar rhythm as the man plodded across the hardscrabble ground. He stopped in front of Richard.

"Hold out your hands," he said as he picked up a knife and started sawing away on something in his cart.

Richard did as he was told. The man lifted something from the cart and tossed it to Richard. To his surprise, it was a hefty slice of ham.

"What's this? A last good meal before tomorrow's fateful game?"

The man lifted the handles on his cart. "Supplies came in. Everyone eats."

Richard stared at the soldier's back as he wheeled his cart up the row to feed the other men. Not far away, Johnrock, his face and body covered with the network of lines in red paint, whistled with satisfaction to find himself getting something other than eggs. This was the first time since they'd been in camp that they had been given any quantity of meat. Up until now they had usually been fed eggs. Sometimes they'd been given stew with precious few chunks of lamb. Once it had been beef stew.

Richard wondered how supplies had gotten through to the encampment. The D'Haran army was supposed to stop any supplies from reaching the Order's army. Starving Jagang's men was their only real chance to stop them.

If Richard hadn't already been worried enough, the thick slice of ham in his hand represented a grave new concern. He supposed that it only made sense that an occasional supply convoy would get through. With food running low, this resupply had been timely.

The Old World was a big place. Richard knew that there was no way that the D'Haran army could cover the whole countryside. On the other hand, he wondered if the ham he was holding could be a sign that things weren't going so well for General Meiffert and the men he had taken south.

Johnrock scooted closer, dragging his chain behind. "Ruben! We get ham! Isn't that wonderful?"

"Being free would be wonderful. Eating well as a slave is not my idea of wonderful."

Johnrock's face sagged a little, then brightened. "But being a slave eating ham is better than being a slave eating eggs, don't you think?"

Richard wasn't in the mood to discuss it. "I guess you have a point."

Johnrock grinned. "I thought so too."

In the gathering gloom of dusk the two of them ate in silence. Savoring the ham, Richard had to admit to himself that Johnrock did indeed have a point. He'd almost forgotten how good something other than eggs could be. This, too, would help give him and his team strength. They were going to need it.

Johnrock, chewing a big mouthful of ham, scooted just a little closer. He swallowed and then sucked juice off his fingers. "Say, Ruben, is there something wrong?"

Richard glanced over at his big right wing man. "What do you mean?"

Johnrock pulled off a strip of meat. "Well, you didn't do so good today."

"We won by five points."

Johnrock looked up from under his thick brow. "But we used to win by more."

"The competition is getting tougher."

Johnrock shrugged with one shoulder. "If you say so, Ruben." He thought it over a moment, clearly not satisfied. "But we won by more points against that one big team . . . back a few days. Remember? The ones who called us names and started the fight with Bruce before the game even started."

Richard remembered the team. Bruce was the new left wing man, replacing the original man, who had been killed during the game Jagang and Kahlan had been at. Richard had at first worried that a regular Imperial Order soldier would not do as well serving under a captive point man, but Bruce had risen to the occasion.

On the day Johnrock was talking about, the other team's wing man had called the regular soldiers on Richard's team names for serving under a captive. Bruce had answered the insults by calmly walking over and breaking the man's arm. The fight that ensued had been ugly but it had been quickly broken up by the referee.

"I remember. What of it?"

"I think they were tougher than the team today and we beat them by eleven points."

"We won today's match. That's what matters."

"But you told us how we must crush all opposition if we are to get to play the emperor's team."

Richard took a deep breath. "You all did good, Johnrock. I guess I just let everyone down."

"No, Ruben—you haven't let us down." Johnrock grunted a laugh and smacked the side of Richard's shoulder with the back of his big hand. "Like you say, we won. If we win tomorrow then we play the emperor's team."

If nothing else, Richard was counting on Jagang at least showing up to watch his own team play for the camp championship. Surely, he would never miss seeing that game.

Commander Karg had told Richard that the emperor was well aware of their team's growing reputation. Richard worried about why Jagang hadn't come to see for himself. Richard had thought that the man would want to size up the likely challengers to his team and so would attend at least the last few games before the final match.

"Don't worry, Johnrock. We're going to beat that team tomorrow and then we're going to get to play the emperor's team."

Johnrock shot Richard a lopsided grin. "And then, when we win, we get our choice of a woman. Snake-face promised us."

Richard chewed ham as he watched the man covered in designs meant to increase strength and power intertwined with symbols of aggression and conquest.

"There are more important things than that."

"Maybe so, but what other rewards are there for us in life?" Johnrock's grin returned. "If we win against the emperor's team, we get a woman."

"Have you ever thought that your reward might be nothing but a terrifying nightmare for the woman you choose?"

Johnrock frowned, staring at Richard a moment. In silence, he went back to eating ham.

"Why would you say that?" Johnrock finally asked, unable to contain his annoyance. "I wouldn't hurt a woman."

Richard glanced over at the man's sour expression. "What do you think of the camp followers?"

"The camp followers?" Johnrock, surprised by the question, scratched his shoulder as he considered. "Most of them are ugly old hags."

"Well, if you aren't interested in them, then that leaves the captive women, the women taken from their homes, their families, their husbands, their children, everything they ever loved. The ones forced to serve as whores for soldiers who very likely were the same ones who slaughtered those fathers, husbands, and children."

"Well, I . . ."

"The women we often hear crying out at night. The ones we hear weeping."

Johnrock's gaze fell away. He picked at his piece of ham. "It keeps me awake, sometimes, listening to the sounds of those women sobbing."

Richard looked out between the wagons and guards at the camp beyond. In the distance the work on the ramp continued. He imagined that the people up in the People's Palace, the last holdout against the Imperial Order, could do nothing but wait for the horde to come. There was nothing they could do. There was nowhere safe left for them to go. The beliefs driving the Imperial Order were swallowing all of mankind.

Down in the encampment knots of men were gathering around cook fires. Among the shadows and gloom Richard could see a woman being dragged to a tent. She'd once had her own dreams and hope for her future; now that the Order was prescribing their vision for mankind, she was merely chattel. Already men were lining up outside, the victors waiting for their reward in return for serving the Imperial Order. Ultimately, despite all the grand pretensions, this was all that it was really about: the lust of some to rule over all others, to impose their will, the pretension of a moral licence that they believed gave them the right to take, by any means, what they wanted.

In other places Richard could see men were gathered around drinking and gambling. The supply train must have brought liquor. It was going to be a noisy night.

Kahlan was somewhere out in that sea of men.

"Well then," Richard said, "unless you want to be a party to the abuse of those women, that leaves the camp followers, who are willing."

Johnrock thought in silence for a time as he nibbled at his ham. If quiet anger could cut steel, Richard would have his collar off and he would be doing something to get Kahlan out of this place and to safety—to what safety there was left in a world gone mad over a cause.

"You know, Ruben, you have a way of spoiling things."

Richard glanced over at the man. "Would you rather I lie? Make up something just to soothe your conscience?"

Johnrock sighed. "No. But still . . ."

Richard realized then that he had better not discourage his right wing man or the man might very well not play his best. If they lost the next game there would be no chance to play the emperor's team and then Richard might not get a chance to see Kahlan again.

"Well, you are getting pretty famous, Johnrock. Men are beginning to cheer when they see you come on the field. It could be that there will be a lot of pretty women who will be eager to be with the big, handsome wing man on the champion team."

Johnrock finally grinned. "That's true. We are winning a lot of soldiers over to our side. Men are beginning to cheer for us." He waved his ham at Richard. "You are the point man. You will have a lot of pretty women who will want to be with you."

"There is only one I want."

"And you think she will be willing? What if she wants nothing to do with you?"

Richard opened his mouth, but then closed it. Kahlan didn't know him. If he did get a chance to try to get her away from

Jagang, what was he going to do if she thought he was just another stranger trying to capture her? After all, why wouldn't she? What if she wasn't willing to go along with him? What if she resisted? There would certainly be no time to try to explain things to her.

Richard sighed. Now he had another thing to keep him awake with worry.

CHAPTER 28

Kahlan sat quietly in the shadows to the side of the outer room in a low, leather chair, her hands nested in her lap. Jillian sat cross-legged on the floor nearby. From time to time Kahlan glanced at Sisters Ulicia and Armina as they worked at their assigned task of comparing the books that were the key to opening the boxes of Orden. They were going through each volume word by word, searching for any variance.

Some of Jagang's other captive Sisters had found a third book down in the catacombs below the Palace of the Prophets, so Sisters Ulicia and Armina now had an additional copy they could cheek against the two books they already had—the one from the Palace of the Prophets, which Jagang had long had in his possession, and the one he'd found in the catacombs in Caska, where he had captured Sisters Ulicia, Armina, and Cecilia, as well as Kahlan.

The books were supposed to be *The Book of Counted Shadows*. The titles on the spines of the latter two, however, didn't say *Shadows*, but instead said *Shadow*. There was disagreement between Sisters Ulicia and Armina if that was meaningful or not.

From what Kahlan had pieced together from bits and pieces she'd overheard, there was the original of *The Book of Counted Shadows*, one true copy, and four false copies. Jagang now had in his possession three of those five copies. Getting their hands on all the copies was a top priority. From what Kahlan could gather, there were people whose lives were devoted solely to that task.

The mystery had deepened when the book found in the

recently discovered catacombs under the People's Palace had turned out to say *Shadows* in the title on the spine, as it was supposed to say. The titles alone would suggest that the first two were false copies—as Kahlan had said they were—and the latest one was possibly the true copy. As of yet, though, there was no way for them to prove any of it.

Kahlan worried about what she would do if Jagang demanded that she rule on whether the latest find was a true copy or not.

From what the Sisters had pointed out to Jagang, the books themselves said that a Confessor was needed to verify if the book was a true version or not. Kahlan had overheard that she was this person, a Confessor, but, along with the rest of her forgotten past, she didn't know what a Confessor was. She had no idea how she was supposed to be able to identify the true copy. Jagang hadn't cared if she knew the way or not; he simply expected her to do it.

With the first two the title being wrong had given her a plausible reason to proclaim them false. With the latest edition, though, she would have nothing to go on, since the title was correct and the text itself could offer her no help because magic prevented her from being able to see it. With his attention focused on Nicci, Jagang hadn't asked for Kahlan's determination on the latest volume's validity.

If he did, and Kahlan couldn't give him an answer that satisfied him, Jillian would be the one to pay the price.

So far the Sisters had not been able to find any dissimilarities between the three copies. Of course, as they had hesitantly pointed out to the emperor, dissimilarities would prove nothing. All three could be different and still be false copies. How were they to know? There was nothing to say that the newest book, even if it turned out to be different from the other two, was a true copy. Being different, in and of itself, didn't prove anything.

As far as Kahlan could see, the only real way to identify the one true copy would be if they had the original and all five copies. Despite his bluster and demands, Jagang had to know that as well. That was undoubtedly why he had people dedicated to locating the other books.

Be that as it may, Jagang still wanted the books checked for any discrepancy, so the Sisters were checking—one word at a time.

Jagang had given them ample time to go over the books. While he was greatly interested in discovering the truth of *The Book of Counted Shadows*, for the time being he was more interested in Nicci.

Ever since Nicci had been captured he had been obsessed with her. He had not taken another woman to his bed and had even forgone the Ja'La matches. It almost seemed to Kahlan as if he thought that if he could satisfactorily demonstrate to Nicci how profound his lust for her really was, then she would be convinced of his true feelings for her, and her defiance would melt away as she was won over.

For her part, Nicci had only become more detached.

Her dispassionate, distant attitude strangely attracted Jagang, but her defiance provoked him to violence and only made her ordeal worse. Kahlan couldn't imagine, though, when her turn came, being anything but defiant.

Several times, after a fit of wild rage, Jagang's anger had died out when he suddenly realized that he might have gone too far. On those occasions Sisters had been rushed in to try to revive Nicci. All the while as they worked desperately to save her life and heal her, Jagang paced with a worried, guilty look. Later, after she had been healed, he would regain his indignation and blame Nicci for driving him to such violence in the first place.

Sometimes, like the night before, he would leave Kahlan and Jillian in the outer room while he took Nicci inside to be alone with her for the night. Kahlan supposed that such privacy was his idea of tender romance. As Nicci had been led to the bedchamber she had shared a brief, covert gaze with Kahlan. It had been a look of shared understanding of the utter madness that gripped the world.

Jagang had been so distracted since having Nicci back that he had ignored just about everything else, from *The Book of Counted Shadows* to the Ja'La matches. Kahlan didn't like the Ja'La games, but she desperately wanted to see the man everyone called Ruben. She knew from daily reports shared between the guards that Commander Karg's team had so far won all their matches, but Kahlan wanted to see the point man with the strange designs painted on him, the man with the gray eyes, the man who knew her.

"Look here," Sister Ulicia said, tapping the page in one of the books. "This formula is different from those two."

Kahlan watched their backs as both hunched over the table, comparing the books laid open before them. Jagang's two big bodyguards standing across the room, near the entrance to the tent, also kept an eye on the Sisters. The two regular soldiers—Kahlan's special guards—didn't appear to be interested in the Sisters; they were watching Kahlan. Kahlan, her face going red when she realized what they were looking at, pulled a thick skein of hair over the view provided by the missing top button of her shirt.

"Yes . . ." Sister Armina said in a drawl. "The constellation is different. Isn't that odd."

"It certainly makes the differences difficult to spot. Not only that, but look here. The azimuth angels are dissimilar." Sister Ulicia pulled one of the oil lamps closer. "They're different in all three copies."

Sister Armina was nodding as she looked between the books. "We never caught that before in the first two books. I always thought they were the same, but they're not."

"Being such a small thing it's easy to see why we missed it." Sister Ulicia gestured at the books. "This makes all three different."

"What do you think it means?"

Sister Ulicia folded her arms. "It can only mean that at least two have to be false copies, but in reality, for all we know, all three could be."

Sister Armina heaved an unhappy sigh. "So now we know something new, but it doesn't really tell us anything useful."

Sister Ulicia cast the other woman a sidelong glance. "His Excellency has a way of coming up with things I would never have expected him to find. Perhaps he will uncover the other copies and then we will at last have a means to be able to tell something for certain."

The cover over the door abruptly lifted to the side. Jagang shoved Nicci through the opening. She stumbled and fell at Kahlan's feet. The woman's eyes briefly turned up, but she pretended not to see Kahlan right there in front of her. It was a deception that had not changed since Jagang had captured her.

Kahlan could see the rage in Nicci's eyes. She could see the pain, too. She could also see the desperate despair.

Kahlan wanted to hold her, comfort her, and tell her that it would be all right. But she couldn't do such a thing. And, she certainly couldn't tell her that it would be all right.

"What have you found out?" Jagang asked the two Sisters as he stepped up behind them.

Sister Ulicia tapped one of the books. He leaned over her shoulder, peering down at where she pointed.

"Right here, Excellency. They are all three different in this place right here."

"Which one is correct?"

Both sisters shrank back a little.

"Excellency," Sister Ulicia said in a hesitant voice, "it is still too early to tell."

"We must have the other copies if we are to know for sure," Sister Armina blurted out.

Jagang turned his gaze on her for a moment and then, uncharacteristically, merely grunted indifferently. He glanced around, checking that Kahlan was still in the chair where he'd told her to stay. He saw, too, that Jillian was on the floor and guards were watching over all of them.

"Keep studying the books," Jagang told the two Sisters. "I'm going to the Ja'La games. Watch the girl."

He shoved Nicci out ahead of him and then snapped his fingers at Kahlan, indicating that he expected her to come along as well, and that he expected her to stay close to him. Kahlan snatched up her cloak and followed after him. She was at least glad that Jillian would not have to be anywhere near the mobs of soldiers, or Jagang. Of course, Jagang could exert his control through the Sisters and thus harm Jillian in any way he wished, anywhere he wished, any time he wished.

After throwing her cloak around her shoulders, Kahlan gave the worried Jillian a hand gesture to urge her to stay put. The girl's copper-colored eyes stared up at Kahlan as she returned a nod. She was afraid to be left alone. Kahlan sympathized, but she could offer no real protection even if Jillian was with her.

Outside the tent a few hundred well-armed guards quickly assembled into ranks, ready to escort the emperor. Such big men, with chain-mail armor and gleaming weapons, were an intimidating presence. Half a dozen of Kahlan's special guards, looking somewhat less intimidating but no less brutish, formed up around her. Jagang's meaty hand gripped Nicci's slender white arm, steering her through the spaces that opened in overlapping walls of the men.

Most of those men took a good long look at Nicci. She might have been Jagang's woman, but they still wanted a look. They were careful, though, to make sure that the emperor didn't see them leering. Those looks left Kahlan relieved that most of these men couldn't see her.

Although it was overcast, the clouds didn't look thick enough to threaten rain. It hadn't rained in quite a while and the ground had turned to dusty hardpan. In the flat, gray light the army camp looked all the darker, all that much grimier. Smoke from cook fires hung in the air, masking the stench to a degree.

As they marched through endless, noisy clusters of men and equipment, Jagang asked one of his more trusted personal guards about the Ja'La games. The man filled the emperor in on the various matches that had taken place since the last report, giving Jagang a rundown on each of the teams as he asked about them.

"Karg's team?" Jagang asked. "Have they been doing well?"

The guard nodded. "Undefeated so far. Their margin of victory yesterday wasn't as great as it has been, though."

Jagang's steely smile was as cold and the sky. "I hope they win today. Of all the teams come to challenge me, I hope my team gets to crush that team."

The guard gestured off to the left. "They're playing today—

over that way. This is the final game for them. With the way the matches have gone so far, if they win today then they alone will advance to the head of all the teams and you will have your wish, Excellency. If not, then there will have to be elimination games. But your team will play them if they are the winner of this match."

As they walked, with Jagang conversing with his guard, Nicci cast a brief glance back over her shoulder at Kahlan. Kahlan knew that she was thinking about the man Kahlan had told her about. Kahlan felt a flutter of anxiety.

As they took a course through the jumble of the camp in the direction the guard indicated, pushing their way though tightly packed throngs of men as they got ever closer to the Ja'La field, Kahlan could hear soldiers in the distance cheering and shouting encouragement to their favored team. Even this far back, with no chance to see the action, men waited for word on the score to be relayed back to them.

There were far more spectators than Kahlan had seen at the previous games. This was obviously an important match and she could see the excitement of the crowd. When a deafening roar suddenly went up she knew that one of the teams had scored. Men pushed in closer, jostling each other, eager for word on which team had scored.

As the guards growled orders or shoved men, the tight press of soldiers looked over their shoulders and then reluctantly parted to let the emperor's party through. With a wedge of big guards opening a pathway, they finally made it to an area that had been roped off for the emperor next to the field. Yet more of Jagang's guards who had gone on ahead had already formed a wall to each side to keep the men back.

Through the screen of spectators Kahlan caught flashes of men running across the field. The yells and shouts from the crowd made it hard for her to hear her own thoughts. She caught brief flashes of red paint. With the press of soldiers watching the game, and the wall of royal guards to each side, to say nothing of the bull of an emperor in front of her flanked by his huge personal guards, it was difficult to see anything other than short snatches of the action on the field.

Another wild cry rose from the crowd as a team scored. The roar shook the ground beneath Kahlan's feet.

Through the small gaps between guards, she spotted something different about this game. All the way around the edge of the field, in front of the spectators, men stood at even intervals, feet spread, hands clasped behind their backs. None wore shirts, apparently to display their powerful builds.

Kahlan had rarely seen the likes of such men. Each was a huge specimen. They all looked like statues, as if they had been smelted from the same iron ore and forged from ingots of white-hot steel.

As Jagang moved out in front, going to the edge of the field to see what was happening, Nicci, seeing the grim men Kahlan was looking at, leaned closer. "Jagang's team," she said under her breath.

Kahlan understood, then, what they were doing. The winner of this match would play the emperor's team. These men were not merely there to watch the tactics of the team they would face. They were there to intimidate the men before them, the men who would win the chance to play them. It was an open threat of pain to come.

Commander Karg spotted the newly arrived emperor and squeezed his way through the wall of guards. Kahlan had come to recognize the man by his unique pattern of snake-scale tattoos. He and Jagang exchanged pleasantries as cheers of encouragement went up for another play on the field.

"Your team seems to be faring well," Jagang said when the cheering died down a little.

Commander Karg glanced back over his shoulder at Nicci like a snake considering its prey. Her glare was already on the man. His knowing gaze swept over the length of her before his attention returned to Jagang.

"Well, Excellency, despite how good my team is, I'm well aware that your team is not merely good, but unbeaten. They are the best, of course."

The back of Jagang's shaved head and bull neck creased as he nodded. "Your team is unbeaten as well, but not truly tested against real competition. My men will easily defeat them. There is no doubt in my mind."

Commander Karg folded his arms, watching the play for a time. The crowd screamed with excitement as a cluster of men raced past, only to moan with disappointment as they apparently failed to make the score. Karg turned once more to the emperor.

"But if they do win against your team—"

"If they do," Jagang interrupted.

Karg smiled as he bowed his head. "If they do, then it would be a great accomplishment for a humble challenger, such as myself."

Jagang viewed his commander with good-natured suspicion. "A great accomplishment worthy of a great reward?"

Karg gestured out at the men on the field. "Well, Excellency, if my team were to win each of them would have a reward. Each would have the woman of his choice." He clasped his hands behind his back as he shrugged. "It seems only right that as the one who handpicked each player and runs such an accomplished team I would have a similar reward."

Jagang's deep chuckle was so lewd that it gave Kahlan a shiver.

"I suppose you're right," Jagang said. "Name her, then, and if you win, she is yours."

Karg rocked on his heels a moment, as if considering his choices.

"Excellency, if my team wins"—Commander Karg turned a sly smile back over his shoulder—"I would like to have Nicci in my bed."

Nicci's cold glare could have cut steel.

His amusement dying out, Jagang glanced back over his shoulder at the woman who had had his recent undivided attention.

"Nicci is not available."

The commander nodded as he went back to watching the game for a time. After the cheering for another play out on the field died down, he regarded Jagang with a sidelong glance.

"Since you are sure to win, Excellency, it's really only an insignificant promise of a reward, an idle bet. If you really believe that your team will certainly triumph, then I wouldn't have the pleasure of ever collecting such a reward."

"Then there would be no point in such a bet."

Karg gestured out at the Ja'La field. "You are sure of your team's success, aren't you, Excellency? Or are you having doubts?"

"All right, Karg," Jagang said at last, "if you win, she is yours for a time. But only for a time."

Commander bowed his head again. "Of course, Excellency. But, as we all know, you have no need to actually fear your team losing."

"No, I don't." Jagang's black eyes turned to Nicci. "You don't mind my little wager, do you, darlin?" His grin returned. "After all, it's only hypothetical, since my team does not lose."

Nicci arched an eyebrow. "As I told you when I first arrived, it doesn't really matter what I want, now, does it?"

Jagang's smile remained as he watched her for a moment. It was a smile that looked like it covered thoughts of bloody murder at her public insolence.

As the intensity of the play on the field built, the crowd all around started pushing forward, trying to get a better view. Jagang's guards reacted by driving men back, giving the emperor even more room. They wanted to be sure that they had the space they needed to protect him. The spectators, seeing the guards' ill humor, reluctantly moved back.

As Jagang and Commander Karg watched the game, becoming completely absorbed by the action of the field, Kahlan checked on her special guards and saw that they, too, were getting caught up in the game. They kept moving up, a little at a time, craning their necks, trying to get a better view. Kahlan edged closer to Nicci. As the royal guards put muscle in their effort and moved the spectators back, it gave Kahlan and Nicci a wider angle of view so that they could see more of both the field and the players.

"The team with the red paint is run by the man I told you about," Kahlan whispered. "I think he painted himself and all his men with the red paint so that no one would recognize him."

As players ran past they got their first clear view of the wild designs painted on all the men of the red team.

When Nicci saw those designs, she looked startled. "Dear spirits . . ."

She took a step forward to get a better look. Kahlan, concerned by Nicci's abrupt change in demeanor and obvious alarm, went with her.

That was when Kahlan spotted the man everyone called Ruben. He was running up from the left with the broe tucked tightly in against his chest as he dodged men diving for him.

Kahlan leaned closer to Nicci and gestured to the left, drawing her attention to the man called Ruben.

"That's him," Kahlan said.

Nicci leaned out a little to look where Kahlan pointed. When she saw him, the blood drained from her face. Kahlan had never seen anyone go so ashen so fast.

"Richard . . ."

The instant Kahlan heard the name she knew it was right. The name fit the man. She didn't know why, but it just fit him.

There was no doubt in her mind that Nicci was right. His name was not Ruben, it was Richard. She felt a strange sense of relief just to know his name, to know his real name.

Kahlan, fearing that Nicci might faint, put a supporting hand to the small of the woman's back. Beneath that hand she could feel Nicci's whole body trembling.

Dodging men as he ran headlong up the field, his wing men to each side, the man she now knew was named Richard saw Jagang out of the corner of his eye. As he ran, his gaze swept behind the emperor and met Kahlan's gaze. The connection, that recognition in his eyes, lifted her heart.

When Richard spotted Nicci standing next to her, he missed a step.

That instant of hesitation gave the men chasing him their chance. They smashed into him, slamming him to the ground. The impact was so violent that the broc went flying.

Richard's right wing man dropped his shoulder, plowing into the rivals, sending them sprawling.

Richard lay facedown, unmoving.

Kahlan's heart felt as if it rose up into her throat.

Just in time, the other wing man used an elbow to the head of a man about to crash down on top of Richard. As the opponent tumbled down to the side, Richard finally began to move. Seeing men flying past above him, he rolled away from the battle as he caught his breath.

In a moment he was on his feet, if somewhat wobbly at first.

It was the first mistake Kahlan had ever seen the man make.

Nicci's lower lip trembled as she stood frozen, staring at Richard. Tears had welled up in her blue eyes.

Kahlan suddenly wondered if it could be.

She discounted the possibility.

It simply wasn't possible.

CHAPTER 29

As he sat in the fading light, knees pulled up to his chest, listening to the ceaseless sounds of the enemy encampment out beyond the ring of wagons and guards, Richard heaved a despondent sigh. He ran the fingers of one hand back through his hair. He could hardly believe that Jagang had somehow captured Nicci. He couldn't imagine how such a thing could have happened. Seeing her with a Rada'Han around her neck made him sick.

It felt to Richard like the whole world was coming apart.

As much as he dreaded even considering the thought, it seemed like the Imperial Order was unstoppable. Those who wanted to decide for themselves how they would live their own lives were being methodically subjugated by the Order's uncountable followers, followers fanatically devoted to depressingly deluded beliefs, followers eager to enforce their faith on everyone else. Such a concept violated the very nature of faith, but that didn't matter to the true believers; all men had to bow and believe as they did, or die.

The believers in the teachings of the Order went where they wanted, when they wanted, slaughtering anyone in their way. They now controlled most of the New World as well as all of the Old World. The had even infiltrated far-off Westland, the place where he had grown up.

It felt to Richard like the whole world had gone mad.

Worse yet, Jagang also had at least two of the boxes of Orden. He always seemed to have everything well in hand.

Now he had Nicci.

But if it broke Richard's heart to see Nicci with the gold

ring of a slave through her lower lip, once again the captive of a man who had abused her so terribly in the past, it made his blood boil to see Kahlan also a captive of that same man.

Richard was also deeply dispirited to know that Kahlan didn't remember him. She mattered to him more than anything else in the world—she was his world. But now she didn't even remember his name.

Her strength and courage, her compassion, her intelligence, her wit, her special smile that she showed no one but him, were always in his thoughts and in his heart and would be until the day he died. He remembered the day they were married, remembered how much she loved him and how happy she had been just to be in his arms. But now she didn't remember any of it.

He would do anything to save her, to return her to who she really was, to give her back her life—to have her back in his. But who she was, was no longer there, within her. Chainfire had taken everything from them both.

It didn't really matter how much he wanted to live his own life with Kahlan, or how much he wanted other people to be able to live their own lives. The people of the Imperial Order had their own designs for mankind.

Right then, Richard could see only a bleak future.

Out of the corner of his eye he saw Johnrock scooting toward him. The heavy chain clattered as the big man pulled it across the hard, rocky ground.

"Ruben, you need to eat."

"I did eat."

Johnrock gestured to the half-eaten piece of ham balancing on Richard's knee. "Only half. You need your strength for tomorrow's game. You should eat."

Thinking about what was going to happen the next day only further served to tighten Richard's stomach with anxiety.

He picked up the thick piece of ham and held it out, offering it to Johnrock.

"I've had all I want. If you want it you can have the rest."

Johnrock grinned at his unexpected luck. His hand paused, his grin faltering. He looked up into Richard's eyes.

"You sure, Ruben?"

Richard nodded. Johnrock finally took the ham and tore off a big bite in his teeth. After he swallowed, he nudged Richard with an elbow.

"Are you all right, Ruben?"

Richard sighed. "I'm a prisoner, Johnrock. How could I be fine?"

Johnrock grinned, thinking Richard was just being funny. When Richard didn't smile, Johnrock turned serious.

"You got knocked in the head pretty good today." He leaned a little closer, lifting an eyebrow at Richard. "Not too smart of you."

Richard glanced over at the man. "What's that supposed to mean?"

"We nearly lost today."

"Nearly doesn't count. There are no ties on Ja'La. You either win or you lose. We won. That's what matters."

Johnrock backed away a little at Richard's tone. "If you say so, Ruben. But if you don't mind my asking, what happened?"

"I made a mistake."

Richard picked at a small stone half buried in the hard, dry ground. Johnrock chewed while he thought it over.

"I never saw you make a mistake like that before."

"It happens." Richard was angry at himself for making such a mistake—for letting his focus slip like that. He should have known better. He should have done better. "Hopefully, I won't make a mistake tomorrow. Tomorrow is the important day, the day that counts. I hope not to make a mistake tomorrow."

"I hope so, too. We've come a long way." Johnrock shook the stubby piece of ham at Richard to add emphasis to his point. "We're not just winning games but winning fans at the games. A lot of men root for us now. One more win and we will be champions. Then the whole crowd will cheer for us."

Richard glanced over at his wing man. "Did you see the size of those men on Jagang's team?"

"You don't need to be afraid." Johnrock flashed a crooked smile. "I'm big, too. I will protect you, Ruben."

Richard couldn't help smiling with his big wing man. "Thanks, Johnrock. I know you will. You always do."

"Bruce will, too."

Richard suspected he very well might. The man was an Imperial Order soldier, but he was also a member of a powerful team with a reputation—Ruben's team, as most of his men called it. They didn't call it that in front of Commander Karg, though. The spectators called them the red team, and Commander Karg called it his team, but among themselves the players called it "Ruben's team." He was their point man. They had come to trust him. Bruce, like some of the other soldiers on the team, had at first been reluctant to wear the symbols in red paint, but now he wore them proudly. Other soldiers cheered him when he came out onto the field.

"Tomorrow's game is going to be . . . dangerous, Johnrock."

Johnrock nodded knowingly. "I intend to make it so."

Richard smiled again. "You watch yourself, will you?"

"My job is to watch you."

Richard rolled the small stone he'd pried up from the ground around in his loose fist as he chose his words carefully.

"A time comes when a man has to watch out for himself. There are times when—"

"Snake-face is coming."

Richard's cut off his words at the low warning. He looked up and saw Commander Karg marching through the line of guards. The man did not look happy.

Richard tossed the stone away and leaned back on his hands as Commander Karg came to a halt right above him. Dust rose around the man's boots. He glared down at Richard as he planted his fists on his hips.

"What was that all about today, Ruben?"

Richard peered up at the tattoos of snake scales that were just still visible in the fading light. "You didn't appreciate that we won?"

Instead of answering, the commander turned the glare on Johnrock. Johnrock got the message and scooted away, back past the opposite end of the wagon, until he reached the end of his chain tether and could go no farther. The commander squatted down in front of Richard. The tattoos of scales moved in a way that looked to Richard like real snake skin.

"You know what I mean. What was that foolishness all about?"

"I got clobbered. It's what the other team is always trying to do. It's bound to happen occasionally."

"I've seen you try your best and come up just a little short and not be able to make a score, or make every effort to evade a charge of blockers and not quite make it clear, but I've never seen you make a foolish mistake."

"Sorry," Richard said. He couldn't see the point in arguing about it.

"I want to know why."

Richard shrugged. "Like you said, it was a foolish mistake." Richard was more angry with himself than the commander could ever understand. He couldn't afford a mistake like that tomorrow. "We won, though, so that means we will play the emperor's team. That's what I promised you—that I would get your team to a match with the emperor's team."

The commander's eyes turned up, gazing at the first stars of the night for a moment, before speaking. "You do remember being captured, don't you?"

"I remember."

His eyes turned back down to fix a stare on Richard. "Then you remember that by all rights you should have been killed that day. I let you live on the condition that you do your best to win my team this championship. Today, that was not your best. You nearly threw away my team's chance to win with a stupid move."

Richard didn't shy away from the man's gaze. "Don't worry, Commander. Tomorrow I will do my best. I promise."

"Good." Snake-face finally smiled, though it was a cold curve of his mouth. "Good. You win tomorrow, Ruben, and you get your woman."

"I know."

The smile turned sly. "You win tomorrow and I get my woman."

Richard wasn't really interested. "Is that right?"

Commander Karg nodded. "If we win, that shapely blonde with Emperor Jagang will be mine."

Richard looked up with a dark frown of his own. "What are you talking about? Jagang isn't going to let you have someone like that, a woman marked as his."

"It's a little wager with the emperor. He's so confident that his team will win that I got him to bet his most prized woman on the outcome. Her name is Nicci. He calls her his slave queen. Jagang doesn't want to lose her to me, she's rather . . . an obsession of his. But I think you can win her for me." His eyes focused into his own distant, lustful thoughts. "I would like that very much—as much as Jagang wouldn't like it, I expect." He returned to the matter at hand and shook a finger at Richard's face. "You had better win for your own sake as well."

"So that I can have my choice of a woman?"

"So that you can live. You lose tomorrow and you will have the death you should have had after you killed all of those men of mine." Commander Karg's sly smile returned. "But if you win, you will have your choice of a woman, as promised."

Richard met the man's gaze with a glare. "I already promised that I would do my best tomorrow. I always keep my promises."

The commander nodded. "Good. You win tomorrow, Ruben, and we'll all be happy." He chuckled. "Well, Jagang won't be happy—not one bit. Come to think of it, I don't think Nicci will be any too happy, either, but then that's not really my concern."

"And the emperor? Don't you think he will care?"

"Oh he will care, all right." Karg chuckled. "Jagang will go crazy when he has to let me have Nicci for my bed. I have a few scores to settle with that woman. I intend to enjoy it."

Richard managed to remain silent and look composed, despite the fact that he wanted to whip the chain around the man's neck and strangle him.

Commander Karg rose up. "You win that game, Ruben."

Richard glared at the man's back as he watched him striding away.

After he was sure that the commander was gone, Johnrock held a length of chain slack to keep it from pulling on the collar around his neck, and scooted back close to Richard.

"What did he say, Ruben?"

"He wants us to win."

Johnrock snorted a laugh. "I bet he does. As the owner of a champion team he can have whatever he wants."

"That's what I'm afraid of."

"What?"

"Get some rest, Johnrock. Tomorrow is going to be an eventful day."

CHAPTER 30

Richard woke abruptly from a light sleep. Even in the dead of night the camp was alive with sound and activity. Everywhere, it seemed, there were men yelling, laughing, and swearing. Metal clanged, horses whinnied, and mules brayed. In the distance Richard could see the ramp, along with lines of men and wagons, lit by torches. Even in the middle of the night the construction continued without pause.

But none of that was what had awakened him. Something closer in had caught his attention.

He saw shadows slipping through the ring of guards and the circle of low supply wagons that marked out his prison. He counted four of the dark figures stealing silently through the darkness. A quick check to the sides revealed another off to the right. He wondered if they had really snuck through unseen or if the guards had allowed them to pass.

By their size, Richard knew who they were. After what Commander Karg had told him about his bet with Jagang, Richard had been expecting visitors. It was the last thing he needed, but it wasn't like he had any choice in the matter.

What really worried him was that, chained to the wagon, his options were limited. He could hardly hide. He certainly couldn't run. Fighting five men, maybe more, was not something he wanted to have to do before the game the next day. He couldn't afford to be injured—least of all now.

He glanced to the side and saw that Johnrock was not close. The big man was lying on his side, facing away, sound asleep. Calling out to his sleeping wing man would cost Richard the only thing he had going for him: surprise. The men coming for him thought he was asleep. For all Richard knew, if he called out to Johnrock the five might first go over and cut Johnrock's throat so that they could go to work on Richard without worry of interruption.

The four big men slipped in close, forming a semicircle. They obviously knew that his chain would keep him from escaping, and blocking him would keep him from having room to maneuver. By how quiet they were being, they appeared to still think he was asleep.

One of the men, arms straight out to each side for balance, took a long step in and threw a kick at Richard's head as if he were kicking the broc in an effort to keep it away from an opponent. Richard was ready. He rolled to the side and then whipped the length of chain around the man's ankle. With all his might he yanked back the chain. It pulled the man's feet out from under him. He landed on his back with a heavy thud, banging his head on the ground.

"On your feet," one of the other men growled now that he knew Richard was awake.

Richard gripped a folded length of chain on the ground behind him, keeping it out of sight, but he didn't get up.

"Or?" he asked.

"Or we kick your head in where you sit. Your choice, standing or sitting, you're going to get hurt just the same."

"So, you really are afraid—just like everyone says."

The man paused for a moment. "What are you talking about?"

"You're afraid that you'll lose to us tomorrow," Richard said.

"We're afraid of nothing," another of the shadowy figures said.

"You wouldn't be here unless you were afraid."

"It has nothing to do with us being afraid of anything," the first man said. "We're only doing as His Excellency asks of us."

"Ah," Richard said. "So it's Jagang who fears that we'll beat you. That tells me a lot. It should tell you something, too—that we're better than you and you can't win in a fair match. Jagang knows it as well, that's why he sent you—because you're not good enough to beat us at Ja'La."

As another man, cursing under his breath at the delay, reached out to grab him, Richard swung the looped section of chain from behind his back as hard as he could. It caught the man square in the side of his face. He spun away, crying out from the unexpected shock of pain.

As a third man charged in, Richard dropped back onto his shoulders. With all his strength he kicked up into the center of the man's gut, using the man's falling weight against him. The blow rammed the man back at the same time as it drove the wind from his lungs.

The first man was already on his feet again. The man who had taken the chain across his face was still writhing on the ground. The other, holding an arm across his middle, rolled to his feet, catching his breath, eager for revenge. The fourth and fifth men came in from opposite sides.

Two of the downed men were up, eager to rejoin the fight. Now four strong, the men charged in all at once. There were too many hands grabbing for the chain all at once for Richard to keep them from getting ahold of it. As he tried to whip it out of their reach, one of the men lunged and managed to capture the heavy links in both hands.

Richard swung his leg around, knocking one of the remaining men's feet out from under him. He landed heavily on a shoulder. The other two seized the chain and then grunted with mighty effort as they yanked it back. The slack in the chain snapped taut. The sudden jerk felt like it might rip Richard's head off as it flung him sprawling on his face. The choking pain in his throat was so severe that for a second he thought the iron collar might have crushed his windpipe.

While Richard was momentarily stunned, fighting the rising sense of panic, one of the men kicked him in the ribs. The blow felt like it might have broken a rib. Richard tried to spin away but they again yanked the chain back from the other direction, twisting the iron collar around his neck and flipping him over backward. The iron burned as it bit into his flesh.

The guards in the distance remained where they were, watching. They would not be eager to get involved. After all, these were men from the emperor's team.

As it snapped taut, Richard seized the chain as he got to his knees, holding tight, trying to keep the men from using the chain and collar to break his neck. Three of the men gave a mighty pull. They managed to yank Richard off balance and over onto his back.

A boot came down toward his face. Richard turned his head aside just in time. Dust and dirt flew. Fists and boots came crashing in from all directions.

Holding the chain with one hand, Richard used his other to knock one man back. He blocked the punch from another and elbowed a third in the thigh, momentarily dropping the man to a knee. Still, as fast as he could block or escape their blows, yet more rained in. With the men holding tension on the chain he couldn't maneuver and he dared not let go of the chain altogether.

Richard pulled himself into a defensive crouch, protecting his midsection, making himself as small a target as he could, getting as much of a lead in the chain as he could. One of the men cocked an arm and threw a punch. Richard let go of the chain and used his left forearm to deflect the blow. At the same time he sprang up inside the man's defenses and rammed an elbow up into the attacker's jaw with bone-cracking force. The man staggered back.

Now that he had a little more slack in the chain, Richard ducked under a punch and kicked sideways into the man's knee. The blow did enough damage to draw a cry of pain and cause the man to start to hobble back to get out of danger, but Richard immediately used the opportunity to kick the side of the man's other knee, folding his legs under. As he came crashing down, Richard brought his knee up into the man's face.

As another punch flew in, Richard dodged to the left and grabbed the man's wrist. With an iron grip on the wrist, he slammed the heel of his left hand into the back of the man's elbow. The joint popped. The man screamed as he pulled his dislocated arm away.

Another punch flew in. Richard deflected it across, past his face, then, as the man quickly punched with the other fist, Richard deflected the arm in the opposite direction, over the attacker's other arm. With the man's arms crossed and tension on the elbow preventing any escape, Richard used the leverage on the crooked arm to flip the big man over.

Even with the success he was having, it was difficult to fight the men off, because the chain around his neck prevented him from moving effectively. He knew, though, that, despite the difficulty, he had no choice but to think of what he could do, not what he couldn't do.

It was also difficult for Richard to fight the men because he dared not use the kinds of blows he would have liked to do. If he killed any of the emperor's players it would, in all likelihood, be an excuse for Jagang to charge Richard with murder and have him put to death. Jagang hardly needed an excuse to execute a man, but Richard's team was becoming well known and if Richard was executed the soldiers in the camp would suspect that it was because Jagang knew his team couldn't beat Richard's team. Richard doubted that Jagang cared a great deal about what anyone said, but the excuse of murder would certainly give him justification.

If Commander Karg's point man was dead, Jagang wouldn't have to worry about losing Nicci to him. Jagang's team was formidable, and stood a good chance of winning, but without Richard as point man there was no doubt that the emperor's team would be victorious.

At the same time, Jagang might not need to bother having Richard executed. His men seemed intent on accomplishing the task themselves. They wouldn't be punished if they killed Richard in a fight. Who with any authority would ever even know, except Commander Karg, and Richard didn't think that even Karg would dare to make an issue of a captive man dying in a fight. Men in the camp died in fights all the time. Such fights were common enough and, as far as Richard knew, only rarely punished. This would just be passed off as an argument gone bad.

Worse, though, if Richard was killed then Kahlan would have no chance. She would be forever lost to the Chainfire spell, a living phantom of her former self.

That thought alone made Richard fight with a fury, even if

he had to be careful to strike with the intent of stopping rather than killing. Pulling blows wasn't at all easy to do in the heat of a fight for his own life and Richard was taking nearly as much punishment as he was dealing out.

When one of the men again threw a punch, Richard seized the man's arm. Grunting with the effort, he ducked under the extended arm, twisting it around, and flipped the man to the ground.

As Richard himself was knocked to the ground, he scooped up a length of chain and spun, whipping it across the face of one of the men. The sound of steel against flesh and bone was sickening. Another man kicked Richard hard enough to drive the wind from his lungs.

The blows Richard was taking were wearing him down. Even though the fight had only started moments before it seemed like hours. The furious effort to defend himself was exhausting him.

Just as another man lunged at him, the man was suddenly jerked back.

Johnrock had thrown a loop of his own chain around the man's neck. As the man clawed at the chain, struggling to breathe, Johnrock pulled him back away from Richard. In a fury of fists, feet, and flailing chain, Johnrock helped Richard drive the men back.

Someone else, yelling angry threats, appeared in the darkness, running in through the ring of guards. Richard was so busy fighting off the men, trying to deflect a flurry of fists, he couldn't tell who it was.

All of a sudden the new man seized one of the attackers by the hair and threw him back. In the light from nearby torches Richard saw the tattoos of scales. Commander Karg yelled that the five men were cowards and threatened to have them beheaded. He kicked at them as he ordered them to get out of his team's quarters.

All five scrambled to their feet and abruptly vanished back into the night. It was suddenly over. Richard lay in the dirt, not even trying to get up.

Commander Karg angrily pointed a finger at the guards.

"If you men let anyone else get through, I'll have you all skinned alive! Do you understand?"

The guards back by the ring of wagons, looking sheepish and worried, all answered that they understood. They swore that no one else would get through.

As he lay panting in pain, trying to catch his breath, Richard hardly heard the commander's yelling. The fight had been brief, but the blows the powerful men from Jagang's team had landed had done damage.

Johnrock knelt down, easing Richard over onto his back. "Ruben, are you all right?"

Richard carefully moved his arms, lifted his knees, and gingerly rolled his foot, testing his throbbing ankle, taking appraisal of his limbs, checking to see if they all worked, checking to see if he could move everything. He hurt all over. He was pretty sure that he wasn't crippled, but he didn't try to get up just yet. He didn't think that right then he could have.

"I think so," he said.

"What was that all about?" Johnrock demanded of Snake-face.

Commander Karg shrugged. "Ja'La dh Jin."

Johnrock paused in surprise at the answer. "Ja'La dh Jin?"

"It's the Game of Life. What do you expect?"

By his deepening frown, Johnrock apparently didn't understand. Richard did.

The Game of Life was about more than just what happened on the field. It included everything that surrounded the game—what came before and what came after. It was strategy and intimidation beforehand, the play itself out on the field, and what resulted from the outcome of that game. Because of the rewards after the game, what took place before became part of the game itself. Ja'La dh Jin wasn't just the game on the field, it encompassed everything.

Life was about survival. If you lived, if you died, all depended on what you did in life. Survival was what mattered. That made everything all a part of the game, just as everything in life mattered. A woman camp follower stabbing a player on an opposing team so that her team would win, painting the men with red paint, or cracking the skull of the point man on the other team in the middle of the night was all part of the game of life.

If you were to live, then you had to fight to live. It was as simple as that. That was the Game of Life. Life and death were the reality that counted, not how someone followed a prescribed set of rules. If you died because you failed to protect yourself, you couldn't cry foul after you were dead. You had to fight for your own life, fight to win, no matter the circumstances.

Commander Karg stood. "Get some rest—both of you. Tomorrow decides if you live or if you die."

The man headed for the ring of guards, yelling at them as he went.

"Thanks, Johnrock," Richard said after the commander had gone. "You showed up just in time."

"I told you that I'd watch out for you."

"You did good, Johnrock."

Johnrock grinned. "You just do good tomorrow. Eh, Ruben?"

Richard nodded as he gulped air. "I promise."

CHAPTER 31

Verna glanced up when the Mord-Sith marched up to the other side of the small desk and came to a halt.

"What is it, Cara?"

"Any word in the journey book?"

Verna sighed heavily as she set down the watch reports she had been studying. They indicated that there was increasing activity surrounding the Ja'La matches down in the Order's encampment. Verna remembered what seemed like a lifetime ago, back at the Palace of the Prophets, when Warren had first told her all about Ja'La Day, about how Emperor Jagang was bringing Ja'La dh Jin to all of the Old World. Like so many things, Warren had studied Ja'La dh Jin and knew a great deal about it.

She supposed that she wasn't so much reading the reports as she was reminiscing about Warren. How she missed him. How she missed so many people who had been lost in this war.

"No, I'm afraid not," Verna said. "I left a message in the journey book in case Ann should happen to take a look in hers, but she hasn't answered, yet."

Cara tapped an insistent finger on the desktop. "It's obvious that something has happened to Nicci and Ann."

"I don't disagree." Verna spread her hands. "But we can't do anything about it if we don't even know what happened to them. What are we to do? Where are we to look? We've searched the palace but the place is so vast that there is no telling how many places we might have overlooked."

Cara's expression was part anger, part worry, and part impatience. With this on top of Richard being nowhere to be found, Verna understood all too well how the woman felt.

"Have your Sisters found anything at all unusual?"

Verna shook her head. "The other Mord-Sith?"

"Nothing," Cara said under her breath as she went back to pacing. She mulled over the situation for a moment, then turned back to Verna. "I still think that whatever happened had to have happened the night they went down to the tomb."

"I'm not saying that you're wrong, Cara, but we're not even sure that they ever made it down to the tombs. What if they changed their mind for some reason and went somewhere else first? What if someone brought a message or something to Ann, and they rushed off somewhere else? What if something happened before they even went down to the tomb?

"I don't think so," Cara said as she folded her arms and paced. "I still think something down there is wrong. Something down in the tombs just feels wrong."

Verna didn't question what could be "wrong." She had already done that to no avail. Cara didn't know what was wrong. She simply had a vague feeling that something was not right down in the tombs.

"Your feeling doesn't give us much to go on. Maybe if it was something a little more specific."

"Don't you think I've tried to think of what could be the cause of it?"

Verna watched Cara slowly pace. "Well, if you don't know what's giving you this feeling about the place, maybe there is someone else who would know why you think something is wrong down there."

"That sounds like Lord Rahl. He always says to think of the solution, not the problem." Cara sighed. "But no one ever goes down—" She spun around and snapped her fingers. "That's it!"

Verna frowned suspiciously. "What's it?"

"Someone who knows the place."

"Who?"

Cara put both hands on the desk and leaned in with a cunning grin. "The crypt staff. Darken Rahl had people who took care of the tombs—took care of his father's tomb, anyway."

"What's this about the tombs?" Berdine asked as she strolled into the room.

Nyda, a tall, blond, blue-eyed Mord-Sith, was with her. Verna saw Adie bringing up the rear.

"It just occurred to me that the crypt staff would know about the tombs," Cara said.

Berdine nodded. "You're probably right. Some of the writing down in the tombs is in High D'Haran, so Darken Rahl sometimes took me with him down there to help him with things he was having difficulty translating.

"Darken Rahl was quite picky about how his father's tomb was cared for. He had people put to death for failing to properly care for the place. His father's tomb, anyway."

"It's just stone vaults." Verna was incredulous. "There's nothing down there—no furniture, drapes, or carpeting. What is there to be picky about?"

Berdine rested a hip against the desk as she folded her arms and leaned in as if she was full of gossip.

"Well, for one thing he insisted that fresh white roses always fill the vases. They had to be pure white. He also demanded that the torches always be kept burning. The crypt staff was not suppose to allow a rose petal to remain on the floor, or a torch that went out to go cold without being replaced with a fresh, burning one.

"If Darken Rahl was visiting his father's crypt and he saw a rose petal on the floor, or if one of the torches burned out, he would get furious. People on the crypt staff were beheaded for such infractions, so, as you can imagine, they were quite attentive to their duties down there. They would be familiar with the place."

"Then we need to go have a talk with the crypt staff," Verna said.

"You can try," Berdine said, "but I don't think they will have much to say."

Verna stood. "Why not?"

"Darken Rahl feared that they might speak ill of his dead father while down in the crypt"—Berdine made a snipping motion with two fingers—"so he had their tongues cut out."

"Dear Creator," Verna muttered as she touched her fingers to her forehead. "That man was a monster."

"Darken Rahl is long dead," Cara said, "but the crypt staff must still be around. They would know the place better than anyone." She started for the door. "Let's go see what we can find out."

"I think you're right," Verna said as she made her way around the desk. "If we're able to get any information out of them it will at least settle the matter. If there really is anything wrong down there we need to know about it. If not, then we need to put our efforts elsewhere."

Adie caught Verna's arm. "I only came to tell you that I be leaving."

Verna blinked in surprise. "Leaving? Why?"

"It has been troubling me that there be no one at the Wizard's Keep. What if Richard goes there seeking our help? He will need to know what be happening. He will need to know that the Keep be shut down. He will need to know what Nicci has done by putting the boxes in play in his name. He will need to know about Ann and Nicci vanishing. He may even need gifted help. There should be someone there if he shows up at the Keep."

Verna gestured off to the west before staring into Adie's completely white eyes. "But the Keep is closed up. Where would you stay?"

Adie's broad smile pushed aside a network of fine wrinkles. "Aydindril be deserted. The Confessors' Palace be empty. I will hardly want for a roof. Besides, I be at home in the woods, not in this"—she waggled a finger at her surroundings—"this place. It weakens my gift the same as any other gifted person but a Rahl. I have difficulty using my gift here so that I might see. It be uncomfortable for me here. I would rather do something than sit here, useless in the darkness this place imposes."

"You are hardly useless," Verna objected. "You helped with a number of things we found in the books."

Adie held up a hand to silence her. "You would have figured it out without me. I be useless here. I be an old woman who be underfoot."

"That's hardly true, Adie. All of the Sisters value your knowledge. They're told me so."

"Maybe, but I would feel better if I felt I had a purpose rather than wandering around this, this"—she again gestured vaguely around her—"great stone maze."

Verna sadly relented. "I understand."

"I'll miss you," Berdine said.

Adie nodded. "True. And I shall miss you, too, child, and the talks we've had."

Cara cast a suspicious look at Berdine but said nothing.

Adie reached out and gripped Nyda's shoulder. "Nyda be here for you."

"Don't worry, I'll keep her company," Nyda said as she gazed at Berdine. "I won't let her get lonely."

Berdine smiled appreciatively at Nyda and nodded to Adie.

"We're surrounded by more enemy men than stars in the sky," Cara said. "How do you expect that a blind woman is going to get through all of them?"

Adie pursed her lips as she gathered her thoughts. "Richard Rahl be a smart man, hmm?"

Cara looked surprised by the question, but she answered it anyway. "Yes." She folded her arms. "Sometimes too smart for his own good."

Adie smiled at the last part. "He be smart, so you always follow his orders?"

Cara snorted a brief laugh. "Of course not."

Adie's eyebrows lifted in mock wonder. "No? Why not? He be your leader. You just said that he be a smart man."

"Smart, yes. But he doesn't always see the danger around him."

"But you do?"

Cara nodded. "I can see danger he cannot."

"Ah. So you can see dangers that his sighted eyes cannot?"

Cara smiled. "Sometimes Lord Rahl is as blind as a bat."

"Bats also see in the dark, do they not?"

Cara sighed unhappily. "I suppose so." She went back to the subject at hand. "But Lord Rahl needs me to see the dangers all around him that he can't see."

With a long, thin finger, Adie tapped Cara's temple. "You see with this, yes? See the dangers to him?" Adie arched an eyebrow. "See dangers that eyes alone cannot see? Sometimes not having eyes lets me see more."

Cara frowned. "That may all be well and good, but still, how do you think you are going to be able to get past the Order's army? Surely you can't be thinking of trying to walk through the camp."

"That be exactly what I must do." Adie waved a finger toward the ceiling. "There be clouds today. Tonight will be a dark night. With the thick overcast, once the sun goes down and before the moon rises, it be black as pitch. On such a night, those with eyes cannot see, but I be sighted in the darkness in ways they are not. I will be able to walk among them and they will not see me. If I keep to myself, and keep away from those who are awake and watchful, I will be no more than a shadow among shadows. No one will pay me any mind."

"They have fires," Berdine pointed out.

"The fire will blind their eyes to what be in the darkness. When there is fire men watch what is in the light, not what is in the darkness."

"And what if by chance some of those soldiers do happen to see you, or hear you, or something?" Cara asked. "Then what?"

Adie smiled just a little as she leaned toward the Mord-Sith. "You would not want to meet a sorceress in the dark, child."

Cara looked worried enough by the answer not to object.

"I don't know, Adie," Verna said. "I really would like you to be here, and safe."

"Let her go," Cara said.

When everyone looked at her in surprise, she went on. "What if she's right? What if Lord Rahl does show up at the Keep? He will need to know everything that has happened. He will need to know that he shouldn't enter the Keep or he could get himself killed by the traps Zedd set in the place.

"What if Lord Rahl needs her help? If she thinks he might need her, then she should be there for him. I wouldn't want anyone to stop me from helping him."

"Besides," Berdine said as she shared a sad look with the old sorceress, "there is nothing safe about this place. She will probably be safer than any of us here. When that army down there finally gets in the palace, it's going to be anything but safe in here. It's going to be one long bloody nightmare."

Adie smiled as she reached out and touched Berdine's cheek. "The good spirits will watch over you, child, and all those here."

Verna wished she believed that.

She wondered what she was doing being the Prelate of the Sisters of the Light if she didn't.

CHAPTER 32

As he finished touching up their red battle paint, Richard tried not to let the men see how painful his injuries really were. He didn't want anything to distract them from the job ahead.

His ankle throbbed, his left shoulder was sore, and the hits he'd taken to his head had left his neck muscles aching. After the brief but furious fight he hadn't been able to get much sleep. As far as he could tell, though, nothing was broken.

He mentally set the pain and weariness aside. It didn't matter if he hurt, or if he was tired. He had a job to do. It only mattered if he did it, if he succeeded.

If he failed he would have all eternity to sleep.

"Today we have our chance for glory," Johnrock said.

Richard, holding Johnrock's chin, turned the man's head to the side a little so that he could see better in the failing light. He didn't say anything. He leaned to the side and dunked his finger in the bucket of red paint and then added a symbol for watchfulness above the one for power that was already there. He wished he knew a symbol for common sense so he could paint it all over Johnrock's skull.

"Don't you think, Ruben?" Johnrock pressed. "Today we have our chance for glory?"

The rest of the men all listened quietly for what Richard might say.

"You know better, Johnrock. Get those thoughts out of your head."

Richard paused in his work and swept the finger, coated in fresh red paint, around at all the eyes watching him.

"All of you know better, or at least you should. Forget

thoughts of glory. Those men on the emperor's team aren't thinking of glory right now—they're thinking of killing you. Do you understand that? They want to kill you.

"This is a day we have to fight to stay alive. That's the glory I want: life. That's the glory I want for all of you. I want you to live."

Johnrock's face twisted in disbelief. "But Ruben, after those men tried to bash in your head last night you must want to settle the score."

The men all knew about the attack. Johnrock had told them all about it—told them how their point man had fought off five of the big men all by himself. Richard hadn't disputed the account, but he wasn't letting on as to how much he hurt. He wanted them worrying about their own necks, not wondering if he could hold up his end.

"Yes, I want to win," Richard said, "but not for glory, or to settle a score. I'm a captive. I was brought here to play. If we win I live—simple as that. That's all that really matters: living. Ja'La players—both captives and soldiers—die in games all the time; in that sense we are equals. The only true glory in winning in these games is the part about living."

Some of the other captive men nodded their understanding.

"Aren't you just a little worried about defeating the emperor's team?" Bruce, his left wing man, asked. "Beating the emperor's team might not be the right thing to do. After all, they represent the power of the Imperial Order, and the emperor. Beating them might be seen as prideful and arrogant, even sacrilegious."

All eyes turned to Richard.

Richard met the man's gaze. "I thought that under the Order's teachings everyone was equal."

Bruce stared back a moment. A smile finally spread across his face. "You have a point, Ruben. They are just men, like us. I guess we ought to win, then."

"I guess so," Richard said.

At that, just as Richard had taught them, the men, as one, let out a collective bellow of agreement, a brief, deep roar of team spirit. It was a small thing, but it served to bond the men, to make them feel that, while they were all very different individuals, they all had a common goal.

"Now," Richard went on, "we haven't seen the emperor's team play, so we don't know their tacties, but they've watched us play. As far as I've been able to tell, teams don't usually change the way they play, so they will be expecting us to do the same things they've seen us do in the past, That's going to be one of our advantages.

"Remember the new plays we devised for each signal. Don't fall back to the old plays for a signal or it will cross us up. Those new tactics are our best chance to keep them off balance. Concentrate on doing your part in each of those moves. That's what will get us points.

"Remember, too, that these men, besides wanting to win, are going to be trying to hurt us. The teams we've been playing knew that what they gave they got back double. These men are different. They know that if they lose they will be put to death, just like the the emperor's last team was when they lost. They have no incentive to play clean. They have every incentive to try to tear our heads off.

"There is no doubt in my mind that they're going to try to take out our players, so be ready for it."

"You're the one they're going to be trying to take down," Bruce pointed out. "You're the point man. You're the one they need to stop. They even tried to eliminate you last night before you could reach the Ja'La field."

"That's all true, but as point man I at least have you and Johnrock protecting me. Most of you men have no protection but your wits and your skill. I think they're just as likely to go after one of you, first, so don't let your guard down for a second. Keep an eye on each other and intervene if need be."

In the distance Richard could hear the rhythmic chanting of countless soldiers eager for the match to start. It sounded like the entire camp was chanting. Richard suspected that every man not forced to work on the ramp, while if not all able to actually see the match, would probably at least be waiting for word to relay back to them.

More men than usual were going to be able to see this game

because the emperor had directed the work gangs, who needed material for the ramp anyway, to scoop dirt from a large area to create a bowl in the Azrith Plain. The new Ja'La field, with its vast, gently sloped sides, would enable far more men than ever before to be able to watch Ja'La games.

Richard had thought that their game with the emperor's team would have been held that afternoon, that it would have already taken place, but the day had worn on as other teams played in games leading up to the match for the championship. The games, after all, were show for the soldiers. The new Ja'La field was the emperor's statement—right below the People's Palace—that the Order was here to stay and now owned the place.

Richard glanced up at the iron gray overcast. The last feathery violets of the sunset had vanished. It was going to be a dark night.

Richard hadn't counted on it being this late when the game started, but night suited him just fine. In fact, it was the one unexpected bit of good fortune in the face of the monumental obstacles that lay before him. He was used to the dark. As a woods guide he often walked the trails of his woods with only the moon and stars to light his way. Sometimes it was just stars. Richard was comfortable in darkness.

There was more to seeing than just using one's eyes.

While in some ways those times in the woods seemed like only days ago, in other ways it also seemed like forever ago, almost like another life. He was a long way from his Hartland woods. A long way from the peace and security he had known.

A long way from having the woman he loved back in his arms.

As Richard was finishing with Johnrock's paint, he spotted Commander Karg making his way through the ring of guards. After their complicity in the treachery of the night before, the men involved stayed well clear of the scowling officer. There were a few new faces among the guards, no doubt more trusted overseers. Commander Karg was leading an escort of troops, men dedicated to watching over the captive players to make sure that they played Ja'La and nothing more.

Mostly, though, the soldiers were there to watch over Richard. They were his special guards.

Last in line to be freed from his bonds, Richard was finally able to rub his sore neck after Commander Karg finally unlocked his iron collar. Without the heavy chain weighing him down, Richard felt light, almost as if he might float up into the air. It gave him a feeling of being weightless and inhumanly fast. He embraced the sensation, making it part of him.

The chanting of the soldiers in the distance had a primeval feel to it. It was beyond eerie. It gave Richard goose bumps.

The spectators were expecting blood.

This night, they were going to get their wish.

As he followed Commander Karg, leading his team toward the Ja'La field, Richard put the growing noise out of his mind. He found a quiet center of focus.

As they moved through passages in the encampment lined with throngs of soldiers, hands all around reached out, wanting to touch the members of the team as they passed. Some of the men on Richard's team smiled, waved, and touched the extended hands of the soldiers. Johnrock, being the biggest man and easy to spot, was the center of much of the attention. He grinned, waved, shook hands, and soaked it all in as he marched along. It seemed to Richard that what Johnrock had always wanted more than anything else was the adoration of the crowd. He loved pleasing them.

Words of both encouragement and hatred cascaded in from all sides. Richard turned his eyes ahead, ignoring the soldiers and shouting as he passed.

"Are you nervous, Ruben?" Commander Karg asked over his shoulder.

"Yes."

Karg gave him a patronizing smile. "That will go away when it starts."

"I know," Richard said as he glared out from under his brow.

The vast depression of the Ja'La field was a cauldron of noise, the spectators a froth of faces over a churning sea of black.

The crowd out beyond the dense ring of flickering torches

at the edge of the field chanted—not words, but a guttural grunt meant to express not only encouragement for the players but for the spectacle itself. In time with the chanting the throng stamped a foot. The deep, primordial noise could be not only heard, but felt in the ground beneath Richard's feet, almost like rolling thunder. The effect was deafening and, in a way, intoxicating.

It was a primal call to violence.

Richard was already lost to those feelings. He let the raw, savage sounds feed those passions he had already unleashed within himself. As he made his way through the seething masses of men, he was in his own private world, lost to inner drives.

Commander Karg brought the team to a halt at one end of the field just before the torches. Richard saw archers, with arrows nocked, stationed all around the field. Near midfield, to his right, he spotted the area reserved for the emperor.

Jagang wasn't there.

Richard's insides tightened with a knot of panic. He had thought that, surely, Jagang would be at this game, that Kahlan would be near.

But the roped-off section was vacant.

Richard schooled his emotions, setting aside his dismay. Jagang would not miss this game. Sooner or later he would show up.

When the emperor's team strode onto the opposite end of the field the crowd erupted in a thunderous roar. These men were the best the Order had to offer. They were heroes to countless thousands of spectators. These were the men who could vanquish all who came before them, the players who crushed all opposition, the champions who were most deserving of victory. Many regarded the team as a tangible representation of their own power and virility.

As Richard and his men waited outside the torches, the other team, looking not merely determined but dangerous, stalked around the perimeter of the field, acknowledging the roar of the crowd with nothing more than bloodthirsty looks. The crowd loved such a visage of hate and menace, of things to come.

When the emperor's team finished circling the field and finally gathered toward the other side of the field to wait for the challengers, the archers and other dedicated guards parted. Commander Karg waved Richard and his team through the gap in the line. As Richard passed, the commander whispered a warning to Richard that he had better win.

Richard stepped out onto the field. His concern for his plan was eased when the resounding cheers for his team were nearly as deafening as they had been for the emperor's team. In the many games they had played since coming to the Imperial Order's encampment, Richard's team had won every game, and in so doing the respect of many. It didn't hurt that Richard was well known for having killed an opposing point man. Probably even more than that, though, was the sight of the team covered with frightening designs in red paint. It was theater that fit the games. Richard was counting on that support.

He was also troubled when he finally got a good look at all of his opponents. They were some of the biggest men Richard had ever seen. They reminded him of Egan and Ulic, the personal guards to the Lord Rahl. It occurred to Richard that he could use Egan and Ulic right about then.

Leaving his men gathered at the end of the field, Richard crossed the empty ground alone to the referee at center field with the fistful of straws. The point man for the emperor's team waiting beside the referee looked to be nearly a foot taller than Richard. His neck started at his ears and just kept getting wider until it met shoulders half again as wide as Richard's.

A neat row of red, swollen marks running diagonally up along the side of his face recorded where the links of the chain had caught him. As Richard waited, the towering point man, glaring at Richard the entire time, drew a straw first.

When Richard drew, he came up with a shorter straw. The onlookers roared their approval that the emperor's team would have the first chance to score. The man shot Richard a smirk before taking the broc and heading to his side of the field.

As Richard returned to his players waiting at their end of the field, his gaze swept over the endless masses of men, fists raised in wild emotion, all wanting the blood of either one side or the other. Men with arrows at the ready watched Richard's solitary walk back to his team. He could feel the fevered emotions of hundreds of thousands of men all pressing in, trying to see what would happen—men who had gotten where they were by trampling over endless corpses of innocent men, women, and children who had only wanted to live their own lives, to better themselves and their families.

Richard felt caught up in a world gone mad.

His gaze passed over the empty space where the emperor was supposed to be. Where Kahlan was supposed to be. Without Kahlan, even a Kahlan who didn't know him, the world was a cold and empty place.

Right then, Richard felt very small and alone.

In a numb haze, he took his place in the line with his men. When the horn blew and the enemy, bunched together in a tight formation, started coming, being down in the bowl of the Ja'La field was like standing in a valley, watching an avalanche descending on him. Right then, in that moment of desolation, Richard didn't know what he would do.

The collision was brutal. Gritting his teeth with the effort, he tried to turn the men protecting their point man, but they plowed right through Richard and his team.

With little ceremony their point man reached the scoring zone and threw the broc. Defenders painted with red symbols leaped to try to deflect the throw, but the attackers rolled over them. The broc landed solidly in the net, scoring the first point.

The crowd erupted with a deafening roar of approval.

Richard had just learned something. The emperor's team appeared to rely on their superior size and weight to grind their way through their opponents' defense. They had no real need for finesse. He gave his men a stealthy hand signal as the other team formed up for their second charge.

When they came, all of Richard's team hooked across the blocking line, using low tackles to take the legs out from under the big men in the center. It wasn't elegant, but it served the purpose of opening a hole. Before the hole could close, Richard was through. The point man didn't deviate course, confident in his size to smash Richard out of his way.

Richard pivoted, abruptly cutting across the front of the man, sweeping a leg at his ankles. As the man stumbled to maintain his balance, Richard snatched the broc out from his arms when they loosened in a natural reaction to falling face-first.

Richard dodged and darted his way through a loose line of men. As yet more men converged on him, he tossed the broc to Johnrock, already positioned behind the line of men. To the wild cheers of his supporters, Johnrock briefly held up the broc for all to see as he ran from a clutch of pursuers. Johnrock, enjoying the moment, turned backward as he ran so he could laugh at the men chasing him, then threw the broc over their heads to Richard.

Men dove in from every direction as Richard caught the broc. He twisted away from one man, dodged another, and pushed himself away from a third, reversing direction wildly in an effort to keep from the clutches of the big men. Despite his own players tackling men, or blocking them out of Richard's way, the opponents closed in all around. As Richard tried to miss one man, another seized him around his shoulders and, as if he were a small child, tossed him to the ground. Richard knew that he wasn't going to be able to keep the broc from these men, and he didn't want them all piling on top of him and breaking his bones, so as soon as he hit the ground he heaved the broc. Bruce was running in the right place at the right time. He caught the broc but was then tackled.

The horn blew, ending the time of play for the emperor's team. They had scored a point, and Richard was fortunate to have kept them from getting two.

As he trotted to his side of the field, he reprimanded himself for letting his feelings get the better of him. He wasn't paying enough attention. His mind wasn't in what he was doing. He was going to get himself killed.

He couldn't do anything to help Kahlan unless he shaped up.

His men were panting, most resting by leaning over with their hands on their knees. They looked despondent.

"All right," Richard said as he reached them, "we've let them have their moment of glory. Now let's take them down."

That brought grins all around. All the men brightened at his words.

As Richard caught the broc when the referee tossed it his way, he glanced around at his men. "Let's show them who they're dealing with. Play one-three then reverse it." He quickly showed them one finger, then three, in case they couldn't hear him over all the noise. "Go."

As one the men broke into a dead run, immediately clustering into a knot of men around Richard. No blockers went out front, no wing men went to the sides. Instead, all the men compacted together into as tight of a formation as they could and still be able to run at full speed.

The other team looked pleased by the tactic. It was their kind of play—brute force. With their supporters cheering them on they ran headlong at the cluster of Richard's team.

All of Richard's men watched Jagang's team, waiting until they reached the prescribed square. Moments from impact, as the defenders reached that spot, Richard's entire team suddenly broke in every direction at once.

It was such a startling move that the other players faltered, turning one way, then the other, unsure what to do as the men they were about to clobber were unexpectedly bolting every which way. Each of Richard's men ran in a crazy zigzag course that appeared to have no rhyme or reason. The men on Jagang's team didn't know who to grab, who to chase, or where they were going. In an instant, the massive, focused charge had scattered like so many fireflies.

The crowd roared with delighted laughter.

Richard ran a wild course the same as the other men, except he was the one with the broc. By the time that fact sank in for the other team, Richard was already around most of them and deep into enemy territory. As two of the blockers went after him he ran for his life.

When he reached the scoring zone he heaved the broc. As soon as it left his fingers he was hit from behind, but it was too late to stop the throw. The broc sailed into the goal. Richard hit the ground with a man atop him. It was fortunate that the man had been running at full speed because his momentum tumbled him over Richard's back.

Richard scrambled to his feet and trotted back toward his side of the field to the wild cheers of the crowd. The score was tied, but he wasn't interested in a tie. He needed to press the advantage. The play he had devised wasn't finished, yet. He needed to complete it.

His men, all smiles, gathered as quickly as possible. Richard didn't need to give them a signal; he had already given them the whole play the first time. When the referee tossed him the broc they all immediately broke into a run.

Again, they formed into a tight formation as they charged across the field. This time, though, Jagang's team, as they raced to meet them, scattered at the last minute, ready this time to intercept all the men as they tried to take off in every direction. The crowd cheered and screamed their approval.

Rather than break apart, though, Richard's team remained tightly packed together as they charged right up the middle of the field. The few dispersed players left within range to intercept them were mowed down by the full weight of the team. The minor defense of first two, followed by a third defender, didn't slow Richard's men at all. The other team, suddenly realizing what was happening, took up the pursuit. They were too late. Richard steered his men to the right goal.

As he reached the scoring zone and his men fell back into a protective shield, Richard threw the broc. He watched it in the torchlight as it arced through the night air and then went in. The crowd erupted in cheering. The horn blew, signaling the end of the play.

The referee at center field announced the score, one for the champions—Jagang's team—and two for the challengers.

But then, before the referee had finished with the announcement and the hourglass was turned over, Richard saw him turn to something on the sidelines. It was Jagang. He was in the area that had been roped off for him. Nicci was at his side. Kahlan stood back a short distance. Jillian was with her.

As everyone waited, the referee went to the sideline and

listened to the emperor a moment. He nodded and returned to center field, where he announced that the second score was ruled to have gone in after the horn blew, so it didn't count. The score, the referee announced in a loud voice, was tied.

Part of the crowd yelled in anger, while others screamed with joy at their fortune.

Richard's men started shouting angry objections, disputing the call. Richard strode in front of them. The noise of the uproar of the crowd was so loud that he feared his men wouldn't be able to hear him, so he pulled a thumb across his throat, cutting off their objections.

"You can't change it!" he yelled at them. "Settle down! Focus!"

They stopped protesting but they weren't happy. Richard wasn't, either, but he knew that he couldn't do anything about it. It had been the order of the emperor, after all, that had reversed their goal. Richard was going to have to alter his plans.

"We need to stop these men," he said as he paced in front of his team. "When it's our turn again, go to play two-five." He showed them first two fingers, then five. Men nodded. "You can't stop what just happened, but you can stop them from scoring. Then we can run our play and get back what was taken unfairly. Stop fixating on what's done and over and put your minds ahead to what we must do."

His men all nodded as they formed up, preparing for the other team's charge. They were still angry but now they were ready to focus that anger on the other team.

The charge by the emperor's team was sloppy. They were still caught up in the jubilation over their reversal of fortune. In a bone-crushing impact their point man was shaken by a coordinated block. Richard was proud of his men for the way they turned their anger around and made use of it.

In the furious struggle after the collision Johnrock came up with the broc. He tossed it to Bruce when the men chasing him got close. Bruce in turn passed the broc to Richard. Richard ran up the field and, to the delight of the crowd, used all his strength to throw from the two-point line. The broc went in. It didn't count, of course, but the crowd roared as if it had.

The cheers shook the ground. It was vindication for the stolen goal. It was as close to snubbing his nose at Jagang as Richard could come.

Their supporters in the crowd started chanting, "Four to one! Four to one! Four to one!"

The score was still officially one to one, but in the view of those who were cheering it was now four to one.

On their next charge, when the point man for the emperor's team ran into the scoring zone and threw the broc, one of Richard's men leaped up high and managed to deflect the broc just enough to cause it to go wide and miss the goal. When the horn blew, the score remained one to one.

On their first play, Richard was almost to the scoring zone when he was tackled. The man caught his legs in a viselike grip. As Richard hit the ground, he tossed the broc in Johnrock's direction. Johnrock scooped it up just before a man on the other team was able to grab it.

Johnrock reached the scoring zone and threw. From the ground Richard watched as the broe went into the net, scoring a point.

Johnrock, overjoyed, waved both hands high in the air as he jumped up and down like a boy. The crowd loved it. Richard couldn't help smiling as he untangled himself from his tackler, who delivered a painful punch in Richard's back just before parting. Richard didn't take the bait. He knew better than to let himself be drawn into a fight when the broc wasn't in play.

As he caught up with Johnrock and they ran together back toward the starting zone for their next run, Richard clapped his wing man on the shoulder.

"You did good, Johnrock," Richard yelled over the cheering.

"I brought us glory!"

Richard couldn't help laughing. "Glory," he agreed as he again clapped Johnrock on the back. "And a point that counts."

As they formed up while waiting for the referee to deliver the broc, all of the men shouted their congratulations to a beaming Johnrock. He pumped his fist, eliciting a mighty team shout, before he took his usual place at Richard's right. Bruce took his left wing. The blockers formed a wedge heavily weighted out ahead of Johnrock. The play was meant to draw the defenders to the left side, where the defense was weakest.

As they charged up the field, the emperor's team started going to Richard's left, as he wanted, but at the last moment they hooked and crashed through the center of the heaviest part of the wedge. Such a tactic would not stop Richard or get them the broc. They were after something else. Richard knew there was going to be trouble when tacklers leaped over the forward blockers.

"Johnrock!" Richard yelled. "Cut right!"

Johnrock, instead, dropped his big shoulder into the teeth of the attack. Three tacklers dove low. The fourth hooked an arm around Johnrock's neck. A fifth man, racing at full speed, hit him from the side, applying force to the fulcrum at Johnrock's neck.

Richard felt like he was in a dream and couldn't make his legs move fast enough.

Even as he was running with all his strength, he could hear bone break.

CHAPTER 33

Her heart heavy, Kahlan watched as Richard knelt beside his fallen right wing man. The horn blew. The men from Jagang's team quickly left their victim slumped on his side to return to their end of the field to be ready to defend.

"Is he dead?" Jillian asked.

Kahlan circled an arm around the shoulders of the girl pressed in against her left side. "I'm afraid so."

"Why would they deliberately do such a thing?"

"It's the way the Order plays Ja'La dh Jin. Killing is a means to get what they want."

Kahlan could see the tears in Richard's eyes as his men hooked their arms under his and dragged him back away from the body. If he didn't go back to play immediately he would be ejected for delaying the game. Referee's assistants quickly set to work dragging the lifeless form of the big man off the field.

Kahlan could hear Jagang, half a dozen paces ahead of her, chuckle.

Nicci, at his side, briefly glanced back over her shoulder. Kahlan didn't quite know what to make of the liquid look in her blue eyes. It seemed part sadness for Richard, part bottled rage, and, somehow, part warning to Kahlan.

Kahlan hadn't been able to speak with Nicci again since that night after she had been so terribly hurt. Ever since Jagang had made his bet with Commander Karg he had been moody and short-tempered.

Last evening, as Nicci waited in the bedehamber and Kahlan waited in the outer room of his tent, he'd met outside with some of the members of his team. Kahlan hadn't heard everything, but it had sounded like he had given them orders that he wanted them to see to it that the point man for Karg's team didn't cause them any trouble.

Kahlan had had a sleepless night, worried that Richard might not live to see morning. Whatever had been planned had Jagang in a lusty mood for Nicci. Kahlan and Jillian had been ordered to stay where they were on the floor in the outer room. He wanted to be alone with his Slave Queen, as he called her.

Kahlan hadn't known what Jagang was doing to her. No matter what he was doing to her, Nicci never screamed. In his bed she always seemed to simply go numb, staring unblinking at nothing in this world as he went about his business. Kahlan understood what Nicci was doing. It was the only defense she had. As she drew inward, her outward indifference was her protection for her sanity. It would do her no good to let herself pay attention to everything that the brute was doing to her. On the other hand, her indifference enraged Jagang, often sending him into fits of violence.

Kahlan wondered if, when he started in on her, she would have the strength Nicci had.

That morning, Kahlan had wondered if the Sisters were going to have to be called yet again to save Nicci, or to heal her at least. When Jagang had emerged from the bedchamber, though, he had Nicci by her hair. He tossed her to the floor in front of him, looking pleased with himself, with her helplessness. Kahlan had been relieved that, while she looked a bit battered and bruised, at least she hadn't appeared grievously injured.

Out on the field Richard's team gathered, preparing for the next play. Kahlan glanced around as legions of men still cheered their satisfaction at the man's death. Others, though, yelled in anger, shaking fists at the emperor's team. The air fairly crackled with tension. As the game quickly went back into action, the crowd began to settle down, at least to a degree.

Kahlan could sense, though, that the mood of the onlookers had changed. What had been universal approval of the match at hand finally getting under way had turned restless and was even in some ways beginning to look malcontent. It had started to change when Jagang had intervened over the last point Richard had scored. Jagang had overruled the referees, saying the goal had been made after the horn blew. The referees had acquiesced and voided the point, but everyone knew that the broc had clearly gone in before the horn.

None of that mattered, though. The emperor had made the call.

The red team seemed determined to play on as if they hadn't just lost their biggest man. Out on the field they muscled their way through a line of blockers. Richard deftly sidestepped several attempts to snare him. A number of other men, though, were closing in.

Richard abruptly halted on the safe square, a place that was rarely used, preventing the man who had been about to tackle him from doing so. It was the man who had broken the wing man's neck.

Kahlan couldn't imagine what Richard was up to. Being on that square prevented him from being attacked as long as he remained there, but it also trapped him on an island that was swiftly being surrounded by opponents. While temporarily safe, he couldn't score from that spot. He would eventually have to move, but with every passing moment the territory all around him was becoming ever more unhealthy.

As the man turned to check on his teammates, who were quickly closing in, Richard shouted something to get his attention. The man turned back.

Richard, holding the broc pressed back against his chest, with his hands on either side of it, suddenly released it in an explosive throw. The heavy broc smashed squarely into the man's face so hard that it rebounded back into Richard's hands.

The blow had been powerful enough to partially cave in the man's face. With his nose completely driven back into his skull, the man went limp and dropped straight down in a heap.

The crowd gasped at the unexpected turn of events.

In a rage, another man to Richard's right lunged, even though Richard was on the safe square. The referee didn't look inclined to step in to call a foul. Richard rolled the broc back under his left arm as he ducked to that side a little. Turning all the while to keep faced to the attack, he swung his right arm. The thick bone of his forearm chopped the man across the throat. The man grabbed for his throat as he stumbled back and collapsed. One leg kicked reflexively as he desperately gasped for air. His windpipe apparently crushed, his face began turning from red to blue.

Without pause, another towering man charged in from the left with a fist raised. Richard twisted toward him, going inside the punch and the opening in the man's defenses, and used his momentum to help him thrust straight in with lightning speed. The powerful strike focused in the heel of his hand hit he man right over his heart. The blow was enough to stagger him back. The big man clutched his chest, looking dazed and confused, and then, as his eyes began to roll back, he crumpled to the ground.

Without any help, Richard had taken out three men who were all considerably bigger than him. She could easily see why there were so many arrows around the field pointed at him at all times.

Kahlan couldn't begin to imagine what would happen if Richard ever got his hands on a blade.

Richard wasted no time. He bolted through the opening he had just created and headed for the goals. His men looked to have been prepared for the move. They were already stationed along his route, ready to block the tacklers going after him. Everywhere across the field men crashed together.

Kahlan could see all the faces on the entire hillside across on the other side of the field turn in unison as they watched Richard running toward the opponent's goals, dodging some men, his blockers knocking others out of his way.

Richard, with no one close enough to bring him down, raced into the scoring zone. In the clear, he heaved the broc into the net, scoring another point. His team was once again ahead.

The crowd was swept up in the frenzy of the fast-paced action. Even Jagang had stepped forward, closer to the edge of the field, to watch, one hand fisted in anxiety at his side. His guards, too, all leaned out to watch as Richard's team, still with time on their turn, got the broc from the referee and started another charge.

As they made it into their opponent's territory, Richard cut left, only to be tackled. Kahlan thought that it almost looked deliberate. It reminded her of way he had fallen in the mud so that no one would recognize him that first time they had gone to see his team.

When Richard hit the ground the broc shot from his arms. This, too, looked to her to be a little less than natural. It struck her that it looked to be part of a scheme. His left wing man, who was racing up the field, just happened to be in the right place at the right time. He dipped and scooped up the broc as it rolled past. In an instant he was in the scoring zone and took the throw. With Richard down, it was a legal play for a wing man to attempt a score.

The broc went in the goal, setting off thunderous cheers.

The wing man threw his arms up in joy at having scored. It was something that wing men rarely had the chance to attempt, and even more rarely accomplished. While Kahlan knew that it was permitted, she'd never actually seen it done before.

As the horn blew, signaling the end of the timed turn, Richard caught up with his left wing man and, with a proud smile, clapped him on the back. Judging by the way the wing man looked at Richard, Kahlan thought that recognition from Richard had meant just as much to the man as the goal.

The wing man was an Imperial Order soldier, not a captive like some of the other members of Richard's team. She wondered why Richard would be so amiable with an Order soldier. Every time she started to have hopeful confidence in the man, something would happen that made her caution return.

Since the last game they had attended, when Nicci had seen the man called Ruben and spoke the name Richard, Kahlan knew that Richard was his real name. She hadn't been able to speak a word with Nicci since then, though, so she couldn't ask, but she suspected that Richard was really Richard Rahl—Lord Rahl.

She didn't know if it was true, but it would certainly explain a lot, like why the man fell in the mud that first day, and why he painted his face with wild designs meant to disguise who he was, and why he told people that his name was Ruben.

It just seemed impossible, though—the Lord Rahl himself being a captive of the Imperial Order, playing on a Ja'La team against the emperor's team.

What really troubled her, though, was that he knew her. He had called out her name that first day he had been in a cage on a wagon in the supply train rolling into camp. She supposed it was possible that the Order had captured him without realizing who they had. The coincidence of it all, though, struck her as pretty far-fetched. She knew, though, there was likely more to it than she realized. Maybe Richard had gotten himself caught, somehow, in order to get close to her. To rescue her.

Now, she told herself, she was just being silly.

Still, she wondered why she kept finding herself at the center of so many things.

She wished she could get a chance to talk with Nicci again so that she could ask if it really was Richard Rahl.

But then, by Nicci's reaction, by her tears at seeing him, Kahlan didn't need to ask. Kahlan could see it written on her face.

This was the man Nicci loved.

Out of the corner of her eye, Kahlan kept track of her special guards as they looked between her and the Ja'La field. When the crowd roared, jamming fists in the air with expectant excitement, her guards leaned this way and that to see between the royal guard and out to the field as the emperor's team took the broc for their turn to try to score. Three of their players, who had just been dragged to the sidelines, had been replaced by substitute players. By the way the three were abandoned off to the side, Kahlan knew that all three had died. Richard had killed three men in a heartbeat without any help.

She didn't think that was going to be the end of it, either.

The emperor's team looked to be in a blind rage as they began their charge. Bunched into a gang, they went straight up the middle, determined to mow down anyone who got in their way. Richard's team parted for them, then from both sides swiftly moved in behind and attacked from the rear, seizing men's legs. Tackled in that fashion, they fell face-first in the direction they were running, making the impact all the more jarring.

One of the tackles was violent enough to break the ankle of the man on the emperor's team. He screamed in pain. The point man, hearing the scream, was distracted for a split second. It was just long enough for him to get hit from the side by two men. He was thrown to the ground so viciously that it knocked the wind out of him and rattled his teeth. A brawl broke out over possession of the broc.

As the emperor's team recovered, they muscled men aside and managed to keep the broc. On their feet again, they fought to get past the defenders. Several men on Richard's team were left on the ground, rolling in pain. The crowd yelled frenzied encouragement to the emperor's team. Their point man dodged this way and that, going around some men, knocking others aside.

Kahlan's guards, hearing the rabid cheering, inched ever forward, trying to see what was happening. That left more empty space back away from the sideline, where Kahlan was. The press of spectators lining the slope behind, all their weight pushing forward, down toward the field, was causing the area reserved for the emperor to be squeezed in from both sides. Toward the front, where Jagang was, the royal guards kept the excited crowds to each side back, but even they were caught up in the frantic struggle on the Ja'La field; they weren't paying as much attention behind, where the space was slowly shrinking.

Kahlan tightened her left arm protectively around Jillian, keeping her close as the special guards, having less and less space, started to inch forward where there was more room up closer to the action. The ones who had been behind her pressed in close, squeezing past as they slowly, steadily moved toward the front.

Nicci, having been forgotten by the emperor as he became completely caught up in the action, took a step back, out of the way. That allowed Kahlan's guards space to move forward.

It looked natural, like she was merely trying not to interfere with what they wanted.

Jagang, like everyone else, cheered, groaned, cursed, and yelled at the teams on the field. Darkness had long ago settled in, lending an otherworldly mood to the event. Torches lining the edge of the field cast flickering light to the open patch of ground surrounded by a sea of black. Between many of the torches archers watched with arrows nocked. But even they were caught up in the emotions of the game, watching the action more than they seemed to be watching the captives.

Kahlan felt as if she were at the center of a boiling, churning, frenzied ritual dedicated to violence. The crowd not only yelled and cheered, but they began to chant, stamping feet in time to those chants as their team raced across the field. The ground shook under those hundreds of thousands of boots all slamming down together. The night, dark and overcast, felt like it was filled with continuous, booming thunder.

The mood was bewitching. It even caught Kahlan up in it.

She, along with all those watching, felt as if she were out there, on the field, running with the men. Her heart pounded as she watched Richard dodge tackles, duck under an outstretched arm, and slip between men diving for him. She winced, half turning away when men were hit. Many of the spectators groaned, almost as if they themselves had taken the blow.

As the hourglass marked the turns, the score went back and forth. As she watched, though, Kahlan saw Richard fail to make scores that she felt sure he could have made. He would seem to slow just enough so that a man could catch and tackle him. One time he threw and missed.

He was falling in the mud again, so to speak. This time, she didn't know why.

As the game wore on it became ever more clear to her that he was manipulating the score, keeping it close. When the emperor's team would score, it wouldn't be long before he would make an answering score to stay even, but then he would fail to follow up and make another—until the emperor's team scored again. Turn after turn of the hourglass went scoreless. It stood at seven points each.

She could tell by the way he moved that he was not merely holding back for some reason, but he was also saving his energy. The other team was wearing themselves out. Richard did what was necessary but no more.

Such a close match only served to heat the emotions of the hillsides of spectators into fevered expectations. Many of them cheered, clapped, whistled, and yelled for the team they favored, while others shook fists and shouted curses at the team they opposed. Here and there fights broke out among the spectators. They ended up being brief because everyone wanted to watch the game.

Kahlan, having watched Nicci's slow progress, saw that she had managed to ease herself half a dozen steps behind Jagang. No one was paying any attention to her. Jagang had glanced back twice, only half looking, satisfied that she was close enough at hand.

Kahlan could see women camp followers, out near the edge of the field, just as wildly excited as the vast crowd, beginning to bare their breasts as men ran past. While the territory up close to the sidelines was highly prized, and often fought over, women at the matches were freely allowed access right up to the edge of the field. Throngs of men, knowing how worked up the women were, how eager they were to catch the attention of the players, egged them on. The women seemed to crave the attention. Over the deafening noise of the crowd Kahlan could hear some of the nearby women up at sidelines yell lewd promises for the victors as players ran by.

Ordinarily, women behaving in such a manner among the men of the Order would not be free for long, but the soldiers were far more interested in the game on the field. The conduct of the women only added to the debauched atmosphere. It was all part of Ja'La dh Jin.

When Nicci slipped close enough, Jillian reached out and touched her hand. "Are you all right?" she whispered just loud enough to be heard over the noise of the crowd. "We were so worried for you."

Cupping the girl's cheek, Nicci smiled briefly as she nodded in answer.

"He's up to something," Nicci said under her breath as she leaned a little closer to Kahlan.

"I know."

"This may be a chance for you to escape. I'll do all I can to help you. Be ready."

With the collar around her neck Kahlan didn't know what chance she could possible have to escape. She was heartened by the sentiment, though, even if she thought it was completely unrealistic. While Kahlan didn't believe that she had any real chance of escape, it might be an opportunity for something else, something that could save others.

When Nicci glanced over again, Kahlan lifted out her hand just a little, hiding what was underneath, in her palm.

"Here. Take this."

When Nicci only frowned, Kahlan turned the hand over briefly, just long enough for Nicci to see the handle of the knife. The blade was pressed up along Kahlan's wrist, under the sleeve of her shirt.

"Keep it," Nicci said. "You may need it."

"I still have two."

Nicci stared for a moment in surprise, then tilted her head, indicating that Kahlan should give the knife to Jillian. Jillian pulled her cloak open just enough to show Nicci the knife Kahlan had already given her.

Nicci looked up at Kahlan. "Knives are not my talent."

"It's not hard," Kahlan said as she pressed the handle into Nicci's hand. "When the time is right, just stick the pointed end somewhere important in someone you really don't like."

Nicci's blue eyes stole a glance at Jagang. "I think I can do that much."

Kahlan thought that Nicci, standing there in the soft torch-light, her blond hair tumbled down over her strong shoulders, was probably the most beautiful woman she had ever seen. It wasn't just that she was beautiful, though. Despite what Jagang did to her, she remained undaunted. There was an inner strength about her, a nobility.

"Is he Richard Rahl?" Kahlan asked.

Nicci's blue eyes turned back to Kahlan and stared for a moment.

"Yes."

"What's he doing here?"

The slightest smile curved Nicci's mouth. "He's Richard Rahl."

"Do you know what he's up to?"

Nicci shook her head the slightest bit as her gaze swept over all the guards, checking to make sure none were paying any attention to either of them. Through gaps they could see men painted with wild red designs race past.

"That's really Richard out there?" Jillian asked.

Nicci nodded.

"How can you tell? I mean, with the paint all over them, how can you be sure? I know Richard and I can't tell."

Nicci glanced down at Jillian. "It's him."

Her tone was of such calm certainty that it left no reason to question. Kahlan thought that Nicci would probably be able to recognize the man in total darkness.

"How does he know me?" she asked.

Nicci again stared into Kahlan's eyes for a long moment. "This is not the place for a conversation. Just be ready."

"For what?" Kahlan asked. "What do you think he's going to do? What do you think he *can* do?"

"If I know Richard, I expect that he's about to start a war."

Kahlan blinked in surprise. "All by himself?"

"If he has to."

Out on the field, the emperor's team scored a point just before the horn blew, signaling the end of their turn. The crowd went crazy. Kahlan winced at the roar. The level of noise was withering.

Richard's team was now behind by one point.

Waiting for the men to take their place and the horn to start the play for Richard's team, the entire crowd started in chanting in a deep, harsh, rhythmic grunt. The horde stamped a boot between each of those grunts.

Who-ah. Thump. *Who-ah*. Thump. *Who-ah*. Thump.

It seemed like the whole world moved with each of those *Who-ahs.* The ground shook with each thump. Even Jagang and his royal guards joined in. It gave the night an eerie, savage, primeval feel, as if everything civilized had been abandoned to the spectacle of raw savagery.

The supporters of the emperor's team wanted the men to rip the challengers apart rather than let them score. The supporters of Richard's team wanted their men to crush those trying to stop them.

The chanting was a call for blood.

With only one timed turn left, Richard's team had to score during this play or they would lose. If they scored only one point during their time at play, though, the game would be tied and go into overtime.

Kahlan caught glimpses of Richard, showing no emotion, as he gathered with his men. He gave them a brief, covert hand signal. As he turned, his gaze swept past. For an instant, their eyes met.

The power in that connection made Kahlan's heart pound and her knees weak.

Just as fast as it had come, Richard's scrutiny moved on. No one but Kahlan would have known that he had looked directly at her or, if they had, they wouldn't have understood why.

Kahlan understood.

He was checking her position.

This was the moment for which he had painted himself with those strange symbols. This was the moment for which he had kept the score even. He had crushed every other team they had come up against so that he could be sure that he was here, in this place, at this moment.

She couldn't imagine why, but it was for this moment.

He abruptly yelled a battle cry and started the charge.

Seeing him covered in the frightening red symbols, his muscles tense, his raptor glare, his focused power, his fluid movement . . . Kahlan thought that surely her hammering heart might burst.

CHAPTER 34

Every eye was on Richard as he ran with the broc tucked under his left arm. Kahlan, too, having taken a step forward, stood transfixed. The crowd, in tense expectation, held its collective breath.

Jagang's team, at the other end of the field, began their rush across open ground to stop the charge. If they could keep Richard's team from scoring they would win the championship. They were experienced players who knew that victory was within their grasp and they didn't intend to let anything change that.

Richard, screened by blockers and his remaining wing man, cut to the right. He hugged the right boundary of the field as he ran at breakneck speed. The flames of torches whooshed and flapped as he flew by. Women reached out to try to touch him as they yelled along with everyone else.

Richard was suddenly right there, right of front of them, racing past the emperor. Jagang looked like he wanted to tackle Richard himself as he ran past.

Kahlan expected Richard to stop, to wheel on the emperor, and kill the man as he had so efficiently killed others, but he didn't. He didn't even glance to the side as he flew by.

Richard had his chance to attempt an assassination and hadn't taken it.

Kahlan couldn't imagine why not, if as Nicci thought, he really had intended to do something. Perhaps it was only wishful thinking on Nicci's part . . . and on Kahlan's.

In an instant Richard and his men were past and gone, charging up the field.

The men of Jagang's team, watching them come and seeing that they were relatively close together in their headlong rush, rather than scattered all over the field as they sometimes had been in the past, converged to form into an impenetrable wall of bone and muscle sure to stop their advance.

In past turns at play the emperor's team had kept Richard's team from scoring. They knew that they would win if they merely contained their adversary and kept them from scoring during this turn. They appeared to want more, though. They didn't simply want to win; they wanted to punish the challengers. They looked fiereely determined to end it in as brutal a fashion as possible.

As they ran, Richard's men, rather than scattering, or even moving into positions designed to try to engage the formation of waiting blockers, instead suddenly and inexplicably came together. Even more surprising, they meshed into a single column. As the men ran they all stacked in close together, with the largest men in the front. At the same time, each man reached out and fastened a hand on the shoulder of the man in front of him, locking the entire column together. Their long, breakneck strides moved in unison.

In an instant, Richard's entire team had connected itself together into a solid, human battering ram.

That column, Richard near the back, wasn't moving as fast as each of the men could have run by himself, but they didn't need to be fast, and what they gave up in a little speed was more than offset by their massive collective weight giving them staggering momentum.

Even though the individual big men of Jagang's team braced themselves, the runaway line of men crashed through them like a tree trunk through a pauper's door.

Jagang's men were all accustomed to their huge size serving them in good stead but, despite how big they were, they were no match for the prodigious weight of Richard's entire team body-slamming into them in such a focused manner. With such overpowering weight, the column punched through without being slowed, transferring the power of the collision to the defending blockers, sending them flying.

Some of Richard's men in the front were peeled away by the violence of the contact, but as each broke off it exposed a new man in the lead so that the file itself remained intact as it plunged through the defending wall of men.

Once they were in the defenders' territory and at the first scoring line, long before they reached the regular scoring zone, the column of men burst apart, crashing into the blockers converging on them. For an instant, it opened a pocket of safety for Richard.

He heaved the broc from that rear line. It was a long way to the goal. As the broc arced through the night air, illuminated by torches, the crowd leaned forward as one, all holding their breath, all eyes watching.

With a thunk, the broc landed solidly in the net, scoring two points.

The crowed exploded with a thunderous roar that made the air tremble and the ground shudder.

Richard's team was now ahead by one point. The emperor's team had no more turns of the hourglass; there was no way for them to win. Even though there was time left on the play for Richard's team, they didn't need it. The game was as good as won, even though it wasn't yet over and the sand in the hourglass continued to drizzle down.

Emperor Jagang stood stone-faced. His guards, looking grim, put their weight into holding back the excited crowds to each side as the cheering went on unabated.

Jagang finally thrust an arm up high. The wild celebration began to die out as attention turned to see what the emperor would do. Jagang signaled for the referee.

Kahlan shared a brief look with Nicci. They couldn't hear as the men conferred, heads together.

The referee, looking a little pale, gave the emperor a nod and then ran out to the center of the field, holding up a hand to indicate a ruling.

"The challenger went out of bounds as he ran along the sideline," the referee called into the still night air. "The points don't count. His excellency's team still leads by one. Play must resume until time runs out."

If the crowd had gone wild when Richard had scored, they now went berserk. The entire army watching the game was in turmoil.

Richard, though, didn't look at all moved by the ruling. In fact, he was already down at his end along with his men, as if he had expected it. His men, looking all business, didn't seem discouraged, either.

As the referee tossed them the broc, they were ready. In Ja'La, play couldn't be interrupted. Jagang's team, however, had been celebrating their sudden turn of fortune and weren't yet formed up to defend their goals. Richard's team, having little time left, didn't waste any and charged away immediately.

As they raced up the field they went to their left this time, to the opposite side of the field from where Kahlan stood watching. Again, they formed into the same tight column, the hand of each man resting on the shoulder of the man in front of him. They were running the same play, but reversing it.

The other difference was that this time they kept well away from the sideline—far enough away that anyone, especially the crowd on that side of the field, could see that they were nowhere near the side boundary.

Jagang's team saw what was coming but hadn't yet organized a defense to stop the formation bearing down on them. They realized the jeopardy and raced to block the advancing team.

When Richard's team plowed through the loose net of blockers and reached the same scoring line as the play before, to the rear of the regular scoring zone, the men again scattered to create a pocket to protect their point man. In that instant, clear of defenders, Richard heaved the broc.

It sailed over the outstretched arms of Jagang's team and thunked into the net for two points.

The crowd erupted in wild cheering.

The horn blew, hardly heard over the thunderous roar.

The game was over. Richard's team had won the championship—several times over.

Jagang, his face red with rage, took a long step back, reached out, seized Nicci's upper arm, and then yanked her forward to his side.

He thrust his other arm into the air to halt the proceedings. The referee and his assistants stood frozen, watching Jagang. The cheering faltered and the dismayed crowd slowly fell to silence.

"Their point man stepped over the boundary line!" Jagang roared into the cold night air. "He ran out of bounds!"

When he had run the play before last, since he had been so close, Kahlan had been able to see that he was not over the boundary line. In fact, people standing right along the boundary line had been reaching out, trying to touch him, and he'd been out of reach. This time, even if Richard really had run out of bounds, there was no way Jagang could have seen it all the way across the field.

"The play was dead!" Jagang yelled. "No points scored! Game over! The royal team wins the championship!"

The hillsides of men stared in disbelief.

"Jagang the Just has spoken!" Nicci shouted out to the crowd, mocking Jagang's decree.

Richard had just forced Jagang the Just to demonstrate to all that under the Order justice was a meaningless slogan. And Nicci had twisted the knife for him.

Jagang backhanded her hard enough to send her sprawling at Kahlan's feet.

The supporters of the emperor's team went crazy with jubilation. Men jumped up and down as they shouted and cheered, as if they themselves had actually accomplished something.

The supporters of Richard's team went crazy with rage.

Kahlan, holding her breath, gripped the knife tightly in her fist, checking the position of her guards as Jillian bent to help the woman bleeding on the ground at their feet.

Supporters of Jagang's team shouted taunts at men who shouted back that their team were cheats and had lost. Men started shoving one another. Fists started flying. Men everywhere sided with one group or the other as weapons were drawn.

In an instant the entire camp was in riot.

The hillsides of men seemed to break, then suddenly begin to avalanche down toward the Ja'La field. In the frantic melee it seemed the entire army was unexpectedly caught up in pitched battle.

Kahlan wouldn't have believed it was possible, but Nicci was right.

Richard had just started a war.

CHAPTER 35

Jagang's royal guard strained, putting their backs into the struggle to hold back the mob to each side. An enraged emperor watched as a fierce battle broke out all around him. He made no move to retreat to safety. If anything, he looked like he wanted nothing more than to join the battle. His guards did their best to keep that battle as far away from him as possible.

Kahlan spotted Richard on the far side of the field. In the torchlight his red paint stood out like a warning that the underworld itself was about to open up and swallow them all. Behind him and the men of his team the entire hillside was in full riot. The drunken rampage, unleashed hatred, and hunge for blood ran unchecked.

Kahlan began to worry that the red paint Richard wore would mark him as a target of all the supporters of the emperor's team. All those spectators knew very well who he was and what he had just done. He was the object of both adoration and hatred. She feared that what had started as a way to hide him would end up being the thing that made him easy to spot by those who wanted to kill him.

Taking appraisal of her half-dozen special guards in attendance and seeing that at the moment they were more worried about protecting the life of the emperor than watching her, Kahlan quickly squatted down beside Jillian. Strings of blood lay across Nicci's face. A line of welts from Jagang's rings ran at an angle up the side of her cheek. She was dazed but seemed to be awakening.

"Nicci," Kahlan whispered urgently as she gently lifted the woman's shoulders and head, "are you badly hurt?"

Nicci's blue eyes blinked, trying to make out Kahlan's face. "What?"

"Are you hurt bad?" With a finger, Kahlan lifted a few strands of blond hair back from Nicci's eyes. "Is anything broken?"

Nicci reached up and felt the side of her face. She moved her jaw side to side, testing how it worked.

"I think I'm all right."

"You need to get up. I don't think we're going to be able to stay here for long. Richard started his war."

Through obvious pain, Nicci smiled. She had never doubted that he would.

Kahlan stood, helping Jillian pull a still unsteady Nicci to her feet. Jillian put her arm around Nicci's waist, helping steady her. Nicci draped an arm over the girl's shoulders for support.

Jagang, glancing back at Kahlan, saw her helping Nicci up. He pointed at Kahlan with one hand while with the other seizing the shirt of one of the special guards. He shoved the man in Kahlan's direction.

"Keep your eye on her," he growled. "All of you!"

The men, the only ones there who could see her—besides Jagang and Richard—abandoned their efforts in helping to hold back the droves of brawling soldiers and scrambled to do the emperor's bidding.

In the confusion and chaos, Jagang's regular guards, along with a contingent of his ever-present personal bodyguards, were furiously fending off the churning, yelling, battling throng all around them. Jagang's guards were all big, muscular men, yet it was all they could do to try to keep the regular soldiers pushed back. Inch by inch, though, they were beginning to lose ground.

Those regular soldiers weren't really interested in battling with Jagang's guards, or with the emperor for that matter—they were fully occupied with fighting one another, lost to the passions of the drunken brawl—but that fight was nonetheless pressing steadily in toward the emperor.

Jagang shouted at his guards, angry that they were being too indulgent with men who clearly weren't heeding commands.

He ordered the guards to gut the men if they didn't move back. Kahlan didn't think that Jagang was at all worried about his safety. It was more a matter of indignation at their lack of veneration for their emperor.

The guards didn't hesitate. Big, experienced men who had been busy pushing soldiers back switched instead to killing those who pressed in toward them. Jagang snatched up a short sword when one of his bodyguards, concerned that it might come to a matter of self-defense, offered it to him. Jagang vented his rage by hacking at men to either side. Over the roar of combat, their screams could hardly be heard.

It wasn't so much that the nearby soldiers involved in the riot were deliberately disobeying the orders to move back—the reality was they had no real choice in the matter. They were being compressed by the weight of the hillside of men flowing downward. As the entire crowd was completely consumed in battle, the men at the bottom near the Ja'La field were caught in that downward crush and were being helplessly carried into the deadly blades of Jagang's guards.

Kahlan glanced out at the riot on the Ja'La field. She blinked at what she saw.

Richard had a bow.

He already had an arrow nocked. He had a second arrow held at the ready in his teeth.

Jagang stood in the center of his guards, a bloody short sword gripped tightly in a fist hanging at his side as he shouted commands. He glared with black eyes at the soldiers out beyond, a great many of them belligerently drunk, as they fought and died over who had won Ja'La dh Jin. Jagang pointed with his free hand, yelling orders to his guards, directing individuals into gaps in the effort to keep the mob back.

Kahlan looked beyond and saw Richard with the bowstring drawn back to his cheek. In another blink, the arrow was away.

She held her breath as she watched the razor-sharp, steel-bladed arrow fly. Almost as fast as the first was away, another followed.

Just before the first could hit home, one of Jagang's guards turned to urgent calls for assistance from other guards fighting back a knot of soldiers who had broken through their lines on the other side. The man dashed past in front of the emperor to help. As he ran past he took the first arrow meant for the emperor. It hit under his right arm, in the side of the chest, between the front and back plate of thick leather armor. The arrow penetrated deep enough to have reached his heart. Judging from the way the man faltered, it had.

In surprise, Jagang turned a little, taking a half a step back when the man gasped as he collapsed. That half step turned out to be enough to save the emperor's life, because the second arrow hit Jagang in the right side of his chest. Had he not moved when the first man was hit, he would have taken the second arrow dead center in his heart.

Kahlan couldn't believe that with such clamor, disorder, confusion, furious fighting, rage, fear, pain, and death all around, Richard could make such a shot.

At the same time she couldn't imagine him missing.

With an arrow buried deep in his chest, Jagang staggered back. As he dropped to his knees, his guards frantically rushed to surround him and form a wall shielding him from the possibility of any more arrows finding their way in. Kahlan lost sight of the emperor behind the tight screen of bodyguards.

She used the moment of frozen shock on the faces of her special guards to slam the knife in her right hand into the right kidney of one of these guards as he watched Jagang's fate unfolding. She thrust the blade in her left hand into the gut of a man to her left as he turned to her. She pulled the knife up, slicing him open. A third guard turned from the emperor's struggle and charged toward her. Jillian tripped him as he rushed forward. Kahlan caught his throat with her knife as he fell past, and with one quick pull cut it open from ear to ear.

She turned and saw Richard across the field.

He had a sword.

As another guard stepped in, his hands reaching out to disarm her, Nicci slammed her knife into his back. He twisted around, crying out in shock as he reached back over his shoulder at the wound. She stabbed him twice in the chest—rapid, heavy blows. He stumbled and fell, trying to throw his arms around her to hold himself up, but couldn't and toppled to the ground. For not being an expert in using knives, Nicci appeared to have worked it out.

A fifth man grabbed Jillian, intending to use her as a shield as he came for Kahlan. Kahlan slashed the forearm wrapped around Jillian's neck, cutting through muscle and tendons down to bone. When he flinched with a cry of pain, Jillian swiftly pulled away from him. As he lunged at Kahlan, she used his forward momentum to impale him on the knife in her other hand. She jerked the blade upward until it hit ribs. His eyes opened wide in surprise. She stepped aside as he fell past her, his insides spilling out when he hit the cold hard ground. In all the confusion she didn't see the sixth special guard, but she knew there was one.

The mass of men on the slope behind Richard was continually slipping downward, flooding into the bowl of the Ja'La field. Clusters of soldiers, as they fought, swarmed out onto the flat field. Most of the men with bows had already been rolled under by the churning throng. Because many of the men with the torches had long since been plowed down as well by the battle descending on them, it was getting darker. It was becoming difficult to see.

The Ja'La field was being inundated with combatants. Men fought for their lives while others fought to take life. Yet others, drunk after a day of celebrating at Ja'La matches, fought for the sake of fighting. Men grievously injured littered the ground. Everywhere men who had been hurt screamed in pain. No one helped them.

There were soon so many men with their faces covered in red that it was becoming difficult to keep track of Richard. What only a brief time ago made him stand out now served to hide him. Only moments ago he was conspicuous; now he was a phantom among the chaos.

None of the soldiers appeared to be slowing down or holding back. They were enraged and in the mood to kill anyone and everyone. Men swinging axes took off arms, split skulls, and chopped chests open. Men with swords ran others through.

Despite how increasingly difficult it was, Kahlan kept

Richard in sight as soldiers attacked him. For many, he was the object of their wrath. He was responsible for the blasphemy against the Imperial Order. He was the one who had dared to think he could defeat the emperor's team.

He had accomplished the unthinkable. They hated him for it. They hated him for what they saw as his arrogance.

Kahlan supposed that they believed that he should have failed—deliberately if he had to—and then everything would have been fine. Failure was a talisman for such men, a grudge they kept close. It brought out their hatred whenever someone succeeded at something, at anything. Success had to be crushed. These were the brutes of the Order, steeped in the Order's teachings, being brutes. The beliefs of the Order, after all, needed brutes to enforce the faith.

As Richard steadily crossed the field, coming toward Kahlan, men continually attacked him. He cut them down with summary composure. He was methodical in the way he made his way across the field. Those who tried to stop him died.

"What should we do?" a frightened Jillian asked.

Kahlan glanced around. There was nowhere to escape. The Imperial Order Army was all around them. There was no route out. Kahlan, being invisible to most of them, could escape on her own, but she wasn't about to leave Jillian and Nicci to fend for themselves among such brutes. Even if she wanted to, though, there was the matter of the collar around her neck.

"We need to stay here," Nicci said.

Kahlan, knowing that there was no real way for them to get away, still puzzled at the woman. "Why?"

"Because Richard will have a difficult time finding us if we go far from this spot."

Kahlan didn't really think there was anything he could do. After all, she and Nicci both had collars around their necks. Jagang might have been hurt, but he was still conscious. If they tried to leave he would stop them with those collars—or worse. She was willing to test it, but not until she saw a worthwhile opportunity.

It was always possible that Richard would be able to finish off Jagang. Then they would have a chance—as long as Sister Ulicia or Armina didn't show up in the meantime. Jagang was a dream walker. For all Kahlan knew, he might have already used his control of their minds to bring them running to his aid.

Holding Jillian close, Kahlan glanced around. Nicci protected the girl from the other side. In every direction men were in a frenzy of killing.

Kahlan nodded. "For the moment we're safer here, protected by Jagang's guards. The way things are going, though, that may not last long."

All around men fought on. Jagang was on his knees, in the center of his guards, clutching his chest. Some of the guards had knelt down beside him to support him in case they had to get him on his feet and fight their way out. Other men shouted urgent orders to get a Sister. Other royal guards savagely slashed at the soldiers who came within range, trying to keep the mob back. The ground all around the emperor's observation area was becoming slick with blood and gore.

Kahlan stood transfixed, watching Richard.

Men from every side rushed in, trying to kill him. He moved among them as if he really were a phantom. In much the same way he had evaded blockers, he ducked aside when blades swung at him, sidestepped thrusts when he had to, slipping between men when they tried to wall him in. When he thrust his sword it was swift and sure and men died. He was a picture of economy of motion, never doing more than was necessary as he fought his way across the Ja'La field. All around tens of thousands of men fought in a noisy, tumultuous battle.

Richard was a point of serenity in the sea of chaos.

His sword flashed and men fell. He didn't even bother to kill many, he simply shoved them out of his way after they had thrust or swung their swords at him. When a man charged in with a knife, Richard set his stance and with a lightning strike to the side took the attacker's head off.

Kahlan watched spellbound.

She understood the way he used a blade.

It was completely unlike the way any of the men around them did. It was, in a way, like watching herself in the heat of battle. Even though the soldiers were taken by surprise, she often knew what Richard was going to do before he did it.

In some ways he fought differently from the way she fought, but in many ways there was much in common with the way she used a blade. He was stronger than she was, and so he used his strength when it was to his advantage, but he still had more in common with her than anyone she had ever seen.

Of course, she couldn't remember anything before the Sisters had captured her and used the Chainfire spell on her, so she supposed that she had to have learned from someone, and that someone had fought like Richard.

Even though he was strong, he conserved his strength by using only the amount of force necessary. He didn't go to others. He waited until they came to him. He didn't make large movements, he instead used their momentum against them, putting his blade where it needed to be so that when they arrived they ran themselves through. He seemed to know what they were going to do and where they would be before they did, and used that knowledge against them.

Even as he fought his way through the fray, his gaze was never far from her.

Despite how he fought men off as he steadily made his way across the field, though, he was still but a man, and like the way he used the weight of his team as a ram to break through stronger men and win the game, the weight of the army around him was not something he could so easily overcome. Despite how valiantly he fought, the weight of that army of men was swirling in around him, inundating him.

In another moment Kahlan could no longer see him.

"What are we going to do?" Jillian asked.

Kahlan saw that Jagang was coughing blood and laboring to breathe.

"I think we need to try to start moving."

"We can't," Nicci said. "If Richard can't find us, we're lost."

Kahlan gestured around at the chaos. "What do you think he's going to be able to do?"

"By now," Nicci said, "I would think that you would have learned not to underestimate him."

"Nicci's right," Jillian said. "I've even seen him come back from the world of the dead."

C H A P T E R 36

Kahlan could only wonder at Jillian's claim. She now knew that the man could indeed start a war, but she didn't really believe that he could go to the underworld and come back. Watching the perilous turmoil unfolding all around them, though, she knew that this was not the time or place to discuss it.

She scanned the confusion of runaway violence, searching for a way out. If Jagang died, or even if he were only to pass out, she might be able to use such an opportunity to get Jillian, Nicci, and herself away from there. She wondered if it mattered if Jagang, being a dream walker, was unconscious or not. She worried that even in an unconscious state he might still be able to control them through their collars.

If Jagang did die or lose consciousness, and wasn't able to stop Nicci and Kahlan through their collars, there was still the matter of the vast army all around them. Kahlan was invisible to virtually all of the men around them, but Jillian and Nicci certainly weren't. Getting a woman who looked like Nicci and the tempting target of a girl like Jillian through all these men would not be easy. Nicci certainly put a lot of faith in Richard, though.

"Do you really think Richard can get us out of here?" she asked Nicci.

Nicci nodded. "With my help. I think I know a way."

Kahlan didn't think that Nicci was the kind of woman who would put her faith in a hope and a prayer. During her ordeal with Jagang she had never tried to latch on to delusions or false hope for salvation. If she said she knew a way, then Kahlan was inclined to think that there was something to it.

Off through a gap in the battle, Kahlan spotted Richard. He thrust the sword forward, running a man through before the soldier could complete the swing of his own sword. Richard, covered in the bloodred symbols, immediately pulled the sword back out of the man and on the backswing smashed the pommel into the face of the man coming at him from behind.

"This may be our only chance, then," Kahlan said.

Nicci stretched her neck to check on Richard's progress before again glancing to the confusion swirling around the injured emperor. "I don't think we'll get a better one. I think it's now or never. With these collars, though . . ."

"If Jagang is distracted enough he might not use our collars to stop us."

Nicci shot Kahlan a look that suggested how foolish the thought was. "Now, listen to me," she said. "If anything goes wrong, I'll do what I can to see to it that you, Jillian, and Richard have a chance to get away." Nicci held up a cautionary finger. "If it comes to that, you take that chance—you hear me? If it comes to that, don't you dare waste the opportunity I gain you. Do you understand?"

Kahlan didn't like that Nicci was thinking of sacrificing her life to give them a chance to get away. She also wondered why Nicci would think it more important that Kahlan live than her.

"If you promise that you won't even consider doing such a thing unless there's absolutely no other way. I'd rather find a way to get us all out of this."

"It's the only life I have," Nicci said. "I want to keep it, if that's what you're wondering."

Kahlan smiled at that and put a hand on Jillian's shoulder. "Stay close, but don't get in the way if I have to use a knife. And don't be afraid to use yours if you have to."

Jillian nodded as Kahlan ushered her in the direction of the Ja'La field where she'd last seen Richard. Nicci stayed close behind Jillian.

Before Kahlan had taken a dozen steps, Commander Karg, atop a huge warhorse, broke through the wall of combat behind them. The big horse snorted its displeasure at the men in its way.

The commander, leading a large force of royal guards, looked around in appraisal of the situation. Like the men guarding Jagang, these were elite combat soldiers. They were all big, powerfully built, and armed to the teeth—and there looked to be thousands of them. The violence they brought to bear was extraordinary to witness. They poured through the soldiers on a wave of blood.

Not far off in the distance behind the royal guards Kahlan saw gouts of flame rise up into the night sky. The harsh red glow lit the straining faces of men fighting for their lives. Who the men were fighting seemed to have lost its importance. The soldiers seemed to have gone mad in a world gone mad. It was every man for himself, except for the royal guard, who did have a very clear idea of who they were fighting—anyone but them.

"Sisters are coming," Nicci said as she watched the flames and smoke boiling up into the black sky. "We don't have much time before it's too late. Try to stay out of sight and out of the way of the guard."

Kahlan nodded as she eased her way along with Jillian in a direction away from the main force fighting their way in. Nicci had a plan to get them away. Richard would be searching for them, so Kahlan didn't want to get too far away from where he had last seen them.

Her aim was to skirt the main confrontation between the regular soldiers and the royal guard while moving toward where she'd last seen Richard, hoping that as they moved off to the side she didn't get too far away from Richard's approach. At the same time she wanted to stay out of the new confrontation. The elite guard would be a very different foe from the regular soldiers.

Commander Karg leaped down off the horse among the original royal guard contingent. "Where's Jagang?" he called out to the wall of guards protecting the injured emperor.

"He's been shot with an arrow," one of the guard officers said as he signaled his men to open a path for the commander.

Kahlan saw Jagang, then, still on his knees, being supported by a big man squatting down to each side of him. He was pale, but conscious. He was having difficulty breathing, occasionally coughing, leaving little dark spots of blood on his chin and down the front of him. One hand clutched the arrow jutting from the right side of his chest.

"An arrow!" Karg yelled. "How in the name of Creation did that happen?"

The officer seized Karg by his chain mail and yanked him close. "Your man shot him!"

Commander Karg glared as he lifted the officer's chin with the point of a knife. "Get your hands off me."

The man released the commander, but returned the glare in kind.

"Now, what are you talking about it being my man?" Karg asked.

"It was your point man. He shot the emperor with an arrow."

Karg's expression darkened. "Then I'll kill him myself."

"If we don't kill him first."

"Fine. You do it, then. I don't really care who kills him—as long as he's dead that's all that matters. The man is dangerous. I don't want him running around loose to do any more damage. Just bring me his head so that I know that it's finished."

"Consider it done," the officer said.

Karg ignored the man's boast as he started pushing other men out of his way. "Get the emperor on his feet!" he yelled at the wall of men around Jagang. "We're getting him back to his compound. There are Sisters there who can help him. We can't do anything here."

No one argued. Guards helped Jagang to his feet. Two men, one to each side, put shoulders under his arms, supporting him.

"Karg," Jagang said in a weak voice.

The commander stepped close. "Yes, Excellency?"

A grin spread on Jagang's face. "Glad to see you. I guess you earned her for a while."

Commander Karg shared in a brief, sly smile with the emperor before turning and yelling at the guards. "Let's go!"

Jillian clutched Kahlan tightly on one side, Nicci on the other as they continued to slip away to the side, trying not to be seen. The guards helping Jagang started moving him out.

The men Commander Karg had brought with him hacked and slashed their way back through the battle.

Kahlan dreaded the thought of being back in Jagang's tent. As she kept an eye on the guards, she looked back over her shoulder, searching, but she didn't see Richard.

Drunken, angry soldiers fought on all around the three of them as Kahlan watched the emperor's guards start to organize a forward wedge to clear a path to get them back away from the Ja'La field and toward the emperor's compound.

Almost all of the torches had long since gone dark in the fighting. The guards had brought some of their own, but they weren't close. As dark as it was with the heavy overcast, Kahlan couldn't even see the Ja'La field anymore. Even the plateau rising up above the Azrith Plain seemed to have vanished in the blackness. She had to use the distant ramp, lit by torchlight, to get her bearings.

With a thud that shook the ground, fire boiled up as Sisters apparently used their power to blast their way through the vast army in order to get to Jagang's rescue. There had been hundreds of thousands of men at the Ja'La match. It didn't seem like any were fleeing. Now the guards protecting the emperor needed to escape that mob.

Kahlan, Jillian, and Nicci, too, needed to escape through the mob, but they didn't have thousands of heavily armed guards to help them. They relied, instead, on trying to be as inconspicuous as possible. Hunching to look harmless, they avoided looking directly at the men around them. They kept the hoods of their cloaks up and their heads down as they slowly slipped through pockets of relative calm amid the chaos. It was slow going. They still hadn't managed to get clear of the guards engaged in hand-to-hand fighting with the mob. Somehow, they had to make it through that line of guards, and then through the army beyond.

Commander Karg, a wicked grin on his snake-face, abruptly appeared out of the darkness and seized Nicci by the upper arm. "There you are." He pulled the hood of her cloak back to get a good look at her. "You're coming with me." He gestured to one of his men. "Take the girl along, too. Since we're going to have a party, we might as well make it a proper affair with a young lady for my men."

Jillian screamed as the man ripped her out of Kahlan's grip and pulled her along as he followed after Commander Karg and Nicci. When Jillian tried to stab the man, he wrenched the blade from her hand. The men couldn't see Kahlan, or they would have grabbed her as well.

Kahlan stepped in close behind the man holding Jillian. She started to lift her knife, but a powerful hand grabbed her wrist. It was one of her special guards—the sixth man, whom she'd lost track of. He towered behind her. Kahlan knew him. He was one of the smarter men. He wasn't as careless as the others. He still had all his weapons.

As Nicci and a screaming Jillian were being dragged farther and farther away from Kahlan, the man twisted her arm behind her back until her fingers went numb. She cried out in pain. His expression was grim and indifferent to her torment as he stripped the knife out of her hand. She kicked back at his shins, trying to make him let go of her. Rather than let up, the man twisted her arm all the more until the pain made it impossible for her to struggle. He muscled her in the direction the emperor was going.

Nicci looked back at Kahlan as Commander Karg dragged her through the confusion of men. Kahlan could see only glimpses of blond hair between the churning bodies.

The hand holding her let go of her wrist. Instead it grabbed her upper arm. That hand abruptly pulled her back through the battling men, back into the darkness. Kahlan turned, ready to fight what the brute obviously intended.

Richard was standing right there instead.

The world seemed to stop.

His gray eyes were staring into her soul.

Up close like this, the strange bloodred designs painted on his face were terrifying. But the smile on his face made him look like the gentlest, kindest man in all the world.

He seemed to be unable to do anything but smile as he stared into her eyes. It took Kahlan a moment to remember how to breathe.

She finally glanced down and saw the special guard who had been holding her wrist. He was on the ground; his head was twisted around at an unnatural angle. He didn't look to be breathing. With bodies sprawled everywhere, no one paid any attention to one more. After all, he was just a regular soldier, like all the men battling each other.

Except that he had been able to see her.

Kahlan's thoughts came rushing back in. The thought of that man having Nicci and Jillian made Kahlan feel dizzy and sick. She flicked her hand in a quick gesture.

"We have to help Nicci and Jillian. Commander Karg has them."

Richard didn't hesitate. His gray eyes turned toward where Nicci had vanished. "Hurry. Stay close."

Within a dozen steps they were back in the thick of battle. This time, though, it was not the regular soldiers that Richard had to fight—it was the royal guard. It didn't seem to matter. He moved through them, cutting men down to clear a path for her when he had to, avoiding them when possible.

As a man thrust his sword, Richard stepped back, out of the way, and severed the man's arm, catching the sword before it hit the ground. He tossed the sword to Kahlan. She caught it and immediately had to use it to stop a man going for Richard.

It felt good to have a sword in her hands. It felt good to be able to defend herself. The two of them cut their way onward through the royal guards.

Commander Karg glanced back and saw Richard coming. He let go of Nicci as he turned to his point man, grinning, ready to do battle. The guards all around saw that the commander wanted to handle this himself, so they turned back to their own problems.

"Well, Ruben, it seems—"

Richard swung, decapitating the snake without ceremony. He wasn't interested in anything but what needed to be done. He was a man who didn't need to teach the enemy a lesson. He was only interested in climinating them.

A guard who had seen what happened started for Richard. Nicci swiftly reached around and pulled her knife across his throat. The man's face registered complete surprise as he clutched at the gaping wound, dropping first to one knee before falling face-first to the ground.

In an instant, they were in the middle of a furious battle. With so many experienced men coming after them, Richard could no longer hold back. He cut into the royal guard with a vengeance.

Worried that there were too many for him, Kahlan couldn't let him do it alone. She now had the advantage of being invisible. She could move among the men attacking Richard and do her own damage. Men expecting to fight Richard fell to her blade coming from nowhere. Between the two of them, they were slaughtering the guard.

Nicci, too, immediately went on the attack. The three of them now had a single purpose—to fight their way out of the midst of the royal guards.

"We need to get to the ramp!" Nicci shouted at Richard.

He pulled his sword out of a man falling past him and frowned at Nicci. "The ramp? Are you sure?"

"Yes!"

Richard didn't argue. He changed the direction of the fight, covering Jillian as he battled his way through the endless mass of big men, making sure that none of them could get at her.

As they stabbed and hacked their way through, Kahlan knew that she had to stay clear of Richard so that he would have the room he needed. Most of the men were going after him. None could see Kahlan, so she pulled Jillian well back out of Richard's way so that the guards couldn't snatch her to use as a shield to get at Richard. Kahlan was better able to protect her than Nicci. Kahlan tried to shield Jillian while she also covered Nicci's back as she went after men who weren't paying attention.

As one of the men behind lifted a sword on Jillian, someone ran him though from behind.

As the dying man fell away, Kahlan found herself staring into the smiling face of a man with the strangest golden eyes.

"I'm here to help you, pretty lady."

Even in the near darkness, the man's sword gleamed.

He was dressed like an Order soldier, but he wasn't one of them. As Jillian backed against Kahlan when another man stabbed at her with a sword, the man with the golden eyes spun and with a backhanded swing caught the attacker along the side of the head. When the gleaming sword hit, the guard's head exploded in bits of bone and brain.

Kahlan blinked in astonishment.

Richard saw what was happening and rushed up. The stranger, suddenly looking enraged, thrust that gleaming sword right at Richard.

Richard then did the strangest thing: he just stood there.

Kahlan knew for certain that this time Richard was going to be run through, but the blade, which only an instant before had shattered a man's head, this time did the most bewildering thing. Just before it impaled Richard, it veered off to the side of him, as if he'd been been protected by an invisible shield of some sort.

The man, even more enraged, thrust again, but again the sword simply turned aside, slipping right by Richard. The stranger looked not only surprised, but worried. The worry turned to a look of cold rage.

"It's mine!"

Kahlan couldn't imagine what the man was talking about. Before she had a chance to wonder at it, she saw Nicci collapse, holding her throat.

A new clot of royal guards charged in with such speed and numbers that Richard was forced to turn and engage them or be killed. A new battle was suddenly in full force. Men yelling battle cries rushed in, swords swinging. Richard fought furiously, but he was forced to fall back. As the wave of men poured in, the space between Richard and Kahlan began to widen.

Kahlan started to attack the men swarming in around Richard, but the stranger grabbed her upper arm, pulling her back away. "We have to go. Now. He can handle those men. He's giving us a chance to get away. We have to take it."

"I'm not leaving him to—"

Kahlan suddenly gasped in a breath as the pain came on with full force. The sword fell from her grip. Her hands went to her throat, clawing at the collar. She screamed even though she tried not to. The searing pain was so sharp, so violent, that it was impossible not to scream.

She dropped to her knees, just as Nicci had done. Tears of agony streamed from her eyes.

"Come on!" the stranger yelled. "We have to get away—hurry!"

Kahlan was incapable of doing anything to get away. It was all she could do to pull a breath through the ripping agony.

Through vision blurred by tears, she could see the horror, the rage, on Richard's face as he tried in vain to get to her.

Yet more of the elite royal guard poured in, intent on taking out the point man who had humiliated the emperor and started the riot. Even as his sword killed with every thrust and men fell dying all around him, more and more men charged in and Richard was driven back.

Kahlan fell face-first onto the hard ground. The pain seared down the nerves of her back and then her legs, making them twitch. She had no control over her muscles.

The stranger grabbed Kahlan's arm. "Come on! We have to get away now!"

When she was unable to respond, he started dragging her.

CHAPTER 37

Richard could see Kahlan crying out in pain, clawing at the collar around her neck. His heart hammered in dread as he fought. Despite his frantic attempts to break through the wall of men in leather and chain mail it was proving impossible for him to get to her. In fact, it was all he could do to hold his own against the increasing numbers of men descending on him.

A deadly variety of weapons came in at him from every direction—swords, knives, axes, and spears. He had to shift his tactics to fend off each of them. He stabbed a man wielding a sword and on the backswing broke a spear. He ducked under an axe as it whistled past just overhead. He knew that if he made even one mistake it could cost him his life.

Through it all, despite fighting as hard as he had ever fought in his life, he was increasingly forced to give ground. It was the only way to keep from being overpowered. Time and again he went back on attack with wild fury, cutting into the enemy line, but as he did ever more men appeared to take the place of those who fell to his blade. In those flurries of frantic exertion the best he could do was to hold his ground. Whenever he took a breath he lost ground.

Kahlan was so close, but so far.

Now, Jagang was taking her from him again.

Richard reprimanded himself for not doing more to try to take out Jagang. He should have tried harder. If only that man hadn't stepped in front of Jagang at exactly the wrong moment, Richard's arrow would have done its job. But even as he told himself that he should have done more, should have tried something else, he knew that he couldn't dwell on what he might have done differently. He had to come up with something that he could do now.

In all-too-brief glimpses he could see Nicci on the ground as well. Like Kahlan, she was also in desperate distress. Richard knew that it was urgent that he help them. Samuel certainly wasn't doing anything worthwhile.

The distraction of Richard's concern was throwing his timing off. He missed connecting with a thrust, leaving the man alive to come back at him. Only swift action saved him from the blade doing more than making a shallow slash across the side of his shoulder. Several times he nearly lost his life as he tried to catch a glimpse of Kahlan. He had nearly missed a move until it was almost too late. He knew that he had to focus. He couldn't help Kahlan, Nicci, and Jillian if he was dead.

His arms, though, felt like lead.

His hands were slick with blood. His grip in his sword kept slipping.

A man spun an axe in his fingers as he lifted it, as if to show Richard that he was now up against an expert. The man caught the handle and started to swing the axe down with lethal intent. At the last instant, Richard ducked to the side, then, with a cry of effort, swung his own weapon. The strike took the man's arm off. Richard used his foot to topple the startled man back out of the way, then ducked under a wild swing of a sword at his head and thrust his own weapon into the man's lower abdomen.

The sword he was using worked, but it was not his sword. Samuel had his sword.

What Samuel was doing there Richard feared to imagine. Seeing him standing over Kahlan, though, he didn't really have to imagine.

Richard remembered Zedd telling him, when he had first given him the Sword of Truth, that he couldn't use it against Darken Rahl because he had put the boxes of Orden in play. Zedd said that during that year long period the power of Orden protected Darken Rahl from the Sword of Truth.

Richard knew that it was foolish to do what he'd just done, but he had to test his theory. He had to know the truth of it if he was to succeed in what lay ahead. The boxes of Orden really were in play in his name, and the Sword of Truth couldn't harm him for that reason.

When he thought he couldn't go on, he used the sheer rage he felt for Kahlan's dire jeopardy to force himself to continue anyway. He didn't know how long he could sustain such an effort. He knew only that when he stopped, he would die.

Just then, another man cut his way in from behind Richard, protecting his left side from a trio of men attacking from that direction. Out of the corner of his eye Richard saw red paint.

He slashed his blade down across the face of a man as soon as the man made the mistake of cocking back his arm. As he fell to the side with a cry, Richard used the opening to snatch a quick glance to his left.

It was Bruce.

"What are you doing here?" Richard yelled over at the man between the clash of steel.

"What I'm always doing—protecting you!"

Richard could hardly believe that Bruce, a regular Imperial Order soldier, was fighting beside him, fighting off the emperor's royal guard. The man was committing treason to fight beside Richard. He supposed that winning against the emperor's team was the bigger treason. Bruce fought with a fury of his own. He knew that this was a game that they couldn't afford to lose. What he lacked in finesse he made up for in sheer tenacity.

Richard stole another look and saw that Samuel was starting to drag Kahlan away. Her face was a picture of terrified distress. Her fingers were bloody from clawing at the collar.

With an abrupt flash and heavy thud to the air, the soldiers all around Richard, including Bruce, were blown back as if by a blast. Yet there was no flame, no smoke, no flying debris, no ringing noise from a blast. Standing at the core of the event, Richard was left with his vision blurred and his flesh stinging from the force of the concussion.

In every direction, the forest of big royal guards lay felled across the dark ground, like toppled trees. In the distance the roar of battle raged on, but closer in it was eerily quiet. Most of the men looked to be unconscious. A few moaned as they tried to move, but their arms dropped after briefly lifting, as if even that much was an effort too great.

A spike of pain suddenly slammed into the base of Richard's skull. It felt like he'd been hit from behind with an iron bar. The stunning pain dropped him to his knees. He recognized the sensation. He hadn't been hit with iron; it was magic. Beside him, Bruce lay facedown on the ground.

Still on his knees, Richard saw, off in the distant darkness, a gaunt woman stalking toward him through the downed soldiers. She moved like a vulture watching wounded prey. Her shabby appearance made Richard suspect that she was one of Jagang's Sisters.

Unable to endure the ringing pain in his head, Richard toppled over face-first. Hot agony flashed through every nerve in his body. Little clouds of dust were forced up into the night air with each of his panting breaths. He couldn't move his legs. He strained with all his might to get up, but he simply couldn't make his body respond. With the greatest of effort he was finally able to move his head just a little.

As he lay on his belly, he tried desperately to push himself to his knees at least, but simply couldn't. He looked across the battlefield scattered with fallen men at Kahlan. Even in obvious pain, she was looking back at him, worried for what was happening to him.

The Sister was still some distance off, but Richard knew that he was running out of time to do something.

"Samuel!" Richard yelled.

Samuel, trying to drag Kahlan by her arm, stopped in his tracks and looked back at Richard, his golden eyes blinking. Richard couldn't help Kahlan. At least, not in the way he wanted to help her.

"Samuel, you idiot! Use the sword to cut the collar off her neck."

Samuel, one hand holding Kahlan's arm, with his other hand lifted the sword he coveted so much, frowning at it.

Richard watched as the Sister off through the darkness stalked ever closer. He remembered once, when being taken to the Palace of the Prophets, using the Sword of Truth to cut through an iron collar around Du Chaillu's neck. He also remembered being in Tamarang with Kahlan and using the sword to slash through the prison bars. He knew the Sword of Truth could cut steel.

He also knew from when the Sisters had put the collar around his neck that the sword couldn't cut through a Rada'Han. The collar had been locked on and held tight with the power of his own gift. It wasn't so much the steel that the sword couldn't cut, Richard suspected, but the binding power of the magic itself. The Rada'Han when used as intended became, in a sense, a part of the person it was locked on to. For that reason he knew that the sword wouldn't be able to cut through Nicci's collar.

But the collar around Kahlan's neck was different. Her own gift wasn't what bound it to her. It had simply been locked around her neck and used to control her. Richard also suspected that Six might have provided Samuel with a bit of extra help. It certainly wasn't his wits that had gotten him this far. Any additional ability she'd given him might aid in this as well. Richard wasn't sure that it would work, but he was sure that it was Kahlan's only chance. He had to get Samuel to at least try.

"Hurry!" Richard screamed. "Slide the blade under the collar and pull! Hurry!"

Samuel frowned suspiciously at Richard for a moment. He looked down at Kahlan's agony, then dropped to a knee and hurriedly slipped the sword under the collar.

Some of the soldiers on the ground looked like they might be starting to come around. They groaned as they held their heads in their hands.

Samuel gave the Sword of Truth a mighty pull. The night rang with the sound of steel shattering. Kahlan, free of the collar, collapsed in relief.

As she lay on the ground panting, recovering from the ordeal, Samuel ran a short distance to the big warhorse that

Commander Karg had ridden in on. He reached under the horse's neck and caught the reins. After he had led the horse close, he hooked a hand under Kahlan's arm.

Kahlan lay limp on the ground, still stunned from the pain of the collar, but she was beginning to move her legs, trying to get up. With Samuel pulling on her arm, she was finally hauled to her feet.

Richard, still unable to get up himself, looked to the side and saw the Sister, holding the tattered shawl closed, stepping over downed men as she came ever closer.

Kahlan staggered unsteadily, but then recovered enough to bend and snatch up a sword. She intended to come to Richard's aid.

Richard couldn't allow that.

"Run!" he yelled at her. "Run! There's nothing you can do here! Get away while you still can!"

Samuel stuffed a boot in a stirrup and sprang up into the saddle.

Kahlan stood staring at Richard, tears in her beautiful green eyes.

"Hurry!" Samuel called down to her.

She didn't seem to even hear Samuel. She couldn't take her eyes off Richard. She knew she was leaving him there to die.

"Go!" Richard yelled with all his strength. "Go!"

Tears stung his own eyes. Despite how much he tried, he couldn't even rise up on his hands and knees. The magic searing through him wouldn't allow it.

The Sister cast a hand out at Samuel. A flare of light shot through the night.

Samuel used the sword to deflect the flash of light. It arced off into the night sky. The Sister looked surprised.

In the distance all around, the battle raged on. Closer in, the guards stunned by the initial blast of the Sister's power still hadn't recovered enough to get up. Apparently, the Sister didn't want them interfering. She had plans of her own.

The big warhorse tossed its head as it pawed the ground. Kahlan looked over at Nicci. She was curled up in a ball, shuddering in pain. Jillian lay on the ground beside her, stunned by the same blast of the Sister's magic. Despite her chance to escape, Richard knew that Kahlan was going to throw that chance away to try to help them.

He knew that there was nothing Kahlan could do for Nicci. If Kahlan stayed, she would die. It was as simple as that. As much as he hated the thought, at the moment Samuel was her only salvation.

"Run!" Richard cried out, his voice choked with tears.

"But I have to help Nicci and—"

"There's nothing you can do for her! You'll die! Run while you still can!"

Samuel reached down and seized her arm, helping to pull her up onto the horse behind him. As soon as she was up, Samuel wasted no time in kicking his heels against the horse. The horse bounded away at a dead gallop, throwing up dirt and rocks in its wake.

As the horse disappeared into the darkness, Kahlan looked back over her shoulder.

He never took his eyes off her, knowing that it was the last time he would ever see her.

In a moment, still looking back at Richard, she vanished into the dark confusion of the camp and was gone.

Richard sagged against the cold, hard ground, tears dripping from his face.

Out of the darkness, the Sister, making her way among the hundreds of stunned royal guards rolling on the ground, finally arrived to stand over him. He felt the level of pain increase, making it difficult to pull each breath. She wanted to make absolutely certain that he wasn't able to lift so much as a finger against her.

She peered down at him in surprised wonder. "Well, well, as I live and breathe, if it isn't Richard Rahl himself."

Richard didn't remember the Sister. She looked haggard. Her graying hair was unkempt. Her clothes were little more than rags. She looked more like a beggar than a Sister of the Light—or a Sister of the Dark, he didn't know which.

"His Excellency is going to be very pleased with me for bringing him such a prize. I think he will be more than pleased, as well, to have a chance at last to extract vengeance on you, my boy. I imagine that before the night is finished you will be just beginning a very long ordeal in the torture tents."

Memories of Denna flashed through Richard's mind.

CHAPTER 38

Even in his agony, unable to get up off the ground, Richard couldn't help being joyful that Kahlan no longer had that terrible collar around her neck. She was free of Jagang.

Richard knew that even if Samuel got himself caught or killed before they could escape the camp, Kahlan was invisible to these men. She would still be able to get away on her own. Knowing Kahlan, she would probably use that advantage to annihilate half the camp on her way out. No matter what happened to Richard, now, his relief for Kahlan was what mattered most to him.

Kahlan didn't know who she was, and she wouldn't know where to go, but she would be alive and out of immediate danger. Richard had come to the Order's encampment to help free her. He had succeeded in that much of it. Despite the peril he was now in, it was worth it to him to have managed to help her get away.

He looked beyond the Sister standing above him to Nicci. It was going very badly for her. He'd had one of those collars around his neck. He knew well the lonely agony she was in. Richard wished that he could help her as well, or at least let her know that she wasn't alone and abandoned. But he could do nothing.

He knew that Jillian was not going to fare any better. He reminded himself not to fixate on such terrible thoughts.

One problem at a time, he told himself. He had to find some way to help them both.

The pain abruptly lifted from his arms and legs. The rest of him still felt on fire. Even though he could at last begin to move, his head was still in so much pain that everything looked blurred and distorted.

"On your feet," the Sister above him said.

She sounded like she was in a vile mood. She had professed to be pleased that catching Richard would gain her a reward from Jagang, but she certainly didn't sound like a woman in good spirits over her unexpected luck.

She had to be a Sister of the Dark, he decided. He supposed that it didn't really matter.

"I bet you're not too happy to see my face again," she said in a tone of smug satisfaction.

She probably thought she had been important, thought the whole world would know her haughty scowl, her condescending attitude, her sharp tongue. Some people thought they could gain prominence, prestige, and renown through pompous arrogance. They mistook fear for respect. Richard really didn't remember the woman, though, and saw no point in humoring her.

"Can't say that I really remember you. Should I, for some reason?"

"Liar! Everybody at the palace knew me!"

"That's nice," Richard said, trying to stall so that he could recover some of his strength.

"On your feet!"

Richard did his best to try to comply. It wasn't easy. His limbs didn't work as well as he would have liked.

Once he was up onto his hands and knees she kicked him in the ribs. Richard winced at the blow. Fortunately, she didn't have the weight or power to make the kick damaging, merely painful. It was her gift that was dangerous.

"Now!" she screamed.

Richard staggered to his feet. His arms and leg were beginning to shake off the searing pain. His head wasn't.

The men all around were still down, but some of them looked like they were beginning to regain consciousness. Bruce rolled over, groaning as he clutched his head.

The Sister's gaze flicked across at a rise in the noise of the battle in the darkness beyond. Richard used the opportunity to take a quick glance, surveying the weapons on the ground. If she turned her back on him he had to take the chance. Once Jagang had him strapped down in the torture tents Richard knew that he would never see the light of day again.

As much as that fate terrified him, a part of him couldn't help feeling lighthearted knowing that Kahlan had gotten away. He swallowed back his anguish at the tears he had seen in her eyes as she had made good her escape. It reminded him of how much she loved him, but she no longer remembered that.

"You don't know how long I've waited for something like this, something that could gain me the emperor's favor. At last the Creator has answered my prayers and delivered you into my grasp."

"So," Richard said, "your Creator is in the habit of delivering victims to you in answer to prayers? He is so giddy at the flattery of your grimy hands pressed together in supplication to him that he is only too eager to help you fill the torture tents?"

She watched him with a slow, cunning smile. "Your flippant tongue will shortly be cut out so humble servants of the Creator will not have to hear you spout your blasphemy."

"A few people have told me that my flippant tongue is one of my shortcomings, so you will only be doing me a service by removing it."

Her cunning smile curdled with bile. She turned to the side, gesturing expansively out at the camp. "You think that you—"

Richard slammed a kick to the side of her face with all the force he could muster. The powerful blow completely caught her off guard, lifting her feet clear of the ground as it smashed into her. Teeth and blood flew off into the darkness. She landed on her side with a hard thud. The stunning impact of his boot looked to have shattered her jaw.

Richard dove for a sword. He knew that he dared not underestimate such a woman. Until she was dead, she could kill him—or make him wish that he was dead. His fingers seized the hilt of a sword. He spun around to plunge it into her.

The air exploded with light. Richard landed on his back so hard that it drove the air from his lungs.

She was up, blood streaming from the bottom of her face in long strings that whipped around as she lifted both hands. Richard could hardly believe that she was able to stand. She looked like the freshly dead come back to life. He knew that she couldn't last for long, but she could very well last long enough to kill him.

The shock of the blow had obviously done horrific damage, yet that sudden shock in the heat of battle also kept her from feeling the pain right then. While for all he knew she might shortly begin to feel it and collapse screaming in agony, at the moment she wasn't feeling it and a moment was all she was going to need.

Murder filled her eyes.

Richard tried to scramble to his feet to finish her, but it felt like a bull had lain down on his chest. The air was being squeezed out of him.

She took a step toward him, then paused, looking confused. Her eyes went out of focus. She abruptly clutched her chest.

Richard blinked in surprise as he watched her stumble forward another step and topple face-first, slamming hard onto the ground without even trying to break her fall. He stared for an instant, not sure if it was a trick of some kind. She didn't move. The weight had lifted from his chest.

Not wanting to waste the opportunity, he grabbed the sword he'd dropped.

Something caught Richard's attention. He looked up and could not believe who he thought he saw standing in the darkness behind where the Sister had been only a moment before.

"Adie?"

The old woman smiled.

"Adie—am I ever glad to see you," Richard said as he scrambled to his feet.

"True," she said, nodding.

"What are you doing here?"

"I be headed out to go to the Keep when I saw the strangest Ja'La game with players all painted with very, very dangerous things. That be when I knew it could only be you. Since then, I tried to reach you. It be a bit of trouble."

He could only imagine.

Richard didn't take the time to consider the whole thing or question the old sorceress. He ran to where Nicci lay on the ground convulsing in pain. Her eyes stared up at him in terror, as if pleading for help. She was lost in a world of agony. It was the collar, he knew, that was inflicting the torture. He didn't know what to do.

"Can you help her?" Richard asked over his shoulder.

Adie knelt next to him. She shook her head. "It be the Rada'Han. That not be something I can get off."

"Do you have any idea who can?"

"Nathan, maybe."

"Lord Rahl, we need to hurry," an approaching voice said. "These men are waking up."

Richard frowned up at the man appearing out of the darkness, sword in hand. It was Benjamin Meiffert. He was dressed like one of Jagang's more trusted guards.

"General, what in the world are you doing here?" The recent supply convoy came to Richard's mind. "You're supposed to be down in the Old World laying waste to the Order's ability to keep this army alive."

He was nodding. "I know. I needed to come back to give you a report. We've run into a problem. A big problem."

Richard knew the man well enough to know that the trouble would have to be more than merely serious for him to abandon his mission to return to report to Richard what was going wrong. This was hardly the place to discuss it, though.

"I wasn't sure where I could find you," the general said, "but I figured that the last time I saw you it was near here, so I thought this would be my best bet. I reasoned that if you weren't here, they at least might know where you were. I've been trying to figure out a way to get up into the palace.

"A little while ago Adie and I came across each other. She told me that you were down here in the middle of this mess. I wasn't sure I believed her—believed it was possible. Turns out she was right."

Richard didn't take the time to ask how he'd managed to come up with the uniform of one of Jagang's guards. That uniform was obviously how he had been able to move around in the camp without getting himself captured or killed.

"How did you get down here?" the general asked Adie. "Maybe we can get back in the palace that way."

Adie was shaking her head. "I came down the road. It be dark and I be alone. I used my ability to help hide my presence as I reached the army guarding at the bottom of the road.

"We cannot go back that way. There be too many guards. They have gifted there with webs in place to detect those who try to slip through. Those shields not be powerful, but they be enough to snare us."

"But with your power—"

"No," she said cutting off the general. "My power be weak in the palace. Even near the plateau it still not be as it should. All those with the gift be weaker there, but they use their ability together to make it stronger. I have no other gifted to help me. I could help hide myself from them when I came through, but I not be strong enough to help all of us, especially not with the burden of Nicci in such grave condition. If we try to go back that way, we will die."

"The great inner doors are closed," the man said, thinking out loud as he considered. "They're heavily guarded as well. Even if we could get through we certainly couldn't get those doors opened."

"Nicci said she knew a way to get up into the palace," Richard told them. "She told me that we have to get to the ramp. I don't know what she was talking about, but we need to find a fast way out of this camp before we get caught. I don't think Nicci has much time, either."

Adie, leaning close, touched her slender fingers to Nicci's forehead. "True."

Richard scooped Nicci up in his arms. "Let's go."

General Meiffert stepped forward. "I can carry her, Lord Rahl."

"I've got her." Richard tilted his head. "Get Jillian."

The man hurriedly lifted the groggy girl.

"What I don't understand," Adie said as she smoothed a hand across Nicci's brow, trying to give her some comfort, "is how she was captured in the first place. She be up in the palace, the last we all saw her."

Richard felt the weight of responsibility. "Knowing Nicci, she was probably trying to find me."

"Ann be missing as well," Adie said as she touched the first two fingers of her right hand to the underside of Nicci's chin.

"I haven't seen Ann," Richard said.

Whatever Adie was doing for Nicci didn't look to be helping. Richard didn't think that Nicci could last much longer unless they found a way to get the collar off her neck. Nathan was the closest hope.

"Adie," Richard said, pointing with his chin back to where he had been on the ground when the Sister had first appeared. "That man over there, with the red paint on him. Can you help him?"

Adie peered over at the man on the ground. "Perhaps."

Adie hurried to Bruce and knelt beside him. He was only partially conscious, the same as all the other men the Sister had blasted down. Adie's straight gray and black hair hung down around her face as she bent forward, pressing her fingers to the red symbols painted across the man's temples. Bruce gasped. His eyes opened wide. He pulled a few more deep breaths as Adie removed her hand from one side.

In a moment Bruce sat up, twisting his head, trying to stretch cramped and obviously sore muscles in his neck. "What's going on?"

"Bruce, hurry up," Richard said. "We need to get out of here."

Richard's left wing man peered around at the men on the ground, at Benjamin, holding Jillian and dressed as one of Jagang's royal guards, at Adie, and finally at Richard standing a few paces away with Nicci draped in his arms.

Bruce snatched up a sword. "Ruben, what's going on?"

"It's a long story. You came to help me. You saved my life. It's time for you to decide whose side you're on."

Bruce frowned at the question. "I'm your wing man. I'm with you. Don't you know that?"

Richard looked the man in the eye. "My name's Richard."

"Well, I knew it wasn't Ruben. That's a silly name for a point man."

"Richard Rahl," Richard said.

"Lord Rahl," General Meiffert corrected, looking ready for trouble even as he held Jillian in his arms.

Bruce glanced from face to face. "Well, if you all want to die, then you can stand around here until these fellows wake up. If that's the case, then I'm not with you. If you're of a mind to live, then I'm with you."

"Ramp," Nicci said in a gasp.

Richard pulled her a little tighter. "Are you sure, Nicci? We could try for the road up the plateau." He was reluctant to trade a way he knew for the vague possibility of another route. "I know it's heavily guarded but maybe we could fight our way through. Adie could help some. We might be able to make it."

Nicci clutched his neck, pulling his head down toward her. Her blue eyes focused intently on his face. "Ramp," she whispered with all her strength.

That look in her eyes was all he needed.

"Let's go," he said to the others. "We have to get to the ramp."

"How are we going to get through all the men still fighting?" Bruce asked as they started off into the night. "It's a long way to the ramp."

With all the guards down, the area they were in was relatively calm. Out beyond, though, it was still chaos.

The general shifted Jillian's weight a little and pointed with his sword. "There's a small supply wagon just over there. We can hide Jillian and Nicci inside. With that paint on you two, you're not going to make it far before a few hundred thousand of these men decide to cut you down. No slight intended, Lord Rahl, but those odds are pretty poor. I want the two of you to hide inside with Jillian and Nicci. Adie and I will lead the wagon. Anyone will think that I'm one of the emperor's guards and Adie is a Sister. We can say that we're on urgent business for the emperor."

Richard was nodding. "Good. I like the idea. Let's hurry."

"Who is this fellow?" Bruce asked as he leaned toward Richard.

"He's my top general," Richard said.

"Benjamin Meiffert," the general said with a quick smile as they all started for the wagon. "You've earned the gratitude of a lot of good people for stepping into the teeth of death to fight beside Lord Rahl like you did."

"Never knew a general before," Bruce muttered as he hurried after the others.

CHAPTER 39

Verna clasped her hands loosely in front of her and sighed quietly as she watched Cara plant her fists on her red-leather-clad hips. The gaggle of men and women in white robes shuffled farther down the hall, gazing at the white marble walls, trailing their fingers across it, stopping here and there to peer closely at it as if they were searching for a message from the world of the dead.

"Well?" Cara asked.

An older man, Dario Daraya, laid a finger lightly across his lips. He frowned thoughtfully for another long moment as he watched the cluster of people bobbing and swaying down the corridor like corks in a river, then swiveled toward the Mord-Sith. He ran his fingers down the sky blue silk edging running down the front of his crisp white robes. He frowned at Cara, his features twisting a little as he scratched the fringe of white hair encircling his bald head.

"I'm not sure, Mistress."

"Not sure about what? Not sure that I'm right, or not sure of what they think about it?"

"No, no, Mistress Cara. I agree with you. Something is wrong down here."

Verna stepped forward. "You agree with her?"

The man nodded earnestly. "I'm just not sure what it could be."

"Like something just feels out of place?" Cara suggested.

He waggled a finger skyward. "Yes, I think that's it. Rather like in one of those dreams where you get lost in a place because the rooms are all mixed around from where they belong."

Cara nodded absently as she watched the crypt staff gliding along close to the opposite wall. They moved on down the corridor, their heads weaving up and down as they peered at the walls. They reminded Verna a little of hounds hunting through brush.

"You run the crypt staff," Verna said to the man. "Wouldn't you know if something was out of place?"

She couldn't imagine how anything could be out of place. There were carpets in a few places, a chair or two in small, side rooms, but other than that there wasn't much of anything to be out of place.

Dario watched his people for a moment, then turned back to Cara and Verna. "I take care of everything surrounding their service. There are quarters to see to, meals, clothes, supplies—all that sort of thing. I run the crypt staff. They are the ones who actually attend to the work down here."

"What kind of work, exactly?" Verna asked.

"Well, in general, sweeping, cleaning, dusting—that sort of thing. There are miles of corridors down here. The staff replaces lamp oil and candles in some places, keeps fresh torches in others. Occasionally a piece of stone will crack and need to be repaired or replaced. The caskets that aren't entombed within walls or in the floor have to be kept in good condition—the metal on some polished, on others kept free of rust, and the carved wooden ones need to be waxed to keep the wood from drying excessively. There have occasionally been leaks down here, so the exterior of the caskets must be carefully inspected to make sure they aren't getting damp or moldy.

"The crypt staff is ultimately at the service of the Lord Rahl. They see to his specific wishes, if he has any. Those entombed down here, after all, are his ancestors.

"It used to be, when Darken Rahl was alive, that the staff primarily carried out his wishes having to do with his father's tomb. Darken Rahl was the one who ordered that the tongues of the crypt staff be cut out. He feared that, while they were down here alone, they might speak ill of his dead father."

"And what if they did?" Verna asked. "What could it hurt?"

The man shrugged. "I'm sorry, but I wasn't about to question the man. When he was alive there was a constant stream of new staff workers replacing those who had been executed for various reasons. It was unhealthy to be anywhere near the man, and the crypt staff often found themselves the object of his rages. New staff were rounded up from time to time and pressed into service.

"Darken Rahl only left me with my tongue because my work didn't take me down here very often. I oversaw the staff. I need to interact with others on the palace staff, so I need to be able to talk with people. The rest of the staff, in Darken Rahl's view, didn't have anything worthwhile they needed to say, and no need for a tongue."

"How do you communicate with them?" Cara asked.

Dario touched his lips again as he glanced at his staff slowly making their way farther on down the hall. "Well, the way you would imagine. They use signs. Grunt a little, or nod, to make their thoughts known. They can hear, of course, so I don't need to use signs to speak to them.

"They share the same quarters and work together, so they are almost always alonc among themselves. For that reason they've come to be quite conversant with signs they've invented among themselves. I'm not nearly as familiar with their unique language as they are among themselves, but for the most part I've come to be able to understand them. Enough to get by, anyway.

"Most of them are quite bright. People sometimes think they're stupid because they can't talk. In some ways they are more aware of the goings-on in the palace than most of the other members of the palace staff. Since people know that they're mute, they often don't even consider that they listen just fine. These people often know what's happening around the place long before I do."

Verna found their little world down in the tombs a remarkable, if somewhat unsettling, revelation. "Well, what about down here? What do they think is going on down here."

Dario shook his head with a look of concern. "They haven't brought anything to my attention, yet."

"Why not?" Cara asked.

"Fear, probably. In the past crypt staff were frequently executed for the most trivial things. Such executions never made any real sense. They learned that to stay alive it was best to be part of the background, to be as invisible as possible. Bringing up problems was not the way to live a long life.

"To this day, they even feared to come and tell me things. Once, there had been a leak staining a wall. They never said a word, probably because they feared they would be put to death for the stain tainting the tombs of the ancestors of Lord Rahl. I only found out about the stain because one night I went to see them in their quarters and they were gone. I found them down here, all working feverishly to scrub the stain away before anyone saw it."

"What a way to live," Cara murmured to herself.

"What are they doing, anyway?" Verna asked as she watched several of the staff running their hands along the wall, as if feeling for something hidden in the smooth, white marble.

"I'm not sure," Dario said. "Let's ask them."

Some distance back down the corridor a force of the First File waited. Some of them had their crossbows loaded with the special red-fletched arrows that Nathan had found for them. Verna didn't like being anywhere near those wicked things. Their deadly magic made her sweat.

The crypt staff, made up of both women and men, was gathered in a clutch, inspecting the walls and every intersection along the way. They had all been down in the various tomb levels most of the day and Verna was tired. She was usually in bed by this time. That was where she wanted to be. As far as she was concerned, the meticulous inspection of nothing at all could wait until the next day.

Cara didn't look tired. She looked intense. She had this "problem down in the tombs" bone in her teeth and she wasn't going to let go for anything.

Verna would have left Cara to it, except that when they had searched out Dario Daraya, the man in charge of the crypt staff, to ask what he could tell them, he had not dismissed the inquiry, as Verna had expected. He seemed nervous that they had even asked the question. It turned out that he shared Cara's uneasy suspicion but as of yet hadn't mentioned it to anyone. He told Verna and Cara that he strongly suspected that the members of his staf were also aware of something being amiss.

Verna had learned that among the vast force that was the palace staff, the members of the crypt staff were considered the lowest of the low. Those with responsibility over important sections of the palace dismissed the work down in the tomb areas as simple, menial work for mutes. The crypt workers were also shunned because they spent their existence working among the dead, thus carrying the invisible taint of superstition.

Dario had explained that such attitudes had left them a shy and withdrawn lot. They didn't eat in the common areas with other people on the staff. They kept to themselves and kept their own counsel.

Verna watched them down the corridor a ways, conversing among themselves in their strange language of signs. Having developed the language among themselves, no one else understood them except, perhaps, for Dario Daraya.

As much as Verna, and especially Cara, wanted to question the staff directly, they were forced to allow Dario to do it. The mere close proximity of an outsider—especially a Mord-Sith—sent the silent group into trembling and even tears. These were people who had been treated very badly by the last Lord Rahl, and probably the one before that. Many of their number, no doubt close friends and loved ones, had been put to death for allowing the petal of a white rose to lie too long on the floor of the tomb of Darken Rahl's father. They had lived and died by the decree of a madman.

These people were, understandably, quite terrified of authority.

Verna had cautioned Cara that if she really wanted to get answers then she had to stay back and let Dario get those answers for them.

Verna watched Dario, standing in their midst, quietly asking questions. The people surrounding him became excited at certain points, pointing this way and that, and making signs to him. Dario nodded from time to time and gently asked more questions, which drew more of the silent language from some of the staff.

Dario at last returned. "They say that there is no problem in this corridor. Everything here is fine."

Cara spoke through gritted teeth. "Well then if they don't—"

"But," Dario interrupted, "they say that in that corridor there"—he pointed ahead to the right—"there is something wrong."

Cara studied the man's face for a moment. "Come on, then, let's have a look."

Before Verna could hold her back, Cara marched in long strides right up to the knot of a dozen and a half people. Verna thought that several of them might faint of fright as they cringed back, fearful of what she was going to do to them.

"Dario says that you think there is something wrong in that corridor up there." Cara gestured to the intersection ahead. "I think there's something wrong, too. That's why I wanted to have all of you come show me what you think. I'm the one who called for you. I called for you because I know that you people know more about this place than anyone."

They looked uneasy about her intentions.

Cara looked around at the faces watching her. "When I was a little girl, Darken Rahl came to our home and captured my family. He tortured my mother and father to death. He locked me up for years. He tortured me to make me be a Mord-Sith."

Cara turned a little and lifted the red leather at her waist, showing them a long scar along her side and back. "He did this to me. See?"

The people all leaned in ogling the scar. One man reached out and tentatively touched it. Cara turned his way to let him. She took a woman's hand and rubbed her finger along the bumpy length of the scar.

"Here, look at this," she said, pulling her sleeves up and holding out her wrists for them to see. "These are left from the shackles when he hung me up—chained to the ceiling."

The people all leaned in looking. Some of them gently touched the scars on her wrists.

"He hurt you, too, didn't he?" Cara knew the answer, but she had asked anyway. When they all nodded, she said, "Show me."

The people all opened their mouths wide for her to see their missing tongues. Cara looked in each mouth, nodding at what she saw. Some held a cheek aside, turning their heads to be sure she saw their scars. Cara carefully looked at each one until they were satisfied that she had really wanted to see.

"I'm glad that Darken Rahl is dead," she finally told them. "I'm sorry for what he did to all of you. You all have suffered. I understand; I've suffered, too. He can't hurt us anymore."

They stood listening carefully as she went on. "His son, Richard Rahl, is not at all like his father. Richard Rahl would never hurt me. In fact, when I was hurt and dying, he risked his own life to use magic to save me. Can you imagine that?

"He would never hurt any of you, either. He cares that all people can have a chance to live their own lives. He even told me that I am free to leave my service to him any time I want and he will wish me well. I know that he's telling me the truth. I stay because I want to help him. I want to help a good man for a change instead of being a slave to a bad one.

"I've seen Richard Rahl weep for Mord-Sith who have died." She tapped her chest over her heart with a finger. "Do you understand what that means to me? In here? In my heart?

"I think Richard Rahl is in trouble. I want to help him and those fighting with him against people who harm others. We want to protect your lives from all those men outside, on the Azrith Plain, who would harm or enslave you all over again."

The people were blinking tearfully at her story, a story they could understand in a way that others couldn't.

"Will you help me? Please?"

Verna knew how heartfelt Cara's words really were.

She felt shame that she had never really thought Cara could be kind and understanding, that she mistook Cara's steadfast defense of Richard as merely a Mord-Sith's aggressive nature. It was much more than that. It was appreciation. Richard had done more than save her life. He had taught her how to live her life. Verna wondered if, as Prelate, she could ever hope to do as much.

Two of the women, one to each side, took up Cara's hands and started leading her down the corridor. Verna shared a look with Dario. He lifted an eyebrow, as if to say that now he'd seen everything.

The two of them followed after the shuffling group of people who had adopted Cara as a patron sister. A number of the people reached out as they made their way down the corridor to touch her, to run a hand down the red leather of her arm, to rest a hand on her back as if to say that they understood the pain and abuse she had endured and were sorry that they had misjudged her.

As they went down the next corridor, Verna realized that she was no longer sure where they were. The tomb area was a confusing maze that occupied several levels. In addition to that, most of the corridors were identical. They were all the same width and height and all made of the same white marble with gray veining through it. She knew that they were down in the lowest level, but other than that, she was depending on the others to know exactly where they were.

Behind, keeping their distance so as not to interfere, the soldiers, ever watchful, followed as quietly as possible.

The group of people in white robes finally came to a halt along a section of the corridor where there wasn't an intersection. Farther down there were a number of halls going off in both directions, but in this place there were none.

Several of the staff placed the flats of their hands on the white marble. They glanced back at Cara as they lightly ran their hands over the walls.

"Here?" Cara asked.

The staff, most of them gathered around her like chicks around a mother hen, were all nods.

"What is it about this place, this corridor, that is strange to you?" she asked them.

Several people, with their hands held uniformly apart, made back and forth gestures toward the wall.

Cara didn't understand. Neither did Verna. Dario scratched his fringe of white hair. Even he was puzzling at the strange show. The staff huddled a moment, using their signs, silently discussing the problem among themselves.

The people all turned back to Cara. Three of them pointed at the wall, then shook their heads. They all turned and looked at Cara again to gauge her reaction and understanding.

"You don't like the way the wall looks?" Cara guessed.

The people all shook their heads side to side. Cara cast a questioning look back at Verna and Dario. Dario turned his palms up and shrugged. Verna could offer no suggestion either.

"I still don't understand," Cara said. "I know you think something is wrong with the wall"—heads nodded—"but I don't know what." She sighed. "I'm sorry. It's not your fault. It's my failing. I just don't know much about walls. Can you help me understand?"

One of the men in the group took Cara's hand and gently pulled her closer to the wall. He reached out and with the finger of his other hand touched the stone. He looked back at Cara.

"Go on," she said, "I'm listening."

The man smiled at the way she'd put it and then returned his attention to the wall. He began tracing some of the gray veining. Cara leaned in a little and frowned as she watched. He looked back over his shoulder. When he saw her frowning in concentration, he went back to tracing the gray swirl. He did it several times, over and over in the same place, to make Cara pay attention.

"It looks like a face," Cara said in quiet wonder.

The man nodded furiously. Others nodded with him. They all rejoiced silently. A woman reached out and eagerly traced the same gray whorl. Her finger followed a curl, an arc. She then punctuated it the same as the man, by touching the center in two places. Eyes.

Cara reached out and traced the same face in the stone, just as they had done, following the gray eddies with a finger, tracing out the mouth, the nose, then the eyes.

The white-robed group made happy-sounding grunts,

clapping her on the back, thrilled that they had been able to make her see the face.

Verna couldn't imagine what it could mean.

One man from the group motioned, then hurried to a spot across and a little farther down the corridor. He quickly traced out something in the gray veining. From where Verna stood she couldn't see it, but she assumed that it was probably another face. He rushed to another spot along the corridor and traced out a small face there in the stone looking out at them. He rushed to another place and pointed out a larger face.

Verna was beginning to understand. These people were down here all the time. They had learned the individual markings in what appeared at first glance as indistinguishable slabs of white marble. But they weren't indistinguishable to these people. To the crypt staff, who spent their lives down here cleaning and caring for the place, these markings were like street signs. They recognized them all.

Comprehension had come onto Cara's face as well. She was also looking more worried.

"Show me again what's wrong," she said in a serious but quiet voice.

The people, excited that Cara was now following along with what they were telling her, all rushed back over to the section of wall where they had shown her the first face. Standing before the wall, all of them moved both hands back and forth, toward and away from the wall.

They paused, the whole group turning to Cara to see if she understood. She watched them.

One of the men then pointed at the wall and beyond in an arcing movement, as if indicating something away over a hill in the distance. Verna was confused again.

Cara stared at the face in the wall. Her brow drew down. She was suddenly looking gravely concerned. Verna was still in the dark, as was Dario, but Cara's blue eyes were alive with dawning comprehension.

Cara suddenly circled her arms around the backs of several of the group and ushered them on their way back toward Verna and Dario. She put a hand on the backs of others and gently pushed, herding them away from the troubling wall. At the rear of the group, arms out, she shepherded the rest of them back up the corridor.

Along the way, Cara gathered up Verna and Dario, turning them around and moving them along. The mute crypt staff all followed close on her heels, looking both concerned that Cara was alarmed about something, and proud of themselves at the same time.

Cara leaned close to Verna when they had retreated up the corridor and around the corner of the intersection.

"Get Nathan," she said in a tone of clear command.

Verna's brow twitched. "Does it need to be tonight? Don't you think that we—"

"Get him now," Cara said in a deadly calm voice of authority.

Her blue eyes were cold fire. Verna knew that, as kind and understanding as Cara had been with the staff, she was not to be argued with now. She was now in charge of the situation. Verna had no idea what the situation was, but she trusted the woman and knew that she needed not to question Cara's word in this.

Cara snapped her fingers at the men waiting nearby. The commander rushed forward to see what she wanted. As soon as he arrived, he stood leaning close, focused on what she might say.

"Yes, Mistress?"

"Get General Trimack down here. Tell him it's urgent. Tell him to bring men. Lots of men. Alert the Mord-Sith. I want them down here, too. Do it now."

Without question the man clapped a fist to his heart and raced away.

Verna clutched the Mord-Sith's arm. "Cara, what's going on?"

"I'm not sure."

"We're about to throw the palace into full alert, drag hundreds if not thousands of people all the way down here—General Trimack, the First File, Nathan—and you don't know why?"

"Didn't say I didn't know why. Said I wasn't sure. I think there are faces looking at us that shouldn't be looking at us."

Cara turned to the faces all watching her.

"Am I right?"

The crypt staff broke out in excited, mute grins, thrilled to have someone understand and believe them.

CHAPTER 40

Richard peered out from under the canvas tarp as the wagon rolled through the outer fringes of the Order's camp. Every time a gust of wind buffeted the wagon he had to keep a good hold on the tarp to keep it down. The towering monstrosity of the ramp loomed overhead. Up this close he could see just how immense it had already become. It didn't seem a false hope that it could eventually reach the palace at the top of the plateau.

After Adie had used her gift to help them make it through the fighting around the Ja'La field, it had been a relatively uneventful journey across the rest of the vast Imperial Order encampment. Regular soldiers wanted nothing to do with the potential trouble offered by a small wagon escorted by what appeared to be a high-ranking royal guard and a Sister. Men mostly ignored them as they passed.

The riot, as large as it was, had primarily been confined to the spectators at the Ja'La match. While it seemed that perhaps hundreds of thousands of men were involved in the fight over the outcome of the game, and it was a vast, gruesome bloodbath, the trouble was still limited to a fraction of the encampment. In much of the rest of the camp commanders had rushed armed men in to clamp down on movement and contain the trouble.

Despite that effort, the turmoil had spread to a certain extent. Most of these men had not joined a struggle to be cold, hungry, and spend their lives digging dirt. They were becoming resentful of having to work at menial labor rather than being about the business of murder, rape, and plunder. Waiting for the prospect of conquest was one thing, but now the remaining spoils looked rather limited and the work of getting to them was considerable. It seemed that self-sacrifice for the cause of the Order had its limits. The line appeared to have been drawn at actually having to work.

Authorities, though, were not only quick but brutal in crushing pockets of trouble as they broke out. As unhappy as many of the men were with their conditions, when they saw what happened to some of those who stirred up unrest, they lost the stomach to join in.

Several times General Meiffert had had to bluff his way through groups of men. Once his bluster had needed to be reinforced by killing a man with a swift slash across the side of his neck. Other times Adie had quietly used her powers to ease their way through potential trouble. Having the soldiers think she was one of Jagang's Sisters ended a lot of questions before they even began. Several times, when she had been stopped and questioned by soldiers foraging for loot, she merely stared at the men without answering. Looking into her completely white eyes as she glared at them, they lost their nerve and vanished back into the darkness.

Far behind them at the Ja'La field there were pockets within the riot that were finally being brought under control, but for the most part the night there had been abandoned to chaotic battles between drunken soldiers. The emperor's guard hadn't really cared about restoring order; they had only been interested in saving the life of the emperor.

Nicci's trembling pain told Richard that Jagang was still alive and able to exert his influence. That didn't mean he was conscious, though. What Richard didn't know was if Jagang at some point, when unable to force her to return, might decide to kill her through the collar. If he did, there was nothing Richard could do to stop him. Getting the collar off from around her neck was the only solution, and to do that they needed to get to Nathan up in the palace.

Peeking out from under the tarp, Richard spotted a confusion of vast pits spread out ahead in the torchlight. Richard could see lines of men, animals, and wagons leading out of pits where material was being dug up. Clouds of dust streamed away from areas where men were actively digging. The lines of men and wagons coming out of those pits stretched all the way to the ramp. Those lines were all in constant motion as they conveyed the dirt and rock to the construction site.

Richard again glanced at Nicci, lying in the low wagon bed right beside him. She had his hand in a death grip. Her whole body trembled. He ached with sympathy for her agony. He knew what it felt like. He had endured the same magic from a collar. His ordeal hadn't lasted as long, though. He didn't know how long she could live through such pain.

Jillian lay on the other side of Nicci, holding her other hand. Bruce lay beyond Jillian, carefully peering out from under the tarp on that side from time to time, sword at the ready in case he had to help them fight their way out of trouble.

Richard wasn't sure how much he could trust the man. Bruce had more than once stepped in to protect Richard at great risk to his own life. Richard knew that not every single man in the Order's camp would choose the Order, if really given the choice. There had to be some, even if only a few, who would rather have nothing to do with the Order. Richard didn't really know Bruce all that well, so he didn't know what experiences the man had lived through that would cause him to take this chance to side with him, but Richard was glad that he had. In a small way it gave him hope that not the whole world had gone mad. There were still some people who valued their own lives and wanted the freedom to live those lives as they saw fit. They were even willing to fight for it.

As the wagon wobbled to a halt, Adie stepped close, laying an elbow casually over the short sidewall beside Richard. She glanced over. "We be here."

Richard nodded, then leaned close to Nicci. "We're here. We're near the ramp."

Her brow was tightly creased in agony. She seemed to be in a faraway world of suffering. With great effort she released some of the pressure on his hand, then squeezed again to let him know that she'd heard him.

Despite how cold it was, she was drenched in sweat. Her

eyes were closed most of the time. Occasionally they opened wide as she gasped from a terrible twist of pain.

It was making Richard crazy that he couldn't help her right then and there, that she had to wait, suffering in her isolated world of torment, enduring the dragging eternity it seemed to be taking to get her to Nathan.

"Nicci, can you tell me what we need to do? We're here, but I don't know why. Why did you want us to go to the ramp?"

He gently pulled back hair that was plastered to her beaded brow. Her eyes opened wide with a stitch of overpowering pain.

"Please . . ." she whispered.

Richard leaned closer yet so he could hear her. "What is it?"

He put his ear closer to her mouth.

"Please . . . end it. Kill me."

She shook with a moan as another bout of pain cascaded through her. She started to sob.

Richard, terror rising in his throat, clutched her close. "We're almost there. Hold on. If we can get inside the palace I think Nathan can get that collar off. Just hold on."

"Can't," she wept.

Richard pressed his hand against the side of her face. "I'll help you get it off. I promise. We just need to get inside. I need to know how do we get in."

"Catacombs," she said in a gasp as her back arched.

Catacombs? Richard blinked at the word. Catacombs?

He lifted the flapping canvas tarp a little and peered out again. The ramp stood nearby. Beyond the ramp the black wall of the plateau, only some of the fringe at the bottom visible in the torchlight, soared up into the night.

As he looked at the plateau, it made sense.

Jillian leaned over Nicci. "Could she mean catacombs like at my homeland?" She looked down at Nicci. "Catacombs like in Caska?"

Nicci nodded.

Richard again looked out from under the tarp, searching for anything that looked different, for any sign of where the entrance could be. He went over in his mind everything he could remember about the ancient catacombs in Caska. Deep within those underground rooms was where they'd found the *Chainfire* book. The maze of ancient tunnels and chambers had run on for miles. Richard had spent nearly the whole night searching through the catacombs and he knew that he'd only seen a fraction of them.

Finding the entrance, though, had been difficult. It had been a only small opening that had led him down into the hidden underground world of the catacombs. Finding such an opening out here in the open, with all these men around, was going to be far more than merely difficult.

He turned back. "Nicci, how did you find catacombs down in the palace?"

She shook her head. "Found us."

"They found you?" Richard peered out again as the realization hit him. "Dear spirits . . ."

It all started to make sense to him. Jagang's men, digging the pits, had uncovered ancient catacombs. They must have used those tunnels to get up into the palace.

"They got up into the palace and captured you? Is that what you mean?"

Nicci nodded.

But if they had gotten up into the palace, then why would they still be working on the ramp? He realized that if the catacombs were anything like the ones in Caska they would need more than those tunnels to get an army up into the People's Palace. It would be like trying to force sand through an hourglass.

It could also be that the ramp was a diversion to buy them time to do just that.

Diversion or not, Jagang might have gotten spies up into the palace through the catacombs. If there was a way in, there was no telling the damage such a breach could cause.

It had to be Sisters who had snuck in. It would have taken Sisters to have captured Nicci. With their powers weakened by the spell of the palace, he knew that it would have taken more than one.

"The crews digging dirt for the ramp discovered catacombs," Richard guessed out loud to Nicci. "Sisters went through the catacombs and found a way to get up into the palace. That's how they captured you."

Though the trembling and pain, Nicci squeezed his hand in confirmation.

Richard leaned close to Nicci. "Does anyone up there know that Jagang has a way in?"

She rocked her head from side to side. "Gathering inside," she managed.

Richard's heart missed a beat. "They're gathering men inside to attack the palace?"

She nodded again.

"Then we'd better get in there and warn them," Bruce said.

"Adie," Richard said to the old woman standing right beside the wagon, "did you hear all that?"

"Yes. The general be right here. He heard as well."

Richard looked out from under the tarp. Off in the distance to the right a little he saw a pit where there were no lines of men and wagons.

Richard pointed out from under the tarp. "Look there, around that pit. There are men standing evenly spaced around the entire area."

"Guards," General Meiffert confirmed.

"That has to be where they found the catacombs—down in that pit. Look at the way they've halted all digging between there and the plateau."

"Why would they do that?" the general asked.

"The catacombs would be ancient. There's no telling what condition they might be in. They don't want to risk caving in any of the tunnels running in under the palace."

"It must be so," Adie said.

"How are we going to get down into the pit?" General Meiffert asked.

"If we had more royal-guard uniforms we might be able to get down in there," Bruce suggested.

"Maybe," Richard said, "but what about Nicci and Jillian?"

Bruce didn't have an answer.

"They certainly couldn't walk in there," General Meiffert agreed, "and a wagon going down into a guarded pit would obviously be cause for suspicion."

"Maybe," Richard said, thinking out loud. "Maybe not."

General Meiffert looked back over his shoulder. "What do you have in mind?"

Richard gently shook Nicci's shoulders. "Are there books down in the catacombs?"

"Yes," she managed.

Richard turned back to the general. "We could tell the guards that, with all the trouble in the camp tonight, the emperor wants to bring a load of important books back to his compound to be sure that they're safe. He sent this Sister along to see to getting the books he's concerned about. You tell them that you need them to organize a contingent of guards to escort the wagon back to the compound."

"They'll want to know why we didn't bring guards with us."

"Because of the trouble," Bruce suggested. "Tell them that with the rioting the officers didn't want to risk any guards taken from the duty of protecting the emperor."

Richard nodded at the idea. "While they're busy going off to gather us some men, we slip down into the catacombs."

"Not all the guards are going to leave the site to go gathering up men for you," Bruce said. "It would sound awfully suspicious if we even suggested such a thing. Any men left in the area will see the two women—especially since we'll have to help Nicci.

"Don't underestimate these guards. See their uniforms? These are men the emperor trusts. I know what these men are like. They aren't fools and they're not lazy. They don't miss much."

"That makes sense," Richard said as he considered Bruce's advice. He frowned in thought as an idea came to him. He turned to Adie. "It's windy out tonight. Do you think you could help the wind?"

"Help the wind?" Her completely white eyes gazed at him in the dim torchlight. "What be your idea?"

"To have you use your gift to stir up the air. Some random

gusts, that sort of thing. Make it appear that the wind is kicking up stronger all the time. After General Meiffert has told them to begin gathering some of their men to serve as escorts, we move the wagon down into the pit. Then an even bigger gust of wind comes through and blows out the nearby torches. When it goes dark, and before the guards can bring more torches down there to relight the ones that went out, we slip Nicci and Jillian down into the tunnels."

"All right, so we get down into the tunnels," General Meiffert said. "There will still be guards down there and who knows how many troops. What do you propose about that?"

Richard shared a troubled look with the man. "We have to get past them, one way or another. But you're right, there are liable to be a lot of them."

Bruce propped himself up on an elbow. "It will be difficult to fight in tunnels. That helps to even the odds."

"You have a point," General Meiffert said. "To a certain extent it doesn't matter how many guards are down in there. They can't swarm over us. In such confined spaces they can only have a few men at a time fighting us."

Richard let out a sigh. "But that's still trouble we don't need. We'd have to walk over every guard we kill and every one of the men down there will be trying to stop us. As we force our way farther in they can surround us from behind. There are sure to be countless chambers, giving them the opportunity to come in from the sides as we advance. It's a long way. What with helping Nicci it's going to be more than difficult to fight our way through."

"What choice do we have?" General Meiffert asked. "We need to get through and the only way is to eliminate anyone who tries to stop us. It won't be easy, but it's our only hope."

"Catacombs be black as pitch," Adie said in her raspy voice. "If I use my gift to snuff out all the lights down there they not be able to see us."

"But then how can we see?" Bruce asked.

"Your gift," Richard said to Adie as he realized her plan. "You see with your gift."

She nodded. "I be our eyes. My eyes be blinded when I

be young. I see by my gift, not by light. I use my gift to snuff out their lights, then go first into the blackness. You all follow. We be as quiet as mice. They not even know that we be slipping through their midst. If I encounter guards, I find a way to slip around them by other routes so they not know we be there. If we must, we kill them, but it be better to sneak past them."

"That sounds to me like our best chance." Richard glanced at Nicci before looking to each of them in turn. No one offered any objections, so he went on.

"It's set, then. General Meiffert talks to the captain of the guards. We take the wagon down into the pit while he goes after men for an escort. Once down in the pit Adie uses her gift to bring up a gust of wind to blow out the torches. In the confusion before they can light the torches we climb down into the catacombs. They'll probably just assume that we started in on our work of collecting the books for the emperor. Once down inside, Adie leads the way and extinguishes any light we come across. She guides us through by the safest route. Anyone in the way who tries to stop us dies."

"Just be ready if the captain of the guard is suspicious and wants to give us trouble," the general said.

"If need be," Adie said, "there be trouble. I make sure of it."

Richard nodded. "We need to hurry, though. It's going to be light soon. We need darkness to get down in the catacombs without any of the guards seeing Nicci and Jillian. After we're down inside it won't matter, but out here we need to make this happen while we still have the night."

"Then let's get going," the general said as he headed forward to lead the horses.

Richard glanced quickly to the eastern sky. Dawn was not far off. He and Bruce pulled the tarp down tight as the wagon began to rumble forward. Richard hoped they could get down into the eternal night of the catacombs in time.

Next to him, Nicci wept softly, unable to endure the agony, unable to summon death.

Her suffering was breaking Richard's heart. All he could do was to squeeze her hand to let her know that she was not alone.

Richard listened to the wind howl as General Meiffert spoke in muffled words to the captain of the guard.

Richard leaned close to Nicci and whispered to her, "Hold on. It won't be much longer."

"I don't think she can hear you anymore," Jillian whispered from just on the other side of Nicci.

"She can hear me," Richard said.

She had to hear him. She had to live. Richard needed her help. He didn't know how to open the right box of Orden. He didn't know anyone who could be more help to him than Nicci.

More important than that, though, Nicci was his friend. He cared deeply for her. He could always find other solutions if it came to that, but he couldn't bear to lose her.

Nicci had often been the only person he could turn to, the person who had helped keep him focused, who had reminded him to trust in himself. In many ways she had been his only confidant since Kahlan had been taken.

He couldn't stand the thought of losing her.

CHAPTER 41

On the northeast bank above the stream, Rachel slipped down off the horse, clutching the reins as she peered all around, watching for any movement. In the early dawn light the dark humps of the barren hills made it look like she was in the midst of a pack of slumbering monsters.

She knew better, though. They were just hills. But there were real things that weren't harmless figments of her imagination.

The ghostie gobblies were real, they were close, and they were coming for her.

White cliffs of twin hills rose up, facing each other across the banks of the stream. Sumac, their leaves already lost to the season, lined the narrow foot trail where she stood, trembling in the cold. The tall mouth of the cave stood close, waiting, like the open mouth of some great monster waiting to swallow her.

Rachel tied the reins of the horse to a sumac and scrambled along the loose dirt and gravel of the trail toward that waiting, dark maw. She peeked inside, looking to see if Queen Violet or Six was hiding there. She expected that Violet might leap out and slap her, then laugh in that haughty way of hers.

The cave was dark and empty.

Rachel twisted her fingers together as she again scanned the round hills. Her heart beat wildly as she looked for any movement. The ghostie gobblies were getting closer. They were coming for her. They were going to get her.

Inside the cave she saw the familiar drawings that she had seen so many times before. There were thousands of sketches covering every inch of the walls. Between large drawings, small ones were squeezed into the available space. Each one was different. Most looked like they had been drawn by different people. Some were so simple that they almost looked like they'd been drawn by children. Some were detailed and remarkably realistic-looking.

Rachel didn't know how to judge such things, but to her it seemed that the drawings had to represent many generations of people. Considering the many different styles and various levels of refinement, they could easily represent dozens and dozens of generations of artists, maybe hundreds.

All the drawings had people in them. All the people in the drawings were being hurt, or troubled, or starved, or poisoned, or stabbed, or lying broken at the bottom of cliffs, or grieved over graves. The drawings gave Rachel nightmares.

She squatted down and felt the oil lamps. They were cold. No one had been in the caves. She retrieved a flint and steel from a small niche cut into the wall of the cave and used it to strike a spark at the wick of a lamp.

She tried a number of times and was able to get a good spark, but not a flame in the wick. She glanced back over her shoulder between tries. She was running out of time. They were coming. They were getting close now.

Rachel shook the lamp to get more oil on the wick then frantically struck the flint and steel together. It took half a dozen tries but to her great relief she finally got a flame going.

She picked the lamp up by the loop handle and stood. She stared out of the mouth of the cave, looking for any movement, looking for the ghostie gobblies. She didn't see them, but she knew they were coming. She thought she could hear them, out in the scrub brush. She was sure she could feel them looking at her.

With the lamp in hand she rushed back into the darkness, away from the ghostie gobblies, to safety . . . she hoped. She had to get away. They were coming. They could get her everywhere else. This was her only chance.

Knowing how close they were she was frantic with fright.

Tears stung her eyes as she ran back into the cave, past all the drawings of people being hurt.

It was a long way back into the darkness. A long way to where she thought she might find the only place where she could be safe. The lamplight raced over the face of the rock all around, lighting the faces drawn on the walls.

Deep into the cave the light from the cave's opening was only a distant soft glow. Crawling over a jutting outcropping of rock, she could see her breath as she panted not only with effort but with gathering panic. She didn't know how far she had to go to be safe. She only knew that the ghostie gobblies were coming for her and she had to keep going, had to get away.

She came to the drawing she remembered all too well. It was a drawing that Rachel had watched Queen Violet make with Six's help. Although they had never mentioned his name, Rachel knew that it was a drawing of Richard. With all the things drawn around the central figure it was the biggest drawing in all of the cave. It was also the most complex.

Unlike all the rest of the pictures, Violet's had been done with colored chalk. Rachel remembered all the time Queen Violet had spent on it—back when she had been the queen—all the careful instruction Six had given her, all the careful sequences of lines and angles and elements. Rachel remembered having to stand there for hours at a time, listening as Six explained the why and how of everything Violet was to draw before she had been allowed to put chalk to the stone wall.

Rachel stared at the drawing of Richard for a moment, thinking that it had to be one of the most awful, sinister things she had ever seen.

But then, ever terrified of what was coming for her, she rushed onward, scrambling over rock and along ledges, going deeper back into the darkness.

Whenever Six had directed Violet in practice drawings, or when they had wanted to draw something new, they had always had to go deeper and deeper back into the cave to find fresh walls to draw on. Rachel remembered all too well that the picture of Richard was the last thing they had drawn, so she knew that beyond it the walls would be barren.

As she went past the colored network of lines and symbols radiating out all around Richard, Rachel was startled to see something she had never seen before. She came to a halt. There was a new drawing.

She stared in astonishment. It was a drawing of her.

All around the picture of her were swirling creatures. Rachel recognized the symbols that forced them in toward her. The awful beasts were like ghosts made of shadow and smoke. Except they had teeth. Sharp teeth. Teeth made to rip and tear.

Without any doubt whatsoever, Rachel knew what they were. They were the ghostie gobblies.

She stood frozen staring at the picture of the terrible deadly things that had been sicced on her by vicious spells drawn there on the cave wall.

She knew from the long hours spent listening to Six lecture Violet what many of the symbols represented. Six had called them "terminal elements." They were designed to eliminate the principal agents of the spell after the end of the sequence of events the drawing was meant to start. She understood the nature of the picture, and what it all meant. It meant that after the ghostie gobblies got her, they would melt away out of existence.

In the drawing the things made out of nightmares were all around her, coming ever in toward her. She could see, now, that there was no escape. The safety she had thought she was running toward was merely the center where they had been chasing her toward, the center where she would be trapped, unable to ever escape.

She heard a sound and looked toward the dim glow of light from the cave's entrance. For the first time she saw the shadows and swirls. They were in the cave. They were gathering, just like in the drawing on the wall. They were coming for her.

Rachel stood frozen in terror. She realized that she could no longer get out of the cave. She could only go deeper. But by looking at the drawing she could see that going deeper into the cave would not save her—there were ghostic gobblies back there, too. She was trapped, unable to go deeper, unable to get out. She was at the center of a spell that was designed to continually close in around her.

"Like it?" someone called out.

Rachel gasped and spun toward the voice echoing in the blackness.

"Queen Violet."

The face, faintly lit in the light of the oil lamp, grinned out from the darkness. Violet was there to watch, to see the ghostie gobblies get her, to witness the results of her handiwork.

"I thought you might like to come and see where they came from before they rip you apart. I wanted you to know who was getting even with you." She gestured to the wall. "So I drew it in a way that would make you have to come here in the end. I made this the place where they would finally have you trapped." She leaned out a little from the darkness. "Where they would finally get you."

Rachel didn't bother to ask Violet why she would do such a thing. She knew why. Violet blamed her for everything bad that ever happened to her. She never blamed herself for the trouble she brought upon herself; she blamed others, blamed Rachel.

"Where is Six?"

Violet gestured dismissively. "Who knows. She doesn't tell me her business." Violet's glare turned as dark as the cave itself. "She is queen now. No one listens to me anymore. They do what she says. They call her queen. Queen Six."

"What about you?"

"She only keeps me around to draw for her." Violet pointed a finger at Rachel. "It's all your fault. It's all because of you."

Violet's glare twisted into the smile that had always given Rachel chills. "But now you will pay for your disrespect, your evil ways. Now you will pay." The smile widened with satisfaction. "I made them so that they will tear the flesh from your bones. Pick you clean."

Rachel swallowed in terror.

She wondered if she could fight her way past the smirking

Violet. But what good would that do? They would soon be coming out of the deeper darkness as well.

Chase had taught her never to give up, to fight for her life. She knew that she had to do that now. But how? How could she fight such creatures? She had to think of something.

She glanced around. There was no chalk anywhere.

At the sound of a screeching howl she gasped and looked up to see the ghostie gobblies floating closer, like smoke swimming and swirling in through the length of the dark cave. Rachel could see the sharp little teeth in the open mouths of the things—teeth made to rip and tear her flesh from her bones.

"I want you to say you're sorry."

Rachel blinked as she turned back to Violet. "What?"

"Tell me you're sorry. Get down on a knee and tell your queen that you're sorry for betraying her. Maybe if you do I'll help you."

Grasping desperately for any hope, Violet quickly went to a knee and bowed her head forward, using the moment it took to think.

"I'm sorry."

"You're sorry . . . what?"

"I'm sorry, Queen Violet."

"That's right. I am your queen. While Six is gone, I am the queen around here. The queen! Say it!"

"You are the queen, Queen Violet."

Violet smiled in satisfaction. "Good. I want you to remember that as you die."

Rachel looked up. "But you said that you would help me."

Queen Violet, laughing to herself, retreated farther back into the darkness. "I only said maybe. I've decided you don't deserve my help. You're a nobody."

Behind her, rasping little growls were coming closer. Rachel thought she might faint from her clawing fright.

She reached into the pocket of her dress and felt something there—the thing her mother had given her. She pulled it out and stared at it in the lamplight. Now she knew what it was.

It was a piece of chalk.

When her mother had given it to her Rachel had been in

such a hurry to get away from the ghostie gobblies that she hadn't really paid attention to what it was.

Her mother had told her that when she needed it she would know what to do.

Rachel glanced back into the darkness. She could see the back of Violet's head as she retreated farther back into the cave, away from the violent death that she knew was about to take her.

Rachel looked back the other way and saw the snarling things swimming through the air, coming closer, their mouths opening wide, their needle-sharp teeth snapping and snapping.

She immediately stepped to the drawing Violet had done to trap her. Rachel used the chalk to swiftly add lines and shading, making the figure thicker, rounder. She made the face rounder, and then put a hateful scowl on it. The chalk flew across the stone as she filled in frilly a dress, the kind of dresses that Violet always liked to wear. Finally, remembering what Violet liked to wear in the jewel room, Rachel drew a crown on the head, changing the picture for good from her, into Queen Violet.

Violet claimed to be the queen. Rachel had just crowned her, giving her what she demanded.

She heard a scream from the darkness.

When she saw them coming from the other side, Rachel pressed her back up against the wall as the creatures floated, wriggled, and swam through the air, making their way back into the darkness.

Rachel, her eyes wide, held her breath as the snarling, snapping wispy forms floated past her.

Her heart hammering, Rachel listened to Violet scream hysterically.

"What have you done!" she cried out from the darkness.

Violet rushed forward into the light. Rachel could see Violet through the ghostly things going back into the cave toward her. Violet's eyes grew big as she saw them coming for her.

"What have you done!" Violet screamed again.

Rachel didn't answer. She was too terrified as she watched.

"Rachel—help me! I've always loved you! How could you do this to me!"

"You did it to yourself, Queen Violet."

"I've always been a kind and loving person!"

"Kind and loving?" Rachel could hardly believe her ears. "Your life has been devoted to hate, Queen Violet."

"I only hated those who did me wrong, who were evil and selfish! I always did what was best for my people. I treated you well. I gave you food and shelter. I gave you more than a nobody like you would ever have had without my help. I showed you only generosity. Help me, Rachel. Help me and I will reward you."

"I want to live. That is my reward."

"How can you be so cruel—so hateful? How can you allow this to happen to another human being? How can you be a party to such a thing?"

"You are the one who created the ghostie gobblies."

"You've betrayed me! I hate you! I hate the air you breathe!"

Rachel nodded. "You made your own choices, Violet. You always chose to embrace hate instead of life. You came down into this cave because you chose to hate. You betrayed yourself with that hate."

When the ghostie gobblies got closer to Violet, they howled in voices that Rachel could only imagine must sound like the cries of the dead in the underworld. It made her flesh prickle.

She pressed her back against the stone wall of the cave and stood frozen in fright as she saw those teeth that had been meant for her rip into a shrieking Queen Violet.

Rachel knew that only when they were finished and the bones had been picked clean would their summoning born of hate be complete. Only then would they finally vanish for good.

CHAPTER 42

Verna glanced up when she heard the commotion. It was Nathan, at last, his arms swinging in time with his long legs, his light cape billowing out behind as he marched briskly toward them. General Trimack was close on the prophet's heels.

Cara, pacing impatiently, finally stopped to watch the approaching prophet and cluster of people following in his wake. As vast as the palace complex was, it had taken a considerable length of time to find Nathan and get him and the others down to the tombs.

Nathan came to an abrupt halt. "I'm going to have to bring a horse into this place to get around faster. First I'm wanted here, then I'm wanted there." He flourished an arm, indicating the grand scale of the palace. "I spend most of my day rushing from one end of this sprawling monstrosity to another." He scowled at those watching him. "What's this about, anyway? No one will tell me anything. Have you found something? Is it Ann and Nicci?"

"Keep your voice down," Cara said.

"Why? Afraid I'll wake the dead?" he snapped.

Verna expected Cara to meet his sarcasm with something caustic of her own, but she didn't. "We don't know what we've found," she said, her worry clearly evident in her demeanor.

Nathan's brow only bunched all the more at her cryptic answer. "What do you mean?"

"We need your ability," Verna explained. "My gift doesn't work very well in this place. We need the use of the gift to help us in this."

His suspicion growing, he took in General Trimack standing

beside him, and then Berdine and Nyda waiting behind Cara. Finally, he glanced around the rest of the Mord-Sith scattered among soldiers throughout the corridor. The Mord-Sith were all wearing their red leather outfits.

"All right," he said, considerably more circumspect. "What is the problem and what do you have in mind?"

"The crypt staff—" Cara started.

"The crypt staff?" Nathan interrupted. "Who are they?"

Cara gestured to several people in white robes far off back up the corridor, well behind the armed and ready men of the First File. "They take care of this place. As you know, I think something is wrong down here."

"So you've said, but for all the searching I still don't see anything wrong down here."

Cara gestured around. "You don't know this place very well. I've lived here most of my life and even I'm not familiar with the maze of passageways down here. In the past the tombs were usually only visited by the Lord Rahl. The crypt staff, though, spends a great deal of their time down here keeping it always ready for those visits, so they know the place better than anyone."

Nathan rubbed his chin as he again cast a look over his shoulder, back up the corridor at the white-robed figures huddled in the distance. "That makes sense." He turned back to Cara. "So, what do they have to say?"

"They're mute. Darken Rahl selected only illiterate people from the countryside to be members of the crypt staff, so they can't read or write, either."

"Selected. You mean he captured people and pressed them into service."

"Exactly," Berdine said as she moved up a little to stand beside Cara. "In much the same way he would acquire young women to be trained as Mord-Sith."

Cara gestured off in the direction of Panis Rahl's tomb. "Darken Rahl wanted a crypt staff who would not speak ill of his dead father, so he cut out their tongues. Since they can't read or write, they also can't secretly write anything offensive about the dead leaders."

Nathan sighed. "He was a harsh man."

"He was an evil man," Cara said.

Nathan nodded. "I've never heard anything to dispute it."

"Then how do you know what the crypt staff thinks about anything that might be wrong down here?" General Trimack asked Cara. "After all, they can't tell you or even write it down."

"You use hand signals to direct your men when silence is critical, or when in the heat of battle they can't hear you. These people do similar things. They use signs they've made up over the years to communicate with each other. I've questioned them and to a certain extent they've been able to make themselves understood. As I'm sure you can well imagine, they are very observant."

"And wait until you hear what they think," Verna said.

The whole thing seemed preposterous to her, but the implications were serious enough that she wanted to know for sure. Verna had learned since becoming prelate that, despite how she might be inclined to view a matter, it was always a good idea to keep an open mind. In matters so serious it would be foolish not to at least make sure there was no real problem. Still, she didn't have to be happy about it.

Nathan's suspicious look returned. "So, what do they think?"

Cara pointed toward an intersection down the corridor. "Back around there they found a place that isn't right."

"Isn't right?" In exasperation, Nathan put his hands on his hips. "Isn't right in what way?"

"The stone down here all has veining in it." Cara turned and pointed out various patterns on the wall behind her. "See? All the people on the crypt staff recognize the veining. They keep track of where they are down here by those unique patterns."

Nathan peered closely at the veining.

"It's a language of symbols," Cara added.

Nathan looked away from the veining and back at Cara. "That makes sense. Go on."

"In that corridor there, down a ways, is a slab of marble wall that belongs somewhere else."

Nathan's suspicion returned as he viewed her askance, as if

playing along but not liking it one bit. "So, where does it belong, then?"

"That's just it," Cara said. "They can't find the hall where it belongs. Near as I can understand, what they're trying to tell me is that there is a corridor missing."

"Missing?" Nathan heaved a deep sigh. He scratched his head as he glanced around. "Where could a corridor be hiding?"

Cara leaned toward him just a little. "Behind that piece of marble."

He stared at her silently as he looked to be thinking it through.

"So we want you to use your gift and see if you can sense anyone behind that wall," Verna said.

Concern etched Nathan's Rahl features as he glanced around at all the faces watching him. "Someone hiding behind the wall?"

Cara nodded. "That's right. Someone hiding behind the wall."

Nathan ran his hand over the back of his neck as he looked down the corridor toward the intersection. "Well, as crazy as that theory sounds, at least it's simple enough to test." He flicked a hand, indicating General Trimack standing beside him. "And you think the First File might be necessary?"

Cara shrugged. "Depends on if there is anything unpleasant on the other side of the wall."

The general was looking not just concerned, but alarmed. He was responsible for guarding the palace and everyone in it—especially the Lord Rahl. He was dead serious about his job.

The general waggled a hand in the direction of the suspected trouble. "And you think there is?"

Cara didn't shy from the general's formidable stare. "Nicci and Ann disappeared somewhere down here."

The scar running down the side of the man's face stood out white. He hooked his thumbs behind his weapon belt as he turned to the side. One of his men rushed forward to take his orders.

"I want all of you to stay close, but be very quiet."

The officer nodded and then trotted silently back to the other men to relay the orders.

"Just who do you think it is that could be hiding behind the wall?" the general asked as he looked between all the women.

"Don't look at me," Verna said. "I'm concerned, but I can't imagine who or what could be there, if anyone. I don't know that I believe any of this, but at the Palace of the Prophets I knew people on the staff who would pick up on the strangest things, things that no one else had been aware of. I have no idea what this is about, but I don't dismiss the worries of people who know this place better than I."

"That makes sense," the general said.

Nathan started out. "Let's go have a look, then."

As she followed behind, Verna was relieved that she'd been able to convince Nathan of the seriousness of the matter. She didn't necessarily believe it herself, but she wanted to support Cara. Cara was the sort of person who deserved to be given the benefit of the doubt. The Mord-Sith had been frantic with worry for Nicci. She hadn't slept much recently. As far as Cara was concerned, Nicci was not just a friend, but a link to finding Richard.

They all moved as silently as possible. Cara led the way, with Nathan following. Verna stayed back a little with Berdine and Nyda. General Trimack, with his large force of men, brought up the rear.

Around the corner and down the suspect corridor, a few torches farther down hissed and sputtered. One of them appeared to be about spent. The staff, though, had been kept away. The general signaled his men. Half a dozen of them collected torches from back up the hall and brought them along.

Cara snapped her fingers to get the general's attention. She motioned for half the men to go past and guard the corridor from the other side. She apparently wanted the place sealed off. Cara sent some of the other Mord-Sith with the soldiers.

At the marble wall Cara traced a finger along the lines of

the face in the stone. By now, even Verna recognized that particular face.

"They say that this face doesn't belong here," Cara whispered when Nathan leaned close to her.

Nathan nodded and then stood up straight. He waved a hand, urging Cara to stay back out of his way.

Cara frowned and gave Verna a puzzled look. She didn't know quite what the old wizard was doing. Verna knew. He was using his ability to sense beyond the stone. He was using his gift to search for life. Verna could do a similar thing, although not with the same level of success as a wizard, but she couldn't do it at all in the palace. In the People's Palace any gift but a Rahl's was suppressed. Verna had tried to sense beyond the wall when they had first been told of the place by the crypt staff, but she hadn't been at all successful.

Cara returned to stand beside Verna. She leaned close, speaking in little more than a whisper.

"What do you think?"

"I think Nathan will tell us when he knows anything."

General Trimack leaned in. "How long?"

"Not long," Verna told him.

As Verna watched, Nathan's face suddenly went white. He staggered back a step.

Seeing his reaction brought Cara's Agiel up into her fist. Berdine and Nyda spun their weapons up to hand as well.

Nathan staggered back another step. His hand went to his face in shock. He turned to them, his mouth agape.

In a rush of movement, being as quiet as possible, he raced back to them.

"Dear spirits." He ran his fingers back through his hair as he looked back at the face on the wall.

"Dear spirits, what?" Cara growled.

Nathan, his face nearly as white as his hair, turned his azure eyes on the Mord-Sith.

"There are hundreds of people on the other side of that wall."

Cara was speechless for only an instant. "Hundreds? Are you sure?"

He nodded vigorously. "Maybe thousands."

Verna finally recovered her own voice. "What people? Who are they?"

"Don't know," Nathan said, his head swiveling back and forth between their faces and the face in the marble wall. "I can't begin to imagine. But I can tell you that they have a lot of steel with them."

General Trimack leaned in. "Steel?"

"Weapons," Verna said.

Nathan's expression was grave. "That's right. Down here there isn't much steel, so it stands out when I use the gift to sense what is beyond the wall. There are a lot of people and they have a lot of steel with them."

"They can only be armed men," the general said as he quietly drew his sword. He signaled to his men. They all did the same. In a heartbeat they all had weapons to hand.

"Any idea who they could be?" Berdine asked in a whisper.

Nathan, looking as worried as Verna had ever seen him, shook his head. "None. I can't tell who they are, only that they are back there."

Cara started across the corridor. "I say we find out."

The general gave quick hand signals to all his men. They quietly started moving in from both sides.

"Just how do you think you can find out?" Verna asked, following on Cara's heels.

Cara paused and looked back at her a moment. She turned to Nathan.

"Can you use your gift to, to, I don't know—knock the wall down, or something."

"Of course."

"Then I think we—"

Cara fell silent when Nathan held up his hand. He cocked his head, listening.

"They're talking. Something about light."

"Light?" Verna asked. "What do you mean?"

Nathan's brow lowered as he concentrated as if trying to hear. She knew that he was listening with his gift, not his ears. It was frustrating in the extreme that she couldn't do the same.

"The light went out for them," he said in a low voice. "Their lamps all of a sudden went dark."

Everyone turned to the wall when muffled voices came from beyond. There was no gift needed to hear them. Men were complaining about not being able to see, wanting to know what was happening.

Then they heard a scream. It lasted only an instant before abruptly going silent. Muffled shouts rose in dismay and growing panic.

"Break it down!" Cara called to Nathan.

Suddenly shrieks erupted from the other side of the wall—men crying out now not only in terror but in shock and pain.

Nathan lifted his arms to cast a web that would bring down the wall.

Before he could act, the white marble exploded out toward them. Fragments of stone blew apart with a deafening noise. A big man, bloody sword in hand, came crashing shoulder-first through the wall at a dead run from the other side. He fell sliding across the floor.

Pieces of white stone of every size and shape sailed through the corridor. Large sections of marble broke free and came crashing down. Beyond the chaos of flying stone shards and boiling dust Verna saw snatches of darkly armored men with weapons in hand. They looked to be in a state of bewildered battle, fighting an unseen enemy. Their roar of voices rose in anger, confusion, and terror.

Through the cloud of dust and debris Verna could see that there was a dark corridor beyond filled with a massive jumble of Imperial Order soldiers.

Through the thundering noise and turmoil, people fell through the breach in the wall. Big tattooed men wearing dark leather armor, straps, studs, and chain mail, several with missing arms, others with their faces cleaved open, crashed heavily to the ground. A head, greasy ropes of hair flailing, tumbled through the chalky stone dust. Men missing a leg toppled out. Others, their middles ripped asunder, stumbled through the mess.

Great gouts of crimson blood splashed across the white marble floor.

In the middle of all the flying stone, billowing dust, disembodied heads tumbling across shattered marble, men falling, screaming, dying, and the confusion of blood and bodies spilling out into the corridor, Richard, with mortally wounded men toppling away to either side, sweeping his sword with one hand, holding an unconscious-looking Nicci up with his other arm around her waist, plunged through the breach in the dark wall of soldiers.

CHAPTER 43

Cara planted a foot on the back of a fallen Imperial Order soldier and leaped into the air toward Richard as he used his momentum to help carry him through the confusion of dust and stone smashed apart by Bruce when he'd charged through the marble veneer as if he were hitting a line of blockers. As Richard slid under the flying blades and blood, he laid Nicci on the floor, letting her limp form, atop a layer of slick stone dust covering the polished stone, slide the rest of the way across the hall and out of harm's way.

Richard immediately spun around, bringing his sword to bear on the wall of men descending on him as they spilled out of the dark corridor and into the torchlit halls. He sliced mercilessly into every opening. They fought fiercely to get at him and bring him down. Blade slashed muscle and hit bone. The noise was deafening as men growled, some yelled battle cries, and others screamed in mortal pain.

Richard evaded their fierce attacks, and at every opportunity thrust his blade through the onslaught. Every one of his swift strikes found its mark. For every man he killed, though, it seemed three more replaced him.

Cara crashed into a big man with a shaved head as he went for Richard. Using both hands, she slammed her Agiel across his throat. For an instant Richard saw the shock of pain in the man's eyes before he went down. Richard used the opening to turn and thrust his sword into another soldier to the side.

All the men who had been quietly gathering in the dark corridor appeared to be experienced fighters. The battle had come sooner than they had planned, but now that it was upon them they fought with wild fury. These weren't the regular Imperial Order soldiers, the men who had joined for glory and plunder. These were professional warriors, well-trained and experienced men who knew what they were doing. They were universally powerful men, all wearing at least leather armor. Some were additionally outfitted with chain mail. All of them were carrying well-made weapons. They fought with measured moves meant to tear through an enemy defensive line.

As good as they were, they'd been caught off guard and surprised by the sudden darkness followed by swift violence. They had believed that as they quietly crept into enemy territory they were safely hidden. In a moment of confusion and alarm when it had gone dark in the corridor they had been gripped by overpowering fear of the unknown. In those brief bewildering moments men had begun dying without understanding how or why.

Richard had used that surprise to tear through their ranks as swiftly as possible. The last thing he had wanted to do was get bogged down in hand-to-hand fighting. His purpose had been to get through, not to engage the enemy. With Nicci, Jillian, and Adie to escort, it was all he, Bruce, and General Meiffert could do to cut their way through without slowing when confronted. Within the palace Adie's ability to help them had diminished.

That had been trouble.

As surprised as the hiding Order troops had been when in the dark, they had quickly recovered and were now in their element: battle. These were the men the Order typically used to lead an invasion, to overwhelm an opponent in a powerful attack meant to slice all opposition to pieces.

Fortunately for Richard, he, Bruce, and General Meiffert at last didn't have to fight alone. Cara dropped any men she could get near and climbed over others to get at those trying to hack Richard to pieces. These men were familiar with armed opposition; they knew little about Mord-Sith. Already they were trying to back away from Cara, only to have other Mord-Sith spring up and take them down. Richard saw Berdine and Nyda ramming their Agiel to the backs of heads or thrusting and twisting them against big chests to kill instantly. Everywhere men screamed in agony.

Not far away the First File charged into the Imperial Order soldiers from both sides at once. Richard saw General Trimack leading his men into the teeth of the battle. The First File were the elite of the elite, more than a match for the Order soldiers not only in size but in ability. The D'Haran troops were all battle-hardened men who were well versed in deadly tactics that gave them a feared and well-deserved reputation.

Several men in dark leather armor, their faces twisted in hate and rage, rushed toward Richard. Before he could bring his sword to bear, yet other big men stepped right in front of them, blocking their ability to get to Richard. With lightning strikes from the elbows of the two men, the necks of the Order soldiers were ripped open, severing carotid arteries.

Richard blinked when he saw that it was Ulie and Egan, two great blond-headed bodyguards to the Lord Rahl. The dark leather straps, plates, and belts of their uniforms were molded to fit like a second skin over the prominent contours of their muscles. Incised in the leather at the center of their chests was an ornate letter "R," and beneath that were two crossed swords. They wore metal bands just above the elbows specially designed for close-quarters fighting. Those bands had razor-sharp projections. It soon became apparent to the invading soldiers that anyone close enough to encounter Ulie and Egan was not just going to die, but going to die in a most gruesome manner.

Yet other troops pouring out of the breach in the wall were cut down by gifted means cast at them by Nathan. Flashes of explosive light sliced through men in chain mail, sending shards of hot steel ricocheting off the walls, floors, and ceilings. It was a grim, one-sided contest, with the soldiers never having a chance to even raise their swords against the tall prophet before they were torn apart by a focused use of his gift.

General Meiffert ducked under swinging axes as he charged through the smoke, Jillian cowering behind the cover of his sword with Adie being held up by his other arm.

Richard saw that Adie was covered in blood.

Cara froze in her tracks. "Benjamin?"

"Here! Take Adie!"

"I have to protect Lord Rahl."

"Do as you're told!" he yelled at her over the roar of the battle. "Help her!"

Richard was surprised to see Cara immediately abandon her argument to help lift Adie from General Meiffert's care. He seized Jillian with his newly freed hand and pulled her around to the other side of him, away from two men who were charging in from his right. He ducked as he thrust his sword, running one man through. Bruce was right there, but down low so as not to get in the way of the general's blade. From that low position Bruce cut the second attacker down at the knees. When a third man reached for the general, Egan wrapped a muscled arm around the soldier's neck and wrenched it around. The man went limp. Egan tossed him aside like a rag doll and immediately went after another Order soldier.

"Get back!" General Meiffert yelled at Cara when she returned to rush back into the thick of the battle.

"I have to—"

"Move!" he yelled at her at the same time he rammed her back with a hand. "I said move!"

"Nathan!" Richard cried out over the roar of noise when he saw the opportunity that General Meiffert had just opened up by forcing Cara back out of the way with him. When the prophet turned to his name, Richard pointed to the dark corridor the general had just cleared. "That's all of us! Do it!"

Nathan understood and didn't waste an instant. He immediately brought his hands up. Light ignited between his palms. Wizard's fire erupted into life from the gathering light, sending glimmering colors and light flickering over the scene of the pitched battle.

Without pause Nathan cast the wizard's fire into the enemy.

The deadly sphere of bubbling, boiling, liquid light tumbled away. The white-hot inferno expanded as it hurtled through the air. Even over the noise of the battle echoing through the stone halls Richard could hear the wail of it flying toward the dark corridor full of Imperial Order troops all pushing forward to get into the palace and join the battle.

The wizard's fire shot down the corridor, casting an orange-red light across the white marble. The sound alone was enough to stiffen men in panic.

It was a horrific sight as burning death splattered across living flesh. The growing sphere of liquid fire stayed aloft as it skipped across the heads of the men, all the while spilling death down on them until the tumbling inferno burst into a cascade of molten light and flame splashing down into the terrified mass of men.

The shrieks of agony drowned out the clash of steel in the battle.

Nathan conjured yet more wizard's fire. In an instant it, too, was away.

The sphere of fire tumbled down the dark corridor, careening off walls and men, spilling flames, catching everything ablaze. The liquid flame was so tenacious, so sticky, so fiercely alive with searing heat that it melted its way through tough leather armor and sloshed right through chain mail to cling to flesh as it burned. Men on fire tore at their clothes, trying to get the fire off them, but they couldn't. Wizard's fire, once on a person, would often burn down to bone before it went out. Even as men started to pull off leather armor plates that the sticky, liquid tire was burning through, it was too late. Their clothes were already melted to their skin and they only ended up pulling off their own flesh.

Fire enveloped faces. Gasping in shock, men sucked swirling flames into their lungs. The stench of burning flesh was overpowering. The sound of the screams was horrifying.

The men already in the hall knew that they would have no one coming from behind to help them. The men of the First File were already bearing in, rolling them under, spearing men who couldn't move in the crushing weight pressing in from both sides.

They had no choice but to fight for their lives. In this battle, there would be no surrender allowed.

General Meiffert hacked a man across the shoulder. Bruce used both hands on the hilt of his sword to thrust it down into a man who fell sprawling on the floor at his feet. As another man, his face twisted with rage and hate, went for Richard, Richard swung, burying his sword halfway through the man's head just below his eyes. He yanked his sword back as the man dropped to his knees crying out in unexpected fright. Berdine, in her red leather like all the Mord-Sith, stepped in and pressed her Agiel to the base of his skull, finishing him off.

Nathan launched another expanding, lumbling, twistling sphere of wizard's fire down the hall. The relentless inferno of death was sickening to behold as it splashed down through crowds of men who had thus far avoided it. Men on fire frantically tried to escape the growing conflagration. There was no escape. They were trapped not just by the flames, but by their numbers and by the dead all around them. They had no choice but to scream in agony and desperate panic as they burned alive. Whorls of flame curled in the open mouths of those shrieks. Richard was certain that near the back men would have abandoned the attack and already be racing back to the safety of the catacombs.

What only a moment before had been a frantic battle was suddenly dying down. Imperial Order soldiers still alive were shown no mercy as they were finished off by the First File.

Cara shoved over a man she had just killed. He toppled backward and landed with a numb thud. General Meiffert was close by. She looked more angry at him than at the man she had just killed.

"What do you think you're doing yelling at me—telling me what to do?"

"My job. You were in the way of what Lord Rahl was attempting to do. I needed you out of the way."

Cara glanced back. "Well, I don't care—"

"I don't have time for debate." His anger looked the match of hers. "As long as I'm in charge, you will do as you're told. That's the way it has to be."

She turned her scowl to the corridor where men still moved

as they burned alive. Arms become torches waved slowly, uselessly, in the inferno.

Richard had known that there had been too many soldiers filling the corridors to fight them all. He had been trying to get the general, Bruce, Jillian, and Adie out of the way so that Nathan could bring wizard's fire to bear. The general had realized Richard's intention. Cara had been in the way. Being a general in charge, he couldn't allow anyone to question his authority—especially not in the midst of a battle.

Once Cara realized the truth of it, she abandoned the dispute and immediately turned to join Richard as he scrambled across the blood-slick floor to Nicci, who was lying on her back against the wall.

"Nicci?" Richard gently slipped a hand behind her neck. "Hold on. Nathan is here."

Her eyes were rolled up in her head. She was convulsing in pain. Richard could only imagine that Jagang was trying to kill her, but the spell around the palace was impeding that effort. It was putting her through a slow and agonizing death.

He turned. "Nathan! We need you!"

Past the fallen forms of dead Imperial Order soldiers, Richard saw Nathan kneeling beside someone. Richard had a terrible feeling that he knew who it was. Nathan looked up, staring sadly, helplessly at Richard.

"Nicci—hold on. Help is coming. I promise I'll get that collar off you. Hold on." He seized Cara's arm and pulled her close. "Stay with her. I don't want her to think she's alone. I don't want her to give up."

Cara nodded, her blue eyes looking liquid. "Lord Rahl, I'm really glad to see you."

He laid a hand on her shoulder as he stood. "I know. Let me tell you, I'm pretty glad to see you, too."

Richard raced over the top of dead Order soldiers rather than taking the time to find a clear path. It felt surreal to see so many corpses, dismembered limbs and heads, so much blood, defiling the sacred white marble corridors of the palace.

As he swiftly made his way across the tangle of dead, his

fears were confirmed when he saw that Nathan was kneeling beside Adie. The old sorceress was hardly breathing.

Richard bent down beside the prophet. "Nathan, you have to help her."

General Meiffert and Jillian knelt on the other side of the old woman. Jillian took up Adie's hand and held it to her breast.

Nathan stared with tired, watery eyes. "I'm sorry, Richard, but this may be beyond my ability."

Richard swallowed back the lump in his throat as he looked down at Adie. She gazed up at him with her completely white eyes, looking very much at peace despite what had to be terrible pain.

"Adie, we made it. Your plan worked. You did it. You got us through."

"I be pleased, Richard." She smiled just a little. "But now you must help Nicci."

"Worry about yourself for now."

She clutched his arm, pulling him a little closer. "You must help her. My part be done. She be your only chance, now, to save all we hold dear in this world."

"But—"

"Help Nicci. She be your only hope now. Promise me you will help her."

Richard nodded as he felt a tear run down his cheek. "I promise."

Her smile widened, pushing back the fine wrinkles of her cheeks.

Richard couldn't help smiling at realizing what she had just done. Zedd had once told him about how sorceresses never tell all they know and in that way lull you into agreeing to things you might not otherwise accept.

"I don't need a sorceress's trick to keep my promise to help Nicci. Nathan will get the collar off her neck."

As she smiled at him, Richard felt her hand tighten just a little. "I not be so sure, Richard. She need help only you can give."

Richard didn't know what he could do that Nathan couldn't. Even if he knew how to use his gift, Richard had long ago lost his connection to it. When Adie's eyes slipped closed and Jillian started to cry with worry, General Meiffert put an arm around her shoulders.

"Lord Rahl!" Cara called.

Both Richard and Nathan looked back at the Mord-Sith hunched over Nicci.

"Hurry!"

"Hold on," Nathan whispered to Adie.

He touched a finger to her forehead. Adie sighed, her muscles slackening.

"That will comfort her for the moment," Nathan said in a confidential tone to Richard. "Maybe with the help of some Sisters I can do something more for her."

Richard nodded, then seized Nathan under the arm and helped pull the man to his feet. On their way to Nicci's side they rushed past tangled figures of the dead. Most of the slain were Imperial Order soldiers, but there were also men of the First File scattered throughout the corridor.

Nicci, if it was possible, looked worse. She shook from the unseen power trying to crush the life out of her.

"You have to get the collar off her," Richard told Nathan. "Jagang has been using the Rada'Han to control her. Now I think he's trying to kill her with it."

Nathan, nodding as he lifted Nicci's eyelid, swiftly evaluated her condition. He reached out, then, and placed both hands on the smooth metal collar around her neck. He closed his eyes for a moment, his brow drawing down with the effort of using unseen powers. The air all around seemed to hum with a soft vibration. After a moment the discordant sensation died away.

"I'm sorry, Richard," he said in a quiet voice as he finally straightened.

"What do you mean, you're sorry? It's still locked on her. You have to get this thing off before it kills her."

Nathan glanced around at all the dead, his azure eyes looking a little wetter than they had a moment before. His sorrowful gaze finally returned to Richard.

"I'm sorry, my boy, but there's nothing I can do."

"Yes there is," Cara said. "You can get the collar off her!"

"I would if I could"—with a dejected look he shook his head—"but I can't. It's held on with both sides of her gift. I have only Additive."

Richard couldn't accept it. "The palace amplifies your ability. You're a Rahl. Your power is greater in this place. You have more power here. Use it!"

"My Additive side is strengthened here . . . but I have no Subtractive ability to amplify. Without the Subtractive side to counter the lock, I can do nothing."

"You can try!"

Nathan rested a hand on Richard's shoulder. "I already tried. My ability is not enough. I'm sorry, my boy. I'm afraid that I can do nothing."

"But if you don't, she'll die."

Looking into Richard's eyes, Nathan slowly nodded. "I know."

General Meiffert appeared behind Nathan. "Lord Rahl."

Both Nathan and Richard looked up.

He hesitated for an instant, looking between them both. "We have to do something before they can send more men through those tunnels. There's no telling how many soldiers are still down there in the other halls and rooms, waiting to come up and renew the attack. We must act now."

"Purge the tunnels," Richard said, his own voice sounding hollow to him.

"What?" Nathan asked.

"Clear the corridors first—make sure there are no more Order soldiers up here. Then use wizard's fire. Send it down through the catacombs. The catacombs are places of the dead. Purge them of the living."

Nathan nodded. "I'll see to it at once."

As he stood, Richard, tightly gripping Nicci's hand, looked up at the tall wizard. "Nathan, there has to be something you can do."

"I can keep any more of them from getting through."

"I mean for Nicci. What can we do to help her?"

From the desolate depths of his own inner torment, Nathan

gazed down at Richard. "Stay with her, Richard. Be with her until she's gone. Don't let her be alone in the last moments. That's all you can do now."

With a flourish of his cape he turned and rushed after General Meiffert.

CHAPTER 44

Cara, sitting on her heels beside him, laid a hand compassionately on Richard's shoulder as he bent over Nicci.

He felt dead himself.

He wrapped Nicci protectively in his arms, unable to offer her any real protection, any salvation—unable to offer her redemption from Jagang's claim on her life.

The totality of the events that had carried him to that point in his life seemed to overwhelm him. No matter what he did, the believers in the Imperial Order advanced their cause steadily onward. In their fanaticism, they were determined to wipe all joy from life, to squeeze any meaning from it, to curdle existence itself into unbearable misery.

Devoted to their mindless faith in a perfect, eternal afterlife gained through sacrifice of this life, the followers of the Order lusted to see to it that everyone who dared to want to exist for the sake of this life alone was made to suffer immeasurably for that singular, intolerable, sinful desire.

Richard hated them. He hated them passionately for all the harm they inflicted on others.

He wished he could wipe them all from the world of life.

Nicci, despite being largely unresponsive, tightened an arm around his neck as if to comfort him in his grief, as if to tell him that it was all right, that she too, like so many all around who had fought and died to defend their way of life, the right of their loved ones to live safe from violence brought against them for simply desiring to live free, would soon be at eternal peace beyond the reach of pain. Even though he knew that she would at last be free of terrible suffering, and out of Jagang's reach, Richard couldn't bear the thought of her leaving the world of life.

At that moment, everything seemed futile to Richard. Everything good in life was being methodically destroyed by people who fervently believed that their pious purpose in life was to murder those who would not bow down and submit to the Order's beliefs.

The world was in the grip of utter madness.

So many had already died, so many more would die. Richard felt as if he were caught in a whirlpool, forever being sucked down into the depths of despair. There seemed no end to the senseless slaughter, no escape from it but death.

And now Nicci was taking that final journey.

He had just wanted to live his life with the woman he loved, the same as so many others. Instead, Kahlan's mind had been stolen from her, leaving her a tool of those with a burning desire to either impose their beliefs on everyone or to destroy them all. While he might have helped Kahlan get away for the moment, Jagang's minions would be hunting her. None of them would ever give up. Unless they were stopped, the Order would have Kahlan just as it would have everyone.

Now Nicci was being slowly drained of her life as well.

As Richard turned inward, turned away from everyone and everything, he felt a sudden, violent, wrenching jolt within. For a moment it held him gripped in a strange and silent netherworld before tumbling him once again into an inner storm.

He didn't know the source of the inner disorientation, but it suddenly felt as if he had become lost among a million meteors. And then they all exploded outward from somewhere within the unfathomable depths of his being.

Cara grabbed his arm and shook him. "Lord Rahl! What's wrong? Lord Rahl!"

He realized that he was screaming. He couldn't stop himself.

Amid the incandescence, understanding overcame him.

He suddenly knew without a doubt the cause of the sensation.

It was an awakening.

The glorious power of that rebirth was staggering. Every fiber of his being was suddenly on fire with the life of it. At the same time, the marrow of every bone rang out in pain so monumental that it nearly rendered him senseless.

He could feel his birthright burning again within, feel himself whole again for the first time in what seemed forever. It was almost as if he had forgotten who he was, what he was, as if he'd lost his way and it had all suddenly returned in one blinding instant.

His gift had returned. He had no idea why or how, but it had returned.

The thing that kept him conscious, though, kept his mind focused, was his seething rage at those who through the self-justification of their own twisted beliefs harmed others who didn't think as they did.

In that moment as his blinding rage at all those who existed to hate and hurt others again flowed through that integral connection with his gift, he heard a metallic pop.

Nicci gasped.

Richard, almost unaware of what was happening, realized that her arms were around him, and she was gasping to catch her breath.

"Lord Rahl," Cara said, shaking him, "look! The collar came off! And the gold ring that was in her lip is gone."

Richard backed away to peer down into Nicci's blue eyes. She was staring up at him. The Rada'Han had burst apart and was lying broken behind her neck.

"Your gift is back," Nicci whispered, barely conscious. "I can sense it."

He knew without doubt that it was true. His gift had inexplicably returned.

He noticed a forest of legs as he glanced around. Men of the First File, weapons in hand, had surrounded him. Ulic and Egan stood between them and Richard. Between Ulic and Egan was a wall of red leather.

Richard realized that when the burning pain of it had exploded through him he had screamed. They had probably thought he was being murdered.

"Richard," Nicci said, drawing his attention. Her voice was little more than a weak whisper. "Are you out of your mind?"

She had to force her eyes open several times. Her brow was beaded with sweat. Richard knew that she was spent from the ordeal and needed time to rest if she was to fully recover. Still, it was profoundly heartening to see the life in her eyes again.

"What do you mean?"

"Why in the world would you paint those symbols in red all over yourself?"

Cara glanced over at him. "I like the look."

Berdine nodded from above. "Me too. Kind of reminds me of our red leather, but without the leather."

"It's a good look for him," Nyda agreed.

Even through her exhaustion, Nicci's expression revealed that she was not amused. "Where did you ever learn to do that? Do you have any idea of the danger those symbols represent?"

Richard shrugged. "Of course. Why do you think I painted them?"

Nicci sagged back, looking too weak to argue. "Listen to me," she said. "If I don't . . . if anything . . . listen—you can't tell Kahlan about the two of you."

Richard frowned as he leaned close, trying to hear her clearly. "What are you talking about?"

"It needs a sterile field. If anything happens to me, if I don't make it, you need to know. You can't tell her about the two of you. If you tell Kahlan about her past with you, it won't work."

"What won't work?"

"Orden. If you ever get the chance to invoke the power of Orden, it needs a sterile field to work. That means that Kahlan can't have foreknowledge about the love between the two of you or the memories can't be rebuilt. If you tell her, she will be forever lost to you."

Richard nodded, not sure what she was talking about, but greatly concerned nonetheless. He feared that Nicci might be delirious from the ordeal of the collar. She wasn't really making any sense, but he knew that it was not the time or place to get into it. He needed her fully recovered and thinking clearly, first.

"Are you listening?" she asked, her eyes sliding closed as she struggled to remain conscious.

Richard wasn't sure if he had actually gotten the collar off in time. He knew that, at the least, she was not yet herself.

"Yes, all right. I'm listening. Sterile field. Got it. Now, just relax until we can get you to a place where you can rest. Then you can explain it all to me. You're safe, now."

Richard stood as Cara and Berdine helped Nicci up.

"She needs a quiet place where she can rest," he told them.

Berdine put an arm around Nicci's waist. "I'll see to it, Lord Rahl."

It had been quite a while since he'd heard himself referred to as "Lord Rahl." The thought struck him that Nathan might be a little resentful of suddenly being displaced as the Lord Rahl. This had not been the first time that he'd been pressed into service as the Lord Rahl, protector of the bond, only to have Richard return to reclaim the title.

Before he could really think about it, he heard an odd noise. It sounded like something crackling, possibly burning, followed by a thump. As the men around him parted to let Richard and Nicci through, he saw a man moving toward them.

At second glance, Richard wasn't sure what he was seeing. It seemed like a soldier of the First File, but then again it didn't. The uniform looked somehow indistinct.

General Trimack, concerned with helping Richard, extended an arm, easing some of his men back out of the way to let Richard get past. Richard, though, had paused. He was looking at the soldier not too far away making his way through the carnage.

The man didn't have a face.

The first thought that struck him was that maybe the man had been horribly burned, that his face had been melted away. But his uniform was intact and his skin didn't look at all burned or blistered. Instead, it was smooth and healthy-looking. He also didn't walk as if he were hurt.

But he didn't have a face.

Where there should have been eyes there were only slight depressions in the smooth skin, and above them the hint of a brow ridge. Where there should have been a nose there was only a slight, vertical rise, a mere indication of a nose. There was no mouth. He looked as if his face was made of clay but hadn't yet been sculpted into features. His hands, too, were unfinished. He had no individual fingers, only thumbs. The hands looked more like flesh mittens.

It was so startling a sight that it was instantly terrifying to behold.

A soldier of the First File, helping an injured man and seeing only the semblance of a First File uniform approaching from behind and the side, straightened. He turned a little, lifting an arm out as if to ask the man in his peripheral vision to stay back. The faceless man reached up and touched the soldier's arm.

The soldier's face and hands blackened and cracked, as if intense heat had instantaneously crisped his flesh to a blackened crust. He never even had time to cry out before he'd been charred beyond recognition. He fell, landing with a thump—the noise Richard had heard only a moment before.

The faceless man had taken on a more distinct appearance. His nose had gained definition. He now had the indication of a slit for a mouth. It was as if he had drawn the features out of the life he had just taken.

In an instant, other soldiers of the First File stepped in front of the approaching threat. The faceless man touched them as he walked through their defensive line. Their faces, too, instantly crinkled into black, burnt folds that no longer even looked human, and they crumbled lifeless to the ground.

"Beast," Nicci said from right beside Richard. He was helping to hold her up. Her arm was around his shoulder. "Beast," she whispered again, a little louder, in case he hadn't heard her the first time. "Your gift is back. The beast can find you."

General Trimack was already leading a half-dozen men toward the new threat. That threat continued to walk toward Richard, unconcerned by the men rushing to meet it.

General Trimack bellowed with the exertion of a mighty swing as he brought his sword whistling down on the advancing threat. The man made no effort to evade the blow. The sword sliced down a good foot into the shoulder, right beside the neck, nearly cleaving the shoulder off the body. It was a wound that would have stopped anyone. Anyone alive.

The general, his hands still on the sword, in an instant decomposed into crumpled, charred, cracked and bleeding flesh that started sloughing away. General Trimack collapsed to the floor without so much as a wince or a cry. Other than his uniform, the body was unrecognizable.

The faceless man, the general's sword still cleaved deeply into his body, never missed a stride. His face had gained yet more definition. Now there were rudimentary eyes peering out from the depressions. Along the side the face a hint of a scar had appeared, similar to the one General Trimack had.

The blade of the sword, where it stuck from the man, began to smoke as it turned white-hot as if freshly pulled from a blacksmith's forge; then both ends sagged as it melted in two, falling away from where it had been embedded in the man's chest. The point of the sword, behind the back, clattered to the floor while the hilt end fell and bounced once, landing hissing and smoking on a nearby body.

Men rushed in from every direction to stop the approaching threat.

"Get back!" Richard yelled. "All of you! Get back!"

One of the Mord-Sith slammed her Agiel into the base of the man's neck. She instantly sizzled and smoked into a blackened, charred corpse and toppled back.

What had been only the indication of hair on the beast refined into blond strands, as hers had been only an instant before.

Everyone at last skidded to a stop and then started backing away, trying to confine the threat while at the same time staying out of reach.

Richard seized a crossbow from a nearby soldier of the First File. The weapon was already armed with one of the deadly red-fletched arrows that Nathan had found for them.

As the man with the evolving face stepped purposefully toward him, Richard raised the bow and pulled the release.

A red-fletched bolt slammed into the center of the chest. The man—the beast—halted. Its smooth skin began to blacken and crisp just like the men it had touched. The knees folded and the beast went down in a smoking heap, looking for all the world the same as the men it had killed.

Unlike the others, though, it continued to smolder. No flames erupted, but the whole thing, including the uniform that Richard could now see was not actually a uniform of cloth, leather, and armor, but actually a part of the beast itself, melted and bubbled. The dissolving mass began to coagulate into a blackened mass. As everyone stood stunned, watching, it burned without flame, drying and cracking and curling until only ashes were left.

"You used your gift," Nicci said, her head hanging. "It found you."

Richard nodded to no one in particular. "Berdine, please get Nicci to somewhere where she can get some rest."

Richard hoped that she could recover, that she would be all right. He didn't just care about her, he needed her. Adie had said that Nicci was his only hope.

CHAPTER 45

My, my, my. Aren't you the clever one."

Rachel jumped, letting out a squeak as she spun to the wire-thin voice.

The unblinking gaze of blanched blue eyes was fixed on her.

It was Six.

Rachel's instinct was to run, but she knew that it would do no good to run farther back into the rear of the cave, and Six was blocking the way out, so there was nowhere to run. Rachel had a knife, but even a knife suddenly felt ridiculously inadequate.

All alone with her like this, the witch woman was even more frightening than Rachel remembered. Her black hair looked as if it had been woven by a thousand black widow spiders. Her tight skin looked ready to split open over her knobby cheekbones. Her black dress was almost invisible in the shadows, leaving the pallid face and hands looking as if they were floating all by themselves in the dead-still cave.

She almost would rather have the ghostie gobblies after her than Six.

Rachel wondered how long the witch woman had been standing in the darkness watching. She knew that Six could move as silently as a snake, and that she had no difficulty getting around in complete darkness. It wouldn't surprise Rachel in the least if she found out that the woman had a forked tongue as well.

Rachel had been so deep in concentration as she'd worked on the drawing of Richard that she had not just lost track of time, but she had, to a degree, forgotten where she was. She had been so absorbed in what she'd been doing that she had forgotten her sense of caution. She didn't know that she could be so absorbed in anything.

She felt stupid for being careless and getting herself caught, for making such a foolish mistake. Chase would have shaken his head in shame and asked if she hadn't paid any attention at all to the things he'd taught her.

But she had desperately wanted to undo what had been done to Richard. She knew what it was like to be at the center of one of these spells. She knew how terrifying it was. She knew how helpless it made you feel. She didn't want that to happen to Richard, and he'd had that spell around him a lot longer than she'd had a spell around her. She had wanted to help him escape the hold of these evil drawings.

She had known that she was taking a risk, but Richard was her friend. Richard had helped her so many times that she wanted to help him for once.

Six glanced to the darkness farther back in the cave, the darkness beyond the oil lamp, the darkness where Violet's bones lay.

"Yes, quite clever."

Rachel swallowed. "What?"

"The way you dispatched the old queen," Six said in a silky hiss.

Rachel couldn't help glancing over her shoulder in confusion. "Old queen?" She looked back at the witch woman. "Violet wasn't old."

Six smiled that smile she had that made Rachel nearly wet herself. "The moment she died she was as old as she would ever be, don't you suppose?"

Rachel didn't try to untangle the riddle. She was too scared to think.

Six abruptly stepped into the light. "How old do you suppose you are at this moment, little one?"

"I don't know, for sure," Rachel said as honestly as she could. She swallowed in terror. "I'm an orphan. I don't know how old I am."

Rachel thought of the visit from her mother—if it really had been her mother. As she thought back on it now, it didn't seem to make sense the way it had at the time. She wondered why her mother would leave her in an orphanage. If it was really her mother, why would she leave Rachel to be all alone? Why would she find her in the middle of nowhere and then just leave her? At the time she walked into Rachel's camp it had seemed perfectly natural, but now Rachel didn't know what to think.

Six only smiled at the answer. It was not a happy smile, though. Rachel didn't think that Six had a happy smile, just that clever one, the one that let people know she was thinking dark, witchy things.

The witch woman aimed a long bony finger at the drawing of Richard. "That was a great deal of work, you know."

Rachel nodded. "I know. I was here when you and Violet did it."

"Yes," Six drawled as she watched Rachel the way a spider watched a fly buzzing in its web. "You certainly were, weren't you?"

The woman stepped closer to the drawing. "This here"—she waggled the finger at one of the places Rachel had altered—"how did you do this?"

"Well, I remembered what you told Violet about terminal elements." Rachel didn't say that she knew what a "terminal element" was, but she did. "I remember you saying how that junction locked it, by means of the azimuth angle, to the person to enable the spell to locate them and then attach the proper parcels. I figured that would make it essential to the function of the whole thing. I altered the ratio so that it would change the position linking it to the subject."

Six was nodding slightly as she listened. "Thus interrupting a fundamental support for the positional structure," Six said to herself. "My, my, my." She shook her head thoughtfully as she peered closer at the drawing. She turned a frown on Rachel. "You are not only quite talented, little one, but quite inventive."

Rachel didn't think she had better say thank you. Six, despite the smile on her thin lips, was probably not at all happy to discover all the damage Rachel had done to the drawing—and Rachel understood pretty well how much damage she really had done.

Six pointed the bony finger. "This here. Why did you add that line? Why didn't you simply erase the junction?"

"Because I reasoned that it would only weaken the hold of the spell if I did that." Rachel pointed at several other elements. "These here support the main elements as well, so if I erased that junction it would have still held. Near as I could figure, if I added that variance to it, instead, then it would redirect the link it had established and in that way break it, rather than merely loosen it."

Six shook her head to herself. "What good ears you have. I never knew a child could pick such things up so quickly."

"It wasn't quick," Rachel said. "You had to keep telling Violet those same things over and over. It would be pretty hard not to catch on after a while."

Six chuckled to herself. "Yes, she was quite stupid, wasn't she?"

Rachel didn't answer. She wasn't feeling very smart herself at the moment, what with being so easily caught and all.

Six folded her arms as she paced before the huge drawing, inspecting Rachel's handiwork. She made little noises to herself as she carefully looked over the whole thing. Rachel was disheartened to see that she looked right at every alteration Rachel had made. The witch woman didn't miss a single one.

"Quite impressive," she said without looking back. She flicked a hand in the air. "You've completely undone the whole thing." Six turned to Rachel. "You ruined the entire spell."

"I'm not sorry I did it."

"No, I don't expect you are." She heaved a sigh. "Well, no harm done, really. It served its purpose. I suppose there is no further need for it."

Rachel was disappointed to hear that.

"This hasn't been a total loss, however." Six, her arms still folded, directed a sly look at Rachel. "I've gained myself a new artist. One who is quicker to learn than the last one. You might very well prove to be quite useful. I think I'll keep you alive for the time being. What do you say to that?"

Rachel stiffened her courage. "I won't draw things that hurt people."

The smile returned, wider yet. "Oh, we will see about that."

CHAPTER 46

Exhausted, Kahlan was about ready to fall off the back of the big horse. She could tell by its uneven stride that the lathered horse, too, was ready to drop. Her rescuer, though, appeared determined to ride the horse to death.

"The horse is not going to last at this pace. Don't you think we should stop?"

"No," he said back over his shoulder.

In the faint light of false dawn, Kahlan could at last see the black shapes of a few trees beginning to appear. It was a relief to know that they would soon be free of the open Azrith Plain. Out on the plain, once the sun was up, they could be spotted for miles from any direction. She didn't know if they were being followed, but even if they weren't there were liable to be patrols that could easily catch sight of them.

She really didn't think, though, that Jagang was simply going to allow her to race away without sending special soldiers to hunt her down. He had some grand plan that involved extracting revenge, and he was not simply going to give up on that plan. As soon as the Sisters healed the emperor, he would no doubt be in an ugly mood and determined to do whatever he had to do in order to get her back. Jagang was not a man who tolerated being denied what he wanted.

No doubt the Sisters would be coming after her as well. For all Kahlan knew it was possible they were already on her heels. Even without being able to spot her and Samuel the Sisters could probably use their powers to follow Kahlan's trail.

Perhaps Samuel was wise not to stop.

But if they killed the horse, that would only put them in worse peril.

She wished they could have gotten another horse. It wouldn't have been all that difficult, as far as Kahlan was concerned. She was, after all, invisible to almost all the men in the camp. She could have slipped down off the horse when they'd ridden near others and collected one. Samuel was dressed as one of them—that was how he'd gotten through the camp in the first place. No one would have raised an eyebrow if he had stopped, and they couldn't see Kahlan. She could have gotten another horse. For that matter she could easily have collected some spare mounts so that they could have rotated and had fresher animals to carry them away all the faster.

Samuel, though, had been adamant that she not even attempt such a thing. He thought the risk was too great. He feared that they would be throwing away their best chance to escape.

Considering what had been at risk, she supposed that she couldn't blame him for wanting to get away as fast as possible.

She wondered why she wasn't invisible to Samuel. Like Richard, he appeared to have come to the camp specifically with the intention of helping her to escape.

Kahlan felt sick that Richard hadn't been able to get away as well. The memory of seeing him there, on the ground, not only haunted her, but broke her heart. She felt ashamed that she hadn't stayed and helped him. Even now, as frightening as the thought was, she felt the urge to go back. Being invisible, she might be able to do something. She desperately wanted to try.

And it wasn't only Richard whom Kahlan was sick about leaving, it was Nicci and Jillian as well. Nicci had already been through so much and now it was probably only going to go worse for her, if that was even possible. Jagang had also threatened to hurt Jillian if Kahlan ever again caused him trouble or disobeyed his orders. She hoped that, without her there for Jagang to torment, hurting Jillian would be pointless.

As much as she wished she would have stayed and helped them, there was just something about Richard's command for Kahlan to leave that moved her to do as he said. It was as if he had given up everything to see her get away, and if she threw away the chance he had bought with his life it would have made everything he'd done all go for nothing. It would have rendered everything he'd sacrificed meaningless.

She couldn't remember ever being so torn over anything.

Kahlan knew that the Sister would not have treated him well. The soldiers, too, would have been all too eager for his blood. She wondered if he was already dead . . . or being tortured.

Tears ran down her cheeks as they rode.

She couldn't put her thoughts of him out of her mind, and she couldn't stop her tears as long as she thought about him. She simply couldn't get that image of Richard there on the ground, helpless, out of her mind.

What made it even worse was that she had been so close to having answers. She knew that Richard would have been able to fill in many of the blanks. He seemed to know so much about her. He even seemed to know about Samuel and the magnificent sword that Samuel carried. She remembered Richard yelling at Samuel.

"Samuel, you idiot! Use the sword to cut the collar off her neck."

Those words still rang in Kahlan's memory.

No sword could cut through metal. But Richard knew that the sword Samuel had could.

More than that, though, it told Kahlan what Richard thought of Samuel. It also told her that even with as little as Richard thought of the man, he wanted to see her safe badly enough that he was even willing to let it be Samuel who helped get her away.

"What do you know about Richard?" she asked.

Samuel rode in silence for a moment. Finally he answered.

"Richard is a thief. Someone not to be trusted for any reason. He hurts people."

"How did you know him," she asked the man she had her arms around.

He half looked back over his shoulder. "Now is not the time to discuss it, pretty lady."

* * *

Richard, flanked by Mord-Sith, Ulic and Egan, and men of the First File, hurried toward the tomb room that had been the breach into the palace from the catacombs beneath.

Nicci was at his side. Despite the fact that she was far from recovered, she insisted that she be there close to him. Richard knew that she was worried about the beast returning and that the next time he might not be able to stop it without her help. She wanted to be near in order to provide that help if need be. Cara, despite her concern for Nicci, had been won over by Nicci's argument for Richard's safety. Nicci had promised that as soon as Richard saw to this, she would rest. Richard thought that her promises to rest would soon be irrelevant because he expected that she very well might collapse.

As they moved onward through the broad corridors, they passed countless burned corpses frozen in grotesque poses. The white marble walls bore scorch marks where men, on fire, had crashed blindly into them and left their impression. Those sooty silhouettes looked a little like manifestations of ghosts, except for the smears of blood that stood as mute evidence that it had been men who had made the marks, not apparitions.

In the rooms and passageways to the sides Richard saw yet more dead Imperial Order soldiers. They had been using the blocked-off corridors as hidden staging areas.

"You kept your promise," Nicci said in a tired tone of not simply gratitude but amazement.

"My promise?"

She smiled through her crippling weariness. "You promised that you would get that thing off my neck. When you said it I never believed you. I couldn't answer, but I never believed you could do it."

"Lord Rahl always keeps his promises," Berdine said.

Nicci smiled as best she could. "I guess he does."

Nathan spotted them all making their way down the corridor so he stopped at an intersection and waited for them to catch up. He had been coming from a hallway to the right.

Astonishment overcame him. "Nicci! What happened?"

"Richard's gift returned. He was able to get the collar off my neck."

"And then a beast appeared," Cara added.

Nathan's brow drew tight as he peered at Richard. "The beast that's after you? What happened to it, then?"

"Lord Rahl shot it," Berdine said. "Those special bolts for the crossbows that you found worked."

"This time," Nicci said under her breath.

"I'm relieved they ended up being of use," Nathan said as he laid a hand on Nicci's head. "I had thought they might," he mumbled absently as his thumb lifted Nicci's eyelid. As he looked closely into her eye he made a sound in his throat that said he wasn't entirely pleased by what he saw there. "You need to rest," he finally announced.

"I know. I will, soon."

"What about all the corridors down here?" Richard asked Nathan.

"We've just finished clearing them all. Found quite a few Order soldiers trying to hide. Fortunately, the area they had blocked off with the slab of stone had no other way up into the palace. It was a dead end."

"That's a relief," Richard said.

One of the officers of the First File leaned out past Nathan. "We eliminated them all. Fortunately they hadn't yet gotten vast numbers up into the palace. We've cleared everything all the way to the tomb room where they got in. We have men there, waiting for us."

"I was just about to do as you suggested," Nathan said, "and purge the catacombs of any more of them."

"Then we need to collapse some tunnels, or something, to make sure that no one else can get in." Richard knew that enemy soldiers were not their biggest worry. Sisters of the Dark getting into the palace could be far worse.

"I'm not sure that's possible," Nicci said.

Richard glanced over at her. "Why not?"

"Because we don't know how extensive the catacombs actually are. We can shut off the place where they got in, but they very well might find another passageway that we're unaware of in a completely different area. There could be miles and miles of tunnels down there. The whole network down there is not just vast but a complete unknown."

Richard sighed. "We need to think of something."

No one spoke up to argue.

As they made their way through the white marble corridor Nicci glanced over at Richard with a look that he recognized. It was the look of a disapproving teacher.

"We need to talk about those symbols in red paint all over you."

"Yes," Nathan said with a frown. "I would like to be a part of that conversation."

Richard cast a look Nicci's way. "Good. While we're having those discussions, I'd like to hear all about how you put the boxes of Orden in play in my name."

Nicci winced just a little. "Oh, that."

Richard leaned toward her a little. "Yes, that."

"Well, like you said, we'll have to talk about it. As a matter of fact, some of those symbols painted on you have a direct bearing on the boxes of Orden."

Richard wasn't at all surprised by that. He knew that some of the symbols had to do with the power of Orden. He even knew what they meant. That was, after all, why he had painted them on his men and on himself in the first place.

Nicci pointed. "Here it is. This is where they got in—in that tomb."

Richard gazed around as they entered the rather simple room. Words in High D'Haran were inscribed in the stone walls, words about those long buried. The casket had been pushed aside, exposing the stairway down. When they had rushed up, getting back into the palace from the catacombs, it had been pitch black, so Richard hadn't seen their surroundings. Adie had been leading them in total darkness. Richard hadn't even known where they were once they'd gotten back in the palace.

Nicci gestured down into the darkness. "This is where the Sisters first got in."

"So they still have Ann, then," Nathan said after looking down the dark well.

Nicci hesitated. "I'm sorry, Nathan. I thought you knew."

His frown darkened. "Knew what?"

She clasped her hands loosely before herself. Her gaze dropped away. "Ann was killed."

Nathan stared for a moment. Richard hadn't known about Ann's death, either. He felt terrible for Nathan, for the shock of Nicci's news. Richard knew how close the prophet was to the prelate. It almost seemed impossible that Ann was actually gone.

"How?" was all Nathan could ask.

"The last time I was here—when Ann and I came down here. We were surprised by three Sisters. They had linked their gift so that they would be able to use their power in here. Ann was killed before we even realized they were there. Jagang wanted me captured alive, or I'm sure they would have been only too happy to kill me, too."

Nicci laid a hand lightly on the prophet's arm. "She didn't suffer, Nathan. I don't think she was even aware of it as it happened. She died in an instant. She didn't suffer."

Nathan, staring off into distant memories, nodded.

Richard put a hand on Nathan's shoulder. "I'm so sorry."

Nathan's brow drew down with what looked to be dark thoughts. By the iron edge in his glare, Richard didn't have any trouble imagining the kinds of things the prophet was contemplating. Richard thought they must be the same sorts of things he often contemplated.

In the awkward silence, Richard gestured down inside the exposed stairwell. "I think we need to insure that there are none of them hiding down there."

"Gladly," Nathan said.

Wizard's fire ignited between his inward-turned palms. The angry ball of liquid flame began turning, throwing hot light around the room as it slowly rotated, waiting to do his bidding.

Nathan leaned over the dark opening and released the deadly inferno. It dropped away into the darkness, howling with fury as it went, lighting the carved stone walls along its swift flight.

"After it does its work," Nathan said, "I'll go down there

and collapse the tunnel where they got in to make sure that at least they can't get in that same place again."

"I'll help put up some shields of Subtractive Magic to insure they don't just dig it out again," Nicci offered.

Nathan nodded absently, lost in his own thoughts.

"Lord Rahl," Cara asked in a low voice, "what is Benjamin doing here?"

Richard looked out into the corridor where the general stood, patiently waiting. "I don't know. He hasn't had time to tell me yet."

Leaving Nathan to his private thoughts as he stared down into the catacombs, Richard, with Cara and Nicci at his side, stepped out of the room to a waiting General Meiffert.

"What are you doing here, Benjamin?" Cara asked before Richard had the chance. "I thought you were supposed to be in the Old World laying waste to the Order."

"That's right," Richard said. "Not that I don't appreciate the help, but why are you here? You said before that you needed to find me to give me a report about some kind of trouble you've run into."

He pressed his lips tightly together for a moment. "That's right, Lord Rahl. We've run into a big problem."

"A big problem? What sort of big problem?"

"A red one. With wings. Ridden by a witch woman."

CHAPTER 47

Richard, elbows resting on the mahogany tabletop, ran his fingers back into his hair. He was so tired that the book in front of him was starting to swim in his vision. He had read so many books recently that he had long ago lost track of how many days it had been since returning to the People's Palace.

The Ja'La match, the riots, Kahlan escaping with Samuel, getting back into the palace, and the ensuing battle already seemed a lifetime ago. With the help of Verna and several other Sisters, Nathan had been able to heal Adie. After she had rested, though, she insisted on once again setting out on her solitary journey. Because the place diminished her power, she was virtually blind inside the palace.

Richard could understand why she would want to leave, but he wondered if, through her powers as a sorceress, she saw no future in staying in the palace. Richard wasn't sure that there would be a future anywhere to worry about.

After what General Meiffert had told him about a witch woman on a huge red dragon hunting down D'Haran troops in the Old World, things were suddenly looking very grim. With men who had been sent to destroy the ability of the Order to support their army in the New World now themselves under such withering attack, Richard didn't know how much time they had left before the Order was finally going to be able to crush all resistance to their new vision for mankind.

The general had been confident in the plan to hit the strength of the Order at its source, and for a time it had been working to great effect. They had hunted down and destroyed supply trains before they could even get out of the Old World.

They had turned recruiting areas and training facilities into desolate forests of stakes with soldiers' heads. Along the way they'd demolished supply depots, ruined crops, and hunted down and killed the men who preached the Order's vile beliefs.

The people of the Old World had begun to understand the bitter reality of the war they had been eager to set loose on others. Their smug gloating over the way their troops were bringing the heathens to the north to heel had turned to sleepless fear that those heathens might be about to visit vengeance on them. Crowds for those who preached the teachings of the Order were thinner. There were even places where revolts against the rule of the Order had broken out.

Jagang, however, did several things to counter that effort. First, he had authorities clamp down swiftly on any hint of insurrection. Towns that were suspected of sympathizing with the cause of freedom were torched, all the people were tortured to extract confessions, and executions by the thousands were ordered. Questioning the rule of the Order brought terrible consequences. Actual guilt was only a minor consideration. Punishment and the exertion of authority were the objectives, so suspicion was enough to bring brutal treatment. People had quickly shrunk into fearful obedience, only too eager to provide anything demanded by the new dictates for supplies.

That widespread fear of being suspected of treason to the cause of the Order had dramatically increased the amount of supplies available to be sent north, so the additional supply trains had no difficulty collecting what was needed. Since the Old World was so vast, that massive effort insured that, despite the efforts of the D'Haran troops, enough supplies were still getting through. Richard remembered the sudden new stocks of food, like the ham, so he knew that the tactic was working, at least for the time being.

All of those issues were obstacles that the D'Haran troops sent south understood and were addressing. Given time, they would have adjusted their methods to address the new problems. That's what warriors did; they adjusted their plans to fit the circumstances they encountered. The enemy made adjustments, you had to counter.

The last thing Jagang had done, however, was a different matter. He sent a dragon and a witch woman—from the descriptions it sounded like Six—to hunt the D'Harans as they went after the supply trains and other facilities. Richard knew from personal experience that from high in the air it was much easier to locate and spot troops. It was an effective hunting technique. With a witch woman's talent, it was all the more deadly.

The tactic had not only reduced the effectiveness of the attacks in the Old World, it had been killing a great many D'Haran troops for nothing gained, making the work for the ones still fighting all that much more difficult. With the increased supplies and the attacks from above, Jagang appeared, despite the greater cost in lives and supplies, to be getting what he needed to continue the siege of the People's Palace. That was all that mattered to him.

It now appeared that it would be those in the palace who would not be able to hold out. Once the ramp was completed, and if they discovered other catacombs to also get through, then the Order's legions could attack the palace from both the top and bottom. Even the ramp alone, though, would prove enough in the end. Such an attack would be costly to the Imperial Order, but Jagang didn't care about the cost in lives to his army, he only cared about his objective. Sooner or later he would take his objective.

When that happened, and Richard knew that it was inevitable, the cause of freedom would be ended. They would be finished.

Richard's only hope now was to find a way to use the boxes of Orden. Of course, he didn't have any of the boxes, but even if he did he didn't yet know how to use them. He needed to learn how to do that, first. Knowledge was now his best weapon. He was determined to arm himself well.

The room he and Nicci were in was a private library that, according to Berdine, was filled with forbidden volumes—books meant for the Lord Rahl alone. Powerful shields protected the mahogany double doors of the arched entrance. Darken Rahl had sometimes asked Berdine to help him translate High D'Haran, but she said that this room was one she rarely visited. She said that he usually came here alone. Richard and Nicci had decided that this was a good place for them to start.

Berdine was searching other libraries, along with Verna and nearly all of her Sisters. Anything deemed to be of possible help was brought to Nicci. She personally checked everything brought in to see if it was something Richard needed to concern himself with. Some of the more experienced Sisters were proving quite valuable at ferreting out important sources of relevant information.

Nicci also kept people away from Richard so he could concentrate on reading and on the wide array of things she was leaching him. In some ways he felt like a recluse. But it also left the mood in the quiet retreat focused, which was just what Richard needed.

Low bookshelves in the private sanctuary were placed near the richly paneled walls, leaving the center open for couches and chairs. It made the room look more like a quiet study than a library. Small statues decorated the tops of some of the shelves, helping them to appear to be display stands rather than bookshelves.

Richard hadn't yet ventured up the narrow, iron spiral stairs to the small balcony on the opposite wall, but Nicci had. As he read, she'd brought books that she thought were important down to add to the stacks awaiting his attention. Although the room didn't have the look of one of the typical libraries filled with row upon row of books, the discreet shelves in the room still had to contain thousands of volumes. The ones they were interested in, though, were somewhat rare, even for this place.

Still, the heavy mahogany table he sat before was piled high with books Nicci had laid out. From within the library there was no way to tell if it was day or night. The heavy, dark blue velvet draperies were closed. Opening them wouldn't have helped since there was only wood paneling behind. The curtains were only meant to give the illusion of windows and to quiet the room. There were ample lamps, though, along with a fireplace. They gave the place a warm glow, making it look cozy and inviting. Richard felt neither.

They worked without pause as much as possible. Food was brought in so they wouldn't have to stop. When they could keep their eyes open no longer, they slept for a time on the couches.

Nicci, never far from him, paced through the shadows and shafts of light from the reflector lamps hung on the polished, dark brown, white-veined marble pillars standing at uniform intervals throughout the library. She scanned yet another book, seeing if it was something he needed to read, only to walk back to the shelves and replace it.

Richard's burning urge was to act. He desperately wanted to go after Kahlan. He knew, though, that it wasn't that simple. To really go after her he had to learn how to use the power of Orden before it was too late to ever get her back. He knew that it would be impossible for him to do such a thing on his own. Nicci had, without hesitation, agreed to be his teacher.

The first thing she had done had been to explain the complexities of sterile fields. She wanted him to fully understand the implications. Richard was no expert in magic, and he certainly didn't know how to use his ability at will, but Nicci had made the principles understandable to him. At first, he found it hard to grasp. He couldn't understand what harm such foreknowledge could really do.

Nicci insisted that the wizards who had created Orden to counter a Chainfire event were convinced that foreknowledge of a certain emotional nature would taint the magic they were creating and thus taint Orden itself. Richard had been dubious.

She told him how Zedd was the one who had explained to her that foreknowledge tainting magic was no theory, but that it was true. He had told her that Richard himself had proven it by falling in love with Kahlan without her Confessor's power harming him. Any foreknowledge that it could be done would have destroyed Richard's ability to overcome the problem because her magic, when she first unleashed it on him even without intending to, would have taken him. While he never revealed the solution to Nicci, Zedd did tell her that Richard had to be totally unaware of a solution even existing, or that solution would not have worked, so she was sworn to secrecy on even that small part of it.

Zedd had told Nicci that Richard himself had proven the central question of Ordenic theory—that foreknowledge can affect the functioning of magic. He had proven it with Kahlan.

Richard knew all too well what Nicci was talking about, even if she was in the dark about parts of it. Because of experiencing such a thing firsthand, he recognized the true gravity of the situation. He knew that, just as his foreknowledge of a solution to loving a Confessor would have made that solution fail, Kahlan having foreknowledge of his profound emotional connection to her would make Orden fail.

It was no theory, as the wizards who created Orden had thought. It was true: foreknowledge tainted a sterile field. Richard, of all people, grasped that concept on a visceral level.

To know in his heart, and to also fully comprehend, that he couldn't allow Kahlan to learn about the two of them being in love tied his insides in knots. At the moment, though, that eventuality was only a distant concern. It was one problem that he sincerely hoped to someday have. He had a lot more to learn before he ever reached that point.

Through reading a number of historical accounts in the library and from books some of the Sisters had found that dated back to the time before the great war, Nicci had been able to form a theory about his gift and how it functioned. It wasn't, in her opinion, so much a matter of Richard not growing up learning about magic that made it difficult for him to control his ability, but that the gift of a war wizard actually functioned differently from a sorceress's or a typical wizard's gift. Richard's power wasn't simply tapped, she'd explained, but worked through intent via his feelings in much the same way that the Sword of Truth functioned.

In this sense, the Sword of Truth turned out to be a kind of primer on how his own ability worked. The sword functioned according to what the person wielding it believed. It wouldn't harm a person who they believed to be a friend, but it would destroy anyone they believed was an enemy. The reality didn't matter; it was what the person believed to be true that drove the magic of the sword. That was the critical concept at the center of both the sword and his gift as war wizard.

Feelings—emotions—were the internal sums of what one had collected, observed, experienced, and grasped about life all delivered in an instant: an interior life viewpoint thrust forward as emotion. That didn't mean, however, that those concluding judgments, in and of themselves, were correct. Just as with the sword, his gift worked in conjunction with what he valued. It was incumbent upon the intellect to sift out legitimate values and provide well-reasoned justification to make those emotions not only true but moral.

That was why it was vital that the right person be selected to wield the Sword of Truth. That person had to be someone with the ability to make those judgments for sound reasons.

Also much like the sword, his gift worked through anger. Anger was actually a projection of his values in that it was a reaction to threats to those values. Thus, his gift was ignited by his anger at whatever threatened what he valued—for example those he loved, or even the ultimate human value of life itself.

Nicci had told him that for all she knew he might never learn to control his ability directly, the way other gifted people did. She said that she suspected that the reason for this was that a war wizard's gift was fundamentally different, serving a different purpose than the gift in others, such as the gift to be a healer, or a prophet. The implication in everything she'd learned was that anger was a key element in the ability of a war wizard. After all, war was not properly entered into out of joy or a lust for conquest, but in response to a threat to values.

Of more immediate concern to Richard, however, was learning to use the power of Orden to reverse the Chainfire spell.

Nicci had been shocked to see the designs and symbols Richard had painted on himself and the other men. She recognized that he had combined familiar elements into completely new forms. But she also wanted to know how he had managed to integrate elements pertaining to Orden.

Richard had explained that he had come to learn that some

of the parts of the spells Darken Rahl had drawn to open the boxes of Orden were also parts of the dance with death, and he knew the symbols relating to the dance with death quite well.

In a way, that association made sense. Zedd had once told him that the power of Orden was the power of life itself. The dance with death, used with the Sword of Truth, was really about preserving life, and Orden was itself drawn from the power of life and centered around preserving it from the rampages of the Chainfire spell.

In a way, the Sword of Truth, the ability of a war wizard, and the power of Orden were all inextricably linked.

Those links brought to Richard's mind First Wizard Baraccus, the man who had thousands of years before written a book, *Secrets of a War Wizard's Power*, for Richard. That book was meant to help him in this quest. That book was still hidden in Tamarang, where Richard had stashed it when Six had held him prisoner for a brief time. Richard knew that Zedd had been headed there to see if he could get the spell drawn in the sacred caves removed from Richard. Since Richard's gift had returned, his grandfather had obviously been successful.

Now that Richard was reconnected with his gift, he remembered every word of *The Book of Counted Shadows*. Nicci was convinced, and had convinced Richard, that the book he had memorized could only have been a false copy that could not be used to open the correct box of Orden.

She believed, however, that even being a false copy it very likely still contained all, or most all, of the elements necessary to open and use the correct box of Orden. To make the version Richard had memorized a false copy would have required only a single sequence of necessary elements being out of order, but that didn't mean that the elements themselves weren't valid and therefore important and necessary.

To that end, Richard had recited the entire book for her. They had made note of every element from the book. If he learned how to create or draw each of those elements, then when they got their hands on the true copy of *The Book of Counted Shadows*, he would simply have to use those components that were actually necessary by rearranging them in the proper order as revealed by the true copy of the book.

For this reason, Nicci now knew what she needed to teach him. And Richard was farther along this path than she would have thought because he already understood many of the key elements involved. He already knew a vast array of the basic parts used in the spell-forms. He had, in fact, drawn them on his whole team and himself. The dance with death had already taught him the basics of those designs, making them by now seem almost intuitive to him.

Richard had discovered that drawing the spell-forms was in fact a natural extension of not just the symbols employed in the depiction of the dance with death, but how he fought with a blade, and how he carved statues. At their base, all of those seemingly different things had basic parts in common. All of them shared movement and flow.

For Richard it was astonishing to discover how it all fit together into a larger picture. As he drew the spell-forms Nicci was teaching him it didn't feel awkward or difficult. It felt natural. He already knew the forms. He recognized in those forms not only the dance with death, but movements with a blade, both from fighting and from carving statues.

Nicci, too, was unique as a teacher because she understood not only how much Richard knew about his varied abilities, but how he used his ability. She grasped, unlike anyone else, how he saw the use of magic. She recognized how different it was from the conventional wisdom and wasn't in the least bit stymied by the way he viewed such things. If anything, it energized her.

She also comprehended his concept of the the creative aspects of magic itself and so she didn't try to correct what he did, but instead guided him to accomplishing what was needed. She didn't just pile on things to memorize; she instead built on what he already knew and the way he saw things. Because she intuitively sensed what he already grasped on his own, in his own way, she didn't waste time dwelling on lessons covering what he already understood, and instead helped him add things he needed, at the place he needed them, when he needed them.

Nicci strolled to the table. "How are you doing?"

Richard yawned. "I don't know anymore. It's all running together in my head."

Nicci nodded absently as she read something in the book she was holding. "What you think is running together may mean that your interior mind is simply beginning to make associations and connections—organizing what you are adding to your knowledge."

Richard sighed. "Could be."

Nicci closed the book and tossed it on the table to the side. "There are some useful things in here. You should take a look."

"I don't think I can see straight to read any more right now."

"Good," she said. She gestured to the pen resting in a holder to the side. "Draw, then. You need to be able to draw those elements from the book you just finished. If the real *Book of Counted Shadows* has similar elements, you will be ahead of the game."

Richard wanted to argue with her, to tell her that he was too tired, but then he thought about Kahlan. Weariness became irrelevant in that light. Besides, he had agreed that Nicci was going to teach him and he would not only do as she instructed but put his every effort into it.

She was a sorceress with invaluable knowledge, experience, and ability that Zedd had said amazed him. Even Verna had taken him aside and advised him to listen carefully to Nicci, that she was in many areas smarter than any of them. Richard knew that this was his only true opportunity to learn what he needed. He was not about to waste that opportunity.

He pulled a piece of paper close and then dunked the pen in the ink. He leaned close and started drawing spell-forms from a book laid open nearby.

One big problem they had not yet solved was the issue of sorcerer's sand. According to *The Book of Counted Shadows* that he'd memorized, the spell-forms needed to open the correct box of Orden had to be drawn in sorcerer's sand. Nicci had told him that even though the book he'd memorized was a false copy, the issue of needing to draw the spell-forms in sorcerer's sand when the time came was true. Whatever spells turned out to be the ones necessary simply wouldn't work without it.

Richard had told her how when Darken Rahl had opened the box of Orden he had been sucked down into the underworld—along with all the sorcerer's sand he'd used to draw the spells. Up in the garden of life there was no more of that precious commodity. There was only dirt left where the sorcerer's sand had been.

Nicci looked up from another book she was thumbing through. "This has some information about the Temple of the Winds."

Richard looked up. "Really?"

She nodded. "You know, the thing that baffles me about that is how you said you crossed the world of the dead to get to it."

It had appeared during the lightning and Richard had crossed over on a road while it was visible.

"I'm sorry, Nicci, but I told you everything I know on the subject."

"According to this, and to what you told me you learned from studying accounts in old books, the Temple of the Winds was sent to the underworld. Because it was banished for protection, it resides somewhere distant across that great void. The whole purpose is to make it far away and impossible to get to."

"But it was right there when the conditions were right. I stepped right across into the temple."

She nodded absently as she went back to reading and pacing. She finally stopped again, looking impatient.

"It still doesn't make sense. It's impossible to get from here to there across the world of the dead. Crossing the void of the underworld is something like crossing the ocean. It would be like walking to the shoreline and stepping onto an island that's on the other side of the world without having to travel across the intervening ocean."

"Maybe the Temple of the Winds isn't really that far away in the underworld. Maybe it's like the island isn't really across the ocean, but just right there, close to the shoreline."

Nicci shook her head. "Not according to this, and not according to the things you told me. Every reference says that to banish the temple to safety they sent it across the underworld—rather like sending it across the universe itself."

"Lord Rahl," Cara called from the doorway.

Richard yawned again. "What is it, Cara?"

"I have some people here with me who need to see you."

As much as he would like a break, Richard didn't want to stop. He needed to learn all of it if he was ever to get Kahlan back.

"It seems to be important," Cara added when she saw him hesitating.

"All right, bring them in."

Cara led a group of six people in pristine white robes into the room. In the somewhat dark library, the white-robed figures almost glowed like good spirits. They all came to a halt on the other side of the massive mahogany table. They looked to Richard more like people fearing they might be executed than like people who wanted to see him.

Richard looked from the six nervous people, five men and one woman, to Cara.

"These are some of the crypt staff," she said.

"Crypt staff?"

"Yes, Lord Rahl. They take care of the tombs and such."

Richard looked at their faces again. They all looked away from his gaze to stare at the floor as they remained silent.

"Yes, I remember seeing some of you when I first came back—when we had the battle down there with the Imperial Order soldiers."

He couldn't imagine the horrific mess that would have had to be cleaned up. He had ordered that the bodies of the Order soldiers be thrown over the side of the plateau. They had more important things to worry about than caring for the remains of murderers.

The people nodded.

"What is it you wish to tell me?"

Cara waved a hand to dissuade him from that notion. "Lord Rahl, they are all mute."

Richard gestured with the pen in his hand as he leaned back in his chair. "All of you?"

The six people nodded together.

"Darken Rahl cut out the tongues of all the crypt staff so that they couldn't speak ill of his dead father."

Richard sighed at hearing such a terrible thing. "I'm sorry you were abused like that. If it makes you feel any better I share your feelings about the man."

Cara smiled as she looked at her six charges. "I told them of your part in his death."

The six smiled a little and nodded.

"So, what's this about? Can you help me understand what you want me to know?" he asked the six.

One of them reached out and carefully placed a folded, pristinely white cloth on the table. The man slid it toward Richard.

As Richard reached for it, a drop of ink dripped from his pen onto the white cloth.

"Sorry," he mumbled as he set the pen aside.

He pulled the cloth closer. He looked up at the six. "So, what is it?"

When they made no attempt to explain, he glanced at Cara. She only shrugged. "They were insistent that you see it."

One of them gestured with his hands held out flat, almost as if they were the pages of a book as it opened, then repeated the gesture.

"You want me to open it?"

All six nodded.

It didn't really feel like it could contain anything at all, but Richard carefully started opening the folds of cloth back onto the table. Nicci, standing beside the six, leaned over the table watching.

When Richard laid back the final fold, there, in the center of the cloth, lay a single grain of white sand.

He looked up sharply. "Where did you get this?"

All six pointed down.

"Dear spirits," Nicci whispered.

"What?" Cara asked, leaning over to look at the single grain of white sand sitting in the center of the cloth. "What is it?"

Richard glanced up at the Mord-Sith. "Sorcerer's sand."

The people were crypt staff, so that had to mean that they had found it down in the crypt somewhere. The sorcerer's sand shone with prismatic light, but he was still somewhat astonished that they would have found a single grain of it.

He also wondered where they had come across it—and if there was more.

"Can you show me where you found this?"

All six nodded vigorously.

Richard carefully folded up the cloth back around the grain of sorcerer's sand. He noticed as he did so that the place where the drop of ink had fallen had, because the cloth had been folded at the time, made two identical spots of ink on opposite ends of the cloth. When the cloth had been folded they had been together, touching, but when the cloth was opened the two spots were on opposite sides.

He stared at it a moment, thinking.

"Let's go," he finally said as he stuffed the cloth into his pocket. "Take me there."

CHAPTER 48

Richard stepped over the melted white stone and into Panis Rahl's tomb. The crypt staff waited outside in the hallway. They had urged Richard to go in alone, first, wanting him to visit the tomb before they dared to enter. It was the tomb, after all, of his grandfather. These were people who had lived and died by the incomprehensible protocol of the previous Lord Rahl visiting his venerated ancestors.

Richard, though, reserved his reverence for those who deserved it. Panis Rahl had been a tyrant with ambitions of conquest little different from those of his son, Darken Rahl. Panis Rahl might not have managed to accomplish the level of evil his son had, but it wasn't for lack of trying.

In the war Panis Rahl had started against neighboring lands, Zedd, as a young man, had been the one called upon to lead free people against D'Haran aggression. In the end, Zedd, acting as First Wizard, had killed Panis Rahl and put up the boundaries that had for most of Richard's life walled off D'Hara.

Even though many had eagerly supported Panis Rahl's lust for conquest, Zedd had not wanted to kill all of the people of D'Hara. Many of them, after all, were also the victims of that tyranny; having been unfortunate enough to be born under a tyrant was not a willful act on their part. So instead of killing all the D'Haran people, Zedd had put up the boundaries.

He said that, in the end, leaving them to suffer the consequences of their own actions was the worst punishment he could inflict upon them. It also gave them the chance to choose to change and make something of their lives. But with the boundaries, they would not be able to continue their aggression against others.

It would have worked, and Richard would still be living in peace back in Westland, had those boundaries not failed. Darken Rahl had helped them along in that deterioration by traveling through the underworld to get past them. Had the boundaries not come down, though, Richard would not have met Kahlan. Kahlan made his life worthwhile. She was his life.

Richard remembered years before, shortly after Darken Rahl had opened the box of Orden and been taken by its power, that one of the palace staff had come to tell Zedd that Panis Rahl's crypt was melting. Zedd had told the man to use specific white stone to seal the tomb before the condition spread to the rest of the palace.

That stopgap of white stone sealing the entrance of the tomb had since mostly melted and the strange condition was beginning to damage the entire room. The walls were beginning to distort, causing the slabs of pink granite to be pushed out of their former flat plane. In the hallway outside, the joints between the ceiling and walls were coming apart from the deformation within the room. If it wasn't stopped, it looked like it could continue to twist support walls until the structure of the palace eventually started falling in on itself.

Richard looked all around, taking appraisal of everything as he crossed the room. The light of fifty-seven torches reflected off his grandfather's gold-enshrouded coffin sitting on a pedestal, making it not only glow in the center of the cavernous room, but almost look as if it were floating above the white marble floor. Words were inscribed not only on the coffin, but into the granite walls all around the room.

"I hate pink," Nicci murmured to herself as she peered around at the polished pink granite walls and vaulted ceiling.

"Any idea why the walls would be melting?" Richard asked Nicci as she walked slowly around the room, carefully inspecting everything.

"That is what really frightens me," Nicci said.

"What do you mean?" Richard asked as he started reading the High D'Haran words cut into the granite walls.

"Verna told me that when I came to the palace, just before I was captured, I had been on my way down here with Ann. Verna said that I told her that I knew why the walls down here were melting."

Richard looked back over his shoulder at her. "And so why are they melting?"

Nicci looked strangely confused and worried. "I don't know. I don't remember."

"Don't remember . . . what?"

"Why I was coming down here, or why the walls were melting. I asked Verna if she remembered anything I might have said, but she said that she didn't."

Richard lightly dragged a finger along his grandfather's casket. "Chainfire."

Nicci looked up, even more concerned. "Do you really think that's the reason?"

"You don't remember any of it?"

She shook her head. "No. I don't remember ever telling Verna that I knew the cause of the problem, but what's worse is that I don't remember ever knowing why the walls were melting. How could I forget something important like that?"

Richard stared into her troubled blue eyes for a moment. "I don't think you could, if things were normal."

"That can only mean that the damage from Chainfire is spreading beyond the original target of the spell."

"It's the contamination," Richard said in a quiet voice.

"If that's true, then that means that whatever is going on in here is connected to what we must do to reverse Chainfire. The contamination in the chimes is erasing memory to protect itself."

Such a frightening concept gave Richard pause. He knew, though, that it made sense. Now he had to worry not only about how Jagang might be one step ahead of him, but about how the contamination with Chainfire might also be acting to defend itself from extermination.

It didn't need to be sentient to react to preserve itself and continue its purpose. To the chimes, eliminating magic was a value, and the contamination they left in their wake was their method of accomplishing that value, so such self-defensive measures were probably integral, much as thorns were sometimes a bush or tree's means of self-defense. Having thorns didn't mean the tree was able to think of how to hurt anyone who came near; it was merely its integral means of protecting itself so that it could continue to exist.

"We have to reverse Chainfire or it's only going to continue to grow worse," Richard finally said to Nicci. "It won't be long before we even forget why we have to reverse it. I must invoke the power of Orden to counter the spell before it's too late."

"We need the boxes of Orden to do that," she reminded him.

"Well, Jagang has two, and the witch woman took the third. Somehow we need to get them back."

"Since Six is doing Jagang's bidding by attacking our troops down in the Old World, I think we must assume that she intends to give him the third box."

Richard traced a finger along some of the lettering on Panis Rahl's casket. "I think you're right. It's only a matter of time before Jagang has all three boxes, if he doesn't already."

"We have something they need, though," Nicci said.

"We do? What?"

"The Garden of Life. Since translating *The Book of Life* I've come to see the Garden of Life in a different way. The book confirmed some of the conclusions I had previously come to, after the last time I saw the garden.

"I now understand the Garden of Life through the context of the magic of Orden. I've studied the position of the room, the amount of light, the angles in relation to various star charts and how the sun and moon traverse the place. I've also analyzed the area within the room where the spells relating to Orden had been invoked—their specific placement in relation to the other elements."

Richard was intrigued. "You mean to say that you really think that the Garden of Life is necessary to open one of the boxes?"

"Yes. The Garden of Life was constructed specifically to provide the controlled conditions necessary to open one of the boxes of Orden."

Richard had to run that through his mind a second time before he was sure that he'd heard her right. "You mean to say that Jagang must get into that room in order to open the correct box?"

Nicci shrugged. "Unless he wants to construct his own room just like it. That certainly isn't out of the realm of possibility, but the elements all brought together in that room are very exacting. Re-creating it would be a complex undertaking."

"But it would be possible for him to do such a thing?"

"He would need the original references from which the plans for the Garden of Life were derived. He would also need the aid not only of sorceresses, but wizards. Lacking everything necessary to do it on his own, he would have to study the Garden of Life itself in order to know how to construct a new one. The only practical solution would be to duplicate what was already built here, since all that preliminary work has already been successfully carried out."

"Well, if he could get into here to do that, he might as well use this one."

Nicci leveled a look at him. "Exactly."

Richard sighed with grasping just how far behind Jagang's true motives they truly were. "No wonder he hasn't been worried about opening the boxes before now. He needed to get here, first. Taking the People's Palace has been part of his larger goal all along. He's known all this time what he needed to do."

"Seems that way," she admitted.

Berdine stepped through the melted opening into the tomb. "Lord Rahl, there you are."

Richard turned. "What is it?"

"I found this book," she said, holding it up as she strode across the room, as if waving the book would explain everything. "It's in High D'Haran. When I translated some if it and realized what it was, Verna told me to get it to you right away."

Nicci took the book from Berdine when the Mord-Sith held it out to her. She opened the cover and started scanning the text.

"So, what is the book about?" Richard asked Berdine.

"It's about Jillian's people. Her ancestors from Caska, anyway."

"The dreameasters . . ." Nicci whispered to herself as she followed along in the book.

Richard frowned. "What?"

"Nicci's right," Berdine said. "It's about how the people in Caska were able to cast dreams. Verna said to tell you that."

"All right, thanks."

"Well, I need to get back. There are some other books Verna needs to have translated. And don't forget," she said over her shoulder as she started away, "sometime I need to tell you the things I found out for you before—about Baraccus."

Richard nodded to the Mord-Sith's quick smile.

Nicci tucked the book under her arm. "Thanks, Berdine. As soon as we're finished here, we'll look into it."

Richard watched Berdine leaving for a moment, then gestured to the inscriptions on the walls. "This all looks rather disturbing. Do you know the exact nature of the spells outlined here? A number of the elements look vaguely familiar."

"They should," Nicci answered cryptically. She pointed out one of the inscriptions on the far wall. "See there? It's instructions from a father to a son on the process of going to the underworld and returning."

"You mean, Panis Rahl wanted to pass these spells down to Darken Rahl, so they were chiseled in the walls of his tomb?"

"No," Nicci said, shaking her head. "I believe that these spells have been passed down through the House of Rahl for countless generations—from each father to his gifted offspring who would become the next Lord Rahl. From each father to his son. They are, in a way, your birthright."

Richard felt rather overwhelmed with the thought of it. "How old do you think they are? And why pass down spells on going to the underworld?"

"From the composition of these spells, my guess is that they have existed from the time Orden itself was created." Nicci looked over out of the corner of her eye. "I believe that to use the power of Orden, these spells may be necessary."

Richard rounded on her. "What?"

"Well, from what I read in the books that explained Orden, like *The Book of Life*, and some of the books on Ordenic theory, I've come to believe that the purpose of such a requirement has to do with the problem of how Subtractive Magic was used in the ignition of a Chainfire event."

"You mean the problem with memories being eliminated?"

Nicci nodded. "Why can't the rest of us remember Kahlan? Why can't she remember who she was? Why can't we use our gift to heal people who have forgotten Kahlan, or heal Kahlan? Why can't our gift restore those memories?"

Richard recognized Nicci, the instructor, asking her student to provide the answer on his own. Richard was more than familiar with the technique. Zedd had used it on Richard his whole life.

"Because those memories are gone. There is nothing to restore."

"And how were they taken?" Nicci asked, lifting a questioning eyebrow.

Richard thought it was obvious. "Though Subtractive Magic."

Nicci only stared at him, as if waiting for more.

Understanding dawned on him.

"Dear spirits," he said in a whisper. "Subtractive Magic is the magic of the underworld." He stepped closer to her. "Are you saying that in order to use the power of Orden, going to the underworld is necessary because those things that were taken with Subtractive Magic are only able to be recovered there?"

"If memories are to be rebuilt, there must be a kernel to grow them from. The memory you have of her is your memory, not Kahlan's missing memory, not Zedd's, not Cara's—not anyone else's. The substance of their missing memory is what is gone from this world. It no longer exists. Not here, anyway."

Richard couldn't even blink. "And that core of the memory taken from the minds of the victims of Chainfire was taken away by Subtractive Magic. So if it still exists at all, it only exists in the underworld."

Nicci gestured around at the High D'Haran words cut into

the granite walls and on the casket. "*The Book of Life*, which Darken Rahl had to have read to have put the boxes of Orden in play, says that part of the process of invoking Orden is going to the underworld."

"But what memory would Darken Rahl have recovered when he traveled to the underworld?"

"Invoking Orden requires prescribed steps. Going to the underworld is one of the steps to be performed in the sequence of invoking Orden." She gestured to the walls. "Those steps."

"But those references say only that going to the underworld is required. Why don't they lay out the purpose of the journey?"

"The purpose of that journey is to recover the core of memories, but Orden doesn't know what is necessary, or who the object of Chainfire was going to be, so it only provided for the step to be undertaken. It doesn't say what must be done there. It is just a tool for the person trying to reverse Chainfire. It is up to them to do what is necessary when undertaking that journey.

"Berdine is the one who first showed me *The Book of Life*. She knew where it was because she had seen Darken Rahl using it. He went to the underworld. These inscriptions here are part of the formula for invoking the spells necessary to do that."

"But Darken Rahl wasn't trying to restore memories lost to Chainfire."

Nicci shrugged. "No, he was using Orden to gain power for himself. It was up to him what he would do once he was there. He probably didn't understand the true purpose of going to the underworld. He probably assumed that it was merely a step to be performed, a part of a complex ritual."

Richard ran his fingers back through his hair. "Kahlan told me that he had traveled the underworld."

Nicci again gestured to the inscriptions. "This is part of how he did it."

"But how in the world am I to do such a thing?"

"According to this, you can't do it by yourself. It requires a guide. Not just a guide, but a guide whom the person embarking on such a journey had to win over and who is now absolutely loyal—even in death."

"A good spirit I can trust with my life."

She nodded and then pointed at a place in the inscriptions. "See here? This is a spell for calling the guide from the underworld to come and take you where you must go."

Feeling rather sick at the thought, Richard looked around at the writing. He pointed to one of the places in the High D'Haran script, then another place on a different wall. "Look here, at these references. These spells require sorcerer's sand."

"They certainly do. Perhaps we had better ask the crypt staff where they found that grain of it you have in your pocket."

Overwhelmed by the things he was learning, Richard had almost forgotten why they had come down to the tomb in the first place.

"You're right," Richard said as he signaled Cara to bring the six people in white robes into the tomb.

The six hurried to follow after her like chicks following a mother quail. Richard waited for the covey to gather. They all peered up at him expectantly.

"You all did a great service by finding that grain of sand. Thank you for being so attentive."

By the way they beamed, Richard didn't think that a Lord Rahl had ever thanked them before.

He laid a hand gently on the shoulder of the one woman. "Can you show me where you found the grain of sand you brought me?"

She looked to the others and then knelt down before the gold casket in the center of the room. She pointed at the floor under one corner of the casket resting a few feet up on a pedestal. She crooked the finger at Richard.

He knelt down beside her, ducking his head under the casket when she did so. She pointed up at a corner on the bottom of the casket that was separating.

Richard rapped on the corner with the heel of his hand. Some sand poured out, the tiny grains bouncing across the white marble floor.

Richard stood in a rush. He shared a startled look with Nicci.

"Bring me your axe," he called to one of the First File watching from the hallway just outside the room.

The man quickly dipped his head through the melted opening and rushed over to hand Richard his axe.

Richard forced the razor-sharp edge into the tight joint where the top was fitted to the rest of the casket. He wiggled the blade, forcing it in deeper. As he rocked the handle, the top began to loosen and lift.

With Nicci's help, he raised the top off the casket. When he signaled with a tilt of his head, the crypt staff and the soldier took the weight of it from Richard and Nicci and set it aside.

The inside of the casket was filled to the brim with sorcerer's sand.

Richard stood staring down at it a moment. Light from the torches reflected from the sand in a broad spectrum of tiny sparkles of color.

He gently brushed the sand away from the body beneath. There, embedded in the sorcerer's sand, appeared the charred skull of Panis Rahl, his grandfather, still bearing the burns of wizard's fire that Zedd, his other grandfather, used to destroy the tyrant. A few drops of that living fire had splashed onto the young Darken Rahl, engendering in him a burning hatred for Zedd and all who opposed the rule of the House of Rahl.

"Now I know why this place is melting," Nicci said. "It's a sympathetic reaction to the Subtractive Magic that was used to open one of the boxes of Orden up in the Garden of Life."

Richard looked over at her. "So it's a harmonic response after having been in the vicinity of that specific power."

With the edge of a finger Nicci carefully pushed some stray grains back inside the coffin. "That's right. This was the safest place Darken Rahl could find to store sorcerer's sand in case he needed more. He died before ever using this here, so it was left hidden here for the last several years. But it's still hot from the sympathetic reaction. That's why the room started to melt. This place isn't a proper containment field for this."

"Don't tell me—the Garden of Life is constructed as a containment field for such things."

Nicci blinked at him as if he had just suggested that water was wet. "Of course."

"Then we need to get this up to the Garden of Life."

Nicci nodded. "Verna and her Sisters can do it, with Nathan's help. They can get this moved for us." Nicci took hold of his arm with a fierce urgency. "Now that we have the sorcerer's sand in which to draw the spells, we need to get back to our studies. We may not have much time left."

"I'm not arguing. Let's go."

CHAPTER 49

I don't feel anything," Richard said.

Sitting cross-legged on a wedge of white stone set in the otherwise complete ring of grass that swept in a circle around the sorcerer's sand, he looked up at Nicci standing behind him with her arms folded, watching him draw the spells.

"You're not supposed to feel anything. You're constructing spells, not making love to a woman."

"Oh. I thought I would . . . I don't know . . ."

"Swoon?"

"No, I mean feel some connection to my gift, some kind of nervous fervor, or delirium . . . or something."

Her blue eyes slowly surveyed the latest components. "Some people like to add in emotional elements when they draw spell-forms because they like to feel the rush of their heart pounding, the pit of their stomach tightening, or their skin crawling—that sort of thing—but it's entirely unnecessary. Mere theatrics. They think they should moan and sway when they're doing such things."

Her eyes turned to him, an eyebrow arching with a taunting expression. "If you want, I can show you how. It might make a long night a little more entertaining."

Richard knew she was just trying to teach him something about the reality of what he was doing by making him feel silly for interjecting the remnants of superstition into what she was trying to teach him was an exacting methodology. It was the kind of lesson that Zedd used to use, the kind of lesson that stuck, that wouldn't be forgotten as so often happened with an equivocal response.

"Some people like to be naked every time they draw the spell-forms," she added.

"No, thanks." Richard cleared his throat. "I can do without moaning, or my heart racing, or my skin crawling, or being naked as I draw."

"I thought you might feel that way. That's why I never suggested such additions to the basics." She gestured to the drawings in the sand. "Whether or not you feel anything, your gift contributes what is essential. The spell-forms do what they need to do as long as you give them the correct elements, in the right order, added at the right time. Don't worry, though, there will be things you must draw naked," she added.

Richard knew about those spell-forms. He didn't like to dwell on them any more than necessary.

Nicci cocked her head a little as she gazed down critically at the angled double lines he was drawing. "Kind of like making bread. If you add the right things, in the right way, the dough does what it's supposed to do. Shivering and shaking doesn't help the dough rise or the bread bake."

"Uh-huh," Richard said as he went back to dragging a finger through the sorcerer's sand, folding an arc around the angled element. "Just like bread. Except that if you do it wrong it can kill you."

"Well, I've had bread that I thought might kill me," she murmured absently as she carefully watched what he was doing, her body leaning almost as if to help him curve the line just so.

Nicci had been able to re-create some of the elements he was drawing from the book Berdine had brought to them when they'd been in Panis Rahl's tomb. Some of the spell-forms had been broken down and diagrammed in the book. For others, Nicci's understanding and experience were invaluable, enabling her to infer some of the remaining parts of the spell-forms from the text alone. In that way she had re-created everything necessary.

Richard had been worried that the book didn't actually illustrate everything that the process needed, and that Nicci might be inferring wrongly. She had told him that they had a great many very real things to worry about, but that particular concern wasn't one of them.

For Richard, this was also a practical test, a chance to use the things he had been studying day and night before the challenge that was to come, the one that would take him into the world of the dead. They didn't have the boxes, of course, but once the boxes were in play there were preliminary procedures that could be done without them. Those measures, considering how dangerous they were, were not something that Richard was looking forward to, but he had no choice. If he wanted to get Kahlan back, along with everything else he needed to accomplish, then there were things he was simply going to have to do, no matter how much he feared them.

At least his ancient benefactor, First Wizard Baraccus, had left a number of clues to help him. Now that Richard had been reconnected with his gift, he also needed to recover the book that Baraccus had left for him: *Secrets of a War Wizard's Power*. If there was ever a time that he needed the information that would be contained in that book, now was that time.

The book, along with the war wizard outfit, much of which also used to belong to Baraccus, was hidden in the castle down in Tamarang, not far from the wilds. Unfortunately that was also where Richard had last seen Six, just before Commander Karg had captured him and taken him to the Imperial Order encampment.

As Richard carefully drew the spell-forms, he was also impatient for the emperor to start losing sleep, start feeling tense and distracted. He had been confident and sure of himself for long enough. It was time for Jagang to start having nightmares.

Richard could just hear the harsh croaks coming through the glass above them. He glanced up and saw Jillian's raven, Lokey, perched on the framework of the glass, watching them. From high in the sky the raven had followed his lifelong friend throughout her captivity, feasting on the ample refuse throughout the camp. Lokey had seemed to consider the whole thing, as he considered most things in life, nothing more than a curious holiday.

Jillian had known that Lokey was there, but she never let

on lest one of Jagang's guards shoot the bird with an arrow. Lokey was a wary bird, though, and seemed to vanish whenever anyone took notice of him. Jillian said that a few times when she came out of Jagang's tent she saw the raven fly high above and do stunts to show off for her.

Being a captive of Jagang, though, Jillian hadn't been cheered by the antics of her raven. She had been in a state of constant terror.

A few flakes of snow were beginning to collect in the corners of the leaded glass. Against the night sky the inky black bird was mostly invisible. Sometimes only its bill and its eyes reflecting the torchlight could be seen, giving it the appearance of a ghostly apparition watching them.

From time to time the raven tilted its head as if it, too, were evaluating Richard's tedious work. As it flapped its wings to animate its raucous caws, moonlight appearing from time to time between the scudding clouds reflected off its glossy black feathers.

The raven was impatiently waiting to do its part.

"Are you ready?" Richard asked, still concentrating as he drew a line in the sorcerer's sand.

Jillian nodded nervously. She had been waiting her whole life for this moment.

Sitting in the center of a place cleared for her in the sorcerer's sand, with spells drawn all around her, she was looking very solemn. She knew that this was the purpose for which her grandfather had selected her, trained her. She was the priestess of the bones, meant to cast dreams to protect her people.

Torches ringing the sand in the center of the lawn softly hissed. Their flames slowly wavered in the dead-still air. The dark band painted across Jillian's face, across her copper-colored eyes, was meant to hide her from evil spirits.

As the priestess of the bones, she was now Richard's servant. Richard, as the Lord Rahl, was now the one meant to help her cast the dreams. It was an ancient connection between their people, meant for mutual protection. What they were casting, however, was not exactly dreams.

They were casting nightmares.

Jillian's people were from Caska. She had been learning to be a teller, someone respected for their knowledge of the ancient times and her people's heritage. Her grandfather was the living teller, the one teaching her the old knowledge, the lore of their past. Someday that legacy would be passed to Jillian.

Her ancestors, a gentle people who had hoped to evade conflicts by settling in a wasteland no one else would covet, had cast dreams to keep potential trouble away. Then, as now, they had cast dreams to repel the horde from the Old World to the south. In that great war they had failed and been all but destroyed.

Richard and Nicci had listened carefully to the tellings, to everything Jillian knew about those ancestral times. Between that, the book, and his own knowledge of the relevant history, Richard had pieced together what had happened.

Most of Jillian's ancestors had been killed, but a number had been captured and turned over to the wizards from the Old World, who coveted their unique ability. Those people were used by the wizards as the raw material to create human weapons. What those wizards had conjured from the captives had become the dreamwalkers—men used not to cast dreams, but to invade them.

Now Jagang was the only living dreamwalker, the living link to the great war from three thousand years before, the war that had reignited. From what Richard had learned, a dreamwalker had been born into the world again because an enemy spy had gotten into the Temple of the Winds and tampered with magic banished there. Wizard Baraccus had found a solution—insuring that Richard would be born with both sides of the gift in order to counter that threat. Jillian's people were descended from the same slock Jagang had come from. His ancestors had once been dreamcasters, like Jillian.

And now Jillian was once again, as the priestess of the bones, about to fulfill her ancient calling of casting dreams to repel the invaders . . . with one exception.

Back in the great war Jillian's ancestors had failed. Everything Jillian knew from the tellings spoke of casting dreams.

Richard thought that might have been why they failed.

He, instead, intended to cast nightmares.

"Do you have the nightmares fixed in your mind?" he asked in a quiet voice.

Jillian's copper-colored eyes opened, appearing in the blackness of the painted band. "Yes, Father Rahl. I never had nightmares before these cruel people from the Old World returned. I only had dreams. I never really knew what nightmares were." She swallowed. "Now I know nightmares."

"Someday, Jillian," Richard said as he bent and drew a starburst symbol before her, "I hope you can forget what nightmares are, but for now I need you to keep your thoughts focused on them."

"I promise, Lord Rahl. But I'm only a girl. Are you really sure that I can cast nightmares to all those men?"

Richard looked up into her eyes. "Those men have come to kill everything you love. You think up the nightmares, and Lokey will carry them to the men down in that camp—I will see to it."

Nicci squatted down beside Richard. "Jillian, don't think about how many men there are down there. It doesn't matter. Honestly. Where Lokey goes, he carries your dreams. As he flies over the camp, the nightmares will be dropping from his midnight black wings like an icy rain. It may not touch every man, but that doesn't matter. It will touch a great many, and that's all that counts."

Nicci gestured to the spell-forms before the girl. "These are the power, not you. These spells do the work of planting the nightmare over and over in those men, not you. Your only job is to think of the nightmare. See this spell here?" Nicci asked as she gestured to a continuous loop that folded in on itself. "This part endlessly multiplies your nightmare over and over."

"But it seems like it would take more effort than I can do."

With a small smile of reassurance, Richard reached out and laid a hand on Jillian's arm. "It is I who helps you cast the dreams, remember? You must only think them; it is I who casts them as needed. It's your thoughts along with my strength that does it."

"I can sure enough think of nightmares." She smiled a little, then. "And you're sure enough strong, Lord Rahl. I guess it makes sense when you both put it like that. Now I understand why I've needed you to cast dreams. That's why the priestess of the bones had to wait for you to return to us."

Richard patted her arm. "The other thing you need to remember is that after Lokey flies around the camp, you must send him to land on Jagang's tent. We want to give nightmares to as many men as possible, but Jagang is the focus of those nightmares, and that special dream with which I want to torment him, so when I whisper to you that it's time for Lokey to land, you think about Jagang in his tent. This spell here"—he pointed—"will send Lokey to perch by the man. When I tell you, all you have to do is to remember Jagang and Lokey will go to his tent."

Jillian nodded. "I remember that awful tent." Her copper-colored eyes, filling with tears, turned to Nicci. "And I sure enough know the nightmares that happen there."

Overhead, Lokey cawed and flapped his wings, eager to be away with his cargo of nightmares.

CHAPTER 50

Jennsen winced as the muscular guard twisted her arm and shoved her through the tent's opening. She stumbled but was able to keep herself from falling. After riding through the sprawling camp in the bright winter sunlight, she found it difficult to see in the somber royal quarters. She squinted, waiting for her eyes to adjust to the dim light. She could see the hulking shapes of guards to either side.

Jennsen turned to a commotion behind her and saw the same big soldiers pushing Anson, Owen, and Marilee, Owen's wife, through the opening and into the tent as if they were herding animals to slaughter. Jennsen hadn't seen much of the others over the course of their swift journey north. All of them had been kept gagged and blindfolded for most of the way to make sure that they were little more trouble to bring along than the rest of the baggage and supplies. It made Jennsen's heart ache to see her friends back in the clutches of such evil people. It felt like a recurring nightmare.

In the distance, on the other side of the tent's large outer room, Jennsen saw Emperor Jagang sitting behind a heavy table, eating. Dozens of candles standing to each side of the table gave that end of the room the appearance of an altar in the inner sanctum. Slaves waited in a line against the back wall behind the emperor. The table was spread with an abundance of food, enough for a banquet. Jagang looked to be eating alone.

The emperor's black eyes were watching Jennsen as if she were a pheasant he was considering beheading, gutting, and roasting for the reclusive feast. He lifted a hand and with two fingers glistening with grease signaled her closer. Large rings on his fingers, as well as long jewel-encrusted chains around his neck, glimmered in the candlelight.

Followed closely by a frightened Anson, Owen, and Marilee, Jennsen crossed the thick carpets to stand before the emperor's table. The candle stands lit a table spread with ham, fowl, beef, and sauces of every sort. There were nuts and fruits, as well as a variety of cheeses.

His terrible gaze never leaving her, Jagang used the fingers of one hand to twist the breast off a small roasted bird. He held a silver goblet in the other hand. He took a big bite, then washed it down with red wine from the goblet. She knew it was red wine because much of it rolled down from the sides of his mouth to drip all over his sleeveless lamb's-wool vest.

"Well, well," he said as he plunked the goblet down on the table, "if it isn't Richard Rahl's little sister come for another visit."

The last time she had come to the emperor's table she had been with Sebastian. The last time she had been a guest. The last time she had not known that she was being used. She had grown up a lot since that day.

"Hungry, darlin?"

Jennsen was starving. "No," she lied.

Jagang smiled. "I don't need to be a dreamwalker to be able to tell that you're lying."

Jennsen flinched when the man's big fist slammed down on the table. Plates jumped. Bottles fell over. Goblets spilled. The three people behind her gasped.

Jagang shot to his feet. "I don't like being lied to!"

Fright flashed through Jennsen at his sudden rage. Veins stood out in his forehead. His whole face had gone red. She thought he might strike her dead where she stood.

Before he was able to act on his rage, a shaft of light slashed into the room. Two women ducked through the opening in the tent. The heavy wool flap hanging over the opening lowered, allowing the gloom to settle back in.

Jagang turned his attention from Jennsen to the two women. "Ulicia, Armina, any word of Nicci?"

The two, obviously taken off guard by the question, shared a brief look with each other.

"Answer me, Ulicia! I'm in no mood for games!"

"No, Excellency, there has been no word about Nicci." The woman cleared her throat. "If I may ask, Excellency, do you have reason to believe she may be alive?"

Jagang cooled visibly. "Yes." He sank down into his elaborately carved chair. "I've had dreams of her."

"But, the link to the Rada'Han went dead. There is no way she could have gotten it off without help. Perhaps they were nothing more than dreams."

"She's alive!"

Sister Ulicia dipped her head in a bow. "Of course, Excellency. You would know better than I about such things."

He rubbed his forehead with the tips of his fingers. "I haven't been sleeping well of late. I grow weary of sitting in this miserable place, waiting for progress. I should have the men building the ramp whipped, as slow as they are. I thought the executions after the riots would spur them into being more devoted to their duty. This is for our cause, after all. Perhaps if I throw some of the slower workers from the top of the ramp that would hurry the rest of them."

"Well, Excellency," Sister Ulicia said as she stepped forward, looking eager to turn his attention away from his dark and violent thoughts, "we have something that we think may make you feel a great deal better about our progress."

He looked up sharply, then scooped his goblet off the table and took a long drink. He set the goblet back down and squeezed off a fistful of ham from the large platter of it sitting just to his right.

After taking a bite from the meat in his hand, he gestured to the two Sisters. "What is it, then?"

"A number of books were brought back with Jennsen. One in particular is . . . well, Excellency, we think you should see it for yourself."

Jagang was looking impatient again. He rolled a hand.

Both women rushed forward at the command. Sister Armina held up the book Jennsen remembered seeing brought up from the secret underground room in the graveyard.

"*The Book of Counted Shadows*," she said.

Jagang looked to each woman's eyes, then held both hands out to the side. A slave immediately stepped forward with a towel and started cleaning the emperor's hands. When Jagang tilted his head toward the table, other slaves stepped in to start clearing platters and bowls away. After they had cleared space on the table a young woman, dressed in an outfit that revealed far more than it concealed, rushed in to wipe the wooden tabletop.

As Jagang was still having his hands cleaned, Sister Armina set the book down before the emperor. He slapped the slave's hands away and turned to the book. He leaned over as he opened the cover and began inspecting the text inside.

"Well," he finally asked as he turned pages, "what do you think? Is it the true copy or a false one?"

"It's not a copy, Excellency."

He looked up with a frown that seemed like it might turn lethal. "What do you mean it's not a copy?"

"It's the original, Excellency."

Jagang blinked, unsure that he'd heard her right. He leaned back in his chair to stare up at the woman.

"The original?"

Sister Ulicia stepped close. She leaned across the table and turned the pages back to the beginning.

"Look at this, here, Excellency." She tapped a place to show him. "This is the maker's mark. It's his seal containing a spell to signify that this is original."

"So what? Maybe the seal is false."

Sister Ulicia was shaking her head. "No, Excellency. That's just not the way it works. When a prophet writes down prophecies in a book he puts this kind of mark in the front of his writings to signify that it's the original, that it's his work, in his own hand, and not a copy.

"You have many books of prophecy, Excellency, but with a couple of exceptions, they are all copies of the original. Most have no seal at all. Sometimes the man who copies the original makes his own mark so that his work can be identified and to make sure it is recognized as a copy. Such a seal to signify a copy is never like this. This is a unique sort of mark that is never put in a copy, only in the original.

"This is a maker's mark left in the form of a spell. It's how originals are identified. This is the original *Book of Counted Shadows*." She closed the book and showed him the spine. "See? 'Shadows,' not 'Shadow.' It has the maker's mark. It was found hidden behind barriers and shields. This is the original."

"What about the others?"

"None have a seal like this. Not one of the three even has a mark of the man who made the copy. In fact, none have any kind of mark at all. They are simply copies. This is the original."

Jagang, leaning a hand on the table, tapped the side of his thumb as he considered.

"I still don't see why it couldn't be a false copy. If they made a false copy and wanted to make it look real they could have put a fraudulent mark in the book to fool people."

"Technically, it's possible, but there are a number of things that point to it not being a fraud. There are also a variety of tests we can do to verify the authenticity of the maker's mark. That, after all, is why he leaves a mark in a spell-form: so that it can be tested. We've done a few tests, and the results have shown that it is genuine, but there are some more complex verification webs we could still use to test it."

Sister Armina waved a hand at the book. "There is also the matter of what it says in the beginning, Excellency, the part about being verified by a Confessor."

Sister Ulicia tsked impatiently. This was apparently an argument they'd already had. She shot Sister Armina a murderous scowl before once again turning her attention to the emperor.

"The book says that a Confessor is in essence used to verify the copy, Excellency, not the original. For that reason we can't reliably trust her to identify the original—that isn't what she is meant to do. The maker's mark does that, and we can do further tests on the mark. I'm confident those tests will confirm what we already know to be true."

Jagang tapped a finger on the table as he considered her words. "Where was this found?"

"In Bandakar, Excellency," Sister Ulicia said.

"You mean it was behind those barriers of magic for all this time?"

"Yes, Excellency," Sister ulicia said with obvious excitement. "That alone is evidence that this is the original manuscript."

"Why?"

"Because, if the original could be identified by the mark, where would you hide it?"

"Behind barriers of magic," he answered, thoughtfully.

"Excellency, this is the original of *The Book of Counted Shadows*. I'm sure of it."

He peered up at her with his black eyes. "Are you willing to stake your life on that being true?"

"Yes, Excellency," Sister Ulicia answered without hesitation.

Jennsen woke suddenly to the strangest sound. As she came out of a dead sleep it seemed like a roaring noise of some sort. At first she thought that it must be Emperor Jagang having another of his nightmares, but the sound was followed by a great commotion outside. Men shouted for others to get out of the way, or in fear. Metal clattered in what sounded like stacked lances being tipped over by scattering men. She heard the roar again, closer, and more shouting.

Jennsen saw the guards at the entrance to the tent peek out from the edge of the hanging covering the opening. She feared to get up from her spot on the floor. Jagang had told her to stay there. As violent as the man could become in an instant, she knew better than to test him.

Anson looked questioningly to her. Jennsen shrugged. Owen took Marilee's hand. The three of them were obviously frightened. Jennsen shared the feeling.

Jagang stormed out of his bedchamber, still buttoning his trousers. He looked tired and groggy. Jennsen knew that with the nightmares tormenting him he was not getting much sleep.

He was about to speak when the flap over the opening pulled to the side. The noise of the pandemonium flooded into the tent.

A thin woman stepped through the opening. In the noise and confusion, she moved with the cool, deliberate demeanor of a snake.

Just from the sight of her alone, Jennsen wished she could crawl under a carpet and hide.

The woman's pale eyes took in the four people on the floor before looking up at the emperor. She ignored the guards. Her pallid skin stood out white against her black dress.

"Six!" Jagang said. "What are you doing here in the middle of the night!"

She regarded him almost contemptuously. "Your bidding."

Jagang glared at her. "Well, what is it, then?"

"A matter of something I agreed to obtain for you."

She lifted out something that she'd had under her arm. Jennsen hadn't seen it because it was so black that it was almost impossible to see in the dimly lit tent, to say nothing of being held against her black dress.

As he stared at the thing she held out, his mood began to brighten.

Jagang's eyes were black. Six's dress was black. Midnight on a moonless night in a cave in a thick forest was black. None of those things, though, could compare to the black of what the woman was holding. It was black beyond anything Jennsen had ever seen before. The thought occurred to her that when a person died, that was the kind of blackness that must enshroud them.

Jagang stared, his eyes wide with delight, a smile settling into his features. "The third box . . ."

Six didn't look to share his abrupt good humor. "I have kept my bargain."

"So you have," Jagang said as he reverently lifted the box from her. "So you have."

He finally set the inky black box on a chest. "What of the other matters?" he asked over a shoulder.

"I burned into their forces, scattering them. I have eliminated patrols when I found them. I scouted the routes for supply trains and insured that they could safely pass."

"Yes, they have been getting through—and none too soon."

"It will be vastly better simply to end this," the woman said. "Have you been able to find the true copy of *The Book of Counted Shadows*?"

"No." He grinned. "I believe, though, that I have the original."

She gazed at him for a long time, as if weighing the truth of his words, or maybe just wondering if he was drunk.

"You *believe* you have found the original?" A humorless smile spread on her thin lips. "Why don't you simply use your Confessor?"

"We had some . . . trouble. She managed to escape."

Whatever Six was thinking she didn't reveal it on her gaunt face. "Well, she is of limited use to you anyway."

Jagang's expression darkened. "Limited use or not, I have plans for her. Do you think you could find her and bring her to me? I would make it worth your while."

Six shrugged. "If you wish. Let me see the book."

Jagang went to a chest and pulled open a drawer. He recovered the book and handed it to her. Six held it between the flats of her hands for a long moment.

"Let me see the others."

Jagang went to a different drawer in the chest and pulled out three more books, all looking to be the same size. He laid them side by side on a marble-topped table, then set an oil lamp beside them.

Six glided close, her arms folded, peering down at the three books one at a time. She placed the tips of her long, thin fingers on one of them. Her hand moved to a second book, pausing on it before finally going on to the third.

She gestured to the books on the table. "These three came after." She pulled the original book he'd given her out from where she was holding it under an arm and waggled it before setting it down atop the other three. "This one came first."

"Came first—as in original? Can you be sure?"

"I don't take foolish chances. If it were a false copy, and

because of that your Sister opened the wrong box, then I would lose everything I have planned and worked for and, considering my part in this, even my life."

"That still doesn't answer my question."

She shrugged. "I am a witch woman. I have talents. This is the original book. Use it. Open the correct box and your nightmares will end."

Jagang stared for a moment, looking unhappy at the mention of his nightmares, but then he finally smiled. "Bring me the Confessor."

Six smiled in a deadly sort of way. "You get everything ready, all set up, spells cast, callings done, and I will bring the Confessor to the party."

Jagang nodded. "Sister Ulicia tells me that we need to get up into the Garden of Life."

"While it's not the only way, it would be the best way to insure success. You should take your Sister seriously."

"I do take her seriously. Since she is the one who will open the box, with me within her mind of course, anything but getting it correct would be very unfortunate her. If the Keeper of the underworld snatched her in that way, it would be the worst possible outcome for her, therefore getting it right is in her own best interest. I think that's why she is so insistent on opening the box in the Garden of Life instead of doing it here."

Six turned an intent look on Jennsen. "Use her. She's Richard Rahl's sister. One by one, everything is turning against him. Adding her life to the mix will only help to tip the balance."

Jagang turned his black eyes on Jennsen. "Why do you think I had her brought here?"

Six shrugged. "I thought it was revenge."

"I want to end this resistance to the will of the Order. If revenge was my goal with her, she would already be in the torture tents, screaming her life away. She is more use to the Order in other ways. My goal is for the Fellowship of Order to at last rule over mankind as they should by right."

"Except for my portion of it," Six said with a deadly glare.

Jagang smiled indulgently. "You are not a greedy partner in this, Six. Your request is quite modest. You can do as you wish with your little part of the world, under the guiding authority of the Order, of course."

"Of course."

"If the life of his sister doesn't sway him, feel free to mention my name. Tell him that I would be happy to let fire rain down on him."

Jagang looked inspired by the idea. "Good idea. As I always suspected of you from the first, you are proving to be quite a valuable ally, Six."

"It is Queen Six, if you don't mind."

Jagang shrugged. "Not at all. I'm happy to give you your due. Queen Six."

CHAPTER 51

Sitting in the darkness, leaning against the stone wall, nodding off from time to time, Rachel heard a sound outside the cell door that brought her head up. She sat up straighter, listening. She thought it sounded like distant footsteps.

She sank back against the cold stone of the wall. It was probably Six, come to take her back to the cave to start making her draw pictures in order to hurt people. In the stone room barren of even furniture there was nowhere to run, nowhere to hide.

Rachel didn't know what she was going do when Six told her to draw awful things to harm people. She didn't want to do it, didn't want to make pictures that she knew would hurt innocent people, but she knew that a witch woman would have ways to make her do those things. Rachel was afraid of Six, afraid of the woman hurting her.

There was no more awful feeling in the whole world than being all alone with someone who wanted to hurt you and knowing that you could do nothing to stop them.

She was starting to get tears just thinking about what might be coming, imagining what Six would do to her. She wiped away the tears, trying to think of something, anything, that could help her.

It had been a while since she'd seen the witch woman. It might not even be Six—it might be some of the guards bringing her a meal. A couple of the guards were men from before, from when Queen Milena had been alive. Rachel didn't know their names, but she remembered seeing them in the past.

There were other men, though, that she didn't recognize. They were soldiers from the Imperial Order. The old guards were never mean to her on purpose, but the new soldiers were different. They were wild-looking men. When they looked at her, Rachel just knew that they were thinking of doing unimaginably vile things to her. They were not the kind of men who didn't seem at all worried about anyone stopping them—except maybe Six. They always stayed out of the witch woman's way. She ignored them, expecting them to get out of her way.

Those men, though, watched Rachel in a way that scared her down to the marrow in her bones. Rachel worried about them catching her alone like this, without Six to keep them away. But the thought of Six coming to hurt her wasn't much better.

Rachel had always hated it when she had lived at the castle before, when Queen Milena had been alive. She had lived in fear most of the time. She was hungry most of the time.

But this was different. This was worse—and she had never thought it could be worse.

She listened carefully to the footsteps outside as they came closer. She realized that it wasn't the sound of a man's boots she heard, but a lighter step. It was a woman's footsteps.

That meant that it would be Six. That meant that it was the day she had been dreading. Six had promised that when she returned she would start having Rachel draw for her.

The lock clanged as the key turned. Rachel pushed back against the wall, wanting to run but knowing she couldn't. The heavy iron door squeaked as it opened. Light from a lantern flooded into Rachel's stone prison.

A form glided in, carrying the lantern. Rachel blinked when she saw the smile.

It was her mother.

Rachel jumped up in a rush. With tears suddenly flooding down her cheeks, she ran to the woman and threw her arms around her waist. She felt comforting hands come around her in a warm hug. Rachel wept with the joy of that unexpected hug.

"There, there. It's all right, now, Rachel."

And Rachel knew that it was. With her mother there everything was suddenly all right. The scary men, the witch woman, none of it mattered anymore. It was all right, now.

"Thank you for coming," she said through her tears. "I've been so scared."

Her mother squatted down, hugging her close. "I see that you used what I gave you the last time."

Rachel nodded against her mother's shoulder. "It saved me. It saved my life. Thank you."

A comforting hand patted her back as her mother laughed softly at Rachel's unrestrained happiness.

Rachel pushed away. "We must get away. Before that awful witch woman comes back, we have to get away. And there are soldiers—mean soldiers. You mustn't let them see you. They might do terrible things to you."

Wearing a radiant smile, her mother gazed at her. "We're safe for right now."

"But we have to get away from here."

Still smiling, her mother nodded. "Yes, we must. But I need you to do something for me."

Rachel swallowed back her tears. "Anything. You saved my life. The chalk you gave me saved me from the ghostie gobblies. They would have torn me apart. What you gave me saved my life."

Her mother cupped her cheek. "You saved your own life, Rachel. You used your head and you saved your own life. I just gave you a little help when I knew you would need it."

"But it was the help I needed."

"I'm so very glad, Rachel. Now, I need your help."

Rachel shrugged. "What could I do to help you? I'm not big enough to do much."

Her mother smiled in a way that gave Rachel pause. "You are just the right size."

Rachel couldn't imagine what she could be the right size for. "What is it, then?"

Her mother picked up the lantern and stood. She reached out for Rachel's hand. "Come. I will show you. I need you to carry a very important message to save someone else."

As they moved out into the stone hallway, the lantern showed that the stone hallway was empty. The guards were nowhere to be seen.

Rachel liked the idea of helping someone else. She knew what it was like to be afraid and need help.

"You want me to carry a message?"

"That's right. I know you're brave, but I need you not to be frightened by what you see. There is nothing to fear, I promise."

As they hurried through the halls, Rachel began to worry. She knew that her mother had helped her before. She wanted to return the favor. Still, it sounded like it might be scary. When people said not to be afraid, that meant that there was something to be afraid of. Still, it couldn't be more scary than the mean-looking men who stared at her, or as scary as a witch woman.

Chase had taught her that it was normal to be afraid, but that to survive you had to be the master of your fear in order to help yourself. Fear, he always said, couldn't save you, but mastering it could.

Rachel looked up at her beautiful mother. "Who is the message for?"

"It's to help a friend. Richard."

"Richard Rahl? You know Richard?"

Her mother glanced down. "You know him, that's what matters. You know that he is trying to help everyone."

Rachel nodded. "I know."

"Well, he is going to need some help. I need you to carry a message for me to see if we can get him the help he will need."

"All right," Rachel said. "I'd like to help him. I love Richard."

Her mother nodded. "Good. He is a man worthy of your love."

She paused before a heavy door to the side, then squeezed Rachel's hand. "Don't be afraid, now. All right?"

Rachel stared up at her mother, feeling flutters in her stomach. "All right."

"There is nothing to fear. I promise. And I'll be right here with you."

Rachel nodded. Her mother pushed the door open out into the cold night air.

Rachel could see out through the doorway that the moon was up. Because Rachel had been in a dark cell, and there had only been the lamplight, she could see everything outside pretty well. It looked like a courtyard, with stone walls surrounding it. The courtyard appeared to be big enough not only for bushes, but for trees.

Together they stepped out into the chilly darkness.

Rachel froze stiff when she saw the glowing green eyes staring down at her.

Her breath caught in her throat, preventing the scream locked inside her from escaping.

Huge wings snapped open, spreading wide. With the moon behind those wings, Rachel could see veins pulsing in the skin stretched across the wings.

It was a gar.

Rachel just knew that in an instant the beast was going to tear both of them apart.

"Rachel, don't be afraid," her mother said in a gentle voice.

Rachel couldn't move her legs. "What?"

"This is Gratch. Gratch is a friend of Richard's." She turned to the deadly beast and laid a hand on the great furry arm, giving it a soothing stroke. "Aren't you, Gratch?"

The mouth split wide. Huge fangs glistened in the light of the lantern. The vapor of its breath hissed out between those fangs up into the cold air.

"Grrratch luuug Raaaach aaarg," the creature growled.

Rachel blinked. It wasn't a growl, exactly. It sounded like it had actually been words.

"Did it just say that it loved Richard?"

Gratch nodded earnestly. Rachel's mother nodded.

"That's right. Gratch loves Richard. The same as you."

"Grrratch luuug Raaaach aaarg," the beast repeated.

This time, Rachel could recognize better what Gratch had said.

"Gratch is here to help Richard. But we need you, too."

Rachel finally took her eyes off the huge beast to look over at her mother.

"What can I do? I'm not big, like Gratch."

"No, you aren't. That's why Gratch can carry you. And you, in turn, can carry a message."

CHAPTER 52

Updrafts buffeted Richard as he stood on the narrow road leading from the People's Palace down the side of the plateau. Nathan, standing to his left, leaned over the edge to take a look down the precipitous drop. Even at a time like this the prophet had the curiosity of a child. A thousand-year-old child, no less. Richard supposed that being kept as a prisoner one's whole life could do that to a person.

Nicci, to Richard's right, was in a quiet mood. Richard couldn't say that he blamed her. Cara and Verna waited behind him. Both looked to be in a mood to throw someone off the side of the cliff. Richard knew, despite appearances, that it was really Nathan who was in the mood to do such a thing. Since he'd found out that Ann had been killed he had been quietly seething. Richard could easily understand such silent rage.

Gears squeaked and the heavy catch clattered as the guards worked to turn the crank to lower the bridge. As the heavy beams and planks slowly descended, Richard could finally begin to see the face of the solitary soldier standing on the other side, waiting. The first thing he saw were the dark eyes, glaring across the abyss.

The young man was big, just coming into his prime, with a massive chest and arms. Greasy strands of hair hung down to his powerful shoulders. He didn't look to have bathed in his life. Richard could smell him from across the chasm.

The young man looked to be developing into a fine brute for the Imperial Order. He was an excellent example of a common Order soldier: a contemptuous, undisciplined thug, a young man governed by his lusts and emotions, and not in the least bit interested in the damage and suffering he caused in order to have what he wanted. He would be without mercy, compassion, or empathy for those he hurt. Their suffering would mean nothing to him. He was completely self-absorbed and devoted entirely to his own wants, not caring what he had to do to satisfy his desires.

He was typical of the regular Imperial Order soldiers Richard had seen.

Unaccustomed to consequences, he was a youth whose muscles had developed far in advance of his intellect, and so he would be only vaguely familiar with what it meant to be a civilized man. Worse, the concept would hold no interest for him, since it offered no immediate gratification of his urges.

He had been selected specifically to send a message. He was a reminder—in all his savage glory—of just what sort of men waited below on the Azrith Plain.

Still, the individual standing there by himself, in his dark leather armor plates, straps, studs, tattoos, and belts laden with crude weapons, really meant nothing. It was the mind of the man that mattered.

And that mind was infused, possessed, and commanded by a dreamwalker, Emperor Jagang.

The emperor had made contact with them through the journey book that Verna still carried. Ann had for many years carried the twin of that journey book, but it was now in the possession of Sister Ulicia and, therefore, Jagang.

Verna had been been totally surprised by the contact. Richard had not. He had been expecting it. In fact, he was the one who had asked Verna to check in her journey book for a message.

Jagang had wanted a meeting. He said he would come alone, but for his own safety in the mind of one of his men. He said that Richard could bring whoever he wanted to the meeting—as many as he wanted, a whole army if he wanted. Jagang was hardly worried about the life of the soldier. The emperor had said that even if they decided to kill the soldier, he didn't care.

Richard knew not only from his own experience but from Kahlan's as well that catching the dreamwalker in the mind of another person was impossible. She'd said that she had touched such a person possessed by Jagang with her power, but even as it took them, the emperor was effortlessly able to escape the danger. Despite the talented people with Richard, he did not delude himself that any of them might just be able to catch the dreamwalker.

Of course, the soldier would be dead. But that was just the sacrifice the man would have to make for the cause, as far as Jagang was concerned.

No, the people Richard had with him had not been brought to try to kill Jagang through the mind of the surrogate; Richard knew better. They each had been brought for other reasons.

The bridge finally thudded down in place. Richard had already given the bridge crew and guards their instructions, so once the bridge had been lowered he gave them the signal and they all started back up the road.

Once the crew and guards were out of hearing distance, Richard started across. His entourage was quick to stay close to him. The man on the other side stood for a moment, his thumbs hooked in his weapon belt, before casually advancing to the middle of the bridge and striking an arrogant pose.

As they came to a halt, the man's dark eyes—Jagang's dark vision—were fixed on Nicci. While the master looking through those eyes was no doubt angry, the young man himself was quite open about his lust for what he saw. He ignored everyone else but the blond woman standing before him in a revealing black dress. The neckline at the top of the bodice was loose and open and the man was quite interested in what he was seeing.

"What is it you want?" Richard asked in a businesslike voice.

The man's eyes—Jagang's vision—turned to Richard, but then went back to Nicci.

"Well, darlin'," the deep voice said, "I see you have managed once again to betray me."

Nicci returned only an indifferent expression.

"You said that you wanted to meet with me," Richard said, keeping his voice calm. "What's so important to you?"

The contemptuous gaze slid to Richard. "Not so important to me, boy. To you."

Richard shrugged. "All right, to me, then."

"Do you care about all those people back there behind you?"

"You know I do," Richard said with a sigh. "What of it?"

"Well, I am going to give you a chance to prove it. Listen carefully, for I'm not in the mood to trade insults."

Richard wanted to ask the man—ask Jagang—if he was having trouble sleeping, but he resisted the urge for sarcasm. They were there for a purpose.

"State your offer, then."

The soldier lifted an arm, rather haltingly, Richard thought, to gesture back up at the palace towering behind them. "You have many thousands of people in there, awaiting their fate. That fate now is entirely in your hands."

"That's why they call me Lord Rahl."

"Well, Lord Rahl, while you only stand for yourself, I represent the collective wisdom of all of the people of the Order."

"Collective wisdom?" Again, Richard had to force himself not to make a flippant remark.

"Collective wisdom is what guides our people. Together, because we are many, we are wiser than the few."

Richard looked down, picking at a fingernail. "Well, I've already played the collective wisdom of your Ja'La team and beat them up one side and down the other."

The man lurched forward half a step, as if about to attack. Richard stood his ground, folding his arms as he finally looked up to stare into Jagang's eyes.

The man halted. "That was you?"

Richard nodded. "What is your offer?"

"When we get in there—and we will get in—men like my young soldier, here, the pride of the people of the Old World come to crush the heathens of the New World, will be set free in the place. I will leave to your imagination what such men will do to the fine people in the palace."

"I already know how the pride of the Order treats innocent people. I've already seen the results of their collective wisdom. No imagining is necessary."

"Well, if you would like that to be repeated here, only tenfold worse just because they're angry at your bullheaded defiance, at having to sit down there building their own way in, then you have to do nothing. They will come, they will get in, and they will extract their vengeance for all that you have done to the people of their homeland."

"I already know all that," Richard said. "It's pretty obvious, after all."

"And would you like to spare your people that pain?"

"You know I would."

The man straightened a little, taking on Jagang's smile. "And do you know that I have your sister, Jennsen?"

Richard blinked in surprise. "What?"

"I have Jennsen. She's quite nice on the eyes, actually. She was brought back after we visited a graveyard in Bandakar to pay our respects to the deceased."

Richard was losing track of what Jagang was talking about. "What deceased?"

"Why, Nathan Rahl, of course."

Richard's eyes slid closed as he remembered that grave marker. "Dear spirits," he whispered to himself.

"While they were paying our respects to the tomb of Nathan Rahl, my representatives came across the most interesting books. One in particular I believe you've heard of: *The Book of Counted Shadows*."

Richard glared, but said nothing.

"Now, as I'm sure you are aware, there are five copies of that particular book. In fact, I have three of them. From what my good Sisters tell me, you have memorized another copy. I'm not sure where the fifth is, but I suppose that it could be any of a number of places.

"The thing is, it doesn't really matter. You see, *The Book of Counted Shadows* that came into my possession, along with your beautiful little sister and a few of her friends, is not a copy."

Richard puzzled at the man. "Not a copy? Then what is it?"

"It's the original," Jagang said in his deep voice, sounding quite amused with himself. "Because it's the original, I don't have to worry about which of the five is the one true copy and which four are the false copies. That no longer concerns me, since I now have the original."

Richard heaved a sigh. "I see."

"Besides that, I now also have all three boxes of Orden. My friend Six was kind enough to bring me the third." The dark eyes turned toward Nicci. "She got it from the Wizard's Keep. Just ask Nicci. Fortunately, Nicci recovered from the touch of the witch woman. I would have been so very displeased had she died."

Richard folded his arms again. "So you have *The Book of Counted Shadows*, and now you have all three boxes. Sounds like you have Ja'La dh Jin well in hand. What is it you want from me?"

The soldier wagged an admonishing finger. "You know what I want, Richard Rahl. I want into the Garden of Life."

"I suppose you do, but I don't think it would be very healthy for me to allow that."

"I suggest that you think about all those people in there, and ask yourself how healthy it will be for them if you don't agree. You see, we are going to get in. It's just a matter of when and what happens when we do get in. If you force me to fight my way in, then, as I said, I will have to let my men extract their revenge on every single person in there—every man, woman, and child. I expect that it will be terrifying beyond their wildest imagination.

"But, if you surrender—"

"Surrender!" Verna shouted. "Are you out of your mind!"

Richard silenced her by easing her back. He turned again to Jagang. "Go on."

"If you surrender, I will not harm the palace."

"If we were to surrender, why in the world would you spare it? I certainly hope you don't expect me to believe that you have it in you to honor such a bargain."

"Well, you see, we were planning to build a grand palace to be the headquarters of the Imperial Order. Brother Narev himself was overseeing the project. But you ended that dream for our people.

"We could start over and build such a palace . . ." The man gestured indulgently. "But it would be so much more fitting, since you took our palace, for us in the end to take yours and rule from it to show all who would defy the Fellowship of Order what comes of such foolish resistance. This seat of the Order would be a statement to all.

"Of course, after you witness the opening of the correct box of Orden I would have you put to death."

"Of course," Richard said.

"A relatively quick death, but not too quick. I would want you to pay for some of your crimes, after all."

"How appealing."

"Well, your people would live. Aren't you concerned for them? Have you no compassion? They would have to bow to the beliefs of the Order, which is, after all, the moral law of the Creator Himself, but they would not be molested by my men."

"Still doesn't sound very appealing," Richard said, his arms still folded.

The soldier shrugged, an awkward movement, like a puppet whose strings had been pulled. "Well, those are your only two choices. Either we eventually smash our way in on a river of blood, letting my men have what they want of your people and your palace while my Sisters and myself do what we must in the Garden of Life, or else you come to your senses and allow your people to live in peace, while my Sisters and myself do what we must in the Garden of Life.

"Either way, I will have the Garden of Life to use as I must. The only question is how soon, and how much blood and suffering it will cost your people."

"You may never get in. You think you will, but you may not. I have that possibility to consider."

"Not really," Jagang said with a surrogate smile. "You see, I always have the additional option of Six helping us. She wouldn't have to fight her way up through the palace. She can just . . . drop us in, as it were. Beyond that, if I grow too impatient I could always go ahead and do it the easy way by simply using the book the way it was intended to open the correct box."

"You need the Garden of Life."

The man gestured dismissively. "The boxes predate the

Garden of Life. There is nothing that says they must be opened in such a place—a containment field, as my Sisters explained it. My Sisters, as well as Six, also advised me that while the Garden of Life was built as a containment field specific to the boxes of Orden, the boxes can still be opened from right where they are."

Richard glared at the man before him. "Without the specific containment field offered by the Garden of Life it would be extremely dangerous to attempt to open one of the boxes. Any number of otherwise inconsequential errors would risk destroying the world of life."

Jagang again smiled a very wicked smile. "This world, this life, is transient. It is the next world that matters. Destroying this vile, wretched world, this miserable life, would be doing the Creator a great service. Those of us who have served His cause through the Fellowship of Order will be rewarded in that eternal afterlife. Those of you who have opposed us will fall into the eternal darkness beneath the Keeper. Ending this wretched world in the cause of saving it would be a noble act worthy of great reward.

"So, you see, Richard Rahl, in this round of Ja'La dh Jin I am going to win it all, one way or the other. I am merely offering you the chance to decide how you wish it to end."

The wind carried a sheet of dust past as Richard watched the man. He knew from the things he'd studied, and the things that Nicci had told him, that Jagang wasn't bluffing about being able to open the boxes without the Garden of Life. He also knew how dangerous it would be. Unfortunately, he also knew that the Order didn't really care if all life ended. They valued death, not life. Even if they could somehow eliminate Jagang it would make no difference, really. He represented the beliefs of the Order, he did not shape them.

In the end, he was hardly the most dangerous part of the Order. It was the evil beliefs the Fellowship of Order taught that were dangerous. Jagang was merely the brute who enforced those beliefs.

"I don't know that I can make such a decision immediately."

"I understand. I will give you some time to think it over.

Some time to walk the halls of the palace and look into the eyes of those women and children under your care."

Richard nodded. "This is the kind of thing I will have to think about. There is much to consider. It will take time."

The man smiled. "Of course. Take your time. I give you a few weeks. I will give you until the new moon."

The man started to turn away, but then turned back. "Oh, one other thing." His dark gaze slid to Nicci. "You will have to surrender Nicci to me as part of the bargain. She belongs with me. She must be given back."

"What if she doesn't want to return to your side?"

"Perhaps I didn't make myself clear. It doesn't matter what she wants. She is to be returned to me. Is that clear enough?"

"It is."

"Good," he said with a condescending smile. "That concludes our talk, then. You have until the new moon to surrender the palace—and Nicci."

The man turned to gaze out at the army spread out below; then he walked woodenly to the edge of the planks and, without a word, stepped out into space. He didn't even scream as he tumbled down through the buffeting updrafts.

Jagang wanted Richard to understand just how little he cared about life, and how easily he was willing to take it.

Verna and Cara started shouting objections and angry arguments.

Richard held up a hand. "Now now. I have things I must do."

He signaled to the bridge crew. "Raise the bridge," he called out on his way up the road as he met them on their way back down.

Fists clapped to hearts in salute.

CHAPTER 53

In the flickering torchlight, lost in deep concentration, Richard used his finger to draw the next element in the sorcerer's sand. Running through the words silently to himself first, he finally looked up to the dark windows, then began murmuring the incantations aloud in High D'Haran.

Through the leaded windows, in his distant awareness, he saw the moonlight. Only the day before, Jagang had given him until the new moon to surrender the palace. That moonlight would day by day continue to dwindle until they were enveloped in complete darkness.

Richard had listened to Verna, General Meiffert, and Cara's strong sentiment that they should not surrender. Verna thought that surrender would be giving moral sanction to criminal beliefs and they should fight such evil to the death; General Meiffert thought that it was little more than a trick and it would be foolish to believe Jagang would keep his word, so they should never surrender; Cara thought that they were going to die one way or the other, so they might as well fight to the death and in the process kill as many of the enemy as possible. Nathan and Nicci had only listened to the arguments, undecided on whether it would be best to surrender or fight.

Richard had pointed out that they were only offering ideas on how they should die, not on how they could prevail. They were thinking of the problem, not the solution.

He knew that there was only one realistic way he could ever expect to get close to the boxes of Orden, but it was not something that the others had wanted to hear.

Moment by moment time was slipping through his fingers.

He knew that he would not be granted more. Richard felt the crushing weight of the responsibility he alone had to bear. He had decided that he could wait no longer; ready or not he had to begin.

He felt nothing as he spoke the proper incantations, just as he felt nothing when he drew the spell-forms. His emotions were entirely driven by his thoughts of Kahlan, the people he cared dearly about, and the choices he had left open to him.

He had to keep reminding himself not to waste time allowing his thoughts to drift to what was about to be lost, but instead to use what time he had to think of a way to prevail.

While he didn't have access to the boxes of Orden, or the true copy or original of *The Book of Counted Shadows*, he knew from the books Nicci had studied, especially *The Book of Life*, which explained how to initiate the use of the boxes of Orden, that this ritual was a necessary component to using Orden to counter Chainfire. Countering Chainfire was central. If Richard ever did get the chance to use the boxes, he had to be ready to use that opportunity. This was one of the those things that he had no choice about. Either he did it, or he could never open the boxes—simple as that.

The sooner he made the attempt, the sooner they would know if it would work. Either he lived or he died. If he didn't survive then it was better to let Nicci, Nathan, and Verna have as much time as possible to try to think of another way to avoid the inevitable.

The emperor had a variety of options. Richard didn't.

Jagang, since he would be opening the boxes through Sister Ulicia, wouldn't have to travel to the underworld. Sister Ulicia was a Sister of the Dark. She already had all the connection with the underworld that she would need to make Orden function for them. Richard would have to create his own connection and find a way to accomplish what was necessary in order to make Orden work to counter the Chainfire event.

The incantations, Nicci had told him, like the spell-forms, were cause and effect. He was the proper person, with the required power, drawing the proper spells, reciting the necessary words. His gift would add what was needed to the elements as he brought those elements into being in the sorcerer's sand. Cause and effect, Nicci had assured him. There was no need for him to feel anything.

He was counting on her being right. They were all counting on her being right.

Nathan, too, was more than concerned about her being right. The prophet was more worried than ever about the great void and how close they were to it.

Richard remembered how Warren had always referred to the boxes of Orden as the "gateway." At the time, when Richard had been at the Palace of the Prophets, Warren had said that the danger was that the boxes, the gateway, had breached the veil and would allow the Keeper of the underworld through into the world of life. Because the boxes were a gateway into the world of life for the Keeper, a way through the veil, they were also a gateway going in the other direction—into the world of the dead.

It had occurred to Richard that the boxes might very well be the gateway to the great void that so concerned Nathan.

Since the powers Richard was invoking were an integral part of Orden itself, Richard was aware that in attempting to journey to the underworld he very well might be about to be swallowed up into his own great void.

Richard thought again about the long talk he had had with Nathan. If Richard was successful this night, then Nathan was once again going to have to step into the role of the Lord Rahl. They couldn't afford to leave everyone without a Lord Rahl for even the short time Richard would be gone. Richard had told the prophet that if anything went wrong then he was going to have to do what was necessary on his own.

Richard, hunched naked before the white sorcerer's sand, used his forearm to smooth the next section, creating a field for the motifs to come. He began to draw the complex enchantments radiating out from the center axis of the larger spell-form. Each of those elements branched into intricate symbols of its own that he had spent countless hours practicing on paper. Nicci had stood over his shoulder as he'd drawn those symbols, guiding his every movement. Nicci could not help him now, though. This, he had to do by himself, without any help. He was the one who had been named the player. It had to be his own work, touched exclusively by his gift.

The torches, their flames wavering slowly in the still air, lit the sand, throwing off sparkles of prismatic light. Those tiny flares of colored light were riveting, spellbinding. They made him feel lost in his own private world.

In a way, he really was lost in his own world.

As he began drawing the abutting spell-forms, Richard gave himself over to the act of drawing. He focused exclusively on the creation of each component as he drew it, making it fit into the larger context of the spell-form not only conceptually, but physically. Back when he had painted the designs on himself and his team, he had discovered that drawing those elements had much in common with using his sword. There was a movement to it, a rhythm, a flow.

Since he was, after all, now conjuring things from the underworld itself, each spell contained elements of the dance with death. It not only had to be the right element at the right time, but had to be carried out with precision.

In many ways, drawing the spells was the dance with death.

In much the way he fought with the sword to stay alive, bringing death to those he battled, the spells were bringing him closer to that cusp between life and death. When he fought with the sword, he knew that any error would result in his swift death. The moves he made with the sword not only had to be the right moves, but they had to be done at precisely the right time and done properly. Drawing the spell-forms was no different. Each move had to be executed properly. Any error would result in swift death.

At the same time, it was an exhilarating experience. He had practiced long hours. He knew the forms. He had painted them on himself and his team. Now he lost himself in the movement of drawing those forms, the strokes, slashes, and points, all the while moving with the constant flow of coming close to death but avoiding annihilation. He existed on the cusp of life, the very outer edge of existence. He moved among the forms as if moving among an enemy, moving among death stalking him.

It was an all-consuming experience that felt to him just like using the Sword of Truth.

In fact, it was all one and the same.

From that first day when Zedd had handed Richard the sword across the table outside his house, Richard had in reality been preparing for this.

He could feel sweat dripping off his face as he worked. As he drew each form, worked each element to completion without allowing anything to distract him into making a mistake, he lost all sense of time. He was part of the drawings. He was, in a very real sense, in the drawings just as he was in a sword fight when he used the Sword of Truth. His brow wrinkled with the intensity of it. He added each element, laid down each stroke and curve with the precision of a cut with his sword—or with the precision of his chisel when he had sculpted. It was the same skill he applied when using a blade. He was destroying and creating all at the same time.

When he at last realized that he had drawn every symbol, completed every spell-form, connected every element, he sat up straighter. His gaze swept over the sorcerer's sand and he at last realized the full horror of what lay ahead.

He looked around at the Garden of Life. He wanted to see beauty before he faced the world of the dead.

At last, he sat cross-legged and rested his hands palm-up on his knees. His eyes slid closed. He took deep breaths. This was his last chance to stop. In another moment it would be too late to change the course of events.

Richard raised his head and opened his eyes.

In High D'Haran, he whispered, "*Come to me.*"

There was a moment of dead silence in which he could hear only the soft burning of the torches all around the sorcerer's sand, and then the air itself shook with a sudden wailing roar. The ground shook.

From the center of the sparkling white sand, from the center of the spell-forms, a white shape, like white smoke, began to rise. It spiraled around itself in tumbling swirls and eddies as it slowly ascended through the sand, as if drawing itself upward out of the spells themselves. As it came, as it lifted ever upward, the sorcerer's sand beneath it was rent open, allowing the blackness of death to establish a void in the world of life.

Richard watched as the white form ascended out of that void, forming into the shape of a figure in flowing white robes. The figure opened its arms, the way a flower would open itself to the world of life and light, until the gossamer robes hung in flowing folds from those widespread arms. The figure floated, suspended above the black void in the white sand.

Richard rose up before the figure.

"Thank you for coming, Denna."

She smiled a beautiful, radiant, and yet longingly sad smile.

As Richard gazed at the spirit, she reached out and touched his cheek. It was as loving a touch as Richard had ever felt. In that touch he knew that he would be safe with her . . . as safe as he could be in the world of the dead.

From the shadows of the trees where Richard had asked her to wait, Nicci watched in wonder as Richard stood before the soft glow of an ethereal figure.

She was an achingly beautiful creature, a spirit of quiet purity and dignity.

Nicci felt tears run down her cheeks at actually seeing a good spirit there before her. It filled her with joy, and at the same time terror for Richard, for where that spirit would be taking him.

As the glowing figure in white robes circled a sheltering arm around Richard, closing him off from the world of life, Nicci stepped forward into the light of the torches. Her forehead beaded with sweat as she watched the gossamer glow gently spiral down into the darkness with her charge.

"Safe journey, my friend," she whispered, "safe journey."

And then, before the opening had completely closed, before the sparkling white sorcerer's sand had healed itself over again, a dark form came together in the air above. The thing whirled itself into a tight funnel as it followed them down into darkness.

The beast had been attracted to Richard through the use of his gift, and now it was pursuing him down into its own realm.

CHAPTER 54

Kahlan added another stick to the fire. Sparks swirled up into the late-evening air as if eager to follow after the departing vestiges of red-orange just visible through the bare branches in the western sky. She warmed her hands toward the building flames and then shivered as she rubbed her arms. It was going to be a cold night.

Short on gear, they each had only one blanket. At least she also had her cloak. Lying on the cold ground made for a miserable, sleepless night. Spruce trees were plentiful, though, so she had cut a number of boughs for bedding. Even as thick as the woods were they wouldn't have offered good protection from any wind, but since the clear night was dead calm at least they wouldn't need to build a shelter. Kahlan just wanted to have something to eat and then get some sleep.

Before they had built the fire she had taken the opportunity to set a couple of snares, hoping to catch a rabbit, if not to eat that night then maybe in the morning before they started out again. Samuel had collected a good supply of firewood to last the night, then built the fire. After finishing with that he had gone off to a nearby stream down a rocky bank to collect water.

Kahlan was bone-weary as well as hungry. They were nearly out of the food they'd brought from the Imperial Order's camp—not that they'd stopped all that often to eat, or rest. Unless they caught a rabbit it would be dried biscuits and dried meat again. At least they had that. It wasn't going to last much longer, though.

Samuel hadn't wanted to stop to try to see if they could

get more food. He seemed in a frantic urgency to get somewhere. They had a few coins they'd found in the bottom of the saddlebags, but rather than venturing into one of the several small towns they had passed near in order to try to get more supplies, Samuel had insisted that they stay well clear of any people.

He was convinced that Imperial Order soldiers would be hunting them. Considering how much Jagang apparently hated her and how keen he was to extract vengeance, Kahlan couldn't really offer any argument against Samuel's theory. For all she knew soldiers might be hot on her heels. The thought added an uneasy edge to her chill.

When Kahlan asked Samuel where they were going he was vague about it, simply pointing west-southwest. He assured her, though, that they were going someplace where they would be safe.

He was proving to be a strange traveling companion. He spoke very little when they rode and even less at camp. Whenever they stopped he rarely ventured far from her. She imagined that he simply wanted to protect her, to keep her safe, but she wondered if it was more that he was watching over his prize. While he had come into the Order's camp to rescue her, he never wanted to talk about his reasons for doing so. One time when she had pressed him he said it had been because he wanted to help her. On the surface it seemed a nice sentiment, yet he never explained how he knew her, or how he knew that she had been held captive.

By the way that he was always glancing at her when he didn't think she was watching she thought that maybe he was just bashful. If she pressed him about anything he would typically pull his head down between his shoulders and shrug. She sometimes came to feel that she was torturing the poor man with her questions, and so she would stop and let him be. It was only then that he would seem to relax.

Still, all of the unanswered questions gave her pause. Despite everything he had done, and how he helped her at every turn, she didn't trust him. She didn't like that he wouldn't answer such simple questions—such important questions. Having so much of her own life a mystery to her left her rather sensitive to the relevance of unanswered questions.

She knew, too, that Samuel was fascinated by her. He often seemed eager to do things to please her. He would cut pieces of sausage, giving her one slice at a time until she had to stop him, telling him that she'd had enough, and that he should eat, too. At other times, though, like when he was distracted by his own hunger, he would forget to offer her anything until she asked.

Sometimes she would glance over and see him staring at her with those strange golden eyes. In those moments, she thought that she saw the cunning countenance of a thief. She tried to keep a hand on the handle of her knife when she went to sleep.

At other times, when she would try to ask questions, he seemed too shy even to look her in the eye, much less answer her, and would hunch back toward the fire as if hoping he could be invisible. Most of the time she had trouble getting more than a yes or no out of him. His reticence never seemed to be out of cruelty, arrogance, or indifference, though. In the end, since it was so difficult getting him to talk and the answers she did get were virtually useless, she had stopped trying.

He was either painfully shy, or he was hiding something.

In those long periods of silence, Kahlan's mind would turn to thoughts about Richard. She wondered if he was alive or dead. She feared that she knew the answer but was reluctant to accept the finality of his death. She was still astonished recalling the sight of him using weapons, the way his blade moved, the way he moved. He had done so much to help her escape. She feared that he had paid the ultimate price for it.

In the still air, thinking about Richard, Kahlan felt a chill that was not from the cold. It was a strange night. Something about it felt out-of-sorts and empty. The world felt like an even more lonely place than usual.

That was the thing that bothered her the most—the constant, gnawing emptiness she felt, the terrible loneliness of being isolated from almost everyone else in the world. A part of her life was missing, too, and she didn't know what it was. She didn't even know who she was, other than her name and that she was the Mother Confessor. When she had asked Samuel what a Confessor was he had stared a long moment and then shrugged. She got the clear impression that he knew but didn't want to say.

Kahlan felt cut off not only from the world, but from herself. She wanted her life back.

In the fading light she made her way over to the exhausted horse as he cropped at the clumps of long grass. There was no currycomb to brush out his coat, so she stroked her hand over the huge animal, cleaning it as best she could, checking for any injuries or burrs. She used her fingers to pry off dried clumps of mud from his legs and then the side of his belly. The horse turned his head back, watching her cleaning off the caked mud.

The horse liked her care and gentle touch. He was an animal kept by men who were little more than animals themselves and wasn't used to being treated with kindness and respect, so he knew the value of both.

When she finished picking his hooves clean, she gave the horse a good scratch behind the ears. He neighed softly, nuzzling his head against her. Kahlan smiled and scratched some more, which pleased the horse just fine. His big eyes closed as he soaked in the attention. She felt closer to the horse than to Samuel.

To Samuel, the horse was just a horse. He wanted to hurry, and the horse was his means of covering ground. Kahlan wasn't sure if it was so much that he had somewhere to go, or if he simply wanted to put as much distance between them and the Imperial Order as possible.

Since he kept to a steady course she supposed that he must have a real destination. If that was the case, then he had some reason to get there in a hurry. If he had a destination, and was eager to get there, then why wouldn't he at least tell her where they were going?

As she rubbed behind the horse's ears, he pressed his head a little tighter against her in appreciation. She smiled at the nudge the horse gave her when she paused, urging her to continue. She thought that he was falling in love with her.

Kahlan wondered if she was being less kind to Samuel. She didn't mean to be deliberately cold toward him, but since he was being less than candid—and likely evasive—she had decided to trust her instincts and remain businesslike with him.

Back at the fire, as Kahlan, sitting on her heels, fed another stick into the flames, she heard Samuel rushing back. She checked the knife at her belt.

"Got one!" he called as he came into the light of the campfire.

He held up a rabbit by its hind legs. She didn't think that she'd ever seen Samuel so excited. He had to be hungry.

She sat back, smiling. "I guess we get a hot meal tonight."

Samuel, grasping the hind legs in both hands, hastily ripped the rabbit apart. Kahlan sat up in surprise as he laid a bleeding half of a rabbit before her.

Samuel squatted not far away, hunched down facing the fire, and began devouring the other half of the rabbit.

Kahlan stared in shock as she watched him eating the raw catch. He tore off a bite of fur with his teeth and swallowed it down. He crunched right through bones. As blood ran down his chin he even ate the entrails.

The sight was making her sick. Kahlan looked away to stare into the fire.

"Eat," Samuel said. "It's good."

Kahlan picked up the hind leg and tossed her half to him. "I'm not very hungry."

Samuel didn't argue. He tore into her half.

Kahlan lay back, resting her head against the saddle, and watched the stars. To take her mind off Samuel she thought again about Richard, wondering who he really was, and what his connection to her was. She thought about how he fought with a blade. In many ways it reminded her of the way she fought. She didn't know where she had learned what she knew. As she wandered through an internal landscape of shadowy uncertainties, she watched the moon slowly rise.

She began wondering why she should continue to stay with

Samuel. He had saved her life, after a fashion, after Richard told him how. She supposed that she did owe him some gratitude. But why stay with him? He wasn't providing her any answers or real solutions. She didn't owe him her dogged allegiance. She wondered if she should strike out on her own.

She realized that even if she left Samuel and struck out on her own, without knowing who she was where would she go? She saw trees and mountains as they rode past, but she didn't know where she was. She didn't know where she grew up, where she lived, where she belonged. She didn't recognize the land or even remember any towns or cities, other than the places of the dead that she'd gone through after the Sisters had captured her. She was lost in a world that didn't know her and she didn't remember.

When she realized that the moon had risen above the trees, she looked over at Samuel. He had long ago finished his meal.

He was polishing his sword as it lay in his lap.

"Samuel," she called. He looked up as if being yanked out of a trance. "Samuel, I need to know where we're going."

"To a place where we will be safe."

"You've told me that before. If I'm going to continue to travel with you—"

"You must! You must come with me! Please!"

Kahlan was taken aback by his outburst of emotion. His eyes wide and round, he looked genuinely panicked.

"Why?"

"Because I will take us to safety."

"Maybe I can take myself to safety."

"But I can take you to someone who can help you get your memory back."

He had her attention. She sat up.

"You know someone who can help me get my memory back?"

Samuel nodded vigorously.

"Who?"

"A friend."

"How can I believe that you're telling me the truth?"

Samuel gazed down at the gleaming weapon in his lap. He ran adoring fingers over its curves.

"I am the Seeker of Truth. You have a spell that has taken your memory. I have a friend who can help you recover your past, recover yourself."

Kahlan's heart pounded with the abruptly unexpected prospect of having her memory back. All of her other questions seemed suddenly insignificant.

Samuel had never told her that he was the Seeker of Truth. She didn't know what the Seeker of Truth was, but she had seen the word TRUTH in gold wire woven through the silver wire of the hilt. It seemed an odd title for someone so reluctant to offer any information about anything.

"When will I meet this person?"

"Soon. She is close."

"How do you know?"

Samuel looked up. His yellow eyes stared at her, looking like twin lanterns in the darkness.

"I can feel her. You must stay if you want to recover your past."

Kahlan thought about Richard with those strange symbols painted all over him. That was the past she was really interested in. She wanted to know her connection to that man with the gray eyes.

Richard knew that it was his only chance.

Darkness unlike anything he had ever known pressed in all around him. It was suffocating, terrifying, crushing.

Denna tried to protect him, but even she had no power to stop such a thing. No one did.

"*You can't,*" came Denna's whispering voice in his mind. "*This is a place of nothing. You can't do that.*"

Richard knew that it was his only chance.

"I have to try."

"*If you do that, you will be naked to this place. Your protection will be stripped from you. You will not be able to be here any longer.*"

"I've done what I must."

"*But you will not be able to find your way back.*"

Richard cried out in agony. The protective structure of the spell-forms that he had created was being shredded. The blackness all around was seeping in and crushing the life from him. This was a place that did not tolerate life. This was a place that existed to draw life itself away into the dark eternity of nothing.

The beast had followed him into that void of the underworld, and now it had him trapped in its own domain.

Finding his way back was no longer what concerned him. That option was already lost to him. His connection to the entry point was gone, broken away by the beast as it tore apart the fabric of the protective spells. There was no way back to the Garden of Life, no way to find something in the middle of nothing.

Now escape was all that mattered.

The beast was a thing created of Subtractive Magic and it was in a Subtractive world. Richard was caught in its lair.

In this place there was no help to be had. Denna could do nothing against a conjured creature of this sort, a creature in its own element.

There was no way he could even make it back to the Hall of Sky, where the ceiling of stone was like a window showing the sky across its surface. Even that now seemed forever ago, forever distant across the eternity of nothing. His connection to it was lost somewhere in the blackness.

As he felt the tormenting claws of death itself tearing to get at him he only wanted out.

His mind held those essential elements he had come for in a death grip. The beast was trying to strip them away from him. even if it cost him his life, he could not let those things go. If he lost those ephemeral aspects, there would be no point in going back to the world of life.

"I have to do it," he cried through the stunning pain of what was ripping at his very soul.

Denna's arms tightened protectively, desperately, around him, but there was no protection to be had in that embrace. Despite how much she wanted to help him, this was a thing she could not fight. She was his protector in this world, but only in the sense of being his guide to help him find what he needed while keeping him from straying into dangers that would suck him forever downward into darker places yet. She was not his guardian from what might come out of that darkness, and she had no ability to stop a conjured creature that did not exist.

"I have to!" he cried out, knowing that there was nothing else to try.

Shimmering tears traced their way down Denna's beautiful, glowing face. "*If you do this, I can't protect you.*"

"If I don't, what do you suppose will happen to me?"

She smiled sadly. "*You will die here.*"

"Then what choice do I have?"

She began floating away, only her hand holding his.

"*None,*" her silken voice said in his mind. "*But I can't be with you if you do this.*"

Twisting in pain as the beast tightened around him, Richard managed to nod. "I know, Denna. Thank you for all you have done. It was a true gift."

Her sad smile widened as she drifted farther away. "*For me, too, Richard. I love you.*"

Richard felt her fingers still touching his. He nodded as best he could. "One way or another, you will always be in my heart."

He felt her kiss on his cheek. "*Thank you, Richard, for that above all else.*"

And then she was gone.

When she vanished, and Richard was suddenly alone, enveloped in incomparable solitude and darkness, in the absence of everything, he released Additive Magic into the beast in a world where it could not exist.

In that instant, as the concussion of the Additive came into being in the heart of nowhere, the beast, unable to endure such an irreconcilable clash between what was and what was not, between the world of life and the world of the dead, between suddenly containing without any protective buffers an element of Additive in a world of Subtractive, disintegrated out of existence in both worlds.

At the same time, Richard felt a stunning blow from every direction at once.

There was suddenly ground under his feet.

Unable to stand, he collapsed among skulls.

Naked men, painted in wild designs, sat in a circle all around him.

Shaking with pain and shock, he felt comforting, calming hands on him. From all around he heard words he didn't understand.

But then he began to see faces he recognized. He saw his friend Savidlin. At the head of the circle he saw the Bird Man.

"Welcome back to the world of life, Richard with the Temper," a familiar voice said. It was Chandalen.

Still catching his breath, Richard blinked at the grim faces watching him. They were all painted in wild designs with black and white mud. He realized that he understood the symbols. When he had first come to these people and asked for a gathering, he had thought the black and white mud was simply random patterns. He knew now that it wasn't. It had meaning.

"Where am I?"

"You are in the spirit house," Chandalen said in his deep, grim-sounding voice.

The men all around him speaking in the strange language were the Mud People elders. It was a gathering.

Richard looked around at the spirit house. This was the village where he and Kahlan had been married. This was the place where they had spent their first night as husband and wife.

The men helped Richard stand.

"But what am I doing here?" he asked Chandalen, still not sure if he was dreaming . . . or dead.

The man turned to the Bird Man. They exchanged brief words. Chandalen turned back to Richard.

"We thought you would know, and that you could tell us. We were asked to have a gathering for you. We were told that it was a matter of life or death."

Richard frowned as he carefully stepped out of the collection of skulls of ancestors. "Who asked you to have a gathering?"

Chandalen cleared his throat. "Well, at first we thought it might be a spirit."

"A spirit," Richard said as he stared.

Chandalen nodded. "But then we realized it was a stranger."

Richard tilted his head toward the man. "A stranger?"

"She flew here on a beast, and then—" He stopped when he saw the look on Richard's face. "Come, they will explain it."

"They?"

"Yes, the strangers. Come."

"I'm naked."

Chandalen nodded. "We knew you were coming, so we brought clothes for you. Come, they are just outside, and you can talk to the strangers. They are eager to see you. They feared you would never come. We have been in here for two nights, waiting."

Richard wondered if it was Nicci and maybe Nathan. Who but Nicci could have known to do such a thing?

"Two nights . . ." Richard mumbled as he was funneled out the door among all the elders as they touched him, patted his shoulder, and jabbered greetings. Despite the unexpected circumstances, they were pleased to see him. He was, after all, one of them, one of the Mud People.

It was dark outside. Richard noticed the slender crescent of the moon. Attendants waited with clothes for all the elders. One of the men handed Richard buckskin trousers, and then a buckskin pullover shirt.

Once Richard was dressed, the group of men swept him through the narrow passageways. Richard felt as if he had awakened in some past life. He remembered all these passageways through the buildings.

Richard was eager to see Nicci. He couldn't wait to find out what had happened, how she knew to help him escape. It was probably the prophet who had known of the problem he would face, and she must have figured a way to help him by providing a way for him to step back into the world of life. He couldn't wait to tell her what he had managed to do in the underworld.

The Bird Man laid an arm around Richard's shoulder and spoke in the words Richard didn't understand.

Chandalen answered him, and then spoke to Richard. "The

Bird Man wants you to know that he has spoken with many ancestors in a gathering, but in all his life he has never seen one of our people return from the spirit world."

Richard glanced over at the smiling Bird Man.

"It's a first for me as well," he assured Chandalen.

In the open center of the village large fires were burning, lighting the crowds attending the feast. Children ran through the legs of adults, enjoying the festivities. People were gathered on and around the platforms.

"Richard!" a girl shouted.

Richard turned to the sound and saw Rachel jump off a platform and run toward him. She threw her arms around his waist. She seemed a head taller than the last time he'd seen her. As he embraced her, he couldn't help laughing with the joy of seeing her again.

When he looked up, Chase was standing there as well. Chase made the largest among the Mud People look the size of children.

"Chase, what are you doing here?"

He folded his arms, looking unhappy. "It's too incredible. You wouldn't believe me if I told you."

Richard gave him a look. "I just came back from the underworld. I think I have you beat for incredible."

Chase thought it over. "Maybe. I was at camp. I'd been searching for Rachel. My mother visited me."

"Your mother? Your mother passed away years ago."

Chase made a face as if to say he knew that better than Richard. "That kind of thing gets your attention."

"Well," Richard said, trying to grasp what was going on, "it obviously wasn't your mother. Didn't you think to ask who she really was?"

Chase, his arms still folded, shrugged. "No." He glanced off into the darkness. "It was a rather emotional experience. You would have had to have been there."

"I imagine you're right," Richard said. "Did she tell you why she had come to visit you?"

"She told me that I had to come here as fast as I could. She said that Rachel would be here, and that you needed help."

Richard was dumbfounded. "Did she tell you what sort of help I needed?"

Chase nodded. "Horses. Fast horses."

"My mother came to me, too," Rachel said.

Richard looked from the girl back up at Chase. Chase shrugged as if to say he had no answer.

"Your mother?" Richard asked Rachel. "You mean Emma?"

"No, not my new mother. My old mother. My mother who gave birth to me."

Richard didn't quite know what to say. "What did she want with you?"

"She told me that I had to help you by coming here. She said that I needed to tell these people that you were in the spirit world and they had to have a gathering so that you would have a way to get back."

"Really" was all Richard could think to say.

Rachel nodded. "She said I had to hurry, that there was little time, so she had a gar fly me here. His name was Gratch. He was real nice. Gratch told me that he loves you. But he had to go home after we came here."

Richard could only stare.

"That was a few days back," Chase said. "We've been waiting for you. The Mud People had to prepare for the gathering. I brought you three fast horses. We have food packed up for you. They're ready to go."

"Ready to go?"

Chase nodded. "As much as I'd like to visit, and believe me, I think we have some things to talk about, my . . . mother said that you would be in a hurry to get to Tamarang."

"Tamarang," Richard repeated. "Zedd was going to Tamarang."

That wasn't all that was there. The book that Baraccus had written for Richard and then hidden for him three thousand years before was in Tamarang. Richard had found the book but then been captured by Six. The book, *Secrets of a War Wizard's Power*, was hidden in a stone cell in Tamarang.

He needed that book now more than ever. Baraccus had already provided invaluable help. If Richard was to open the boxes of Orden, though, that book might well provide the things he needed.

"Tamarang," Richard said again in thought. "There was a spell there that cut me off from my gift."

Rachel nodded. "I fixed it."

Richard stared down at her. "You fixed it?"

Chase gave Richard a look. "Like I said, there are some things we need to talk about, but now is not the time. As I hear it told, you're in a big hurry. You only have until the new moon."

With a feeling of sinking dread, Richard glanced at the sliver of a moon. "I can't get back to the People's Palace by the new moon. It's too far away."

"You aren't going to the Peoples' Palace," Chase reminded him. "You're going to Tamarang."

Richard grasped Chase by the arm. "Take me to the horses. I'm running out of time."

Chase nodded. "So my mother told me."

CHAPTER 55

Zedd winced in pain. He heard someone calling his name again. The voice sounded like it was drifting into him from some distant world. He didn't want to answer the call, didn't want to open his eyes, didn't want to be fully conscious and have to feel the full brunt of awareness.

"Zedd," the voice called again.

A big hand shook him, gently rocking his body back and forth. Zedd forced his eyes open just a little, squinting with the full dread of consciousness. Rikka and Tom, hunched over him, were both looking down with intent worry. Zedd saw the that the side of Tom's blond hair was matted with blood.

"Zedd, are you all right?"

It was Rikka's voice, he realized. He blinked, trying to tell if every bone in his body was broken or if it only felt that way. Fear lurking in the shadows of his mind whispered that this might be the end of everything.

His middle hurt. That was where Six's spell had caught him.

He felt like a fool. Having taken the measure of her before, he had been prepared. He had been sure that he could counter the woman's ability—and he would have been able to, except that she had caught him off guard with a form of constructed spell, a little surprise that she'd had drawn in the caves, patiently waiting for his arrival should he ever enter her domain. Even though it was the type of thing he'd never known a witch woman to do, he should have considered that possibility. He should have been ready for a trick.

She was a witch woman, not a sorceress or wizard, and she knew that, while she had considerable talents of her own, she was vulnerable to certain things Zedd could do. He had revealed some of those things back at the Wizard's Keep by preventing her from killing him and the others when she tried. She had learned from that experience and found a way to construct a counter—something that was simply out of character for a witch woman. It was quite brilliant, actually, but right then he wasn't exactly in the mood to marvel at her accomplishment.

"Zedd," Rikka said, "are you all right?"

"I think so," he managed. "You?"

Rikka grunted with a note of displeasure. "They were certainly ready for us. Whatever she did kept me from being able to stop her."

"Well, don't feel bad, she did the same to me."

"With you unconscious all those soldiers were more than I could handle," Tom added. "Sorry, Zedd, but I let you down when you needed me the most. I should have been the steel against steel for you."

Zedd squinted up at the man. "Don't be silly. Steel has its limits. It was I who shouldn't have allowed us to be taken in such a way. I should have known better and been prepared for it."

"I guess we all failed," Rikka said.

"Worse, we failed Richard. We didn't even make it into the cave to help him. We need to get into the cave to break that spell keeping him from his gift."

"Not much hope of that, now," Rikka said.

"We'll see about that," Zedd grumbled. "At least it appears we're safe for the moment."

"Unless Six returns to finish us."

Zedd peered up at the man. "You're a comfort."

With the help of both of them pulling on his arms, Zedd sat up. "Where are we, anyway?" he asked as he looked around in the dim light.

"Some sort of prison room," Tom said. "The walls are entirely stone, except for the door. The hallway outside is filled with guards."

It wasn't especially large. A lantern burned on a small table. There was a single chair. Other than that the room was barren.

"The ceiling is beams and planks," Zedd observed. "I wonder

if I could breach them with my power, enough for us to sneak out of here."

With their help he staggered to his feet. Rikka steadied him as he lifted an arm to use his gift to probe the ceiling.

"Bags," he muttered. "When she used that constructed spell she also put some kind of barrier around this room. It keeps me from breaching it with my gift. We're sealed in."

"Something else," Tom said. "The guards are mostly Imperial Order soldiers. It appears that Six is working on the same side as Jagang."

Zedd scratched his scalp. "Great, that's all we need."

"At least she didn't kill us," Tom offered.

"Yet," Rikka added.

Zedd squinted as he looked up at the ceiling. He pointed. "What's that?"

"What?" Tom said, looking up.

"That there. At the edge of the ceiling, up against the wall. There is something wedged between that last beam and the top of the wall."

Tom pulled the chair over and used it to reach the dark bundle hidden in the shadow of the beam. He tugged on it until it suddenly fell to the floor. Some of the things inside tumbled out.

"Dear spirits," Zedd said, "that's Richard's pack."

He recognized some of the things that had fallen out. He bent to right the pack, inspecting the clothes briefly before stuffing them back inside the pack.

When he lifted the black shirt trimmed in gold and returned it to the pack, he spotted a book lying on the floor. He picked it up, squinting in the dim light of the lantern.

"What sort of book is it?" Rikka asked.

Tom leaned closer to see. "What does it say?"

Zedd could hardly believe what he was seeing. "The little says *Secrets of a War Wizard's Power*."

Rikka let out a low whistle.

"My sentiment as well," Zedd muttered as he inspected the front and back covers. "Where in the world would Richard have gotten such a thing? This could be invaluable."

"What does it say about his powers?" Rikka asked, as if eager for gossip.

Zedd opened the cover and turned over a page, then another. He blinked in surprise.

"Dear spirits . . ." he murmured in astonishment.

Nicci looked up when she saw a shadow fill the doorway. It was Cara.

"How are you doing?" the Mord-Sith asked in a quiet voice that seemed to get lost in the somber room.

Nicci's gaze wandered off to stare into space. She couldn't really see the relevance of the question. She supposed that Cara was just trying to find something to say, something that reflected her genuine concern. It struck Nicci as tragic that a Mord-Sith would come to finally possess such simple, decent qualities when it was too late to matter.

"I don't know anymore, Cara."

"Have you figured out what went wrong?"

Nicci looked up from the padded leather chair she was in. "What went wrong? Isn't it pretty obvious?"

Cara stepped closer and idly stroked a finger along the other side of the mahogany table. In the dimly lit library her red leather stood out like a splash of blood.

"But Lord Rahl will find a way back."

It sounded to Nicci like a plea rather than a statement.

"Cara, if Richard was coming back he would have been back ten days ago," Nicci said in a dejected voice, unable to summon a lie. Cara deserved more than to have the truth obscured with the deceit of false hope.

"Well, maybe it took longer than the two of you thought it would take."

Nicci wished it were that simple. She shook her head. "He should have been back by the next morning. Since he never returned that means he didn't survive what he—"

"But he has to come back!" Cara shouted as she leaned over the table, unwilling to allow Nicci to finish such a thought.

Nicci watched the anxiety on Cara's face for a moment. What was there to say? How could she explain such a thing to a person who didn't really understand the things that were involved?

"Believe me, Cara," Nicci said at last. "I want him to return just as much as you do, but if he was able to survive the spell and the journey to the underworld, he would have been back long ago. He couldn't stay there this long."

"Why not?"

"You might say that it's a little like diving to the bottom of a lake. You can hold your breath for a time, but you need to come back out of the water within a certain amount of time. If you get your foot caught under a log at the bottom of the water, you will drown. He couldn't survive there this long. Since he didn't return when he should have . . ."

"Well, maybe he came out somewhere else. Maybe he came up for air in another place."

Nicci shook her head. "Imagine that the lake is covered with ice. The hole he went through—that's the spells in the sorcerer's sand—is the only way back out. The boxes of Orden are a gateway. This part of it was using elements of Orden, of that gateway. The underworld is just emptiness."

She knew she was getting tangled up trying to make it understandable to Cara. Nicci didn't even fully grasp the nature of the underworld herself. "Let's just say that if he tried to come up somewhere else under the ice of the frozen lake, he couldn't break through. He needs to come back through that hole he cut, the hole he created into the underworld, through the gateway. Does that make any sense?"

"In a way, but it should have worked." She gestured to all the books lying open all over the table. "The two of you had it all figured out. Darken Rahl did it. There is no reason this wouldn't have worked just the same. There's no reason it shouldn't have worked for Richard just as well."

Nicci looked away from Cara's intent blue eyes. "Yes, there is."

Cara straightened. "What do you mean? What reason?"

"The beast."

Cara stared for a long moment. "The beast. You think the beast might have found him there, in the underworld?"

Nicci shook her head. "No. The beast found him here, in this world, as he drew the spell. When Richard finally went through that gateway he'd created, it was waiting and ready. The beast followed him into the underworld."

Cara's expression was somewhere between horrified and enraged. "But he would have fought it."

Nicci looked up from under her brow. "How?"

"I don't know. I'm no expert on such things."

"Neither is Richard. In the underworld it would be different than here. In the past he used his sword or the shields to stop it. When the beast appeared the last time, he was able to shoot it with one of those special arrows. What was he going to do to fight it in the underworld? He had to go naked. He had no weapons, no way to fight it."

Cara's expression tipped toward enraged. "Then why would you allow him to go?"

"He had already gone into the underworld when I saw the beast. It went down after him. There was simply no way to stop the beast or even to warn Richard."

"There had to be some way you could have stopped him."

Nicci stood. "Going to the underworld is something he had to do if he was to have had a chance to use the power of Orden. Without going he can't counter Chainfire and if he can't counter Chainfire we're all lost. Besides, I couldn't have stopped him if I wanted to."

Cara paced before the table. "But it's going to be the new moon in a few days. We're running out of time. There has to be something you can try. There has to be a chance that he's still trapped there, holding his breath. Lord Rahl has never given up on us. Lord Rahl would fight with his last breath for us."

Nicci nodded as she stepped around the table. "You're right. I'll go back to the Garden of Life and cast some calling spells."

She knew it was a silly idea. She knew that such a thing was not only impossible, but a waste of time. Still, she felt like she needed to do something or she would go mad, and it would at least make Cara feel better until the end came. Besides, what else was there to do, now.

"Good idea," Cara said. "Do some calling spells until you pull Lord Rahl back."

Out in the hallway, Nicci saw that in both directions it was blocked off by men of the First File. They each had a crossbow armed with a red-fletched bolt. It looked like the men were deliberately sealing off the library area.

Nicci saw the top of Nathan's head of white hair as he made his way through the dense wall of men. The prophet finally stepped through all the soldiers. Spotting Nicci, he immediately headed toward her.

His face looked more than grim. Just seeing the look on his face made Nicci's mouth go dry.

"Nathan, what is it?" she asked as he came to an abrupt halt before her.

His azure eyes looked tired. "I'm sorry, Nicci, but this is the only way."

Nicci blinked in confusion. She glanced briefly to the soldiers standing shoulder-to-shoulder across the hallway. They, too, looked bleak about being there.

"What is the only way?" she asked.

He looked away from her eyes to wipe a weary hand across his face. "Richard and I had an earnest talk before he left on his dangerous journey. He told me that if he failed to return I should do what must be done to save the people here from the horrors Jagang would set loose upon them. Without Richard, prophecy says that we will lose in this final battle."

"We have always known that."

"I know a thing or two about going to the underworld, Nicci. I am familiar with the spell-forms he used. I've been up to the Garden of Life. I've studied the things he did. Richard got it all correct. It should have worked."

"The beast chased him into the underworld," Cara said.

Nathan sighed heavily, but didn't look all too surprised. "I figured it had to be something like that. The thing is, I've studied the methods Richard used."

Cara appeared hopeful that the prophet could offer an answer that Nicci couldn't provide. "Good. Have you figured out a way to get him back from the underworld? Nicci's going to cast calling webs. Maybe you could help her. The two of you together . . ."

Her voice trailed off. Nathan didn't look in the mood to entertain such nonsense.

"There is no such thing, Cara. We can't get him back from the underworld after this amount of time. Richard is lost to us."

Cara blinked away tears, unable to abide such a proclamation.

"The emperor is going to get in here," Nathan said. "It's only going to be a matter of time. The great void will shortly be upon us. All we can do now is hope to spare as many people in the palace as possible."

Nicci held up her chin. "I understand."

"The only way to do that is to surrender the palace as soon as the new moon arrives—and to do it in the way that Jagang has demanded."

Nicci swallowed. "I can't say that I know any other way, Nathan."

"I'm sorry, Nicci." His voice revealed just how sincere his words were. "But I need to prepare a number of things, so I'm going to have to put you under arrest and have you securely locked up until Jagang comes on the new moon to collect you."

Nicci felt a tear roll down her cheek, not for herself, but for the loss of Richard to all the people who had been depending on him to turn the tide, to fight the final battle, to at last do what only Richard could do.

"You don't need all the guards with those arrows." She managed to keep her voice from breaking. "I will go peacefully."

Nathan nodded. "Thank you for not making this any more difficult than it already is."

CHAPTER 56

Kahlan woke in a flash of icy fright.

She was lying slightly on her right side, her head turned all the way to the right, her jaw lying against the pillow of a saddlebag. She took a careful peek through the narrow slits of her eyelids. The overcast was just blushing with a hint of the approaching dawn.

While she hadn't known why she'd awakened so abruptly, she soon realized the reason.

Out of the corner of her eye she could see that Samuel was right above her—hovering over her. He was still and silent, mere inches away, like a mountain lion poised over prey.

He was completely naked.

Kahlan was so startled that for an instant she lay frozen in confusion, wondering if she really was awake or if she was having some kind of bizarre nightmare. Her disorientation evaporated in urgent alarm as her instincts took charge.

Without letting on that she was awake, she inched her hand downward toward her belt to get at her knife. Since she was turned to the right the sheath for her knife was somewhat under her. She had to squirm her fingers under her to get at the knife, trying not to betray the fact that she was awake. She counted on her blanket to help hide the movement of her hand.

The knife wasn't there.

She glanced down a little, hoping it had fallen out somehow and that it would be on the ground nearby. It wasn't. As she was feeling around under the blanket, trying to find her knife, she saw the pile of Samuel's clothes not far away. Then she saw the knife. It had been tossed beyond his clothes, well out of reach.

She was sickened by the mental image of him stealthily removing his clothes as he stared at her while she slept. She was appalled by the thought that he had been so close to her, watching her, taking her knife, preparing for the obscene things he wanted to do to her, and that she hadn't even been aware of it. Besides being appalled, she was angry at herself for letting him get this far.

While Samuel had always seemed timid and shy, and sometimes eager to curry favor, this didn't entirely surprise her. She remembered all too well the times she'd caught him staring at her. Those looks had always seemed to contain a sneaky craving that he never otherwise betrayed. She controlled her outrage, focusing instead on survival.

Being hesitant and indecisive, Samuel was moving ever so slowly, inching into position, skulking in close rather than boldly pouncing. He apparently wanted to get completely over her, and then when he felt he was close enough to be sure that she couldn't get away, he would muscle her under control and then live out the dark thoughts that had always been hidden behind his golden-yellow eyes.

Samuel wasn't a big man, but he was muscular. He was certainly stronger than she was. There was no way she could escape without a fight, and she was in a poor position to grapple with him. From this close she couldn't even punch effectively. In this close, without a knife, without anyone to help her, she had little hope of fending him off.

Even though he was considerably stronger and she had been asleep, he had been wary. His mistake had been in not acting swiftly to incapacitate her. It hadn't been a question of lack of ability or advantage, but a lack of courage. Her only edge at that moment was that he hadn't acted swiftly and he didn't know she was awake. She didn't want to squander that advantage. When she acted, that surprise would help even the equation and give her an opportunity she would not get again.

Her mind raced through a list of options. She would have only one chance to strike first. She would have to make it count.

Her first thought was to bring her knee up where it would hurt him most, but the way she was lying, turned to her right, her legs trapped under a blanket, and with the way he was positioned over her pinning that blanket down, she deemed it a poor choice for a first strike.

Her left hand was free, though, just outside the blanket. That seemed her best choice. Without further delay, before it was too late, she struck hard and fast, as quick as a viper, trying to gouge out his eye with her thumb. She pressed with all her strength into the soft tissue of his eye.

He cried out in fright, immediately jerking his face back and away. Quickly regaining his wits, he used his arm to slam hers away as she clawed at his face. At the same time he dropped his weight down, driving the air from her lungs in a whoosh.

Before she could draw a breath he rammed his other forearm across her throat, both pinning her head to the ground and preventing her from getting a breath. Kahlan kicked and twisted with all her might, trying to get away. It was like trying to fight off a bear. She was no match for his strength and weight, especially not in the vulnerable position she was in. She had no leverage to push him away and no effective way to strike.

Kahlan twisted her head more to the right to get her windpipe out from the direct weight his forearm was putting across her throat. Her straining neck muscles at least took the full load off her throat long enough for her to get a breath.

As she gasped in that needed breath, her sight was focused on his clothes lying not far away. She spotted the hilt of the sword just sticking out from under his trousers. She could see the early-morning light glinting off the gold word TRUTH on the silver wire of the hilt.

Kahlan desperately grasped for the hilt of the sword. It was just beyond the reach of her fingers. She knew that, since she was on the ground and didn't have full use of her arm, even if she could get ahold of it she had no chance to draw the blade from its scabbard in order to stab Samuel or even slash at him. Her aim was simply to get her hand around the hilt and then bash the point of the pommel into his face or skull. A sword was heavy enough to do substantial damage in that manner.

A good hit in the right place, such as his temple, could even kill her attacker.

But the hilt of the sword was just out of reach.

At the same time she was desperately stretching, trying to reach the sword, Samuel was having difficulty having his way with her. The blanket was interfering with his lust to get at her. Crouching on top of her to keep her down was proving a troublesome complication. It seemed he hadn't taken the practical aspects of the procedure into consideration. He was quite effectively pinning her down, but the blanket was part of the means by which he was keeping her arms and legs under control. At the same time it was preventing him from getting to his ultimate goal.

She knew that it was going to be only a moment until it dawned on him to simply knock her unconscious.

As if reading her mind, she saw his right arm cock back. She could see his big fist tighten. As he drove the fist down toward her face, she used all her strength to twist her body and lunge away from the blow.

His fist slammed the ground just behind her head.

Her fingers found the gold wire spelling out TRUTH on the hilt of the sword.

The world seemed to come to an abrupt halt.

In an instant, she was flooded with understanding.

Things within her that had been entirely lost were suddenly right there.

She didn't remember who she was, but she instantly remembered what she was.

A Confessor.

It was far from a complete joining with her past, but in that thread of linkage she knew what being a Confessor meant. It had been a complete mystery for so long, but now she not only remembered all that it meant, she felt that birthright within her, felt its bond to her.

She still didn't know who she was, who Kahlan Amnell was, and she didn't remember anything of her past, but she remembered what it meant to be a Confessor.

Samuel drew back his arm to punch at her again.

Kahlan pressed her hand to his chest. It no longer felt like there was a powerful man atop her, controlling her. She no longer felt panic or fury. She no longer struggled. She felt as if she were as light as a breath of air and that he no longer had any power over her.

There was no longer any frantic rush, any sense of desperation.

Time was hers.

She didn't need to consider, evaluate, or decide. She knew with complete certainty what to do. She didn't even have to think it through.

It was not necessary for Kahlan to invoke her birthright, but merely to withdraw her restraint of it.

She could see his furious, focused expression frozen above her. His fist remained poised unmoving in an ever-expanding spark of time, as it would until this was finished.

She had no need to hope, or expect, or act. She knew that time was hers. She knew what was going to be, almost as if it had already happened.

Samuel had come into the Imperial Order camp not to rescue her but—for reasons she would know before this was finished—to capture her.

This was not her savior.

This was the enemy.

The inner violence of her power's cold coiled force slipping its bounds was breathtaking. It surged up from that deep dark core within, obediently inundating every fiber of her being.

Time was hers.

She could have counted every whisker on his frozen face had she wanted to and he still would not have moved an inch in his headlong rush to hit her.

Her fear was gone; the calm of purpose and control had replaced it. There was no hate; the cold appraisal of justice had taken over.

In a state of profound peace born of the command of her own ability, and through it her own destiny, she contained no hate, no rage, no horror . . . nor any sorrow. She saw the truth of what was. This man had condemned himself. He had made the choice; now he would have to encounter the immutable consequence of his choices. In that infinitesimal spark of existence, her mind was in a void where the all-consuming rush of time seemed suspended.

He had no chance. He was hers.

Even though she had all the time she could want, doubt did not exist.

Kahlan unleashed her power.

From her innermost being, that power became all.

Thunder without sound jolted the air—exquisite, violent, and for that pristine instant, sovereign.

The memory of that instant of effect was an island of sanity for her in the dark river of her unknown self.

Samuel's face was frozen in twisted hate for that which he had hoped to possess.

Kahlan stared up into his golden-yellow eyes, knowing that he saw only her merciless eyes.

In the twist of that instant, his mind, who he was, who he had been, was already gone.

Trees all around in the frigid early-morning air shook from the violent blow of the concussion. Small twigs and dry bark dropped from branches and boughs. The profound shock to the air lifted a ring of dust and dirt all around that raced away in an ever-expanding circle.

Samuel's strange eyes went wide. "Mistress," he whispered, "command me."

"Get off me."

He immediately rolled away to end up on his knees, his hands pressed together in supplication as his gaze remained fixed on her.

As Kahlan sat up, she realized that the sword was still gripped in her right hand. She let go of it. She needed no sword to deal with Samuel.

Deeply distressed as he waited, Samuel looked on the verge of tears. "Please . . . how may I serve you?"

Kahlan tossed the blanket aside. "Who am I?"

"Kahlan Amnell, the Mother Confessor," he answered immediately.

Kahlan already knew that much. She thought a moment.

"Where did you get that sword?"

"I stole it."

"Who does it rightfully belong to?"

"Before, or now?"

She was a bit confused by the response. "Before."

Samuel became distraught by the question. He began to cry in earnest as he wrung his hands.

"I don't know his name, Mistress. I swear, I don't know his name. I never knew his name." He fell to sobbing. "I'm so sorry, Mistress, I don't know, I don't, I swear I don't know—"

"How did you get it away from him?"

"I snuck up and cut his throat while he was asleep—but I swear I don't know his name."

Those touched by a Confessor confessed without the slightest hesitation anything they had done—anything. Their only concern was their constant, torturous dread that they might not please the woman who had touched them with her power. Their mind's only remaining purpose was to do her bidding.

"Have you murdered other people?"

Samuel looked up sharply with the sudden joy of having a question he could fully answer. His face beamed with a smile.

"Oh, yes, Mistress. Many. Please, may I kill someone for you? Anyone. Just name them. Just tell me who I am to kill. I will do it as quickly as possible. Please, Mistress, tell me who and I will do your bidding and dispatch them for you."

"Who does the sword belong to now?"

He paused at the change of subject. "It belongs to Richard Rahl."

Kahlan was not surprised.

"How does Richard Rahl know me?"

"He is your husband."

Kahlan froze with the shock of what she thought she had just heard. She blinked, her thoughts suddenly scattered in every direction at once.

"What?"

"Richard Rahl is your husband."

She stood staring for a long moment, unable to reconcile

it all in her mind. In one way it was a stunning shock. At the same time, it made sense in a way she couldn't begin to fathom.

Kahlan stood struck speechless.

Finding that she was married to Richard Rahl was a terrifying revelation. In another way . . . it made her heart swell with profound joy. She thought of his gray eyes, thought of the way he looked at her, and the frightening aspect of it seemed to evaporate. It was if all the dreams she had not dared to dream had just come true.

She felt a tear roll down her cheek. With her fingers she wiped it away, but it was quickly followed by another. She almost let out a jubilant laugh.

"My husband?"

Samuel nodded furiously. "Yes, Mistress. You are the Mother Confessor. He is the Lord Rahl. He is married to you. He is your husband."

Feeling herself trembling. Kahlan tried to think, but her mind just didn't respond, as if it had so many thoughts all at once that they simply jumbled together in a tangled mess.

She suddenly remembered Richard lying on the ground in the Order's camp, crying out for her to get away.

Richard was a captive of the Order at best, but more likely, he was dead.

She had only just learned her connection to him, and now he was lost to her.

She felt a tear roll down her cheek, but this time there was no joy behind it, only horror.

She finally collected herself and focused her attention on the man on his knees before her. "Where were you taking me?"

"To Tamarang. To my . . . my other mistress."

"Other mistress?"

He nodded hurriedly. "Six."

She recalled Jagang talking about her. Kahlan frowned. "The witch woman?"

Samuel looked terrified to answer, but he did. "Yes, Mistress. I was told to bring you and to give you over to her."

She gestured to where she had been sleeping. "Did she tell you to do that?"

Even more reluctantly, Samuel licked his lips. Confessing to murder was one thing, but this was entirely different.

"I asked if I could have you," he whined. "She said that if I wanted to take you I could, as my reward for my service, but that I was to bring you to her alive."

"And what did she want with me?"

"I believe she wanted you as a bargaining tool."

"With who?"

"Emperor Jagang."

"But I was already with Jagang."

"Jagang wants you very badly. She knows how valuable you are to him. She wanted to take possession of you and then trade you back to Jagang in return for favors for herself."

"How far are we from Tamarang, from the witch woman?"

"Not far." Samuel pointed southwest. "If we don't delay, we can get there by the end of tomorrow, Mistress."

Kahlan suddenly felt very vulnerable being this close to a woman as powerful as that. She knew without doubt that she had to get out of the area or she might be located without the benefit of Samuel dragging her right up to Six's feet.

"And since you were to turn me over tomorrow, you knew that your time with me was running out. You were going to rape me."

It wasn't a question, but a statement of fact.

Samuel wrung his hands, tears streaming down his red face. "Yes, Mistress." In the terrible silence he became even more distraught as she stood staring down at him. Kahlan knew that a person touched was no longer who they were, no longer had all the mind they once had. Once taken, they were completely devoted to the Confessor.

It occurred to her that something very much like that had been done to her. She wondered if her memory was as lost to her as Samuel's past was now forever lost to him. It was a terrifying thought.

"Please, Mistress . . . forgive me?"

In the dragging silence he could not endure the guilt of his intent. He began to cry hysterically, unable to endure the condemnation in her eyes.

"Please, Mistress, find mercy for me in your heart."

"Mercy is a contingency plan devised by the guilty in the eventuality that they are caught. Justice is the domain of the just. This is about justice."

"Then please, Mistress, please . . . forgive me?"

Kahlan stared into his eyes to be sure that he would not mistake her words or her intent.

"No. That would be a corruption of the concept of justice. I will not forgive you, not now, not ever—not out of hate but because you are guilty of more crimes than those against me."

"I know, but you could forgive me of my crimes against you. Please, Mistress, just those things. Just forgive me for what I have done to you, and for what I intended to do to you?"

"No."

The reality of the finality of that proclamation settled into his eyes. He gasped in horror at the realization that his actions, the choices he had made, were irredeemable. He felt nothing for his other crimes, but he felt the full weight of responsibility for his crimes against her.

He saw himself, probably for the first time in his life, for what he really was—the way she saw him.

Samuel gasped again as he clutched his chest, and then crumpled onto his side, dead.

Without delay, Kahlan began gathering up her things. With the witch woman this close she had to get away as fast as possible. She didn't know where she would go, but she knew where she couldn't go.

She suddenly realized that she should have thought more about it and asked Samuel a great many more questions. She had let those many answers slip through her fingers.

The news about Richard—about Richard being her husband—had so scrambled her thoughts that she simply hadn't considered asking Samuel anything else. She suddenly felt like a monumental fool for missing such an invaluable opportunity.

Done was done. She had to concentrate on what to do now. She rushed over in the dim, early light to saddle the horse.

She found the horse on the ground, dead. Its throat had

been cut. Samuel, probably fearing that she might use the horse to somehow escape before he could have his way with her, had cut the poor animal's throat.

Without delay she rolled as much as she could carry into her blanket and stuffed it into the saddlebags. She tossed the saddlebags over a shoulder and picked up the Sword of Truth in its scabbard. Sword in hand, Kahlan started away, in the opposite direction of Tamarang.

CHAPTER 57

In crushing loneliness, Kahlan plodded northeast. She began to wonder why she bothered. What was the point of fighting for her life if there could be no future? What could there be to a life without her own mind in a world dominated by the fanatical beliefs of the Imperial Order, by people who defined their existence through a filter of hatred for those who wanted to live and accomplish for themselves? They didn't want to accomplish anything; they simply wanted to murder anyone else who did, as if by destroying productive accomplishment they could revoke reality and live a life made of wishes.

All those who defined their existence by that burning hatred of others were smothering all joy out of life, and in the process suffocating life itself out of existence. It would be easy to simply give up. No one would care. No one would know.

But she would care. She would know. Reality was what it was. It was the only life she would ever have. In the end, that precious life was all she had, all anyone had.

It had been up to Samuel to decide how he would live his life, and he had made his choices. It was no less true for her. She had to make the most of what she had in life, even if her choices were limited, and even if that life itself was to be cut short.

She had walked for less than an hour when she began to hear the distant rumble of galloping hooves. She paused as she saw horses break from a line of trees ahead. They were coming right toward her.

She glanced around the bottomland she was crossing. In the gloomy light of a leaden sky she could see that the trees covering the foothills to each side were too far for her to reach their cover in time. The grass, long since brown as winter closed in, had been flattened by wind and weather. It didn't provide anywhere for her to hide.

Besides, it looked like she might have been spotted. Even if she hadn't, at the speed the horses were closing they soon would catch up to her, and she had no hope of running across their line of sight and not being seen.

She tossed the saddlebag on the ground. The gentle breeze lifted her hair back off her shoulders as she gripped the scabbard of the sword in her left hand. Her only choice was to stand and fight.

She realized, then, that she was invisible to most everyone. She almost laughed aloud with relief. This was one of those rare times when she was thankful to be invisible. She stood her ground, remaining quiet, hoping the riders wouldn't see her and would simply ride by and be gone.

But in the back of her mind she remembered Samuel telling her that Jagang would send men after them. Jagang had men who could see her. If that was who was riding toward her, then she was going to have to fight.

She didn't pull the sword free in case the riders, on the off chance they could see her, weren't hostile. She didn't want to start a battle unless she really had no choice. She knew she could draw the blade in an instant if need be. She had two knives as well, but she knew that she could handle a sword. She didn't know where she'd learned, but she knew she was good with a sword.

She remembered seeing Richard fight with a blade. She recalled thinking at the time that it reminded her somewhat of the way in which she fought with a blade. She wondered if it had been Richard—her husband—who had taught her to use a sword the way she did.

She noticed then that while there were three horses, only one had a rider. That was good news. It cut the odds to even.

As the galloping horses bore down on her, she was astonished to recognize the rider.

"Richard!"

He leaped off the horse before it had skidded to a halt. It snorted, tossing its head. All three horses were lathered and hot.

"Are you all right?" he asked as he rushed toward her.

"Yes."

"You used your power."

She nodded, unable to take her gaze off his gray eyes. "How did you know?"

"I thought I felt it." He looked giddy with excitement. "You can't imagine how glad I am to see you."

As she stared at him she wished that she could remember their past, remember all they meant to each other.

"I was afraid you were dead. I didn't want to leave you there. I was so afraid that you were dead."

He stood gazing at her, seeming unable to speak. He looked like she felt, as if he had a thousand things all bottled up, all wanting out first.

Kahlan remembered the way he had fought when he had started the war Nicci had said he would start. She remembered the way he had moved so fluidly among the other Ja'La players, and then among lumbering brutes as they hacked away with swords and axes, desperately trying to kill him.

She remembered the way the blade had seemed to be a part of him, almost an extension of his body, an extension of his mind. She had been spellbound that day as she'd watched him fighting his way toward her. It had been like watching a dance with death, and death had not been able to touch him.

She held the sword out. "Every weapon needs a master."

Richard's warm smile broke through like sunshine on a cold, cloudy day. It warmed her heart. He gazed at her a moment, still unable to look away, then gently lifted the weapon from her hands.

He ducked his head under the baldric, laying it over his right shoulder so that the sword rested against his left hip. The sword looked completely natural with him, unlike the way it had looked with Samuel.

"Samuel is dead."

"When I felt you use your power I thought as much." He

rested his left palm on the hilt of the sword. "Thank goodness he didn't hurt you."

"He tried. That's why he's dead."

Richard nodded. "Kahlan, I can't explain it all right now, but there is a great deal happening that—"

"You missed all the excitement."

"Excitement?"

"Yes. Samuel confessed. He told me that we're married."

Richard went stiff as stone. A look akin to terror passed across his face.

She thought that maybe he should take her in his arms and tell her how happy he was to have her back, but he just stood there, looking like he was afraid to breathe.

"We were in love, then?" she asked, trying to prompt him.

His face lost some of its color. "Kahlan, now is not the time to talk about this. We're in more trouble than you can imagine. I don't have time to explain it but—"

"So, you're saying that we weren't in love?"

She hadn't expected this. She hadn't even considered it. She suddenly had difficulty making her voice work.

She couldn't understand why he just stood there, why he wouldn't say anything. She supposed that there was nothing for him to say.

"It was just some kind of arranged thing, then?" She swallowed back the lump rising in her throat. "The Mother Confessor marrying the Lord Rahl for the good of their respective people? An alliance of convenience. Something like that?"

Richard looked more terrified than Samuel had when she had been questioning him. He drew his lower lip through his teeth as if trying to think how to answer.

"It's all right," Kahlan said. "You won't hurt my feelings. I don't remember any of it. So, that's what it was, then? Just a marriage of convenience?"

"Kahlan . . ."

"We're not in love, then? Please, answer me, Richard."

"Look, Kahlan, it's more complicated than that. I have responsibilities."

That was what Nicci had said when Kahlan had asked if she

loved Richard. It was more complicated than that. She had responsibilities.

Kahlan wondered how she could she have been so blind. It was Nicci he loved.

"You have to trust me," he said when she could only stare at him. "There are important things at stake."

She nodded, holding back the tears, putting on a blank face, hiding behind the mask of it. She didn't try to test her voice just then.

She didn't know why she had let her heart get ahead of her head. She didn't know if her legs were going to hold.

Richard squeezed his temples between a finger and a thumb, his gaze going to the ground for a moment. "Kahlan . . . listen to me. I'll explain everything to you—everything—I promise, but I can't right now. Please, just trust me."

She wanted to ask why she should trust a man who married her without loving her, but right then she was not sure that she would be able to summon her voice.

"Please," he repeated. "I promise I'll explain everything when I can, but right now we have to get to Tamarang."

She cleared her throat, finally gathering the ability to speak. "We can't go there. Samuel said that Six was there."

He was nodding as she spoke. "I know. But I have to go there."

"I don't."

He paused, gazing at her.

"I don't want anything else to happen to you," he finally said. "Please, you need to come with me. I'll explain later. I promise."

"Why is later better than now?"

"Because we'll be dead if we don't hurry. Jagang is going to open the boxes of Orden. I have to try to stop him."

She didn't buy the excuse. Had he wanted to, he could have already answered her.

"I'll go with you if you answer one question. Did you love me when you married me?"

His gray eyes studied her face a moment before he finally answered in a quiet voice.

"You were the right person for me to marry."

Kahlan swallowed back the pain, the cry wanting to escape. She turned away, not wanting him to see her tears, and started toward where Samuel had been taking her.

It was well after nightfall when they were finally forced to stop. Richard would have kept going but the terrain, thickly wooded, rocky, and becoming uneven as ridgelines rose up around them, was simply too treacherous to negotiate in the dark. The nearly new moon would have come up at sunset but the narrow crescent didn't provide enough illumination to brighten the inky cloud cover in the least. Even the light that would have been provided by meager starlight was hidden by the thick clouds. The darkness was so complete that it was simply impossible to go on.

Kahlan was tired, but as Richard started a fire in the fluff of cattails he'd broken open for tinder, she could see that he was in far worse condition. She wondered if he'd slept in recent days. After he had a fire going, he set fishing lines and then started to collect enough firewood to last them through the cold night. Up against a rocky rise they at least had some protection from the biting wind.

Kahlan did her best to care for the horses, fetching them water in a canvas bucket among the supplies Richard had with him. When he'd finished collecting firewood he found that they had some brook trout on his lines. As she watched him cleaning the fish, throwing the innards on the fire so they wouldn't attract animals, she decided not to ask any more questions about the two of them. She couldn't endure the pain of the answers. Besides, he had already told her what she had asked: she was simply the right person for him to marry.

She wondered if he'd even met her before he agreed to marry her. She realized that it must have been heartbreaking for Nicci to see the man she loved marry someone else for unromantic, practical reasons.

Kahlan forced her mind away from that whole line of thought.

"Why are we going to Tamarang?" she asked.

Richard glanced up from his work at cleaning the fish. "Well, a long time ago, back in the great war three thousand years ago, the people back then were fighting this same war we're fighting now, a war to defend ourselves against those who want to eliminate magic and all other forms of freedom.

"The people defending against such aggression took a number of extremely valuable things of magic—things they had created over many centuries—and put those things in a place called the Temple of the Winds. Then, to protect it all from falling into the hands of the enemy, they sent the temple into the underworld."

"They sent it into the world of the dead?"

Richard nodded as he laid out some big leaves. "During the war, wizards on both sides had conjured terrible weapons—constructed spells and such. But some of those weapons were made out of people. That's how the dreamwalkers came to be. They were created out of people captured in Caska—Jillian's ancestors."

"And that was when they created the Chainfire event?" she asked. "During that great war.

"That's right," he said as he spread a layer of mud on the leaves. "Other wizards were constantly working to counter the things that had been created from magic. The boxes of Orden, for example, were created during that great war in order to counter the Chainfire spell."

"I remember the Sisters talking to Jagang about that."

"Well, the whole thing is quite complicated but, basically, a traitor named Lothain went to the Temple of the Winds where it was hidden away in the underworld. He secretly did things to one day aid the basic cause of the Order when it eventually rekindled."

"They thought the war would reignite?"

"There have always been, and always will be, those who are driven by hate and want to blame those who are happy, creative, and productive for their misery."

"What sort of things did this Lothain do?"

Richard looked up. "Among other things, he made sure that

a dreamwalker would one day again be born into the world of life. Jagang is that dreamwalker."

Richard finished wrapping the fish in leaves and mud and set the little bundles in the glowing coals at the edge of the fire.

"After that, the people on our side sent the First Wizard to the Temple of the Winds. His name was Baraccus. He was a war wizard. He made sure that another war wizard would be born to try to stop the forces trying to take mankind into a dark age."

Kahlan pulled her knees up and drew her blanket around herself to keep warm as she listened to the story. "You mean that there haven't been any war wizards since that time?"

Richard shook his head. "I'm the first one in nearly three thousand years. Baraccus, though, did something at the temple to insure that another would one day be born to carry on the struggle. I'm the one born because of what he did back then.

"Realizing that such a person wouldn't know anything about his ability, Baraccus came back and wrote a book called *Secrets of a War Wizard's Power*. He had his wife, Magda Searus, who he loved very much, take that book away and hide it for me. He was very careful to make sure that no one but me would get ahold of the book.

"While Magda Searus was on that journey to hide *Secrets of a War Wizard's Power*, Baraccus killed himself."

Kahlan was astonished to hear this news. "But why would he do such a thing? If he loved Magda Searus, why would he do that and leave her all alone?"

Richard looked over in the flickering firelight. "I think that he had just seen so much pain and suffering in the war, as well as treason and betrayal, to say nothing of the experience of traveling through the underworld, that he just couldn't stand it any longer." His eyes looked haunted. "I've been through the veil. I can understand what he did."

Kahlan rested her chin on her knees. "After spending time in the Order's camp, I guess I know how disheartened a person can get about everything." She looked over at him. "So, you need this book to help stop the Imperial Order?"

"I do. I found it, but I had to hide it again when I was taken to the Order's camp."

To rescue her. "Don't tell me, the book is in Tamarang."

He smiled. "Why else would we be going there?"

Kahlan sighed. Now she could see why it was so important. She stared into the flames, thinking about Baraccus.

"Do you know what ever happened to Magda Searus?"

Richard used a stick to drag a wrapped fish out of the fire. He opened it and tested it with his knife. When he saw that it was flaky and done, he set it beside her.

"Careful, it's hot." He dragged out the other baking bundle. "Well, Magda Searus was heartbroken. After the war they needed to get the truth out of Lothain, the traitor who had betrayed them. A wizard at the time, Merritt, came up with a way to do that."

Richard stared into the flames for a moment before he went on. "He created a Confessor to get the truth."

Kahlan paused at nibbling at the fish. "Really? That was where the Confessors came from?" When he nodded, she asked, "Do you know who she was?"

"Magda Searus. She was so heartbroken about her husband being dead that she volunteered for the experiment. It was extremely dangerous, but it worked. The Confessors were created. She was the first. Eventually she fell in love with Merritt and they married."

Being a Confessor was the only part of her past to which Kahlan felt connected. Now she knew where Confessors had come from. They had come from a woman who had lost the man she loved.

Richard picked up a fat piece of wood and was about to loss it into the fire, but instead he paused and held it in a hand, turning it around, staring at it. He finally set it aside and tossed a different piece in the fire.

"You'd better get some sleep," he said when they'd finished. "I want to be out of here as soon as it's light enough to see."

Kahlan could tell that he was more exhausted than she was, but she could also tell that something was deeply troubling him, so she didn't argue. She wrapped herself in her blanket close enough to the fire to stay warm.

As she glanced up at Richard, she saw him still sitting before the fire, staring at the piece of firewood he'd set beside before. She had thought that he would be more interested in looking at his sword now that he finally had it back.

Kahlan woke softly. It was a good feeling not to wake the way she had the day before with Samuel on top of her. She rubbed her eyes and saw that Richard was still sitting before the fire. He looked terrible. She couldn't imagine what must be going through his head with the responsibilities on his shoulders, with all the people depending on him.

"I have something I'd like to give you," he said in a quiet voice that felt so soothing to hear when she first woke.

Kahlan sat up, stretching for a moment. She saw that there was just a hint of light in the sky. They would need to be on their way soon.

"What is it?" she asked as she folded her blanket and set it aside.

"You don't have to take it, but it would mean a great deal to me if you would."

He finally looked away from the flames and into her eyes. "I know that you don't know what's going on, or even who you are, much less what you're doing here with me. I wish more than anything in the world that I could explain it all to you. You've been through a nightmare and you deserve to know everything, but I just can't tell you right now. I'm asking you to trust me."

She looked away from his eyes. She couldn't bear to look into those eyes of his.

"In the meantime, I'd like you to have something."

Kahlan swallowed. "What is it?"

Richard reached around on the other side of him and pulled something out. He held it out to her in the dim firelight.

It was the statue she had before, the statue she had left in the Garden of Life when she had taken the boxes for the Sisters.

It was a carving of a woman with her back arched, her head thrown back, and her hands fisted at her sides. It was the embodiment of the spirit of defiance against forces that would subdue her. It was a carving of nobility and strength.

It was the statue she had before. It had been the most precious thing she had, and she'd had to leave it behind. This was not the same one, yet it was. She remembered every curve and turn of that one. This one was the same, but a little smaller.

She saw then the wood shavings all over the ground. He had spent the night carving it for her.

"It's called *Spirit*," he said in a voice that broke with emotion. "Would you accept it from me?"

Kahlan reverently lifted it from his hands and clutched it to her heart as she broke down in tears.

CHAPTER 58

Before we start a war," Richard said in a near whisper, "I need to get into the place where I hid the book. I have to get it back first, in case anything goes wrong."

Kahlan let out a breath as she appraised the look of determination in his eyes. "All right, but I don't like it. It just feels like a trap. Once we get in there we're liable to be snared. We may have to fight a war to get out."

"If we have to, we will."

Kahlan remembered the way Richard fought with a sword—or with a broc, for that matter. But this was different.

"And if we get caught in here do you think that sword of yours is going to be any good against a witch woman who could be lurking anywhere?"

He looked away from her eyes to check the hallway again. "The world is about to end for a great many good people who love life and just want to live it. That includes you, and me. I don't have any choice. I have to get that book."

He leaned out to check the other direction down the dimly lit hallway. Kahlan could hear the approaching echo of boots as soldiers patrolled. So far they had been able to evade a number of them. Richard was very good at moving in dark passages and hiding in plain sight.

They pressed back into the shallow shadow of the recessed doorway, trying to make themselves as flat as possible. The four guards, talking about the women in town, rounded the nearby corner and strolled by, too eager to brag about their conquests to notice Richard and Kahlan hiding in the dark doorway. Kahlan, holding her breath, could hardly believe that they hadn't been spotted. She kept a tight grip on the handle of her knife. As soon as the guards turned the far corner Richard grabbed her hand and pulled her after him into the hallway.

Down another dark corridor he came to an abrupt halt before a heavy door. The hasp had a lock in it.

Richard, his sword already in his hand, slipped the blade through the bar. Pressing his lips tight, he strained to twist the sword. With a muffled metallic pop the lock broke. Pieces of steel bounced across the stone floor. Kahlan winced at the sound, sure that it would bring guards running. They heard nothing.

Richard slipped in through the doorway.

"Zedd!" she heard him call in a loud whisper.

Kahlan stuck her head into the room. There were three people inside the small stone cell: an old man with disheveled white hair, a big blond-headed man, and a woman with her blond hair in the single braid of a Mord-Sith.

"Richard!" the old man shouted. "Dear spirits—you're alive!"

Richard crossed his lips with a finger as he pulled Kahlan in behind him. He quietly shut the door. The three people looked tired and bedraggled. It looked to have been a harsh confinement.

"Keep your voice down," Richard whispered. "There are guards all over this place."

"How in the world did you know we were here?" the old man asked.

"I didn't," Richard said.

"Well, I can tell you, my boy, that we have a great many things to—"

"Zedd, be quiet and listen to me."

The old man's mouth snapped shut. Then he pointed. "How did you get your sword back?"

"Kahlan gave it back to me."

Zedd's bushy brow drew down. "You saw her?"

Richard nodded. He held out his sword. "Put your hand around the hilt."

Zedd's frown grew. "Why? Richard, there are a great many more important—"

"Do it!" Richard growled.

Zedd blinked at the command. He straightened and he did as Richard had told him to do.

Zedd's gaze shot to Kahlan. A light seemed to come on in his hazel eyes as they went wide.

"Dear spirits . . . Kahlan."

As Zedd stood frozen in shock, Richard held the sword out to the woman. She touched the handle. Recognition dawned in her eyes as she stared at Kahlan, who had just suddenly seemed to magically appear before her. The big man, when he touched the hilt, was no less astonished.

"I know you," Zedd said to her. "I can see you."

"Do you remember me?" Kahlan asked.

Zedd shook his head. "No. The sword must interrupt the ongoing nature of the Chainfire event. It can't restore my lost memory—that's gone—but it stops the ongoing effect. I can see you. I recognize who you are. I don't recall you, but I know you. It's rather like seeing a face you know but not being able to place it."

"Same with me," the big man said.

The woman nodded her agreement.

Zedd grabbed Richard's sleeve. "We have to get out of here. Six will be back. We dare not get caught here and have to tangle with her. She's more than a handful."

Richard started across the room. "I have to get something first."

"The book?" Zedd asked.

Richard stopped and turned back. "You saw it?"

"I should say I did. Where in the world did you ever come across such a thing?"

Richard climbed up on the chair and pulled down a pack stuffed up behind a beam. "First Wizard Baraccus—"

"From the great war? That Baraccus?"

"That's right." Richard hopped down from the chair. "He wrote the book and then had it hidden for me to find. He is responsible for me being born with both sides of the gift, so he wanted to help me with my abilities. He had his wife, Magda Searus, hide it after he came back from the Temple of the

Winds. It's a long story, but the book has been waiting for me for three thousand years."

Zedd appeared dumbfounded. They gathered around the table as Richard dug around in the pack until he found the book and pulled it out. He held up the book for Zedd to see.

"The problem was, at the time I was cut off from my gift, so I couldn't read it. It just looked like blank pages. I don't know what Baraccus wanted to tell me about my ability."

Zedd shared a look with the other two captives. "Richard, I need to talk to you about what Baraccus left for you."

"Yes, in a moment."

A frown grew on Richard's face as he thumbed through the book. "It's still blank." He looked up in confusion. "Zedd, it's still blank. The block on my gift was broken—I know it was. Why would this still appear blank to me?"

Zedd laid a hand on Richard's shoulder. "Because it is blank."

"To me. But you can read it." He held the book open before the old man. "What does it say?"

"It's blank," Zedd repeated. "There is no writing at all in the book—only the title on the cover."

Richard puzzled at the old man. "What do you mean it's blank? It can't be blank. It's supposed to be the *Secrets of a War Wizard's Power*."

"It is," Zedd said in a grave tone.

Richard looked heartbroken, angry, and puzzled all at once. "I don't understand."

"Wizard Baraccus left you a wizard's rule."

"What wizard's rule?"

"The rule of all rules. The rule unwritten. The rule unspoken since the dawn of history."

Richard ran his fingers back through his hair. "We don't have time for riddles. What did he want me to know? What is the rule!"

Zedd shrugged. "I don't know. It's never been spoken, and has never been written.

"But Baraccus wanted you to know that it's the secret to using a war wizard's power. The only way to express it, to make sure that you would grasp what he was intending to tell you, was to give you a book unwritten to signify the rule unwritten."

"How am I supposed to use it if I don't know what it is?"

"That's a question for yourself, Richard. If you are the one Baraccus thought you were, then you will know how to use what he left for you. He obviously thought it was exceptionally important and worth all the trouble he went to, so I would say that it must be what you need."

Richard took a deep breath to steady himself. Kahlan felt so sorry for him. He looked at his wits' end. He looked on the verge of tears.

"My, my, my," came a voice from behind.

They all spun around.

A reed-thin woman in black smiled a sly smile. Her hair was a tangled nest of black. Her bloodless flesh and blanched eyes made her look cadaverous.

"Six . . ." Zedd said.

"What do you know, if it isn't the Mother Confessor. And won't the emperor be pleased when I bring him Lord Rahl as well, all tied up in a nice bundle."

Kahlan saw Zedd press his hands to his head, in obvious pain. He staggered back and crumpled to the ground. Richard's sword made a ringing sound as he drew it. He charged the woman but was stopped short and driven back by forces Kahlan couldn't see. His sword clattered across the stone floor.

The woman held out a thin finger toward Kahlan. "Not a good idea, Mother Confessor. Not that I care if you fry your own brain trying to turn mine to mush, but you are much more valuable to me alive."

Kahlan felt the pain of the unseen power forcing her back, just as Richard had been forced back. The debilitating agony was something like the pain from the collar, but sharper, deeper down in her ears. It made the back of her jaw hurt so much that she had to open her mouth. All five of them were cringing back, holding their ears with the pain of it.

"This is going to make things so much easier," Six said in a self-satisfied manner as she glided toward them, like death itself.

"Six," a stern voice called from the doorway.

Six spun to a voice she obviously recognized. The pain lifted from Kahlan's head. She saw the others recovering as well.

"Mother . . . ?" Six said in emotional confusion.

"You have disappointed me, Six," the old woman said as she stepped forward into the room. "Disappointed me greatly."

She was slender, much like Six, but stooped with age. Her black hair flared out from her face in much the same way, but it was streaked with white. Her eyes, too, were a blanched blue.

Six backed up a couple of steps. "But I, I . . ."

"You what?" the old woman demanded in a venomous tone of displeasure. This woman was a commanding presence who feared nothing, least of all Six.

Six cowered back a step. "I don't understand . . ."

Kahlan's jaw dropped as she saw the tight, pale flesh of Six's face and hands begin to move, as if bubbling from beneath.

Six started screaming in pain, her bony hands groping the crawling flesh of her face.

"Mother, what do you want!"

"It's quite simple," the old woman said, stepping closer yet to the witch woman as she shrank away. "I want you to die."

At that, Six's whole body jerked about violently as her skin convulsed and churned, looking like it was separating from the turbulent muscle and sinew beneath. She almost looked like she was boiling from within.

The old woman grabbed the suddenly slack skin at the back of Six's neck. As Six began to crumple downward the old woman gave a mighty pull.

The skin, mostly in one piece, pulled right off the stricken witch woman. She collapsed, a bloody, unrecognizable mess barely contained by the sack of a black dress, to the stone floor. It was about as sickening a sight as Kahlan could imagine.

The old woman, holding the sagging remains of Six's skin, smiled at them.

They all stood frozen in shock as the old woman seemed to shimmer, her appearance wavering and flickering. Kahlan stared in astonishment. The old woman was no longer old, but young and beautiful, with long, wavy, auburn hair. Her variegated gray dress did little to conceal her sensuous figure. Points of the airy fabric floated as if in a gentle breeze.

"Shota . . ." Richard said, a grin splitting his face.

She dropped the bloody hide in a sloppy pile, then smiled a coy, teasing smile as she stepped forward and tenderly cupped his cheek with her other hand. Kahlan could feel her own face going red.

"Shota, what are you doing here?" Richard asked.

"Saving your hide, obviously." She smiled even wider as she glanced down to the remains in the black dress. "I guess it cost Six hers."

"But, but I don't understand."

"Neither did Six," Shota said. "She expected me to scurry away with my tail between my legs to forever hide in trembling fear that she might find me, so she never expected a visit from her mother. Such a thing was not among her otherwise considerable talents, or her limited imagination, since she had no comprehension of the value of a mother and no empathy with those who do. She could not imagine the power and meaning of such a bond, so such a thing blinded her. Her connection to her mother was loathing schooled by fear."

Kahlan could feel her face heating even more as she watched Shota run a long lacquered fingernail down the front of Richard's shirt.

"I don't like it when someone takes what I have worked for and created," Shota said to Richard in an intimate voice. "She had no right to what is mine. It took me a great deal of time and effort to reverse all that she had done to sink her treacherous tentacles into my domain, but I did."

"I think there was more to it, Shota. I think you wanted to help us all."

Shota stepped away, flicking a hand in acknowledgment as she turned her back on Richard. "The boxes are in play. If the Sisters of the Dark open them a great many people who have done no wrong will die. I, too, will be cast to the Keeper like a scrap of meat."

Richard could only nod at the truth of that. He bent and picked up his sword. He held the hilt out. "Here."

"My dear boy, I've no need for a sword."

Kahlan didn't know how anyone could have such a beautiful, silken voice. Shota didn't act like she even knew that there was anyone else in the room. Except when she cast a brief, warning glare at Zedd, her almond eyes rarely left Richard.

"Just humor me and touch it."

Her whole face softened with a flirtatious smile. "If you say so."

Her graceful fingers curled around the hilt. Her eyes suddenly turned to see Kahlan standing right there beside him.

"The sword interrupts the ongoing effect of the Chainfire spell," Richard explained. "It doesn't reverse it, but it enables you to now see what is before you."

Her gaze lingered a moment before returning to Richard. "So it does." Her voice turned serious. "Right now, though, all of us in this room are about to be taken by the power of Orden and given over for all eternity to the Keeper of the dead in the underworld." Her fingers touched the side of Richard's face. "As I've told you before, you need to stop that from happening."

"And how am I to do that?"

Shota gave him a scolding look. "We've had this discussion before, Richard. You are the player. It is up to you to put the boxes in play."

Richard heaved a sigh. "We're a long way from the boxes. Jagang will have them in play long before we can get back."

Shota smiled at him. "I have a way for you to get back."

"How?"

Shota pointed a finger skyward. "You can fly."

Richard cocked his head. "Fly?"

"The dragon that Six had bewitched and was using is up on the rampart."

"A dragon!" Zedd exclaimed. "You expect Richard to fly on a dragon? What sort of dragon?"

"An angry one."

"Angry?" Richard asked.

"I'm afraid that I'm not very good at appearing as a dragon's mother, but I've gentled it." Shota shrugged. "A little, anyway."

* * *

Richard had them all wait in the hallway as he quickly changed into the things from his pack. When he emerged, Kahlan's breath was taken by what she saw.

Over a black shirt he wore a black, open-sided tunic decorated with strange symbols snaking along a wide gold band running all the way around its squared edges. A wide, multilayered leather belt bearing more of the emblems cinched the magnificent tunic at his waist. The ancient, tooled-leather baldric holding the gold- and silver-wrought scabbard for the Sword of Truth crossed over his right shoulder. At each wrist was a wide, leather-padded silver band bearing linked rings encompassing more of the strange symbols. Black boots over his black trousers also had pins with yet more of the rounded designs. His broad shoulders bore a cape that appeared to be made of spun gold.

He looked like Kahlan's idea of what a war wizard should look like. He looked like a commander of kings. He looked like Lord Rahl.

Kahlan had no trouble at all understanding why Nicci was in love with him. She was just about the luckiest woman in the world. She was also a woman worthy of this man.

"Let's hurry," he said to Shota.

Shota, strolling at a steady pace down the center of the halls, her filmy gray dress flowing out behind, led them though secondary, unadorned passageways in the castle as if it were deserted. From time to time she waved a hand toward a door or a passageway, as if to ward off anyone from bothering them. That must have been exactly what she was doing, because no one intercepted the small company of people hurrying through the hallways.

They all paused behind the witch woman when she finally stopped at a heavy oak door. She gave them all a look as if to ask if they were ready, then threw open the heavy oak door. When they went through the doorway into the overcast day, Richard's cape billowed out behind. Out on the rampart they were confronted by a huge beast with glossy red scales and a forest of black-tipped spikes on its back.

Flame roared across the rampart, kicking dirt and gravel in every direction. They all shrank back.

"That's not Scarlet," Richard said. "I thought it might be Scarlet."

"You know a dragon?" Kahlan asked.

"Yes, so do you, but not this one. This one is bigger, and a whole lot meaner-looking."

The heat from rolling flames again drove them back. Shota, unconcerned, singing a soft song, casually walked forward. The flames stopped. The dragon brought its head floating downward toward her, tilting it to the side, as if curious. As Shota whispered things Kahlan couldn't hear, the dragon snorted softly in a contented manner.

Shota, stroking her fingers under the dragon's chin, turned back to them. "Richard, come speak with this handsome fellow."

The dragon almost sounded like it was purring at her words.

Richard hurried forward. "I have a dragon friend," he said up to the beast. "Maybe you know her. Her name is Scarlet."

The massive creature threw its head back and fired a column of flame skyward. Its spiked tail swished across the rampart, knocking large blocks off the stone wall over the side.

The red head swung back down. The lips drew back in a snarl to reveal wicked-looking fangs.

"Scarlet is my mother," the dragon growled.

Richard looked pleasantly surprised. "Scarlet is your mother? Are you Gregory?"

The dragon drew closer yet, sniffing at Richard as it frowned. Richard's cape billowed up with each puff of air.

"Who are you, little man?"

"I'm Richard Rahl. The last time I saw you, you were an egg." Richard, as if talking to an old friend, made a half circle with his arms. "You were this big."

"Richard Rahl." Gregory grinned, its hostility evaporating. "My mother has told me of you."

Richard laid a hand on Gregory's snout. His voice turned gentle with concern. "Is she all right? Magic is failing. I've been worried how it might harm her."

Gregory snorted a puff of smoke. "She is very sick. She grows weaker by the day. I am stronger and still able to fly. I bring her food, but the witch woman kept me from being able to do so. I don't know how to help her. I worry that she will be lost to me."

Richard nodded sadly. "It's the taint caused by the chimes having been in this world. That taint is destroying all magic."

Gregory nodded his huge head. "Then the red dragons are doomed."

"As are we all. Unless I can stop that taint."

The big head cocked to the side so that Gregory could peer at Richard with one yellow eye. "You can do that?"

"Possibly, but I'm not sure how, yet. I do know that I need to get to the People's Palace if I am to try."

"The People's Palace? Where the dark army waits?"

Richard nodded. "That's right. I may be the only one who can stop that taint. Will you take us there?"

"I am free, now. A free dragon does not serve man."

"I'm not asking you to be my servant, only to fly us to D'Hara so that I can try to save all of us who want to live free, including you and your mother."

Gregory's head glided closer to Zedd, Tom, and Rikka. He thought it over briefly, looking back at Richard.

"All of you?"

"All of us," Richard said. "I need the help of my friends, here. It's our only chance to stop all the terrible things that are about to happen."

Gregory's head came down close until his snout nudged Richard's chest, pushing him back a half step. "My mother told me the story of how you saved me when I was but an egg. If I do this, we will be even."

"Even," Richard agreed.

Gregory lowered his body down onto the rampart as much as possible. "Let us be off, then."

Richard told the rest of them how to get up and how to hold on to the spikes and projections. He went up first, settling himself astride the dragon's back at the base of its long neck, then helped pull Zedd, Tom, and Rikka up behind him. Zedd muttered under his breath the whole time. Richard told him to stop cursing.

Kahlan was last. Richard leaned down, took her hand, and

pulled her up behind him. As she adjusted herself on the dragon's back behind him, she saw him pull a white cloth out of his pocket, looking at it.

Kahlan, her arms around him, whispered in his ear. "I'm afraid."

He smiled over his shoulder. "You get dizzy flying on dragons, but you don't get sick. Just hold on tight and close your eyes if you want."

It struck her how easy it was being close to him, and how gentle and natural he was with her. He seemed to come alive when she was near him.

"What's that you have?" she asked, tilting her head toward the white cloth. It had an ink spot on one side and another just like it on the opposite side.

"Something from before," he said in a distracted sort of way. He was obviously not thinking about her question. He was thinking about the white cloth with the two ink spots.

He stuffed the cloth back in his pocket and looked down at the rampart. "Shota, are you coming?"

"No. I'm returning to Agaden Reach, to my home. I will wait there for the end, or for you to stop that end from coming."

Richard nodded. Kahlan didn't think that he looked at all confident. "Thank you for all you've done, Shota."

"Make me proud, Richard."

He smiled at her briefly. "I'll do my best."

"That's all any of us can do," she said.

Richard patted the dragon's glossy red scales. "Gregory, let's get going. We don't have much time."

Gregory let out a brief blast of flame. As it curled away into black smoke, the dragon's immense wings lifted and then snapped down with tremendous yet graceful force. Kahlan felt them lift into the air. It felt like her stomach turned upside down.

CHAPTER 59

As they marched through the empty, magnificent marble halls of the People's Palace, Richard knew where everyone had gone because he could hear the soft chanting echoing through the passageways.

"*Master Rahl guide us. Master Rahl teach us. Master Rahl protect us. In your light we thrive. In your mercy we are sheltered. In your wisdom we are humbled. We live only to serve. Our lives are yours.*"

It was the devotion to the Lord Rahl. Even at a time like this, even when their world was about to end, everyone at the People's Palace went to the devotion when they heard the call of the bell. He supposed that this was a time when these people needed him the most and the devotion was their way to acknowledge that bond. Or maybe it was meant to remind him of his part in that bond and his responsibilities to protect them.

"*Master Rahl guide us. Master Rahl teach us. Master Rahl protect us. In your light we thrive. In your mercy we are sheltered. In your wisdom we are humbled. We live only to serve. Our lives are yours.*"

Richard put his feelings about the devotion out of his mind. He felt like he was juggling a thousand thoughts all at once. He didn't know what to do. There were so many different questions overwhelming him all at once that he just couldn't seem to organize the mountain of problems into meaningful order. He didn't know where to start that arduous climb.

He felt inadequate to be the Master Rahl.

He did believe, though, that the seemingly endless problems

were connected, that they were all pieces of the same puzzle, and that if he could just figure out what was at the core of what was bothering him, it would all begin to fit together.

He just needed a few years to figure it out. He would be lucky to have a few hours.

Once again he forced his mind back to the relevant issues. Baraccus had left him a message in a three-thousand-year-old book, a rule unwritten, and Richard didn't know what it meant. Now that he once again had access to his gift, he did at least now recall all of *The Book of Counted Shadows*, but it was most likely a false copy. Jagang had the original. Jagang had the boxes.

Why was a Confessor central in it all? Was it because a Confessor was central to the boxes of Orden if one of the copies of *The Book of Counted Shadows* was used? Or was he just imagining it? Was he just thinking that a Confessor was central because Kahlan was a Confessor and she was central in his life?

Just the thought of Kahlan sent his mind off track and racked him with anguish. Having to keep from telling her all the things he so desperately wanted to tell her was crushing his heart. Having to keep from taking her in his arms and kissing her was killing him. He just wanted to hold her tight.

But he knew that if he destroyed the sterile field of her mind, then there was no chance for the power of Orden to restore her to who she was. He had to remain distant and vague.

What terrified him the most was the thought that it was too late, that Samuel had already tainted that sterile field.

He could feel Kahlan walking beside him. He recognized the sound of her footsteps, the scent of her, the presence of her. One instant he was overjoyed that he had her back, and the next he was panicked that he was going to lose her.

He had to stop letting his mind drift to the problem and focus instead on the solution. He had to find the answer.

If there really was an answer.

"Master Rahl guide us. Master Rahl teach us. Master Rahl

protect us. In your light we thrive. In your mercy we are sheltered. In your wisdom we are humbled. We live only to serve. Our lives are yours."

All these people would die unless he helped them by finding that answer. But how in the world was he to do that?

He returned to what he thought had to be the heart of the solution. He would need to open the boxes of Orden if he was to reverse all the damage done—that was all there was to it. Unless he did that the world of life, damaged by the Chainfire event and its subsequent taint, would spiral out of control. Unless he opened the right box Jagang's Sisters would. But he didn't know how to open the boxes and besides he didn't have control of them, Jagang did.

Richard reminded himself that at least he had accomplished a number of the steps he had to accomplish if he was to have a chance to open the right box. At least he had been successful in his journey through the veil. And he had been successful in returning what he had brought back in the manner required. That in itself had been a puzzle, but he had found the solution. Now Orden was needed to actually restore it.

Kahlan had accepted the carving he did of *Spirit.*

He reminded himself that he also had the Confessor that was needed.

Confessor. Something was wrong about that, but he couldn't figure out what it could be.

But he did know that there was only one way to get close to the boxes of Orden. That was his only chance—if he could figure it out before Sister Ulicia opened one of them.

When he heard the whisper of hurried footsteps he looked up and saw Verna and Nathan rushing toward him. Cara and General Meiffert were close on their heels. Zedd, Tom, and Rikka were close on Richard's.

At a bridge covered in beautifully veined green marble overlooking a devotion square and a conjunction of wide halls, Richard came to a halt as Verna and Nathan rushed up. The people below were all on their knees, bent forward with their foreheads to the tile as they chanted. They were unaware of what he was about to do.

"Richard!" Verna gasped, catching her breath.

"Glad to see you back," Nathan said to Richard with an additional nod to Zedd.

"Six will no longer be a problem," Zedd told the prophet.

Nathan let out a sigh. "One less hornet, but I'm afraid that there's no shortage of them."

Verna, ignoring the tall wizard beside her, waved her journey book urgently at Richard. "Jagang says that it's the new moon. He demands your answer. He says that if he doesn't get that answer then you know the consequences."

Richard glanced at Nathan. The prophet looked more than grim. Cara and General Meiffert looked tense as well. They were the helpless guardians of a place with tens of thousands of people who were all on the verge of being slaughtered.

Soft chanting drifted up from below.

"*Master Rahl guide us. Master Rahl teach us. Master Rahl protect us.* In your light we thrive. In your mercy we are sheltered. In your wisdom we are humbled. We live only to serve. Our lives are yours."

Richard rubbed his fingertips on his forehead as he swallowed back the lump rising in his throat. He had no choice—for more reasons than the one.

He looked up at Verna with forbidding finality. "Tell Jagang that I agree to his terms."

Verna's face went scarlet. "You agree?"

"What are you talking about?" Kahlan, at his right, asked. Richard was distantly heartened to hear the tone of awakened authority in her voice. But he ignored her and directed himself to Verna.

With great effort, Richard controlled his voice. "Tell him that I have decided to give them what they want. I agree to his terms."

"Are you serious?" Verna was bottled rage. "You want me to tell him that we surrender?"

"Yes."

"What!" Kahlan said, seizing a fistful of his shirtsleeve to pull him around toward her. "You can't surrender to him."

"I have to. It's the only way I have to keep all those people down there from being tortured and killed. If I surrender the palace he will allow them to live."

"And you're going to take Jagang's word for that?" Kahlan demanded.

"I have no choice. This is the only way."

"You brought me back here to turn me over to that monster?" Kahlan's green eyes brimmed with tears born of anger and hurt. "Is that why you wanted to find me?"

Richard looked away. He would have given just about anything to tell her how much he really loved her. If he was to go to his death, he at least would want her to know his true feelings and not think that he had married her out of a duty to an arrangement and was now using her as treasure to be turned over in a surrender. It was crushing his heart that she thought that.

But he had no choice. If he corrupted the sterile field then the Kahlan that he knew would be forever lost—if it hadn't already been corrupted by Samuel, if she wasn't already lost to him.

Richard turned his attention elsewhere. "Where's Nicci?" he asked Nathan.

"Locked up like you told me to do until Jagang can collect her."

Kahlan rounded on him. "And now you're also giving the woman you love over to—"

Richard lifted a hand, commanding silence.

He unclenched his jaw as he turned to Verna. "Do as I say." His tone of voice made it clear that it was an order not to be discussed, much less defied.

As everyone stood in stunned silence, Richard started away. "I will be in the Garden of Life, waiting."

He needed to think.

Only Kahlan followed him.

Ever-waning daylight slanted in through the leaded glass overhead. This would be the night of the new moon—the darkest night of the month. Richard had heard it said that such darkness brought the world of life closer to the underworld.

In the hours waiting for Jagang to make it up the plateau and to the Garden of Life, Richard had paced the whole time, deep in thought, thinking about those two worlds—the world of life and the world of the dead.

There was something about the whole thing that didn't make sense to him. He went through *The Book of Counted Shadows* that he had memorized, knowing that there was probably some flaw in it that would make it impossible to use it to open the power of Orden, but also knowing that the elements would still be largely true, if out of order. It would take nothing more than changing a single detail to have made it a false copy. He knew that there was a flaw in the copy he had memorized, but he didn't know how to identify the specific deviation from the original.

Jagang had the original. He wouldn't have to worry about there being errors in his book. Sister Ulicia, with Jagang in her mind the whole time, would be reading the original directly, so they would be using the actual, true version of the book. Therefore, they wouldn't need a Confessor.

He came to a halt before Kahlan. "Copies of *The Book of Counted Shadows* have to be verified through the use of a Confessor. If you had the text to *The Book of Counted Shadows*, if I recited it for you, do you think you would be able to verify the true parts?"

Kahlan, deep in her own thoughts, looked up. "I've asked myself that same question countless times. I'm sorry, Richard, but I just don't know how.

"It's too bad that the first Confessor, Magda Searus, didn't leave me a book on how to use my powers, like her first husband left for you."

A lot of good that book was doing him. Richard let out a despondent sigh and went back to pacing.

He turned his thoughts back to the book that Baraccus had so desperately wanted him to have: *Secrets of a War Wizard's Power*. Baraccus had thought that it was vital that Richard have that book with the rule unwritten. The whole thing was so bizarre that Richard was left stunned and not knowing what to think. It had been a monumental effort to recover that book. It had to have also been a great effort on the part of Baraccus to see to it that only Richard would eventually be able to find it.

Why leave him a book that said nothing?

Unless it actually said everything.

Richard glanced to his silent grandfather sitting on the short, vine-covered wall nearby. Zedd met his gaze but his sadness at not being able to help Richard was evident.

"I'm sorry," Kahlan said.

Richard glanced over. "What?"

"I'm sorry. It had to be a terrible decision. I know that you are only trying to keep Jagang's brutes from slaughtering all the people here. I wish I could touch Jagang with my Confessor power."

Confessor power. First brought into existence in Magda Searus. The woman who had been married to Baraccus. But she had been married to Baraccus back during the great war, long before she became a Confessor . . .

"Dear spirits," Richard whispered to himself, icy realization flashing through his veins.

Baraccus had left Richard *Secrets of a War Wizard's Power* to tell him what he needed to know.

That was exactly what Baraccus had done.

He had given Richard the rule unspoken, the rule unwritten, since the dawn of time.

In that instant, as he grasped the *Secrets of a War Wizard's Power*, Richard was able to fit the other pieces together and understand it all.

He grasped the totality of it, how it all worked, why they had done what they had done, why they had done everything.

With trembling fingers, he pulled out the piece of white cloth with the two ink stains. He unfolded it and stared at the two spots on opposite sides.

"I understand," he said. "Dear spirits, I understand what I have to do."

Kahlan leaned close, looking down at the cloth. "Understand what?"

Richard understood it all.

He almost laughed maniacally. He understood the whole thing.

Zedd was watching him, frowning at him. Zedd knew Richard well enough to tell that he had figured it out. As Richard stared at him, his grandfather gave him the slightest smile and nod of pride, even if he had no idea of what Richard had figured out.

They all looked up at the sudden clamor of people entering the garden. The few men of the First File present, as instructed, fell back out of the way without offering any resistance. Richard saw Jagang at the head of the wave of people pouring in the doors. Sister Ulicia was right beside him. Other Sisters followed behind carrying the three boxes of Orden. Heavily armed guards, their boots all striking in unison, marched in the double doors, spreading into the garden like a dark flood.

Jagang's presence, his burning, enduring hate, not only defiled the Garden of Life but defined him.

Richard smiled inwardly.

The gaze of Jagang's completely black eyes was fixed on Richard as the emperor marched down the path between the trees, past beds of long-dead flowers and past the short vine-covered walls. His royal guards were spread out behind, pouring through the shrubs as they established a defensive perimeter.

Jagang wore a condescending smile as he passed the sorcerer's sand and crossed the sweep of lawn.

His hate defined him.

The Sisters set the three inky black boxes on the broad granite slab that was supported by two short, fluted pedestals. Sister Ulicia ignored the people in the garden. Focused on the job at hand, she only glanced briefly at Richard before setting the book on the granite altar in front of the boxes. Without delay, she cast a hand out, igniting a fire in the pit, adding to the light given off by the torches.

Night was falling. The new moon was rising. Darkness was coming, darkness beyond what anyone living had ever experienced. Richard knew that darkness. He had been there.

Jagang strode right up to stand close in front of Richard, as if challenging him to a fight. Richard stood his ground.

"Glad you came to your senses." His gaze slid to Kahlan. He regarded her with a leeherous look. "And I'm glad you brought me your woman. I'll deal with her later." He looked back into Richard's eyes. "I'm sure you aren't going to like what I have in mind."

Richard returned a glare but said nothing. There was nothing to say, really.

Jagang, for all his intimidating presence, his completely black eyes, his shaved head, the way he displayed his muscles as well as his plundered jewels, looked more than tired. He looked frazzled. Richard knew that the emperor was having nightmares and even more than that, haunting dreams about Nicci. Richard knew because they were nightmares and dreams that Richard had given him, through Jillian, the priestess of the bones, the dreamcaster who was descended from the same people as Jagang.

The emperor stormed over to where Sister Ulicia stood waiting before the sorcerer's sand. "What are you waiting for? Get started. The sooner this is finished the sooner we can get on with finishing all resistance to the rule of the Order."

"Now I understand," Kahlan, standing close beside him, whispered to herself as if she, too, had had her own revelation. "Now I see who he wants to hurt through me, and why it would be so terrible."

She looked up into Richard's eyes with a countenance of sudden comprehension.

Richard couldn't afford to be distracted right then. He returned his attention to the Sisters. He still had a few things he needed to reason out. He needed to make sure it all made sense, or else they would all die—by his hand.

Several Sisters knelt before the sorcerer's sand, smoothing it out in preparation. By the way they were working as a team, Richard figured that they had already studied the original of *The Book of Counted Shadows* in preparation and had all the procedures and enchantments memorized.

He was surprised to see them all starting to draw the

required elements. He recognized them from *The Book of Counted Shadows* that he'd memorized as a young man. He had expected Sister Ulicia, the one who had put the boxes in play, to be the one to draw those elements, but as they worked, Sister Ulicia instead went from one symbol to the next, finishing the final part that completed it. Richard realized that it made sense; it was only necessary that the elements be done, and this saved a great deal of time. Since Sister Ulicia was the one finishing each element, Richard guessed that the book had some requirement that the player be involved, probably requiring that they be the one to complete the spell-forms.

She was the one invoking Orden. She was the player. Jagang, though, possessed her mind and thus ultimately would control Orden.

Richard remembered well how long it had taken Darken Rahl to run through all the procedures. The way they were doing it the Sisters were not going to take anywhere near that long. By working together they were able to divide the work into simpler components.

Jagang paced back to Richard. "Where's Nicci?" he growled as his black eyes glared.

Richard had been wondering how long it would be before he asked that question. It was even sooner than Richard expected.

"She is being held for you, as promised."

Jagang's heated expression turned to a grin. "Too bad you don't really know how to play Ja'La dh Jin."

"I beat you."

Jagang's grin only widened. "Not in the end."

As the emperor went back to his impatient pacing, Sister Ulicia directed the elements from the book, reading pertinent parts when necessary. Richard understood the things they were drawing. Parts were the dance with death. When Darken Rahl had first drawn them they had seemed so mysterious, but now the language of them all made sense.

Jagang was looking more and more edgy by the moment. Richard knew why.

"Ulicia," the emperor finally said, "I'm going to go get Nicci. There is no reason for me to stand here while you work. I can watch this through your eyes just as well."

Sister Ulicia bowed her head. "Yes, Excellency."

Jagang turned his glare on Richard. "Where is she?"

Richard gestured to one of the officers of the First File standing not far away, the man Richard had ready for this purpose. There were only a few of the First File present, all having waited with Richard for the Imperial Order to arrive. They were there to guard him until the bitter end.

"Take the emperor down to Nicci's cell," Richard told the officer.

The man saluted with a fist to his heart. Before leading Jagang away, the contented-looking emperor turned back to Richard.

"Looks like you lose at the final turn at Ja'La dh Jin this time as well."

Richard wanted to say that the time had not run out and the game was not yet over, but instead he simply watched the man leaving as he waited for the nightmare to begin in earnest.

Kahlan stood silently at his side. The way she glanced up at him made him uneasy.

Zedd and Nathan looked lost in their own thoughts. Verna looked angry and bitter that it had come to this. Richard couldn't blame her. Cara, standing beside Benjamin, took hold of his hand. Along with the rest of his party, Jagang had brought Jennsen into the Garden of Life. The royal guards kept her on the other side of the room. Tom's gaze was fixed on her. She stared back at him, unable to say all the things she obviously wanted to say.

Cara inched closer. "Whatever happens now, Lord Rahl, I'm with you until my last breath."

Richard returned a smile of appreciation.

Zedd, not far away, nodded his agreement with Cara's sentiment. Benjamin lightly clapped his fist to his heart. Even Verna finally smiled and gave him a single nod. They were all with him.

Kahlan, close at his side, whispered, "Would it be all right if you just held my hand?"

Richard could not imagine how alone she must feel at that moment. With a heavy heart that he couldn't say anything, he took her hand.

CHAPTER 60

Nicci sat in the near darkness on the bench carved out of the same stone as the walls. The outer room, a second layer of protection guarding the room hollowed out of solid rock, was shielded. The only way in or out was through the double set of iron doors with the shielded room between them. This was where the most dangerous of prisoners were held, prisoners who could command magic.

There was no telling how many people had sat in this very room as they awaited their appointment with death, or worse.

Nicci could hear footsteps in the outer passageway beyond the two iron doors. Someone was coming.

She had known that it was only a matter of time until he came.

Nicci was in a state of utter calm. She knew why she was there. She knew why Richard had told Nathan to have her locked in this cell.

She heard the lock in the outer door clang open, the metallic sound echoing through the network of low corridors. She could hear someone grunting as they tugged in a series of muscular pulls, forcing the door bound up on rusty hinges to open enough to get through. When she saw shadows through the small opening in the door to her inner cell, Nicci blew out the flame on the lamp beside her on the stone bench that was the room's bed and only furnishing.

A key scraped and then the lock to her cell sprang open. After being in complete silence for so long, she found the strident sound exceptionally loud. As the door grated open the light from a lantern flooded in. Dust from the rusty door floated up in that harsh yellow light.

Emperor Jagang ducked down as he stepped over the high sill to squeeze in through the doorway. Nicci stood.

He was wearing his sleeveless vest so as to display his muscular bulk. His shaved head reflected the single flame of the lantern he'd brought. His black eyes looked entirely at home in the depths of the dark hole in the rock. Those black eyes gleamed as he took in the sight of her. She had made sure to loosen the top of her dress so that he would have something to catch his attention. It worked.

"I've been dreaming of you, darlin'," he said as if he thought it would impress her.

He always had believed that his lust proved something to her, as if his lack of civility or restraint only demonstrated how overwhelmingly appealing she was to him. To Nicci it only served to prove that he was an unprincipled savage.

Nicci stood tall, saying nothing, refusing to shy away as Jagang moved in close. He circled his muscular arm around her waist, pulling her tight against his powerful bulk, demonstrating his command of her, his virility, his unchallenged authority.

Nicci had no desire to drag it out.

She casually reached her arms up around him and snapped the Rada'Han closed around his bull neck.

He staggered back a step in confusion.

She knew that he would feel the power of the collar piercing into every fiber of his being.

"What have you done?" he asked in a tone of anger bordering on a kind of horror she had never heard out of him before.

She had no desire to discuss the matter, so she simply exerted her control through the collar to prevent him from talking. If she knew Jagang, and she did, then Sister Ulicia would be up in the Garden of Life working to open the right box of Orden. She didn't want Ulicia to realize what had just happened.

Jagang would have been impatient to get at Nicci. The nightmares Richard had sent had plagued him, but the dreams Richard had given him of Nicci had turned his obsession for her into a passion, a mania, that had slowly grown to the point where it was nearly intolerable. Jagang had always desired her, but after the dreams Richard had crafted, Jagang could think of little else but possessing her.

He had even been willing to leave Sister Ulicia to her work to come down to the dungeon and personally recover her.

It was a small gift Richard had given her. When Nathan had locked her in the cell, he had explained, from behind the shields that protected his words from the ears of any spies, that Richard had devised the scheme as his last gift for Nicci. Richard knew that they would have to surrender the palace. He knew that they were all going to die. The one thing he could give Nicci was Jagang.

The Rada'Han had been in the cell. It was the collar that Ann had left there when she had been imprisoned by Nathan for a time. That was what had been so important that Ann had been trying to tell Nicci before she had been killed.

Nathan had known that the Rada'Han was in the cell, behind the shields of the room. Richard wanted Nicci to have it, and to have a way to bring final justice to Jagang the Just.

Richard had no illusions that it defeated the Imperial Order. The corrupt beliefs of the Order tainted the minds of millions. Jagang was not its architect. That communal hatred would burn on without one man.

Nicci understood that as well. She had grown up with the teachings of the Order. She knew how they attempted to perform the alchemy turning suffering into virtue, wrongdoing into righteousness, death into salvation.

Such beliefs were born in man's willful refusal to use his mind, in his lust for the unearned, his wish for success without effort. Such beliefs were the embodiment of hatred for all that was good, a hatred for virtue, hatred for value. It was ultimately a hatred of themselves, of life, of existence. It was that hate, that dedication to death, that was the true manifestation of evil.

Killing Jagang would not cure mankind of such irrational zealotry. The beliefs of the Order were not driven by one man. The Order would go on without Jagang.

Nor would killing Jagang stop those who had put the boxes of Orden in play, or the Chainfire spell, or the taint from the chimes, or the vast army who lay in wait, surrounding the palace, so eager for blood and plunder. This would not change any of that.

But Richard had wanted to give her the last gift of being able to see this small bit of justice done before her own life was snuffed out, along with the rest of them, by the Sisters invoking the power of Orden in service to the army devoted to the beliefs of the Fellowship of Order.

It was Richard's only way to thank her for all she had done, to allow her this one small bit of final salvation from the man who had so terribly abused her.

Nicci stepped over the high sill. Her prisoner, unable to protest, followed. While her gift was limited within the People's Palace, it was enough to easily use the unique nature of the Rada'Han. She could have dropped Jagang to the ground in overwhelming agony, but she used only the power necessary to overcome his unwillingness to follow her silent directives.

Outside the second door several officers of the First File, men who had brought Jagang down to his caged prize, waited. The passageway was so low and cramped that the men had to hunch under the low ceiling and stand in a line because they wouldn't fit side by side.

They were shocked to see Nicci now in command of the emperor.

A big man in a uniform, the captain of the prison guards, was there with them. The man had been kind to her, offering to bring her anything she wanted. She now had what she wanted.

"Captain Lerner," she said, "if you would be so kind as to show us out of this maze?"

He gazed at the muscular man behind her in a collar and then smiled at her. "I would be only too happy to do so."

Once up into the immense halls of the palace, Nicci made Jagang lead the way. She followed close behind him, making sure that he kept going, that he talked to no one, that he acknowledged no one. He tried mightily to overcome the power of the collar. It was ridiculously easy for Nicci to overwhelm all of his resistance, all of his might and fury. He was as helpless as a puppet.

Throughout the palace, men of the Imperial Order bowed to him as he passed. Nicci didn't allow Jagang to acknowledge them. The men of the Order were used to his superior arrogance, his indifference to them, so they thought nothing of seeing him march past without so much as a look.

There was no easy way to get to the Garden of Life. The entire palace was laid out in the form of a power spell, designed to enhance the gift of the Lord Rahl and interfere with the gift of any other. To get anywhere, one had to navigate hallways that were really elements of the spell-form. The major lines of the form were the vast corridors. The subordinate elements were formed by smaller halls.

The entire palace was a maze of corridors with columns and halls guarded by rows of statues. Much of the interior of the palace was done in stone beautifully crafted in extravagant designs. The whole palace, while being a spell-form, was also a city, with streets made of the spell's corridors and halls.

But getting anywhere required maneuvering through the complex lines of that spell-form. That made getting anywhere time-consuming. The journey from the dungeons up to the Garden of Life was a long one. As they made their way past places with skylights, Nicci saw that the sky was just beginning to take on a hint of blue.

By the time they reached the garden level of the palace, the sun was just up. The first warm rays coming in through the east windows were touching the white marble on the opposite walls.

Nicci's intention was to go into the garden with Jagang to see Richard one last time. She had found out from brief questions that Richard had somehow made it back. Jagang didn't know how. Nicci supposed that it didn't really matter, now. He was back, and she wanted to see him one last time before the end. She wanted to let him see Jagang so that he would know that at least the emperor would not enjoy the terrible fruit of the long war he had carried into the new world. After all he had done, Richard deserved at least to know of that small victory.

When they went through the double doors into the Garden of Life, Nicci could see between the trees that the sun was just touching the altar. Half a dozen Sisters were gathered around Sister Ulicia. She was standing before the boxes.

Even as the boxes were bathed in the sunlight, it looked like they were black voids in the world. The sunlight did nothing to illuminate the boxes. They, instead, looked like they were pulling that sunlight in, taking it down to where it would never be seen again.

Jagang struggled mightily to move closer, to fight off the control of the collar, but he couldn't. Nicci kept him in place, in the back, where his guards thought he was merely watching and didn't want to be disturbed.

Nicci knew that she could end Jagang's life in an instant. When the time came, she would. No one had any chance to rescue their emperor, even if they had known that he was in mortal trouble. He was hers now.

Nicci could see Richard in his magnificent war wizard's outfit. The sight of him made her heart ache.

Kahlan stood quietly beside him. If Richard had preserved the sterile field in order to have a chance to counter Chainfire, she wouldn't even know his true feelings for her. Now it looked like Richard would never get that chance, and she would die without ever knowing the truth.

Richard spotted Nicci. He saw Jagang beside her and understood that she had succeeded in using the gift he had given her. He gave her a small, private smile.

Sister Ulicia tapped the box on the right. "This one."

The other Sisters were beaming at their success. They would now be able to deliver the power of Orden to the emperor. They didn't know that he would never be able to celebrate their victory.

Sister Ulicia lifted the lid on the box on the right. Golden light flowed from within, almost as if it were liquid. It enveloped the Sisters standing before the stone altar.

They all smiled with exhilaration at what they had accomplished, even if it was to be put into service of the Imperial Order, and not themselves. Of course, they would put it to that service without even realizing that Jagang was no longer controlling their minds.

If Nicci made them aware of that, though, then the Sisters would use the gateway to free the Keeper of the underworld. Nicci's choice was to allow them to give the world over to the Order, or to the Keeper.

She knew that was no real choice. At least life under the Imperial Order would be life. If Sisters of the Dark were allowed to do as they would prefer, there would be no real life.

Nicci did not want to live to see what was going to come of the new world brought into being by hate.

She supposed that she would not have to worry about it. She expected that she had mere moments to live.

But Jagang would die before she did. She would make sure of that.

Justice would finally visit Jagang the Just.

The one thing Nicci couldn't understand was why Richard was smiling.

CHAPTER 61

Richard watched as the golden light coming from the box of Orden lifted the seven Sisters.

Kahlan's hand tightened on his. The others in the room watched with a mix of awe and terror. This was something unlike anything that any of them had ever seen, or would ever see again.

Richard glanced at Nicci. Even she was transfixed by the sparkling light that swirled around the Sisters. Jagang, standing beside her, was smiling. Richard could just see the metal of the collar peeking though the front of the vest. Jagang knew that his cause would have the power of Orden, even if he didn't live to see it. He believed that was all that mattered. He believed in their cause.

The Sisters within the golden glow appeared to be delighted by the heady power of Orden.

It was short-lived.

The light darkened as it swept them all up into the air, carrying them toward the darkening sea of sorcerer's sand.

The floating Sisters glided together, collecting in a tight cluster above the ground. They all began to rotate helplessly in the sparkling amber light. The room darkened as a few flashes of lightning began to flicker about over their heads. Several Sisters screamed. A low roar grew to fill the room.

The ground trembled as the tight clump of seven Sisters floated out over the sorcerer's sand.

The sand beneath them began to rotate along with the light. The sparkles within the light connected with the fits of lightning dancing around the room, giving the sisters a flickering appearance.

"What's going on!" Sister Ulicia screamed.

Richard let go of Kahlan's hand and walked across the grass to the edge of the sorcerer's sand that was slowly darkening from honey-colored to amber to a burnt brown. Richard could smell it burning.

"What's going on!" Sister Ulicia again demanded as her panicked gaze found him.

"Did you read *The Book of Life*?" he calmly asked her.

"Of course! You have to use *The Book of Life* to put the boxes of Orden in play. We all read it! We followed every formula and instruction exactly!"

"You may have followed the instructions contained within the book, but you didn't abide by its meaning. You read what you wanted to read—the formulas and spell-forms."

Several of the Sisters screamed as lightning cracked through the air right near their faces.

Sister Ulicia was enraged. "What are you talking about!"

Richard clasped his hands behind his back. "At the very beginning there was only one thing all by itself on the first page to emphasize how important—how central—it was. It wasn't a formula, or a spell-form, but it was the first thing *The Book of Life* said. It was first for a very important reason. In your arrogance, your greed to have what you wanted, you ignored it.

"The introductory statement to *The Book of Life* is a warning to anyone who would use the book.

"It says, 'Those who have come here to hate should leave now, for in their hatred they only betray themselves.'"

"What are you babbling about?" one of the other Sisters asked, not concerned with what they saw as a dusty aphorism.

"I'm talking about a book of instruction on using the power of Orden. *The Book of Life* is the very first thing needed to use that power. Such power is dangerous almost beyond measure. Those who created it wanted to protect it. Most dangerous things of magic are protected by guards, defensive shields, and fail-safes.

"Orden was designed to counter Chainfire, but because it needed to be profoundly powerful to do that, that also made it profoundly dangerous. Those who created it came up with a fail-safe that is at once both striking in its simplicity, and foolproof.

"That safeguard says, 'Those who have come here to hate should leave now, for in their hatred they only betray themselves.'"

"So what!" Sister Ulicia screamed.

"So," Richard said with a shrug, "it's a warning—about as deadly a warning as there can be. It's telling you that hate will trigger a deadly reaction from the power of Orden. If you want to use Orden to cause harm then that can only mean that you would have to be someone who hates. Only those with hate in their hearts would scheme to use such a thing to harm others."

"That doesn't make any sense! How would it harm someone who is evil?" she asked. "How could you use Orden to stop us? You hate us, you would be using Orden for hate."

Richard shook his head. "You mistake hate and justice. Eliminating those like you who harm innocent people is not done out of hate, but out of love for those who have done no wrong and are being hurt and killed. It's love and respect for innocent life.

"Eliminating such people is not hate. It is a product of reasoned justice."

"But we don't hate!" another Sister cried out. "We want to eliminate those who are heathens, sinners, and are only selfishly concerned with themselves."

"No," Richard said, "you hate those you envy. You hate that they are happy."

"But we used *The Book of Counted Shadows*!" Sister Ulicia cried in desperation. "We followed the original exactly. It still should have worked."

"Well," Richard said as he strolled before the blackening sorcerer's sand, "even if you disregard the safeguard in *The Book of Life*, I'm afraid that you made a mistake thinking that *The Book of Counted Shadows* would be of any use."

"But it's the real book! The original!"

Richard smiled as he nodded. "It's the original of yet another fail-safe. Didn't you read the first thing in that book as well? It also put the important warning first."

"What warning!"

"The warning to use a Confessor."

"But we had the original! We had no need of a Confessor!"

"The warning wasn't that you need a Confessor. The warning was the mention of a Confessor at all."

Zedd, unable to contain himself, held up a hand. "Richard, what in the world are you talking about?"

Richard smiled at his grandfather. "Who was the first Confessor?"

"Magda Searus."

Richard nodded. "The woman who had been married to Baraccus. That was during the war. After the great barrier was up and the war was over the wizards up here discovered that the prosecutor in the trial over the Temple of the Winds, Lothain, was a traitor. To discover how he betrayed them, Wizard Merritt used Magda Searus to create a Confessor."

"Yes, yes," Zedd said, nodding. "So what?"

"The boxes of Orden were created during the great war. The first Confessor was not brought into being until long after the war. How could *The Book of Counted Shadows* be the key created to open the boxes if Confessors had not even been dreamed up when Orden was created?"

Zedd blinked in surprise. "*The Book of Counted Shadows* couldn't possibly be a key to open the boxes of Orden."

"That's right," Richard said. "They were merely a trick to prevent the misuse of the power of Orden. Using them, even the original can only get you killed. *The Book of Counted Shadows* is not the key to opening the power of Orden."

Richard turned to the pandemonium of a building rumble. Vapor, smoke, shadows, and light spun with a roar. The ground shook violently. The sorcerer's sand, now black as pitch, was sucked into the vortex. With a grating sound the whole of it rotated over the abyss. The sounds of the world of life and the underworld mixed in a terrible howl.

The Sisters spun in the maelstrom, arms and legs sticking

out in every direction, their screams lost in the thundering clamor.

Blinding light ignited in the center of the spinning mass. Beams of white-hot light shot upward through the windows overhead and downward into the blackness of the abyss. The air shimmered with heat, light, and a piercing shriek.

With a wailing roar the blackened sand under the Sisters ripped open. Violet light shot up to engulf the terrified women. The rotating light, black sand, and lightning tightened as it built momentum.

Without the benefit of a spirit guide, the Sisters spiraled down into the world of the dead. They went still alive. They went screaming.

A flash lit everything to a blinding white, and then there was silence as everything went black as death.

When the light gradually returned, the Garden of Life was silent. The hole in the ground was gone. The sorcerer's sand was gone. The Sisters were gone.

Jagang's personal guard who had been in the Garden of Life were also gone. Being in the room with the power of Orden had been fatal to them as well as the Sisters.

Jagang, wearing the collar that was under the dominion of Nicci, was still there, looking even more angry, if that was possible.

Men of the First File streamed through the double doors into the Garden of Life to protect Richard.

"Close and bolt the doors," Richard ordered.

The men rushed to do his bidding.

Richard went to the altar and flipped the open box of Orden closed.

"You may have had your little success," Jagang said with a sneer, "but it means little. It changes nothing."

When he fell silent with a choking sound, Richard held up a hand. "Let him speak, Nicci."

She brought the emperor forward.

"The Imperial Order will still get in here and rip this place and all you miserable people apart," Jagang said. "They do not need me to pursue the just cause we fight for. The Order will cleanse mankind of the scourge of you selfish people. Our cause is not only moral but divine. The Creator is on our side. Our faith proves it."

"Truth has advocates who seek understanding," Richard said. "Corrupt ideas have miserable little fanatics who attempt to enforce their beliefs through intimidation and brutality . . . through faith. Savage force is faith's obedient servant. Violence on an apocalyptic scale can only be born of faith because reason, by its very nature, disarms senseless cruelty. Only faith thinks to justify it."

Jagang's face went red. "We do the Creator's work! Devout devotion to the Creator is the only true and moral way of this life. Strict adherence to our pious duties will bring us salvation and everlasting life! It is the blood of nonbelievers like your people that lifts us to the side of the Creator Himself."

Richard made a face. "That doesn't even make sense."

"You are a fool! Our faith alone proves us right! We alone will be rewarded in the afterlife for our reverence to Him. We are his true children, and will live forever in his Light."

Richard sighed as he shook his head. "It's always been difficult for me to believe that a grown man could actually believe such nonsense."

Jagang ground his teeth in fury. "Put me to your tortures! I accept your hatred of me because I have faithfully performed my duties to a greater good for mankind."

"You will not serve some grand place on the stage of life," Nicci said. "You will not be paraded in chains. You will not serve as a martyr or be venerated for a glorious death.

"You are irrelevant. You will simply die and be buried, and in that way no longer be able to threaten decent, innocent people. You are irrelevant to the future of mankind."

"You must extract your revenge on me for all to see!"

Richard leaned close to the man. "There will be other problems, as there always are in life, but you will not be one of them. You will be yesterday's garbage, rotting back to dust, your life having meant nothing worthwhile."

Jagang tried to lunge at Richard, but Nicci's control of him through the collar kept him back like a chained animal. "You arrogantly think you are better than us, but you are not. You too are but a miserable creature that the Creator placed in this vile world. You are no different than us except that you refuse to repent and worship Him. This is about hatred. That's all it is. It's just about you venting your hatred of the Order."

Richard rested the palm of his left hand on the hilt of his sword. "Justice is not the exercise of hatred, it is the celebration of civilization."

"You can't simply—"

With a signal from Richard, Nicci opened a flow of her power into the collar. Jagang's black eyes opened wide as he felt death fill his empty soul. He toppled face-first to the ground.

Nicci gestured to several men of the First File. "I'm sure that there are soon going to be a great many dead. Throw his corpse in the mass grave with the others of his kind."

As simply as that, the emperor of the Imperial Order was gone. As Richard had commanded, there was no grand end. There would be no celebration through violence and mutilation, no torture, no forced confessions of wrongdoing. Reasoned people understood the wrongdoing quite well enough. The threat to reasoned people was removed; that was all that mattered. Jagang's death was no more significant than that.

CHAPTER 62

Without delay, Richard went to the stone altar where the boxes of Orden sat.

He drew his sword.

The distinct metallic ring filled the Garden of Life.

"Richard," Zedd said in a rising tone of warning, "what do you think you're doing?"

Richard ignored his grandfather. He instead gazed into Kahlan's eyes.

"Are you with me, Kahlan?"

She stepped to within a few paces of him.

"I have always been with you, Richard. I love you, and I know you love me."

Richard's eyes closed for a moment.

He had no choice.

He turned to the boxes of Orden and closed his eyes as he lifted the blade to touch his forehead.

"Blade," he whispered, "be true this day."

He brought the Sword of Truth down and drew it across the inside of his arm, letting blood run down until it dripped off the tip.

He placed the blade on top of the box on the right, the one that Sister Ulicia had opened.

The blade turned as black as the box itself.

He withdrew the blade and it returned to its shiny state.

He placed the sword on the box on the left. Again, it turned as black as the underworld itself.

He withdrew it, letting it return to its normal state.

Richard took a deep breath, and then laid the flat of the

blade on the center box. He thought about all the innocent people who simply wanted to live their lives. He thought about all those like Cara and the other Mord-Sith who had been driven mad until they would serve a tyrant. He thought about Nicci, indoctrinated her whole life with hate, driven to a miserable life of sacrificing herself to twisted beliefs. He thought about Bruce, his left wing man, who, when he saw strength without hate, was drawn to it.

He thought about Denna.

When he opened his eyes, the blade had turned white. The box beneath it was just as white.

Gripping the hilt in both hands, Richard lifted the point of the Sword of Truth high over the white box . . . and with the killing thrust from the dance with death, drove it down, pinning the box to the altar.

The Garden of Life went white. The entire world of life went white. Time stopped.

In that moment, Richard stood in the center of a white world with nothing around him. He looked around, but there was no one there, and at the same time everyone was there with him—every individual in the world of life was there with him.

He understood. This was in many ways the opposite of the last journey he had taken in this room when he went into the world of darkness and in a way every soul there had been with him.

In this place, in this state, he had the conscious awareness of every living person. In this moment, in this place, they all waited for what the man who commanded the power of Orden would say, and what he would do. This was Orden, the power of life itself.

"Every person makes choices as to how they will live," Richard began.

"Evil does not exist independent of man. Men do evil by choice. Choice involves the requirement to think, even if ineffectually. The most basic choice you can make is to think or not to think, to let others do the thinking and tell you what to do, even if they tell you to do evil.

"Wise choices require more, they require rational thinking. Refusal to think rationally affords one the ability to maintain the illusion of knowledge, wisdom, even sanctity while committing evil. If you follow the teaching of others who do your thinking for you and who have you do evil, the innocent victims are harmed just the same as if you choose to harm them yourself.

"Dead is dead. Their life is over.

"Teachings that defy reason defy reality; what defies reality defies life. Defying life is embracing death.

"Celebrating faith over reason is merely a way of denying what is, in favor of embracing any whim that strikes your fancy.

"The followers of the Fellowship of Order have decided how they wish to live their lives. If it stopped there, none of us who value our individual liberty would care how they choose to live, but they have made the choice—made a conscious choice—that they will not allow others to live their own lives as they wish.

"It is that choice, made of their own free will, which we cannot abide. We will not allow them to impose their evil choice on us. It ends here, now.

"I give them their wish for a world in which they can live as they have chosen. I grant them the thing they want most in life—the life they choose.

"I could condemn them to no worse fate.

"From this moment on there are now two worlds, twins in most ways. This world will remain as it is.

"The power of Orden has just duplicated, in many ways, this world, giving them a world of their own. Their world will be theirs.

"They may not ever come to realize the foolishness of their choice, but they will certainly suffer for it. They will have the lives of misery they so fervently cling to. They will have the lives of suffering they piously embrace. They will have the lives of hopeless dread and fear they have chosen to impose on themselves by refusing to use their own minds to think rationally.

"They have chosen to throw their lives into the caldron of all-consuming hatred. I grant them their wish. It is the last time wishing will ever bring them anything. They will live out their existence wishing and hoping, endlessly lost in the darkness they have imposed on their own minds—in their own self-loathing. But they will never be able to harm us again.

"They believe that those who are free cause all of their hardship. They blame us for their woes. They attack us, saying we are the root of evil because we exist, because we are prosperous, because we are happy. They wish to destroy us so that they may have the world be the way they wish it."

Richard turned his attention to the followers of the Order already in that other world, already at the other end of the gateway that was open. Those in his world could hear as well.

"I grant you your wish.

"You now have what you always claimed to want, a world in which your beliefs rule. A world without magic, without free men and free minds. You can believe as you wish, live as you wish.

"But you will not have us as the excuse for the misery you create for yourselves. You will not have us as an excuse to fuel your hate.

"You will be without any enemy but your miserable selves. Your world will be yours to rule as you see fit, to crumble around you as you wallow in your own hate.

"Your children, witness to the senseless cruelty of your willfully ignorant beliefs, will in time hopefully change your world for the better, will make their own adult lives worthwhile and joyful. But that will be entirely up to them. They will have to choose for themselves to use reason rather than force to deal with each other. Like anyone else, they will have to make choices as to how they will live their only life.

"This world will be ours.

"This will be a world without the teachings of the Imperial Order. Without those who wish to use force to impose those beliefs on us. Without those who would murder us for wanting to choose how to live our own lives.

"This world will be a world with all the imperfections and uncertainty of life, with all the consequences of poor choices, with all the hardships and failures that life presents, but it will be a world in which we have a chance to make what we will of our lives, a world in which our lives are our own and our achievements are our own, a world in which man can learn, create, accomplish, and keep the products of his mind and labors. This will be a world of liberty, a world in which people have the right to live their life as they wish, to believe as they wish, as long as they follow reasoned laws and do not use force to impose their will on others.

"Not everyone in this world will succeed, or be happy, or even understand how to make a moral life for themselves. For now, though, for those of us who are living, it will be a world without the followers of the Order.

"This is a world of life. Life is what we make of it. We may fail. But for the time being, we will have the freedom to succeed or to fail. How we honor that freedom will be up to each of us.

"Perhaps our children will throw all this away, wanting to sink back into the misery of faith, of wishing, of force, but that, too, will be the world they create anew for themselves. That will be their choice, their life. They, too, will have to suffer the consequences if they fail to mind the lessons learned through our struggle. That is their responsibility to themselves, to their own lives.

"But for now, for those of us actually alive, those of us who exist now, this will be a world where reason is free to allow us to live our lives, lives without the beliefs of the Imperial Order to blight us.

"Despite the harm those in that newly distant world have inflicted on us, I will not kill them. I don't need to kill them. My responsibility to myself and those I love is to remove the threat so that we may live. I have done that.

"Our revenge will be to live lives filled with love, laughter, and joy.

"We will turn our attention and precious lives to the meaningful matters of life, to those we love and care about, to our future.

"Those of you in the newly distant world can look forward to what you would have brought us: a thousand years of darkness.

"I expect that you shall forever worship that to which you no longer will have any connection, or any possibility of a connection, that you will forever pray for an afterlife with the Creator in the spirit world, but you will be forever cut off from any world but your own. In that distant world you will have your own lives, and after you die you will be dead. Your spirits will no longer exist. Your souls will extinguish along with your lives.

"You will have your lives, and if you waste them by continuing to worship other worlds, wishing for invented visions of eternal salvation, wanting an escape from the reality of existence, you will reap only the emptiness of death after enduring lives unlived. You will have a chance at life; it will be up to you to value those precious lives or to cast them away for nothing.

"You wanted a new dawn of mankind. You wanted a world of life in which pining for other realms invented in your minds alone was the righteous cause of mankind. I grant you your wish. Now you must live with it.

"We will be free of you.

"Your world will be yours. You can never return to this world, for there will be no way back. Once this gateway closes, there will be no underworld for you as a conduit back, no other world for you but your own. There will be no means to get to this world and whatever worlds layer it.

"Those of us who remain behind will continue in our world as it has been, with whatever other realms have always existed around this world, the world of life.

"Your world will be surrounded by no other realms. It will be an island of life. Eternity will separate you from everything here. That means that you will be cut off from the underworld, the world of the dead.

"Your existence in your world is finite. You will have your lives, but when you die your souls will cease to exist. You have only one existence—in your world of life. If you continue to waste it, if you fail to use your minds to properly grasp the reality of your world, your singular existence, you will lose out on the priceless value of your only life.

"You have life. You now have your own world. You can never return to this one. You can never again harm us. I give you what you have wanted: a world without dragons . . . and without all that goes with magic. You will forever be left longing for what you no longer can have.

"I am sure that every new day will bring us challenges to overcome, but the beliefs of the Order will not be one of them. As Nicci said, you are irrelevant."

CHAPTER 63

In the pure white void, his sister, Jennsen, stepped into view. Tom was with her, his arm reassuringly resting around her shoulders. Anson, Owen, and Marilee were there as well. Except for Tom, they were all pristinely ungifted—pillars of Creation.

"Richard," Jennsen said, "we want to go to that new world."

A tear rolled down Richard's cheek. He knew that every one of those like her was listening, and they were all in agreement.

"You all have every right to stay and live free here."

"I know," she said for them all.

"But you have taught me the value of life, and of respecting the lives of others. This is a world with magic. We don't want our lives to be at the expense of this world, or of lives here whose existence depends on magic. We are pillars of Creation. We need to grow and build, to create our own world, a world without magic. This is your world. That distant world is ours."

Richard cupped her cheek. "As much as I would want you to stay, I understand."

More than understanding, he had known that they would want to go to that other world.

Richard smiled at how beautiful she truly was, at how good a person she truly was. "I think you will find a safe home for yourself and your friends."

"Do you think we will be safe, Lord Rahl?" Tom asked. "I mean, considering the nature of the people you sent to inhabit that distant world?"

Richard nodded. "Movements like the Order, which only degrades and destroys the lives of its believers, needs an enemy to divert attention from the profound misery it produces. A great demon gives them an excuse for their misery. Such an enemy, as we have been, is the glue that binds their flailing suffering together. Without the excuse of a powerful evil enemy to blame, their ideas, even if they burn out of control for a thousand years, eventually collapse in on themselves. Simple tyranny usually rises up from those ashes to spring back to smoldering flame over and over throughout history in endless cycles of blaming people in the past.

"The pristinely ungifted will be far too small an enemy for the Order to be aware of, or to notice, or to blame. You will simply be too small and insignificant in numbers to be a worthy excuse."

"We will be safe," Jennsen said, answering the concern still in Richard's eyes. "Without an enemy like they had here to blame, to battle, to conquer, the people of the Order will turn their hatred inward. They will prey on their own. We will see to it that we don't bring too much attention to ourselves. We will be fine."

Richard nodded. "If you get in their way, in their sight, they will crush you, but I'm hoping that you and your people can find a place—perhaps in the area there that is known as Bandakar here in this world. You can live your own lives, there. I wish it were otherwise, but I know it must be this way.

"I have sent the Chainfire spell to that distant, new world," he told her. "It will work its way through all the people there, erasing the memory of this world, of what you have left behind. I must leave it infected with the chimes to insure that any magic carried into that distant world will be destroyed.

"Along with magic, memories of this place will be destroyed.

"I have no idea how the voids in the memories of people will be filled in—what they will eventually substitute for their real history, their real memories. Those created memories will by definition be more tenacious than the reality of what once was, of what was here. Those created memories will link together in the mind of man through the Chainfire spell, becoming a common conviction, a shared certainty. Those beliefs will hold sway over future generations despite all else. Any memory of us will eventually be lost in that distant world.

"But I can't count on the Chainfire spell and the contamination destroying all magic the way I believe it will. I simply can't count on those who will still have magic there for a time not finding a way around it."

Richard laid a hand on Jennsen's shoulder. "You, and those like you, will be the insurance for the future of your world, insurance that magic will forever be erased from existence in that world, from future generations. Once your descendants eventually touch everyone born, there will be no more magic in that distant world, even if some try to preserve it, secret it away for their own despotic ambitions. Time, and all those pillars of Creation who are born, will spread your trait of having no spark of the gift so that in the future, no one in that world can ever again be born with any spark of the gift, none will ever be able to bring back magic. But it will live on here.

"I know that you will remember me, Jennsen, but I also know that after time, that memory, along with all of this world, all that was in it, will slip away and come to be nothing more than legend."

Richard turned to Tom, the big, blond-headed D'Haran. "You are not pristinely ungifted."

Tom nodded. "I know, but I love Jennsen and wish to be with her more than anything in life. Wherever we are together is wonderful, and we will have a wonderful life together. I'm rather excited about the prospect of helping to build a world for us, a world where Jennsen and all the other ungifted will not be different, but simply people.

"I ask, Lord Rahl, that you release me from service to you so that I may devote my life to loving and protecting your sister, as well as our people there in our new world."

Richard smiled as he clasped hands with the man. "There is no need for me to release you, Tom. You have always served me by your own grace. I will be eternally thankful that you have made Jennsen happy."

Tom saluted with a fist to his heart, then, grinning, embraced Richard briefly. Owen, Anson, and Marilee, also grinning with the excitement of their lives ahead, clasped hands with Richard, thanking him for teaching them to embrace life.

"I love you," Jennsen whispered as she gave him a tight hug. "Thank you, Richard, for helping me love life. Even if I forget you, you will always be in my heart."

As she stepped away, she and the others began to slip away into the white void of the gateway.

All alone in the white void, Richard gripped the Sword of Truth to withdraw it from the box of Orden, to pull the key from the gateway. He could only think that even if everything had worked as he had planned, the one thing he had hoped for the most for himself had failed.

The sterile field he had needed to allow the power of Orden to succeed had been tainted. Kahlan had known that he loved her.

"You are a rare person, Richard Rahl," came the most beautiful voice in the world.

Richard turned to see her standing there before him. Her green eyes sparkled. She wore her special smile that she wore for no other.

Richard stood frozen, one hand still gripping the sword so hard that he could feel the word TRUTH pressing into his hand.

Kahlan stepped close, slipping an arm around his neck. "Richard, I love you."

Richard circled an arm around her waist, his feelings overwhelming him.

"I don't understand. It wouldn't work if the sterile field was breached with foreknowledge."

"I was protected," she said with a crooked smile.

Richard frowned. "Protected? How?"

"I had already fallen in love with you all over again. I didn't need a sterile field. I think that from the first moment I saw you in that cage as it rolled into the Order's camp I started falling in love with you. In everything you did, you revealed just what kind of man you are—the man I fell in love with so long ago, the man I married in the Mud People's village.

"When you gave me that carving of Spirit, it confirmed everything I had come to know all over again.

"Art reveals the artist's inner self. Art reveals a man's ideals, what he values. Anyone with that much reverence, that much passion for the nobility of the human spirit, could only be a man who shares my passion for life."

Richard smiled as he felt a tear roll down his cheek. "I went to the underworld to get the memories taken by the Subtractive Magic of Chainfire. There, I learned that the core of those memories could only be restored if you accepted them of your own free will. I put them into that carving.

"When you accepted it, you accepted everyone's memories. You broke the Chainfire spell that had taken so much from so many. By being so willing to embrace all that is good, to value the beauty of life and hold it to your heart, you gave everyone back their memories."

She gazed into his eyes for the longest moment.

And then he kissed his wife, the woman he loved, the woman who meant everything to him. The woman who loved him.

The woman he had gone to the underworld and back for.

As he lost himself in that kiss, as her arms tightened around him, he pulled the Sword of Truth from the box of Orden, closing the gateway for all time.

When Richard finally opened his eyes, the world had returned. Zedd was standing nearby, watching them, grinning.

"Zedd," Richard said, blinking at all the others also there.

"No need to apologize, my boy."

"I wasn't apologizing."

Zedd gestured for them to continue. "Well, you have a right to kiss your wife after all this time. I always knew that you two belonged together for all time.

"I just wish it hadn't taken you so long to figure all this out."

Richard scowled at his grandfather. "Sorry to have inconvenienced you. Maybe you should have taught me a little better in the beginning and it wouldn't have taken me so long."

Zedd shrugged. "I must have been a good teacher—you got it all right."

"Richard," Nathan said as he stepped forward. "Do you realize what you have just done?"

Richard glanced around. "Well, I believe so."

"You just fulfilled prophecy!"

Richard skeptically cocked his head at the prophet. "What prophecy?"

"The prophecy about the great void!"

Richard made a face. "But I just saved us from the great void you warned us was the threat in prophecy."

Nathan threw his arms up in excitement. "No, no, don't you see? You just created a world where magic doesn't exist. That's why prophecy sees that other world as a void—because prophecy can't see into a world without magic! Prophecy was actually predicting what you would do. When you split the worlds, that was the fork in prophecy. The great void is prophecy's prediction of that other world."

Richard sighed. "If you say so, Nathan."

"I don't understand something," Zedd said. "How did you know that the Sword of Truth was the key to opening the boxes of Orden? I mean, you knew that *The Book of Counted Shadows* couldn't be the real key because Orden predated the existence of the Confessors. But Orden also predated the Sword of Truth. How could it be the key?"

"The sword protected my mind from the Chainfire spell because the boxes of Orden are the counter to the Chainfire spell, and the Sword of Truth—or, more correctly, the magic invested in it—is the key to the boxes, so it's part of Orden. That was the spark of insight that made me realize that the sword is the key—because I was holding it when the Sisters ignited the spell, it protected my memories of Kahlan, and the sword interrupted the ongoing effects of the spell for those who touched it."

Zedd planted his hands on his hips. "But the sword was created after Orden."

"That was a trick."

"A trick!"

"What better way to protect something of such profound power than with a trick, rather than a complex, extravagant construction of magic, like everyone thought of *The Book of Counted Shadows.*

"After all, a trick, if properly done, is magic," Richard smiled. "You taught me that, remember? That's what the wizards back then did. The whole thing with *The Book of Counted Shadows* was a trick to disguise the real key: the Sword of Truth. The sword was invested with the magic to unlock Orden; the book was a ruse, a trick, to send everyone off track.

"The true key—the sword—has elements of magic that complete the constructed magic of Orden. The sword contains those necessary elements—magic invested in it by hundreds of wizards. The sword may have been created later, but the magic invested in it was the magic created by the same wizards who created Orden. It was right under everyone's nose all the time.

"That was the reason that the Sword of Truth has always been the responsibility of the First Wizard. It was beyond priceless.

"You, Zedd, were a proper caretaker for the sword. You found the right person for it, the right person to be the true Seeker of Truth.

"The reason it was so important to find the right person to be the Seeker is because only that kind of person, with the love of life and empathy for others, would be able to turn the blade white. Only that person, when touching it to the correct box, could have turned the blade white.

"Only a true Seeker of Truth can use the Sword of Truth and thus the power of Orden.

"It's tied in to the admonition at the beginning of *The Book of Life* that says 'Those who have come here to hate should leave now, for they only betray themselves.' The Sword of Truth requires compassion to work. Hate will not turn the blade white—only compassion will. That is the final fail-safe for Orden. At the same time, it works this way in order to be the key to the boxes of Orden.

"You can't use hate to make Orden work. Hate is not a part of the solution. *The Book of Life* warns of that very thing. Once you grasp the concept, it's all pretty simple."

"Yes, I can see how simple it is," Zedd muttered to himself as he poked a finger through his thatch of unruly white hair to scratch his scalp.

Nathan snapped his fingers as he turned to Zedd. "Now I also understand that other prophecy."

Zedd looked up. "Which one?"

Nathan leaned close. "You remember: 'Someday, someone born not of this world will have to save it.' Now it makes more sense."

Zedd frowned. "Not to me."

Nathan flicked a hand. "Well, we'll have to work out the details later."

Zedd turned an intent look on Richard. "There are a lot of questions remaining, a lot to understand. As First Wizard I need to know everything so I can tell if you got all the particulars correct. What if you made some sort of miscalculation in some aspect of it? We need to know if—"

"There was no time," Richard said, cutting him off. "Sometimes one has only an instant to do something, and in such circumstances every eventuality can't be considered or addressed. In that cusp of opportunity not every circumstances can be recognized, much less planned for or dealt with.

"Sometimes it's more important to seize the chance and do what you can, even knowing that it won't likely account for everything, every problem, than it is to do nothing.

"Only later can one go over the what-ifs and should-haves."

"I had to act. I did the very best I could before it was too late."

Zedd smiled and then gripped Richard's shoulder, giving it a jostle. "You did good, my boy. You did good."

"Yes, he certainly did," Nicci said.

They all turned to see her making her way down the path, a big smile on her face.

"I just checked. The army of the Imperial Order is gone from the Azrith Plain. There are a few men left, those like Bruce, who want the chance to live free to try to make something of their lives."

A cheer went up from all those in the room at hearing confirmation that the vast army of the Imperial Order was gone.

As soon as Nicci was close, Kahlan immediately embraced her. She finally pushed back and smiled knowingly at Nicci.

"Only someone who truly loves him would do all you did to get me back. You are more than a friend to us."

"Richard taught me that to love someone means that you sometimes are fulfilled the most by putting their deepest desires above your own. I won't deny loving him, Kahlan, but I still couldn't be happier for both of you. To see you both together, and so much in love, brings me profound joy."

Nicci turned her attention to Richard. She was looking serious to the point of disquiet. "I want to know how you could create a distant world on the other side of nowhere and send everyone there."

"Well," he began, "I read in the books on Ordenic theory that the gateway that was created could bend magic around in a way to counter Chainfire. That gave me an idea."

He pulled the folded white cloth from his pocket. "See here? A drop of ink fell here."

Zedd leaned in. "So what?"

Richard unfolded the white cloth. "Look," he said, pointing to the two spots on opposite sides of the cloth. "When the cloth is folded, these two spots are touching. When you unfold it, they are on opposite ends of the cloth.

"The power of Orden is able to bend existence—in effect Orden *is* the bend in existence that is able to undo Chainfire and restore memory. So in effect, I used Orden's power to create an impression of this world. Orden sent those people through the gateway to that other world that was actually right here in the same place, and then when I pulled the sword back out of the box and closed off the gateway, that other world is now on the other side of existence—just like this spot that was once touching the original is now on the other side of the cloth."

"You mean," Zedd said, deep in thought as he rubbed his chin, "Orden created a gateway that momentarily joined the two places in order to allow those who wished a world without magic to step across, and then it separated the worlds forever."

"You're a quick study," Richard said, teasingly.

Zedd swatted Richard's shoulder.

Richard took a few steps to lay a hand on Verna's shoulder.

"It was Warren who gave me the spark of the idea. It was he who first told me that the boxes of Orden were a gateway, a conduit through the underworld. I couldn't have done it without Warren. He helped us all with his knowledge."

Verna, her eyes brimming with tears, rubbed Richard's back affectionately in appreciation.

Richard lifted the amulet he wore around his neck, the one once worn by wizard Baraccus.

"This amulet illustrates the dance with death. It's about more than just fighting with the sword, or even about living life. This emblem also contains what I needed to go to the underworld, the world of the dead. This is part of what Baraccus intended for me to understand.

"But this amulet also represents that final movement of the dance with death, the killing thrust, that was needed to use the boxes of Orden."

Kahlan circled her arm around his waist. "You have done wizard Baracus proud, Richard."

"You have done us all proud," Zedd said.

Nicci's blue eyes sparkled with her smile. "He certainly has."

Zedd smiled in a manner Richard had not seen in a very long time. It was the old Zedd, Richard's grandfather, advisor, and friend. Zedd spoke with quiet pride.

"What all those ancient wizards tried to do with the great barrier to the south, and what I, as First Wizard, tried to do with the boundaries, you actually did, Richard.

"You eliminated the threat to prevent them from ever harming us again, but you left life for the future. All those children of those people will have a chance to learn from the mistakes of their parents and, possibly, they will learn and grow and rise above hatred of others as a way of life. You have given them a world to live out their hatred of life, a world to take into a thousand years of darkness, but you have also given future generations the chance for a rebirth of mankind there, who hopefully will embrace life and the nobility of the human spirit.

"You have given both worlds the gift of life, and you did it through strength without hate."

CHAPTER 64

A balmy breeze lifted Jennsen's red hair as she stared at the ornate letter "R" engraved on the silver handle of her knife.

"Thinking about your brother?" Tom asked as he walked up to her, bringing her out of her memories.

She smiled up at her husband as she hugged him with one arm. "Yes, but only good thoughts."

"I miss Lord Rahl, too."

He pulled out his own knife to gaze at it. It was the twin of Jennsen's. His had the same ornate letter "R" for the House of Rahl. Tom had spent the better portion of his young adult life as a member of the special forces that served covertly to protect the Lord Rahl. That was how he had earned the right to carry that knife.

Jennsen leaned a shoulder against the doorframe. "It seems you only just got a Lord Rahl worth serving when you gave it all up to come here with me."

"You know," he said, smiling as he slipped his knife back in its sheath, "I rather like my new life with my new wife."

She hugged her arms around the bear of a man. "You do, do you?" she asked in a teasing way.

"I like my new name, too," he added. "I'm finally used to it. You know, comfortable with it."

When they married, Tom had taken her name, Rahl, so that they could carry it on in the new world. It seemed only fitting that the man who had given them their new life should be remembered in some fashion.

In every other way he was vanishing from memory.

It was surprising to Jennsen how so many people no longer

even remembered the place they came from, their old world. It was just as Richard said: the Chainfire spell was taking their memory and those blank places were being rebuilt with new memories, new beliefs, about who they were. Since the Chainfire spell and the taint within it were both Subtractive Magic, it had affected even the pristinely ungifted, so even they were continuing to lose track of who and what they had been.

For the most part, magic had become no more than superstition. Wizards and sorceresses were even less important. They had become no more than tales told around campfires to scare people for a good laugh. Dragons were becoming only folklore. In this world there were no dragons.

Any who possessed magic were fading away. Their ability was dying out, smothered by the taint from the chimes. Day by day they became more powerless. Eventually they would merely be old hags living by themselves in swampy places and considered crazy by most folk.

Any trace of the gift that survived, if not withered away by the taint of the chimes they'd brought with them into their world, would eventually be completely eliminated by descendants of the pristinely ungifted. It would be only a matter of generations before there was no trace of the gift left in mankind—just the way the Order had once said they wanted it.

Everyone was concerned with more important things now. Their lives now revolved around the hard work of survival when there was no one who accomplished anything worthwhile. People had forgotten how to do things, how to create things. Even what had once seemed the most common of things, such as construction methods, was being lost. The people here never knew how to create—they had depended on others to build and create. It would take future generations to discover them all over again.

Those from the old life, those who created, who invented, who made life easier for everyone, and who were the object of such hatred, were not in this world to help make life better. The people left, for the most part, were left to eke out an existence as best they could.

For most, living in such a dark age, sickness and death were their constant companion. As they had in the world they had been banished from, they turned to superstition and a grim, fatalistic acceptance of the misery of life and its accompanying devotion to their faith.

It seemed that everywhere Tom and Jennsen traveled to trade for supplies, they saw churches going up as the hope for mankind's salvation from misery. Men of God traveled the countryside to spread the word, and demand devotion to Him.

Jennsen and her people kept mostly to themselves, enjoying the fruits of their own labor and the simple joy of being left alone by tyrants and brutes. Some of them, though, had started keeping the symbols of the religious beliefs pressed on them. It seemed easier for them to go along than to question, to accept prepackaged beliefs than to think for themselves.

Jennsen knew that their world was going to be one that sank into a very dark age, but she also knew that within that dark world, she and those with her could carve out their own small place of happiness, joy, and laughter. The rest of the world was too busy suffering to bother with the remote area of a few quiet people. Some of the pristinely ungifted, though, as their memories of the old world vanished, had left to go out among the cities and far-off places.

Unknowingly, they carried the pristinely ungifted trait. It would continue to spread to the far corners of the world.

"How is the garden coming?" she asked Tom as he knocked mud off his boots.

He scratched his head of blond hair as he grinned. "Things are coming up, Jenn. Can you believe it? I'm growing things—me, Tom Rahl. I'm finding it more than agreeable.

"And I think the sow is going to have her litter any time now. I tell you, Betty is beside herself. The way her tail is wagging, I have the feeling that she thinks the piglets are going to be hers."

Betty, Jennsen's brown goat, loved her new home. She got to be near Tom and Jennsen all the time and she could rule the roost. Betty had a couple of horses she was in love with, a mule she tolerated, and chickens that were beneath her. She would soon have her own kids.

Tom leaned his shoulders back against the wall and folded his arms as he gazed out appreciatively at the beautiful spring countryside. "I think we'll do just fine, Jenn."

She rose up on her tiptoes and kissed his cheek. "Good, because I'm going to have a baby."

He looked thunderstruck for a moment; then he leaped in the air with a wild hoot.

"You are! Jennsen, that's wonderful! We're bringing a new little Rahl into the new world? Really?"

Jennsen laughed, nodding at his enthusiasm.

She wished that Richard and Kahlan knew, that they could come visit once she eventually had her baby.

But Richard and Kahlan were in another world.

She had come to love the broad sunlit fields, the trees, the beautiful mountains beyond, and the cozy house they had built. It was home. A home filled with love and life. She wished that her mother could see her place in the world. She wished Richard and Kahlan could see her new home, the place Tom and she had built out of nothing. She knew how proud Richard would be.

Jennsen knew that Richard was real, but to the rest of her friends in the new world, Richard and all that he embodied, all that he represented, everything they once had known . . . was passing into the shrouded realm of legend and myth.

CHAPTER 65

Kahlan stopped every step, it seemed, to greet people. She rose up on her toes to gaze out over the crowd, trying to see people she was looking for, people she was excited about seeing again. It seemed like the entire world was assembled in the expansive corridors of the People's Palace. She couldn't ever recall seeing so many people come out for anything.

But then, this was a special event, something no one had ever seen before. No one wanted to miss it.

The world was a different place. With so many people devoted to hatred vanished out of this world and into their own, there was a rebirth, it seemed, of spirit. With fewer people to produce by the toil of labor, the need for food and other goods had spurred labor-saving innovation and inventions. Every day she heard of accomplishments, of new things being developed. The opportunities for individuals to create and prosper were no longer restrained. It seemed the world was in flower.

Kahlan stopped when someone caught her arm. She turned to see Jillian, with her grandfather. Kahlan hugged the girl tightly and told her grandfather what a brave young woman she had been, and how she had helped to save them all by casting dreams. Her grandfather beamed with pride.

Kahlan was besieged by people all wanting to take her hand, to tell her how beautiful she looked, to ask if she and Richard were well. The crowds seemed to float her along. It was a delight to see such celebration, such joy and goodwill come together like this.

Several members of the crypt staff stopped her to express

their excitement at being invited. She hugged one of the women to stop her from talking. Since Richard had unleashed the power of Orden and grown them their tongues back, Kahlan didn't think that any of the crypt staff had stopped talking.

Kahlan spotted Nathan strolling through the hallway. His full head of straight white hair hung to broad shoulders holding a blue velvet cape over a ruffled white shirt. He was wearing an elegant sword at his hip—he said that it made him look dashing. He had an attractive woman on each arm, so she guessed that it worked. Kahlan hoped that Richard was as ruggedly handsome wearing his sword when he was a thousand years old.

She waved at Nathan across a sea of people. He pointed, to signify that he would see her with Richard. She headed in that direction. When she spotted Verna, Kahlan caught the prelate's arm.

"Verna, you came!"

Verna smiled like the sunshine. "I wouldn't think of missing such a thing."

"How is life at the Wizard's Keep? Are your Sisters happy there?"

Verna's smile widened. "Kahlan, I can't begin to tell you. We've found a few new gifted boys. They've come to join us and we've been teaching them. It's so much different than before, so much better. It's all so new and exciting with a First Wizard to help. Seeing such young boys coming to know their gift is wondrous."

"And life with Zedd at the Keep?"

"Zedd has never seemed so happy. With a Keep full of people you would think he would be grumpy, but I tell you, Kahlan, the man has come alive. He's like a child himself again to have Chase and Emma living there now, with all their children, and the boys learning their gift. The place is full of life again."

Kahlan was getting choked up just hearing about it. "That sounds wonderful, Verna."

"When are you coming for a visit? Everyone wants to see you and Richard again. Zedd has seen to it that people have come in to repair the damage to the Confessors' Palace. It's looking majestic again. It's ready for you to come back to visit your home whenever you wish. You won't believe all the staff who have returned and are hoping you and Richard will spend some time there."

It was such a joy for Kahlan to know that so many people were sincere in their desire to have her around. She had grown up a Confessor, a woman feared by all. Now, because of Richard and all that had happened, she was loved as herself, and as the Mother Confessor.

"Soon, Verna, soon. Richard has been talking about wanting to get out. The palace is driving him nuts. He is surrounded by marble and the man wants to go look at trees."

Verna kissed Kahlan's cheek before Kahlan started on her way again. She had gone only a short distance when the square-jawed Captain Zimmer saw her and tapped his fist to his chest in salute.

"Have any ears to show me, Captain?"

He smiled knowingly. "Sorry, Mother Confessor. Haven't needed to collect any, lately—thanks to you and Lord Rahl."

She gave his shoulder a squeeze as she moved on.

She finally spotted Richard through the crowd. He turned to look at her, almost as if he could sense her presence. She didn't doubt that he could.

The sight of him, as it always did, made her weak with joy. He looked magnificent in his black war-wizard outfit, fitting attire for the occasion.

When she reached him, and he circled an arm gently around her waist, drawing her close to kiss her, the rest of the world, the thousands of people, most of them no doubt watching, vanished from her mind.

"I love you," he whispered in her ear. "You are the most beautiful woman here."

"I don't know, Lord Rahl," she said with a playful smile, "some more might show up. Better not judge too quickly."

Richard saw Victor Cascella, with his wolfish grin, tap his fist to his heart in salute. Richard, smiling at the blacksmith, returned the salute in kind.

Kahlan spotted Zedd, then. She threw her arms around the old man. "Zedd!"

"Don't squeeze the life out of me."

She pulled back, gripping his arms. "I'm so glad you came!"

His grin was infectious. "Wouldn't miss it for the world, dear one."

"Are you enjoying yourself? Have you had anything to eat?"

"I would be enjoying it more if Richard would leave me be so I could sample a few of the delightful-looking treats."

Richard made a face. "Zedd, the kitchen staff run when they see you."

"Well, if they don't like to cook, they shouldn't have become cooks."

Kahlan felt someone grab her hand. "Rachel!" She bent and hugged the girl. "How are you?"

"Wonderful. Zedd has been teaching me to draw. When he's not eating."

Kahlan laughed. "Do you like living at the Keep?"

Rachel beamed. "It's the most fun ever. I have brothers and sisters and friends. And Chase and Emma, of course. I think Chase really likes being a Keep warden."

"I bet he does," Richard said.

"And someday," Rachel added, "we may move to Tamarang to live in the castle. But Zedd says that I'm a long way from ready for that."

Rachel had been born with royal blood that carried the ability to draw spells in the sacred caves. She was, technically, the queen of Tamarang. Someday, she was going to make a grand queen and draw wonderful things.

"Zedd," Kahlan said, "have you seen Adie?"

"Yes." Zedd smiled to himself. "Friedrich Gilder makes her happy. If ever there was a woman who deserved to find happiness, I think it's Adie. Lucky for her she traveled to the Keep back when the palace was under siege and ran into Friedrich. The two of them just seemed to hit it off. Now that Aydindril is back full of life, Friedrich has more work gilding than he can handle. I can hardly get him to do any work for us at the Keep."

"And you're all right?" Kahlan asked.

His brows lifted. "Well I will be when you and Richard come and stay for a while." He shook a finger at Richard. "I tell you, Richard, sometimes I feel like you've gone off to the underworld, to live at the Temple of the Winds."

Richard leveled an even look at his grandfather. "The Temple of the Winds isn't in the underworld."

"Of course it is. It was banished there during—"

"I brought it back."

Zedd stiffened. "What?"

Richard nodded with the slightest smile. "When I went to the underworld before I opened the power of Orden, I did a few little things. While the gateway of Orden was open I was able to put the temple back where it belongs—in this world. It was designed, created, and built by the mind of man. The things in it were the creations of the mind of man. It belongs to man. I brought it back to those of us who value such genius."

Zedd still hadn't blinked. "But it's dangerous."

"I know. I made sure that for now no one but me can get in. I figured that when you're not busy, you and I can go visit it. It's quite a remarkable place, actually. In the Hall of Sky the ceiling of stone is like a window showing the sky across its surface. It's so beautiful. I'd love to be the one to show you a place that no one else has seen in three thousand years."

Zedd's jaw was hanging. He held up a finger. "Richard, did you do anything else while the gateway of Orden was open?"

Richard shrugged. "A few things."

"Like what?"

"Well, for one thing, I fixed it so that red fruit in the Midlands is no longer poison, just like I promised you I would a long time ago."

"What else?"

"Well, I—oh, look, it's time to start. I have to go. We'll talk later."

Zedd's brow drew down. "You had better believe we will."

Taking Kahlan's hand, Richard ascended the steps to the platform of the devotion square. Egan and Ulie stood with their hands casually clasped, waiting for the Lord Rahl. Richard took his place, Kahlan at his side.

The crowd spread out through the vast hallway quieted.

When Kahlan finally saw her coming, she smiled so broadly that it made her cheeks hurt. The crowd parted along the seemingly endless red carpet for the couple approaching the platform. The escorts followed in a long trail.

Cara, looking positively radiant, ascended the steps with Benjamin at her side, holding his arm. He looked magnificent in his dress uniform. Benjamin was now General Meiffert, Commander of the First File at the People's Palace.

Cara, like all the Mord-Sith following behind, was wearing her white leather. With Benjamin's dark uniform they made a stunning couple. In a way it reminded Kahlan of her in her white Confessor's dress and Richard in his black war-wizard outfit.

Nicci, as beautiful as ever, smiled as she stood among the Mord-Sith to represent Cara as her official witness.

"Are you ready?" Richard asked.

Cara and Benjamin nodded, too giddy to answer, Kahlan thought.

Richard leaned down a little, fixing Benjamin in his raptor glare. "Ben, don't you ever hurt her, do you hear me?"

"Lord Rahl, I don't think I could hurt her if I wanted to."

"You know what I mean."

Benjamin smiled broadly. "I know what you mean, Lord Rahl."

"Good," Richard said with a smile as he straightened.

"But I can still hurt him if I want, right?" Cara asked.

Richard lifted an eyebrow. "No."

Cara grinned.

Richard looked out over the silent crowd. "Ladies and gentlemen, we are gathered here today to be a part of something wonderful: the start of the life of Cara and Benjamin Meiffert together.

"They both have proven themselves to be the finest examples of the kind of people we all hope to be. Strong, wise, loyal to those they care about, and willing to overcome everything to embrace the highest values we have: life. They wish to share that life with each other."

Richard's voice broke just a bit. "No one in this room is more proud of that, or them, than I am.

"Cara, Benjamin, both of you are bound not by these words spoken before us all, but by your own hearts. These are simple words, but in simple things there is great power."

Kahlan recognized the words from their own wedding. She thought that he could offer no greater respect for them than to use some of those same words for Cara and Benjamin.

Richard cleared his throat and paused for a moment to compose himself.

"Cara, will you have Benjamin as your husband, and will you love and honor him for all time?"

"I will," Cara said in a clear voice that carried over the crowd.

"Benjamin," Kahlan said, "will you have Cara as your wife, and will you love and honor her for all time?"

"I will," he said in an equally clear voice.

"Then before your friends and loved ones, your people," Richard said, "you are now wedded for all time."

Cara and Benjamin came together in an embrace, kissing, as the Mord-Sith behind them cried and the crowd went wild.

When the noise finally died down, and the kiss finally ended, Richard held out a hand, inviting them to come and stand beside him and Kahlan. Berdine was still crying tears of joy on Nyda's shoulder. Kahlan saw that Rikka, tears brimming, wore a pink ribbon in her hair that Nicci had given her.

Richard stood tall and proud as he looked out over all the faces watching him. If Kahlan didn't see all the thousands gathered, she would have thought the halls were empty, it was that quiet.

Richard spoke, then, in a voice that all could hear.

"To exist in this vast universe for a speck of time is the great gift of life. Our tiny sliver of time is our gift of life. It is our only life. The universe will go on, indifferent to our brief existence, but while we are here we touch not just part of that vastness, but also the lives around us. Life is the gift each of us has been given. Each life is our own and no one else's. It is precious beyond all counting. It is the greatest value we can have. Cherish it for what it truly is."

Cara put her arms around his neck. "Thank you, Richard, for everything."

"It is my great honor, Cara," he said as he hugged her.

"Oh, by the way," Cara whispered in his ear, "Shota stopped to see me just a little while ago. She wanted me to give you a message."

"Really? What message?"

"She said that if you ever come back to Agaden Reach she will kill you."

Richard pulled back in surprise. "Really? She said that?"

Cara nodded, grinning. "But she was smiling when she said it."

And then the bell calling people to devotion rang.

Before anyone could move, Richard again spoke.

"There will be no more devotions. None of you have to kneel before me or anyone else.

"Your life is yours alone. Rise up and live it."

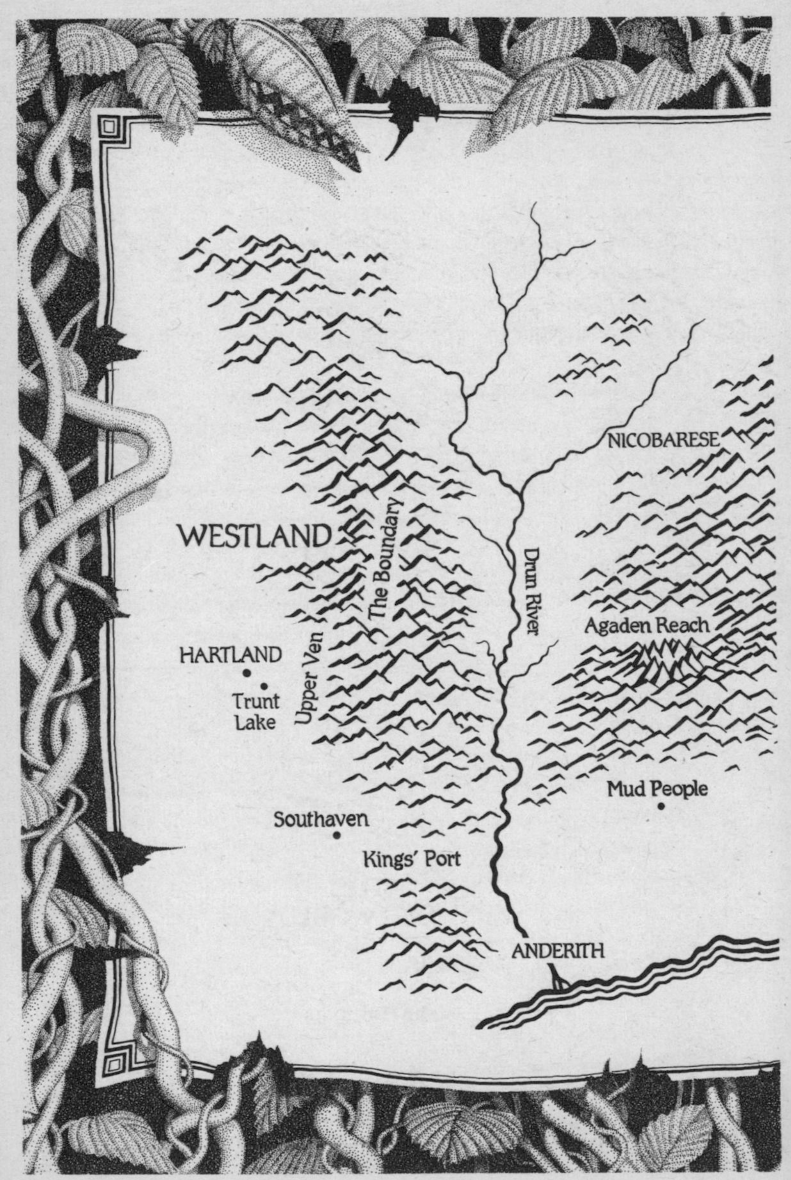

NICOBARESE
WESTLAND
The Boundary
Drun River
Agaden Reach
HARTLAND
Trunt Lake
Upper Ven
Mud People
Southaven
Kings' Port
ANDERITH

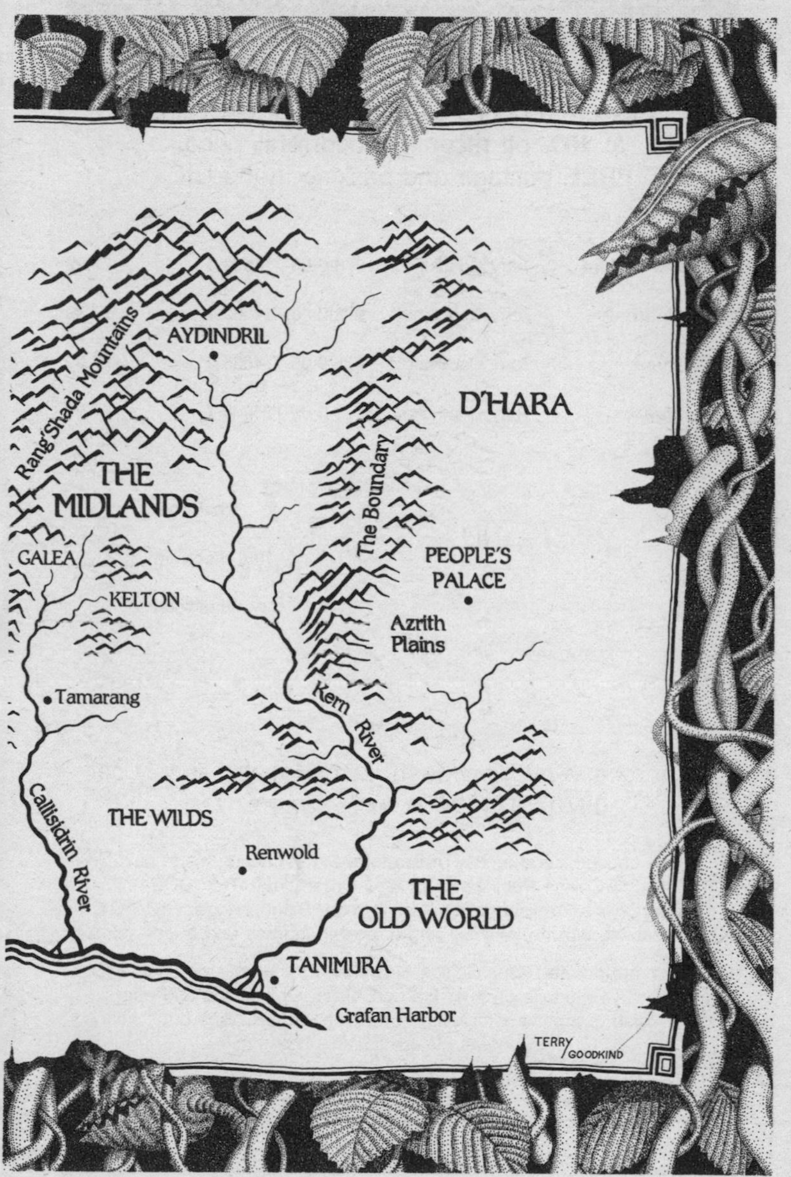
AYDINDRIL
Rang'Shada Mountains
D'HARA
THE MIDLANDS
The Boundary
GALEA
KELTON
PEOPLE'S PALACE
Azrith Plains
Tamarang
Kern River
Callisidrin River
THE WILDS
Renwold
THE OLD WORLD
TANIMURA
Grafan Harbor
TERRY GOODKIND